Katharine King

Our Detachment

A novel

Katharine King

Our Detachment
A novel

ISBN/EAN: 9783337048648

Printed in Europe, USA, Canada, Australia, Japan

Cover: Foto ©Andreas Hilbeck / pixelio.de

More available books at **www.hansebooks.com**

OUR DETACHMENT.

A Novel.

By KATHARINE KING,

AUTHOR OF "THE QUEEN OF THE REGIMENT," &c., &c.

NEW YORK:

HARPER & BROTHERS, PUBLISHERS,

FRANKLIN SQUARE.

1875.

OUR DETACHMENT.

CHAPTER I.

A SUBALTERN ALONE.

I WAS on duty that day, and couldn't get out, and awfully dull work I found it, leaning out of my window, and trying to catch a glimpse of the town and its inhabitants, over the top of the horrid blank wall that bounded our horizon—in an earthward direction I mean, for looking upward, certainly there was plenty of a blue summer sky to be seen, flecked with white fleecy clouds; but I had seen lots of that kind of thing any day this hot summer; and though I won't deny it is pretty, still a fellow can't always be star-gazing; or if he is, he is pretty sure to fall into some desperate grief here below—worse even than the old cove we used to read about in our Grecian history.

Then there were distant mountain-tops in view, looking so sunny and heathery and tempting that they were an aggravation rather than a solace—more particularly as I knew that just under them lay a beautiful lake, renowned for its fishing; and that on that very delicious day my captain, Lord Claude Feversham, had gone to inspect it, and try his luck. "At any rate, it's a bad day for sport," I mused—"too bright altogether; and I'm glad of it, for it's a beastly shame to leave me mewed up here alone, and all the other fellows off amusing themselves. I'd bet five bob Mayleigh will be able to tell, when he comes in, the whole history and antecedents of that pretty pair of feet I saw yesterday as we marched into the town. It is too bad, for it was I saw them first, and pointed them out to him, and now he will take all the credit of the discovery to himself.

"I say, there's an old hag selling gooseberries just outside the gate. I wonder could I hit her with a bit of plaster off the wall here, and make her bring me some. They'll be down on me now for barrack damages, I suppose; but Feversham needn't think he can shut up Madcap Darrell a whole afternoon alone, in such a confounded dull hole as this, without seeing a little alteration in the place when he comes back. Bravo! that hit her. Now she is looking this way. I say, you! Biddy, Peggy, whatever your name is, how do you sell those things?"

"'Two-pence a quart, your honor, bless your purty face, my little master," answered the old thief, with a grin that showed all her toothless gums.

"Confound her impudence!" I thought— "what does she mean by speaking in that way to me, Vivian Darrell, junior ensign in Her Majesty's —th foot." So I answered her stiffly, as I flatter myself I can on occasion:

"Come, I want none of your chaff. Remember, you are addressing an officer in Her Majesty's service, and I'll have you placed under arrest if you don't keep a civil tongue in your head."

"Och! murder, yer honor!" she cried, bobbing a series of courtesies, and crossing herself as she looked up at my window. "Sure it's no offense I meant, my purty dear; but I thought as you were the Captain's little boy, as I'd heard tell about—him as came down a day or two ago, and got a house in town, your honor. Sure and I could only see your head and shoulders, dearie, so I couldn't tell if you were bigger nor him. But don't tell the min to take me up, agra; for a purtier dear I never seen, and I've seen a many, being sixty years old next Lady-day. Devil a lie I'm telling you, yer honor."

There the old harridan stood, gazing up with her blear eyes at my window, and though pretending to put up her wares, evidently not with the least intention of moving as long as I would listen. However, her aspersions on my appearance and dignity were more than I could bear, and I made up my mind I would even do without the gooseberries, and the amusement they might have afforded me, rather than by buying them encourage this woman in the belief I was little Ussher; though why men shouldn't eat gooseberries as well as boys of ten or twelve, I couldn't think. Indeed I knew they did, for I had seen our sergeant-major half an hour before investing in some, which he swallowed skins and all—the beast—if I'm not much mistaken. Indeed, I don't believe I'd have thought of getting them but for his example. So I said, with great dignity and severity,

"You may go now, good woman. I sha'n't take any of your fruit; and you'd better learn to know an officer when you see him before you come into barracks again."

"Sure now, and didn't your honor call me?" she answered, with the greatest assurance. "And may be, if you'll not be afther taking the berries, you'll give me the price of a plaster, Captain dear, for the place where your honor hit me with a stone, when I was sitting there beyant."

"I never threw a stone at you, you fool!" I cried, angrily. I give you my word the thing she called a stone was a bit of mortar about an inch square, and it hit her on the old rag of a shawl she wore round her shoulders. I don't like to be imposed on, and I would give her the money in a minute when she chose to recognize me as an officer in Her Majesty's service, only that she asked for it on that plea, so I went on:

"It was only a bit of plaster off the window here struck you; and it is not for your hurt you want it, for you were not hurt, but to get a glass of whisky, or something. Get along with you out of barracks. Do you think I don't know the whole set of you!"

As I spoke I got up from the chair in which I had been sitting, intending to leave the window, and so end the discussion, as there were several of the men hanging about, and they were rather inclined to laugh, I thought. But when the harridan saw me standing up, perceiving by my height, I suppose, that I really was what I had given myself out to be, she uttered a howl, and catching up her basket, hurried off, crying out,

"Holy Mother of Moses, he's coming afther me! Bad luck to ye, ye yellow-skinned, black-eyed spalpeen, that wouldn't give an old body that's sixty come next Lady-day a penny-piece to cure the blow you gave her! Faix it's meself believes his mammy doesn't give him money yet, till he gets big enough to take care of it."

This was too much; so, putting my head out of the window again, I called out,

"Hold hard there, you old thief! For the credit of Her Majesty's service I suppose I'd better give you something; so take that, and get drunk as soon as you like; only don't let me see you in the barracks again, or I'll have you arrested."

Just as I uttered this threat, and threw half a crown to her at the same time, who should pass across the square but our sergeant-major, and he, overhearing my threat, burst into a most disrespectful laugh.

"Come," I said, turning to him, "let me hear no more of that, Green. Do you think you were sent here to ridicule your officers? I'll let Captain Feversham know how you behave, and we'll see what he says to such conduct. Ah! she's gone now. I say, Green, like a good fellow, don't let her in again. She's an awful old woman, and she'd turn the barracks upside down in no time."

Now perhaps you may think this all very extraordinary, but I'll tell you the whole state of the case, if you will keep it dark; only I don't want the ladies to know, as they would call me a boy, and laugh at me. I am Vivian Darrell, the only son of Viscount Traverscourt, and you see they made such a piece of work about me at home that I was never allowed to go to school, or any of those places, but always had a tutor. He was a good fellow, too, and was up to a lark, so that we got into no end of scrapes together. When Claude Feversham came to spend last Christmas with us, and advised my going up for my examination for the line, I rather think my parents were not quite sorry to have a chance of a quieter house in future. I passed, as you know, or else I should not be here, and was gazetted to the —th, my cousin Claude's regiment. He is my captain, and the jolliest brick going; but I wish I had a way of paying him out for leaving me alone like this, our first day in a strange town.

I always tell our fellows I am twenty, and I think they believe it, because I am very dark, which makes a man look older; but this is what I am going to confess, and which I hope you will keep secret—the truth is, I was only eighteen the other day. I begged Claude not to betray me, and though I could not get him to promise, yet I think he will not, and that is the only thing that keeps me from having my revenge on him for his beastly selfishness in going off to take his pleasure, and leaving me to take care of the barracks. You see he might tell all about me, if I was to be very hard on him, and I don't think it worth while paying a fellow off, unless I can come down on him well.

We marched into this little country town in the south of Ireland yesterday. I don't go in for praising scenery, you know — it looks spoony; but I don't mind allowing the mountains are very fine, and I am told there is fishing both by lake and river, yachting, shooting, and, for ladies' men, croquet and dancing. I am not a lady's man, you understand. I believe I once had a weakness that way just after I joined; but when I proposed, while helping my partner and the object of my admiration to a Champagne-cup at a ball, she answered, with a laugh, "Thank you; but I do find little boys just into jackets so troublesome, and as I have two little brothers of that age to mind, I don't feel equal to undertaking care of a third."

You can imagine what I suffered then, for really the girl was as pretty as any girl could be, with lots of fair hair, like spun glass. After that cruel answer, she went off to dance with a tall, dark fellow in the Blues she was flirting with; and I heard she married him afterward. Can you wonder that since then I have hated the sex, and that a constant puzzle to me, whenever I let my thoughts revert to that painful subject, is how she found out my age? For I had taken good care a few minutes before to tell her I was three-and-twenty.

As I said, we came in here yesterday. On our way from the terminus to the barracks, I pointed out to Mayleigh a pair of the prettiest feet and ankles possible to see, walking a little way in front; but we had not overhauled them when we were obliged to turn up a by-street, and so lost sight of them. Now I know well it is after those feet Mayleigh went out to-day, saying he was just going to see the town, and take a stroll; and Feversham has gone out fishing, as I said; and Ussher is somewhere mooning about with his wife, I suppose: the other two fellows said they were going up the lake, and perhaps they did, but they agreed to come back to lunch, and ordered me to have some for them. Catch me, that's all! I've had no walk to give me an appetite, so I'll let them wait till I get one. I must have some gooseberries.

"I say, Potter," I cried to a soldier passing, "just run and get me a gallon of gooseberries from that old woman; but don't tell whom they are for, as I don't wish to encourage her hanging about the barracks."

So he went and bought me the gallon of gooseberries, and for a time I got on very well, having found a note-book of Mayleigh's, which I began illustrating with extracts from his history, calculated to drive him rabid, when he should see all his little weaknesses figuring in highly-finished etchings, and exhibited round the table. As I drew I sucked my fruit, and worked away till my fingers got stiff; even my liking for the dainty before me could not induce me to finish them. What should I do with them? I would not give them to the others, for I was sure they did not deserve them. Stay! I have it! I rushed off to our mess-man, got a large flat dish, poured what remained on to that, and then proceeded to Feversham's room, where I concocted, for his benefit, a very cleverly constructed bed of the apple-pie kind. My tutor had taught me how to make them, with this difference—he had never used a dish of gooseberries as the foundation of his structures. It would have been impossible, when all was finished, to guess there was any thing unusual in the bed, and I danced a frantic *pas seul* of delight at the success of my stratagem.

It wasn't done much too soon, either; for I had hardly returned to my own room again, and resumed my post by the windows, when Mayleigh, Flower, and Preston entered the square, all together. They were very busy talking, and did not perceive me until I hit Mayleigh in the eye with a gooseberry-skin.

"There is that confounded young monkey, Madcap, at his tricks again!" said Mayleigh, loud enough for me to hear. "I'll spoil his black little figure-head some day for him, if he doesn't mind!"....

"I hope you have not been very dull, Madcap?" called Flower up to me. "I expect the barracks are not the better for being under your care so long. How many fights have you got up since we went out this morning?"

"Stow that chaff, Flower, will you?" I retorted, sulkily. You see, it is a shame to be always bringing up a fellow's old ignorances against him, and this is what Flower was alluding to:

One day, not long after I had first joined, I had been left alone as I was to-day, and roaming in a very idle frame of mind about the square, I came suddenly on two of the men quarreling. They were calling each other no end of bad names, and looked mischievous enough; so I said,

"Well, there's no good in you two fellows going on like that; hard words break no bones, and give no satisfaction either, I think; you are so evenly matched at them. Try a round or two, and I'll be umpire."

No sooner said than done; and they were hard at work at it, the little fellow walking well into the bigger one, when who should turn in, right on to us before we saw him coming, but Flower.

"What on earth is all this?" he cried. "Darrell, what's up?"

"Only these two fellows were abusing each other, and I told them to take a turn with their fists while I acted umpire."

"You two stop this instant," Flower said, turning very sharp on the men; "and mind, if I hear any more of this, you will be punished. And now, for heaven's sake, Madcap, come away, and don't let me hear of your doing this kind of thing again. It can't be allowed, indeed, and you will get into awful hot water if you go on in that way."

"Well, I don't see," I answered, "that it is any worse their pommeling themselves a little, and getting all rancor beaten out of them, than to go on calling each other ill names, and keeping up a constant spite."

This is what he was bringing up at me again, and I don't like it; though still, you see, I think I was right. Besides, as I told him then, my tutor always said every Englishman should know how to use his fists, and should use them too, if occasion required. Now, of course, you know, I understand it wouldn't suit the discipline of a regiment, but I don't think he need always be reminding me of the one or two little mistakes I made on first joining. Indeed, I know he was as bad, for he was always called Baby, and I should like to know which is worst, that name or Madcap? It riles him uncommon to call him Baby, so I put my head out of the window again, and shouted out, so that the sentry and every one should hear,

"I say, Baby, did your nurse take good care of you out? You would have been better, I am sure, in with me, and it would be much more manly than going out in leading-strings."

"You infernal young monkey, won't you catch it if I get at you!" roared Flower, coming in hurriedly, for some of the men about were laughing. "I'll break every bone in your little slippery body, if once I lay hands on you!" As he spoke he turned the key in the lock, so that I might not have the chance of escaping by the door.

Then a frantic chase commenced, which was hard work to him, as I suspect he had always been too good a boy to go robbing orchards and climbing trees for nests, like other fellows. It was a prime lark for me, however, and a good excuse for trying the springs of Mayleigh's arm-chair, which always occupied a comfortable position near the fire; for I had gone down to the ante-room when I saw Flower coming in a rage. Round and round the room we went, without ever, on my part at least, touching the floor—from chair to table, from table back to chair, and so on, till I saw Flower was getting thoroughly pumped; then, making him a profound bow, I called out, "Good-bye, Baby dear; this sort of thing is too much for your constitution, so I think I had better cut it short. I hope it will have got over its fractiousness by dinner-time." So saying, I sprang on to the window-sill, and dropped into the court-yard below. It was not much of a drop, about seven or eight feet, but I knew my friend would not follow me. Fortunately I had snatched up my forage-cap as I left my room, so now the world was before me where to choose, and kissing my hand to Flower, who leaned out of the window in a white heat, I dashed out of the barracks and down the steep, dirty hill that led into the town.

It was not a bad place for an Irish country town, and I assure you I was quite astonished to see how respectable most of the inhabitants looked, my mother having mourned over me as one going among cannibals when she heard we were under orders for Ireland. She even wanted me to exchange into the Guards; but that I refused to do, for I should have lost the society of Claude, and with all his faults I like him; besides, I think it is good for him to have somebody always near to look after him. I think him a little inclined to be susceptible, you know, and am convinced my friendly ridicule saved him from making a regular mess of himself once or twice before now. Besides, I told the mum I wanted to see a little active service, and, if any thing happened to me there I should be nearer home than if I was to go to any other savage country; so, after a good deal of kissing and crying over me, she consented to my going, after making me swear solemnly I would neither get shot nor become so contaminated by bad examples as to shoot any one myself; and also that under no circumstances whatever would I leave off the flannels, of which she had provided me with a stock, or turn Roman Catholic. As I said, I was astonished to see the respectable-look of the inhabitants, and that there were actually two churches, nice-looking ones too, besides schism shops of various denominations, and plenty of the regular religion of the country also. Why do some of those fellows wear petticoats? It is not a compliment to the old women they resemble, for however well it may suit the old women, it is very unbecoming to them.

There were shops too—grocers and butchers and bakers; fruit shops, where, only that I had already had so many gooseberries that morning, I should have been tempted to spend some money on strawberries, which were really very fine. There were also millinery and tailoring establishments, and at length, just after crossing a second bridge, and remarking that the water in the river was very low, I came on the queerest little hole, and the wonderful variety of articles displayed in the window tempted me to enter.

Such an odd fish as I found in possession! He capered round his counter, bowing and scraping the whole time as he did so; then he brought forward a chair, placed it before me, and requested me to sit down. This I did, while he, returning to his seat behind the counter, offered me some chocolate-cream bonbons, which I was pleased to accept. You see, that is another thing I don't like talked about, but I don't mind telling you: I am awfully fond of sweets, though before people I generally pretend I can't bear them—that they spoil one's palate for distinguishing the flavor of wines, olives, and such-like things. I hate olives like poison, you know, but I always eat them when they appear at table; its looks epicurean, and like a *bon-vivant*, who has had his tastes educated at Paris. Mercifully, here in the country they never have them, so I am spared that.

By-the-way, this queer little wretch I had hunted up was called by the most magnificent name, out of those old histories, you know. John Hampden was up over his shop-door, and he assured me every one called him so. Then you must imagine a person five feet nothing in height, yellow-skinned and dried up, with a whining voice, and queer, skipping, hopping, bustling movements; a man, I should say, who devoted more of his energies to the collection of gossip than to the business of his trade.

He told me he kept a pass-book with the barracks, and I might get any thing I liked. Of course it would all be entered in the book at whatever price he chose to put on the articles afterward; but we would not be pressed for payment till the regiment was leaving.

"That is a very convenient way of dealing with gentlemen like the officers," he went on; "for, you see, often, young fellows come here not very flush of money, and if they could not get credit they would buy nothing. You are Captain Ussher's young gentleman, aren't you, sir? Would you ask your papa to favor me with his custom, whenever he wants any thing in my line?"

"I am no connection of Captain Ussher's," I answered stiffly, rising and leaving the chocolate creams behind me, so great was my indignation. "I am one of the officers, and if you are not more respectful in your manner of speaking to me in future, I shall be obliged to give up coming here; it lowers the dignity of the service when its officers are treated with familiarity."

"Oh, surely, sir, you are right," replied the little man, with a face expressive of the deepest concern. My determined conduct had evidently cowed him. "You see, sir, the last regiment was here, sir, they were such nice, friendly gentlemen, and took every thing in good part. I used to have great fun with them, and was always up at the barracks; but, you know, I was the only man in Belmurphy they were so friendly with. Every one's good to John Hampden, however, particularly the ladies; they would not get their things at any other shop in town. Ah! here come the Miss Dashaways. Good-morning, ladies;" and then he began the same bowing performance over again to which he had treated me.

The girls were pretty, certainly, but bad style; one of them tall, with dark hair and a very good complexion; the other dark also, but short, with fine eyes and pretty dark hair; both of them decidedly good-looking, but not the style I care about.

They looked at me for a minute very hard, then turned away and began business with the English patriot, while I rose and went out, determined to see more of the town, and mentally registering a vow that I would twist young Ussher's neck for him some day, if his father kept him down here; and how such a mistake could have been made when I was in undress I could not conceive.

"At any rate," I concluded, "as these fellows can not recognize an officer in Her Majesty's service when they see him, I will take preciously good care never to go out in 'mufti' while I am here, except in the evening."

Having taken this resolution, I wandered on, climbed a high green hill on the outskirts of the town, that commanded a most delicious view of the country around, and finally returned to barracks, meeting, on my way back, several pairs of very pretty girls (I've said before that I don't care for the ladies; but it sounds well to comment on beauty, even if you don't know one face from the other); and I arrived just in time to get ready for mess, where I discovered that Feversham had not yet returned, and that Flower had recovered his wonted good humor.

CHAPTER II.

A RENCONTRE.

Of course they were all down on me the minute I came in, wanting to know what I had seen and done. I had not much to tell them, as you know; they had found out my friend John Hampden before me, but not the feet. No; to my great gratification, Mayleigh was obliged to own he had failed in all his endeavors to unearth the possessor of that captivating pair of understandings.

And Feversham did not come home till late—not that it mattered much, for I knew I must make up my mind to wait some time before I

could see my *ruse* crowned with success. Therefore I was not impatient, when Claude returned in
the highest possible spirits, and evidently greatly
amused with his day's sport, though all that he
had caught, as far as we could see, was one wretched trout, about two inches long.

We used to mess at half-past six, and it was
long after that when Feversham returned. We
were able to question him about his day's adventures, as we sat over our wine afterward. Then
his well-pleased air attracted attention, and Mayleigh asked, in his usual inquisitive manner,

"What's up, Captain? You look as pleased
as if you had discovered a gold mine."

"So I have," answered Feversham, with his
quiet smile, as he passed the decanter before him.
"At least, if it is not a gold mine, it is a mine of
amusement well worth its weight in gold, in this
dull place."

"Tell us all about it," we cried in chorus.
"You would not keep such a treasure-trove to
yourself."

"You will find it out, my good fellows, in
time, even if I tried to keep it ever so dark. It
is not a light that will allow itself to be kept under a bushel, I can assure you." He paused for
a moment, and looked round on our attentive
faces, with an amused glitter in his dark eyes;
then he went on: "You know when I went to
Lough Glenty this morning, I had no permission
to fish there, which I suppose I ought to have
had; however, they told me here in town it belonged to General Bambridge, and that he was
not very particular about preserving it. The day
was too bright for doing much, but I got out my
tackle, set it to rights, and then amused myself
admiring the scenery, which is really magnificent.
The lake is long and narrow, lying in the centre
of a valley, shut in between such steep mountains
that a great part of their height is sheer precipice,
while the lower slopes, though steep enough too,
are clothed with woods that just now are bright
with the young summer green, and scented with
thousands of flowers. Mountain torrents dash
over the frowning cliffs that overhang the woods,
looking like silver streamers, waving in dazzling
white against the cold gray limestone, and losing
themselves in the woods at the base, through which
they glide with a low drowsy murmur into the
lake. Oh! if I was a painter, I could find subjects enough even in that narrow valley to gain
me a name; and as I am, having none of the artist faculty, I made more use of my eyes, watching
the mountain-tops, than looking for the likeliest
hole for fish, or gazing in hopes of a bite as I
made a cast. So absorbed, I heard no one approach me—indeed it almost seemed to me as if
there was no living thing within miles but the
lark singing gayly far up in the blue heavens.
Suddenly a soft voice, with a very merry ring in
it, exclaimed close to my ear,

"'Now I wonder who gave you leave to fish
here, sir? Have you permission?'

"I turned round with a start, for I felt rather guilty when so questioned; besides I was really taken by surprise. Standing before me was a
tall, elegant-looking girl. Her bearing and carriage were most graceful, and I can tell you her
face was to match. Not perhaps strictly beautiful, but sparkling—yes, that is the term to apply
to it; with large, liquid, dark-blue eyes, pale,
clear complexion, and wide, smiling mouth, dis-

playing a most perfect set of teeth. She was
dressed in simple, serviceable attire, well suited
to the country and to the pursuit in which she
seemed to be engaged; yet with an indescribable
air of taste and fashion in every fold of her neat
get-up. In one hand she carried a light driving-
whip, and standing a little way off on the high-
road was the vehicle she had been charioteering
when attracted by my poaching appearance.

"'Come,' she continued, flourishing her whip,
'you must get out of this at once. Do you hear?
My father does not allow poaching in these waters. And sorry as I am to disturb you from
quarters that seem to suit you so exactly, I yet
must beg you will retreat, without compelling me
to take any more energetic steps in the matter.'

"She drew the lash of the whip through her
hand while speaking, in a manner that seemed
to intimate she could use it, if necessity occurred, and a kind of suppressed merriment glittered in her eyes as she made this threatening gesture."

"Well, that is a queer adventure!" burst in
Flower, his mouth wide open in intense astonishment, and his whole expression what the French
call *ébahi*. "Are all the young ladies in the
country like this specimen, I wonder? If they
are, a fellow will have to be cautious how often
he dances with them, and be very sure of his
ground before he ventures to ask for a flower."

"Which will cut at the root of your little
amusements, Baby," went on Claude. "Yes, I
advise you to be careful, especially with Miss
Bambridge, for, by Jove! she is dangerous in
more ways than that one. However, I rose to
go as I was told, and was in the act of winding
up my line, when the young lady, who remained
standing by, as though determined to see the last
of me off the ground, again broke silence.

"'You are one of the officers just come with
"the army" to Belmurphy, are you not? You
are,' she went on, guessing my answer almost
before it was spoken. 'Very well, as you have
behaved properly, and done as you were told
without any demur, I will reward you in a way
I am sure you'll like. Come home to lunch with
us. I will introduce you to my father, who I am
sure will be most happy to give you the permission I denied you, and you shall see my mother,
and Clarissa too. Take care of yourself, however
—Clary's dangerous.'

"An invitation such as this, and given in so
curious and off-hand a manner, I could do no
less than accept. A minute or two more, therefore, saw us beside the vehicle, which turned out
to be a mail-phaeton, drawn by two fine-looking
horses, that I soon saw required plenty of driving, which indeed they got at the hands of my
new acquaintance.

"I found them a pleasant family: General
Bambridge, very fond of field-sports; indeed I
may say the same of Mrs. Bambridge, who is a
mighty fisher, and, I fancy, generally has the best-
filled basket at the end of a day's sport. The
dangerous Clarissa was a very pretty girl, with
the same odd, brusque, frank manner that distinguished her sister. Her prettiness, as regards
mere feature and beauty of coloring, was the
greatest, but she did not take me quite as much
as my first friend. Altogether they are an original family, very far removed from what one sees
generally, and all the more interesting on that ac-

count. We were very jolly, and had the merriest conversation, the most sparkling music, and the heartiest laughing I have enjoyed for some time. They hope to make acquaintance with all of you ere long, and I am sure you will be as charmed with them as I was."

Mayleigh laughed.

"Hard hit, Captain, eh? I didn't think you were the sort to go down so easily, though Madcap will maintain that you are susceptible. I shall begin to believe it now, however."

Claude laughed, and shook his head gayly, with an assumption of indifference that almost imposed on me."

"By Jove!" he went on, "you should have seen that girl's look and manner when she ordered me off!"

"I would rather you had met her than I," I broke in. "I should like to see any woman threaten to turn me off, *nolens volens*. I would let her know Vivian Darrell is not to be insulted with impunity. Claude, I had thought better of you than to imagine you would allow Her Majesty's uniform to be treated with contempt in your person, and all because the offender had dark blue eyes, a merry smile, a fine figure, and perhaps a heavy hand, forsooth. The last was what mastered you, I know. You did not care to have that stinging lash laid across your shoulders."

Claude cast a contemptuous glance at me, while I thought to myself, "Yes, it is all very fine, now you have the laugh on your side, but wait till to-night, and you will wish you had not annoyed me—that you had allowed the couchant lion to slumber in peace, in fact."

There was a pause, which Claude broke by saying,

"How are the horses after their journey, Madcap? Have you been down to see them lately?"

"I went to look at my own," I replied; "but I did not know whether you would care for me to inspect yours."

"I dare say you are right, and it was better to leave them alone," answered Feversham, with a smile. He was thinking of that time at home when I let out a young four-year-old of his; it took every man in the place six hours hard labor to catch the beggar again, but I assure you his escape was an accident. I would not have done so mischievous a thing on purpose on any account.

I can not sit up late, Claude says, because I am not done growing; though why that should make me so sleepy I can not understand. This night, even, when I would willingly have staid up, sleep overpowered me, and I was obliged to turn in long before the captain thought about such a thing. Never mind, I reflected, I shall hear all about it in the morning, and I dare say I shall come in for squalls, as I am quite sure it will be put down to me. Every thing is laid at my door—I am sure I don't know why.

Having settled matters thus in my mind, I was certainly considerably astonished at finding myself taken by the back of the neck, and coolly lifted on to the floor in the middle of the night, while the perpetrator of this outrage proceeded to take possession of my comfortable nest. I was so bewildered by sleep and surprise that I could only gasp out,

"I say, what is this for, my good fellow? and who are you, I should like to know? You will just walk off faster than you came, if you please,"

I went on, proceeding to try to roll out the intruder.

"I say, stop that!" shouted Claude Feversham's voice. "You know well why I am here, and all about it. Did you think you were going to make my cot a mess with your horrid gooseberries, and not catch something for it? I sat down on the bed before I knew they were there, so every thing is in an awful state, and I am going to sleep here for the night; you can take your own handiwork to sleep in. Good-night. I hope you will be wiser next time."

In vain I pulled at him, trying now and then to soften his hard heart by piteous entreaties that he would make a shake-down for himself on the sofa, and leave me my own quarters; he was not to be moved, and pretended to sleep soundly, though I know quite well he was shaking with laughter whenever my pleading was particularly earnest. At last there was nothing for it but that I should take the sofa myself, which I did, mentally registering a vow that my next trick on Feversham should be one which he could not turn against me quite so easily.

I dare say I looked a little foolish—I am sure I felt rather awkward, when next morning the captain told at breakfast every thing that had happened—all about my beautiful plot, how nicely it had been planned and executed, and finally its ignominious failure. How they all laughed, Flower in especial! I hope they may not get hold of the beginning of the story, all my difficulties about obtaining the fruit, etc.

That afternoon, as I went out for a walk, I met, coming up the hill to the barracks on horseback, Miss Bambridge and her father. The gentleman, no doubt, was going to call on us, but what the lady was up to I could not quite make out, unless, being exceptional in every thing, she had decided to inaugurate a fashion of ladies calling on the officers. Well, I will not be hard on her, for as I passed I heard her say,

"What a nice little boy, papa—so gentlemanly and good-looking! I wonder who he is!"

"Thanks for your good opinion!" I mentally exclaimed; "but you shall not think me a little boy very long. And she really is very handsome, this Miss Bambridge. I don't wonder at Claude's admiring her. It is such a gay, sweet face, not at all regularly beautiful, but twice as charming for that."

A most unconventional young lady surely, I thought, as, passing the barracks shortly after, I perceived her riding up and down the street, waiting for her father to come out; she did not seem in the least embarrassed as passers-by gazed curiously on her and her horse; indeed I thought I could perceive a saucy, half-triumphant expression in the smile which curved her lips as she looked nonchalantly around. However, I was amusing myself trying to find out the humors of the place, so I did not waste my time looking at her then, but passed on, mentally determined that before long we should be better acquainted.

I had not long to wait either; an hour or two later, as I was returning from a stroll along the country roads, whom should I see riding toward me but Miss Bambridge, and this time alone, her escort having, as I afterward learned, stopped in town for a game of billiards.

She was riding very slowly, and as I approached she pulled up, leaned toward me, and said,

"Look here, boy! Come round and tighten this strap for me; the saddle feels loose, somehow. See if you can girth it better."

I came round accordingly, and found that, as she said, the saddle was very loosely girthed, and I did not think it well put on either. I therefore offered to settle it as it should be, if she would dismount and allow me to arrange every thing properly.

No sooner said than done. Before I could get round to assist her, she had sprung lightly to the ground, and waited, holding the horse by the head while I set matters right. It was not an easy job for me either, as I dare say she saw, for nothing is more tiresome to any one unaccustomed to the work than girthing a side-saddle properly.

I knew how it ought to be done, however—thanks to the long visits Kate Merriton used to pay us at home, she being a first-rate horsewoman, and very particular about her equipments, on which subject she had given me many a lecture.

It was settled at last, and then came what to many men would have been the most anxious moment of all—namely, the mounting. I had graduated in that too, however—thanks to the same instructress; so when she drew back a little from my proffered assistance, fearing she was too heavy, and that it would be better to lead the horse up to a wall, from which she could seat herself on its back, I said,

"Have no fear. I assure you I can mount you quite easily."

Without any more demur, she placed a very neat foot in my hand, and, light as a bird, sprang to her seat.

"Are you fond of goodies, my little man?" she asked, as she settled herself and gathered up the reins. "I am sure you must be, so take that and get yourself something nice at the shop on the bridge. Many thanks for the trouble you have taken."

Before I could utter a word, she tossed me a shilling, and was off and away at a long, slinging trot.

As for me, I stood for a minute or two dumfounded, wondering what on earth I should do with her money, or whether I should leave it there for the next passer-by to pick up. Suddenly, however, an idea struck me, and acting on it, I took the shilling, tied it carefully in a corner of my handkerchief, and continued my walk home.

They say all men about my age are impressionable, but that they get over impressions easily. I do not know how that may be with others, but of this I am sure—it was not so with me. I was too light-hearted, too mischievous, had, as my comrades said, too much of the monkey in me, to be susceptible; and though at an age when most young fellows have had some fleeting experiences of the tender passion, I had never as yet cared to look round after the prettiest face or the neatest figure that had ever crossed my path in England's gayest assemblies.

Therefore, when, with a half-mischievous, half-tender idea in my head, I stooped to pick up Miss Bambridge's coin, it never occurred to me I was taking the first step along that road which every man follows at least once in his life. It would have made no difference, very likely, had I known; but thus in blissful ignorance of whith-

er I was tending—from the prospect of such a route I should have shrunk in alarm had I but understood, as one more experienced might—I stepped briskly back to town, murmuring merry snatches of song as I went, and drawing in the balmy summer air, with a keener enjoyment of its perfumed sweetness than when I left barracks that afternoon. I do not remember seeing any of our fellows when I came in; indeed I believe I went to my room, and occupied myself piercing a hole in the coin tossed to me by Miss Bambridge so short a time before. It did not take long to do, so that, by the time we assembled at mess, the precious piece of silver was suspended round my neck, and hanging near my heart, where I intended it should remain—at least until I knew the donor better, and got an opportunity of showing her to what use her present had been turned.

"What has happened to Madcap since he went out?" exclaimed Mayleigh, suddenly. "I have never known him silent for so long together, or seen him look so grave since he joined. What mischief are you concocting now, pretty one?"

If there is one thing I hate more than another, it is Mayleigh's odious, inquisitive way of asking people questions whenever he sees they have any thing on their minds. I was not in a mood to bear it now, so I answered,

"Stow that, Mayleigh, will you? You are always poking that sharp nose of yours into other people's business, and neglecting your own."

It was not a civil answer certainly, and I fancy if any other subaltern had so spoken to his senior officer, he would have caught fits for it; but, by common consent, they seemed to have agreed that I should be treated as a spoiled child, and so I gave them plenty of it. It will not do much longer, however—it is high time I should be treated as a man, and I shall insist on being so.

"We had visitors to-day," began Feversham, after a curious look at me, that seemed to say the child is more out of temper now than usual. "General Bambridge—Miss Bambridge waited outside. Did you see her, Mayleigh?"

"Rather," answered the lieutenant, dryly. "A proper flirt, I should say, to judge by the way she glanced about her, and the *empressé* reception she accorded you, Captain, when you went down with her father on leaving."

"Miss Bambridge is a lady, I am sure," I interrupted; "and I think you should refrain from saying any thing disparaging about her, Mayleigh, till you have some certain charge to bring against her."

"Whew!" whistled Mayleigh, in long-drawn intonation. "Is the wind in that quarter, eh? I did not know you were acquainted with the lady, or I would have spared her character, out of consideration for your feelings. By Jove! this is a queer thing! Madcap Darrell in love, and with a girl he has never even seen, as I believe."

"Have I not, then?" I asked, with my most impudent air. "I saw her to-day as she rode up, and I don't mind betting a pony I will cut all you fellows out in her favor, bar one, Claude here, who I think has made strong running with her already."

"By Jove! there is a plucky youngster," said

Flower. "However, I back Mayleigh to win, for I don't think young ladies are generally partial to boys only just out of the nursery."

"We shall see," I replied, quietly. "I don't want you to lose your money, Flower, but I fear you won't win mine. What do you say, Captain?"

"That you are more conceited, Madcap, than I gave you credit for. You count too much on the success you have always had among your mother's friends. But this is quite different, and you may not find yourself so much the spoiled darling of the boudoirs here as there."

"That is hard of you, Claude," I answered. "I see you have not forgiven me the gooseberries yet. But perhaps you may find me a rival some day, though I know at present you can carry all before you. 'That dear Captain Feversham,' I heard Miss Moneybagg say the other day. 'What beautiful eyes he has! Is it not a pity he's so taken up with flirting Miss Wildman. She will never have him. And it is very sad such a delightful man should break his heart about a girl like her.' By-the-bye, I have been intending ever since to ask if Miss Wildman did refuse you? Is it true, old fellow?"

Claude laughed his sly, quizzical smile, and answered slowly,

"It is unfeeling of you, Darrell, to bring up such a subject! A broken-hearted man can not bear his grief to be lightly spoken of."

"You look broken-hearted! I begin to think it was you who were the flirt, and poor Miss Wildman did not deserve all the blame she got. For shame, Claude! A male flirt is the most despicable of his kind, as I have often heard my aunt, Lady Tabitha, say."

"My dear fellow, don't distress yourself; it was a case of diamond cut diamond. Besides, we poor fellows are often forced to flirt in self-defense. Never fear; the young ladies are well able to take care of themselves; and I don't think any broken hearts among the other sex can —at least nowadays—be laid to our charge."

"I don't know that," I answered, more, I must confess, for the sake of contradiction than because I believed a word I was saying; "it seems to me, as far as I have yet studied the female character —and you know, not going in for ladies' society myself, I occupy the position of looker-on, and therefore see most of the game—it seems to me that women are not as susceptible as we are—do not give away their hearts at once and on the spot, charmed by some outward attraction; but when attention and devotion become marked, they gradually, with many doubts and fears, are drawn into the net from which few afterward escape. From the very gradual growth of their feelings arises, I think, the main cause of their constancy. Love, slowly ripened and brought to perfection, stands bravely against the storms and hardships of life, while that which is sudden and fierce, as that of most men is, fades away quickly, and wears out and changes while yet young."

"Well done, youngster!" cried Mayleigh, his wicked eyes sparkling with a satirical meaning that made his ugly face still uglier. "What a devoted squire of dames you will be! You see, my ideas on the subject are not so exalted. I agree with Feversham—the pretty creatures are as well able to take care of themselves as we are —yes, and a precious sight better too. As for this Miss Bambridge, take my word for it, Captain, she is dangerous; let me advise you to keep cool and wary when near her, or you will be brought to book before long."

"Thanks, Mayleigh; I think I can take care of myself. I forgot to tell you, they asked us all to go over there to-morrow, for a little croquet. I said we would go. And now let us take a stroll before it gets dark: this soft twilight is so inviting."

CHAPTER III.

THE CROQUET PARTY.

A LOVELY day was the next; not that glaring, overbearing sun that parches up every thing and makes all exertion impossible, but a soft, gray day, with glimpses of the sunlight lying on the mountain-tops here and there, and a breeze just enough to lift the hair off heated foreheads, and fan the heightened color in fair cheeks refreshingly.

We went to General Bambridge's place—Endley, of course—and found no one but ourselves had been asked.

"A little quiet croquet, just to make acquaintance and learn to know each other," explained Miss Bambridge. "A large party is so stiff, and we should never have become more intimate if you had been lost among a crowd." Just then her eye fell upon me. She blushed a little, with a charming expression of the faintest possible shade of embarrassment, mingled with a great deal of amusement, as she held out her hand, saying, "What! are you here? I did not know you belonged to the barracks." Then, in a low tone, she continued, "Forgive me my rudeness last night; I did not mean any impertinence, being quite in the dark as to who you were."

Feversham and the others would have given their eyes to know what was the meaning of this aside, but I merely smiled at them with my most important air, and stepped back as Miss Bambridge turned to speak to the others.

"Well, little boy, who are you?" asked Miss Clarissa, stopping in front of me, and giving me, for the first time, an opportunity of inspecting her. "You look lost, all alone," she went on, good-naturedly; "come over to the window and tell me all about yourself. You are one of Captain Ussher's children, an't you?"

"You are mistaken, Miss Bambridge," I replied; "I am an officer in this regiment. My name is Darrell, and I am a cousin of Feversham's. That is about all I know of myself. You, I presume, are Miss Bambridge — Clarissa — whom your sister stigmatized as dangerous to Captain Feversham."

"Did she?" laughed the girl, merrily. "Well, and which do you consider the most dangerous of the two? I fancy Gwendoline's fascinations are the most potent, to judge by your captain's face at this moment. Do you think I could cut her out if I made strong running?"

She asked this question so gayly, with so much carelessness and merry indifference to whatever the answer might be, that, though not a little astonished at such a conversation on first acquaintance, I entered into the spirit of it at once, and replied, "If I were to judge his heart from my own, I should say all other visions would be chased from his mind by the one now present before me; but as I fear, if he were attainable, I should be cast aside, I pray sincerely he may find your sister's attractions the most fatal of the two."

"Well done, Mr. Darrell," she laughed, tossing her head gayly. "Look now at that ugly little man talking to my mother. Who is he? Mayleigh, did you say? Isn't he like a ferret? I would not care to be a rabbit near him; and see, he does not half like our chatting together here; he is your senior, I suppose, and thinks he ought to be taken more notice of. Then the other young man, who is looking as if he wished papa in Jericho, in order that he might come and join us. Who is he?"

"Oh! that is Flower; he is just above me, and a good fellow enough, but soft. If it was not for me, he would be terribly put upon."

She smiled, and looked at me all over as she answered, "Well, you do look sharp enough. See, we are going now out to the garden. You like fruit, don't you? I do; so come along."

I followed her as desired, and in a few minutes we were scattered all over the garden, deep in strawberries, and hiding behind gooseberry-trees, gradually separating from each other, till at last I found Miss Bambridge beside me, and Clarissa nowhere to be seen.

"Oh! Mr. Darrell," she said, "how ashamed I am of offering you money yesterday; you must have been rather amused. But I hope you got the goodies, as I told you?"

"I am ashamed to say I did not," I replied; "but would you like to see what I have done with the money? Mind, I would show it to none but you."

"Yes, do let me see," she cried, eagerly. "I was so taken aback when I saw you to-day, but as you are not offended, it does not matter."

"Here it is," I went on, slowing drawing the precious coin from its hiding-place. "I shall wear it against my heart by night and day, while life lasts; and if ever I part with it, I shall no longer be the Vivian Darrell who stood by the roadside looking after you, as you rode away through the soft summer evening."

"You foolish boy," she laughed, seeing by my manner that, solemn as were the words, the affair was a mere jest, "I hope it may prove a talisman to you, and keep you out of danger; turn away bullets from that susceptible heart in battle, and otherwise reward you for your constancy. But, child, you are too young to be romantic: do let me lecture you a little, and do not be angry with what I say. I do not like to see so young a boy talking sentiment—it is out of place, and makes him look ridiculous. I like you, and think it is a pity you should spoil yourself in that way, so take my advice and drop it."

I sulked, or at least would have done so had I thought such a performance manly, and answered, "I am not so young as you think; ask any of our fellows, and they will tell you I am twenty; so I do think I may be as romantic as I have a mind to be. Besides, you know, temptations may be too strong," and I put as much meaning into my glance at her and Miss Clarissa, who just then appeared near us, as I could. She laughed, and shook her head. "Is it possible you are twenty? Then I forgive you; I took you to be between fourteen and fifteen. I am

sorry too, for I can hardly talk in so motherly a strain to one as old as myself."

"Oh, but pray do!" I begged, eagerly. "That need make no difference, and I like being lectured by you; it makes me feel so good—just as if I was a cat, and you stroked my fur the right way."

"Poor pussy!" she said, making a motion with her hand as though she was caressing the animal in question; "does it like it? Then it shall have it sometimes, when it is good. And now let us join the others."

We did join the others, as Miss Bambridge suggested, and again she paired off with the captain, leaving me to the tender mercies of Miss Clarissa. What fun we had that bright summer-day as we walked together to the croquet-ground, and afterward sat about in groups on the short soft turf, chaffing, talking nonsense, pelting each other with balls of daisies, and, in fact, doing every thing in the world but the thing to do which we had been invited to Endley.

No one so much as looked toward the croquet tools, while Miss Clarissa sat enthroned on an old moss-grown stump, like a queen surrounded by her court; at a little distance apart, Feversham and her sister appeared to lose all consciousness of our presence, in the charms of a very earnest flirtation.

What a girl Clarissa Bambridge was! I think I can see her now, and can hear her droll and sometimes very startling sallies, her merry peals of laughter, provoking a response even from innocent Flower, who, as a rule, was more addicted to sentiment than merriment.

How she cut up the oddities of the county notables and imitated their peculiarities!—not ill-naturedly, be it understood, but more, as it seemed, because her sense of the ludicrous was so strong she could not help noticing and remembering traits that would escape others less gifted with the dangerous power of satire. And how pretty she was! The color excitement and high spirits brought to her cheek was like the inside petals of a blush-rose, her long blue eyes were positively dazzling under their dark, curled lashes, her full red lips took the most charming forms as she uttered her daring sallies, while her slight girlish figure, in its simple white dress, was with every change of her attitude more perfect than before.

In spite of all this, however, and though my eye recognized the beauty of the picture-as a boy's eye beauty can recognize while his heart is untouched, my attention wandered incessantly to the pair seated under a wide-spreading beech; their faces were more serious than ours, though now and then a smile would light up the girl's gravity, till her sweet face seemed so ablaze with merriment I felt inclined to think the former soberness must have been assumed in deference to her companion, over whose quiet countenance no trace of amusement passed. I was not astonished at this, as I knew Feversham's turn of mind was almost always serious, when he could find any one to indulge him in that line. I could see plainly he fancied he had now found a kindred spirit, and was going into the affair over head and ears, as is the fashion of such grave, quiet natures.

It annoyed me a little, I must say, when I saw the case promised seriously. First of all, I knew his mother would be perfectly distracted at the mere thought of such a thing; and really I was aware myself it was not desirable he should marry an Irish girl, no matter how good or beautiful she might be, for what would all his friends in England say to such a thing?—and I, being his cousin, could not but feel with all his other relatives, and decide it would not do.

While I thought thus and watched them, they both rose and came toward us.

"How merry you are here!" cried Gwendoline. I was already calling her so in my mind. "I am perfectly bewildered philosophizing with Captain Feversham; finally he has propounded a question I can not solve without help, so I have brought it over here, in the hope that some of you will assist me. The case is this: suppose you had a friend in trouble of any kind; that you were acquainted with the wrong—if wrong there were—and were questioned about it; suppose that, in fact, it became necessary in any way—no matter how—that for the good of a friend you should deny the truth, would you do so? Captain Feversham says not; I said I would, if there was no other way. I dare say I might repent and be very sorry afterward, more particularly if the falsehood did not serve the end I desired; but still, if I saw a friend in dire distress, or with evil, though unknown to himself, impending over him, and knew that a bold and barefaced lie— there is no other name for it," she apologized— "from me would save him, I think I should tell it."

"So would not I," broke in Miss Clarissa, gayly. "My friend ought to be able to face and fight his difficulties himself; and if the thing was discovered, what a nasty mess it would get one into, and what a lot of mischief it would do one in the eyes of the world! No; truth pays best, and though I might be sorry for the unlucky individual, I could not help him at that price."

Feversham smiled.

"My reasons for refusing the lie are quite different from yours, Miss Clarissa. It is because truth ennobles and purifies a man, falsehood debases and degrades him, that I would avoid it. I would refuse to speak what I knew that might injure my friend; I would serve him in any other way, even to the death, but I could not tell a falsehood for him: it would leave a stain on my conscience, that, even though unknown to all the world, would be a constant reproach to me before other men. Besides, a falsehood can not stand alone; it draws others around it, till their name becomes legion. If you did it once, you must either acknowledge your sin afterward, or go on adding to it day by day, till all that once was upright in your character had become obscured by the foul sin."

He looked very noble standing there, with his head up, and his eyes fixed on the distant hills, as he preached his stern moral code; and I could see by a side-glance that Gwendoline Bambridge turned her head, and seemed ashamed of the sentiments she had avowed, while an unconvinced expression still lingered round her mouth. It was as though she said mentally, "I am sorry I let them know my opinion; but if the case arose, I should do it all the same."

Flower and Mayleigh listened silently to the discussion, but evinced no desire to speak; so, after waiting a minute, I broke in:

"You take a very high tone, Claude, and no doubt you are right—for one, at least, who can put a restraint on his feelings strong enough to see trouble come on a beloved head, which he might have averted by the sacrifice of his moral purity in some slight way. To me the end would justify the means, and not only that, but if driven by circumstances to such a resource, I would stand by it—that is to say, if by so acting I could achieve the welfare of one dear to me."

"Pshaw! You don't know what you are talking of, Madcap," answered Feversham, rather angrily. "I should be sorry to think those were really your ideas on the subject. In a man a keen sense of honor is all-important, and once admit that what is untrue can be right in one place, there is no reason why it should not be correct in all."

"No," broke in Miss Bambridge, "I think you wrong both him and me, Captain Feversham. One could not do it for one's self; that would be cowardice, and therefore even more degrading than the breach of truth by itself would be. But for the sake of one who had been true to you, and whom you had loved and believed in, it would be possible. However, it is no good talking over a hypothetical case; only I agree with Mr. Darrell, and could even see a certain nobility in such conduct in a good cause. Let us have some music; Clary and all of you join in the chorus."

Soon we were gay again, but I could see Feversham was startled and uneasy, keeping more apart from us than before, and indulging no longer in têtes-à-tête with Miss Bambridge. I was very glad of this, for she took me up, and we chatted away as merrily as though we had known each other for years. There was a great deal of similarity between her and her sister, not only in manner, but in style of thought and bias of mind, only I could see that where Clarissa was satirical and inclined to be severe, Gwendoline was pitiful, passing over failings in silence, or making allowance for them. She had the most heart, Miss Clarissa the most cleverness.

It was very pleasant wandering by the lake alone with her, while the others followed lazily, their bursts of laughter pealing down to us on the evening breeze, and her low voice talking with the unrestrained confidence of friendship on every topic we lighted upon.

It may seem strange to you that I, Madcap Darrell, should have cared for this kind of thing; to tell the truth, even while I listened to her voice, and followed her ideas with wrapt attention, I wondered now and then, with a curious feeling of anxiety, why I did not find it slow. If Kate Merriton were to see me now, how she would laugh, I thought; but Kate is a goose, not worth a sensible man's attention, and I really do feel like a man to-night.

So I listened and talked in my turn, sometimes nonsense, sometimes sense. At length she asked me, "Is Lord Feversham generally liked? His ideas are noble, but a little severe at times. Do his brother officers care for him?"

"There is not a better fellow going than Feversham," I answered; "he is the jolliest, kindest-hearted, most forgiving man in the world. We all delight in him, for he is up to every thing; riding, driving, shooting—winning the men's hearts that way, for no one thinks of being jealous of him, he is so unassuming; as to the ladies, they all adore him: his dancing is perfection, I am told, and besides, I do not think he objects to a quiet flirtation. You took him on his sternest side to-day, but don't think the worse of him for that. He is a true friend, and, in spite of his talk, I think it would go hardly with him to keep up to his standard in such a case as you described."

"You don't seem a bad friend yourself," she smiled, looking at me approvingly. "He is your cousin," she went on. "Are you fond of him?"

"Rather," I answered. "I would not go into any other regiment than this, because I wished to be with him. He has such a jolly place near ours; you should see it; such trees, such a river for trout, and no end of deer and things of that kind, such as ladies like. I don't like it as well as Longhurst—that is our place—but it is the next best in the county; indeed I don't think there are many such places in England."

She pumped me pretty well, as I must have known, had I not been too much pleased and flattered by the attention she was paying me to think of any thing else; but let me do her the justice to say I don't think it was with any mercenary view she cross-questioned me; rather, I think, it was that her fancy was already attracted by my handsome cousin, and she naturally interested herself in all concerning him. Of course it was pleasant to hear he was a rich man, and owner of a fine place, but the mischief was done before then, and she gave ample proof, in time, of disinterestedness such as I think few women would exhibit.

I see this all now plainly—then I did not, but thought she liked me at least quite as much as she did him, so that by the time I left that night, I was in a kind of delicious dream, not seeing before me the certain shipwreck of all my hopes, which would have been apparent to any of my comrades, had they but known my thoughts. Yet I was not in love, or at least did not know that I was; all that I understood and felt was that she, a bright, clever, intelligent girl, one whom I knew to be courted and sought after in society, had talked to me, and listened to me, as though I was the equal in mind and experience of the men who flocked around her. She had accepted my decision of a vexed question, as one that appeared to her right and just; she had talked confidentially of their life in the country, had confided to me her opinions on numberless subjects—some grave, some gay; in fact she had treated me as a friend, suited to her in mind and habit of thought, till I felt the ladies' society had a charm of which formerly I had been ignorant, and that the loveliest, wittiest, most captivating woman I had ever met was Gwendoline Bambridge. I felt that any thing she commanded me I could perform, and that to win her approval and commendation there was nothing I could not attempt. I was very silent during our drive home, hardly hearing the conversation around me, though the others were criticising our late entertainers, and praising the grace and beauty of the young ladies, with an enthusiasm that I must have agreed in, had I listened; though probably I should not have cared to hear them so freely discussed. Feversham, too, was very quiet, putting in a word now and then, generally by way of silencing Mayleigh's biting re-

marks, but otherwise seeming to be buried in his own thoughts.

"How quiet Madcap is!" cried Mayleigh at length, when, stopped in some ill-natured speech, he sought a fresh object to torment. "Has he fallen head over ears in love with the fair Gwendoline, or have his calf's brains been stolen by the bewitching Clarissa? Poor fellow! What will Lord and Lady Traverscourt say, when they hear the hope of the family is hopelessly in love with a fast Irish siren? Which is it, Darrell?"

"Come, Mayleigh," I answered, with a strange feeling of firmness rising in my breast, "I don't care what you say about me, or how disagreeable you make yourself—it is natural to you, and you can't help it; but I won't have you say any thing nasty of the Misses Bambridge. If they are merry, they are lady-like, and have in no way laid themselves under the lash of your censorious tongue."

"Bravo! young one," cried Feversham. "I did not know you could speak like that. I declare you are getting quite a man. Your mother won't know you when you go home again."

I smiled, but did not answer. It was pleasant to hear that even Feversham recognized the change from a boy to man that I felt within myself. I could not help wondering what had caused it, and if he knew; but a secret jealousy of any prying eye discovering what was hidden from myself restrained me from asking his experience to come to my assistance.

Altogether it had been one of the pleasantest days of my life, and I had jumped off the car at the barracks with a feeling of regret that it was so soon over—regret, however, that did not prevent my locking Mayleigh's room on the outside, and then pushing the key under the door on my way up stairs—a feat which kept that gentleman in a white-heat for half an hour, and called forth sundry unseemly execrations; he had not the least idea how it had happened, as I managed the matter during the two minutes he stopped below talking to the driver, while I dashed up stairs two steps at a time, and was in my own room, and half into my smoking costume, before he found out what had happened.

After this we made acquaintance with no end of county notabilities—went to balls, picnics, croquet parties, every kind of device for making country life pass gayly; and wherever we went we met the Bambridges. Besides, we were at their own place very often, and the more we saw of them the greater grew our infatuation. Gwendoline and Claude had become fast friends—not that she ever neglected me either; her greeting was just as hearty and cordial to me as to him. Had it not been so, I should hardly have dared to build the castles in the air that now occupied all my thoughts, for I could not even think of any person or any thing but of her alone. For her, and to be worthy of the favor I thought she bestowed on me, I cast the boy as much away from me as possible, and strove in all things to think and act not only as a man, but as the man should think and act who could hope to win her. My very nature seemed changed—all the volatile impulsiveness and feverish energy of my character turned to a deep, passionate devotion that centred itself on her, and made all other things subservient to her. I cared nothing that Mayleigh and Flower laughed and said, "The young one is desperately hard hit." I did not even pay any attention to the fact that Feversham was striving for the same prize. I knew it was so, but I thought I had as good a chance as he, and I felt as though I could do battle with a brother even in such a cause. Sometimes indeed my hopes would fail me, as I saw her dark eyes turned to Claude's handsome, manly face, and watched, with hate and jealousy gnawing at my heart, their lengthened converse; then my hopes would spring up at a bound as, with a ringing laugh and a merry gesture, she would turn toward me and say, "Vivian, come and help me to overwhelm your cousin. He talks dreadful nonsense sometimes, and must be put down."

Then she would tease him, and pet me, till his brow would grow dark and angry, and he would walk away, saying sulkily,

"That young scape-grace will get into trouble some day; he talks too much about what he doesn't understand."

Did she know what she was doing, that dark-eyed, sweet-faced girl? Did she know she was waking a passionate man's heart a world too soon in a young, careless breast? Did she know she was sowing distrust and strife between hearts once fondly united? Did she know that the course she was pursuing must end in disappointed hopes and a blighted life, to one at least of those striving for her favor?

Hard questions these to answer, and perhaps the truest solution of them would be that she never thought about them at all, or rather that the boy's devotion seemed to her an absurd and fleeting passion, that would pass away at the sight of the next pretty face, and transfer itself to a new object. In the mean time he was pleasant and lively, and saw no light in earth or heaven but the brilliance of her eyes. She was flattered, amused too; so she encouraged him, and only noticed the look of pain that would cross his face as she talked to his rival, to soothe it away with a fresh dose of captivation, never considering the day must come when the pain would be permanent, the relief beyond her power to administer. Only Miss Clarissa seemed to pity me sometimes. She would draw me away when she saw me watching, with angry, glowering looks, Feversham and her sister chatting confidentially on the seat under the beech-tree, and, calling me after her, would wander off, wasting her wittiest sallies, and indulging in her most daring satires, in the vain hope of calling up a similar spirit in me.

She was very good to me, though I had before said she had no heart. Now I began to think she must have one, and a pitiful heart too, else why did she take so much pains to rally me from my idle dream? All her efforts were vain, however, and she saw they were so. Therefore, one day, as we roamed along by the shore of the lake, Gwendoline and Claude in front, she said,

"Lord Feversham seems to admire Gwen. Don't you think so?"

I was taken by surprise at her putting the question so boldly, though the fact was apparent enough. I stammered and hesitated before replying, then answered,

"Yes, he does admire her. How could he help it? She is very charming!"

I tried to speak calmly, but blushed as only a boy can blush, when speaking of the one dear to his heart for the first time. She glanced at me, and took in all my confusion and my secret, though that, no doubt, she knew well before.

"I think he likes her," she went on, "and I think Gwen likes him—at least as well as any man she knows. I would not care to be a candidate for her hand under the circumstances. He is too dangerous a rival. Don't you think so, Vivian?"

"No," I answered, with my blood up, for I thought I caught a look thrown back to me from the subject of our conversation. "He would indeed be a poor-spirited hound who would give up the chase because the struggle was severe, and the antagonist formidable. All the more honor to the one who wins. It is hard for the vanquished too," I muttered, not thinking, however, even then, that would be my lot.

"You understand, of course," Clarissa continued, "our conversation is quite private. Gwen would never forgive me if she thought I had presumed to guess her feelings."

"You may trust me," I answered, thinking, with satisfaction, "it is but a guess, after all, and one she would not like her sister to know." Then the pair in front turned and joined us, I being at once raised to the highest pitch of hope and happiness by the bright looks and pleasant words of her I loved so dearly.

Yet all this while I never acknowledged to myself that I was in love. I was almost too much of a boy still, lived too entirely in the present to form any schemes for the future, or to think of how all this must end; that some day we would be ordered off, and then all our pleasant intercourse would cease, unless— But I never went as far as that in my day-dreams, or surely my eyes would have been opened.

Sometimes, when a jealous pain rose in my heart, as I watched Claude's attentions and the looks with which they were received, I questioned myself for a minute or two as to what this might mean. Why should she not be pleased at his evident admiration? She smiled equally on me. "Yes," I answered myself; "but I fear she likes him best. If I was only sure her friendship for me was the greater, I would be content."

Foolish boy that I was, cheating myself with the word friendship, and talking of content. What man in love, ay, or boy either, for that matter, was ever satisfied with any thing less than full and absolute possession of his idol? And I was not more wise, or less ardent, than others; only my heart was yet untried, and I was ignorant of its depths.

I can see now, looking back through a vista of years, how foolish and absurd this infatuation of mine must have appeared to dispassionate lookers-on; how intensely aggravating it must have been to my cousin, who, loving her with the love a man should have for the woman he wishes to make his wife, found himself perpetually thwarted and interrupted in his progress in her friendship by a lad of my age; who, however intensely devoted, could not, to the eyes of calm common sense, hope to succeed. But common sense is rarely an attribute cultivated by lovers; and while I refused to see that my pursuit was ridiculous, he was equally unable to comfort himself by knowing that it was so; and many a smothered malediction was showered on my head in consequence.

For all this, and though I thought myself so much of a man, and tried to persuade myself I had left all my school-boy pranks behind me, Flower and Mayleigh often aggravated me with their chaff till I was driven to make reprisals; and then it was amusing to hear them growling and saying, "That young monkey had been at his pranks again," and they wished "Miss Bambridge would teach him better manners."

The mention of that name always sobered me, and I would be profoundly sorry I had been led into any escapade that could give those fellows an excuse for mentioning her, or talking in their light, joking fashion of her influence over me.

Claude saw, as well as the rest, all that was passing within me. I was inexperienced, and had little worldly wisdom. I could not for my life hide my rapture when she called me to her side, or conceal my jealousy and mortification when my captain ousted me; but I think that Feversham, even had he not been my rival, would still have tried to keep me from pursuing this will-o'-the-wisp of my imagination.

He knew no more than I did, I really believe, which of us two she liked best; and he was savagely jealous, with a man's cruel, vindictive jealousy; but he knew also better than any one except myself how young I was, and that, desire it as I might, it would be impossible for me to marry before I came of age. Therefore it seemed to him certain that I stood in his light without any advantage to myself; and one sunny afternoon, meeting me out walking, we both being alone, he turned to accompany me, and began:

"Vivian," he said—and his voice was harsh and stern, as it never used to be in the old days—"when are you going to cease this folly? Dogging Miss Bambridge like her shadow, spending day after day at their house, and never inquiring whether your presence there is welcome or otherwise. I gave you credit for more good sense, thinking that though you are still but a school-boy, yet that you had plenty of the keen Traverscourt wit to show you when you were making a fool of yourself. And remember, though Miss Bambridge may amuse herself with you, you are far too young for her ever to think of you in any other light than as a pleasant pastime for idle hours."

I felt my face glow all over at this speech, reminding me so scornfully of what I felt to be the greatest drawback in my way, and answered hotly,

"I won't ask if Miss Bambridge is your authority for speaking to me in this way. I know she is pleased to see me every day, and at all hours. As to sense, in what particular is mine worse than yours? If it is wise and right you should admire her, why should it be folly in me to do so? She and I are about the same age, and have, therefore, many ideas and pleasures in common, and I might as well, and perhaps with quite as much truth, advise you to beware of wearying her. Until I hear from her own lips that my society is irksome to her, I shall continue my visits there. That is my answer, Feversham. You can act as you choose."

"Thanks for the permission," he replied, haughtily; "but remember, my fine young fellow, I have been letting you off duty since we have been here—have been indulging you in every way, in fact: that is over now. To-morrow is your day in barracks, and we are going to dine at the Bambridges'."

So saying, with a malicious smile he walked off, leaving me overwhelmed at the intelligence. I should have to stay at home on duty, and he would make as much running as he liked with Gwendoline. The thought made my blood rush wildly through my veins; and I determined, come what might, it should not be as he had planned.

But how to prevent it?—that was the rub; and I walked on thoughtfully mile after mile, turning the matter over in my mind, and trying to arrive at a solution of the difficulty. At last a plan shaped itself in my brain. I will not say it was a good one—indeed, if carried into execution, it would entirely rest with my commanding officer whether I should get into great trouble about it or not. But I was wild and reckless; it seemed to me a little matter, losing my commission in exchange for one short evening in her society; and besides, a profession was nothing to me. I, Vivian Darrell, would be wealthier than most of the men around me, and have as good a position, whether I left the army or not. So I made up my mind, and returned to barracks with a defiant, desperate feeling in my heart, and a dash of insolence in my manner whenever I was obliged to address my cousin.

This, however, he would not notice. To do him justice, he was never harsh; and it must have been a wild spasm of jealousy indeed that induced him to act so unkindly by me in this instance.

Next day I was on duty, as Claude had told me I should be. I moped about the barracks, looked as wretched as I could, and otherwise tried to conceal the daring defiance that really reigned in my breast.

So the day wore on till about five o'clock. I knew the car for the others was not ordered until six, but I wished to get a start of them before they returned from their walk. I dressed, therefore, and, slipping a top-coat over all, walked quietly off in the direction of Endley by a back road. I had told a car to be in waiting for me about a mile out of town; but, not wishing to arrive too early at my destination, I had ordered it for six o'clock. I had about half an hour to wait, therefore, when I arrived at the appointed place; but the evening was fine and warm, so I sat down by the roadside to rest, the quiet beauty of the scenery soothing the tumult of angry feelings in my breast.

Every thing went right; the car came at the appointed time, and I arrived at Endley about a quarter of an hour before the others.

"Why have you come alone?" questioned both the sisters in one breath; "where are the others?"

"They are coming after," I answered, with a laugh. "I could not wait any longer; it seems such an age since I have seen you."

"The day before yesterday was the last time we met," laughed Gwendoline; "it is an age, as you say. Why did you not ride over yesterday?"

"I feared to intrude by coming so often," I stammered, but led to speak freely by her manner. "If I thought you wished it I should have been only too happy to come."

"You are always welcome," she replied, with her soft smile. "I'll tell you when I'm tired of you, if that will satisfy you."

"Only I should die if you were to tell me so," I answered, in a low, trembling voice, as I seated myself beside her.

I had never dared to say as much to her before, and now my agitation said a thousand things I could never have found words to utter. I had glanced at her face to see how she took it. She blushed, and there was a slight expression of surprise in her eyes that seemed to say, "You are coming on very fast;" but she answered,

"If you wait for death till then, rest assured you will live to a ripe old age. Ah! here are the others." And rising, she went forward to meet them.

I knew by Claude's expression that he had seen me the instant he entered the room, but he said nothing; and as the rest had always been allowed to go out—even when they were on duty—in our quiet country quarters, they thought my presence there was all right.

After dinner, however, and before we joined the ladies, Feversham took me by the arm and drew me toward the window, leaning out of it to cool his heated brow in the balmy summer twilight.

"Do you know, Vivian," he began gravely, "what you have done? Sometimes I wonder whether it is sheer folly gets you into so many scrapes. Do you know that, if I was to report this last escapade, you would be tried by court-martial for deliberate disobedience of orders?"

"I know it," I answered, with a sullen pride in the admission. "I know you can have me tried, if you please. I counted the cost before I did it. But you don't think I could have sat quietly in barracks, knowing you were here? It was more than my blood could stand; but I am willing to bear any punishment."

Claude looked at me gravely in the dim twilight, and it seemed to me there was a tremor in his voice when at length he answered,

"I can't hurt you, Darrell, and you know it. You acted as I would have done myself; only I wish you had a little more confidence in me. When the time came round I thought the trial was too hard, and went to your room to give you permission to accompany me. You were gone then, however; I guessed whither, and I was right, as I saw at once on entering the drawing-room here. Only be careful, child. Many would not have forgiven such an act of insubordination; and, if any one else had known the state of the case, I should have been obliged to make an example of you. Don't do so again."

"You are too good to me, Claude," I cried, thoroughly overcome by his kindness, now that I was completely in his power. I had hardened myself to bear angry accusation, and threats of court-martial only too likely to be carried into execution, but this I had never expected, though it was like Claude, too, and like none but him. Firm as he could be when it was required, there was none who knew better when gentleness might be used; and kindness was more natural to him than severity. "I wish," I continued, passionately, "I could do something to please you—could make some sacrifice that would show how I feel your goodness; but the only sacrifice you would care for I can not make. It is stronger than I am. You must forgive me still, for, while hope remains, I will fight against you."

He smiled a little sadly as he replied, "So be it, then; but let it not breed a quarrel between us. Was there ever woman yet worth a breach between two hearts that had once known and valued each other?"

I interrupted him hotly.

"You do not know what love is if you ask its worth—it can not be bought or measured. It may prove delusive and false, but while it lasts, the glory, the beauty, the faith with which it surrounds the beloved object are worth more than all the world besides. You who count the cost leave her to me, who would do and dare all for her sake."

"This is the first blind, wild adoration of a fresh young heart," he answered. "What a pity that it can not last!—that as surely as the sun will rise to-morrow over the hill-tops the illusion must fade and pass away, never to return in all its first purity and force. Come, let us go to the ladies."

So we joined them, and passed a merry evening. Gwendoline was most impartial in her attentions; while Clarissa kept the others fully amused, she being quite equal to entertaining any number of people at once. What a pity such pleasant moments pass away so quickly. We bask as it were in the sun for a few short hours, and then begin again the strife and turmoil and bustle, the conflicting emotions that we call life.

CHAPTER IV.

COMING TO AN UNDERSTANDING.

The days passed on, and still the situation remained unaltered between Feversham and me, with the difference of a slight change in Miss Bambridge's manner toward us. She had been accustomed to be equally friendly, equally sociable, equally mirthful in her manner to both; but latterly there had been a change—a change that had excited my buoyant, sanguine nature to the highest pitch, and that aroused Feversham's deep, brooding jealousy more frequently than ever. And the change was this—she avoided him sometimes pointedly, she seemed occasionally ill at ease in his presence, and anxious to escape those têtes-à-tête with him that had at first pleased her apparently so much.

But she never avoided me, she never seemed weary of my society; her eyes would meet mine with the frank, upward look that set all my young blood boiling with passionate adoration; and when she most shunned him, then more than ever she sought my society. She and her sister had both taken to calling me Vivian, without any special conversation on the subject, dropping into it in a casual way that flattered me immensely, and made me think it the prettiest name in the world, when I heard it uttered in their soft, musical accents. If I had been the man I had flattered myself I had become, I should perhaps have known better how to interpret these signs. I should not have been stirred by them into the wild, feverish exultation, the maddening belief in my eventual success, that took possession of me. Rather, if I had read them aright, might I have known that no woman, not even one so fearless and outspoken as Gwendoline Bambridge, would have shown so clearly her preference for the man she loved; and from all this lavishly bestowed favor I would have drawn the true conclusion, that she looked upon me as the boy I was in point of age, and fancied that this devotion of mine would be passing and transient, as boyish passions usually are.

But Feversham was as much deceived as I was —he was too cruelly in earnest to read the real meaning of her new-born shyness and timidity with him. At times still, when they were unavoidably thrown together, she was as kind and friendly and attentive to him as ever—more so even than she was to me, and he knew it. But then again she would shun him, and he would persuade himself either that she loved "the boy" best, or that a mischievous demon of coquetry had possession of her, stirring her up to torment him, and raise the mad devil of jealousy within him, that all his strong self-control could hardly master.

His manner to us both became capricious and variable: at times I know he hated me. I almost think he felt so to her also when deeply stung, but if he did the feeling was transient, and the next minute he would condemn himself savagely for having dared to think harshly of her. She, in her bright, happy ignorance of the wild storm of passion she had raised in two hearts once closely united by friendship, doubtless intended no evil, was not to be blamed for such if it arose; could not, in fact, be judged by the plain, clear laws of conduct, meant to govern people less charming, or more aware of their power. At times he would think leniently of my share in the matter, would acknowledge, perhaps, that I was not to blame for following this temptation, that had proved too strong for him; and then he would try to show his sorrow for former severity to me, by renewed kindness of look and manner, whenever we came across each other. Sometimes, if he had been fortunate, and she had greeted him with a return of their first friendly intimacy, he would brighten up into his own genial self, feel once more that such a mere lad as I could have no possible chance against him, and would even treat me with a kind of pitying manner, that I, blindly secure, allowed to pass without letting it ruffle my temper.

We were sitting over our wine after mess one evening. Claude was in his joyous temper; he had been out the whole day at Endley, and I had not been there. Consequently, as I told myself, Gwendoline had been able to give him her attention, and he was happy because it had been so. I was not uneasy or alarmed; I had told her the day before that I should not be able to see her that day, and she had said she should be sorry, that she should miss me: that was quite enough for me, and I could afford to laugh at my captain's triumph over me.

I am not much of a wine-drinker; of course I give my opinion if I hear wine spoken of, and, thanks to hearing people at Longhurst discussing the subject, I can say something very much to the point on most of the ordinary vintages one meets with in this country; and I think it makes a fellow appear more of a man of the world to know something about the matter. To say the truth, I don't care to support my opinions by drinking much of what I uphold, and so I generally have a good deal of spare time on my hands as we sit round the table of an evening. They do say in our mess that most of the broken wine-glasses at table are due to me, but this is a calumny; and I hope what I am about to relate will not be taken against me in the matter, as it was quite an exceptional occurrence, and not my fault besides. Indeed as you must have seen, the other fellows put all their scrapes down at my door, so that even in this little country town, where I have lived more quietly than I ever lived before, every one talks of Mr. Darrell as being the most unlucky young gent for getting into scrapes that ever was seen in the country. And that is all Mayleigh's fault, as I will show you presently.

The other fellows were talking all round the table, and passing the decanters now and then before me. I was not minding them; I was very busy trying to execute a trick I had seen Cavendish and some other fellows of "ours" perform, and which I was always rather unfortunate over. The thing seemed simple enough, till one came to try it. It was only this: fill your glass, pile three or four wine-glasses on it, one on top of another, and then drink your wine without disturbing the balance and arrangement of your fragile column. As I have said, I had never succeeded well with this trick; but on this particular occasion a serene, triumphant feeling that possessed me seemed to have given an unusual steadiness to my hand, and I really believe I was about to do the trick, and insure to myself lasting satisfaction from the consciousness of possessing so much skill, when a fragment of biscuit well aimed, and thrown hard, hit the topmost glass, and the next minute my elaborately reared structure was strewed, a mass of fragments and splinters, over the table.

"Halloo! young one," cried Mayleigh's sneering voice—and I should have known by his voice, even had I not caught sight of his uplifted hand, that he was the delinquent—"four broken glasses; six times four is twenty-four; just two dozen glasses you owe our mess. It is a good thing for you you have plenty of money, or this kind of work would soon make a hole in your pocket."

"You ought to pay for them all, or at least half," I retorted, raising a rather flushed face, for I was angry. I had long set my heart on accomplishing this trick, and I am sure but for him I should have succeeded on that occasion. Since then I have never again been so much in the vein for that kind of thing. "I would not have broken one," I continued wrathfully, "but for you. Not that I mind the expense, or our good motto, 'Who breaks pays,' but that you are always mixing yourself up with other people's business or amusements, and I tell you I won't stand it much longer."

"Why, I thought you were too much of a man now, Madcap, to set your heart on tricks of that kind, or of course I would not have spoiled your little amusement," laughed Mayleigh. "And, besides, it was so jolly to see the glasses tumbling all down about your absorbed face."

"I don't care," I answered, rather more annoyed than mollified at this allusion to my manhood. You see, I looked at the trick as a trial of skill, and not at all as a childish amusement, and I was not inclined to have him poking fun at me, because I thought I saw Feversham laughing. "Look here, Captain," I continued, "don't you think Mayleigh bound to make good half those glasses?"

I knew Mayleigh was a screw, and would not laugh when he found he had to pay for his cock-shot.

"Well, really," said Feversham, laughing, "I suppose if you go into the right of it he is, since it was he, not you, broke them; but you looked so tempting a mark, I don't wonder he did not resist the temptation. Flower and Preston were in the act of raising their hands to have a go in at you, when his shot took effect; so you see he wasn't singular. But come, I have news for you that I received in a letter that arrived just before dinner. Attention, please, till I make the announcement. The authorities have discovered, or think they have discovered, that this is a very disturbed, unsettled neighborhood, and our head-quarters are to be moved down here. I heard this from Colonel Annesly, so you may be sure it is correct. How will you like that, my boys? No more shirking duty then, no outing for the officers of the day."

He looked with a smile at me as he spoke, and I answered, defiantly,

"No more unfortunate ensigns kept in out of their turns. All share their duties in proper routine then. Hurra! for Captain Annesly and head-quarters!"

"Confound head-quarters and Horse-Guards, say I, for sending them here," growled Flower and Preston. "A man won't be able to call his soul his own, once Annesly puts in an appearance. It will be drill, and marching, and pipe-clay, and drill again, etcetera, everlastingly. What has our regiment done, above all other regiments, to be afflicted with such a colonel?"

"I am sure," added Mayleigh, "Madcap here has done all he can to prevent our being thought a pattern corps, in any respect."

"Oh! never mind Annesly," said Feversham. "I admit he does keep one up to the collar when he is with us, but you know as well as I do he will be getting leave for the partridge shooting presently, and will leave us under Harvey, who is a jolly, easy-going fellow, as we all know."

This was a comforting view of the case, but it would have comforted me much more had I at all been able to fathom the meaning of my cousin's curious and unusual self-content. Content to him meant discontent and pain to me. Clearly he thought he had cause to be pleased with his day, and nothing but Gwendoline having shown him unusual favor would please him, I well knew. What was it that had happened? Long afterward, when Feversham was in trouble from other causes, and thought himself very secure with her, he confided to me what had happened, which I may as well repeat here, in the order in which it occurred; but I knew nothing of it, be it remembered, for some time, and therefore continued to consider myself favored, and my cousin as an unwelcome intruder in all our interviews.

That day, at Endley, Gwendoline, Clarissa, and Feversham had gone out for a walk after lunch. It was a very hot day in the beginning of July. Climbing the mountain was warm work, and presently, having arrived on the brink of a picturesque mountain stream, Gwendoline proposed that they should sit down, and defer the rest of the walk *ad infinitum*. Claude agreed willingly, but Clarissa, after a few minutes' pause, declared she must go on.

"You two lazy ones," she said, "can stop here; I want to find the green-stemmed fern that grows somewhere about, and shall hunt for it while you are resting."

Gwendoline, finding she was about to be left alone with Claude Feversham, tried to rise and follow her sister.

"Let us go on," she said. "I am also interested in the finding of that fern."

"Sit down," he answered, without attempting to stir. Gwendoline then perceived that a corner of the skirt of her dress was under his elbow, on which he was leaning, and he made no movement to allow her to withdraw it. She sat down almost frightened. Lord Feversham had been very odd lately, and she really felt a little alarmed about what he might be going to say, for it was evident he was going to say something. Was it possible he would rebuke her for allowing Vivian Darrell to make such a fool of himself about her? Well, if he was she could not help it, and, what was more, she did not think that Darrell would be easily shaken off, or made to keep aloof, unless she was really to be unkind to him, which she could not be.

"What has made you avoid me of late?" he asked, nervously plucking the long grasses that grew near. "You used to be good friends with me at first—now you never speak to me."

"I—I didn't mean to avoid you," she said, with hesitation; then an irresistible feeling compelled her to look at him, and their eyes met. Under the magic of that look she was impelled to correct herself and speak the truth, and she continued, with downcast eyes and a heightened color: "at least, if I did, it was not because I did not like you."

"Then it was because you did like me," he answered, in a tone of the fullest content, laying his hand for one minute on hers, and then rapidly withdrawing it. He saw she was frightened, uneasy, and he feared to say more just then, for fear of losing his cause from precipitation.

There was silence for a few minutes, Gwendoline looking down into the brown waters of the brook at her feet, apparently studying the outline of the stones, seen clearly through the transparent water, but in reality feeling in every nerve of her body the long, silent, passionate gaze of the man beside her, whose look seemed to pierce into her inmost soul, and there stir up strange feelings, half terror, half rapture, that were altogether new to her; of the possibility of experiencing which she had hitherto been unaware. It was like awakening into a new life; every sense seemed quickened to a tenfold power and keenness of appreciation; and yet she was as one in a mesmeric trance, unable to resist the will of the mesmerizer. When he spoke at last, in a low, murmuring voice of intense happiness, saying, "What a strange way you have of showing liking—I shall want you to try another plan in future," she felt as if no answer was possible to her but to turn and look once more into the handsome brown eyes, that were gazing so eagerly at her face.

There was a smile in those eyes as she met them, and she, though still frightened, feeling that she was just passing through a crisis in her life, could not restrain a faint, timid, answering smile, a mere ghost of the responsive feeling his look should have called up, but her heart was too full to open freely yet, even to him. She wanted to be alone a little with the happy, the joyful discovery she had just made, before she could disclose its full importance to him, even if he were to question her about it. Happily for her, she thought, he did not; he was inexpressibly contented and satisfied; for a while every longing of his heart was silent from pure happiness, and he lay back among the grass and ferns at her feet, gazing to his heart's content on her beautiful downcast face, and following with enraptured eye the graceful outlines of her perfect figure.

One beautiful hand rested among the ferns close to him. How he cursed, mentally, the well-fitting kid glove that concealed its beauties of shape and color. What were gloves made for? They were an outrage on good taste, and a mere profanation of nature. He wondered that Gwendoline Bambridge, superior as she was to the rest of her sex in every thing, stooped to obey the imperious decrees of fashion in such matters. One as beautiful and perfect as she could surely afford to set fashion at defiance, or lead a fashion of her own. He had not courage to ask her to remove her glove, and might have gazed at the pearl-gray covering with ungratified longing for the rest of the evening, had not a happy idea suddenly struck him. Close by grew a low-growing bush of the dog-rose, profusely covered with pinky-white blossoms. Reaching forward suddenly, he gathered two or three of the prettiest buds, and silently presented them to her. Equally silently she took them, thanking him with a hurried, timid look, that would have seemed to him much more delightful had it been more prolonged. Then he discovered that a thorn from one of those happy roses had penetrated his finger deeply, sinking below the surface, so that there was no hope that his unaided efforts could get it out.

"What is the matter?" asked Gwendoline, as he moaned a little over it, pretending to suffer severely from it.

"Only a thorn," he replied—"it has got in deep; but if you had a needle or pin, you might get it out for me. I assure you it smarts painfully."

"Let me see," she answered, "I have only the pin of my brooch; but if the operation is not a difficult one, I might manage to do what you want with that."

As she spoke she drew off her gloves, laid them beside her, and took out her brooch. The wounded finger was held out for inspection, was pitied duly, and after a little probing was pronounced to be an incomprehensible case.

"I don't think there is any thorn in it at all," said Gwendoline, after a careful investigation. "It seems to me there is the mark of a severe prick—a thorn ran in, and was pulled out again as you withdrew your hand — there is nothing there."

"Do you think so?" asked Feversham, anxiously, bending over to inspect the invalided member more closely, and thereby bringing their two heads into a close proximity, the effect of which was immensely amusing to Clarissa, who, perched on a rock higher up the mountain, was looking down with mischievous delight on the scene below. "I am sure it is still there," he continued discontentedly, as Gwendoline gave signs of being about to give up the search. "Do just look again," he pleaded.

Gwendoline complied, but again without discovering any thing. Suddenly looking up, she encountered his eyes fixed upon her—not with the expression of petulant pain he had before assumed, but brimful of a mirthful contentment which at once revealed to her that she was the victim of what Lord Feversham doubtless considered a pious fraud. Coloring a little, with a half-vexed, half-amused expression, she dropped his hand, saying,

"I don't believe there is a thorn there at all, and you knew it. For shame! I thought you were too honorable, too unblemished, to soil your conscience with a falsehood."

He laughed, but colored all over his broad, open brow.

"All's fair in love and war," he answered; "but I must acknowledge you have brought my words against me well. What are you looking for?"

"For my gloves. I laid them down somewhere here."

"I have got them," he answered quietly, as though he were announcing the most ordinary every-day occurrence, drawing them out of his pocket as he spoke, stroking them between his hands, and looking at them with a very different expression from that with which he had regarded them ten minutes before.

"Oh! thank you," she said, holding out her hand for them. "I was afraid they were lost. Give them to me."

"Not yet," he replied, putting them again into his pocket. "You don't want them here; and you might really lose them. I will keep them for you till we are going back to your home."

"But I want to put them on."

"That is exactly what I wish to prevent," he answered with provoking coolness; then they looked at each other again, and Gwendoline did not know whether to be angry or amused. Gradually the expression of Feversham's look changed, and though he had assured himself a few minutes before that the time when he might plead successfully had not yet arrived, and that he must not be precipitate, he now lost all coolness and self-control. Passionate, loving words rushed to his lips, and would next minute have been spoken, when a handful of long tangled grass, neatly fastened round a small stone, fell at their feet, and Clarissa's merry, ringing voice was heard exclaiming,

"A good shot, Gwen, wasn't it? I have found my fern, and as it is now getting late, I think we had better set out, if we wish to be in time for dinner."

"Why, what o'clock is it?" asked Gwendoline, nervously, as though she had been caught committing some enormity. In truth, if it was late, she must feel very guilty, for the time had slipped by as though it were but half an hour, and they had not talked so much either. It was those long treacherous silences that had devoured the hours in such an incomprehensible manner.

"Just five o'clock," sang Clarissa, with a most provoking look; while Feversham drew out his watch, and glanced at it, with the air of one who believes all ladies' watches to be wrong, and is confident he will find this particular one wrong too. "We came out at two o'clock," continued Clarissa, "so we have been here very nearly three mortal hours. What you two people could find to talk about all the time, I can't think—

indeed, I believe you both went to sleep—or at least Lord Feversham did, and you, Gwen, were afraid to awake him. I would not be as quiet as you are, Gwen, about such things—I would waken up any one that treated me in that way, I can tell you."

"How would you do it?" asked Feversham, wishing lively Miss Clarissa a hundred miles away. Gwendoline, he knew, wanted her gloves, and he could not take them out of his pocket under her sister's eyes and present them to her. Yet the more he wished for her absence, the more he felt constrained to be polite, and make himself agreeable, and try to act as though he desired her presence. He paused, looking up for an answer to his question, but in reality speculating whether, if Clarissa kept by them the whole way back to Endley, he might carry off the gloves without returning them to their owner. The thought cheered him, and when Clarissa answered gayly, "Try me in that way, and I will soon show you what I would do," he laughed, as though she had said something intensely witty.

"What did I say that was so amusing?" she asked, looking from one to the other with a puzzled, innocent air. Then, seeing Gwendoline was as bewildered as she was herself, she continued, "I don't believe you know what you are laughing at, Lord Feversham. This is levity, which I never encourage. Come, Gwen, he will recover quickly when he finds himself alone;" so saying, Clarissa caught her sister's hand, and drew her down the narrow path after her, Feversham quickly following, as she had predicted.

In spite of pressing invitations to remain to dinner, Feversham insisted on returning to mess. There were several reasons for this, the principal of which was that he could not hope to have her to himself any more that day, and he had arrived at a stage when, seeing her in company, surrounded by people who prevented private conversation, was more of a penance than a pleasure. Then he was well aware also that he could not trust himself any longer with her alone—he would infallibly say more than at present it was wise he should say, and might fail in obtaining what he desired from over-anxiety to gain it. He was not by any means sure yet that she cared sufficiently for him to insure him against all chance of a refusal, and, like most men, he was morbidly sensitive on that point. It was true she had that day shown very plainly that she liked him, and he could not doubt that she understood he loved her; but for all that, women had been known to lead men on, and refuse them when they had been certain of success, and he did not care to be one of the number so deceived and deluded.

It was rather a selfish kind of pride—one that he would not perhaps have liked to own to, that most men would feel rather ashamed of, if its true causes and bearing were explained to them, and yet that influences most of them immensely in their dealing with women. It would be a curious study for investigators of such curiosities to ascertain how often, since the fashion of proposal and rejection began, have women been vituperated and censured for having encouraged and thrown over men, when the real impediment to a happy and satisfactory arrangement of the case has been that the man, in his intense dread of refusal, has failed to explain his meaning clearly to the object of his love; wrapping up a plain simple demand for marriage in such enigmatical form as would require an Œdipus to unravel.

The woman meanwhile, besides bearing to the man and his fellows the imputation of heartlessness, has had to bear the wearing, aching load of hope deferred, to experience the pangs of a pained wonder, dull at first, but growing every day more keen—as to the reason of the coldness that has sprung up between hearts once so dear to each other. A wonder perhaps doomed never to be satisfied or enlightened—perhaps after long years destined to be relieved, when too late, by the intervention of some common friend, who can throw on trivial words long forgotten some gleam of light gathered from acquaintance with the mind of the man who, once frightened away, can rarely, if ever, be recalled.

Claude Feversham did not think of matters in this light as he drove merrily home, but he did determine to wait a little longer, and make himself more sure of his ground before he ventured on the fatal step. Still matters appeared well for him at present, as he had seen them that day, when that monkey Madcap had not been near to intrude; therefore Feversham had been almost condescending to me when he met me that evening at mess.

Gwendoline Bambridge was sitting alone in her room; she had dressed for dinner, and was absorbed in what seemed to be a pleasant reverie, while waiting for the gong to sound. Suddenly the door opened, and Clarissa flitted into the room: both these girls were peculiar in their manner of moving and walking about a room. Gwendoline always reminded me of a clipper-ship under press of canvas—she literally sailed along the ground, seeming to me also like a swan, piloting itself gracefully over the clear waters of the lake; but Clarissa flitted, or flew—it was more the rapid, graceful motion of the swallow, intensely swift, with nothing of hurry or exertion discernible; she was at the door as you looked at her; the next instant, without your knowing how, she was at your side. They were pretty and distinctive peculiarities, and I had often noticed them, deeming them suggestive and characteristic. In one minute Clarissa had flitted, or skimmed, over to her sister in her rapid, noiseless way, and laying a hand on each of Gwendoline's shoulders, was looking down into her sister's eyes, with her own brimful of fun and merriment.

There was a long pause. Clarissa evidently expected Gwendoline to speak, and Gwendoline remained pertinaciously silent. Isn't it provoking that people always will do exactly what they are not wanted to do?

"Well?" asked Clarissa at length, seeing that her sister would not initiate the conversation.

"Well!" replied Gwendoline, impenetrably.

"Has not our grave and gracious friend proposed this afternoon, Gwen? I am sure I gave him ample time to do it in, and do you know it is slow work fern-hunting alone. I should not have minded, if dear little Vivian had been with me; but then, of course, he would have been miserable at seeing you alone with his cousin. I do wish, Gwen, you would be quick and hook this fish, if you are going to have him, because you draw all the best men in the place, and leave me no chance; if you were married, I should have a little fair play, and begin to do business on my own account. What did he say? Is the matter decided?"

"No," answered Gwendoline, trying to look as if she felt more doleful than was by any means the case. "You know, Clary, I always tell you there is nothing in it; we are not thinking of each other."

"Ha, ha!" laughed Clarissa; "I know very well when you say there's nothing in it, it is sure to be something very serious for the poor man concerned, and he generally gets his dismissal a few days afterward. But he should have proposed to-day, when I did every thing on purpose;" and leaving her sister, Clarissa walked over to a cheval-glass, and began turning herself round and round before it, singing "Why don't the men propose?"

Satisfied with the arrangement of her skirts, she turned away presently, and continued, "That lover of yours is a very handsome fellow, I admit, but not nearly as good-looking as my little darling Madcap. What eyes that boy has, to be sure! If I were you, I should be in love with him, over head and ears. How can you go in for that sentimental, grave, dignified, long-legged stork? I have never made out what animal he is like, for, though I call him a stork, his face is not like one; but one name's as good as another. As for dear little Vivian, in spite of his good looks, any one can see with half an eye he belongs to the monkey tribe. If Mr. Darwin had been acquainted with him, I could forgive him for his theories respecting the origin of man. By-the-bye, I'll ask Vivian if he knows Darwin."

"And he will tell you he does—meaning of course his book. How can you be so absurd, Clarissa?" laughed Gwendoline. "I don't think Vivian like a monkey at all; he is more like a rough Scotch terrier."

"Oh, it is all the same thing; he is a little darling, whatever he is like, and I wish you would throw over the solemn captain for him. I should like him for myself if I could get him, but failing that, he would make a beautiful brother-in-law. Now I am disgracing myself by my levity, I suppose," she added; "old Mother Botters would tell me so, were she here. What a mercy she is not, or I should never be able to resist the temptation of scandalizing her! Ah! there's the gong," and Clarissa, pirouetting two or three times on one toe, vanished suddenly from the room, before Gwendoline had time to get out of her chair.

<hr>

CHAPTER V.

NEW-COMERS.

A FEW days after Feversham had announced to us at mess the forthcoming arrival of our headquarters, the little town of Belmurphy was thrown into a most unusual and unprecedented state of excitement by the incoming of what was, to the inhabitants, a real army, and not the puny representation of military pomp and parade they had been accustomed to dignify by that high-sounding title. You would never have believed the town could have contained such crowds of old women, children, and small boys as it poured forth on that occasion. These all put in an appearance at the station, and afterward accompanied the troops through the streets, keeping up

as best they could, according to their several capacities; the small boys managing best in that line, and varying the monotony of the march by turning wheels, standing on their heads, and such accompaniments to the pomp and circumstance of war as were in vogue in Irish country towns, or were suggested by ready Celtic wit.

I was glad to see some of my old comrades again—not that I had known them very long before being sent down here, but still their faces were familiar. With one of them I had always been friendly; there was one man, whose kindly handsome face I could see beaming on me out of a carriage window before the train drew up in the station; he, next to my cousin Claude, had always been my particular chum in the regiment. In fact, there is no doubt that, in some ways, he was more to me than Claude had ever been, or than it was now likely he ever could be. We were more of an age, had many tastes and ideas in common, which my sterner captain would have looked upon as childish; in fact we suited each other; that is the shortest way of putting it, and no other way explains the matter as well.

But Claude had once asked me why Cecil Egerton suited me, and what I saw in him to like: with the provoking manner of things in general, I could, at that minute, think of no reason for my liking, that Claude could not poke a hole in with one word. According to his account, every other fellow was as good as Egerton, and better too; because they had none of his weakness, which I am bound to admit was his great fault.

Claude's questions and cynical criticisms had the effect of making me think a little about character for the rest of that day. I have never studied human nature much, for though some fellow says "The proper study of mankind is man," still the subject appears to me so deep, there is in it such an infinite variety, that I find it comparatively useless to reason from analogy. If I try to classify my observations, I meet immediately some one who upsets all my pet theories which I have evolved with much cigar-smoke out of my inner consciousness. That is provoking, you know; a fellow does not like having his theories upset, and I have found that mine begin and end in—smoke.

But these observations of Feversham's did make me think a little on the matter, in spite of my preconceived determination not to lose myself in its depths any more; the result of my thought was, I began to perceive that, as no man can be really a great man who has not firmness —a mental backbone to his character—so also none can be great who has many petty weaknesses, no matter how fine an appearance he present to the world. The little flaws, though hardly perceptible, work themselves through the nobler metal, and prevent it ringing true when struck full and hard in the battle of life.

There is Claude, now. He is as perfect as most men—perhaps, in natural character, as great as a man can be—but he has a flaw that often to me, who know him well, spoils all his really good points. He has firmness, uprightness, candor, generosity, good-nature, and no alloy of the petty vanity that so often spoils good-looking and clever men. But the very strength of his nature causes its defects; he has no toleration for weakness, no sympathy or pity for those less strong than himself. He will be helpful and kind to them, but he despises them; and contempt, unless exhibited for something in itself base and unworthy, is a meanness.

Cecil Egerton is Claude's opposite in many things. More clever in some ways, even better looking, he is distrustful of himself, and humble always; as generous, as candid, as upright, where he himself is concerned, but more sympathetic, and weak as water in opposing the wishes of those to whom he is attached; like all such gentle, artistic natures, very loving, very impressionable. Perhaps Claude would not speak or think so hardly of him, were he aware of Egerton's history; and did he know how much that timid, vacillating manner is the result of hardship and toil from early childhood—of a precarious living earned with difficulty.

His father and mother had always been poor ever since he remembered them; but they had been well-bred and refined, in spite of poverty. His mother had been disowned by her family, in consequence of her marriage with Mr. Egerton, who was an artist, a man possessing considerable ability and some genius, which had been almost crushed out of him by the stern band of necessity at the time Cecil began to remember him.

He did not know him long, however; when Cecil was ten years old Mr. Egerton died of overwork and over-anxiety—a combination that has proved fatal to many talented, sensitive men; and then little Cecil and his mother were left to pull on together as best they might, when dependent entirely on the exertions of a feeble, heart-broken woman. But help came to them when they least expected it; and when the burden laid on his mother had become too heavy to be supported by the earth-wearied shoulders, or borne by the toil-worn brain much longer. An elder brother of Mrs. Egerton's, one of those men who had cast her off on the occasion of her marriage, hearing of her husband's death, now came forward, offering to provide for her and the boy in the future.

For her own sake, had she been alone, Mrs. Egerton would have accepted nothing from one who had allowed her husband to die of want, when he could easily have procured him some employment that would have relieved their poverty; but for the sake of the child whose interest she was bound not to neglect, she availed herself of the proffered assistance, and tried to school herself to gratitude. Her time was come, however; pleasures and luxuries arrived too late to one who had worn out her power of living, in stern battle with necessity. Two or three months after she and her son had been established under Mr. Vansittart's roof, she passed away, glad, but for the anguish of parting from her child, to gain the promised rest so long prayed for, so much needed.

It might be thought the boy was too young then to understand much of what was passing, but sorrow is a wonderful sharpener of young wits, and little Cecil comprehended what he had never heard expressed in words: namely, that his uncle Vansittart had hated his dearly loved father, who was gone, that he had let him die without endeavoring to save him, and that his after-attention to his mother and himself had come too late to save her life. He knew that his uncle entertained no liking for him on account of his

resemblance to his dead father, and he hated Mr. Vansittart with an impotent, childish hatred, that was the more bitter because he felt it to be futile and impotent, when he would so gladly have had it active and hurtful. He did not see much of his uncle. He was sent to school immediately after his mother's death, and there he remained—except when some of his school-fellows asked him to their homes for the holidays —from year's end to year's end, until after he was eighteen years of age. Then one day, without any previous warning, he was sent for to appear in the master's room; and he found himself, after the lapse of eight years, standing face to face with his uncle, Roderick Vansittart.

Mr. Vansittart, as he thus came before the eyes of his nephew, now a lad of nearly eighteen years of age, seemed rather a different person from what he had appeared to the boy of ten. Cecil was bound to admit that some of his ideas on the subject had been warped and prejudiced, and that hate had had too much to do with the estimate he had formed of this his only relative, who had taken no notice of him, and had only helped him to live.

Mr. Vansittart was a tall, spare man, with dark hair, very plentifully sprinkled with gray, and iron-gray whiskers; his cold blue eyes were keen and quick, his forehead was high and narrow, and his thin drawn-in lips gave to a rather large mouth a compressed, trap-like appearance. In dress he was scrupulously neat, always attired in perfectly fitting, dark-colored clothes. Ill-natured people had been heard to aver he possessed but one suit, but if that were so, then must that one suit have been made of self-renewing cloth, endowed with perennial youth, for no one ever saw any thing shabby upon him. His large white hands were as spare as his body, and were always wonderfully clean and spotless; they furnished him with a favorite object for contemplation, and he was engaged in minutely inspecting them when his nephew entered the room.

Mr. Vansittart's visit was more to Dr. Percival, the school-principal, than to the lad, and had for its object to ascertain what progress young Egerton had made in his studies, and whether he was likely to be a credit to his uncle, and repay him for the money that had been expended on educational purposes.

"If he promises to turn out well," Mr. Vansittart had explained, "I will place him in the army, and, having interest, I will get him pushed on. We have not in our family favored the military profession; but it has always seemed to me that, with interest, it might turn out a good thing, and a man who rises rapidly in the army always enjoys a certain consideration among outsiders, who may not see how the wires that work the puppets are pulled. There is to be an examination for the line in the course of the next three months: if it is your opinion, Dr. Percival, that Cecil is competent to pass that examination, it would be my wish that he should go up for it."

And in order that this wish should be announced to him, young Egerton had been summoned down from the intense and absorbing labor of composing a poem in Latin verse, that was to be sent in for competition for Dr. Percival's special prize.

Mr. Vansittart did not appear in quite so bad a light for some days after this announcement.

Dr. Percival had expressed his belief that Egerton could not fail to pass, had praised his abilities very highly, and had particularly commended his aptitude for every branch of drawing and design.

"He will make a splendid draughtsman in a few years' time, when he has gained a little more knowledge and experience," continued the good doctor, undisturbed by the gathering frown on Mr. Vansittart's brow. "I am always glad to see a young man exhibit such a talent; it keeps him out of mischief, and gives him an object, when otherwise his life would be aimless and desultory."

"It is at the root of all vagabondage and evildoing!" thundered Mr. Vansittart, startling the doctor out of his prosy platitudes, and the lad out of his dreams of gold and scarlet, cold glittering steel, and bullion embroidery. "Art is another name for meanness of every kind, fortune-hunting and dishonesty included."

"It is false!" shouted Cecil, springing from the window, where he had been standing. "My father was an artist, and you know it. It is his memory you slander when you speak as you spoke just now. Before me you shall never do it, or I will leave you and your hateful benefits, and seek my own livelihood from a world that can not be more cruel than you."

He stopped speaking, and then the spirit that had borne him up in the moment of excitement failed, and he turned again to the window, resting his head against the panes, that the tears that flowed, in spite of his efforts to keep them back, might not be seen.

Mr. Vansittart had almost quailed under the vehemence of the boy's attack. When he finished speaking and turned away, his uncle with difficulty restrained himself; but Egerton's appearance was very striking; the old man had no heir; and it had struck him that if the boy turned out well, and made a figure in the world, he could not do better than adopt him. It was but natural that the lad at first should not see all the advantages that would accrue to him from strict subservience to all his uncle's moods and whims, and the flash of fiery spirit pleased the old man, as being a suitable thing in one who was to succeed in the army, make a figure in the world, and finally inherit the splendid Vansittart property of Beaumanoir, and the Vansittart name. For even the change of name at some future period had already formed part of the old man's scheme.

"Come here, Cecil," he said, after a few minutes' silence, during which the doctor looked from one to the other nervously. "I was wrong to speak before you as I did just now. My zeal for your future welfare led me astray. I will not allude to the matter again; only let me see no artist tendencies in you, and pass your examination in November."

The frank acknowledgment that he had been in the wrong touched the lad's impressionable heart, he being utterly incapable of conceiving how entirely conventional the expressions of regret had been, how little real meaning there was in them. His uncle was raised to a higher place in his esteem forthwith, and he even began to think his conduct in former days might be pardoned, if Mr. Vansittart should really repent the course he had pursued, as the lad's sanguine heart led him to believe was probable. For Cecil was prone to judge every one by himself, and supposing to be possible what was impossible, namely, that he should knowingly act cruelly or unkindly to any one, he would have been afterward overcome with remorse; this exceptional tenderness of conscience the foolish boy believed was common to every one, as well as to himself.

The examination came, and Cecil passed through it triumphantly, taking a very high place — third on the list — to the intense pride and delight of his uncle, who at once wrote him a very friendly letter, asking him to Beaumanoir, there to pass the time that must elapse before he could be gazetted. Cecil had no other home to which he could go, and he therefore accepted the invitation, his ill feelings toward his relative still further dissipated by the really friendly wording of the note.

But once established at Beaumanoir, old associations, familiar scenes, forgotten incidents recalled, and closer acquaintance with his uncle, revealed sentiments, opinions, and characteristics eminently distasteful to a young and ardent mind, full of poetic and Quixotic fancies; and the old dislike not only returned, but deepened. Mr. Vansittart was mean; in fact, he was made up of meannesses, and he, judging others by himself, deemed that every one around him was compounded of the same ingredients. He had a favorite theory that money was every thing in the world. He said it represented not only power, influence, fame, all the many mercenary interests of the world, but that it meant also all those closer and more cherished sentiments that men pretend (according to him) to set such store by. It meant, in his reading of the word, honor, truth, friendship, devotion, constancy, love; all that poetic or heroic souls have ever dreamed was comprised to him in that sordid word. With such a creed, what could the man be? Was it not rather a wonder that he was what he was, that he had not dried up into a miser pure and simple, that he had any feelings left that could prompt him to give his sister's child an education? To him all men were knaves or fools; all women wicked and weak. With a world peopled as he believed it to be around him, it was only a wonder that he had in himself kept up the semblance of an outward respectability, and avoided falling into those glaring sins from which, according to his creed, none were kept, except by a fear of exposure, the result of the hypocrisy he deemed inherent in man.

"I would not trust any man in the world with a woman or gold, or any woman in the world with a man or gold," he said, deliberately, after dinner, on the night of his nephew's arrival, expounding to him his strange doctrines. "Act as if every man in the world were your enemy, whom you must deceive, and as if every woman were your slave, whom you must cow. They act so toward you; do you pay them in their own coin."

Cecil Egerton looked at his uncle's narrow, cunning face with astonishment.

"I don't know much of the world, I suppose," he said, "but still, perhaps, from having been so long poor, I have seen more than most lads of my age; and though I know we rubbed shoulders with many queer characters in those days, still I never thought them as bad as you say.

Indeed, as far as their means went, they were good to me."

"Because they hoped to make something out of you," Mr. Vansittart answered, with his low, self-contained laugh. "And now, with your youth and inexperience, you will be more exposed to the attacks of sharpers than ever. Hold faith with no man, as long as you can escape detection, or where detection will not hurm you; but if you are found out in any mess, I warn you I will not stand by you. I believe in roguery—we are all rogues—but then I will only have to do with clever ones."

"I have only wit enough to be honest," answered the lad, with his frank laugh. "I had rather be the person deceived than be the deceiver. I hope I may never adopt your creed, sir."

"You will in a little time, boy," replied Mr. Vansittart, laughing quietly to himself; "indeed, I doubt not you practice it now on me in a mild way, by trying to make yourself out more honest than you are. Well, that is a paying line; a rogue of unimpeachable integrity will fleece more fools to his one brain in a year than six doubtful characters would in ten years. So, if you can act the thing without believing the cant the character obliges you to talk, you will do well."

"But it is no cant," cried Cecil, earnestly; then, meeting his uncle's cold stare of incredulity, he looked down at his plate and remained silent.

Day by day brought out some trait in the old man's character more and more distasteful to his nephew. The natural result of his views with respect to people in general was that he distrusted every one, imputing bad motives for the most trivial acts of kindliness. Young Egerton soon found, to his disgust and indignation, that his sweet, obliging temper and ready good-nature had caused him to be branded in Mr. Vansittart's eyes merely as a rather more skillful and successful hypocrite than most men.

After this discovery there was very little more friendliness between them: Cecil trying to show by his manner how little he cared for his uncle's opinion, how independent he was of the mercenary motives imputed to him, and Mr. Vansittart endeavoring, by threats and arguments, to coerce him into the state of mind and feeling for which he believed his nephew was formed, and which he approved, as one that frequently led to success in life. Two such ill-assorted characters, brought thus into the close proximity of a country house, could not fail either to quarrel or to influence each other very materially. Egerton was not quarrelsome, but he was weak; he had not sufficient strength of mind and purpose to maintain a steady, silent opposition to the insidious workings of a strong mind over his weaker one, and he would without doubt soon have succumbed, had he not been gazetted to the —th, just two months after he arrived at Beaumanoir.

How delighted he was to receive that long blue, official-looking envelope, marked on the outside, "On Her Majesty's Service!" It was like an order of release to a long pent-up prisoner; he felt as if escaping from the contact of his uncle's vice-imbued mind would be as a breath of air from fresh, heathery mountain-tops to the captive long confined in the close air of a dungeon.

His uncle was with him at the breakfast-table, in the long dining-room at Beaumanoir, when Egerton received the letter. His cheek flushed and his eye sparkled, but he passed over the envelope and its contents without a word. As the old man took the announcement and looked over it, Cecil glanced round the room as though to take the well-remembered furniture that had seen long ago his bitter sorrow into his confidence about his great joy. The low French window at one end of the room was open, and through the opening came the sweet-scented morning air and the golden gleam of the early sun. Every thing looked brighter and more cheerful than it had done an hour before—even his uncle's face was pleasant, he thought, as Mr. Vansittart returned the letter, saying,

"Very good; the —th is a fine corps—a light-infantry regiment, and considered rather fast, I believe. There are some good men in it from the neighborhood around this. By-the-bye, you never met any of my neighbors, I think; it doesn't much matter, as the young men, such as Lord Feversham and some others, are in your regiment, and you will meet them there. They will of course pay you attention, knowing you to be my nephew. I should have liked you to see Longhurst; but it is a very long drive from this —fourteen miles, at least. Some people think it almost as fine as Beaumanoir: I can't say I do. I like land lying toward the south—it gets so much more sun. Longhurst lies westward—a pretty aspect of a summer's evening, but gloomy in winter; and in England, winter certainly claims three-fourths of the year. I hope you will remember all I have been telling you when you enter your regiment: in a society of young men like that, the overreaching principle, the desire to make as much as possible out of every one, is always at work, no matter how skillfully it may be concealed. Don't forget that; and remember, the aggressor always has the best chance: just as the man who tells his story first always makes most way in men's opinions, and often gets a prejudged favorable verdict before the other side of the question has been heard at all."

Cecil looked gloomy; his brilliant ideas and high aspirations were being sadly damped by this view of the companionship he should acquire in exchange for that of his uncle. He had not taken up his uncle's ideas personally, despised them still, and would have resisted any temptation to act on them; but by dint of constant repetition, he had come to think there might be some truth in them, as regarded others. Already the mischievous doctrines he heard propounded every day began to work. He was angry with himself, however, for having allowed them to acquire any hold of his mind, and he did not choose his uncle to see their effect, therefore he remained silent.

Breakfast over, he roamed out to say farewell for a time to the old place, and the haunts of that brief period of his childhood when he and his mother had been all in all to each other here. The sun was shining brightly, and the day was soft and warm, though it was only the end of January. It was one of those few days that come sometimes with the beginning of the year, to delude us with the hopes of the near approach of spring.

Cecil Egerton strode on briskly, stepping out toward the far blue, hazy outline of hills upon the horizon, trying to listen only to the joyful voices in his heart, and not to the dreary calumnies scattered broadcast by his uncle over every true and noble feeling of his nature. He was to leave the next day but one, and sincerely did he rejoice at the prospect. Mr. Vansittart had been kind to him in his way, but the young man felt he was expected to do well, to make a name, in fact, in order that he might merit this kindness, and that it might be continued to him. If the world was such as his uncle described, it was pretty certain he must go to the wall and be nowhere; for, had he the will, Egerton felt in himself he had not the mental force or strength to be a successful man in the manner in which his uncle desired him to be successful.

He was right there, and more right than he knew himself to be. As soon as he walked into our anteroom, after reporting himself, a few days later, Feversham, looking at him, said to Preston, in an under-tone:

"Weak as water; how did he ever find strength of mind enough to pass his exam?"

"I don't see that," answered Preston; "he has an intellectual face. Don't you think so? Look at his brow."

"Follow the line of the jaw and the expression of the mouth rather, and you will see I am right. Do you observe, he seems perpetually about to speak, and then says nothing?"

"Which is, at least, better than if he spoke with nothing to say," Preston returned, laughing.

"Wait a day or two—he will come to that presently," answered Claude, in a cold tone of disapproval. "No man with that face could keep in any idea, no matter how feeble or futile, that came into his head."

"You are too hard, Feversham. How would you like strangers to judge you so?"

Feversham laughed a contented laugh.

"I despise weakness," he said. "Why can't a man know his mind and act on it? At any rate, no one can laugh at me on that score."

Preston thought not, but he was not going to flatter Feversham, so he did not answer him, but went over to speak to the new-comer, who was looking rather ill at ease, surrounded by a crowd of quizzical subs. He did not mean to do any thing, or make fun of him in any way, but sometimes the spirit of mischief gets into young fellows and they can not help themselves; besides he was a good deal younger then than he is now. That is quite six years ago. At any rate, however it happened, or whatever tempted him, he began presently to cram Egerton with some wonderful story about the major, who was a good fellow enough, but eccentric. His anecdote seemed to stir up some recollections in Egerton's mind, for he presently assented to a rather unworthy proposition of Preston's with regard to the major's character, saying that he had heard things were so in the world, and particularly in the army; but that, if the case were so, all he could say was, that he thought the army, and the rest of the world with it, had better be at the bottom of the sea than that men should avow and practice such doctrines.

Preston was a little startled, for he had only been chaffing, and had not imagined any one could really take him to be in earnest. But, from whatever cause it had happened, he had been believed, and it was evident that the supposition of wickedness such as he had described distressed the new-comer, therefore he could not be a bad fellow.

Rather amused and interested, Preston tried to explain that his story was an allegory, a romance, or whatever he liked to call it.

"Ah!" Egerton said, when Preston had finished his explanation, "then you are one of those who like to take advantage of the ignorance of others."

Preston was struck dumb; the rejoinder had a certain truth about it that gave it a bitter flavor, and yet it was good; something might be learned from it, he felt at once, though he was too confused at first to know exactly what.

"I did not mean to take advantage of you in any wrong manner," he stammered, hardly knowing what to say; "I only meant to make a little fun."

"And I was stupid enough to take your random assertions literally, and fancy that things were worse here than they really are. I am too matter-of-fact in any thing concerning every-day life to understand chaff at present," he continued, pleasantly, "and I have had a bad instructor lately on such subjects, so you must pardon me when I make mistakes, and misunderstand you. I have been told lately that truth and honor are unknown in the world, that every man's hand is against his neighbor; and though I had not believed such assertions before, yet your account seeming to ratify and indorse that judgment, I began to fear I had been more incredulous than I should have been."

His look and manner, as he answered, were so frank and winning, that Preston forgot the difficulty in which he had just been placed. He saw also that Egerton was just the character who would soon be a prey to Mayleigh's keen, sarcastic wit, and who would be likely to suffer thereby if he was not warned. He answered, therefore:

"If our fellows find you believe all they tell you so easily, they will not explain things to you, but will probably make matters appear worse and worse. Don't believe them, and do not let any thing they say bias your conduct, or you will become a perfect weather-cock, veering now one way, and now another."

After that they had some more conversation, and every minute Preston was more and more struck by the incongruities his companion's character presented. He had noble, lofty principles, in which he implicitly believed; he had the firm desire and purpose to do right, and a naturally sweet, good disposition; and with all these fine points, an extraordinary weakness of purpose, that allowed him to be swayed from what he knew to be right with every passing word, even if the speaker of that word was a man of whom he knew nothing, or, as I afterward found, whom he knew to be capable of evil. But I liked him when I joined and came to know him, though I could see Claude Feversham sometimes looking up from his paper to listen to our conversation, when he happened to be in the room; and as soon as Egerton left, he would rise from his chair impatiently, saying,

"What a fool that fellow is! How such men are allowed into the army is a puzzle to me. If he was in the act of cutting down an enemy in a skirmish, and any fellow passing by called out ' Let the fellow off,' he would do it, and perhaps be bowled over by the same man half a minute after. Unstable as water, would describe him well."

I would laugh, Claude's disgust was so extreme, but it did not change the opinion I had formed of Egerton, that he was a nice fellow, and clever in all save that one point, which is, I almost think, an essential, if cleverness, or, more properly speaking, talent, is to bear any fruit. He became a great friend of mine; he suited me very well, for though I rather condemned his weakness, still I found it pleasant to have a companion always obedient to my wishes, and who never offered an opinion of his own in contradiction to one of mine. And this man had now arrived at Belmurphy, and into his sympathetic ear I promised myself I would pour all my hopes and fears as soon as he had got comfortably settled in his new quarters.

I do not think Cecil had ever been in love, but he was of a romantic, poetical turn of mind, that made me often wonder he had not at least fancied himself smitten often before now; at any rate, this tendency to romance made him sympathetic, and I was certain he would listen with interest to all I had to tell him.

And I was right; he listened to my sorrows eagerly and intently, and was inclined to pass a harsh judgment on Feversham for interfering. He and Feversham were cruelly distrustful of each other. They had never taken to each other or become friends, which to me seemed strange, as they had many tastes in common; and Claude, though always contemptuous on the score of my new chum, admitted that he only wanted a mental backbone to turn out a splendid fellow. Cecil, I think, was afraid of Feversham, feeling his captain's hardly concealed contempt, and avoiding him in consequence; always regarding him with a feeling approaching to reverence and awe. Of late they had become better friends, and Claude was always kind to him. None of the other fellows were as intimate friends of mine as this man, though I got on well with all of them. I am afraid this was not due to my own merit, because I know I was often a troublesome monkey; but it had been unanimously agreed that it was no good correcting Madcap; he might steady in time, but until then it would be necessary to put up with him. They were very good to me— much more so than I deserved; and just at this time, not being at all happy, I am sure I was not pleasant to them very often; indeed Cecil told me they all wondered what had happened to Madcap, to make him so captious and irritable, particularly with his chum and Captain Claude Feversham.

Cecil soon understood why it was so, but unless questioned, he was not very talkative, and therefore kept my secret well. I often blamed myself, however, thinking I had been indiscreet in telling him; fearing that, when he heard conjectures afloat about me, he might perhaps be tempted to say what he knew. My fears were unnecessary, however; to me Cecil was true as steel.

CHAPTER VI

CLARISSA'S CONQUEST.

OF all the new-comers to Belmurphy belonging to "ours," the most important personage in the eyes of the neighborhood, and the one who also ought undoubtedly to have been the most important in our eyes, was Lieutenant-colonel Dropmore, the officer at that time in command. He was a widower, but, before I joined, his wife and he had been great characters in the regiment. She had been a person of tart, severe disposition, of whom the subs stood greatly in awe, and whom Mayleigh had named one day, in an inspired moment, Acid Drops. The name was a good one, and it stuck; the colonel, a good-natured fellow himself, going by the name of Acid Drop's husband, or more generally, for shortness, A. D.'s husband. She, poor soul, had been dead for two years; and though it might be thought such an experience would have cured Dropmore of any fancy toward matrimony, it was now well known that he was very anxious to make a second trial, and generally offered himself to every eligible young lady that appeared upon the scene.

He was a short, stout man, with a handsome, good-humored face, in which, however, all the indications of a quick, hot temper were visible. Indeed, Acid Drops (the name, though a misnomer, had descended to him) was a very peppery individual, but his fits of passion blew over very quickly.

He and several other of the new-comers were asked to dinner at the Bewleys' the day after they arrived in Belmurphy. We were to follow them later in the evening, and have some dancing. We knew most of our lady-friends would be there, and we were quite curious to see which of them all would make an impression on old Drops's susceptible heart. Claude and I had very little doubt who must be the attraction to every body, and I am sure both our hearts beat faster at the thought. Claude ought to have been certain enough, as I knew afterward; but I was entirely in the dark as to the position I occupied; and I fancied it was quite possible our handsome colonel, in spite of his stumpy figure and choleric disposition, might prove more attractive than an ensign, so very juvenile as to be constantly mistaken for a boy.

All the same I felt almost inclined to quarrel with old Drops for his bad taste, when I arrived at Bayview next evening, and found him a declared admirer of Miss Clarissa. It was such outrageous stupidity of the man to look at her, when her sister was near. I felt quite angry at first, but presently became very much amused, watching how she managed him, and twisted him round her finger, and laughed at him all the time, without his for one minute suspecting she did not admire him quite as much as he did her.

"He is such fun, that colonel of yours," she said to me later in the evening. "He has been telling me all about the late Mrs. Dropmore— how sincerely he was attached to her, how long they were married, how he lamented her loss, what a good wife she made him, ending by pointing out that a good wife makes a good husband, and *vice versa*. That seemed to be a special point with him, and matrimony is evidently his hobby. You call him Acid Drops, but after the conversation to-night I would recommend you to change his name to Pear Drops, only I am afraid you will be shocked at such a frightful pun."

I laughed.

"I suspect that conversation had serious intentions, Miss Clarissa, and that you will find he designs for you the honor of asking you to be the second Mrs. Drops. It is an honor that has been offered to a good many, so that you will not even have the gratification of thinking you are alone in your glory."

"You provoking boy! Why could not you have left me that illusion? You will rob life of all enchantment to me, if you insist on bringing me behind the scenes, and making me see the *rouge* and pearl-powder on the actors' faces, and the care-worn expressions that there take the place of the fascinating stage smile."

"You talk so feelingly, one would think you were an actress yourself," I answered.

"So I am. We are all actors; every one is. Hamlet discovered that for us a long while ago. But I am more of an actress than most people. It is an irresistible temptation to me to mislead and bamboozle, by seeming to be something different from what I am. No, you need not look frightened. In the first place, you would not be alarmed if I was ever so great a deception; and, in the second place, I never act to you. You are too much of a friend for me to find any amusement in wearing the mask with you; but with Colonel Drops it is different, and I intend to make him give me a little amusement."

"Don't be too hard on him, Miss Clarissa," I said; "he is such a good old fellow, though a trifle hot at times. I should be sorry if you hit him hard—and you know you do sometimes."

"Poor little thing! has it felt the truth of that remark?" she said, laughing. "If it was hit hard, it was not by me; and, unfortunately, in this warfare it is only the hand that strikes the blow that can cure. Dear me, what a queer place the world is! I wonder shall I ever feel inclined to heal any wound I make?"

"Heal old Drops," I answered. "It would be such fun to have you at the head of the regiment, for you would make a first-rate coloneless, and we should all think it unutterably jolly."

"Yes, and call me Clarified Drops, I suppose?" she cried, laughing. "Thank you—you are all too kind; but though I feel extremely grateful, I fear I must decline such a glorious destiny. Have you been dancing with Gwen to-night? Doesn't she look handsome now?"

I followed the direction of her eyes, and saw Gwendoline Bambridge leaning back in a low chair talking to Claude, who sat on the end of a sofa quite close to her. She was indeed looking splendidly handsome, and unutterably happy. If I had not been an infatuated fool, I should have known the truth then; as it was, for a few short minutes I guessed it, and a dull, cold pain took possession of me, making the lights seem pale and dim, the music sound faint and distant, and even the merry voice of my companion lose its silvery tone. Has any one, in a moment of supreme pain, the power to grasp and realize his anguish? I think not; and I believe that it is so arranged by wise and merciful dispensation. Afterward, when the shock is over and the mind begins to recover its force, we know where the wound has penetrated, and can tell how and why we suffer pain, and what the intensity of our suffering is; but at first we know nothing of all this, and can not even frame words to express our feeling, can only moan and writhe, and rebel inarticulately against our misery, like the dumb beasts, with whom we have more affinity in suffering than in joy.

But as I stood like one stunned beside Clarissa Bambridge, and watched with a fixed stare, the intensity and direction of which was beyond my control, the couple at the other side of the room, Gwendoline looked over at me, smiled, and signed to me to come to her. The painful deadness that had taken possession of me was banished by that look. I heard the merry measure of the galop we had been dancing still ringing out through the ball-room; so, passing my arm round Clarissa's waist, we took a few turns round the room and stopped near her sister.

"You wanted me?" I asked, stopping at length beside Gwendoline Bambridge, and waiting, with my heart in my eyes and ears, for her answer.

"I wanted to ask you when you are going to dance with me. I know," she continued, "that you say I am *passée*; but I never allow any one to flirt with Clary who does not also pay her dear sister a little attention. So you see what you have to go in for."

She laughed with an intensely mischievous expression, while I, utterly miserable and fiercely indignant, answered,

"I never said you were *passée*; I never even thought it, I assure you."

Here I almost choked from the intensity of my feelings; the mere idea of such a term in connection with that bright and beautiful being was sacrilege.

"Oh, it is no good your denying it," she persisted. "I know you said I was *passée*, and that you admired Clary much more than you did me; but I will forgive you, if you promise to dance the next waltz with me."

"I am engaged for the next," I answered, ruefully; "but I don't mind. I will throw her over, if you will promise to tell me who it was who said I had spoken in that way of you."

I was quite ready to speak out then and there, and tell her I regarded her sister Clarissa's beauty as a mere foil to her peerless loveliness, though I knew Clarissa was standing by listening to all this, and with difficulty restraining her desire to laugh. The fear of offending my divinity alone restrained me. Besides, I could feel Claude's eye fixed on me with a cold, sarcastic expression.

I turned away hurriedly, saying I would be sure and come in time for the next dance; but as I went off with Miss Clarissa, I heard Feversham say, in a cool, clear voice, that I was certain he meant should reach me,

"The young one seems rather off his head at present. Nothing betrays age so much as the style in which a man conducts himself when in love."

I turned and looked at him for one minute—it was but a minute, but he understood my look; he knew I had detected him in the meanness of trying to make me appear badly in the eyes of the woman we both loved, and he had still sufficient good feeling left to be ashamed of himself. He colored all over his bronzed face, and bent his head to avoid my gaze, and I passed on, thinking bitterly that Claude was changed indeed to act thus, to stoop to a baseness that, even in my wildest moments, I would not have sullied myself with.

But I forgot all annoyance, all pain, when my dance with Gwendoline came round. She was as kind, as merry, as perfectly friendly as ever, and my poor, sore heart was soothed by the magic of her bright smiles, and the caressing tones of her soft voice.

"Who is that tall, handsome young man standing in the door-way?" she asked, presently. "I never saw him before to-night, yet he came with your party. I suppose he is one of the new arrivals. He is very good-looking. Introduce him to me."

I looked in the direction she mentioned, and saw Cecil Egerton leaning against the door-post, and talking in his quiet manner to Miss Graham. Now and then he laughed, as that young lady said something that amused him, and I could tell by the expression of his face he was enjoying himself, but in a way peculiar to him, and very different from our frank, outspoken merriment. He always seemed to me as if he felt things so far down below the surface that, except for his irresolution how to act, one would hardly know whether he had felt them at all. At the minute we looked at him we both could perceive he was laboring under the difficulty of deciding whether he should ask Miss Graham to continue the dance, or whether he should remain there listening to her talk. Fortunately for him, the young lady herself decided the matter, for, as she finished speaking, she put her hand on his shoulder, and he whirled her away among the dancers.

"Who is he? Introduce him to me," repeated Miss Bambridge.

"He is Cecil Egerton, an ensign in our regiment, a good bit senior to me. I will introduce him if you like," I answered, sulkily. It seemed to me as if every thing that evening conspired to annoy me. Why should she want to know him? What business had she to talk of him, and look at him, when she might have talked on subjects more nearly interesting to me, and might have looked at me? I was very savage and very miserable, and began to think all my special friends seemed to have been created for no other purpose than to pain and irritate me. But when the introduction was accomplished, and I saw by Egerton's manner he had no intention of paying particular attention in that quarter, I decided he had no feeling for beauty, and was a kind of outer barbarian, with whom, in spite of his poetic tastes, I could have nothing in common, and with whom it was surprising I could have lived so long on such intimate terms.

What weather-cocks we all are, swayed about by every trivial incident, every unexpected look or word! Why, even Claude Feversham, and I myself, were, in matters of feeling, as unstable and fickle as Egerton was in action. And we had presumed to laugh at him. Before the evening was over I had forgotten that Claude was a traitor, that Egerton was soulless and unfeeling, and that I had almost called Gwendoline a coquette. The thought had tried to take shape in my mind, but I had resisted it; I would not give it place, and finally I drove it forth in triumph. When we set out on our drive home, I remembered nothing but that I had danced three times with Gwendoline, that she had been as kind, and merry, and winning as ever to me, and had laughed a great deal with me over Clarissa's new admirer.

"I shall let Clary keep Colonel Dropmore," she said. "I always make her give up any of her men that I fancy, because, being eldest, I have right of first choice. If Colonel Dropmore was a good catch, it might be worth my while claiming him, but I don't fancy he is. Do you know any thing about it, Vivian?"

"If I did, I would not tell you," I answered boldly, looking up in her laughing face. "I will not encourage you in your evil courses; besides, it isn't fair Miss Clarissa should have nobody."

"Most Quixotic Madcap, Clary is well able to take care of herself. But really it is amusing to watch those two. See how Clary is snubbing him."

I did not care to look at them at all, having something much more interesting to me before my eyes; however, I did as I was told, and watched them for a few minutes. As Gwendoline had said, they were too amusing: Old Drops was touchingly devoted, and Clarissa was divided between saucy triumph and approaching boredom. Now and then I could see she struggled valiantly against a yawn that would come, and then she would turn with a smile to our little colonel, and say something with a serene expression, that could not have been very serene or placid in its wording, to judge by Dropmore's irritated look. It was evident the fish was hooked, and she was playing him skillfully. I suppose that is how we all look when we are caught, so we may comfort ourselves by thinking that even the wisest men in the world have looked at least once in their lives like helpless fools.

That was a consoling reflection to me, knowing, as I did, that I had probably looked just as idiotic, very likely more so, several times that evening.

But we were going home, and I was happy. Matters were as doubtful as ever between Gwendoline and me; yet her manner had given me confidence. One thing, at least, I had determined on, and that was that I would speak to Claude about the way in which I had overheard him allude to me that evening. It was a very foolish resolution on my part, but I was as foolish as most young men in my state of feeling are; I hoped that shame at being convicted in such a pettiness might make my cousin less pushing and forward in his attentions to Gwendoline in future.

Such a fool's hope! For an answer to it, I need only have asked myself, would any shame have availed to keep me away from her if I thought she cared to have me near her? And certainly she had given Claude that excuse during the evening. But one always expects one's friends and neighbors to be obedient to laws that one can not see to be in any way binding on one's self, and I was just as exorbitant in my demands on my cousin's good behavior as we all are usually with regard to those around us.

As Claude was turning into his room, when we arrived at barracks, I followed him.

"I want to speak to you a minute," I said.

"Very well," he answered, with an assumption of indifference that convinced me he knew what was coming. As he spoke, he pulled off his coat, and proceeded to get into his smoking toggery.

"What did you mean by saying to Miss Bambridge that I was off my head to-night? You also hinted very broadly that I was in love. Will you explain your meaning?"

"My good Vivian," he replied, laughing, "don't be absurd; you *were* rather off your head when I spoke—angry about something, I think—and all the world sees you are in love; so there was no harm in mentioning that."

"If I am in love," I retorted, "it is nothing to sneer at, let me tell you; and those who live in glass houses should not throw stones. But I will tell you what it is, Feversham, you have no business to monopolize Miss Bambridge in the way you do, and prevent any other fellow getting near her. I don't believe she likes it."

"And I believe she does," said Claude, slowly, with a half smile. "My dear boy, I don't want to pain you, but you are very mad and very foolish. You are too young to think of marriage. I love Miss Bambridge, and I think she cares for me; we understand each other pretty well, and the sooner you give up this hopeless infatuation of yours, the better it will be for you."

"Have you asked her to marry you yet?"

"Well, not exactly; but I think she knows I intend doing so. I am entirely dependent on my mother for means, and must get her consent and approbation before I can marry comfortably. I intend going over to see her in the beginning of September, telling her all about it, and getting her to make me a good allowance; until then I shall say nothing to Miss Bambridge; it is not much more than a month to wait."

"A most prudent and methodical person," I replied, sarcastically. "Love has not upset prudence, and an eye to the main chance, in your mind."

Claude walked up and down the room impatiently.

"Take care, Vivian," he said; "you may try me too far, patient as I am. Love does not prevent my seeing that it would be desirable I should offer my wife as good a home as that to which she is accustomed; but failing to secure that, I should still ask her to take me, because, putting all other matters aside, I have let her know my intentions too plainly to be able to draw off now. Not that I should do so in any case, Vivian; you underrate my feelings very much if you think that possible; but indeed I fancy you are not capable of understanding them, and that I waste my breath talking to you."

"Well, you will at least let me know your success," I urged.

"Certainly, if you wish it," he replied, with a confident laugh. "But don't build up hopes for yourself, Madcap; they will be in vain, and will cause you pain. I believe solemnly Gwendoline cares for me, and will accept me. I think she is kind to you only because you are my cousin."

This was too much for me; the vanity and conceit of that man, qualities I had never remarked in him before, were becoming unbearable, and I flung out of the room without uttering another word. On my way to my own quarters I met Egerton: we both had to cross the square to get to my rooms, and being bound in the same direction, we walked over together.

"Was that the Miss Bambridge about whom you have been talking so much, to whom you introduced me to-night?" he asked, as we walked over; and on my telling him it was, he remarked in his quiet way, "It is very odd how you fellows get into a state of mind about a girl like that. She is handsome, no doubt, but I don't see half the things you have discovered in her; and what is more curious, though there were such a number of pretty faces there to-night, none of them took possession of me in any way calculated to produce the feeling called falling in love. I suppose I am not capable of that kind of thing: something wanting in my mental organization prevents me from seeing perfection where it does not exist."

I was provoked with this fellow; he had been specially honored by her having asked for him to be introduced to her, and he had the audacity to appear almost bored by the honor.

"I am sure I don't know where you can find any one nearer perfection," I answered, hotly.

"Perhaps so," he replied; "but I admire her sister, Miss Clarissa, more. There is no accounting for taste, my good fellow, so don't enter into a particular explanation of why one sister must be handsomer than the other, as I see you are about to do; but tell me, did you see how old Acid Drops went in for Miss Clarissa? It was first-rate fun watching them—she played him so skillfully. In the end she got tired, and would have liked to get rid of him, but the impression she had made was too deep, and he would not leave her."

"I saw it," I answered, gloomily.

I hated fellows who did admire and run after Gwendoline, and was always seized with an insane longing to do them a mischief; but I never could bear men who had the bad taste not to admire her—it showed at once they were stupid louts, and stupid people are intensely irritating to me.

"Here are my quarters," said Cecil, just as I was about to express this feeling. "Will you come in and have a smoke and chat before you turn in, or are you going straight off?"

"Oh! I am off at once," I answered; and turning away left him, the keen edge of my pleasure in the evening completely blunted by his want of perception and Claude's vanity.

As to that fellow, Egerton—he was sure to suffer for it some day—it was such an absurd thing for him to think that he was not quite as capable of making a fool of himself as any of us. Of course it was only that he had not happened to meet the right person yet, and being always taken up by drawing and painting, for which he displayed remarkable talent, he had not time to waste on foolish flirtations, as most of our young fellows had.

With regard to his artistic abilities, they were wonderful; and though he had had but few lessons, I liked his pictures more than those of many of the swell Academy men. I often asked him why he did not exhibit, and found he had set himself some absurd standard of perfection that he was to attain before doing so—a standard he was never likely to attain, for though his keen perception of the beautiful kept him tolerably straight in the right path, still, in this pursuit, his vacillating nature injured him more than it could have done in any of his ordinary avocations. Every thing he did had to be changed and altered, painted and re-painted dozens of times, the matter generally ending by my taking forcible possession of the canvas until he was absorbed in something else, when it might be restored to its owner without fear of consequences. His ideal standard, consequently, he would never reach, and there were many beautiful things tossing about his rooms that would have won high praise at any exhibition. He was devoted to sketching, and determined to profit by the beautiful country surrounding Belmurphy, it promising to afford him ample opportunity for indulging in his favorite pursuit.

Sometimes he would get leave for a day or two, and start from barracks in a regular artist's get up—portable easel, knapsack, with paint-box and materials, gray tweed clothes, and high felt hat of the brigand shape, so dear to the artist's soul. Particularly handsome he looked in that attire, the dark felt hat suiting the handsome, melancholy cast of his countenance extremely well.

His uncle, he told me, hated this passion of his, and whenever he was at Beaumanoir he was accustomed to steal off without announcing his departure, and remain away for weeks together, returning as suddenly as he had left. His uncle thought he went up to London to amuse himself, and made no objections to these excursions, which he would have forbidden had he known their innocent object. He was even generous enough to offer the young man money occasionally, saying that young men were accustomed to find their allowances too small, and he wished his nephew to do every thing handsomely. Lately he had offered to keep a horse for Cecil. The offer had been accepted, for, though Egerton knew very little of riding, he was fond of it, and found it assisted his sketching trips greatly to be able to go on a quadruped's feet instead of on his own.

I thought of all this as I growled at Egerton's stupidity that night, and would have wondered that, being an artist, he had not found himself compelled to admire Gwendoline, as one would admire a picture, when I remembered that his particular line was landscape—about portrait-painting he knew nothing. Feeling slightly contemptuous over Egerton's short-coming, and reflecting that if he did fall in love he would change his mind every day, I dismissed the subject, and began to dream of Gwendoline's manner to me, and Feversham's abominable egotism in fancying that it was regard for him prompted that manner.

What will become of the world when men are so vain that they can not see another fellow's chance is as good, or better, than their own? And thinking thus, I fell asleep.

———◆———

CHAPTER VII

HOSTILITIES.

DAYS passed on, and matters went much as they had done before our re-enforcement: that is to say, we fished, and boated, and rode, and drove, and croqueted, and danced, and Egerton mooned about the country roads sketching, and a curious state of affairs sprang up between Claude and myself. It was thus it arose:

Though Claude persisted that he had never yet spoken distinctly to Gwendoline Bambridge, he took upon himself all the monopolizing airs of an accepted lover, and was very fond of talking to me about her, and arranging what he would do when they were married, as he seemed to take it for granted they would be. His choice of a confidant was at least singular; he knew the state of my feelings, and should have spared me, and at least not talked of his success to me, if success it was.

Of this I was not quite sure, but I was beginning to be convinced by his manner. He could never have spoken as he did, had not something passed between them that made him certain of his ground. I was wretchedly unhappy. I listened to Claude's confidences because there was a fascination for me in hearing any thing about Gwendoline, even if what I heard was altogether unfavorable to my hopes; I would listen to him moodily, and hate him for talking thus, and myself for being so mean-spirited as to stay and hear what he had to say. Then, perhaps half an hour afterward, if I met Gwendoline, she was so friendly and so particularly anxious for my company, that I would forget all Feversham had been telling me, and give myself up to the happiness of the moment. Cecil Egerton himself could not have been a more utterly weak-minded fool than I was at that time, living alternately on a pinnacle of happiness and in a gulf of gloom and despair.

One thing struck me particularly, and from it, in my inexperience, I drew a favorable augury, when I might have known, had I been older and wiser, that it was the worst sign possible.

Gwendoline now never spoke to me of Claude Feversham, as she had been accustomed to do when we first came to the place. On the contrary, I thought she sometimes avoided mention of him, when she might have been led to allude to him in following a subject. Of course I decided she did not interest herself in him, when in fact it was precisely because her interest in him was great that she kept silence.

Colonel Dropmore had continued his attentions to Clarissa Bambridge. He had explained to her the amount of his income, the settlements he had made on his first wife, and various other little details that showed plainly what his intentions with regard to her were.

She had become alarmed; and from laughing at him, had proceeded to snubbing him regularly, but without much effect. Indeed the poor man seemed to become more and more in earnest the less hope there appeared to be for him. But Clarissa could not keep him from coming to pay visits; could not keep her people from inviting him; could not altogether avoid his attentions when he was there. And thus it happened that, one day, as the whole party were in the garden, gooseberry-picking (as Clarissa afterward observed), Colonel Dropmore managed to discover that young lady in an isolated corner, all alone.

"It was very stupid of me to have gone there," she said afterward, to Gwendoline. "I might have known, with Pear Drops in the place, retirement of any kind was dangerous. But there was a pet plum-tree of mine in that corner, and the plums are just ripe, and I did not think he would find me. That was a mistake, I must confess. He is sharper than I thought. Having found me, he began, in his odious, direct way, to tell me that he had been fascinated by my many charms and virtues, and that he designed me the honor of making me the second Mrs. Dropmore. I can give you no idea of the stilted politeness of his language, or the exquisite composure with which he awaited his answer, quite convinced it would be all he could wish. I was struck dumb at first, and did not recover myself until he tried to take my hand. Then I drew away and put my hand behind my back, saying, 'Excuse me, Colonel Dropmore, but I don't quite see this matter in the same light as you do. I am convinced, from what you tell me, that you would make a most estimable husband, and I know you are the pink of propriety and consideration, but I have set my heart on something much more unruly and scatter-brained. I could never consent to lead the life of dull decorum that would await me as your wife.'"

"'I will be as unruly and scatter-brained as you like,' said the poor old fellow, in answer. 'Indeed, Miss Clarissa, I am very much in earnest, and I think you have hardly a right to refuse me, after all the encouragement you have given me.'

"I was very angry then," continued Clarissa. "Fancy my having encouraged him, when I had been snubbing him all along as hard as I could.

"'I deny that I have encouraged you,' I said. 'I have tried to keep you off, by every means in my power; and if you don't like what I say to you now, remember you drew it on yourself.'

"Then he got very angry, and told me he knew I was in the habit of keeping a whole lot of young fellows dangling after me, and treating them as I had treated him; but he would put a stop to it, at least in part.

"'I will keep them up to their work,' he continued, 'and not let them go racing off here at every hour of the day. We have had a great deal too little work and too much amusement lately; but that must be altered now.'

"And so I believe it will be," added Clarissa, with a fresh burst of laughing, "for I was so annoyed at what he said to me that I told him he need never hope to occupy the same place in my regard as his subalterns, who were, most of them, particularly nice young men. He looked so furious then that I got frightened, and ran back to you, Gwendoline. Do you think he will stay to dinner?"

Gwendoline paused in the act of picking a plum, and looked round cautiously to see that there was no one near, before she answered,

"I don't care about his staying to dinner; indeed I think it would be much better he did not do so. But I hope to goodness he will not be able to prevent our friends coming out to see us; it would be too provoking. I could not exist without seeing Vivian every day."

"In fact, when the —th leave, life will be a burden to you on his account," retorted Clarissa, slyly. "But how about Lord Feversham—does he come in nowhere? I was inclined to think he had quite as much to do as dear Madcap in mitigating the tedium of your existence."

"Don't be absurd, Clary," answered Gwendoline, laughing. "There are some subjects on which even younger sisters have no right to intrude, if it were only possible to teach them so; but you are a hardened offender. Don't think you will get any information out of me, however."

The colonel did go, as Clarissa had expected he would; he told General Bambridge there was urgent business awaiting him at barracks, and he actually hurried away without saying good-bye to the young ladies.

"What have you been doing to Colonel Dropmore, girls?" asked Mrs. Bambridge, noticing this. "It must be your fault, Clarissa, for you were the one he was last seen with."

"Oh! indeed, mamma," laughed Clarissa, gayly, "don't ask me what has taken him away. No one knows what I have gone through the last two weeks, with the defunct Mrs. Dropmore, her settlements, her peculiarities, her devotion, her little touch of spirit, that some ill-natured people called temper, etc. I have lived in hourly terror of being carried off, and made Mrs. Dropmore, *nolens volens*, ever since I first met him; and it is such a relief to me when he takes himself off for a while, that I hope no one will mention his name this evening."

We all obeyed her wishes, and I think if old Drops had known how perfectly we enjoyed ourselves that evening without him, his frame of mind, as he drove back to the barracks, would have been even worse than it undoubtedly was. And then he did not smoke, and of course felt all his grievances a great deal the more for that abstinence. It does soothe a fellow, you know, and is better than drink as a consoler, being less immediately deleterious in its effects, though the doctors do tell us it is quite as certain.

It is all very fine saying the mind is the master of the body; perhaps in very highly organized natures it may be, but with ordinary everyday people like the majority of us, I maintain that bodily indulgence, if it be indulgence in anything for which you have a very strong liking, deadens, and for a time overmasters mental affliction. The indulgence may be drink, smoking, eating, riding a good horse, boating, or athletics; any of those things, in proportion as you enjoy them, make a fellow feel almost jolly as long as they last, and every time the mind is diverted from its trouble the hold of that trouble is weakened.

But our good old man had no such consolation, and even the slashing pace at which the post-horse took him back to town lost the power of gratification it might have possessed, from the fact that the animal that showed such a turn of speed was not his own, but only a wretched hired screw. The colonel's was not a very noble nature, though a good-natured one, and he was sorely ruffled and annoyed at the manner in which he had been treated. It seemed to him quite impossible that his offer could have been refused, and refused in such a manner. It was all the fault of the crowd of foolish boys that followed the girl about everywhere, and that prevented her from thinking seriously of business; but he would settle that—he would give those fellows plenty of work now, find them something to do besides flirtation and love-making.

Of course when one has the fixed intention of making one's self disagreeable, it is not at all difficult to find an opportunity for doing so; and this Colonel Dropmore soon found.

His opportunity occurred in the following way: We were sitting round the table over our wine after mess one evening, a day or two after the Bambridges' party. It was very curious how every one guessed that Acid Drops had failed in getting a second Mrs. Drops. Miss Clarissa had kept her own counsel, and yet we had all read the secret at once, and knew why the colonel was unusually gloomy and taciturn, and why he had not gone near Endley the last two days.

We had been talking of all the dances, and other entertainments we had been at lately, and we had been praising the hospitality of our friends about Belmurphy. Suddenly Feversham looked up from the laborious task of pounding a biscuit into minute fragments, a task that had for some time absorbed all his energies, and said, "It seems to me we ought to do something in return for all their civility. Don't you think we could manage it?"

"What shall it be?" asked several voices.

"A dance, of course," I suggested, boldly; "nothing else gives such general satisfaction. Ask the old fogies to dinner, and it will not only be dull for us, but all the ladies who are really our best friends in Belmurphy will be left out in the cold; give a picnic, and we shall have an immensity of trouble, and the midges will eat up the thin-skinned, and the delicate will get their feet wet, and the salt will get into the claret cup, and the wasps into the sweet dishes; but give a dance, and you are all right—all are safe to enjoy themselves, and it is not nearly so much trouble either to make a thing of that kind pass off well."

"A dance!" cried Mayleigh, joining in, "that will not be much of a return for all the hospitality that has been shown us. We shall have to do something more."

"Why not give a lot of dances?" suggested Preston, languidly, and as if the matter had not much interest for him. He was a sleepy kind of youth, and having shown so much interest in the proceedings, relapsed again into silence.

"That is not a bad idea," cried Flower. "Let us fix a certain night in the week, and give small early bops every time that day comes round. Say, begin at six and end at twelve. That will not entail much dress on the ladies, and people will be more willing to come a distance when they know they can get away early."

"Bravo! Flower," echoed from all sides of the table; "you have got an idea there at last. That is the very thing." A little more talk, and Flower's plan was decided on. Thursday in every week was chosen as the most suitable day; and Colonel Dropmore not being present, having gone that day to dine with the Graces at Fairleigh, it was arranged that Feversham should tell him what had been settled next day, and get him to consent to their messing at three o'clock, on that particular afternoon every week until further notice.

I don't know that any one expected old Drops would oppose this plan for our amusement, and you may be very sure we were all much astonished when, next evening at mess, on the project being mooted by Feversham, he negatived it very decidedly.

"Can't have it," he said, in the quick, excited manner he had when put out. "Can't hear of it at all. Quite impossible to mess at three o'clock; couldn't do it; should get dyspepsia and all kinds of horrors. Let me hear no more talk about it, I beg."

"Well, but colonel, it is not necessary you should dine at three; if we younger fellows like to do it, I am sure we could manage to get you a snug, comfortable little dinner all to yourself, in some room where we should not interfere with you." So spoke Claude Feversham, looking rather anxious.

"You young fellows indeed!" growled Dropmore, irritated anew by such an unlucky expression; "I suppose you think no one is young but yourself, and that it is a proof of youth to dine at impossible hours. It is a proof of folly, if you like. And I know very well what my comfortable little dinner would be: fish cold, soup greasy, chops black and sooty, bad feeding, and worse waiting, and no company to make matters pleasanter. No, I will have no folly here, let me tell you."

"We have a right to the mess-room," I called out, rather imprudently. "We may dance here if we like."

"I was not addressing you, Mr. Darrell; when I want information I will apply to you for it. Yes," he continued, with an ominous chuckle, "the mess-room is yours, and you are welcome to it; much good may it do you. I wish you joy of it, and of your three o'clock dinner."

After this he subsided into a series of suppressed chuckles, which told plainly he was concocting some scheme against our intended amusement. What his plan was we could not divine, and he kept his own secret; it was very provoking, as naturally we imagined he had devised some way of interfering with us, and yet not seeing any move on his part to prevent our design, we proceeded with our preparations.

Thursday came, and we were just sitting down to dinner, when James, the adjutant, came in hurriedly; he had been a little late, and we had sat down without waiting for him. "Just listen to this," he cried, as he entered. "That old fool Drops has sent me a note, which I received this minute, in which he informs me that he has lent the band to the Robinsons at Glenlough for this evening, and that, as the drive is a long one, they must start at five o'clock."

This was a blow indeed; every body stopped eating, and looked up with a helpless, dismayed expression on their countenances. I was in a blazing passion; the idea of that old beast thinking he could spoil our fun at the last minute. Never! we would teach him better than that.

Springing on to my chair, I signed to every one to be silent, and proceeded to harangue the meeting. It was necessary to be impressive, to stir up those around me to rebellion, and to effect this object, I knew that I must keep myself cool. This was a hard task, but the cause was worth it: it would be such a glorious victory if we foiled our adversary with his own weapons.

"Gentlemen," I said, with solemnity, seeing every eye fixed on me, more in astonishment, I am bound to admit, than as recognizing me as a leader whom they would be proud to obey—"gentlemen, this is a case of flagrant tyranny, and one that calls for immediate and decisive action. Colonel Dropmore has taken a mean advantage of us; thinks he will at one stroke please his friends and spoil our pleasure. Let us show him that we will not for one moment submit to such an unjust proceeding. He wants the band—that he shall not have; he is welcome to the bandsmen—they are his; let him take them: the instruments are ours—we will keep them. I am afraid he will not find those fellows as conducive to harmony as he may wish when they arrive without our consent and support. It will give him a lesson, I think, and make him take care in future how he promises the band without our leave. As to our dance—don't despair; I know where we can hire a piano and musicians for to-night. Send the bandsmen, James, by all means; but with my consent not even a cornet shall go with them."

"Bravo! Well spoken, young one!" was shouted in chorus, as I jumped down. "That is the way to do it! Old Drops will find he made a mistake this time. It will be a little more trouble to us to get the musicians before six; but that won't matter; we will have our dance, and perhaps will enjoy it more than the colonel will enjoy his entertainment."

We carried out our plan; the bandsmen went to Glenlough minus their instruments, and we had a jolly dance. I can not say we were all of us quite without misgivings as to what would be Colonel Dropmore's retaliation, but we did not let the thoughts of it interfere with our amusement.

I believe he was absolutely raving when the bandsmen appeared. The band-master, as soon as they arrived, had the sense to send in for him, asking to see him as soon as dinner was over; and on his appearing, handed him a note drawn up by James, and signed by all of us. He stamped, and raged, and swore, and finally, remembering the men were there, told them they might remain at Glenlough for the night. If they went back, those fellows would have the use of them, he reflected.

He then questioned the band-master, to know if the preparations for the dance had been continued, once it was known the bandsmen would not be there. The man did not know very well how matters had been arranged, but he had heard something about Mr. Darrell having gone down to the town to look for musicians—or some people of that sort, added the band-master, with a lofty contempt for any musical talent not embodied in a regimental band.

"Always that young cub!" growled Colonel Dropmore between his teeth. "He is the fellow that is always knocking about with the Bambridges; and now I suppose he will spend the whole night flirting with Clarissa! Young whelp! I should like to horsewhip him soundly!"

With this remark, uttered so as to be perfectly audible to the men, Colonel Dropmore turned away, and went to break the news to the hostess, that the bandsmen had arrived, but not the band. It was too aggravating;· all attempt at dancing had to be given up, as none of the young ladies there present were equal to the task of playing dance music, and there were no musicians attainable at Glenlough, as there had been at Belmurphy.

Our dance, on the contrary, passed off splendidly, and was even kept up a little later than we intended it should be. We issued our invitations for next Thursday before we separated, and retired to rest well pleased with the success of our entertainment.

Next day Colonel Dropmore was moody and silent. He made no mention of the occurrence of the day before, and we did not think it necessary to allude to it in his presence. But we could see he was boiling over with rage, which was all the more dangerous because it was concentrated in a nature where concentration was unusual. Days passed by, and still he made no allusion to what had occurred; and we began to think he was beaten, and was contented to revenge himself by strictness in all the minutiæ of barrack life, and in an excessive overdose of drill which he now laid upon us.

But next Wednesday, just as we had begun to congratulate ourselves that no attempt would be made to interfere with our amusement next day, he said at mess,

"I am going to hold a special parade at three o'clock to-morrow, gentlemen. I tell you this that it may not interfere with your dinner-hour, which, I believe, falls earlier on Thursday than on any other day of the week."

We all looked at each other in dismay. It was necessary we should get mess over early, as otherwise the room would not be ready; and it seemed this provoking old villain was determined to prevent our dining at the only hour that would suit. We had been very gay, talking and laughing, a few minutes before; now we all sat silent and annoyed, wondering how we should get over this new difficulty thrown in our way. We could not talk the matter over then, however, and we waited until old Drops had vanished before any one alluded to the subject. Then there was a perfect Babel of voices, one advising one thing, one another. At length above the clamor rose Claude Feversham's quiet voice, saying,

"It seems to me we should have plenty of time to dine after parade, if we could dine in any room but this; it is only the difficulty of having the room ready in time. That can be arranged, however, I think. We will order dinner at the hotel; those who have to stay in barracks can make shift to dine somewhere, and thus we shall circumvent Drops again. Don't let him know what we are about, or he will keep us longer at work."

This proposal seemed to meet the difficulty, and it was accordingly settled the matter should be thus arranged. Claude and I sauntered down to the hotel at once, to give the proper instructions, and the original arrangements for next day were counter-ordered. It was really great fun, devising how to get round and counteract the old fellow's schemes; one felt as if one was an Indian following a trail, or a detective tracking out a crime. Claude and I laughed over it as we went down the town, and laughed still more at the astonishment of the old lady who kept the hotel when she heard the order. She could not think what was up, and, though no doubt inwardly delighted at a freak that promised to bring her so much custom, was too intensely curious to know the meaning of it to appreciate its benefits fully.

"I have them now," thought Colonel Dropmore next day, when he saw us all assembled on parade at three o'clock. "I will see if they can have things ready in time when I let them go."

And he did keep us a good time indeed, putting us through a whole lot of stupid drill that we knew to the last degree of perfection. We could not satisfy him, however; he growled and scolded, and made us go over things again and again. I think, if the men were aware on whose account they were put through all this business, they must have devoutly wished us all at the bottom of the Red Sea. I caught it particularly heavily; was told I was a negligent, ignorant, brainless officer—a young man who would never make a good soldier, and who had quite mistaken his profession in coming into the army. I felt rather indignant at being so rated, but, knowing the old fellow had enough to try his temper, I listened to it all, with as meek an expression as I could assume. Besides, what had more influence with me than any thing else was that I knew, in his present state of mind, he would be quite capable of ordering me into close arrest in my own quarters, if he thought I looked disrespectful. So I seemed as doleful as I could, and did my best to please; but we had a hard time of it certainly until five o'clock, when, thinking we were too late to get over dinner in time for the dance, he let us off.

He was going out that night himself—going to dine somewhere. He was a *bon-vivant*, and very fond of dining out; since our row he had hardly messed with us once. But this time he had not requested the attendance of the band. We of course kept our plans very secret, and said nothing about our wanting it. The colonel would be gone by six, and, once he was off, we would have it in. There was very little time to go down town to get dinner, but Claude arranged with me, I being unable to leave barracks that day, that I should play host, and entertain any early comers, until he and the others returned.

Every thing went off splendidly. Old Drops cleared out in good time, the band came in as we had arranged, our fellows returned from their dinner just as the first car-load of guests drove up, and we had a very merry and successful evening—an evening that was to me intensely happy, for Gwendoline paid less attention to Claude than she had done for some time past, and the attention she withdrew from him she bestowed on me.

One rather provoking *contretemps* the colonel did contrive to produce in this way: There was a Mrs. Grace and her daughters, who were great friends of ours. They had intended to come to our dance that evening, but meeting Colonel Dropmore in town during the morning, they happened to mention their intention.

"I think," said old Drops, "you will find that there will be no dance at the barracks to-night: I have been obliged to order an extra parade that I am afraid will interfere with the arrangements, and prevent the dance coming off."

"I suppose we shall hear from some of the other officers, if it is not to take place?" said Miss Grace, inquiringly. She knew the colonel had not been at the last dance, and fancied, therefore, that very likely he knew little about the matter.

"I don't know how that will be," replied Colonel Dropmore, "but I am pretty sure there will be no dance. In fact, I do not see how there can be."

That was decisive enough, and the Graces did not appear that evening at our festivities—a great disappointment to some of the party, who looked out for them anxiously, until it was too late for any further hope.

They were dreadfully annoyed next day when they heard that the dance had taken place, and it was a long time before the colonel was forgiven

for what was certainly an unintentional deception on his part. As to old Drops himself, he was rather astonished when he found that, in spite of all he could do, we had carried out our plan; and what irritated him most in it was that the Bambridges were constant attendants at our entertainments, and that Miss Clarissa had a number of admirers, whom she treated with much more favor than she had ever treated him. He could keep us all much harder at work, and prevent us from getting out as much as we used to do, but he could not prevent the young ladies coming to our hops, nor prevent us giving them, and he began to feel himself beaten. He kept up the three o'clock parade, however, for one or two more Thursdays; but at last, finding it completely inefficacious, he gave in, and we were allowed to return to our original plan of early mess, and dancing afterward. Perhaps the only person who regretted the change was the old lady at the hotel, to whom it must have made a considerable difference, as she no longer supplied us with a weekly dinner. I don't think Colonel Dropmore felt on very friendly terms with us for a while after this; it would not have been natural that he should; but by degrees his anger died out, and being a good-natured little fellow, he forgot and forgave the whole matter, only retaining a prejudice against poor Cecil Egerton, whom, in some unaccountable way, he had taken it into his head to consider a ringleader in the rebellion against him, and with whom he continued very sharp and snappish in consequence.

It was now August. Lots of our fellows had got leave to go off to Scotland for the twelfth; Claude would have gone too, I think, but for Miss Bambridge. I being such a very youthful individual, did not get the chance. We were pretty sure to have good shooting where we were, however. It was a good grouse country, and we had many friends who all wanted us to be with them on the twentieth. Indeed we could not divide ourselves among them all, and so accepted General Bambridge's invitation, as being the most attractive. There was something besides grouse in it—the certainty of coming back to dinner after the day's sport, and the possibility of luncheon among the heather, with Gwendoline and Clarissa to brighten the repast with their presence. Besides we heard the shooting was good, so we had a sufficient excuse for yielding to the real attraction, which was not in any way connected with the sport of grouse-shooting.

There is something delightful to me in the balmy, heather-scented mountain air; it raises one's spirits, and makes every thing appear twice as beautiful and exhilarating as the same thing would seem down in the dull, damp lowlands.

I always did love the mountains, though I confess that in this country some of them are execrable walking, and I should like to know how a fellow can be expected to hit a bird when he is balancing on the extreme point of a conical tussock, in a quaking bog, where one false step will plunge him up to his neck in a boghole, from whence, if he be not immediately rescued, he may never be released, as he will settle down into it very quickly, disappearing altogether shortly. I found these little peculiarities in the nature of the ground interfered with my shooting, and what disturbed me still more was the knowledge that, as I anticipated, Mrs. Bam-

bridge and her two daughters would bring up
the luncheon-basket later in the day. A ren-
dezvous had been appointed by a beautiful
mountain lakelet, and, like a fool as I was, I
let fancy pictures of our little forthcoming picnic get between me and all my best shots.
Claude was shooting very well; neither his
mental nor bodily equilibrium was so easily upset as mine, and I looked at him sometimes with
wonder, not unmixed with envy.

We had with us a Scotch gamekeeper in the
employment of a neighboring proprietor, over
whose land we had permission to shoot; and,
besides, we had four Irish fellows, queer chaps,
who told you long stories about packs of birds
they had seen, that we never by any chance
came across, and that we presently became
aware were just as apocryphal as the Scotch-
man's tales of wonderful setters that had belonged to his last employer.

' The heather was a mass of purple bloom, the
walking, as I have said, was execrable, and the
heat of the day intense. Claude and General
Bambridge did not seem to mind it, neither did
Cecil Egerton, who was a wonderful shot—never missed—but spent his whole time regretting
he had not brought his sketching-block, becoming every now and then so absorbed in the view
that the grouse rose almost under his feet without his seeing them. But I must acknowledge
I found the work rather hard, and was very glad
when we arrived at the tarn, and found the ladies
there awaiting us.

They had laid their table at the foot of a high
bank of heather, against which we could rest our
backs, and which afforded us a very welcome shelter from the blazing August sun. ·

Clarissa chaffed me on my fatigue, and on my
want of success.

"I thought you were a good shot," she said;
"but I do believe I could do better myself. Shall
we try after lunch?"

"With all my heart," I answered. "What
shall we try at? Will you join our party and
blaze away at the grouse?"

"Oh no," she laughed. "I don't pretend to
hit any thing unless it will stand still for me.
We will put your hat up on a stick and shoot at
it."

"Willingly," I answered, "if you will put
yours on another, for me to take a shot at.
That is only fair."

She took off her hat and looked at it.

"I bought this hat second-hand," she said,
"from a lady who had nearly done wearing it.
It cost me two shillings and twopence half-penny, and, as it is becoming, I don't think that
dear. How much did yours cost?"

"Clarissa, my dear," interrupted her mother,
"put on your hat, or you will have a sunstroke.
What are you asking Mr. Darrell?"

"I was only asking him what his hat cost,"
replied Clarissa, unconcernedly. "He hasn't
told me yet. How much was it?"

"Ten shillings," I answered, taking off the
article in question, and holding it out toward
her to examine. "Mine is worth more than
yours, it seems, but then I am more likely to do
mischief than you are, so perhaps, after all, it is
pretty fair."

"You will have to give me a nearer range,
though," she continued. "I could not take the

matter up unless you will give it to me at twenty
yards, and you at sixty."

"That is rather long odds in your favor," I
remonstrated. "I don't think I could make
such a bargain."

"All the better for my poor hat, then," she
returned, smoothing down the feathers with her
hand. "Don't you think, Gwen, it was a very
reasonable offer?"

"Very, indeed," replied Gwen, absently, with
her eyes fixed on a piece of white heather Feversham had just offered her. "Indeed," she
added, brightening up suddenly, as though afraid
of letting herself relapse into dream-land, "if
Vivian gives you such a chance, I will take a
shot at it myself."

This decided me. Of course she had only
entered into Clarissa's rather original scheme for
amusing herself in order to please me (so I told
myself), and immediately all the resistance I had
prepared against her sister's claim for a twenty-
yards' range vanished. Gwendoline might have
blown my hat to bits had she felt so disposed,
and I should only have been flattered.

I was the more pleased now because I saw an
impatient frown pass over Claude's face when
Gwendoline announced her intention of shooting
with us. It was evident he perceived her partiality for me, I thought, and was displeased at it.
I think that made me enjoy myself all the more;
it showed that there really was a chance for me,
that I was dangerous, and I rose in my own estimation accordingly.

What a merry luncheon that was to me! How
we laughed and jested, and afterward made the
gamekeepers and gossoons sing for us! Then
Gwendoline and Clarissa sang, and finally we
set about our shooting match.

Mrs. Bambridge insisted on being in it too,
and declared she would beat any of us, Mr.
Egerton excepted. He had earned himself a
wonderful name as a shot (whenever he did
choose to shoot), but, as I said before, he was
generally mooning when his gun should have
been to his shoulder.

And my poor hat was to come in for most of
it, as none of the gentlemen were in the match
but myself; Clarissa vehemently declaring she
would not have her most killing head-gear destroyed by the deadly fire of veteran warriors,
as she was pleased to call Claude and Egerton.

To my surprise and great disgust, they contrived to pepper my new tile in very destructive
fashion, and it did not help me to bear the matter
better to hear Feversham grumble close behind
me :

"Serves the confounded puppy right! I wish
he had come in for a few grains himself!"

A minute's reflection convinced me he would
not have said this but for jealousy; and, encouraged by this idea, I went home that evening
perfectly happy.

CHAPTER VIII

A FAMILY ARRANGEMENT.

ALL this time, while Claude was getting himself more and more involved in the net of Gwendoline Bambridge's fascinations, he seemed to
forget what his mother would say to the whole

affair, and he also ceased to remember a family arrangement that this infatuation of his promised to upset completely.

Not very far from the "Castle," as Feversham's place was called in the county, there lived a family of the name of Prendergast. They were very wealthy, and had one daughter, Mabel, who, as the heiress to such a splendid property, was very much run after. Claude's mother, Lady Feversham, had, however, planned a match between her son and the young lady in question—a match that met with the full approval, not only of Mr. and Mrs. Prendergast, but of Miss Mabel also, the only one who did not see the matter in the most favorable light being the captain himself.

The affair had long been arranged, and he, though not intending to marry at present, had never distinctly refused to have the young lady; only his mother had been unable to work him up to the proposing point, and, until that formality had been gone through, the match could not be regarded as quite settled.

The girl herself was only eighteen, and had not long been out; she had heard, however, quite enough of the plans of the family to know for whom she was destined—an arrangement in which, after meeting and dancing with Claude once or twice, she perfectly coincided.

Mabel Prendergast was tall, dark, and slight, beautifully made, with pretty hands and feet, immense masses of black hair, shaded at the edges with rusty brown, and curious red-brown eyes, that possessed a strange, inscrutable, sphinx-like expression; more the eyes of a wild beast than of a human being, but they were capable of great fascination, probably from their very singularity; a pale complexion, with only the faintest creamy tinge of color in her cheeks, and an indescribable air of coquetry hovering round her pretty mouth, as one who could be saucy and coaxing both, if she thought it worth her while to try.

This was the girl whose very faintly traced image was rapidly being obliterated from Claude's heart by the queenly beauty of Gwendoline Bambridge; and so lightly did he regard the known wishes of the families that he never deemed it possible they might look on his lazy indifference to their schemes in the light of acquiescence, and even think him virtually engaged.

Lady Feversham was fond of Mabel. She liked the girl's strange beauty, she liked her rich, tasteful dress, and, above all, she liked to listen to the piquant stories and quaint witticisms constantly falling, in the softest, most musical tones, from those charming lips.

Therefore Mabel was with her constantly, riding over from The Poplars unattended, and passing hours of the day in walking round the garden with her future mother-in-law, or in the cold weather sitting snugly up to the fire, listening to the latest news from Claude.

"He does not write me very long letters now, dear," complained the elder lady one day; "he seems amusing himself, however. There is a General Bambridge who appears to be civil to them, and they are constantly at his place."

"Has he any daughters?" asked Mabel, with a sudden perception of the truth bursting in on her.

"Yes — two," answered Lady Feversham; "odd, Irish kind of girls, I fancy. I remember his telling me how he first met them. One of them tried to horsewhip him for fishing on her father's ground without leave. Great hoydenish vulgarians, I imagine they must be; but, after all, when you have said they are Irish, that is enough to explain the kind of people they are."

"Do you think so, Lady Feversham?" said Mabel, softly, but with an accent that plainly said such was not her opinion. "I have heard some people say Irish girls are very charming; perhaps your son finds them so too."

"Tush, child! I don't know who can have told you such a thing; but I am convinced a Feversham would find nothing fascinating about them; moreover, my dear, you know my wish with regard to my son and you."

"Yes, I know," answered the girl, with a smile so careless and indifferent that the most skilled physiognomist would have been puzzled to detect any deep feeling beneath it; but your son may not obey your wish in this instance. And do you know," she continued, with more energy, and a faint, saucy smile dawning on her rosy lips, "I am not quite sure that I should care for the fulfillment of your desire either, if it is only to please you he does it. It is foolish, is it not, Lady Feversham?" she went on, taking a rosebud out of a vase and arranging it in front of her dress, "to wish to be married for one's self—not because one has money and it suits the families. But, do you know, I think I am foolish, after all. Let Lord Claude look to it, if he does not want a silly wife."

So saying, she turned away with a rippling laugh that broke from her only on rare occasions, but then, all the more beautiful for its rarity, it pleased the ear like the tinkling of a mountain stream trickling over a mossy bed.

"What a strange child it is!" thought Lady Feversham, watching her as she walked over to a sofa and threw herself on it, still laughing. "I hope she may not be tired of waiting, and that Claude will not lose the bonnie bride I have been keeping for him all these years. As to her idea about those Irish girls, it must be absurd. However, I will write to Lady Longwreath about it; she often goes to that part of the world, and most likely has friends there who give her all the news."

Lady Feversham, once startled, lost no time in endeavoring to find out the way matters were going on in Ireland. She wrote that night to Lady Longwreath, explaining her anxieties, and beseeching her friend to find out if there really was any danger to be apprehended from those Irish Bambridge girls.

She had to wait more than a week before she could possibly hope to get an answer, during which time she petted and caressed Mabel even more than usual, so fearful was she of losing the labor of many years—a contingency she had never even contemplated till after Mabel's curious speech the day before.

As for Mabel, her rosy lips wore their faint, triumphant expression more frequently during those days than ever before. Mentally, she said, "This will decide the matter; something will be arranged; and at least, if he is infatuated about any bog-trotting belle over there, I shall be taken up to London, and shall queen it during the season to my heart's content."

For she was well aware of her power, though

she knew it had done little for her with Claude Feversham: partly because she had never cared to triumph in that quarter, believing the matter secure by family compact. It would have been like making love to one's husband to have shown him any attention, she thought; only, if she had known, perhaps it might have been worth while. For now that the prize was about to slip from her grasp, or seemed ready to do so, she began to have an idea that she had lost something that had been pleasant to her. His face was handsome, his manner gentle; certainly she had seen none she liked better, and she might have grown to like him more, if he had but felt warmly toward her. But that was the annoying part of it all, as she had told Lady Feversham; she was inclined to be foolish, and now more so than ever. It was not that she wanted particularly to care for her husband—she could do without that; but it was imperative he should care for her.

About ten days after, as she sat at breakfast with Lady Feversham, when the post-bag was opened she saw a letter with the Longwreath crest, and waited impatiently while her hostess broke the seal and slowly perused a very lengthy epistle. The red-brown eyes watched Lady Feversham closely as she conned over her friend's letter—so closely, indeed, that before the elder lady had half finished reading it, the younger knew its contents from the expression of her friend's countenance, and knew, moreover, that its purport was unfavorable to her hopes.

"Well," she asked, when Lady Feversham at length looked up, with a very disturbed face, "is this Irish belle as fascinating as I foretold?"

"Do not joke about it, child," groaned the old lady. "This is very serious. Lady Longwreath has not only found out that Claude is really *épris* with this Miss Bambridge, but she also adds she knows the young lady well herself, and can answer for it that, having obtained an influence over any man, she will not be easily forgotten."

Mabel flushed up a little more than her wont; it sounded like a challenge to her, like a slur cast on her powers of captivation, that this girl should be so spoken of before her, and she tapped her saucer impatiently with her spoon as she thought,

"Oh! if only I had him here, he should soon forget his Irish charmer!"

It was never her cue, however, to speak out what she felt; so she asked, carelessly,

"And what will you do now? I am afraid your wishes can hardly be fulfilled as the matter stands, even were I willing."

"Oh! my dear Mabel, don't decide any thing in a hurry," begged Lady Feversham. "It is quite impossible he can marry this girl; she has no money; and you know it was I brought all the late Lord Feversham's property to him, and can leave it entirely and absolutely to whom I choose. Therefore, if I was driven to it, I could disinherit Claude, who would find his title a very empty concern, without the money to keep it up. You know, dear, I am afraid, however badly he treated me in the matter, I could not keep up the quarrel with him long. I can be very determined, none more so, for a short time, but, after that has lasted a little while, my resolutions weaken, and I could forget and forgive any thing. He knows this as well as I do, and therefore I fear any threat of disinheritance from me will

be little regarded. Still I can't allow this marriage. How would you advise me to stop it?"

Mabel mused a while, and Lady Feversham, watching her, could not help being struck by the curious mingling of expressions visible on her countenance. There was a kind of triumphant look, along with determination and cunning, and even a slight shade of tenderness in her smile, as she leaned her head on her hand and gazed thoughtfully out of the window before her. After a few moments' pause, she turned to her companion with a quiet, unmoved manner, and answered,

"If you are determined this is not to be, you must make up your mind to go any lengths in support of your authority. For myself I do not care; my feelings, fortunately, were never engaged in this scheme; but if your objections to the match rest on other grounds, and you are resolved to stop it, I will help you to do so, and can make you almost certain of success, if you will take no step in the matter but such as I advise."

"I wish you would not throw off all personal interest in the match," answered her companion, pettishly; "if you can stop his marrying her, why can't you take him yourself, as you know all your friends wish?"

"No," replied the girl, decidedly; "I will not work in it as a personal affair, and I renounce, at least for the present, all prospect of winning Lord Feversham's affection, or being more to him than I am now. Only under these conditions can I assist you in the matter; I think, if you consider, you will see there is wisdom in it, too. If it should ever come to Lord Claude's ears that I had assisted you in separating him from Miss Bambridge, with the understanding I was to marry him as my reward, do you think I should be one whit nearer gaining him than I am now?"

"If he hears of it, it will tell against you, no matter what your motives may have been," answered the elder lady. "We must take care he knows nothing about it."

"What you say is very true," replied the girl; but she added, with a little hesitation, "Don't you see that, if I do it with no desire to win him, he can not pride himself afterward on having foiled me, if he takes some other girl to whom you can have no objection. Believe me, Lady Feversham, if I help you at all, it must be in my own way."

"Very well," answered her friend, "it shall be as you wish. Now what do you recommend?"

"That you should write to him without delay; tell him what you have heard, point out how dependent he is on you for all the comforts he enjoys at present, and that you not only can but will exercise your power to the uttermost to prevent his marriage with this Miss Bambridge."

There was intense scorn in the accent with which Mabel Prendergast spoke the last three words, as she rose, fetched paper and writing materials, laid them before Lady Feversham, and continued: "I am going to ride over to The Poplars now; papa and mamma will be expecting me; I have not seen them for two or three days. Write your letter, and I can post it in the village as I go through; it will leave a mail sooner. Stay, let me give you a draft of what you ought to say; I am afraid you will not be sufficiently decided."

It was a strange sight to see the pretty, graceful girl, with such a hard, determined look on her delicate face, sit down and dash off the lines that the elder lady waited submissively to copy when she had done. Her part of the business finished, Mabel ran lightly to her room to dress for riding; she was expeditious over her toilet, and when it was finished, paused for a moment before the glass, to survey her own image reflected there. A dainty picture it was; the slight round figure in its neat, well-fitting habit, the plain high hat perched securely on the massive coils of black hair, the tiny edge of white collar tracing the round of her slender throat—all formed a harmonious, workman-like appearance, that suggested irresistibly visions of a light hand and a graceful seat, a fiery steed and daring rider.

But she was not thinking of horses and horsemanship at that minute; she was saying to herself, "I wonder why I am taking so much trouble about this business of Claude Feversham's? Is he worth it? My friends say he is, because he is rich and titled, but that is nothing to me; young De Vaux is richer, and will have a title too some day, and he adores me, which haughty Lord Feversham does not. His mother tells me he is worth it, because a kind son is sure to make a kind husband. Good and true, she calls him. What is that to me, I wonder? I am not good and true, I am sure," she went on, with a short laugh; "if I were, instead of trying to chisel this poor girl out of her lover, I should be helping her to keep him. But I should not object to his liking me, I confess; he is cold, and grave, and gentle; I should like to have power over him, to be able to ruffle that calm of his by my slightest word or smile—to make his heart beat angrily when I was cold, and rapturously when I was kind. Yes, I know now why I care about it; it is the love of power urges me. I should like to have power over a mind like his, and I will yet, if I am not much mistaken. Does Miss Bambridge like him, I wonder, or is her motive the same as mine? If it is, *gare à vous*, mademoiselle, it will be war to the knife between us, and we shall see which is the strongest." As she finished these reflections she turned away, and, catching up her whip and gloves, tripped lightly down to Lady Feversham.

In a minute or two more the note was in the pocket of her saddle, and reining in her fiery horse with a practiced hand, she sauntered down the avenue. The groom stood for a few minutes watching the impetuous animal she was on, as it snatched and pulled at the bit, backing and kicking from exuberance of spirits, in a way that most people would have found unpleasant.

"She's the pluckiest piece, that one, I ever came across," he soliloquized; "see how quietly she takes that beast, that half the men in the county wouldn't mount for their lives. Eh! but she has a rare spice of the devil in her!" The object of this eulogium rode on quietly till she left the domain, then turning into the fields, she set off in a hand-gallop across country, the nearest way to The Poplars, turning neither to the right nor to the left, and riding at every thing with a skill and judgment that betokened long practice. At this pace they soon reached her father's domain, where we will leave her riding slowly up the avenue.

CHAPTER IX.

A MISADVENTURE.

STILL the same routine was going on in Belmurphy; there were the same dances and picnics and croquet-parties, though the summer was almost at an end, and the grouse-shooting had begun some time. Not that the shooting interfered in the least with the flirtations carried on during the time of idleness; on the contrary, it afforded additional opportunities for any thing of the kind. First there was the early breakfast, at which those of the ladies who liked could put in an appearance; then there was the luncheon-party on the hills, where fun and merriment reigned supreme, and where bets were made in the most reckless manner on the luck of individuals. These luncheons also not unfrequently broke up the shooting-party to a fearful degree, for no matter how keen the sportsman might be beforehand, a pair of bright eyes looking entreatingly, when the signal for a move was made, would often produce an entire revulsion in a fellow's feelings, and cause him to pronounce a good day's work confoundedly slow.

Claude and I had no end of fun at the Bambridges', and I am sure, after the first day, my shooting raised me considerably in every body's eyes; they could not persist in thinking me a child when I rarely if ever missed, and brought home twice as many birds as they did.

But though of course I felt a little pleased I was too uneasy and anxious to care much about it. Gwendoline still lured us both on, with so much impartiality, it would have been impossible to say which was most favored. But I feared, and was unhappy; it seemed impossible she should prefer me to one so much more worthy of her in every way as Claude was. How painfully I felt all my short-comings, and how I longed to imitate Feversham's grave, stately ways, and copy his quiet, protecting manner when speaking to her.

But I felt that part was not for me, that I was nothing if I was not natural; and so I held my ground as well as I could, though my usually gay spirit would at times sink very low when I realized how little hope there was before me.

One fine morning, about the end of August, I noticed that Claude seemed worried and anxious, as he came down to breakfast: after a time he turned to me suddenly, and said,

"Madcap, come out for a walk with me this morning; I want you."

"All right," I replied, wondering what he might have to say, for latterly, though he had been kinder than ever to me, we had spoken very little to each other.

I was rather surprised, therefore, when, pulling a letter out of his pocket, he handed it to me, saying, as he did so: "Read that, and tell me what you think of it."

Wondering, I opened it, seeing it was in my aunt Anna's handwriting. I was no doubt astonished when I found she was acquainted with Claude's infatuation (as she called it), but hardly surprised at the light in which she viewed it, not knowing Miss Bambridge or any thing about her. The letter was short, severe, and to the purpose; ordering Claude to renounce all intention of marrying this girl, on pain of being disinherited, a threat which the writer then proceeded to show, in a very business-like manner, it was fully in her power to carry out.

"What shall you do?" I asked, as I handed the letter back to him.

"There is but one course open to me," he answered; "I will not sell my love for a crust of bread and a mess of pottage, as Esau of old sold his birthright. I will take this letter with me to Endley, show it to Gwendoline, tell her how truly I love her; I will ask her if she is willing to share what I have got, which is little more than my captain's pay, or whether she cares so little for me that the prospect of poverty frightens her. I am not quite sure of my ground, and would have preferred putting off this question for some time longer, but now it must come out. Vivian," he continued, after a pause, in a low tone of stern displeasure, "I know that you care, or fancy you care, for Miss Bambridge—that you imagine yourself my rival; but even so, how could you have persuaded yourself to act in this manner? I trusted you, and you have grievously disappointed me."

"How?" I asked, calmly. "In daring to love the same person as yourself, I suppose. Claude, that is too absurd; you are my senior in years and rank both, and I am willing to pay you all requisite deference on that account, but I can not see how you can expect me to yield my own chances of happiness, in order to make yours more certain. It is a demand I should never have expected you to make; that you know well I would never comply with."

"I never made any such demand of you," replied Claude, harshly. "What I allude to is the dishonorable means you have used to try and remove me from your path. Two can play at that game, remember, though I would scorn to soil my hands with such a deed, and therefore you think you are safe; but what would you say were I to write to your mother, and tell her what you are doing here? In your case it would probably have much the same results as in mine, only that Lord Traverscourt can not disinherit you; but no doubt they would take some equally effectual steps to save you from the consequences of what, in your case, they might, with some reason, term your folly."

I stood still with amazement when I saw at what Claude was hinting. How he got the idea into that wise head of his, I can not conceive. It would indeed have been vastly amusing, had it not been so very insulting. I tried to speak several times, but he would go on; so at last I waited patiently till he had finished; then I said, rather angrily,

"Look here, Claude, I take a good deal from you because you are my cousin, and my best friend; but what you have just been saying is not chaff, and I won't stand it. Don't speak to me in that way again."

"If I had been you," answered Claude, "I would not have laid myself open to being spoken to in that way. It is well for you no one but me knows it, or you would have a bad time of it among our fellows. For the sake of your father and mother, and still more for my own sake, as you are my cousin, I will say nothing about it this time; but if I ever catch you meddling with my affairs, I will first horsewhip you within an inch of your life, and then tell the reason I did so, afterward."

"Good heavens, Claude! you must be mad!" I cried, really thinking there must be a screw loose somewhere, to render him capable of such a supposition. "Why, Claude, you ought not to want such an assurance from me, and I ought not to stoop to give it to you; but as I am aware that you are upset by this letter, I will act as kindly toward you as I can, and give you my word that I am as ignorant as you are of how your mother became cognizant of the state of affairs here. If you like, you can verify what I say by asking Aunt Anna if I have ever written to her, or from whom she heard it."

He looked at me hard as I spoke, and I met his glance unflinchingly. I saw that his mind was terribly disordered by the fears that such an interruption to the even course of his love had caused, and I knew that, unless such had been the case, a suspicion of me, such as he now harbored, would never have entered into his head.

After a long pause, during which his look seemed as though it would have penetrated my very soul, he shook his head, as if to dash away unwelcome thoughts, and said,

"You are true, Vivian, and I ought not to have doubted you. But until you are placed in such a position as mine, you can have no idea what crowds of hateful suggestions jealousy and fear bring into one's mind. A day or two ago I thought myself very sure of her, and now I can not see that I have any ground for hope at all. But I must ask her, and that immediately. After all, if she is what I take her to be, this will make no difference."

I had perhaps indulged in a hope that he would have given her up, for my heart seemed to stand still as he announced his intention of asking her at once.

"Why do you tell this to me?" I asked, almost angrily. "You know I do not wish you success."

"Is it still so?" he answered, slowly. "I had hoped you might have seen the matter differently now. Still I thought it fair you should know I was going to speak, and why I do so."

Suddenly a light flashed upon me.

"You will have to wait," I cried; "they go to Dublin to-day, for a week or two. There is something going on there they wish to see."

"True," he replied; "I had forgotten that. Then I must wait till their return. In the mean time, I will write to my mother, and assure her that no threats shall prevent my at least trying to win the woman I love, for my wife. There is some baby-faced miss living near us, who will be a great heiress; and her ladyship has set her mind on my marrying the child. That, I know full well, is the cause of this violent opposition; but she need not have troubled herself so much, for, even if I can not have Gwendoline, I will never take the prim little chit she has chosen for me—a mere wax-doll, a kind of puppet, on which to hang fine clothes and jewelry, with as little soul as her own money-bags!"

I had, of course, heard of Mabel Prendergast, but had never seen her. I could not, therefore, judge whether his accusations against her were correct, but I felt quite inclined to join in condemning one whom Claude so despised, though under all a secret wish that her rival claims might prevail gave me a little more hope and courage than I had for long possessed.

While we were so occupied with our own difficulties and troubles, the others had been amusing themselves more or less well, according to their characters and dispositions. Mayleigh, for instance—keen, cautious, and calculating, with no money but his pay, and a very ready wit—had become welcome in all societies in the place. His forte was to feign a devotion he did not feel, wherever he thought his interests might be furthered by so doing. He had on hand at present a very promising flirtation with the heiress of the district. In that quarter his attentions were unremitting, having a far greater appearance of devotion than much real affection has. We did not scruple, however, to say that the fascinations of her handsome property were in his eyes the real causes of attraction, though she was a pretty and pleasant girl, well worth attention on her own account.

One string to his bow would never have satisfied Mayleigh, who accordingly was very devoted to several others when the chief prize was not by. Where his heart could be among them all, we could not make out; but that was his affair, not ours.

Flower was a susceptible youth, and of course was not long without getting up one of those safe flirtations of which he was so fond. The object in this instance was a remarkably pretty girl, who could hold her own in a ball-room against many beauties of experience and repute. The art of flirtation was not unknown to her; and though, no doubt, had there been higher game unmarked, she would have flown at it, yet she was not disposed to cavil at any thing that promised so much amusement as Flower's infatuation.

There was to be a picnic up the lake the day after my conversation with Claude, given by one of the notabilities of the place; to this poor Flower was looking forward with the full intention of making great play, and taking advantage of every facility afforded him to prosecute his advances in her favor.

Not that it must be for one minute supposed he had the least intention of going in for the prize seriously; no, that was very far from his thoughts; but his was one of those minds that never seem thoroughly happy unless they are balancing themselves, as it were, over an abyss into which the slightest false step will precipitate them on one side or the other.

The day was fine and sunny; the young lady was there looking her brightest and best, Flower and Mayleigh were in their glory, while Claude and I, deprived of our usual service, devoted ourselves assiduously to the general good.

The dinner passed off as picnics generally do, except that nothing was forgotten. It might even have been pleasanter than these out-of-door entertainments generally are, but for the prodigious swarms of biting insects—ants on the ground, midges in the air, rendering any thing like enjoyment of the meal impossible. How we fanned and shook ourselves, and got into a white-heat beating off the intruders! Mosquitoes are a joke to a swarm of lake midges, and some of our party were really disfigured by their attacks.

A few of the ladies, however, seemed quite safe from their importunities, and to these few it must have been rather laughable, watching the frantic gestures of the sufferers. Why are people so fond of picnics? It seems to me such a waste of time and trouble; every thing in the entertainer's house is turned five times more topsy-turvy than if they gave a dinner or a dance; besides which, and over and above the insect plagues, is the fact that people having nothing particular to do, except in the case of very marked flirtations, do not amalgamate well.

After dinner it was the thing to walk round the island, and every one set off accordingly. This was just what Flower wanted—it would be such a good occasion for the soft, half-sentimental nonsense he was so fond of uttering. They set off, therefore, at a quiet pace, and were soon deep in the language of flowers, when Mayleigh, prompted by the spirit of mischief, and angry because a third person had spoiled his tête-à-tête with the heiress, determined to join Flower, and assist the young lady to annihilate him.

For Mayleigh, who got on well with the ladies, knew that Beatrice Graham liked setting down her sentimental squire occasionally, and he guessed by her look there would be some fun to-day.

"Where is the heiress?" demanded Flower, as Mayleigh approached. "You had much better be with her. We don't want you here."

"Oh! pray don't go, Mr. Mayleigh," broke in Beatrice Graham. "Mr. Flower is explaining a bouquet to me so nicely. I had no idea the language of flowers could be so interesting. Do you know any thing of it?"

This question she addressed to Mayleigh, turning her large hazel eyes, brimming over with fun, full upon him.

"I can't say I do," he replied; "but I would like immensely to hear Flower's explanation. It is never too late to learn, and it might be of use to me some day."

"Come up here," cried Flower, anxious to change the subject, and leading the way to a precipitous craggy hill that commanded a wide view of the lake. "It's fearfully steep," he went on, holding out his hand to assist Miss Graham, "but the prospect from the top well repays one for the climb."

He hoped by this manœuvre to shake off Mayleigh, who was of a lazy disposition, and averse to hard walking without an adequate motive. On this occasion, scenting amusement from afar, he would not be shaken off, but clambered up along with them. It was indeed steep, as Flower had observed, and moreover very slippery, so much so that a single false step would send the unlucky climber sliding to the bottom a great deal more quickly than he had got up; but thanks to the gentlemen's sticks, which they dug firmly into the ground at every step, the summit was at last gained.

Here they sat down to recover breath, and felt themselves fully rewarded for their trouble by the scene before them. The lake in its whole extent lay at their feet, nestled in among its shadowy woods, and overhung by lofty mountains, the water glistening like a sheet of silver, the boat they came in moored below, with the crew eating their dinner beside it, a yacht spreading its white sails far away toward the upper end of the lake, while close below them, at the foot of the hill, the greater number of the picnic party had gathered, laughing and talking, and calling up to them, to know if it was worth the climb to get there.

"We don't want them up," cried Flower, impatiently. "Let us say there is nothing worth looking at, and that we are coming down."

As he spoke he set his foot against a tuft of grass before him, and leaned forward to answer. With the pressure of his foot the grass gave way, and the next minute he was sliding rapidly downward. Finding himself going, he caught wildly around for something to hold by, grasped a portion of Beatrice Graham's dress, and holding on to that with the energy of despair, though not knowing in his bewilderment what it was, he pulled her from her seat, and the next moment they would both have been descending the hill pell-mell, when Mayleigh caught her by the arm and drew her back, just in time to save her, but not to save her dress, a pretty light muslin, that, unable to bear the strain put on it, tore with a loud crack, and Flower, once set free, slipped down the hill, gathering impetus every moment, till he glided into the middle of the laughing group at the bottom, dirty, torn, and scratched, very red in the face, very confused, and smeared with earth, but not hurt in any way. As soon as it was ascertained he had not suffered from the adventure, the laughing was long and loud at his expense, and it did not diminish when Miss Graham, who had descended with Mayleigh in a slower and more dignified manner, appeared upon the scene, holding up her tattered dress, and saying,

"How did it feel, Mr. Flower? I hope you are not the worse for it. My poor dress, I fear, has been the greatest sufferer. I think you have some of it in your hand still. Would you give it me?"

"Really, Miss Graham," gasped Flower, hardly yet in full possession of his senses, "I think you might leave it to me as a remembrance of this day."

Shouts of laughter greeted this speech, and the half-devotional, half-convulsive manner in which Flower pressed the tumbled bit of muslin to his heart, while Beatrice Graham answered, smiling,

"I should have thought you might have been able to remember this day without a souvenir, but if the memories connected with it are so very dear, I really think I must allow you to keep the muslin. Whenever you look at it, you may picture yourself once more on this hill, and recall again the pleasant sensations that took possession of you when you grasped my poor dress so firmly."

This answer seemed to reveal to Flower the fact that we were all there, and laughing at him, for, coloring even more than he had already done, he looked from Miss Graham to the fragment in his hand for several minutes, evidently puzzled what to do with it now he had got it. At last a bright idea seemed to strike him.

"You are right, Miss Graham," he began. "I need no remembrance such as this to remind me of a happy day; and you will no doubt want the piece to repair the mischief I have done, though you were kind enough not to refuse me when I asked for it. I will therefore take the liberty of calling to-morrow and returning it to you, if you will allow me."

"Oh, for shame!" cried Miss Graham, laugh-ing—"a gentleman returning a lady's gift in that way! You deserve to be punished for thinking of such a thing, and I have a great mind to forbid you my presence for a week in consequence."

"You couldn't be so cruel," pleaded Flower. "It will be very hard for me to give up this souvenir, though when I thought you might want it I was willing to do so. None but you, however, could obtain it from me, and if you do not require it, I shall keep it and prize it as my most precious treasure."

Flower tried to look very sentimental as he said this; but Beatrice Graham, who had plenty of wit, and always kept her senses about her, began to see that, though as yet the laugh had been against her admirer, if the matter went on much longer she might come in for her share of ridicule; so she answered decisively,

"You are quite right, Mr. Flower — I shall want it. You may as well give it to me now. It is not too much for me to carry home."

So saying, she took the scrap the crestfallen young fellow handed to her, and walked off with Mayleigh, Flower following in gloomy silence at a little distance.

They made it up again before long, however, as I saw them dancing together that evening; the picnic winding up with a small hop given by our entertainers, the Pearces.

CHAPTER X.

MATCH-MAKING.

WHILE relating the events recorded in the last chapters, I have been losing sight of Cecil Egerton, which is strange when I come to remember it, as not only was he my most constant companion whenever Claude was otherwise occupied, but also about this time he became mixed up with people and incidents that afterward exercised a great influence not only on his life, but also on Feversham's and mine.

He had only been a few weeks at Belmurphy, when one morning he came into my room early. I was lazy that day, and was still in bed. We had had very hard work the last few days after the grouse up among the heather, and I was quite worn 'out. Claude was tired too, I know, though he would not allow that it was so. Cecil, of all of us, was the only one who did not seem to mind the severe exercise we had gone through; and he often told me he thought the life of privation he had led when a boy made him more able to support physical fatigue than most men in his position. It was all such child's-play compared to the misery and wretchedness he had then undergone, when helping his parents in their struggle for existence, and there was now none of the mental effort and suffering that had been worse to bear than physical trial.

So he only looked fresher and brighter for his week's exertions, while I was glad to lie an hour or two longer in bed, and Claude and others spent some additional time lounging over letters and papers that a day or two before had been glanced at and then thrown aside for consideration at a more convenient opportunity. But as Cecil came into my room that morning I saw that his face did not wear its usual bright expression; in fact, he seemed perplexed.

"Just read that," he said, tossing me a letter, and sitting down on the foot of the bed.

"Don't you see a fellow's asleep?" I answered, not willing to disturb myself and let the air into my warm nest. "Read it yourself; I'll listen."

He picked up the letter, and proceeded to read as desired. It was from his uncle, reminding him that it was now six years since he had entered the army, and that during all that time he had only once returned to Beaumanoir to see his uncle, or thank him for what he had done for him. Not that the writer expected thanks—at least he said he did not. Gratitude, according to him, was the most foolish of all those foolish perversions of intellect called virtues; in fact, it could only be excused in any rational being by the rendering, "a lively expectation of favors to come;" but in that light it was entitled to consideration: if his nephew had learned any thing by his contact with the world—which Mr. Vansittart was inclined to doubt—in that light he would consider it. His uncle went on to say that he should be glad of his nephew's company for a few weeks: he had some arrangements to propose to him—looking upon him as his possible heir—and he would be glad if Cecil would make it convenient to come to him soon.

When Egerton had finished reading, he looked at me with a very gloomy expression on his generally cheerful countenance.

"A rum old chap the fellow must be that wrote that letter," I said when he had finished; "I wish he would offer to adopt me; I feel convinced his peculiar views, as exemplified by that production, would suit me down to the ground. I wonder you have not made up to him more, Cecil."

"I hate him," replied Egerton, with a kind of suppressed vehemence; "you know how he treated us while my father lived—let him die of neglect to gratify his vindictive spite, and in so acting, caused my mother's death also; but that is not all, though it is enough to make me wish to avoid him, to make me hate the advantages he offers me. Besides that, he would insure my moral death if he could, kill every thing upright or honorable in me, and make me the human reptile he is himself. Surely, Darrell, living in the same county with him, you must have heard something of him; you must know the estimation in which he is held, and which clings to me like Deianira's poisoned shirt, wherever I am introduced as his nephew. I have seen people look at me askance, and whisper, when some kind friend has told them I was brought up by Mr. Vansittart, and am to be his heir; for every one in these parts believes that is to be so, though I myself think he has no such intention, but only holds out the hope of it as a bait to lure me into obedience to his wishes, to conformity with his views."

"I have heard about him," I answered, not caring to pursue that side of the conversation further. I remembered hearing no measured terms of reprobation used when speaking of him, and I could not recollect ever having known any one say a word in his praise. "You will go to Beaumanoir, of course," I continued, hoping to make him look at some brighter aspect of this visit.

"I suppose I must," he answered. "It is true I owe every thing I am to him; I often wish so much I did not; it hangs like a chain round my neck, to think his money has provided for me for so many years. I ought to be able to pay it back some day; I would not try to do so to any one else, but he has no feelings to hurt, and I think it would please him. I know some of my sketches would sell, if I could work myself up to the point of offering them for sale, but foolishly I feel shy about doing so. However, I shall spend a few days in London on leaving Beaumanoir, and will then try what I can do. Mr. Vansittart thinks I have never been on leave all these years, that I am devoted to the army and my comrades, as indeed I am; but he is far from suspecting that I am still an artist at heart, and prosecute my studies in that line as vigorously as ever. He thinks he has quite eradicated the hereditary taint; and if he finds he is mistaken, he would disinherit me without a moment's compunction."

"What an old fool!" I exclaimed; "but really, after all, I don't see what there is to say against your going. The old fellow may just as well leave his money to you, who will make a good use of it, as to any one else; and it by no means follows that because you are in the house he need find out your artist tendency; you concealed it pretty well before."

"It is not that," he answered, "that troubles me," and as he spoke he twisted old Vansittart's letter nervously in his hand; "it is that I am sure these arangements he speaks of are something with which I ought to have nothing to do; something that, if I stand firm, will cause a difference between us; and you know," he added, fixing his eyes upon me with an expression of mute distress that to me always seemed intensely touching, "I find it so hard to be firm, even when I know what is right. In fact, I fear he will tempt me to do wrong, I feel such a strange disinclination to this visit. It is as if I had a presentiment that something bad was going to happen to me."

Cecil had often hinted that he knew of his infirmity of character, but had never spoken of it so plainly as now. I was puzzled what to say. It was evident for some reason he dreaded the visit; yet to ordinary powers of observation, it would have seemed madness that he should risk displeasing his uncle, who certainly appeared to mean well by him, for some foolish caprice that he called a presentiment.

I did not believe in such things myself, and I answered accordingly, "Nonsense, man. You are in low spirits, because you are enjoying yourself here, and know you will not enjoy yourself there; at least you think you will not, but it may be better than you expect. Come, cheer up; I insist on your going. Walk off to James this minute and ask for leave: I dare say he'll be able to give it you; and you take it so seldom, you are really entitled to it now. I believe you will find every thing better than you expect; have some stunning partridge-shooting, and come back quite in love with the old boy. And if you see my mother, just tell her you know her young hopeful, and you will always be welcome at Longhurst after that. I will tell them to ask you over for some shooting, which will help to pass away the time you must spend with your uncle."

So I overruled the poor fellow's wavering mind, and saw him off by the early train next day. He looked quite solemn, and no one would have imagined, to see him, that he was going on leave to a wealthy uncle, and to put up at such a place as Beaumanoir.

His spirits rose, however, as he proceeded on his journey, and by the time he reached the station nearest his uncle's place, and was met by a dog-cart drawn by two dashing bays, he had reasoned himself, or more probably veered round without reasoning, as it was in the nature of his mind to do, into very high spirits, seeing every thing in the best possible light, and quite prepared to think that Mr. Vansittart might have entirely changed in every way, and might be about to appear in the character of an estimable and praiseworthy member of society. His views on this point were certainly a little damped by an incident that occurred on the journey, shortly before they arrived at Deenham station, where he was to get out. There was a fine-looking, middle-aged gentleman traveling in the same carriage with him; they had been together all the way from London, and had fallen into conversation. Egerton was a good talker, a man of many ideas, though they were too often of a chimerical, unpractical nature. They were interesting, however, as exhibiting the workings of an ardent, enthusiastic imagination, which, however, bore the impress of the warping agencies of his early life. Conversation between him and a stranger must always have been suggestive; his accent, manner, education, appearance, dress, all bore the impress of wealth, and of wealth as known among refined, social circles, not as it might have been found among wealthy manufacturing society; yet in every word, look, and tone was expressed an intimate knowledge of, and sympathy with, hardship and suffering. The pain-stricken, miserable early years had left their mark on his impressionable nature, and even were it possible he should ever forget them, he could not efface their traces, which were woven into his existence. You could see there was some sad history written on that grave, thoughtful brow, looking out behind the merriest glance of those gentle, wistful eyes; and seeing thus much, and no farther, strangers were usually both attracted and puzzled by the handsome young soldier.

When they arrived near Deenham, the stranger, seeing they were both about to leave together, said, "We are coming to the same part of the country: it is possible we may meet; I do not know your face in the county, so I suppose you are visiting somewhere. Will you tell me where you are staying?"

"I am going to my uncle, Mr. Vansittart, at Beaumanoir," answered Egerton.

A very perceptible change passed over the stranger's face on hearing Mr. Vansittart's name; he almost seemed to draw back for a minute, as he replied, "Mr. Vansittart's nephew, are you? I should not have thought it. In that case, I fear we are not likely to meet—I do not know him—our places are so far apart. "Good-morning," he added, stepping out, as the train stopped, and hurrying away to a nicely turned-out, quiet-looking dog-cart, that was waiting for him, and on which Cecil, following him to get to his own trap, recognized the Traverscourt crest. "So that is Madcap's father; I thought I knew the face," he mused; "but he would have nothing to say to me, once he knew I belonged to Beau-

manoir. How strange it is that people will visit other people's offenses on innocent heads; my uncle being the man he is, is no reason I should be a social pariah too; but in this county, at least, it is evident we must sink or swim together."

This reflection, though at first bitter to him, presently hardened him a little, as he sped along behind the two dashing bays, with the low August sunshine flinging long shadows of tree, and cottage, and well-filled rick-yard across his path, as they passed swiftly through prosperous English hamlets, and rolled gayly along the wide level road, so different from the irregular, winding, hilly ways he had been used to travel on lately.

The sun had not yet set when he reached Beaumanoir, and all the western windows of the grand old building were ablaze with crimson light as he drove up; but he hardly glanced at a scene that should have charmed his artist eye. He had during the drive persuaded himself that his uncle was not as bad as public opinion would make him out—that he was, in fact, suffering for misdeeds of former years; and that since they two were condemned together, he at least being guiltless, he must endeavor to be more to the old man, to bear more with him, and from him, than he had ever done before; to forget the past, and live only in a noble and better future. Full of these resolves, his eyes dwelt only on a figure that he could discern waiting on the door steps, and that he recognized as that of his uncle. Springing to the ground as soon as he had pulled up, he stepped toward him quickly, holding out an eager hand to meet the one his uncle, somewhat more slowly, extended to him. He had no reason to complain of coldness in that hand-clasp; the old wrinkled fingers closed on his with the strength of steel, as Mr. Vansittart said, with a low laugh,

"I knew you would come. Trust me for being able to fetch any man when I want him. You made sure of the old place, my boy, when I said I wanted to consult you about some arrangements, and you came then fast enough, though you haven't cared to see me all these years, when there has been nothing to gain by it. But it is not that yet, lad, though if you do as I wish it will lead to it. It is something else I have to speak to you about, and which I think you will do for me. I see you are getting more knowledge of the world; you are not quite such a fool as you were—not quite!"

Thus muttering, and laughing at intervals, the low, cunning laugh that had always been so repulsive to Egerton, Mr. Vansittart led him into the house, not leaving him time to say a word to exonerate himself from the suspicion of interested motives that his uncle had chosen to cast upon him. He had not intended his obedience to insure him advantage, and he had not contemplated the possibility of others thinking such a motive had actuated him. He was disgusted; all his good resolutions, all his new-born pity, and desire to like this man, vanished at once; he felt only the old inborn antagonism between their natures, the feeble but pure and good principle in his shrinking with loathing and repulsion from the strong and wicked energy of the other character, which he felt instinctively was powerful enough to destroy and overwhelm his weak resistance in time. His only safety was in silence; he felt himself right, but he dared not express his rectitude, knowing that any such attempt would be sneered at, and his feeble defense torn to shreds, by the keen, ready satire of his opponent.

They stood by the fire in the drawing-room, the young man looking thoughtfully into the flickering blaze, telling himself he had made a great mistake in leaving Belmurphy; the elder, with his back to the fire, gazing sideways with a cunning leer at his nephew's troubled face. Neither spoke for a few minutes; then Mr. Vansittart went on again:

"You don't ask me why I brought you all this way; you don't ask me what I have to say to you. Upon my word, you have very little curiosity. You are right, though, for I should not tell you any thing yet. This is not the time to talk business. After dinner we will do that; when the wine is in the wit is out, remember. I want you to bring your wits out, in a different way from that meant by the proverb, and use them a little on the matter in hand. You know your way to your room. That is the dressing-bell; we will have dinner in half an hour. Tell me if every thing is not comfortable; but I think they know me better here than not to make all my guests comfortable, especially the heir that is to be."

And the old man laughed his low, mocking laugh as he spoke the last words. He seemed to have an unaccountable pleasure in always reverting to that supposition. In point of fact, he believed it to be the chain that held his bond-slave, and he liked to hear it clank. He had pulled it a little too hard then. Egerton turned on him with a white face of intense passion.

"I don't know why you are always taunting me about being your heir, speaking as though I desired it, or thought it was to be. I neither desire it nor think it. You have given me a profession that pleases me; I neither ask nor expect more from you, and for that, so far as circumstances permit me, I am grateful. But you shall not suppose that I am bound to you by hope of further reward. I regret that I came here at all, and I will leave again to-morrow. I will bear insult from no man, least of all from you, to whom, if much beholden in gratitude, I owe also a larger debt of hate."

Mr. Vansittart drew back a little as his nephew spoke, and stood looking at him with a kind of admiration for the spirit that could lead a man to risk so much on account of a few sneering words. He liked Cecil then better than he had ever liked him, and was the more determined to carry out the plan he had formed concerning him.

"Don't be so angry, Cecil," he answered, soothingly. "I had no idea you were such a fire-brand. I was only laughing at the way in which every one about here puts you down as my heir. I don't mean to say that you have ever counted on it, though you may do so, if you please me in the arrangements I wish to propose to you after dinner. You are not a bad-looking fellow, Cecil, and do credit to the family beauty, which was not well represented in my person. You are a little bit of an actor," he added, laughing good-humoredly. "Confess all that tragedy business just now was not quite real, just a little bit made up for the occasion."

"It was real, every bit," answered Cecil, stoutly. "I don't know what you mean by saying I am an actor. I trust, at least, I shall never act what I don't believe in and feel."

He turned into his room as he spoke, shutting the door sharply behind him, and the old man continued his way down the corridor, muttering,

"Acting, certainly, whatever he says; too earnest to be real. Good acting, though—very good; might make his fortune on the stage, if he doesn't turn out to be my heir."

Laughing to himself at this observation, that for some reason or other always appeared to afford him intense amusement, Mr. Vansittart proceeded to his room, leaving Cecil trying in solitude to calm the angry, rebellious feelings that would rise in his heart.

It was hard indeed that the only one in the world with whom he could claim kin, the one with whom he must be intimately associated, was the impersonation of every thing that he had been taught from childhood to scorn and avoid. His mother, gentle in all other things, had been strict in her moral training, and had held up before her child's eyes the highest standard of perfection as the one after which he was to follow. And it had been easier for him to do so than for most people, because all the love he had ever met with, all the affection he had ever bestowed, was intimately connected with, and wound round, purity and goodness, nobility of mind and unswerving truth. In those respects, parental example supported and encouraged him, and the memory of those lost urged him constantly forward in the right way.

Dinner passed over quietly. It seemed that Mr. Vansittart, either frightened at Cecil's outburst on his way up stairs, or desirous of soothing him before approaching the matter in hand, exerted himself to be agreeable, and actually for a time almost succeeded in keeping his hateful philosophy out of sight. The deference thus shown to his opinions, the good dinner, and the handsome, appropriate surroundings, all exercised their influence on young Egerton, who began again to waver in his feelings to his uncle, and grew more sociable and cheerful as time passed on. When they were left alone with their wine and fruit, he had got quite lively, relating anecdotes connected with his regiment, and enjoying the old man's keen wit very fully, now that it was unmixed with the cynicism that had made it so unpleasant. He did not notice that his uncle's keen gray eyes watched him slyly and unceasingly; he did not observe that, as his spirits rose, a triumphant expression overspread the old man's face: he was too much taken up with thoughts of his absent comrades, their sayings and doings, and his as mixed up with theirs, to pay any attention to the sinister expression of his companion's face.

After he had rattled on for some time, however, his uncle interposed.

"Suppose we come to business now, Cecil?" he said. "Of course you know it was not for the pleasure of your society I brought you over here, though I must acknowledge you are more amusing than I expected to find you. No, I had another object, as I told you before; and I think, as we are in a talking humor, I may as well explain it to you; but let us look at your position calmly and clearly, considering first what it is, and secondly what it may be. You are an on-sign in Her Majesty's —th; near the top of the ensigns, you say ? I am glad to hear it; but it doesn't much alter the position with regard to the matter in hand. For your commission, as well as your education, you are indebted to me. I don't want to boast of it—I merely mention it as a fact; and when you want to purchase a step, I must do it for you. So far, so good. You have, we see, absolutely nothing of your own, except your pay, and you have the prospect of nothing, except what I shall choose to give you, either in purchasing your steps or making you my heir, as we were talking of before dinner, when I made you so angry. Don't be annoyed ; I am not telling you this with any desire to irritate you— merely as a matter of business between two men of the world. Well, it now seems that all your future prospects rest with me, and I am willing to do the best I can for you, hoping that you will be a credit to the family, and designing for you this heirship you so indignantly repudiated to-day, if you please me in the matter I shall presently refer to. Situated as you are, the course most natural to a young and good-looking fellow like you, who has not a half-penny he can really call his own, is a wealthy marriage. Have you ever thought of marrying?—and if so, have you considered how important it is that the lady should have money ?'

"Indeed, sir," answered Cecil, the color rising to his brow as he began to see the drift of his uncle's observations, "I have never given either of those subjects any consideration. A fellow of my age is too young to think of marriage."

Mr. Vansittart nodded his head approvingly.

"In an ordinary case you are right," he answered ; "if there was no money to be obtained it would be quite simple — you would wait, perhaps never marry at all ; but where there is money to be had, the matter is different; and it is on this account I asked you over."

"I don't think it likely I shall ever marry for money," replied Egerton, coldly. "Indeed, I may as well say at once I will not ; and besides, I number no heiresses among my acquaintance."

"But what if I do—what if I do ?" repeated Mr. Vansittart, laughing softly. "Of course that first speech of yours is the proper thing to say, and I applaud it, but it is humbug—arrant humbug—all the same ; and you will agree with me that it is so, when you see the young lady in question."

"I have said before, uncle, I will not marry for money, and seeing the young lady will not alter my determination ; besides which, it is hardly possible she would care to buy for a husband such an outcast as I am."

The old man laughed.

"I don't know about that, of course," he said, "though I don't think you look like a fellow a girl would refuse; but the beauty of the whole thing is that, if she will have you, you need not marry her for money at all, but only for love— for love of the prettiest woman in four counties round. It is time enough to say you won't have her when you have seen her; wait till then, my boy, and I have no fear but you will be as anxious for the match as I am. And then, if you two settle it between you, and all goes on well, then I promise to make you my heir; so you need not fear their saying you are looking after her gold, for you will have as much in prospect

as she has. Is that not worth thinking about, young man ?"

And Mr. Vansittart peered cunningly into his nephew's gloomy face as he finished speaking.

"I am not given to falling in love," answered the young man at length, "so it is not probable this young lady will have as powerful an effect on me as you seem to anticipate. But you have not told me her name. I may as well know that, even if the matter does not turn out as you wish."

"Miss Prendergast—Mabel Prendergast," repeated the old man. "A pretty name, but not half as pretty as the woman that owns it."

"But if she is so beautiful and such an heiress, how is it she is not caught already ? Probably there is some one hanging after her to whom she is attached, so I might as well spare myself the pain of seeing her and falling in love with her."

"She is very young—only just out of the school-room, and has been out to none of the county festivities; that is how it happens that she has not a swarm of men after her. Few people as yet know about her; and besides, there is another reason—there is some kind of arrangement between her people and Lady Feversham. Lady Feversham wants her for her son; but I don't know that the young people think any thing of that arrangement, and I fancy you would have as much chance as he. To my mind you are far better-looking, and, if she will take you, will have more money than he, though no title."

"She is intended for Lord Feversham, is she ?" cried Cecil, startled out of the reserve he had intended to maintain in that county respecting his captain's love-affair. "Feversham won't go in for her, I know."

"What do you know about it at all ?" questioned Mr. Vansittart, eagerly. "Oh! I remember —Lord Feversham is in your regiment; but how does that tell you what may be his intentions with regard to Miss Prendergast ?"

"How I know it does not much matter," Cecil replied, "and as it is not my secret, I can not explain further. I ought not to have said so much. But I know quite well he has no intention of marrying her, whatever Lady Feversham intends for him."

"That makes it all the easier for you. You might have tried to persuade me that you had some absurd scruples about cutting out your friend—scruples that I should not have believed, as I think men would rather do a thing of that kind than go in for a woman about whom there was no competition. However, this settles it very comfortably for you, and I am glad to see you are much more reasonable about it than I had expected."

"Don't call me reasonable, please," interrupted Cecil, "for that means that you expect me to do as you wish, and I warn you that it is ten thousand chances to one that I do not do so. I only consent to see this girl that you may not say I did not try, as far as lay in my power, to please you; and if you had not promised to make me her equal in fortune I would have avoided her, and not have laid myself open to the risk of a love which all the world would believe feigned, and impute to mercenary motives."

"Very well," answered the old man. "Of course that is the right thing to say, though how you can believe it, after having been so long knocking about the world, I can not imagine. If it is a blind, you might as well do without it, and speak as freely to me as I to you; but somehow I fancy you really do mean what you say, which is an entirely inconceivable infatuation and folly. The difficulty now is, how you are to meet this girl. The people hereabouts, who are no whit better than myself in reality, but who do not express their opinions as openly, turn up their noses at me generally; not that the gentlemen are not very glad to know me, and come to my little dinners, and ask for my vote at their meetings, and so on, but for the most part they do not introduce me to their ladies. But I think I can get the Pearsons to do it for me. They are very neighborly as a rule, and they know these Prendergasts. I will take you to call there to-morrow. I know they are giving a lot of parties now, and they will be glad to have a handsome young gentleman to put in an appearance at their croquet-parties, and to dance with their young ladies at their balls. And now let us go into the next room to our coffee."

The day after the last recorded conversation between Feversham and myself, he wrote to his mother, and showed me the letter; for curiously enough his knowledge that I cared for the same girl, and also a consciousness that, were my people to get wind of the affair, they would act in precisely the same way toward me as his mother had done toward him, drew us more closely together, causing him to choose me as his confidant on a subject which, under other circumstances, he would have hidden most jealously from a declared rival.

And I felt very strangely about it. His confidence in me pleased and touched me; he did not regard me as a mere boy, evidently, or he would not have taken me into all his secrets, and yet it annoyed me in other respects, showing, as it so plainly did, that he regarded my feelings as being neither deep nor permanent.

I listened to his difficulties, however, and his plans for surmounting them, only buoyed up by this thought, that nothing was known yet of her feelings, and it was but a chance that she would take him; more particularly—I thought, with a little secret pleasure I could not in any way suppress—more particularly now that he was a poor man.

Claude's letter to his mother was manly and determined, though respectful. If I had been obliged to answer such an epistle as hers had been, I am afraid I should hardly have been so calm and deferential; but then Claude tells me I am more passionate than he ever was, and, besides, have not yet been tamed by the world. He told her in every other act of his life he should be happy to receive her advice, and might almost promise to act on it, but in this one matter he, and none other, must be the judge. "Consider," he said, "that it involves the happiness of my life. If I take a wife because you like her and recommend her, or because she has money, or title, or any other worldly advantage, what guarantee is there that we shall be able to get on happily together? But if I choose her because her disposition suits mine, and we love one another, we have at least a fair prospect of happiness. As to Miss Bambridge, you know nothing of her, and if you allow yourself to be prejudiced against her by any aversion to the country of her birth, you are very wrong. Hold over all judgment on the matter until you see her; then if you do not withdraw your opposition I shall be very much surprised. Understand, however, that whether you give your consent or not, if Miss Bambridge will take me, I will marry her; not that I wish to offend you, but that I can not consider any interference in such a matter justifiable, at least when the person is of an age to judge for himself. At present Miss Bambridge is in Dublin, and will be there for a week or two; as soon as she returns, however, I shall show her your letter, and ask her if she will have me, knowing I am a poor man, with nothing to offer her but a true heart."

Something such as this was the purport of Claude's letter, and I could not help thinking what he said very true. It does seem to me hard that parents should interfere in the marriage of their children, since it is not the old people who will have to live with the wife chosen for her money, or good blood, without respect to temper or disposition: they will not be the sufferers if she turns out cold and irritating, or frivolous and extravagant; therefore I think the person who is to suffer from her whims and caprices, or he made happy by her smiles and caresses, should at least be the one to choose the partner with whom he is to live.

When Lady Feversham received this letter she was greatly perplexed. Mabel Prendergast was still with her, and she threw it toward her, saying, "Read that. I knew perfectly well he would not believe my threat of disinheritance, and you can see such is the case, for he takes no notice of it. What shall I do? He seems quite determined to have his own way in the matter."

Mabel picked up the letter, and read it slowly and deliberately. She paused a minute or two after she had finished, while Lady Feversham waited anxiously to hear what advice she would give.

"What is to be done?" she asked at last, as Mabel stirred her coffee absently.

The girl looked up hurriedly. "Ah! I forgot. I should see Miss Bambridge myself if I were you, and represent the matter to her; if she loves him, I should tell her she was ruining his prospects in life if she took him, for that you had designed greater things for him, and would never forgive him if he disobeyed you. If she does not care for him the course is simple enough; she will not take him, once she hears he has no money. Yes; if I were you I should see the girl myself; he says she is in Dublin now. I think the object you have in view would be well worth a trip over there. Don't you?"

"Well, but when I get to Dublin how am I to find her?" asked the old lady, pettishly.

"That is what I was thinking of," continued Mabel, not noticing her friend's tone. "I should say your best plan would be to write a line to Lady Longwreath, asking her to find out their address. She knows numbers of people who know them, and who will tell where they are, and how long they intend to remain in Dublin. Will you do it?"

"I suppose I had better," answered Lady Feversham. "I will do it now. You will be riding this morning, I suppose, and can post it?"

"Yes," answered the girl. "I am going to have a scamper, and the morning is so lovely I have ordered the horse in half an hour. Shall you be ready by that time?"

About an hour after this conversation had taken place, Mabel ran into her mother's boudoir at The Poplars.

"Here I am, mamma," she said, after the first embracing was over, throwing herself negligently on to the sofa, and tapping the tip of her boot with her riding-whip. "Have you been wanting me the last day or two?"

"We are dull without you, Mabel dear. Indeed, your papa was very anxious to send for you a day or two ago, but I stopped him. I said if he ever wished to see you Lady Feversham, he must be content to do without you for a little now, as it pleases her ladyship to have you."

"Well, there does not seem to me to be much chance of my ever being Lord Claude's wife. I told you he had fallen in love with some Irish girl, didn't I?—and that her ladyship had written to tell him if he married her she would disinherit him. She got an answer to her letter to-day, in which he told several truths that are very much against my chances of success. He intends to tell this girl how he stands with his mother, and that if she marries him he will be a poor man, at the same time asking her to take him, if she cares enough for him to bear poverty for his sake. (If I met a man who could say that to me, supposing I was as poor as Miss Bambridge, I should love him for it.) Then he tells his mother she has no right to prevent him pleasing himself in such a matter; that it is he who will have to bear the consequences of a mistake, if a mistake is made in the choice of a wife; and that therefore he considers he should please himself only in the matter. He is quite right, you know, mother. If I did not wish it myself, you'd never get me to take any one you chose; and if I saw any one I liked better than Claude Feversham to-morrow, I would take him, and leave his lordship to be happy with his Irish lady-love."

"Good gracious, child, how you do run on!" cried Mrs. Prendergast, a comely, good-natured-looking woman, who seemed as if she took the world very easily. "I am sure I don't know where you pick up those queer ideas, and those strange, independent manners. I know it is not from me, and your father was never like that since I have known him."

"You took it out of him, mamma dear, as Lord Claude is to take it out of me, I suppose. After all, I wonder why I help Lady Feversham about this. I declare I think it is a love of mischief, and nothing better, drives me on. It is rather pleasant to be making or marring a man's life, when he thinks you are the simplest, most insignificant child going. I told them to have 'Stole Away' ready for me in half an hour—I want to give him a gallop on the hills, up near Farmer Morton's, you know. There he is at the door, the beauty! I will be off; but I shall lunch here before going back to the Castle."

So saying she ran down to the door, where a magnificent brown-black, thorough-bred hunter was waiting for her.

"He's very fresh, miss," said the groom holding him, as she approached. "He threw Jim Matthews a few days ago, and broke his leg. Since then no one has mounted him, miss, and he seems rale wicked to-day."

So he did, indeed, as he rolled his eye, showing the white ominously, and laid back his ears on his smooth, firm neck, as she came forward.

Mabel Prendergast, however, was not easily frightened by such demonstrations, but patted his sleek shoulder before she mounted, with her usual careless indifference as to what might be the temper or disposition of the animal.

Once in the saddle, the reins in hand, and "You may let go," said to the groom, it became apparent that "Stole Away" was not in the most amiable frame of mind. Setting up his powerful back with a squeal, and lashing his hind-quarters viciously, he executed a series of vigorous buck-jumps, varied by violent kicking at intervals. It was pretty evident such was the process by which he had been accustomed to dislodge the grooms, and he hoped to dispose of his young mistress just as effectively.

The lawn before them was open, only a few large trees growing here and there, while at the farther end it was bounded by a sunk fence and wide ditch; once over that, the country was almost open, rising in sunny pasture slopes up to the very summits of the hills that bounded the view in that direction. All this Mabel knew well enough; so, after a few moments, during which she kept her seat like a Centaur, in spite of the furious efforts made to get rid of her, she turned the horse's head in the right direction, and bringing down her whip with stinging force across his quarters, darted forward like an arrow from a bow, and sitting well down, piloted the flying steed through the clumps of timber toward the sunk fence and ditch before mentioned. As she neared the leap, she tried to take a pull on the horse and get him together; he was running away, or would have been had she tried to stop him; but having been left free till then, and seeing what was before him, he steadied a little into his stride on feeling himself taken by the head, and went at it gallantly. There was a great drop over the ditch on the far side, and altogether it was a biggish place; but Mabel had crossed it many a time before, and worse things too, on that same horse "Stole Away." It was not the leap, therefore, that caused her to utter a half-stifled cry as her horse threw himself well forward over it; the object that caused her so much alarm as to startle her out of her usual composure was the figure of a man lying in the ditch close to the spot where she crossed it. But that "Stole Away" swerved in his jump as he caught sight of the prostrate figure, Mabel might not have remarked it; but even in the short glimpse she obtained of it, before her horse carried her wildly onward, she was aware that something was wrong with the man lying there. The confused, huddled-up attitude prompted her to return and find out what assistance was needed. But it was not an easy matter to stop her startled steed or reduce him to obedience, and being in a large pasture-field, she soon found the quickest way to accomplish her purpose would be to give the fiery animal a gallop before taking him back to the fence by which the man was lying. Round the field they went, startling the sleepy herds of cattle into menacing groups; but still "Stole Away," stout of wind and limb, showed no disposition to halt in his wild career. She was too full of a kind of undefined anxiety to be pleased with what, at any other time, she would have enjoyed immensely.

At length, after an apparently interminable gallop, she felt that her steed would be willing to stand should she find it necessary to dismount, and turning, she rode at once to the place where the man lay. He was there still, she could see as she approached, lying without motion or sign of life. Mabel's heart almost stopped beating with apprehension, as she advanced slowly toward him. When she stood beside him, every thing that had puzzled and alarmed her was at once explained.

The fence was one of the kind known as a sunk fence, and the higher side was faced with massive stone-work. The ditch being deep and wide, it was evident the man, who no doubt had intended to cross the fence, had not tried to jump, but had endeavored to climb, and had caught hold of one of the large stones that faced the higher bank, by which to pull himself up. This stone, loosened by action of water or some other cause, had given way, and had rolled on top of him as he fell backward.

It lay a heavy, crushing mass on his chest; but how long it had lain there, and whether the sufferer was dead or not, Mabel could not say; she only remembered that the spot was unfrequented, and, had she not happened to pass, the body might have remained there for days longer; for that he was either dead or insensible was evident. His face was partially hidden by one hand; the only life-like thing about him was his thick brown hair, that fluttered a little in the breeze, his hat having fallen off. Beside him also lay a small book, the leaves of which, turning over with a faint sound, allowed Mabel to catch sight of penciled and colored outlines here and there amidst its pages.

"An artist," she thought. "What shall I do? I must go home for assistance."

Turning the now submissive thorough-bred to a more practicable place, she went over and quickly arrived at the house.

It did not take long to tell her story and send men to the relief of the stranger, who was presently brought in, still insensible, and carried to the room Mabel had already caused to be got ready for him.

"We can do no less, mamma," she answered, when her mother remonstrated, on the ground that they did not know who he was. "I found him: we must do all that lies in our power for him. Send Jacob for the doctor at once," she went on, addressing the footman, who had answered her peremptory peal on the bell.

"It all comes of your riding those frightful horses, my dear," moaned Mrs. Prendergast. "I always thought you would kill yourself, but it seems you have found some one else killed instead."

"Nonsense, mamma; he isn't dead," answered Mabel, rather crossly—all the more crossly because she was horribly afraid her mother spoke the truth. "Ah! here they are with him. He had better be laid on the bed at once, and we must try to bring him round before the doctor comes."

But all their efforts to revive him were for long unavailing, even after the doctor joined them. When at length he did open his eyes, it was only to close them again in another swoon. He seemed weak, the doctor thought, as though he had lain in the field some time; but after a little brandy had been administered his breathing became more regular and his pulse stronger.

When Dr. Sims joined the ladies afterward, he told them he apprehended no danger, if fever did not set in; the most serious injury was the very severe contusion he had received in the chest; but he had no doubt time and care would cure him completely—make him as strong as ever he was; "or indeed stronger," he added, with a laugh. "It seems to me he is a traveling artist —a gentlemanly-looking fellow, for all that."

"What's his name, doctor?" asked Mabel. "Did he tell you?"

"He has not spoken at all yet," replied the doctor—"indeed, the less he speaks the better for some time; but I found a letter in his pocket addressed to Cecil Egerton, Esq., Beaumanoir, Blankshire, so I presume he is staying with Mr. Vansittart. I shall write to that gentleman when I go home, to see if I can find out any thing about him."

"Yes, and you may have his things sent here," said Mabel, eagerly, "as it will be some time before he can move, I imagine."

"Very well," answered Dr. Sims, bustling down to his gig as he spoke. "I will call again to-morrow."

"Now what am I to do, mamma?" asked Mabel, when the village medico had disappeared. "It is not fair to leave you all the burden of this man I have brought home, so I think I had better leave Lady Feversham for the present and return here. He is too much of a gentleman, I think, at least in appearance, to leave him entirely to servants; it would not be kind. It is a great bore, all the same," she went on. "I was advising Lady Feversham about this business of Lord Claude's, and now it will all be in a muddle, unless I ride over there every day."

"Well, you can do that, darling," answered her father, who had come into the room while she was speaking. "I have been looking at this young fellow, and he seems a gentleman from his appearance. He is lying quite quiet, with his eyes closed, but I think not sleeping. He seems to breathe with difficulty; but the doctor says he will get over it soon. Do you know how it happened, dear?"

Then she related how she imagined it had happened, and ended by saying,

"It is most provoking I should have been the person to discover him. It is fearfully disagreeable having a man of whom you know nothing sick in your house, particularly under these circumstances, as it obliges you to be civil. However, it can't last so very long. I suppose a month will see our trouble over. Now I will gallop back to the Castle and explain it all to her ladyship; but I will return in the evening."

Lady Feversham was in great distress when she heard her young ally must leave her. She felt it quite impossible that, without Mabel's assistance, she could bring the matter to a successful termination.

"And besides," she went on, "I really don't see the necessity for your going home; and the man need be no burden to your mother; the housekeeper would take care of him."

"Of course," assented Mabel, somewhat impatiently; "but, you see, he seems rather too much of a gentleman to be left entirely to servants. It will be right for some of us to go and see after him now and then, and it would be rather too much to ask mamma to do it always, when I brought him into the house. As to your business, however, I will ride over every morning, and then we can settle what had best be done. I posted your letter to Lady Longwreath, but we can't have an answer that will be of any use to our plans for at least a week."

So it was arranged that Mabel should return home, but that she was still to be the governing spirit of Lady Feversham's schemes. She rode away that afternoon a little annoyed and worried at her morning's adventure, yet not wholly displeased at it, since it afforded a pretext for leaving the Castle, where she was beginning to get rather bored.

"Stole Away" was quiet enough by this time, and the young girl, laying the reins on his neck, followed the road homeward, absorbed in reverie. It was a lovely evening early in September; the sun, low down in the horizon, threw long shadows of the horse and his rider over bank and hedge-row, as she passed along; the clouds floated high in the still heavens, blazing with crimson and gold; the trees, already beginning to don the richest autumn tints, hardly rustled a leaf in the still evening air; while, all along the white, dusty road, cattle were wending their way homeward, or parties of laborers returning from their work, touched their hats respectfully to the squire's young lady. She was well known to them all, and a favorite with most, for she showed no haughtiness of disposition toward her inferiors; and being of a generous disposition, with plenty of money at her command, she took a pleasure in relieving any want that came under her notice. Besides, she could ride as few even of the men in the county could, and her daring awoke a warm feeling of admiration in the country bumpkins, who sometimes watched her rapid flight across the country.

But this evening she took very little notice of their respectful salutations; her mind was fully occupied with other things. First, there was this business of Claude Feversham's. Should they win, and might she hope some day to have him at her feet? or would he carry his purpose, as, indeed, she well believed he had strength of will to do?

After all, if Lady Feversham could find the girl's address, it would depend more on her character than on Claude's will; but if she loved him as he did her, it was more than probable she would regard her lover's entreaties more than his mother's threats.

Then her thoughts reverted to the morning's adventure.

"So stupid!" she muttered, drawing her whip across her horse's neck with a threatening gesture, but without striking him. "It was your being so wild, you old fool, that caused me to discover him. I must take care to give you plenty of exercise, or you will be mad before the hunting begins."

Then she wondered what the stranger might be like. She had not seen his face, shaded as it was by his hand when she rode up, and afterward, in the bustle and confusion, she had not noticed it.

She only remembered heavy masses of dark, wavy hair, cut rather short, and a white, delicately formed hand; not at all the hand of one accustomed to rough it, and labor for his daily bread—rather it seemed suited to a dreamer or a poet. As she thought of this, Mabel wondered more and more who he could be, and what brought him there.

It was almost dinner-hour when she reached The Poplars. Running up stairs, she began to dress quickly, ringing for her old nurse, who was also her maid, as she did so. Her bell was answered by one of the other servants, whom she asked sharply why nurse did not attend to her. The girl replied that nurse was in the sick gentleman's room, but she would send her to Miss Mabel at once.

"No, no," cried Mabel, hastily; "you will do very well for what I want now. I can stop and speak to nurse as I pass the room. It is rather a bore, having one's maid turned into a sick-nurse," she grumbled, as she went on dressing.

Shortly after, on her way down stairs, she knocked gently at the door of the invalid's room, and looking in noiselessly, asked how he was doing.

"Pretty much the same, miss," replied the nurse. "He has neither spoken nor moved since the doctor saw him last."

"Well, I just came to speak to you about the dress you are making for me," continued Mabel. "I was thinking, when I was out to-day, that I should like little flounces all up the back, and not a bunched-up panier, as every one wears now. Do you think you can manage that? It was better to tell you at once, for fear you might cut the stuff the other way."

"Very well, miss," answered the nurse; "you only just spoke in time, as I had laid out to cut the panier to-night. I have not seen any dresses made that way, but if you can show me one of the fashion pictures, I dare say I shall be able to manage it."

"You'll find *Le Follet* in my room," answered Mabel, "and there is a plate of the very thing I want. I suppose the gentleman is insensible, as you say he has not spoken or moved since he came, nurse. What is he like? I had no opportunity of getting a look at his face."

As she spoke Mabel noiselessly crossed the room and stood by the bedside, while nurse took up again the work she had laid down, and answered:

"He is a nice-looking young gentleman enough, miss, if he was stronger; but he must have been lying out there some time, the doctor thinks, before you found him; and he is that wasted you could blow him away if you had a mind to do so."

Mabel smiled as she listened to nurse's opinion, and mentally passed her own while she looked at his haggard, pallid countenance, which was handsome in spite of suffering. As she stood thus he opened his eyes wearily, and at first there was no meaning or purpose in his gaze; it was simply a vacant stare. By degrees, however, an expression of pleasure dawned over his weary, pain-altered face; he did not attempt to speak, but his look followed Mabel as she turned away. When she left the room he closed his eyes with a sigh, and she went down stairs musing,

"How handsome he is! Who can he be?—a gentleman, evidently, with that face and those hands, but who?"

A question not to be answered, at least at

present, so she descended to the drawing-room, and was rather more meditative even than usual that night; but her parents were used to their little daughter's fits of abstraction, and her absent manner passed unnoticed.

CHAPTER XL.

A FASCINATING ACQUAINTANCE.

In the mean time, we on duty in Ireland began to have rather hard times of it. The Fenian agitation was recommencing in preparation for the winter, at which time they were always most troublesome. We were perpetually being confined to barracks, besides being obliged to be much more strict in the performance of our duties than we had been ever since we entered these jolly country quarters. It was very hard to be up to them; they had so many ways of disguising themselves and going about, and the Government was so awfully frightened of them, a great deal more so than the necessities of the case warranted. We were fearfully bored at not being able to go out at night when we wished, it being necessary always to leave some of us in charge of the barracks. Indeed we seldom got any distance from the town now, for fear of sudden calls being made for us; not that we should have been of much use in case of a rising, I apprehend, as in such a difficulty the orders were that we should shut ourselves up in barracks.

Under these circumstances, it did not so much matter the Bambridges being away, as we could not have got over there often; so we amused ourselves as best we could, playing billiards and lounging about the town.

The billiard-room was in the hotel, and was a very constant resort of ours every afternoon: we generally met some one or two of the country gentlemen there, and really there was nothing better to do than getting up matches between ourselves and them, which was done without much loss on either side, none of us being very first-rate players.

One afternoon, however, when Flower and I entered the billiard-room, we found it occupied by a gentlemanly-looking man, who was knocking about the balls by himself, and who apparently did not find that amusement lively, for on our approach he laid down his cue, and asked if we were about to have a game. Now Flower and I were so ill matched—that is to say, he was such a bad player, that it had become somewhat monotonous my constantly winning; I therefore answered that if the stranger would play a game with me it would give me great pleasure, and Flower would mark for us.

I don't think Baby half liked being ordered to mark, but he was rather afraid of me, so he assented somewhat sullenly, and we set to work. Our unknown friend was not only a splendid player, soon making me repent of my weakness in challenging him, but he was also a very liberal, friendly kind of fellow, called for Champagne, and invited us to drink with him in a way that plainly showed he had money at his command, and was not one of the poor tourists that are most frequently to be seen at country hotels in the west of Ireland.

He beat me, of course; then he played with Flower, giving him a good lot of points, and beat him with equal ease; after that Feversham having come in, they began a game, but here he found himself better matched, and it was a very close struggle between them, ending, however, by the stranger's winning. He was a communicative fellow, called himself Mr. Maguire, and told us all about his family and fortune, where he lived, and what brought him down to Belmurphy. Then he played another game with the police inspector, who had just come in, finished him too, and after that, as it was nearly time for mess, walked part of the way back with us. This went on for some days. He was a most agreeable, gentleman-like fellow, full of fun and anecdote, and did not always win at billiards, which kept us all in a good-humor with him; it was such a triumph when one did manage to defeat a good player. As we got more intimate, he used to ask us to cozy bachelor dinners, and we in return asked him to mess one evening, as we were about to leave the hotel, after a pleasant afternoon spent there.

He accepted willingly, saying it was very lonely dining by himself, and came along with us at once.

"Have you had any trouble about those Fenian fellows lately?" he asked, as we drew near the barracks.

"Well, you know," replied Feversham, "the Government is in an awful funk about them, and really if the barracks all over the country are like these, they could not be very easily defended."

"I don't know," answered Maguire. "You see I have traveled a good deal on the Continent, and have learned something of fortification there, so perhaps, if you are not above taking a hint, I might give you one or two. You see the barracks stand on the summit of a high hill; it is true they are commanded by another hill over there, and you would not have troops enough to occupy that; but then these Fenians have no cannon, and without them the height beyond would serve them little. Then, if I was defending this place, the first thing I should do would be to destroy all these poor houses that come close up to the walls, and that would afford cover to the enemy. Once they were removed, nothing could approach you without being exposed to your fire. However, I suppose you know all this as well as I do. Were not those your plans?"

"Well, yes, in part," answered Feversham, "but I think we might even do a little more;" and then he proceeded to unfold his ideas for fortifying the barracks in case of a rising.

Mr. Maguire listened with attention, suggesting an improvement here, disputing the wisdom of a measure there, until we went in to dinner, when the subject dropped, and was not again resumed. "He is a clever fellow that," whispered Mayleigh to me before we sat down. "He is as well up in fortification as I am myself."

"Which would not be saying much for him," I laughed. "It seems to me he knows more than Feversham, and some of his ideas are original, though he supports them strongly."

When he was about to leave that night, our guest, while shaking us warmly by the hands, said that it was with great regret he bid us good-bye, as he must be off by the early train next day.

"I shall ever think with pleasure of our brief

acquaintance," he added, feelingly. "And even if we don't meet, you will hear of me again."

"I am sorry he is going," we all exclaimed when he had left; "he was such a pleasant companion."

"Yes, it is quite refreshing to meet with such a clever fellow, who is not above joining in ordinary amusements," chimed in Feversham. "He has got no mean talent in the engineering line; he pointed out one or two little defects in the plans we had formed for defending the barracks."

So we all agreed we had lost a most charming acquaintance, and regretted him very much till the next afternoon, when Colonel Dropmore received an official communication, to the effect that the famous Fenian leader, Colonel Kelly, was in the town, residing at the hotel, and that immediate measures must be taken for his arrest. Then followed a description of his *personne*, in which we recognized, with unfeigned astonishment, a most accurate portrait of our agreeable billiard-playing friend.

"Well, if this isn't a pretty go!" cried Mayleigh, going into a fit of laughter; "at any rate the bird has flown now, and he deserved to get safe off, for a bolder or cooler fellow never breathed. How well he walked into us! By Jove, I feel a good deal smaller since I heard how we were taken in!"

"It is very annoying," answered Feversham. "What a confounded set of fools we must appear to him! But, as you say, I am glad he escaped, for he was a plucky fellow after all."

The laugh raised against us, when this became known, gave the county amusement for many days, and we had to stand a heavy fire of chaff from every man we met for a good while after.

But this was not all, even. Shortly after a man was taken up somewhere else on the supposition that he was Colonel Kelly, and several of us had to go over to London to see if we could identify him. It was a great bore, as we were dragged over, confronted with the prisoner, who proved to be the wrong man after all, and then were sent back on the spot, not being even allowed a few days to rest and amuse ourselves among the pleasures of the great city.

"It will teach us to be more careful in choosing our acquaintance in future," said Claude, when, wearied and travel-stained, we returned again to Belmurphy; "not but that he was as good a fellow as you could meet with, and I am glad he got safe off."

In the mean time, while all this was going on down with us, Lady Feversham, after at least ten anxious days of waiting, received the required information from Lady Longwreath. The Bambridges were in Lodgings in Kildare Street, the number was given, and all was ready for Lady Feversham to decide on her course of action. This, however, she could not do without first consulting Mabel Prendergast, who urged her strongly to go over and see Miss Bambridge in person.

"I will not tell you what to say," she went on; "the situation must, of course, suggest that; but if you find she is not afraid of poverty, try and get her pride up in your favor. Insinuate that you look on a match with her as a *mésalliance*, and that it will lower Lord Feversham's position in society. There—I need not tell you

any more; you understand it very well, and if you are determined to succeed, you will do so."

Lady Feversham would have liked greatly to take Mabel with her. It was a long, tiresome journey, with only her maid for a companion, but she could see plainly it would be useless asking such a thing, and so she at last made up her mind to do it by herself, with only a feeble milk-and-water kind of woman—her maid Purcell—as a protector.

"You'll be back in two or three days?" asked Mabel, as she watched her friend get into the train, on her way up to London.

"Yes, certainly," the old lady answered, "and I hope with good news—good for you as well as me, remember."

Mabel nodded her head with a smile, but as she turned away an impatient expression overspread her face.

"Did not I tell her," she thought, "that it was not for myself I was assisting her, and less now than ever? And why less now than ever?" she asked herself, as she took her ponies' reins and turned their heads homeward. "I think I am going mad, or getting softening of the brain, or something dreadful, when I begin to fancy even for a minute I could give up the power I might enjoy as his wife, and all because a face haunts me—as if it was not very natural a face as perfect as that one should do so! Why, it is quite a pleasure to think of it," she mused, smiling, leaning back, and letting the ponies take their own pace homeward. "A picture would please me as well. There is a want somewhere in the face, and yet you never think of that when looking at it. Too much sweetness and tenderness, and too little strength—that is the fault. Well, there is strength enough about Lord Claude's face, but it is nothing to look at, though I believe many people think him handsome."

She was nearly home by this time, and, as she drew near, she whipped up the ponies, as if impatient of every moment until she reached the house; then throwing the reins to the groom, she ran up stairs to a little pleasant morning-room, where Cecil Egerton lay stretched on the sofa. He had been carried in there that day for the first time, and even that exertion seemed to have been too much for his feeble strength, for he lay now with the western sunlight streaming over him, his eyes closed, and appearing hardly to breathe. Suddenly a shadow fell across him, and as he had done on the first night of his arrival, so now he opened his heavy eyes, which lighted up with a look of such unutterable happiness that Mabel Prendergast turned away her head, that she might not behold the unconcealed rapture that shone in his glance.

"I knew it was you," he murmured, and his soft, slow utterance spoke the same tale as his face—passionate, adoring love. "Your step is light as air, but I heard it and knew it. You have been away a long time."

"Not so long," answered Mabel, lightly; and stepping to the window she drew the blind partly down, to shade his face from the sun; then, not trusting herself to look at him, she went on gayly, "As to hearing my step, that is nonsense —it was my shadow between you and the sun aroused you."

"I should know your step among a thousand,"

he persisted, feebly. Then, after a pause, he whispered again, "When shall I be stronger? Does the doctor tell you when I shall be well?"

"Not for two or three weeks yet," she answered. "And you will not be much to boast of even then. Why are you so anxious to be well? Are you tired of being here?"

"Tired!" he repeated; and his glance, which she had turned to meet, startled the careless coquette with its deep meaning. "I am only afraid," he added, "that I shall feel my usual life unbearable after this."

"Well, do not think of it for the present," she replied—"it will be time enough to meet your troubles when they come. In the mean time, rest and be happy. Ah! here is mamma coming to see the patient. He is getting on very slowly, mamma dear, and seems tired by having been moved into this room to-day."

"I was afraid he would," answered Mrs. Prendergast; "but he seemed so very anxious for a change that at last I consented."

So saying, she sat down beside him, talking pleasantly of the little events of the day, not requiring an answer, and striving by every art in her power to cheer and entertain the invalid.

Certainly, as far as kindness and consideration went, Cecil Egerton could not have fallen into better hands, and yet he wished sometimes bitterly that it had been his fate to die where he fell, or be picked up and succored by the meanest laborer in the field, rather than to have been let into this paradise of beauty and love, to be turned out again, in a few short weeks, deprived of the only thing that had hitherto supported him—his light, careless heart. A heavy heart, indeed, he was doomed to carry henceforward, for he told himself again and again it was impossible that he could ever be any thing more to the bright young beauty who formed the light of his life than the stranger whom she had found injured accidentally, and whom her kindness had succored.

So while Mrs. Prendergast chatted away merrily, thinking she was beguiling the weary moments of the invalid, his thoughts flew back to his uncle, and a mental review of his position passed before him. Mr. Vansittart had not come to see him when he heard what had happened, but he had written a note, which was cautiously worded, and not unkind. Cecil could tell from it, however, that his uncle considered the accident a very lucky one, or, in other words, that he fancied it was an accident on purpose, and that he gave his nephew credit for being more than usually mercenary, as being willing to run bodily risk to insure his securing the prize. This added to the sting caused by what he believed to be the hopeless nature of his love. It was bitter to feel that he had given his whole heart to one so incomparably and immeasurably his superior—that she, looking down from the height of a heavenly pity, could never either understand or return his affection; but it was still more bitter that he should, by the accident that had opened to him the door of this paradise, that had filled his heart with this priceless love, have laid himself open to the base insinuations of those whose hearts were too sordid to understand his pure devotion, or her immeasurable distance above him. Mr. Vansittart said in his note he would himself call to see his nephew as soon as he

should hear that Cecil was strong enough to receive him; but the young man determined he would not let his uncle know of his convalescence until he was well enough to leave The Poplars.

The great fault of his character was, as has been said, a weakness that caused him to think ill of himself and of his own endeavors at all times, and to exalt the performances of others unduly. It was a sweet, loving character, with great capabilities for affection, but no energy, no ambition that might urge him on to take the place in the world to which his imaginative powers entitled him.

As an artist or a poet, under favorable circumstances, he would have been great; as a man of action and purpose, he could never have been distinguished. He recognized this fault in himself clearly, as indeed he saw all his faults, without ever perceiving his counterbalancing merits. As he lay back, listening to his hostess's chat, a dull despair stole over his heart when he thought of his love, and the utter improbability of her ever learning to care for him. He thought of her as he saw her when he opened his eyes that first night, and beheld the white-robed figure standing by his bedside, looking so pitiful and tender. He remembered how she appeared to him like an angel of light—like a vision from some happier world—and he had hardly dared to breathe, for fear the enchanting apparition should fade and vanish from his sight.

When she turned and left the room, speaking for an instant to the nurse as she went, he understood that it was no unreal form that had charmed his weary senses and beguiled his pain; satisfied that what he had just seen he should see again, he slept peacefully for the first time since he was injured.

After that day, as he slowly recovered, he thought of her constantly, watched for her approach, and centred every feeling of his passionate heart in her. How he should like to paint her portrait, he thought, assuring himself his devotion was merely artistic admiration. In his mind he drew her for every fair and famous woman noted in the history of every age and clime, always ending by deciding that her own age and character suited her best: he could not associate the actions of any other being with her. As he began to get stronger, and knew that before long he must make an effort to move, and not trespass longer on his entertainers' kindness, he discovered at once and suddenly how deep this ill-fated affection had struck its roots into his heart.

It was not only that he thought of her by night and day, that her strange, expressive eyes haunted him with their changeful meaning, that her fair face hovered always before him, with its indescribable smile, and surrounded by its frame of dark hair, like a picture by some rare old master; it was not this delight of the senses, exquisite though it was, that rendered the agony of parting so keen and unsupportable; it was that with every good, and tender, and noble quality with which nature had gifted him, he had endowed her with lavish imagination; and all that was lofty, and strong, and admirable, in which he was deficient, seemed to him to shine forth in her with greater brilliancy than in any other being he had ever met.

When she sung, it was a pleasure so exquisite

as to be pain; when she talked, with her low, caressing voice, his heart would beat wildly with rapture; and when the red-brown eyes rested on his with that indefinable smile, half coaxing, half triumphant, curving her lips, he felt as though he could die happy, were he but assured that strange sphinx-like smile and the glorious light in the unfathomable eyes were for him, and him alone.

The feelings that rose so wildly in his heart would at times break bounds and betray themselves. Weak in all things, he was weaker yet in this, and would, when alone with Mabel, utter words that revealed plainly all the longing and the passion which was so irrepressible and, as he thought, so hopeless. These outbreaks she affected to treat as expressions of gratitude for the little kindnesses she showed him; or at times, when it was impossible to twist his words so as to render such interpretation probable, she would say, laughing, though but for her back being always turned to him on these occasions, he might have detected the quivering of her lips,

"Nonsense, you foolish boy! We don't talk of such things here, and I can not allow it. Mind, if you disobey me," she would add, holding up a warning finger, "I shall leave you in Mrs. Meek's charge, and never come near you again."

The mere threat of such a fate was sufficient, and the danger would be tided over for a time. Mabel, laughing within herself at his implicit obedience to her word, and believing that she could keep him forever as submissive as he then was, would think no more of the matter, and see as much of him as before any rash words had crossed his lips to her.

In the mean time, what did she think of him? No sooner had she discovered the state of his feelings with regard to her than she asked herself that question, but could give no answer to it.

"He is certainly wonderfully handsome," she thought, as, sitting a little behind him in the shade of the window-curtain, she scanned his clear-cut features, wide forehead, dark violet eyes, and sweet, irresolute mouth, shaded by a heavy dark mustache; "and he loves me as I have never been loved," she mused. "If I would marry him to-morrow, and had nothing in the wide world to call my own, he would take me by the hand and lead me with him as cheerfully as though I brought him thousands of dowry. Why can not I afford to please myself? I know people would say what a fool that girl was to marry the poor soldier she had rescued; but, after all, why should I give my money to a rich man, simply because the world expects it. But then Lord Feversham. If his mother breaks off the match, it will be a fine thing to subdue that man, and teach him the chit he used to look down upon may be a prize to be desired. I do believe I could fascinate him if I tried, and then what a sphere would be open to my ambition as his wife! No, it is folly to think of love when so fine a game is opening before me. As for this poor fellow, I fear he will not like it; but he could not expect to win me, and I have been much kinder to him than he had any reason to hope. I wonder how he will take it! I hope I shall be able to get out of the way when he is leaving."

So thinking, she rose, turned the cushions under his weary head, lingered a little as she bent over him, feeling that his dark dreamy eyes were fixed on her, and that he followed every turn of her graceful figure with undisguised admiration; but she cared little, while she paid him these attentions, whether the result would be life-long misery, or cynical, callous indifference.

CHAPTER XII.

LADY FEVERSHAM IN DUBLIN.

LADY FEVERSHAM arrived in Ireland with less of fatigue and worry than she had anticipated. She might have heard before of the Holyhead boats, or might have been told that the passage was short and safe, but certainly she had expected difficulties and dangers in reaching that barbarous island which did not meet her in reality. She felt almost disappointed that she had not been called upon to go through something much more terrible, which would have given her the right to consider herself a martyr to her son's interests.

However, it was not to be, and she found herself comfortably installed in the Shelbourne before she began to realize that she had indeed crossed the Channel, and was in the much-dreaded sister-island, of the horrors of which she had always entertained such a lively idea. That very afternoon she drove to the number in Kildare Street where the Bambridges were lodging, and asked for the young lady: she did not care to make acquaintance with the rest of the family, and thought she could arrange matters better with Miss Bambridge if quite alone.

Gwendoline was in. She was going to a ball that evening, and was taking a rest, so as to be fresh for the occasion; still she did not refuse to see visitors, and Lady Feversham was admitted. General and Mrs. Bambridge were both out, and every thing favored the enterprising old lady in her mission; nevertheless she felt extremely embarrassed when Miss Bambridge entered the room, looking splendidly handsome, and with an easy, cheerful manner, that showed how little she guessed her visitor's errand. A few commonplaces passed between them, and Lady Feversham was still uncertain how she should begin, when Gwendoline Bambridge opened the subject, saying carelessly,

"I think I met a son of yours in the —th lately."

"Yes, I believe so," replied the old lady, stiffly, feeling the task before her a hard one, and coming to it slowly. "My son is in that regiment, and indeed it is about him I called here to-day."

"Really?" asked Miss Bambridge, with surprise, but coloring a little, for she felt something unpleasant must be coming; and Claude Feversham never having spoken to her of his love, she hardly thought it possible his mother was about to allude to the subject.

"I am afraid," Lady Feversham went on earnestly, "that what I am about to say will pain you, but unwilling as I am to give annoyance, still in this case my duty will not permit me to spare either your feelings or mine."

She paused, as though expecting an answer; but Gwendoline, who began now to see that the business was more disagreeable than she had feared, sat as if carved in stone, waiting to hear more before she would commit herself to a reply.

"I have heard," the old lady went on, after a short silence, "that my son is an admirer of yours—indeed, some say a lover; I have moreover been assured that you encourage him, which is perhaps not unnatural, as in this country your chances of an advantageous settlement must be limited. But I should like you, before the matter goes any farther, to understand distinctly how he is placed with regard to fortune, and what his prospects are."

"Lord Feversham has never done me the honor to speak to me of his love, so I should suppose your ladyship's fears are groundless, and that you have been misinformed," answered Gwendoline, in a hard, dry voice.

"I would willingly think so," replied her ladyship, coldly, "but I know that my information is correct; and though Claude has not yet proposed to you, yet he intends doing so. It is in order to prevent any misconception as to his prospects, and that if you accept him you may do it with your eyes open, that I am here to-day. My son," the old lady went on with rising passion, "is dependent on me for every thing. If he marries to please me, he will have all I possess; but if he opposes my wishes, not one penny of my money shall he ever see; and let me tell you, young lady, in case his title may have some fascination for you, a coronet is a very pretty thing when it is well gilded, but without that it is as useless and insignificant a bauble as can well be. I have written to forbid Claude's marriage with you," she went on, after pausing for a moment to take breath, "and have told him my intentions in case of his disobeying me; in spite of which his infatuation is such that he still persists in his intention of marrying you, if you will have him. It was to show you how very bad a match he would be, and to beg you to relinquish all thoughts of him, that I have come over, and called to-day to see you. You can understand I must be thoroughly in earnest, to have taken so long a journey for this purpose alone."

Still Miss Bambridge sat with her eyes fixed on the ground; but at length, raising her head with a defiant toss, she answered,

"Does Lord Feversham say he will marry me, if I will have him, in spite of poverty and the opposition of his friends? Then I am proud of my love. I always knew he was noble and true, and now that I am more certain of it than ever, do you think I will give him up? No, indeed. While he loves me, and thinks me worth so great a sacrifice, I will be true to him. He loses much, I nothing; but I gain immeasurably, in gaining the heart and name of a man so faithful and fearless as he. Though you are his mother, and as such I would willingly do much to please you, I can not do this, and you ought never to have asked it. You wish to barter your son's happiness for some whim or fancy of your own, and care not how many joyless years you entail on him, so you accomplish your scheme."

"Really, Miss Bambridge, you are most courteous," said Lady Feversham, with a sarcastic smile. "I should have thought a young lady who dresses as you do would have been above the old-world prejudice of love. I am sorry you do not at once see the matter in my light, for I must talk it over a little with you, until I get your promise to abandon the project. It is very natural you should be dazzled by the coronet, my child, though, as I told you before, it is worthless without money. But there is another thing connected with it that I wish to point out to you; for you will blame me, and Feversham too, for that matter, if, after your marriage, you find out disagreeables that you had not thought of before. Among us," she went on, after a minute or two, during which pause Gwendoline Bambridge neither spoke nor moved, "we are very jealous about interlopers and *mésalliances*. Of course you would have to bear this as well as any other person of your class, who, by some fortuitous circumstance, had suddenly become elevated to ours; and I must say, Miss Bambridge, as far as you are concerned, you are not much to be pitied, for you seem to have sufficient self-possession to bear a good amount of snubbing. But though it might not affect *you* much, think of Claude. He has always been accustomed to be treated with the greatest consideration, and perhaps you can conceive how painfully galling it would be to his high spirit to see himself pitied on all sides, while his wife would be treated with undisguised coldness. In how many bad quarrels do you think he would be involved on your account?—how often, as the iron entered into his soul, would he wish that he had never been tempted to descend from his proper sphere in life, and barter his position for the beauty of a woman whom all his efforts could not raise to the place in which he would wish to see her. Think of him dragged down by debt, balked in his military career, his whole future blighted and destroyed by the wife that, instead of being a helpmate, as a wife should be, would more properly be likened to a millstone round his neck, drawing him down into an abyss of misery and ruin."

"Enough, enough!" cried Gwendoline Bambridge, rising, while tears that she was too proud to let fall filled her eyes. "I had not thought of the mischief it would do him. I see only too clearly it would be a sacrifice of every thing — fortune, career, position — and all for a caprice he will outlive in a few short months. It was selfish of me to think of accepting his offer, and you are right. I give you my word he shall never know I loved him; for if he knew he would take me against my will. You may go now," she added, impatiently, as her visitor showed no signs of moving. "You have my promise; you have saved your son and blighted my life. Take your cruel face away from me, and let me try to forget this bitter interview. Go, and let me see you no more. I could tell you what I think of you—a hard, unnatural mother, preferring your gold to your son's happiness—but you are his mother after all, and I spare you; only do not tempt me any longer."

She leaned heavily on the table as she finished speaking, and watched the old lady leave the room with haughty, tranquil steps. When the street-door shut after her, Gwendoline Bambridge threw herself down by the sofa, and clasping her hands on her burning brows tried to think. The tears in her eyes scorched and pained her, but they would not fall—they seemed burned up by the fierceness of her grief—for she had a wild, strong nature, and had a power of suffering greater than weaker characters possess.

The only thought impressed on her brain seemed to be that they must part, that the pleasant days in the meadows and among the mountains could never come again; that all was over; the merry chats, the quiet moonlight strolls, the evenings on the lake—all were over, and forever. Why had she not enjoyed them more while yet she had them? Why had she flirted with that miserable boy, and made her lover unhappy and jealous? How many precious moments of intercourse with him had she lost by such folly!

And then the boy himself. She had been causing him pain, no doubt, for which she was sorry now, and in which she could sympathize; for surely he had loved her too, as well in his fashion as Claude had done in his. But was it all over? She feared there was a greater trial yet in store for her, when he should confess his love and ask for hers, and she must not betray her secret. How could she hide it? How could she bear to conceal what would make him so happy? It seemed impossible she could do so. Yet her word was passed, and it was for his good—for his alone; so it must be done, no matter at what cost. The world must not see she had been wounded, nor chatter of the cause of her sorrow. No, she had another task now before her. She must be bold and brave, show as haughty a front and be as merry as though this had never been.

Thinking thus, she presently pushed the tossed hair back from her throbbing temples, and rose from the sofa, looking round her like one in a dream.

That stern-looking old lady, who called herself Claude's mother, was gone, and every thing was so exactly as usual that for a minute or two it seemed to her as if the terrible interview she had just passed through must have been a delusion. Perhaps she had been dozing, and dreamed it. But no—the pain she suffered was too real and fresh for it to be the result of mere imagination; as she thought thus, a small crimson rose lying near the chair Lady Feversham had occupied attracted her attention. She picked it up mechanically, recognizing it as one out of a small bunch in the front of her late visitor's bonnet. "I will keep it," she thought, "in remembrance of this day. Who knows what service it may render me at some future time?" Then she settled her hair, and tried to look as usual, for she heard her mother and Clarissa coming in from their shopping expedition, and, if possible, she did not wish them to know who had called. She tore Lady Feversham's card into a thousand pieces, and dropped it behind the willow shavings in the grate, pretty certain that the servant who let the lady in would never think of mentioning the visitor, since one of the family had seen her.

And so it proved; for though, in spite of her high-hearted courage, Gwendoline Bambridge's eyes were heavy, and she complained of headache, no one dreamed that any untoward intrusion, while all the rest were out, was the cause of her indisposition.

"Are you glad we are going back to Belmurphy to-morrow?" asked Clarissa, pausing in the act of fastening a water-lily in her hair, while dressing for going out that evening.

"I am," replied her sister. "I feel tired to-night, and I do not think I enjoy these town balls half as much as our little country hops."

"Well, that is all very natural, as far as you are concerned," went on Clarissa. "You have your lover down there; and of course you would rather meet him and dance with him than flirt with the thousand-and-one partners here, who are nothing to you. But as for me, you see, I have no little game going on down in the country, so I can not help enjoying the light, and crowd, and flirtation, and admiration of these affairs a thousand times better. If Lord Feversham was as devoted to me as he is to you, no doubt I should feel as you do."

"Don't talk to me of Lord Feversham," answered Gwendoline, so coldly and quietly that she seemed only intent on the set of a refractory curl. "He is, and never will be, any thing to me; so I don't like our names being coupled together."

"Halloo!" cried Clarissa, turning quickly and looking at her sister; "since when have you given him up? Is there any bigger fish on hand, or have you quarreled?"

"Neither the one nor the other," replied Gwendoline, still calmly, though she was obliged to turn her back, to prevent her inquisitive sister from seeing the quivering of her white lips; "only I think it improbable he will ever ask me to marry him, and if he does I shall not accept him."

"Well, this is a curious state of affairs!" ejaculated Clarissa, forgetting her dressing in her intense astonishment. Then she went on, after a minute's pause: "Will you tell me, is little Darrell the cause of this resolution? I know you have been carrying on a good deal with him, but I thought it was likely to end badly for my poor dear little Madcap, and not for the stately captain."

"What nonsense you do talk, Clarissa!" cried Gwendoline, getting rather cross. "Madcap is a dear little boy, and I am very fond of him, but I could not compare him with Lord Feversham, and certainly should never prefer him."

"You like Madcap?" asked the younger girl, half sadly, half merrily. "Well, so do I. But if you would not care for him as a lover, how would you like him as a brother?"

Gwendoline turned slowly, and, for the first time during this conversation, looked at her sister. "You don't mean to say that is what you are thinking of?" she said slowly, as Clarissa blushed, yet met her look firmly. "How blind I must have been never to see that he cared for you!"

"He does not care for me," answered Clarissa, hanging her head; "he has eyes and ears only for you. But if he would look at me, if he would care for me, I think he would find that I could love him as well, and make him as true a wife as any other woman in the wide world."

"But you are both so young," urged her sister. "You were only seventeen your last birthday; and I am sure he can not be much older. However, I am glad you have let me know how matters stand. I will show him I do not want him now, and then he will begin to think more about you. I dare say," she added, smiling, "that in a week's time he would not return to me if I wanted him."

Clarissa did not answer. Perhaps she thought

so too; but they were already late, so they ceased talking, and devoted themselves vigorously to the business of dressing, to such purpose that they did not keep the carriage waiting more than half an hour.

Next day they returned to the country; but on account of the Fenian disturbances, their friends in barracks were not able to spare time to visit them, so that the days passed dully, or, rather, would have done so, but that General Bambridge determined, in case of a rising and the house being attacked, to defend it to the utmost. With this view he polished up all the old arms about the house, got a stock of revolvers, and taught the girls how to use them; besides which, all the men about the place who could be trusted were brought into the house, armed, drilled, and a regular garrison thus kept up.

There were many other families in the neighborhood who did the same thing, but none had their band so well regulated and organized as General Bambridge's; therefore he was not a little proud of it.

Such was the state of terror and excitement throughout the country at that time that few people went to bed at night at all, and the Bambridges, living in a wild, out-of-the-way place, formed no exception to this rule, the general considering that, with his army, a surprise was the only thing to be feared.

Not so Mrs. Bambridge. She disapproved of the organization altogether—rank nonsense she called it—to think of defending a small country house against a mob of two or three thousand men; and as for those girls and their revolvers, she would say, "It is all very well now, and of course they like popping away at a mark during these dull days when there is nothing else to do; but put them face to face with a sea of shouting, uproarious men, and they will be just as likely to shoot themselves, or you, from sheer terror, as to do the enemy any mischief. No; it is the most foolish thing that can be done, keeping arms in the house, for the first place they will make for will be the country houses, where they know such things are to be had. Any opposition will only exasperate them, and cause them to revenge themselves when they overcome the handful opposed to them; whereas, if there were no arms in the house, or if the arms were given up at once, they would be very civil, and cause you no annoyance."

It was all very true and very sound reasoning, but the general would not give in to it; so night after night the whole family sat up in the gun-room till day dawned, when, pale and worn out, they would retire to rest, the Fenians never choosing the day-time for their exploits.

The girls were very much of their mother's opinion on the matter, but they dared not avow such sentiments before their father, and practiced all day long with their revolvers as though it was the best fun in the world.

Their courage was destined to be put to the test, for one night, as General Bambridge lay peacefully slumbering on the sofa in the gun-room, while they and Mrs. Bambridge worked and read to keep themselves awake, there came a loud ringing at the door-bell.

The three women dropped their work and looked at each other, the gentleman slumbered on. Suddenly rising, with a look of determination lighting up her pale face, Mrs. Bambridge beckoned the girls to leave the room, and going out with them closed the door quietly behind her.

"Now, girls," she said, "if we can give them the arms without disturbing your father, all will be right." By this time the servants were assembled in the hall, armed to the teeth, and Mrs. Bambridge stepping forward addressed them, pointing out eloquently all the dangers to which resistance would expose them, and how safe they would be if the arms were given up quietly. "I will open the door," she went on, "and give them all they want; only you do as I tell you, and make no attempt at opposing them."

By this time another peal rang through the house, and fearful of the general's being awakened, Mrs. Bambridge undid the fastenings of the door with trembling fingers, and opening it said, "Good people, we are ready for you. You shall have every thing you want."

"All right, ma'am," answered the leading figure, saluting respectfully. "Sorry to disturb you at this time of night, but the general told us to call up some evening during our rounds, to see if his people were all alive. Hope you were not alarmed, ma'am, but them was the general's orders. Would you tell him we did as he wished?" and saluting again most respectfully, the head constable and his patrol withdrew, leaving Mrs. Bambridge rather taken aback and very much disturbed at the thought that the police must surely have divined her intention.

The general laughed heartily when he heard of her discomfiture, but mentally promised himself that he would not go to sleep again. He had no intention of being balked of his skirmish in that way, and if he had not been so much amused at the finale of his wife's manœuvre, would have been very angry at it. As it was, it afforded a good subject for chaffing for many a day after, Mrs. Bambridge always maintaining she had acted with great presence of mind and prudence; while the girls felt a little ashamed of having abandoned their colors, and tried to turn the subject whenever it was mentioned.

After a week or two, however, the excitement again subsided: people said there was nothing to be feared till later on in the winter, and all minds reverted to what had occupied their thoughts before other and more engrossing matter had called attention away. It was now the end of September. Gentlemen were getting their horses into condition for the hunting, and those who were not supplied with hunters, but had money enough to keep them, began to search the country high and low, and frequent all the large fairs, with a view to mounting themselves for the coming season.

Among those thus occupied Feversham and I were most conspicuous, for we had determined to come out strong; but having neglected to form our stud early, we found it now a much more difficult matter than we could have expected. What increased the difficulties of the search very much was the fact that we both seemed to imagine the country round Endley must be the most favored haunt of the equine race, for in that direction did we invariably direct our steps, though I can't say we ever came across any thing more likely than a rough mountain pony. But if we did not get the steeds we wanted, at least we were always welcome at the Bambridges', and fell into our usual habit of calling there at least once a day, Claude anxiously waiting for an opportunity of laying his mother's letter before Miss Bambridge, and pleading his cause with her.

The occasion offered at last, one balmy October day, in this way : both Claude and I had remarked that, since Gwendoline's return from Dublin, her manner to both of us was altered—to me it was playful and indifferent, more as if she was speaking to one immeasurably younger than her-self, and not at all like the confidential way in which she used to talk to me, though still kind and pleasant; while with Feversham she was sometimes absent and *distraite*, and always, as it appeared to us, more anxious to avoid a tête-à-tête with him than seemed at all natural, or than she had ever been before.

"Something is up," remarked Claude to me : "she can not have heard of my mother's letter, and taken this way of showing she does not wish me to propose ? I will not believe it of her, unless I hear it from her own lips; and, Vivian, I will try my luck to-day. We will go out for a walk, and do you entice Miss Clarissa off for one of the wild strolls she is so fond of; that will give me an opportunity of saying what I want to her."

"Very well," I answered, feeling that life was very hard on me. I could see now plainly by her manner that she cared nothing for me but as an amusing companion, too young almost to be even considered much of a friend; yet I loved her as well, or better than ever, and my heart was very sore when I thought that Claude might go in and fight his own battle, with at least a probability of success, while I dared not even show that I worshiped the ground she trod on, lest I should be turned away with a half-pitiful, half-scornful refusal, and perhaps a sly laugh of amusement at my boyish folly.

So when we set out for our walk that soft October day, I, in front with Clarissa, proposed that we should go to the glen, and thence climb up the mountain. "It will be so pleasant to-day," I urged; "I like the fallen leaves rustling under one's feet, when they are dry and crisp, as they must be now, and the mountain views will be beautiful under this soft, blue-gray sky. If it is not too far for you, let us go."

Clarissa looked pleased, and answered,

"With all my heart. I like a day such as this in the glen too, and we can have a delightful chat. I want you to tell me what was the story I heard you laughing at the other day—something about Mr. Flower, wasn't it ?"

I told her Flower's last *bêtise*, and we laughed, and climbed, and scrambled, and got ourselves into all manner of dangerous and impossible situations, like a boy and girl let loose from school, more than like an officer in Her Majesty's service, and the belle of brilliant ball-rooms. Gayety is very catching, and she was so naturally and spontaneously merry that I almost forgot my heavy heart, and ceased for a while to envy Claude, as I helped her along, and laughed at her ready wit and dashing repartee.

At length we reached the summit of the mountain, and lay down to rest among deep heather. We were on the brow of a precipice about three hundred feet high, at the foot of which lay the woods, now turning brown, and russet, and orange with their autumnal tints; below them again lay the lake, nestled in between the mount-ain on which we sat, and the frowning mass opposite, yet so steep was the descent that it seemed as if you could throw a stone from where we sat right into the smooth water below.

"Where is Gwen ?" asked Clarissa at length. "How slow they are, to be sure! They have not yet got out of the trees; or perhaps she does not feel up to walking so far."

Her words recalled my recollection of the er-rand on which Claude had set out, and I could form a pretty good guess what had detained them, though my companion did not seem to understand it.

I could not help wondering, with painful anxiety, what answer she would give him; though, after all, what did it matter, for it was evident she did not care in that way for me. I remained silent, thinking, therefore; and Clarissa, unusually quiet for her, did not disturb my troubled reflections, until the lengthening shadows warned us it was time we were going home.

When we reached Endley I did not see Gwendoline, but Mrs. Bambridge gave me a message from Feversham, to say he had suddenly remembered some business in Belmurphy, and had been obliged to go off to see about it, but that he had left the car behind for me. I guessed at once what all this meant, and had Miss Bambridge been visible, and shown any signs of favoring me, there is no knowing what foolish castles in the air I might have built on the strength of it; but she was up stairs, and it was time to leave; so saying good-bye, I started on my lonely drive, wondering greatly what could have happened. For I could not believe that Claude's want of money would influence Miss Bambridge : she seemed a girl quite above mercenary motives.

Long afterward I came to a knowledge of what passed between them. When we walked on so fast, for a time Miss Bambridge tried to keep up with us, but Claude lingered and dawdled till we were far out of sight; and then, being deep in the wooded recesses of the glen, he proposed sitting down to rest for a minute.

"I am not tired," answered Gwendoline, passing on. But Feversham stopped her.

"Wait a moment," he cried; "I want to show you something, and ask your advice about it." Then, drawing the letter from his pocket, he went on : "This is a letter from my mother, which I received a week or two ago, when you were in Dublin. It seems she had found out—how I know not—the most precious secret of my heart. She knows it; therefore it is high time you should. Gwendoline, I love you, as fondly and truly as a man should love the woman he asks to be his wife. I don't ask you yet if you love me, if you will take me," he continued; "not until you have read that letter; then I shall require an answer."

With trembling hands Gwendoline took the folded sheet; her face was white as death, a mist swam before her eyes, and she gasped faintly, "I will sit down; it will be better, as I must read this."

He placed her sitting on a fallen tree-trunk, and stood beside her, looking down on her, his breath coming hard and fast, and his heart beating tumultuously, as he watched her agitation.

It was not the manner of one who is frightened, yet pleased; no, there was an agony of distress in the pallid cheeks and trembling hands that showed she was suffering from some hidden cause.

"I can not read it," she cried, looking up with piteous pleading eyes into his, after several endeavors to decipher her ladyship's very intelligible handwriting. "I think I must be ill to-day," she went on. "I can't see well. Will you read it to me, if indeed it is necessary I should hear it; but I don't think it can influence my answer, and it will perhaps pain you to go over it again."

"You must hear it," he replied. "I can not ask you to be my wife until you know all: it will not take long to read it to you, and it will explain every thing in a few words."

Leaning against a tree that spread its branches over them, he read the hard, stern decision of the woman of the world, while Gwendoline's head bent lower and lower, and the struggle within her became more violent as she listened. Would that she might have looked up and rewarded his love and faith by a happy smile, and the touch of her soft white hand! But her promise bound her, and also she believed, as his mother had said, that it would be ruin to his prospects and career if he married her. So she listened silently, pressing her hands to her heart, to still its beating; and when he had finished she answered, without looking up,

"I could have spared you the pain of reading that, as it in no way affects my decision. Why did you ever think of me in this way? I can never be your wife, and must beg you to forgive me if ever, by word or act of mine, I led you to think you had grounds for hope."

He started, and looked at her as one who had not heard aright; then, in a low broken voice, he murmured,

"Oh! Gwendoline, I did not think this of you. Is it possible that the knowledge of my poverty can have changed you so soon?"

This time she raised her eyes to his, and stretched out her hands toward him, crying, "Think any thing but that of me. If I had intended to take you, your money would have made no difference; but I never thought of you in that way, and this does not change my purpose."

"Never thought of me in that way!" he repeated, scornfully; "then why did you lead me on and encourage me? I could have sworn you loved me at times; yes, and I believe you do so still, but your mercenary nature will not allow your heart to make itself heard. I was deceived in you truly, for I thought that where your affections were concerned you could give up every thing. How vain to expect truth and faith from a woman! I see even now you love me, and yet you send me from you in despair and misery. I can not forgive you, I can not wish you luck in the path you have chosen; you have driven the iron too deep into my soul. I can only pray I may never see your fair, false face again!"

"Stay!" she cried; "do not part from me with such cruel words; you judge me too harshly. If I encouraged you—and, as you say it, I suppose I did—I am to blame; but I am sorry for it, and I did no more to you than to young Vivian Darrell. Why should you think I loved you more than him?"

"That boy!" he cried, with a smothered imprecation. "Oh! this is too dreadful! I see now why I am scorned and refused. That poor child has money, and will have a title; he is a better speculation in every way; and so you

throw aside the man you love (deny it if you can!), and sell yourself to a foolish boy, who can pay a better price for the toy that has caught his fancy!"

"It is not true!" she cried, piteously; "I do not care for Vivian Darrell, and shall never marry him. I shall never marry a man I do not love; and as to you, you say I can not deny my affection for you. If nothing else can satisfy you, I can and do deny it. I do not love you; I will never become your wife."

"Is it so?" he answered, slowly, while he looked long and earnestly on her bent head and drooping form. "Then may God forgive you for playing with a human heart as you have played with mine! I can not forgive you yet, but if you injured me in thoughtlessness I will try to do so, and you on your part try to be more merciful to others than you have been to me. Farewell!" And turning on his heel, Feversham walked away and left her.

Alone in the woods she sat, with the soft autumn air stirring the rich masses of her hair and fanning her fevered cheeks; but she noticed nothing, heard nothing; only the pent-up anguish of her soul found relief in bitter, scalding tears and heart-rending sobs.

It was all over. She had done what she could, she had made the sacrifice required of her, no less a sacrifice than that of her life's happiness; for now she should never love another, and though, if hereafter she saw him successful and prosperous in life, she might with a faint pleasure exclaim, "This is my doing; he would never have been what he is but for me," still the time was far distant, and it was even possible it might never come, if he was to turn in disgust from the pursuits that until now had been dear to him. But no; he was not a man to deem his life a useless burden because his dearest hope had failed; he was more likely to turn to the pursuit of ambition, and draw fame and distinction from his very disappointment.

Only she would be the sufferer, and it would result in good to him. Still, as she clung to this idea, and repeated it to herself over and over again, she felt the misery just as keenly, and derived no comfort from the reflection with which she tried to assuage her grief.

As she thought of the long weary years before her, during which she must live on the remembrance of her short dream of love, her head sank lower and lower, and a wailing cry escaped her lips. "How can I bear it? It is too hard!"

As she uttered the words a low, quick sigh sounded near her. She looked up with a start, and saw Feversham bending over her.

"I can not leave you to return alone," he stammered. "Allow me to conduct you home."

She tried to rise and gulp down her tears, but they came afresh at this token of the kind and thoughtful nature of the man whom she had wounded so deeply. Then he sat down beside her and took her hand in his.

"Can you tell me what grieves you?" he asked, softly. "If it is any thing in which I can be of use to you, do not hesitate to ask me, and I will serve you to the utmost of my power. I spoke very harshly to you just now—forgive me. I was in pain, and I forgot myself."

He waited for her answer, but, though her tears flowed faster, for some time no answer came.

At length she calmed herself by a supreme effort, and replied:

"No one can help me; but I thank you truly for your kind intentions. You have been too good to me, after the trouble I have given you; I shall never forgive myself." And so they got up and walked home.

Thus it happened that, when Clarissa and I came down from the mountain, Gwendoline was not visible, and Feversham had gone back to town.

CHAPTER XIII.

THE RISING.

FOR the next few days we heard nothing of the Bambridges. The Fenians had risen. We were busy late and early, and never off duty for a moment. Clarissa Bambridge described to me afterward what they went through, and as it gives some idea of the real state of a large part of the country at the time, I will relate it as she told me.

As soon as it became known that the Fenians had risen, and were going armed about the country, all the county families that were not in a position to defend themselves took refuge in the neighboring police barrack. Mrs. Bambridge and the young ladies, having no desire to exercise their prowess in arms, insisted on doing so also, and finally General Bambridge accompanied them, in order to assist in the defense.

There they were shut up, to the number of twenty or thirty, for two whole days in a small country police barrack. The children and nurses had one room, the ladies and gentlemen occupied another, and during a great part of the time, while a large Fenian force was attacking the building, the women were obliged to stand with their backs up against one of the walls of the room, that being the only position in which they were protected from the enemy's fire.

During these weary two days and nights their only solace was drinking tea, of which, fortunately, they had a large supply. The only room in which it was possible for the ladies to lie down and take any rest was that occupied by the women and children, and the principal bed in it was in possession of the head constable, who had been up about the country for three days and nights, and who, having been severely wounded a month or two before in capturing a Fenian, a wound from which he had never entirely recovered, was now completely done up, and slept profoundly through the din of crying children, scolding nurses, and the rattle of fire-arms outside.

"Such a miserable two days!" concluded Clarissa, with a shrug of her pretty shoulders. "And poor Gwen, who really was ill and done up, bore it so well, without a murmur. For my part, I should have liked to be cross, but was ashamed to be so, when every one else bore it cheerfully; but, oh! the discomfort of it, and the anxiety, and the pain of the cramped position. I felt several times as if it would be better to come out into range of their shots, and take my chance, than stand flattened up against that hateful wall from morning to night."

We heard nothing of this at the time, but as soon as it was possible for any of us to be spared for a while, Claude called me to him, and said,

"I hear the police barrack near Endley has been attacked. Do you, like a good fellow, ride over there and see how the Bambridges are doing. I fear they must have experienced some annoyance. You can take Fleetfoot; he will not be long carrying you over."

Delighted with my errand, I mounted and rode off. I knew that Claude's suit had been unsuccessful, though he had not told me what had passed between them; therefore a hope sprung up in my heart that it might be in my favor he had been refused. If such were indeed the case, what happiness was in store for me!—and with my foolish heart beating joyfully, I gave Fleetfoot the reins, and sped on my way gayly.

The Bambridges had that day returned to their house, but they were all out in different directions when I arrived, except Gwendoline. I told her how anxious we had all been about them, and that, as soon as any one could be spared, Feversham had sent me over to inquire. At the mention of his name, I saw a hot blush overspread her face, and she twisted her handkerchief nervously as she thanked me for coming, and said it was like Lord Feversham to be so thoughtful. But I did not read these signs as I should have done, and after a few minutes' awkward silence, began timidly,

"Miss Bambridge — Gwendoline, I must call you so, at least for these few minutes—will you be kinder to me than you were to Claude Feversham the other day, if I ask you the same question?"

"I can not," she answered, sadly. "I like you very much as a dear friend—a most amusing companion—but I do not love you with the love you ask for, and which alone would induce me to marry you. You are not angry with me?" she went on, pleadingly. "I never knew it would come to this, and Lord Feversham said I had led him on. If I have done so to you, forgive me."

"It was something very like it," I answered low to myself, for I did not wish to add to her grief, and yet I could not wholly absolve her from blame. My heart was sore, and it seemed to me that, try to hide it as she might, she did care for Claude Feversham. I suppose it was jealousy enabled me to detect the quivering tenderness in her voice when she named his name—at any rate I felt it, and rebelled against it for a minute or two. Then something seemed to speak within me, and to urge me to give up myself and my claims, which I saw plainly were hopeless, and speak up for my friend, if by any means I might benefit him, or discover the reason why he had been refused. So, after a pause, I began again: "My case is hopeless; you do not care for the foolish boy who has given you his whole, untried heart, but you do care for Feversham—I know you do—yet you have refused him. Why is this? It can not surely be that you, whom we have thought so true and womanly, are afraid of poverty with as faithful a heart as his—I could not believe it of you; but what, then, has come between you?"

She pulled her handkerchief even more nervously than before, and her eyes filled with tears as she answered,

"Thanks. I am glad that you, at least, do not think me so base as to sell my love for gold; but I can not tell you my reasons for refusing him, and condemning myself to life-long misery; it is no fault of his, it is none of mine, and yet there is a gulf between us that all our affection can not bridge over. Ask me no more about it, and never let Claude know what you have discovered, for he thinks I never cared for him, and it is better so. We shall still be friends, shall we not?" she went on, holding out her hand to me. "I should be sorry if I thought that you, too, were lost to me. You, being young, will outlive this fancy, and you and your wife, at some future time, will laugh over the remembrance of your attachment to a steady old maid, as I shall be by that time."

I could not laugh, though I tried to smile at her fancy picture, but I was grieved for her, for myself, and for Claude. She was evidently in trouble, yet she loved him, and might have made him happy by a word; therefore, miserable though it would make me, I felt I could be so truly rejoiced in her happiness that I wished that word might be spoken.

No doubt it was presumptuous of me to talk to her on this subject, once I had said my say, and heard her answer; but the sight of her sorrow-stricken face moved me, and I thought, if only I might be the means of bringing them together—if only she could some day say, smiling, "Vivian, I owe every thing to you," it might ease the dull sorrow at my heart, and help me to recover my old boyish gayety.

How long ago it seemed since I had been the harum-scarum boy, Madcap Darrell, the delight of the men, the pet, and, at the same time, the terror of my brother officers! It is true, now and then, when a good opportunity for mischief presented itself, I could not help indulging in it; but these escapades were few and far between, and every one remarked how much quieter I had become of late.

Full of my idea of bringing these two so strangely separated together again, I began:

"Is there no hope for Claude, Miss Bainbridge? He loves you so truly, and you confess you like him. I will not ask the reason of your refusal, as you do not wish me to do so; though I think it could be all explained, if you would tell what influenced your decision. But will you not let me know if there is any hope of your objections being removed at some future time? He would wait so gladly if he had but one ray of hope to cheer him!"

"You are true to your friend," she answered, slowly, "and it is good of you to be so; but I can give you no word of encouragement for him. You will serve him best now by letting him think of me no more."

So saying, she turned to the window, and leaned her head against it, with her back toward me; when she looked round again her face was calm and cold, and after a few commonplace remarks, I left.

Some days after this—the country having become more settled—Feversham obtained leave and went home, leaving me very disconsolate, and under the control of Captain Ussher, a married man and a martinet: an old fellow who had been goodness knows how many years in the army, but, being poor, had never got beyond the rank of captain, and whose temper had been soured by seeing younger and less skillful men purchasing over his head.

About this time Flower was sent, along with another detachment of our regiment, to relieve a small body of the 140th, stationed at the little village of Ballybune, near which the Grahams resided. Of course Flower was nothing loath to go, for though a fearfully dull place for those who had no object in stopping there, it promised a never-failing fund of pleasure to a young fellow whose lady-love lived in the vicinity. Fine times he had of it, too! The Grahams had an immensity of shooting, and though there were no hounds near, his gun and his flirtation kept the mild young fellow well employed.

One day, however, he went out with only a country lad to carry his game-bag, and penetrated deep into the mountains. There was not much game to be seen, yet he trudged on manfully, when suddenly, from behind a huge boulder of rock, there sprang two policemen. Darting on the surprised and unresisting Flower, one of them seized him by the collar of the coat, while the other possessed himself of the unfortunate youth's breech-loader.

"We've cotched you at last, my fine fellow, I think!" said one of them. "Many's the weary tramp we've had after you, and now you'll tramp after us."

At these words the country boy, who had waited for a minute to see if the gentleman would get the best of it, threw away the game-bag, and made off, crying, "Oh! wirrasthru! The polis!" and used his legs to such purpose that in a moment or two more he was out of sight.

"Why didn't you secure him?" asked the policeman holding Flower, of the other.

"Bad luck to him! How was I to know he'd use his legs so handy?" answered the one addressed; "and besides, it was him we wanted. We've got the head of them, and no mistake, with his gun and his game-bag! Small harm he'd do the game, this same chap, for all he's rigged out as if he was after them."

An opinion on his part that was considerably strengthened when, on picking up the bag, nothing was found in it.

"Didn't I tell you so?" he asked, triumphantly, showing it to his companion. "It's not this kind of game he's afther, anyway."

By this time Flower had recovered a little from his surprise; so, drawing himself up, and trying, but in vain, to shake himself clear of his captor's grasp, he said,

"What is the meaning of this, pray? I have leave from Mr. Graham to shoot over these lands, and I have a license also, only I have left it at Ballybune."

"That's all mighty fine," answered the policeman; "but Mr. Graham doesn't give his shooting to every one that way; and gentlemen always takes their license out with them nowadays."

"But I tell you, fellow," broke in Flower, angrily, "I am an officer in Her Majesty's service—Mr. Flower, of the —th, stationed at Ballybune."

"Come, Bill; we won't listen to this nonsense any longer. As if we didn't know that it's the 140th that's at Ballybune just now."

"It left three days ago," cried Flower. "It is the —th that's quartered there now."

"Is it, indeed?" answered his captor. "In that case you can't mind coming with us, as it's just back there we're bringing you. And we'll see what Mr. Graham will say to you when he sees you. Come on."

And so poor Flower was dragged off, and compelled to walk the ten miles back to Bally-bune at a most terrific pace, arriving at last before Mr. Graham's house, decidedly blown, and not looking the better for his exertions.

The laugh was now on his side, as the discomfited policemen were eager in their apologies, and explained that they had taken him for one of the Fenian leaders, whom they had been long hunting over the mountains, having received certain information that he was in hiding somewhere about. This day at least they made sure they had secured the right person; and Flower's astonishment being mistaken by them for alarm, they were all the more convinced they had their man at last.

It was a great sell for them, and raised a tremendous laugh against Flower, in which Beatrice Graham joined so heartily that the flirtation in that quarter was rather damped; and I think after a week or so our soft ensign was glad to return to his duties at Belmurphy.

In the mean time Feversham, quite unconscious of his mother's action in his affairs, had returned home; shortly after their first greetings were over, he said,

"And now, mother, I may as well tell you all your alarm was unnecessary. Miss Bambridge has refused me. It appears I misconceived her manner—she never loved me, and paid me no more attention than she did to young Darrell, so you need not have been so frightened. But you must understand distinctly, if she would have taken me, I would have married her without a farthing, and tried if it were not possible to live on one's pay. I had deceived myself dreadfully," he went on with broken voice—"I could have sworn she cared for me, and I had given her my whole heart before I knew my mistake."

He passed his hand over his face, and looked thoughtfully into the fire, while his mother laid her hand on his arm tenderly. Now that she had gained her point, she could be tender and pitiful.

"My poor boy," she murmured, "she was not worthy of you. How could you have thought of throwing yourself away on an Irishwoman? I am sure you will do better when you get over this. There are many nice English girls who would be proud of your love. Why not look out for one of them, and show this young lady you are well able to do without her?"

"You know nothing about it, mother," answered Claude, indignantly. "She was a girl any man might be proud to win as his wife. Where among the milk-and-water misses round us shall I find another with her daring spirit and unconventional nature? No, no, mother; she may know that she has made a mark on my life not easily to be effaced, if she cares to know it, for I will not marry merely for the purpose of persuading her the wound was light. Rather I should like her to see that quite unconsciously, as I believe, she has pained me to the heart. It may perhaps teach her to be more careful with another at some future time."

Lady Feversham said no more. She saw only too plainly that her son was sore stricken—his very face was changed, his sweet smile rarely

lighted up his countenance, which was uniformly grave and sad, while his voice had acquired a hopeless tone, that told the interest of his life had for a time departed.

There was a few minutes' silence beween mother and son, as they stood beside the fire in the chill autumn dusk, and watched the glowing embers with eyes that saw in them each their own separate visions. Claude's thoughts were busy with that troublesome past that haunted and tortured him constantly. Lady Feversham was building up for him, her only son, a magnificent future, constructed to suit her own views of beauty and magnificence.

Suddenly he looked up and spoke.

"Mother, tell me who it was warned you that I loved Miss Bambridge?"

Lady Feversham started. She had not calculated on being asked this question, and it was most important to her schemes that it should never be truly answered. "I can not tell you," she said. "You would be angry with one who acted so truly a friendly part toward you, and might speak or act ill toward the person. I will not tell you."

"If you are afraid of my conduct toward the person, it must be some one I know, or else that precaution would be unavailing. Tell me, is it so?"

Lady Feversham hesitated. She could write in stern fashion enough to her son, but when he was standing there beside her, asking questions in that cold, dry voice, he seemed to force the answers out of her against her will. She tried to keep silence, but his eyes, fixed on her, forced her to speak, and finally she stammered out,

"Yes, it is some one you know. And now you must not ask me any thing more, for I will not answer you."

His brow clouded over as he heard her answer, but he persisted in his questions, saying:

"Tell me at least it was not Vivian Darrell who played this traitor's part. I believed the boy when he denied it, but your words seem very much as if my suspicions had been correct."

Lady Feversham kept silence. She did not wish to get her young nephew into trouble with his captain, but it would certainly be convenient if Claude's suspicions were to fix themselves very far away from the real object. She would not say what was untrue, even to effect so convenient a result; but if what she said led him to imagine such a thing, she did not choose to take any trouble to undeceive him.

"Tell me," repeated Claude, impatiently, "was it Vivian Darrell, or not?"

"You know very well Vivian never writes to me," replied Lady Feversham, with irritation, "and I have not seen him since he joined. But I will answer no more questions." And she rose and left the room, leaving her son gazing into the fire with a pained, puzzled look on his handsome face.

"She would not answer me straight out 'No,' as she would have done had my suspicion been false. I fear greatly it is true." And the gloom on his brow deepened.

Mabel Prendergast was still at home: Cecil Egerton had not yet left, and except when she rode over, which was pretty regularly, Lady Feversham saw little of her ally.

The very day, however, after Claude Fevershnm's arrival, the young lady rode up, looking very beautiful on her thorough-bred hack, with her fair face a little flushed with exercise, and her brown eyes dancing with excitement.

"So Lord Feversham is at home, I hear," she said, after greeting her friend. "What has brought him? Was it not rather sudden?"

"Yes. He arrived yesterday unexpectedly. That affair is all over. How I wish he would come in now and see you, dear! You are looking lovely!"

Mabel laughed one of her low, musical laughs that were not very frequently heard, and were all the more charming when she did indulge in them. As she did so the door opened, and Claude walked in.

"I was in the yard, Miss Prendergast," he said, "when your horse came round. I knew no one rode such perfect cattle but you about here, so I came to pay my respects at once."

It was a set, polite speech, but Lady Feversham took it as an augury that he was already beginning to look after other young ladies, as she had urged him, while Mabel read it more truly, and answered carelessly,

"Yes, Bonnibel is a pretty creature. But tell me what was the cause of your paying us a visit here so suddenly? I thought you were all so busy in Ireland you could not get leave."

"Oh, the worst of that is over," he replied, seating himself, and doing his best to make himself agreeable during the short time Mabel remained. As for the young lady, she was very merry, even calling up an amused smile several times on Claude's sad face; but after about a quarter of an hour's rattling talk she asked for her horse, and, in spite of Lady Feversham's efforts to detain her, rode away.

Claude went down and put her up; as she nodded and smiled, riding away, she thought to herself,

"Come, I have made a step in advance. He never took the trouble to mount me before. Things look promising. I shall win him yet. After all, it would be very nice to be Lady Feversham, with a splendid fortune, both on my side and his, and a quiet, gentle-mannered husband, over whom a wife might feel sure she could acquire unbounded influence, and who is very good-looking besides. I should have the whole county at my feet then," she mused, "and be able to do any thing I liked. After all, there is nothing like power — lots of it — for making people happy."

As she neared the house, and saw Cecil Egerton sitting out in the garden enjoying the evening air, and looking for her return, her thoughts changed, and she checked her horse suddenly, to gain time to collect herself before meeting him. For he, whose quick ear had caught the ring of the horse's feet on the avenue long before it appeared in sight, had risen and come toward the gate to meet her, dragging his weak, nerveless limbs along with a painful effort, but his whole face brightening up, and becoming radiant at her approach.

"What shall I do?" she thought, with a sudden spasm of pain. "It will kill him, and I could not bear he should think badly of me either. What a pity he is so weak in character! If he would claim me boldly as his, and dare me to abandon him, I feel I should give in; as it is,

I do not know how it will end. He is nobler and higher principled and truer than any lord ever was, be the other who he may, but yet his weakness will lose him to me, for I know I shall betray myself and him, if the other man wishes it."

As she rode up to him, she stopped, sprang from her horse, and walked slowly beside him, listening to his soft, low words, and feeling his ardent, joyful looks fixed upon her, without raising her eyes to his. She could not look on him and determine to be false, so she cast her eyes on the ground, and walked on silently. Presently he said,

"Lord Feversham is at home now. Did you see him to-day?"

"Yes," she answered; "we have known him for many years, and, of course, he came in to see me directly he knew I was there."

If she had been trying to rouse his jealousy, she could hardly have spoken more to the purpose. A wild look sprang up in his eyes as he asked eagerly,

"Do you see much of him when he is at home?"

She laughed. "Don't get so excited; we see him pretty often. Is there any thing else you would like to ask about him?"

"Yes," he replied; "I should like to ask you one more question, but you will be angry, and I could not bear you should be displeased with me, so I dare not say what I wish."

"Do not be afraid," she answered, gently; "I could not be offended at any thing you said."

He looked at her half doubtfully for a moment, and then blurted out, hotly and eagerly,

"You like Lord Feversham, do you not? Are you going to marry him?"

She colored, and looked intensely haughty for a minute or two, while he who watched her as though his very life depended on her answer, felt his heart sink within him at the thought that he had offended her; but after a moment, remembering her promise, she replied,

"I don't know why you should fancy I like Lord Feversham, though certainly I can not say I don't like him. I do not care for him in the way you mean, however," she went on, with a smile; "and to put your mind quite at rest, I may as well tell you he is in trouble because he loves some girl in Ireland that his mother will not allow him to marry. Having satisfied your mind on this score, let me tell you it is very wrong of you to ask such questions, and only that I am a great deal too good-natured, you would get no reply to inquiries you had no right to make."

"Only the right," he answered, slowly, but with a firmness and decision most strange to him — "only the right given by my love for you, which makes me jealous of every man that can meet you on more equal terms than I, and that tortures me until I find how far they engross your attention."

It was the first time he had spoken so plainly of his love to her, and she thrilled all over at the words with secret delight, but answered, rather coldly, "Now you are talking nonsense, which you know I never allow. I have done more than I ought in satisfying you about Lord Feversham; so be reasonable, and do not forget yourself in this way again."

The young man looked down at her; as they stood thus together they would have presented a curious contrast to a beholder: he tall, slender, and dark, with too sweet and soft an expression on the handsome face, now white and worn with illness; she graceful, almost fragile in appearance, yet with a look of firmness unmistakably visible in her beautiful face, and in the carriage of her well-set head. As he looked and marked her downcast eyes, and the quick-flitting blushes that colored her brow, a wild desire seized the young man to hazard all to win her, to dare to speak of his love, and force her by urgency and entreaty to answer him definitely, and put him out of his pain.

The greatness of his anxiety alone gave him strength for once to act with determination; so, laying his hand on Bonnibel's bridle, he stopped her and her mistress, and spoke passionately, and, for him, with a kind of wild vehemence that caused Mabel to fear the game might become dangerous if carried too far.

"You are trying me too much," he cried. "You know what I feel, though I have never spoken out boldly to you; but I will do so now. Listen for one minute while I show you what depths of misery and anguish, or what heights of hope and joy, there may be in the human heart—"

He would have continued, but she drew back angrily, and passed on, saying,

"Silence, sir; you are forgetting yourself most strangely to-day. Is this the return my father and mother are to meet with for their kindness? How do you think they would care to have their daughter married to a poor soldier?—a man without family, kindred, or expectations, so far as I know."

The cruel words were hardly out of her mouth when she wished them unsaid; her heart quailed within her at the expression of his face. Despair, pain, and wondering astonishment were written on it; after a pause he turned away, saying,

"Farewell; I have been cruelly deceived in you. I will endeavor never to meet you again, or offend you any more by my presumptuous words."

As he spoke he turned away in the direction of the house, taking another path, with weary, faltering steps, stopping every now and then to wipe the drops of pain and anguish from his brow.

Mabel stood looking after him; she would have given worlds to have recalled him, but her lips could utter no sound, and she gazed with wide, startled eyes after his retreating figure, feeling in her heart that she loved him better than she had ever thought to care for any human being, and that she must have him back at her feet again at all hazards.

Then she went slowly forward to the house, gave up the mare to a servant, and ran to her room, where she threw herself on her bed and wept the bitterest tears that had ever visited her beautiful eyes. Why had she treated him so, and would he ever forgive her? She feared not; yet she felt if he had offended her she could forgive him over and over again. How could she ever have thought of winning Claude Feversham, since she had seen Cecil Egerton and loved him? She was rightly and fitly punished for her share in injuring Miss Bambridge. Now

she knew her heart, and, if the chance was ever again given her of being true to her love and refusing Lord Feversham, she would show the lesson had not been thrown away.

As she determined thus, a vision of all she renounced in becoming the bride of a poor man, as she imagined him to be, burst upon her, and on the other side she seemed to see the advantages she would enjoy as the mistress of the Castle, and as Lord Feversham's wife; besides, she had as good as promised his mother long ago, and her parents understood also it was to be a match, whatever he might think. It would be hard to undeceive them and give up all she might enjoy; and, after all, was it necessary?

Cecil Egerton, she felt sure, would always love her, and never another—at which thought her tears fell faster, though not so bitterly; but for all that she did not see that he need ever be more to her than a dear friend. Some people said such friendships were dangerous—she did not think so; she was mistress of herself, and could keep herself out of mischief. In time, perhaps, this wild fancy would die out when she saw more clearly the folly of it; in the mean time it would be strange if she could not keep them both hanging after her, playing one off against the other, till she had decided in her own mind what course to pursue.

But first of all it would be necessary to soothe the lover she had so imprudently offended. Her heart died within her as she thought how difficult a matter that might be, for in this instance he had spoken with a firmness and decision she had never observed in him before. She wondered whether his new-born determination might not enable him to resist her entreaties, now that her cruel words had pointed out to him his daring in aspiring to her hand.

He must be pacified and detained, no matter how hard he might try to break from her fetters—yes, even if she had to yield more to him than she had ever intended. Having arrived at this conclusion, she ceased sobbing, dried her eyes, and proceeded to dress for dinner. She had nearly finished her toilet when a knock at her door startled her, and on calling out "Come in," her mother entered, looking rather annoyed.

"My dear Mabel," she began, "I wish you could see what you can do with that impracticable Mr. Egerton. He wants to leave the house to-night—says he has already trespassed too long on our kindness, and in fact will go. He is not fit for it at present; I should be so sorry if he got ill in consequence, and was laid up at his horrid uncle's place, with no one to take care of him. Such a nice young man, too—I never met one I liked so much. Like a good child, finish dressing, and run and speak to him."

Mabel paused while fastening a brooch into her dress, and reflected a moment. It was never her plan to conceal the truth, unless she saw some positive good was to be gained by it. It seemed to her it might be wiser to tell her mother what had passed that day, and see how she took the intelligence, before deciding on any definite course of action. Her mother's expressions of interest in the young man had quite as much to do in influencing her to this decision as any thing else, so after a moment's consideration she answered,

"He did not tell you why he was going, mamma, but I will. He began talking some nonsense about love to me, and I got angry, told him he was requiting your kindness very badly by doing so, and that I would not have it. I do believe I spoke too strongly, but I was annoyed, and could not help it. After that it is for you to decide if I shall ask him to remain."

Good, easy-going Mrs. Prendergast had a most profound respect for Mabel's capabilities of head, and did not feel in the least alarmed at the disclosure. It was but natural the young fellow should love her; even Mrs. Prendergast felt it would have been more natural had Mabel loved him in return; but it was pretty evident she did not. Mrs. Prendergast liked the young man, and did not wish to give him pain, but she did not care to lose a pleasant companion, or one at least to whom she had taken a fancy, so soon. Besides, the best and gentlest means of curing his passion would be to allow him to remain in the house, and see how indifferent Mabel was to his advances. So she replied,

"You were quite right, Mabel dear, to show him he was in the wrong; but, as you are safe, I don't see why he should not stay at least until he is strong. Run and ask him to remain."

As she hurried off to obey, a voice in Mabel's heart seemed to cry to her earnestly,

"Beware, you are not safe. This is dangerous. Have nothing to do with it." But she went on in spite of the warning, and met Cecil Egerton coming out of his room.

That short hour of misery had greatly changed his appearance, she could see, as he tried to pass her with a bow; but she put her hand on his arm and stopped him. As she touched him, she could feel him shrink from her, but he did not speak, only remained waiting in a patient attitude for her to begin.

"I want you to come with me into the morning-room for a minute or two. I can not speak to you here."

He followed her as she moved on, still without answering, till they stood by the window in the quiet room together; then she went on,

"We want you to stay with us some time longer; you are not well enough to move yet, and we could not bear you should leave us before you have quite recovered. Don't go, please. You will not refuse me?"

She tried to put on her usual coaxing manner, which never failed with any one, but for once in his life he looked at her sternly, and answered decidedly,

"You have spoken words to me this afternoon that render it impossible for me to stay. Though they were cruel, they were true, and I forgive you for them; yet I think the same truth might have been told me in a gentler phrase."

"Never mind what I said," she cried; "it is not true, and it was only my evil pride caused me to speak so. I wish you to stay. If you love me as you say, surely that is enough."

The temptation was too strong for him; he seized her hands, and turned her face to the waning light with an eagerness that caused her to shrink from him.

"If I stay now, when you have asked me thus, do you know what it means?" he asked. "Do you know how I must regard it?"

She smiled a faint smile.

"How can I?" she replied. "Every one might attach a different meaning to it."

"Then I will tell you," he answered, drawing her close to him, and though her heart beat fast she did not resist. "It means that you accept the love you rejected so scornfully but little more than an hour ago—it means that you are mine, mine only, and that ever after no earthly power can separate us. This is what it means to me, the only meaning under which I can consent to stay. I do not know that I am right even then," he added; "but with that assurance I can fling every thing except honor to the winds. But I must tell your parents, if you do consent, and then they will order me off quick enough. It would be better I went now, as I had intended."

"No, do not go!" she cried, softly, her heart for once getting the better of her. "Your meaning shall be mine, if you wish it, and my mother knows why you were going, and yet sent me to beg you to stay."

How happy he was as he held her, trembling and submissive, to his heart! He had never dared to hope for such bliss as this, yet it was his; he seemed to himself to be dreaming, and held her tight, fearing that in a minute or two he should awake and find her gone. They sat down and talked, and she forgot for a while her ambitious dreams, and the utter folly of the step she had taken, in her intense happiness. At last the gong sounding for dinner roused them from their fool's paradise, and Mabel, beaming with love and joy, went down with her lover to the drawing-room, where she found her mother, who, in her pleasure at Mabel's success in keeping Cecil, never noticed her daughter's look and manner.

The girl had cautioned her lover before they came down to show nothing by his face of what had passed between them; "because," she explained, "though mamma understands it, papa does not, and it is better to wait a while for a favorable opportunity to win his consent than to act rashly, and be separated forever."

The mere hint of such a contingency was quite enough for the young man, who promised at once to be discreet and cautious. He succeeded in being so sufficiently to escape the observation of Mabel's parents, but not that of the attendants, the butler remarking to his fellow-servants after dinner, "There is some game up between Miss Mabel and the young gent that has been ill in the house so long. How do I know it?" he went on, in reply to the question of an incredulous housemaid—"to be sure I do, when I see him with his eyes always fixed on her, and her looking down on her plate as demure as you please, for all the world like a cat licking her lips after she's been stealing the cream. And what has the like of him to do with such as her?" he went on, warming with his subject—"a fellow picked up out of the fields, and coming from no one knows where; and she is a lovely young lady surely, though a deep one, I take it, by that smile of hers, that you never know whether it means yes or no."

In this opinion the servants' hall unanimously agreed; at least in the sentence that he was not good enough for her, except that the women servants averred the poor young gentleman was so handsome no one would have the heart to refuse him.

When the ladies left the table after dinner, a struggle went on in Mabel's mind, how much of what had passed it would be prudent and safe to tell her mother. That she must tell her something she knew, for she saw her words had awakened in her lover's mind a nervous susceptibility as to whether the course he was pursuing was honorable or not. But it was hard to decide what she should tell and what conceal; so that, after a good deal of deliberation, she determined to disclose every thing, only pointing out that she did not feel bound by such an engagement, and intended to keep it secret, so that, if at any time she wished to break it off, it would only be necessary for her father to hear of it and forbid it, and for her to submit to his will.

"Mamma will not like it, I know," she mused; "but if I can not come round her any other way, I will bully her. I never do it except when I can not help it, but now I must."

However, the matter seemed to be more difficult than she had imagined, for when she told her mother the way in which she had prevailed on Cecil Egerton to remain, Mrs. Prendergast, though not very stern or particular with her daughter, shook her head gravely, and said,

"This will not do, Mabel. I understood from you you did not care for the young man, and therefore never imagined you could delude him with such a promise. It is not," she went on, "that we wish you to marry Lord Feversham, though, of course, such a match would be very desirable, and would please your father and me very much; but we have always determined that, having money enough to afford a poor marriage, you should be allowed to have your own choice, only insisting on the respectability of the man on whom you should set your fancy. It remains for you, therefore, to decide which of the two you really prefer, and though, in Egerton's case, we do not know whether he has any means, his poverty, supposing he is poor, need not be a drawback. I think we could get over that. Now tell me what you wish to do, for, if you will not have him, he should be undeceived immediately."

Mabel mused. It was delightful to be loved as he loved her; for a time, she knew, that would make her quite happy, but how long would that last? She tired of every sensation after a short while; all but one—ambition, love of power, that was her ruling passion, and she feared that a love, meaning a relinquishment of all that promised the influence she coveted, would ere long become irksome to her.

So her sober reason told her, as she stood and pondered, thinking of the position Lord Feversham's wife would occupy, and comparing it with her situation as the wife of Cecil Egerton. Still, after turning it over many times in her mind, and heaving a long-drawn sigh at her fading prospects, she turned to her mother, and said,

"Thanks, dearest, for your assistance. I love Cecil, and would be his wife gladly. But don't you think it would be desirable to keep our engagement secret—at least until he gets his lieutenancy? I should not like to marry before, and be the laughing-stock of all my friends; he must purchase his steps quickly, and it will not be long to wait if the engagement is not known and talked about. What do you say to that plan, mamma dear? Is it not a good one?"

"It seems to me good and prudent in every way," answered her mother, proud of the wisdom evinced by her daughter, in a worldly point of view, at not wishing to marry an ensign in a marching regiment; and equally touched by the disinterested manner in which she gave up her ambitious schemes, when her heart was engaged in another direction.

Mrs. Prendergast had a strong spice of romance in her disposition, and could never have crossed the course of true-love in the way her neighbor, Lady Feversham, had done. As for Mr. Prendergast, the wishes of his wife and child were law to him, and he simply never dreamed of disputing their will.

"I will speak to your father to-night about it," Mrs. Prendergast went on. "Whenever Cecil gets leave, he can spend it here—the only condition we will make being that he must on no account reveal his engagement until he gets his lieutenancy, immediately after which event the marriage may take place."

"Yes, but I should not wish him to leave the army then," put in Mabel. "We shall be very comfortable, and can soldier in an easy fashion, so that I should like him to stick to his profession."

As she spoke, she conjured up before her mind's eye as brilliant a life as the wife of the colonel of a regiment, as that which would have followed her union with Lord Feversham. To her ambitious mind it even seemed very easy that her Cecil should be a general and K.C.B., so that already she was beginning to be not only satisfied, but pleased. When the gentlemen came up after dinner, she beckoned Cecil into the back drawing-room, where only the fire-light relieved the darkness of the room, and sitting there on the floor with her head resting on his knee, she told him all she had arranged while he sat wearily with her father over his wine.

"Now you see the good of being a favorite," she laughed when she had finished; "if mamma had not got so fond of you, I hardly think she would have settled all this. But do you know she likes you so much, I think she would have been dreadfully cut up if I had refused you."

This girl, with all her cold calculations and prudence, when she had once made up her mind that her love and her ambition could go together, did not give herself away by halves. She petted and caressed her lover, letting him see that she really was fond of him, and thought it no sacrifice to promise herself to one of whom she knew as little as she did of him. It would be impossible to say whether this was done with a motive or not; perhaps she feared he might urge their engagement being open, and hoped by her cajoleries to bribe him into submission to her wishes. However this might be, as she looked up into his face with the strange, unfathomable eyes to which love was lending a new beauty, he felt he was indeed a lucky fellow—that more had been done for him than he could ever have dreamed or desired, and that it would be almost ungrateful in him to express a wish that their engagement should be made public; at the same time he felt such a wish very strongly, and thought it the thing wanting to complete his happiness. He ventured to express this very mildly:

"Why, darling," he asked, "do not you like it to be known?"

"Because," she answered, "I hate a long engagement. People would talk about it, and say why with her money does she not marry him at once? then if I did so, every body who now envies me, and covets my advantages, would cry, 'Just look at that girl! With all her money she has only managed to hook a penniless ensign in a marching regiment!' Only that I love you, I would not have married you till you got your company. But I feared you would think it so hard, I determined to keep you in suspense as short a time as possible."

"I did not think you cared so much what people said," he answered, as he expressed his gratitude for her consideration of his feelings in an appropriate manner. "What are they to you, that you should care what they say?"

"After all," she replied, "I dare say it is a matter of habit. I have been accustomed, at least in thinking of marriage, to defer to the opinion of the Mrs. Grundies about; and I do not feel inclined to set them at defiance now; but as you are to spend all your leave with us, it can not matter much."

"I must let my uncle know what has happened at once," he said, presently; "it will please him, I fancy, and he is pretty sure to make me a handsome allowance. I need not continue in the army unless I like."

"Oh! but I wish it," she cried, in some alarm. It would, by no means have suited her that he should settle down into a quiet, easy-going country gentleman. She was determined her husband should be a person of note in the world, and she had decided that nothing was easier than that Cecil should be so in the military line. She told him now very distinctly he must stick by his profession as long as it should be her pleasure that he should do so.

And so the evening wore on as they sat and enjoyed their happiness. Mabel forgot every thing in the present, while Cecil, who had no pleasant past to look back on, and never had a future to look forward to until now, was bewildered with the weight of his good fortune, and gazed on the fair girl he had won, through no exertion or deserving of his own, with a wild idolatry only to be felt by ardent, imaginative natures like his, and which was little short of madness.

When Mr. Prendergast was made aware of what was going on, his placid face expressed decided astonishment. That the young fellow they had picked up, as one might say, by the roadside, and had nursed and tended with as much devotion as though he were their own son—that he should have dared to lift his eyes to the heiress of The Poplars, was a height of presumption his mind at first seemed scarcely capable of taking in; but when he found his astonishment and indignation were not echoed back by either his wife or the object of such presumption, he began to think it would be useless for him to attempt to stem the torrent, and he had better give in with a good grace.

Accordingly matters were arranged as had been decided between Mabel and her mother, and Cecil announced his determination of going over to Beaumanoir and breaking the intelligence to his uncle, as soon as he should be strong enough to undertake so long a drive.

Cecil felt no misgivings about the result of his errand; he knew a great deal better than any of the others how it would be received, and how his present position, as a penniless man, would be improved thereby. He had confided a good deal of his knowledge on this subject to Mabel, who had laughed, and had rather admired Mr. Vansittart's shrewdness.

When Mabel Prendergast rode off that day from the Castle, and Lord Feversham returned slowly to the house, he thought, in a dreamy kind of way, that she was a very pretty girl, and excessively improved since he last saw her. When he returned to his mother, she asked him at once, but in a careless way, "whether he admired her."

"In a critical point of view—yes," he answered. "She is very pretty as regards complexion, features, hair, and figure; in fact, beautiful in every way. But, do you know, what I consider most attractive about her is that faint, incomprehensible smile she has; it sets you thinking what she means, and trying to find out. If it was sarcastic, or haughty, or even sweet, you would not be attracted or care half so much to excite it and study it; but having once seen her smile, you feel perpetually anxious to see it again. I can fancy her very taking, and immensely run after in society.. Though she is not at all my style, I feel her attraction as one might see the beauties of a picture that one did not care for."

Lady Feversham smiled. The spell, she thought, was working, so she let the subject drop, and went on with her worsted-work, while Claude strolled down to the stables.

———◆———

CHAPTER XIV.

A HUNTING MORNING.

MABEL had insisted that her mother should on no account tell any of their neighbors of her engagement; and when Mrs. Prendergast represented that Lady Feversham at least should know that her scheme was impracticable, the girl declared there was no reason for telling her any thing of the kind.

"Lord Feversham has no thought of me, mamma," she urged; "he is wrapped up in this Miss Bambridge; and if we told her ladyship, we might just as well tell every body else in the county. I will not have it, mamma; so talk no more about it."

If Mabel had been asked what were her reasons for keeping her engagement dark, and for being especially anxious it should be concealed from the Fevershams, she would have been puzzled what to say; for at that time she had no thought of being untrue to her love, and had so merged her ambition in her affection that she would even have been unable to see any inducement to be false, in the certainty of winning Lord Feversham, were such a thing possible.

It was more probably a wish to assert her power over a man who had hitherto been superior to its influence. Still such a wish was not declared, even to herself, and wanted opportunity to call it into activity.

Feversham himself wrote to one of our fellows a few days after his return home. I wondered then very much that he had not written to me, but, in default of understanding it, I was rather interested in what he told us. He said in his letter:

"Who do you think has been getting himself

famous here lately? You will never think of him, so I may as well tell you. Our quiet sub, Cecil Egerton. He is a handsome fellow, and a gentleman; but I never knew a man with his expression of countenance who made his mark in the world, or achieved any success in life. He was stopping for a long time with the Prendergasts near us. Miss Prendergast, who, besides having money, is a very beautiful girl, though a most audacious rider, found him half dead under a fence one day, when she was bucketing a violent horse across country, and being on their land her people considered themselves in duty bound to see he was brought through his illness safely."

Such was Feversham's account of the manner in which Cecil had passed his leave; when we saw him again we were all inclined to think that his illness was not over yet. He was in much better spirits—apparently much happier than we had ever known him—but he was wasted, and weak, and hectic-looking, like a man who had been on the brink of the grave, and who had not got very far away from it yet. Indeed it was only his new-found happiness, I really believe, that helped him to live.

Latterly I had never been quite able to fathom Claude's feelings about Miss Bambridge, or find out exactly how he bore her loss. He was very grave and gentle, more so than ever, but at the same time joined in all our sports and amusements, riding a degree harder than was perhaps wise or safe, playing sometimes rather high, though more as if it bored him, than as if he found any relief in the excitement. Indeed he was so constantly lucky that he had no reason to feel the absorbing interest of one whose fortune lies on a turn of the cards. At the numerous balls and parties which he attended in Dublin, whither we had been removed, he would sometimes flirt desperately for half the evening with some pretty girl, whose heart would begin to flutter with pride and pleasure at the thought that she had caught that handsome Lord Feversham; then, perhaps, just when at his gayest, a sudden remembrance would shadow his face, and darken the laughing light in his eyes, and turning away, he would pass the rest of the evening moping in some retired corner.

We, who understood the matter, could see that he was very unhappy, and all the pleasures he had of old delighted in afforded him now but little distraction from the thought of his lost love. Once he spoke to me about it, and said,

"If I could understand it, Vivian, it seems to me I should be more satisfied. I could have sworn she liked me, even when she said she did not. And I do not think it was vanity made me fancy so, either. By Jove! if I saw her, I almost think I should be fool enough to ask her again, even if I got another refusal for my pains."

I knew better than he that she really did love him, and yet I could not for the life of me encourage him to try again. I had tried truly at the time to further his suit; but now, as I saw how ineffectual my effort had been, a new hope sprang up within me. It was true she did not love me now, but might she not in time grow to do so, if I persevered? And I, who had no eyes for the Dublin belles, determined to achieve by patience the fulfillment of my hopes, if such a fulfillment could indeed ever be possible.

What a wild infatuation it was! I saw every day women more beautiful and more highly born, who might have looked on me with no unfavorable eyes, but I never even so much as glanced round after them when they passed. To my mind there was but one woman in the world, the girl that loved my friend, and who was loved by him in return.

If I could but have convinced myself of the utter hopelessness of my suit, how much pain might I not have been spared! Could I but have seen her heart at the time when I was building these vain castles in the air, how different it might all have been!—that is to say, if a man in love can ever be convinced his case is hopeless, as long as the object of his affections is unwon. She, poor girl, I afterward heard, took the matter more seriously to heart than her lover did, in outward appearance. It is certainly more in a woman's nature to do so, and then they have fewer distractions and amusements to divert their minds from their sorrows; besides, she had this sorrow above all his, that she had denied her love, and convinced him, as she thought, that she had acted the part of a heartless coquette. That thought stung her most; if only he could have known how she cared for him, she believed it would have been easier to give him up; but now he fancied she had led him on and encouraged him, either from sheer thoughtlessness, or as an amusement for her idle hours.

When she remembered all this, her brain would reel, and her heart grow sick at the bitterness of her lot, and it was only by a mechanical repetition of the one idea: it was for his good that she could calm herself under such a crushing grief. She kept up bravely, however, only yielding to utter despondency when alone; still her sorrow, being always present before her, undermined her strength, and caused her to get nervous and irritable.

General and Mrs. Bambridge, alarmed at these symptoms, decided on leaving the country, and taking her to London for change of air and scene. The excitement and gayety there, they hoped, would divert her mind, and it would be good for Clarissa also, though that, at present, was a minor consideration. They would have preferred staying in Dublin, but knowing the —th were quartered there, it was not deemed desirable they should run the risk of meeting Lord Feversham everywhere, and London was accordingly settled on.

But Gwendoline Bambridge, though looking pale, thin, and ill, still showed a brave front to the world, and none but those of her own family had the least idea what was the matter with her. She could laugh and talk with an aching heart, as well as the greatest fine lady in the fashionable world, and she did so to such purpose that most of her county friends imagined she was carrying on a successful flirtation in a widely different quarter from that in which her affections really lay.

At first General Bambridge had been inclined to censure Lord Feversham's behavior toward her, and Gwendoline was obliged to explain that he had proposed, and she had refused him, before her father's indignation could be pacified; but the reason of her refusal she would confide to no one, and persisted in asserting she did not love him. So, not being able to discover what was wrong, the Bambridges determined on going to London in April, being convinced, notwithstanding the girl's assertions, that Feversham and the —th were somehow connected with her illness.

About December I went on leave. Claude had not yet returned from his; but Longhurst was a good way from the Castle, so we did not see each other often, except when the hounds with which he used to hunt met near us, and then I generally met them and him too.

The first day I saw him, I noticed there was something odd and constrained in his manner to me, for which I could by no means account; and as I could not ask him for an explanation among a lot of other fellows, I pretended to observe nothing unusual, and was as friendly to him as ever.

One day, about three weeks after my return home, the Harkaway—the pack with which he most generally hunted—met about four miles from us, and I, as was usual on these occasions, attended. There were a good many fellows of our hunt, the Dashington, out that day as I rode up, but as yet Claude had not put in an appearance. There were a few minutes to spare still, and I knew, if he came at all, he was sure to hit off the exact moment. Expecting to see him presently, I turned to speak to some one near me.

"By Jove!" I heard a voice say presently, "isn't that a spicy turn-out—nag and all! Just what I call perfection."

I looked round at this speech, and saw, to my astonishment, Claude Feversham in the act of settling a lady's habit, having, as I imagined, just put her up on a magnificent brown-black hunter—one of the finest animals I ever saw. The lady's face was turned toward me as she bent and assisted in arranging her habit, so that I had a very good view of her, and could see plainly she possessed no small degree of beauty. Indeed, had not my thoughts been all taken up with some one far different, I should have said she was exquisitely pretty; and there was no doubt about her dress being perfection, from the crown of her neat hat to the point of a tiny patent-leather boot I had observed as Claude pulled her habit into its place. All was tasteful and workman-like, while her mount was simply unrivaled.

I had not been much about in my own county, therefore I was quite in the dark as to who this fascinating Diana might be. Riding up to Claude, just as he was about to mount his chestnut, I greeted him warmly.

"You are on duty to-day," I said, after a few moments' conversation, with a glance in the direction of the fair unknown. "Might I ask who is the lady?"

"What! don't you know her? Why, I thought every one in the county had seen Miss Prendergast. She is under my care to-day, as you observe, and has been staying for a day or two at the Castle with my mother."

"Looks as if she could go. Can't she?" I asked, as we rode up to where she was quietly waiting for her escort.

"You shall see, Vivian," replied Claude, with a smile. So saying, he left me and turned to the young lady, who, it seemed to me, paid more attention to my steed and general turn-out than she did to myself—evidently setting me down as a boy not worth attention.

We placed ourselves in what we deemed to be an advantageous position, and waited while the hounds dashed into covert, and only a low whimper now and then, or a crackling among the under-wood, proclaimed their whereabouts. At length a shout from the far end of the covert proclaimed the fact that the fox had been viewed away, and as we looked eagerly in that direction, we could see his agile red body gliding over a grass field in front of us, while the hounds were only just bustling out of covert and settling down on his tracks.

At the bottom of the field in which we were standing was a gate opening into the pasture through which the fox was just speeding.

"This is our way, Miss Prendergast!" cried Claude, excitedly. "We must gallop to get there before the ruck; they are bearing down on it like lightning, and then there will be a block."

While speaking, we were riding down at the gate, doing our best to arrive there before the crowd. We did succeed in getting in front of them, and Claude was just pulling up to open the gate, when, taking her horse by the head, the young lady popped over, and, without looking round, sailed away alongside the hounds, but well out of their way, showing that she combined both daring and judgment, a knowledge of hunting with perfect riding.

We were beside her soon, and I could not but admire the consummate ease with which she rode her powerful thorough-bred, and how completely it seemed to be under the control of her hand, certainly one of the finest and lightest I ever saw. Sir Richard Lewin, our respected master, riding alongside of us, looked at her with unwonted admiration, as she flew over a bullfinch with a stout rail on the far side. Here I nearly came to grief, not being able to clear the rails properly, but fortunately we had chanced on a rotten place, and the timber giving way, Blackfoot picked himself up with a scramble, and on we went again.

On the top of a hill in front of us we checked for a minute, but the pace had been so severe, and the country crossed so stiff, that only the first-flight riders were up, and even one or two well known in that position had come to grief. Our horses were rather glad of the brief respite, I fancy; but I could not help remarking that Miss Prendergast's mount seemed not to be aware of the pace at which he had been hustled along, but looked as cool and composed as if he had only just come out of his stable.

Close below us, at the foot of the hill, we could see the Rush, a sluggish, broad stream winding along between its steep, green banks. Almost before we had time to collect our thoughts the hounds recovered the scent, and went straight down to it at a rattling pace.

This was indeed a startling position; there was no bridge or ford within half a mile, and have it they must who wished to live with the hounds or see the end of the run. At the same time it was more than most people would have cared to look at, being at least twenty feet wide all along that stretch, and in many places more. One thing, however, was favorable to those wishing to cross it—the ground fell gently to the brink on our side, and the farther bank was still a little lower; the advantage was not much, not indeed sufficient to tempt any one but our master and myself. Claude considered himself in duty bound to keep Miss Prendergast out of danger, urging her to strike off at once for the bridge; but she, looking round at him, quietly answered, "I always ride at my own place, Lord Feversham—I have it now; and besides I have crossed the Rush before."

As she spoke, she took hold of her horse, and working him up into his wonderful stride, went down at the water at a pace that left us far behind, and that must get her over or in.

I was so fascinated watching her riding that I quite forgot to think of myself, and could have cheered loudly when the brown-black rose like a bird, and clearing the water with several feet to spare, soon put himself on terms with the hounds in the next field.

Sir Richard was not so fortunate; he was immediately behind her, but his horse, frightened at the sullen, deep waters, refused violently. Claude got over by a fluke, his chestnut getting its fore-legs well landed, but slipping its hind-legs in; and only for Feversham's agility in springing to land and helping it up, horse and rider would have had an ugly ducking. As for me, I was deposited along with my steed about half-way over, and we both had to swim for it.

However, we came out on the right side, and there being a check a field or two farther on, I got up with the hounds, but not a minute too soon, as before I could well draw rein they were off again, heading straight for Burnley Gorse, through some as stiff country as I had ever ridden over. Miss Prendergast, Claude, and I were now alone with the hounds, and the pace continuing severe, it was highly probable that if we could last we should have the honor of seeing the end of it alone also. Whether we could last, however, was the question, the lady being the only one going well within herself, and still at her ease; the chestnut's coat was dark with sweat, and he seemed to lean a little on the hand; while as for my own steed, I confess he was done to a turn, and I knew there would be little more to get out of him. Just as I thought this, and was about to pull up in despair, the hounds stooped to the scent and began to hunt a little—a heavy cloud passing at the minute being probably the cause of this opportune slackening of speed.

They stuck to him well, however, and in about ten minutes more ran into him, on the very outskirts of Burnley Gorse, where he would have been lost to a certainty, had he made good its friendly shelter.

It was a clipping run throughout, and as I turned old Blackfoot's head to the wind, after performing the office of huntsman, *vice* that functionary, who had not yet made his appearance, I congratulated him heartily on having preserved so good a place, during an eleven miles' burst over a stiff country, done in fifty minutes, inclusive of the two slight checks before mentioned.

"What a stayer 'Stole Away' is, to be sure!" said Claude, resting his hand on the neck of the brown-black, who looked as if he had enjoyed his gallop, and was ready for another. "Not that he carries much weight," he added, glancing with evident admiration from the brown's powerful form to the slight figure he carried.

CHAPTER XV.

CATCHING A TARTAR.

To return to Cecil Egerton, who was left ill at The Poplars: when he was at length pronounced convalescent, and allowed to return to Beaumanoir, he tried to work himself up into a fit state of mind to bear the congratulations that he knew his uncle would offer on the occasion. It never struck him that Mr. Vansittart would view the matter in a light that would make him consider his nephew as even a more knowing man of the world than himself. Such was the case, however. Mr. Vansittart had recommended his nephew to fall in love with Miss Prendergast, and to insure that object had tried to effect a meeting between them in a commonplace, every-day manner. But the young man had not only taken up his uncle's idea, though at the time he had almost refused to do so, but he had also, with a far greater knowledge of the workings of the feminine mind than was possessed by the elder man, taken care that their first meeting should be very far from every-day or commonplace.

It was by no accident, his uncle thought, that he had been lying by the sunk fence that day; his return to itinerant sketching was the result of a bold and daring design, and even the accident, though of course its serious nature was unintentional, was to a certain degree preconceived.

It was a clever trick, one of which Mr. Vansittart not unnaturally felt proud, one that convinced him his nephew's cant concealed a very deep fellow indeed; a trick that from its very magnitude and audacity ought, in common justice, to bring forth grand results.

So when Cecil Egerton returned to Beaumanoir, he was hardly prepared for the enthusiasm with which he was greeted, and did not quite understand the jocose way in which the old gentleman laughed at him, and assured him he was a sly dog, and one who knew how to take a hint to some purpose. It was sharp practice, though," he added, "and nearly finishing you off altogether," glancing at the young man's wasted figure as he spoke. "You did not mean to carry it so far, however, and of course accidents will occur, even to the best-laid plans."

Egerton glanced at him wonderingly. "Why, uncle," he said, "you do not mean to say you think I went out sketching there on purpose to meet her! I knew nothing of Miss Prendergast and her ways, and had I known she would have been likely to pass in that direction, I most certainly should have avoided her. Now it has happened I regret neither the accident nor its consequences, but I certainly never intended them."

"Fiddlesticks!" ejaculated Mr. Vansittart; "perhaps you will tell me next you do not admire the girl, and that you will not marry her."

"I will not tell you that," laughed Cecil, "as I should be treating her very badly if I did not marry her. We are engaged, uncle, and I am the happiest man in the world—too happy even to fight with you. But this is a secret; we are not to be married for some time—not at least until I get my next step. No one is to know of the engagement between us but you and her father and mother; do you understand?"

"I hear what you say," replied the old man, gruffly, "but I don't pretend to understand as all. If you are engaged, as you say, what prevents your marrying at once? I told you, if you succeeded in this scheme I would make you my heir, and in this case it would not suit me to break my word; if I did, she has money enough for both of you. What is the meaning, then, of this delay?"

"I am sure I do not know," answered Egerton, his joy a little damped by this allusion to conduct on the part of his betrothed that had puzzled himself. "Mabel does not wish to marry immediately," he continued, "and that is why she has made this excuse, I suppose."

"Just so," grumbled Mr. Vansittart; "some woman's foolery and nonsense. I should have thought a man with as much sense as this business proves you to have, could have easily managed to overcome her scruples."

"Perhaps I did not try," replied Cecil, almost sadly.

He was thinking how wonderful it was that he, a man of obscure origin—at least on one side—and utterly penniless, but for his uncle's bounty, could ever have dared to raise his hopes so high as to aspire to this heiress, the descendant of a long line of well-born ancestors; and how still more wonderful it was that he, having dared so to love, should have won her love in return. He felt so utterly insignificant, so entirely unworthy of her, when he looked at the matter in this light; it was the light in which his position was very frequently before him.

"You did not try," interrupted his uncle, breaking in upon his reverie. "Then you should have tried. Don't you know this delay is only an excuse to give her time, that she may see if she can not hook higher game? Don't you remember I told you Lord Feversham was after her? and I hear he is expected over directly. Unless she is publicly bound to you, she will slip out of her promise as easily as an eel would slip out of your hand. Never trust a woman out of your sight, unless you have the whole world for her keepers; and this one is a deeper sort than common, or I am much mistaken in what I have seen of her."

"I prefer to manage my own affairs myself, sir," returned his nephew, sternly; "let me tell you, if I did not consider Miss Prendergast a woman to be trusted, whether before the world or not, I would never have asked her to be my wife. Let me never hear you apply your hateful worldly code to her; she is as far removed from it as virtue is from vice, and she shall not be named in the same breath with any of its maxims."

Cecil ceased speaking, but his breath came short and quick, and a thick perspiration broke out on his pallid forehead. He was supposed to be convalescent, even well, but he was very weak, and the violent excitement his uncle's speech had caused him did him up completely. He did not know, neither did we—perhaps no one knew but the doctor himself—that that gentleman considered he was as well as he would ever be, but knew that he never would be again the strong, active, hearty young fellow he had been before the accident. More damage had been done internally than had been at first supposed. Perhaps, but for the new interest his love lent him in life, he would never have so far rallied as he had done.

His uncle looked at him anxiously. He was one of those men who have a rooted aversion to and distrust of illness. One reason why he had, in his way, liked Cecil, was because the young man was so healthy and active; a man likely to live long, and keep up the dignity of the family in the old place for many years. But this accident, that had been so wonderfully opportune, and had had such splendid results, was not, after all, an unmitigated piece of good fortune, since Cecil had not recovered from its effects, and something seemed to tell the old man, while he looked, that he might never recover them altogether.

As this conviction stole upon him he experienced a sort of feeling that he had been cheated, that the heir he had desired because of his good looks and strong, robust health, was an imposition after all. Stung by this thought, he spoke harshly.

"What is the good of your working yourself up into that state? You are only doing yourself mischief; and it is confounded nonsense to say that you can not listen to the truth about a girl. You must accustom yourself to hear unpleasant truths, at least from me; and unless you take them more calmly, you will never recover."

"Sometimes I think I never shall be as strong as I was before," answered Cecil; "but I will not hear, not truths, but slanders, from any one, least of all from you. Remember that."

The young man spoke firmly and sternly. It was certain his love lent him a determination and energy that were foreign to his nature; but he trembled while he spoke, and looked about for a chair on which he might sit down.

"There, now you are done up," said his uncle, sullenly, as the young man sank exhausted into a seat. "How can one talk business to a man who goes on like that? Did you tell Mr. Prendergast my intentions with respect to you?"

"I did not. No doubt he thinks you will do something, but it seems that he has some fancy his daughter is to please herself; and as she can afford to marry a poor man, she is to be allowed to do so if she chooses. Of course, even if I had known this, I should never have thought of asking her to be my wife, but for your promise to settle something on me. I ventured to hint that you would do so to her, for I could not bear that she should think I, a penniless man, had dared to talk of love to her, unless I had the prospect of a home to offer her. It would have been too like a proposal to support myself on her money."

"I will write to Mr. Prendergast, then; that will be the best way. He will be able to talk over business better with me than with a young man like you. He would be almost certain to overreach you, or drive too hard a bargain in some way."

Cecil looked at him with a kind of contemptuous amusement. It was very absurd to hear good, honest, generous Mr. Prendergast accused of the design of overreaching his intended son-in-law; but it was useless to think of arguing his uncle out of his views on human nature; they were incorporated into his very being, and there they must remain. It was only to be hoped that, acting in accordance with those ideas, he might not succeed in insulting Mr. Prendergast in some irretrievable and irrevocable manner. That must be left to chance. He was undoubtedly the person who ought to arrange the business matters with Mabel's father, and all that could be done by Cecil was to forbear further discussion, and hope for the best.

Young Egerton by no means comprehended his uncle, or gave him credit for the amount of *finesse* and tact which he possessed, and which he was accustomed to use when dealing with persons whom he could not bully. He hardly understood how it was that all business matters were discussed pleasantly between Mr. Vansittart and Mr. Prendergast, and arranged without any of those differences that make the preliminaries to marriage (especially between people with money) usually so disagreeable.

Mr. Vansittart was for some time very urgent that the engagement should be at once declared, but Mr. Prendergast persisted that was a matter that entirely concerned his daughter, and that he would not interfere with any of her plans. With this answer the old man was, sorely against his will, forced to be content. He had been over at The Poplars one day, and had been particularly urgent with Mabel's father, seeking to make him use his influence either to cause the marriage to be hastened, or to get the relations in which the young people stood to each other made known. He had failed in both attempts, as has been said, and set out on his return to Beaumanoir in rather a discontented frame of mind. He had lunched at The Poplars, but had not met the ladies. They had taken their lunch while the gentlemen were talking business, and were now out. Mr. Vansittart had often noticed that the gentlemen of his acquaintance did not care to introduce him to the ladies of their families, and he had secretly sneered over this particularity, saying to himself that the ladies so carefully secluded from the contamination of association with him were every bit as bad as he, in their way; but he had never regretted this caution. Now, however, it did seem to him that there might be such a thing as overcarefulness, in not allowing him to make acquaintance with his future niece, and he was almost hurt, if such a thing had been possible to his nature, at the opinion of him thus implied.

He would have rejected the lunch thus offered, but that he knew the cellar at The Poplars was famous for its claret, and that it was the thing to be able to speak of the wine in that cellar with the air of familiar knowledge that would become not only a visitor at the house, but also a connoisseur in rare vintages, a character much more valued by Mr. Vansittart than that of an intimate of the family.

The wine maintained its reputation, he was forced to admit; and long experience of the world and its vinous beverages had convinced Mr. Vansittart that such a vindication of report is rarely met with, either in regard to wine or other things. The conviction that such was the case made him less than ever pleased with the policy that practically forbade his often enjoying such wine; for though on an occasion like this, and once in a way, it was possible to pass over the slight offered to him as an accident, he knew a repetition of his visits would lead to the estimation in which he was held becoming painfully apparent, in which case it would be difficult for him to get out of the predicament gracefully.

Thus meditating, he drove his two dashing bays down the avenue, and in his indignation gave them a little more of the whip, and took them over the ground a good deal faster, than was either necessary or usual. The groom in the back seat of the dog-cart noticed this, and muttered, "If Master Cecil drove the 'osses that way, the master would eat his 'ead off when they come in; but as it's himself as does it, it don't matter."

A very true remark, though it was only Mr. Vansittart's groom who made it. We none of us see the harm of what we do ourselves, whether it be unjust, untrue, or cruel, but we detect whatever another does wrong very fast indeed. Is it not strange that we should persist in this error, when we are all so well aware of it? More than eighteen hundred years ago the very highest authority warned us against it; and though we all acknowledge it as a fault to which we are liable, we have not done much to correct it yet. It springs ever new in every successive generation, and is perhaps of all failings the hardest to eradicate in each individual nature.

The road along which Mr. Vansittart drove in his handsome dog-cart was one of those beautiful English country lanes that resemble a green tunnel, so overarched are they by spreading boughs, and fenced in by luxuriant hedges. Though the day was a bright one in the end of September, this particular road was dim, and cool, and shady. Entering it, one seemed to pass at once from the glare of day into a soft green twilight, that was inexpressibly soothing and delightful to eyes that had been tired and strained by the glare outside. Mr. Vansittart did not appreciate natural beauty; he looked upon trees as timber, and on hedges as good fences, when properly treated, for keeping out cattle; but even to him, on a day as hot as this, there was something soothing and refreshing in the cool shadows of the interlacing boughs. He let the good bays take it easier, and began mentally to appraise the value of the timber, whose welcome shade he was enjoying. It was on Mr. Prendergast's property, and he had a kind of right now to take an interest in that property, to be inquisitive about its value, and do little sums about the probable price every thing would fetch if brought into the market. Not that it ever would be. Cecil, thank heaven! was no spendthrift, and the worst fate that was awaiting The Poplars was that of being amalgamated in and swallowed up by the superior size of the Beaumanoir property.

Suddenly, a few hundred yards ahead, just emerging out of the shadow, and crossing a sunlit patch in the road, he saw Mabel Prendergast on horseback. She had gone out with the intention of exercising "Stole Away," the horse that had caused so much mischief, but to whom, strange to say, since the accident, she had been more than ever attached. She had given him a good gallop over some grass-land of her father's, and he was now quiet enough, walking slowly along the road, hardly raising his head to listen when he heard the tramp of Mr. Vansittart's bays behind him.

Mr. Vansittart had nearly overtaken Miss Prendergast; he had been admiring her graceful figure and admirable seat as he drove up behind her, when suddenly a thought struck him. This matter of the engagement and the marriage rested entirely with her; if any body took the trouble to persuade her, she might be induced to alter her mind, and then it would be all right; even if Cecil had to return to his regiment, he might do so confident that every thing would go on well in his absence. Mr. Vansittart had met her here alone; it was most opportune; he would speak to her. He had never met her to speak to, but he knew her well by sight, and she knew him, and of course, considering the relation which they would presently occupy toward each other, there could be no harm in his introducing himself, in default of some one to perform that mystic ceremony for him.

He drove on until he had passed her, setting the brown-black thorough-bred dancing a little, in sympathy with his fretting bays; then, handing the reins to the servant, he said, "Drive them on slowly to the top of the hill in front, and wait for me there." After that he turned and advanced toward Miss Prendergast, who, recognizing him, comprehended at once he wished to speak to her, and, wondering what it was about, rode slowly toward him.

As he approached he lifted his hat, and said, "I have the pleasure of speaking to Miss Prendergast, I believe?"

"Yes," she answered, quietly, "I am Miss Prendergast. Can I do any thing for you?"

It did not suit her to show that she recognized him as her lover's uncle; she was pre-eminently cautious, and such a recognition might have bound her to too many consequences. She therefore affected to regard him as a total stranger—one perhaps who desired information about the country, or some such trifle.

He saw through her very clearly, but nevertheless formed a better opinion of her from her very attempt to blind him. It was evident he had to deal with a woman of the world, one whom he could understand, and not one of those sensitive, imaginative, high-principled humbugs who never looked at things from his point of view, and whose own point of view, if they had any, he found it quite impossible to catch.

"I am Mr. Vansittart," he continued, doing away with the thin veil of formality she had drawn between them, by pronouncing those few words. He looked at her keenly as he spoke, thinking he could judge, by the surprise she would act at this announcement, of the mental calibre of his feminine opponent.

She did not act at all, however; she merely held out her hand, saying,

"You are Cecil's uncle, then. I was beginning to think it must be so. But why is he not with you? Why did he not come over to-day?"

"Because I came to talk over business with Mr. Prendergast. He thought he might be in the way, and he intends to come to-morrow. Now can you guess, Miss Prendergast, why I have taken the liberty of introducing myself, and have stopped you here to speak to you?"

"No, indeed," she replied, this time with perfect truth.

She did think it very odd he should have done so, but she did not know that it would do any good her expressing her wonder, so she kept silence.

Mr. Vansittart paused too. He hardly knew how to begin; he must get on the subject of the marriage first, before he could broach what he wanted to say. Well, there was one easy way of doing that; laying his hand on "Stole Away's"

bridle, by way of steadying him, for he was fidgeting to get after the bays, he went on:

"You know, I suppose, why I came to see your father to-day? May I venture to express my hopes for your future happiness, and my joy at seeing my nephew's dearest wishes about to be realized? He is a good fellow, I believe, as men go. I like him, though many people will tell you that is a bad testimonial in his favor. I do not mean it so, however. I think you will make him happy, and I think he will try to do the same by you. It will not be his fault if he fails."

Mr. Vansittart paused, and Mabel, either thinking, or pretending to think, that he had said all he had to say, answered,

"I should not have accepted Mr. Egerton if I had not had the very highest opinion of him. Of course your praise of him is very pleasant to me, but it would not alter my judgment respecting him if you had abused him. I think we have every chance of being happy together, and I thank you for your good wishes."

The red-brown eyes gleamed with a faint, concealed amusement, and she drew her reins through her hand a little, as if to intimate to her companion that she wished to proceed; but, though the horse shifted his position, Mr. Vansittart took no notice of either movement, and, still keeping his hand on the reins, continued:

"After all, though Cecil is happy, he is not by any means well yet. He wants careful nursing still, and will want it for many a long day, if he is ever again to be the fine, strong, handsome fellow he once was. And it is about that I stopped to speak to you to-day. He will get no care and attention when he returns to his regiment, which he must do soon, and I fear the consequences to him in his present state of health will be very serious."

"Do you really think so?" she asked, earnestly, beginning to feel a little alarm at the thought of her lover suffering and ill when far away from her watchful care. "What is to be done?" she continued. "If it is bad for him, I do not see how it can be helped, unless we get him a doctor's certificate, and make them give him longer leave."

"His health has been so shattered, that it will be a matter of time waiting for his perfect recovery; and it will not be possible to get him leave for so long, I think; besides there are many causes that would militate against the adoption of that plan. The course that seems to me the best, the simplest, the most straightforward, is, that your engagement should be proclaimed at once, that he should sell out, and that you should marry as soon as possible. You would then be able to see that he took care of himself; and happiness alone would further his recovery. At present, though he does not say much, and tries to persuade himself he is contented, I can see he frets at the uncertainty of his future, the length of time he may have to wait before he can claim you, and the false position in which he is placed by not being able to appear as your affianced lover. Consider, if he met you to-morrow at a party, he would have to treat you as the merest acquaintance, or run the risk of causing gossip which would be disagreeable both to you and to him."

Mabel Prendergast shook her head, and laughed.

"If those are the only terms on which I can secure his recovery, he must remain as he is. Did he depute you to act as his ambassador in this matter? For if he did, I think I had better break off the whole affair at once. I have decided every thing is to remain as it is at present; and I allow no one to question the wisdom of my decisions, or to dispute my will. You do not know that yet, Mr. Vansittart, but he does, and he ought to have known better than to send—"

"But he did not send. He knows nothing of what I have been saying," interrupted Mr. Vansittart, in great alarm. "I am the only person to blame, and as you say, not knowing you, I hope my well-meant interference will be excused."

Mr. Vansittart felt very small and very humbled as he made this apology. He had a keen consciousness that he had been beaten with his own weapons—that this girl was more than a match for him, and he knew by the gleam of her eyes that she was aware she had asserted her supremacy, and gloried in the victory she had obtained.

One parting shot he might fire at her, and he did so, hoping that by some chance this, his last arrow, might pierce some joint in her armor of self-complacency.

"Good-bye," he said, raising his hat and moving toward his trap. "Excuse me for troubling you about the matter of which we have been talking. Some girls are so foolish about a man they love. I made a great mistake in thinking you one of such poor, soft-hearted creatures."

Mabel Prendergast sat still for a few minutes in the place where he left her. He would have been pleased, and considered that he had been a little revenged for his defeat, had he known how his last words rankled.

Was it true, then, that she was so different from other girls in her manner of treating her lover? She had long been aware herself that she was not sufficiently overpowered by her infatuation, as she called it, to cease for one minute looking out for the main chance, or to leave off thinking how she might best compass her ambitious hopes; but she had until now thought that she had concealed these peculiarities of her nature so carefully that no one but herself recognized them. However, it seemed she had been read, and that, too, by the last person she would have cared should so read her. Besides she did not like being compared with other girls in a sense unfavorable to herself; it stung her self-esteem, of which she had an unusually large share. She had been accustomed to think herself rather better than other women, no matter from what point of view her character was considered. And this not because she thought herself good, but because, judging by herself, and seeing their little faults and failings in society, she considered them worse than herself. She had by no means an exalted opinion of her sex. It is suggestive that wherever such an attitude of mind is discernible, the person holding it will almost always, if not invariably, be found to be a not very estimable character, seeing every one around through a mental lens, discolored and distorted by the imaginations of an evil nature.

So Mabel Prendergast believed that all her own sex were hypocrites and heartless, though some, no doubt, were fools enough to act parts of tender feeling, and perhaps persuade themselves they felt. She could do that too if she gave way to the anxiety about Cecil's health that Mr. Vansittart's words had aroused. But she was not a fool, and however well it might have looked in some people's eyes, she did not intend to act that rôle. Thus thinking, she gathered up her reins and rode on.

About two months subsequent to this, and just after Claude Feversham went home, Cecil Egerton returned, as I mentioned before, when I stated that his evident weakness excited comment among us. He could still go about and do his work, but he did it with difficulty, and after it was over, was quite done up for the rest of the day. Indeed, when he was subaltern of the day, I often did his work for him, as I pitied him, when I saw the state of prostration to which his duties reduced him. He would say sometimes, in thanking me, "I shall be well again soon, Madcap, and then when you are ill I will do as much for you as you are doing for me." I used to feel stupid, and walk away without answering when he spoke thus. Somehow, I did not believe he was getting stronger.

CHAPTER XVI.

RIVALS.

I HAD gone on leave to England, as I have said, and I had met Claude and Miss Prendergast out hunting. I had noticed before that Claude's manner to me was very strange and stiff, but on the occasion of this hunt he was too excited to be very distant. Now and then he would seem to remember something suddenly, and freeze up into a cold silence; but again, when talking and laughing with Miss Prendergast, he would forget, and include me in the conversation. One thing I remarked as strange, however, and that was that, though I had joined them, and rode entirely with them, he did not attempt to introduce me to the lady with him, and seemed annoyed when she spoke to me, which she did at the end of the first run, probably induced to do so from having observed the good place I and my old friend Blackfoot kept during the run. It was very odd of Claude, and I determined to ask him the reason of it at the first opportunity.

As we rode slowly home that evening after the hunt, Miss Prendergast said, suddenly,

"There is a Mr. Egerton in your regiment, is there not?"

"Yes, but he is on duty at present," I replied, before Claude had time to answer. "Do you know him?"

"He was very ill in our house last autumn," she answered. "How is he liked in the regiment?"

"He is a good sort of fellow," I said; "very easy-going and good-natured—too much so, in fact. I have a kind of idea he will get into trouble some day, simply from not being able to say no. He is a clever fellow too, and does every thing well. He and I are great chums; but I wish he had a little more backbone to his character."

"We liked him very much," answered Mabel, in a little sharp, decisive manner. "We have asked him to come and see us whenever he gets leave."

Claude looked at her a little quickly, and, as I almost fancied, jealously, as she said this; indeed it had struck me my lord was particularly attentive that day — much more so than the young lady required, she being fully as well able to take care of herself as he was of himself. It was not that he seemed the least bit in love with her; no, there was nothing devotional in his manner; simply it showed admiration, and that she certainly deserved in more ways than one.

She looked perfectly charming in her neat-fitting habit, and after a hard run, when we were all glowing with heat, and panting from our exertions, she was prettier than ever, with the faint flush called there by exercise tingeing her usually pale face. Then her riding was perfection; it was a pleasure to see a powerful, headstrong animal so easily handled, and so submissive, with all his strength and spirits, to the light hand that guided him. No place was too big for her; yet, as she told me herself, she never rode for a fall, thinking truly that a lady should never run risks, however hard she is riding. "Not that I would be afraid of a fall, Mr. Darrell," she added; "and were I a man, I should not care how many I got. But gentlemen are so horrified at the sight—and indeed it does look dangerous—that one is often obliged to be more careful than one would wish."

"You are not troubled with too much carefulness, at least," I laughed. "Do you ever refuse a place, Miss Prendergast?"

"Oh!" she said, smiling, "that is a home question, and I really do not know what I should do on any other horse; but 'Stole Away' has never found any thing too much for him yet, so I hope he never may, and ride at many a place on that chance that I would not look at on any other horse. Even my second hunter, 'Hold Hard,' is not to be trusted as he is."

"I do not like ladies hunting generally," broke in Claude; "they are very apt to put themselves in the way, and to spoil one's pleasure; but when they do it as well as you, Miss Prendergast, I must acknowledge I like to see them out. You never look blown, or pulled, or disordered, and, above all, never seem in danger, no matter where you go; that is certainly a great satisfaction to your escort. Besides, you do not keep him behind, every one must allow."

"Flattery," laughed Mabel Prendergast. But I, watching her pretty face, and admiring its puzzling variety of expression, could see she looked pleased, and blushed slightly. "I do not ride," she went on, "for admiration, or that you may praise me; only because it is like the breath of life to me to feel a good horse bounding under me, to glide over the springing turf in a stretching gallop, and feel the rush of the breathless leap. Whatever troubles and annoyances surround and harass me in daily life, let me but feel myself in the saddle, with an impatient steed champing his bit, and arching his neck to my hand, and I am gay and happy again. Troublesome thoughts can not intrude when cantering over a grass country, under a soft gray sky, and with a balmy south wind fanning your cheek. It is glorious! And those who do not care for it lose one of the keenest enjoyments in life."

So we chatted on, till I came to a cross-road that led back to Longhurst, and then we separated; Claude and Miss Prendergast pursuing their tête-à-tête ride back to the Castle.

Lady Feversham was well pleased with the good understanding that evidently existed between them. When, tired and draggled, they met her in the great hall, Claude's manner was most attentive to Miss Prendergast. If it was more courteous than warm, her ladyship did not take notice of so trifling a departure from the course she wished.

"All is going smoothly, it seems," she said to herself, while dressing for dinner. "What a clever girl Mabel is! Now I should never have thought that escorting her out hunting would have such an effect. With many men it would have produced directly contrary feelings. It only shows how good a wife she will make him, when she understands his character so perfectly. It is very stupid of her to persist, however, that her match with him is broken off—that she will not have him; for though I have not a doubt she will change her mind as soon as he asks her, yet it worries me, and prevents me urging him about it just yet."

Notwithstanding which reflection, she asked him into her boudoir next morning after breakfast, while Mabel was out in the greenhouse gathering flowers, and said to him,

"I am glad to see, Claude, that you and Mabel get on so well together. I hope you do not mean to treat the poor girl badly."

He laughed.

"Depend upon it, mother, Mabel Prendergast is well able to take care of herself. I do not think it would be in any one's power to break her heart, because, if she has one, she will contrive never to give it till her fish is hooked. She is a very charming girl, I must allow; clever, intelligent, and amusing; always a lady, yet with a dash of originality. But I think, after all, she is much more likely to use me ill, than ever likely to give me opportunity of so using her."

"Do not be foolish, Claude," answered his mother; "you know what I mean, and what has always been considered a settled thing between the Prendergasts and us. I allude to your marriage with Mabel. She, of course, poor girl, looks upon it as an engagement, having been brought up entirely with that view; so, before paying her any more attention, you should decide on the course you intend to pursue."

"My dear mother, do not be unreasonable," he replied. "If you are so anxious I should marry, why did you interfere to prevent a match that offered me every prospect of happiness? for I can not help thinking that your letter must have had some influence in preventing her taking me. I feel a conviction she liked me, and, had you been favorable, I should be happier now than I ever am likely to be again. If I ever marry—and I suppose I must some day, for the sake of the name and title—it may as well be Miss Prendergast as any one else; only you must give me time, and do not be in a hurry; for, if I thought I could in any way alter Miss Bambridge's decision, no other woman alive should have a look or a word from me that could be construed into a lover's attentions."

"Yes, but you see Miss Bambridge will not have you," his mother answered; "so you might just as well oblige me and take this girl, that I have always intended for you. Will you not do such a little thing to please me, Claude dear? I have never thought any trouble too much, so long as I was furthering your interests, and I think you might repay me by this small sacrifice now."

"A small sacrifice, do you call it?" he said, with a harsh laugh; "it is only that of my love and my life's happiness, and yet you think you have a right to demand it. So be it, then. I will think over the matter; but I warn you it may be months or years before I make up my mind to take the fatal step."

Poor Claude! having made this half promise, he stepped out into the garden on his way down to the stables. Presently, as he walked, he became aware that Mabel was hurrying after him. He heard her step, but did not turn to look, and angry as he was with his mother, himself, and her as the cause of all, he quickened his pace; and soon knew he was leaving her behind. Then a feeling of compunction began to steal over him; after all, it was not the fault of the girl that his mother should consider her a good match, and desire him to marry her; it was not civil his walking away from her. Perhaps she wanted his assistance or help in something.

The moment this idea struck him he halted, and facing about, saw Mabel walking slowly after him at some distance, and carrying in her hand a beautiful bunch of hot-house flowers, which she arranged with due attention to color and form as she walked.

She did not look up until she was close beside him, and then as he stepped toward her she started a little, and said:

"I had no idea you were so near; I saw you passing through the garden just now, and knew you were going to the stables. I thought perhaps you would take me with you, as I want to see 'Stole Away,' after his run yesterday, and do not like going alone; but you walked so fast, I thought I should never overtake you."

"I saw you, and stopped," he explained; and then they walked on together to see the horses, and satisfy themselves they were all right after yesterday's exertions.

As they walked back together Claude looked at Mabel, and listened to her merry sallies, wondering whether this beautiful, clever girl might be his if he chose. His mother said so, yet somehow he fancied the girl thought differently, and would give him no opportunity of proposing, even if he wished to do so. Her manner was friendly, but there was a kind of line drawn in her advances, that seemed to say, "I am willing to be your companion up to a certain point, but not beyond." He admired her all the more for that; it was such a relief to feel that here at least he was not expected to commit himself, that he yielded to the enjoyment of such a feeling, and really made more advance in the line his mother wished than he ever would have done had the girl been sentimental and self-conscious. So things went on for a week or two, Claude admiring his beautiful, lively companion more and more every day, feeling very friendly toward her, but not a bit lover-like; at the same time often thinking, "Well, if I must marry some day, and can not have the one I care for, this girl Mabel will at least make me a beautiful and pleasant wife; one of whom I may be proud, and with whom I

can get on well, even though I may not be passionately attached to her."

Mabel was far too keen an observer of character not to perceive very soon the state of his feelings. Lady Feversham having told her of their conversation and his half promise, she began to reflect that she was placed in an awkward position, as it was quite possible he might at any time take it into his head to obey his mother's commands and propose to her. Much as she had once wished for this, it did not now suit her at all; her love for young Egerton was as fresh and strong as ever, but her ambition was even more active. If she could be certain her betrothed had it in him to be a great and successful man, she could be true to him, and wait for him, years if necessary; but if it was not so, then she felt she had it in her to throw him over, even at the expense of many a pang, for Lord Feversham's assured position. She could not make up her mind to do so yet; she must wait and see how matters went; in the mean time it was quite possible to keep him by her, working on his feelings, if possible exciting him to love her, but preventing any actual explanation until she had herself decided what course to pursue.

She became more friendly than ever with him after she decided thus; she walked and rode with him, played and sung to him, courted him sometimes, laughed at and scouted him at others, till an interest was raised in his heart that closely resembled love, though after all it was only a counterfeit of the real thing. He sometimes sighed when he thought of Gwendoline Bambridge, and wondered if this feverish infatuation for Mabel Prendergast would ever obliterate her image from his mind. His mother saw with approval that Claude's manner to the heiress was totally changed. Now he was never from her side if she was staying at the Castle; if she was at The Poplars he rode over nearly every day, and when he had no excuse for going there he was restless and uneasy. Still, when she urged him to speak out and ask the decisive question, he would shake his head and declare she gave him no opportunity to do so.

"Indeed I think she is right," he would continue, "for though I admire her more than any woman but one I ever saw, and though I am fond enough of her in an uncertain way, yet it is not an affection with any repose in it. I never feel sure of her for two minutes together, and sometimes think that if I was given my choice of having her for my wife or forgetting her altogether, I would prefer the latter course."

Thus matters went on quietly until Cecil Egerton came to The Poplars on leave. It was near Claude's time for returning to his regiment, and he was making the most of his stay by spending it constantly with the Prendergasts. The very day after Egerton arrived, when Feversham rode up for his daily visit, the first sight that greeted his eyes was the slight, well-proportioned figure of his subaltern.

Both men looked at each other mistrustfully, and seemed to divine instinctively that they were rivals; only there was no uncertainty in Cecil's case to sharpen his jealousy: no—even that very morning he had held his loved one in his arms, and she had whispered fondly that he was more dear to her than ever. He permitted a feeling of amusement to dart through his mind, therefore, as his captain rode up, and he advanced to meet him.

"You here, Egerton?" asked Feversham, with an assumption of friendliness he did not feel. "I did not know you were expected so soon."

"I had promised Mrs. Prendergast my first visit should be here," he answered; "so as soon as I got leave I came on straight. I did not know you lived so near, or rather I had forgotten it."

He said this in a confused manner, as he remembered the scene last autumn, when he first became acquainted with Lord Feversham's being a neighbor of the Prendergasts. It was a scene that ended happily for him, yet he could not help remembering he had been jealous then; and at the thought he seemed to feel a return of the forgotten sensation.

Just then Mabel appeared on the steps in her riding-habit. She colored when she saw Claude, but advanced to him without embarrassment, and explained that she and Mr. Egerton were going out for a ride—"in which I hope you will join us," she continued, with her most winning smile.

If she wished it truly, Cecil did not, and he scowled ferociously on his senior when he accepted the invitation. Claude, however, was too busy talking to Mabel to notice this, and just then the horses were led up.

It has been said that since Cecil joined the army his uncle had allowed him to keep a horse; but though an animal was thus provided for him, Egerton had never cared much about riding, and had not become a very experienced horseman. He looked very well on the road, if the animal was gentle and well-trained, but, as we were all well aware, he knew nothing about riding across country—in fact had probably never taken a jump in his life. He was perfectly mounted that day, on Mabel's hack Bonnibell, and enjoyed himself very much as he rode along, almost ignoring his captain's presence, and monopolizing a large share of the conversation.

Now Feversham, with all his many good qualities, was inclined to be rather impatient, and perhaps a trifle overbearing, when any one interfered with his plans or amusements. He was greatly nettled at Cecil's accompanying them, and still more at the favor with which Mabel treated him. Besides, he had always entertained a slight contempt for his handsome subaltern, who had not sufficient strength of character to fight his way in the world with the energy and persistence that distinguished other men in the battle of life. He felt, therefore, the less compunction at trying to oust the young man from the position he evidently occupied in Mabel's regard. He knew that perhaps the quickest and easiest way by which to weaken a lover's hold on a woman's mind is to make him appear ridiculous, not only in her eyes—that she might possibly forgive—but also in the eyes of other people. If he could contrive to put Egerton in some absurd scrape, in which he would show up badly, he was sure a girl like Mabel Prendergast would pay very little more attention to him.

In this surmise he exhibited more knowledge of this particular woman's character than could by any means have been expected from a man, and a great deal less knowledge of his subaltern than can be accounted for, except by remembering that he had been accustomed to think of the young man as a kind of amiable nonentity not worth studying.

It must not be imagined that Feversham deliberately set himself to consider how he could put Egerton in a ridiculous position, and thus make him unworthy of notice in the eyes of a woman for whom he evidently felt something warmer than mere admiration, which was the name by which Feversham designated *his* feelings; but it flashed on him suddenly, not only that he should like to eclipse Egerton, who was in his way, but also that the means and method of doing it with such a girl as Mabel Prendergast were ready and open before him.

It was infallible that a girl who rode as she did should feel a little contempt for a man who could not ride. Egerton looked very well on the road, but none knew better than Claude how he would probably appear across a country. Before he had time to consider his thought twice he acted upon it.

"At any rate," he thought, "I will have it all my own way to-morrow." And he forthwith asked Mabel if she would accompany him to the hunt at Moorsfield next day.

"I did intend," she answered, "to have ridden to the meet with Mr. Egerton, taking James to follow me in the field; but if you will join us at the cross-roads, we can ride on together, and I shall be glad of your escort when the hunting begins. Mr. Egerton does not feel quite up to crossing country yet."

"I do not know," cried Cecil, whose blood was beginning to get up at the thought of Lord Feversham escorting his betrothed, with the most favorable opportunities for making himself agreeable constantly presenting themselves. "I think if I tried I could do it. Suppose we attempt something now, and, if I get on well, there is no reason why I should not follow to-morrow."

Claude pricked up his ears at this proposition—it gave him such a good opportunity for placing the man he felt must be his rival in a ridiculous light; for it was hardly possible he could escape getting a tumble, if Claude chose the places big and made the pace fast.

"A very good idea, Egerton," he cried, looking out, as he spoke, for something sufficiently difficult to try the learner's powers to the utmost. "What do you say to this bank, Miss Prendergast, then over the gate at the end of the field, and so on up to the top of the hill, where there is a bridle-path that leads down to the road again? It will make a nice little steeple-chase; and this bank is so easy it is almost a walk over."

"I hardly know what to say," Mabel answered, feeling perfectly sure Cecil would come to grief, and thinking she had much rather he did not make a fool of himself before the captain. "However," she went on, "if Mr. Egerton wishes it, I have no objection to make. Bonnibell can jump as well as trot, and you will find her perfectly safe. All you have to do is to stick on."

Egerton replied eagerly, quite forgetful of the foolish appearance he would make if unsuccessful before Lord Feversham's sarcastic eyes,

"Do let us try. I should like it of all things, and feel as if I could do wonders."

"Indeed you do not seem as if you wanted jumping power," answered Claude, half-admiringly, for he could not help being struck by the young fellow's pluck. "At it we go, then!" and turning his horse, he went quietly over the bank to the other side.

It was little more than a walk over, as he had said, and Cecil, following Mabel's advice, and leaving the reins entirely to Bonnibell, got over very easily, being hardly stirred in his saddle. Then they all rattled up the pasture, in high spirits with the excitement of the rapid motion, and, in Cecil's case, with the consciousness that he had made a good beginning.

The next fence, however, was of a very different character—being a ditch, a thorn hedge, and flight of ox-rails on the far side. The gate, although strong and stiff, promised a better exit, and for it they made accordingly, allowing Claude to go first, in order that Cecil might see from his example what it was necessary he should do.

"She is very good at timber," said Mabel to Egerton, just as Claude cleared the gate. "Steady her a little till she is close to it, then give her her head. I will follow you."

He went at it manfully, though with some misgivings; his fears were realized, for though the clever little mare hopped over it like a bird her rider lost his balance, and after clutching frantically at the pommel of the saddle, and then at her neck, measured his length on the soft sloppy ground.

A very rueful spectacle he presented as he got up and shook the wet from his clothes. When he looked around him, he saw Feversham had just succeeded in catching the mare, and was bringing her up to him, while on the other side of the gate Mabel was watching him with anxious eyes. He thought she was afraid he had been hurt, and walked toward his horse quickly, to show that he was uninjured; but, if the truth must be told, her cause of anxiety was different. She saw Claude Feversham choking with suppressed laughter, which was not unnatural, as the upset, and Egerton's frantic effort to save himself, had been sufficiently ludicrous, and a fear dawned upon her that Cecil might object to going on with his ride, for fear of another accident.

In that case she knew what a fine story Claude would make out of the affair, a story that would not redound to the credit of his subaltern in the regiment, and that would, she could not help feeling, affect her liking for him very severely.

For ridicule has the most wonderful power in clearing away the veil love casts over the eyes, even when the one whose eyes are thus opened is not as ambitious a young lady as Mabel Prendergast. She watched, therefore, with a beating heart while he mounted, intending then to cross the gate, and, if he was still willing, continue their ride over the field; but before she had time to carry out her intentions, she saw Egerton gather up his reins and ride back again toward her, with a determined air and bearing that delighted her, and raised him tenfold in her esteem.

Feversham called to him to stop. "Let us come on to the next fence," he said; "that gate is too high for schooling over." But the only answer he received was the heavy thud of the mare's feet in the soft ground, and the next moment she was over the gate like a bird, and landed this time with her rider on her back, though it could not be said his attitude was very graceful. That did not matter. Mabel was proud of his determination, and praised him freely as they went back to Claude, doing the leap this time in fine style, Egerton getting more into the thing every turn.

As for Feversham, he felt disappointed. He could not help acknowledging that, for so inexperienced a rider, his subaltern had made a very good beginning; he had shown pluck and determination not to be beaten, besides a great aptitude for the noble science of horsemanship. Claude began to admit there was more in his junior than he had ever been disposed to allow, and that after all he was not an unlikely fellow to please a girl's fancy. This was not at all satisfactory to Claude, who, now that his leave was so nearly up, and that he had to return the next day but one, found himself more *intrigué* about this incomprehensible girl than he would have liked to acknowledge even to himself.

He did not feel the same true, deep love for her that he did for Gwendoline Bambridge, but she perplexed and interested him; and now that the real object of his affections was not attainable, he felt a wish to monopolize this girl and keep her for his own, a wish she seemed by no means inclined to allow him to carry out.

Egerton, staying in the house with her, would have every thing his own way; he had even succeeded in taking the edge off the weapon of ridicule with which the captain had calculated on annihilating his pretensions forever. As they turned their horses' heads homeward, Claude Feversham began to think his mother made a little too sure of the heiress; and this thought made her seem to him a much more desirable prize than she had ever done before.

It is probable that if he had had the chance then, he would have put the important question to her without further dallying; but she, as if aware of what was passing in his mind, divided her attentions with laudable equality between her two cavaliers—taking care that neither of them left her side for an instant, and feeling, as she went up to her room on her return, more puzzled than ever what distinctive course to take, and more pleased and proud of Cecil than she had ever been before. She knew that Claude Feversham only waited an opportunity to ask her to marry him; that opportunity she was determined he should not have next day at the hunt; the day after he must join his regiment, which would relieve her of anxiety for a good time to come. Indeed she might then feel herself safe till they should meet in London in the spring.

She succeeded in settling matters just as she had laid out in her own mind, giving Claude no chance of speaking to her privately at the hunt, and bestowing a good deal of friendly encouragement on Cecil, who rode in dashing style, until his horse got pumped, which, the run being a severe one, and he having no experience, happened early in the day. His fault, however, was merely want of knowledge when to spare his horse, and when to let him out, an ignorance that Mabel very easily forgave him, in consideration of the really brilliant style of his performance, as long as he could live with the hounds.

As they were returning home, all three together—Cecil on getting his second horse having managed better, the run not being so severe—his animal got a stone in its foot, and while he got down to knock it out, the other two rode on slowly. They had only a minute or two together, but even in that short time Claude managed to say, "I have to join to-morrow; I fear I shall not see you again till we meet in London, in the spring."

"I suppose not," she answered, trying not to look glad, which in truth she was, as she found two lovers rather hard to manage. "I am sorry you are going," she added, with more politeness than truth.

"Dare I hope you will not forget me before we meet again?" he asked, bending toward her, as he heard the hoof-strokes of Egerton's horse close behind them.

"How could I?" she murmured, with a delightful blush; "we have had so many happy days together. Oh! Mr. Egerton, is it you? What was the matter?"

When Mabel went up to dress for dinner that evening she gave a long sigh of relief, like one who has escaped a danger; as she smiled at her reflection in the glass, while her maid brushed and coiled up her hair, she said to herself, "It was touch-and-go that time; but I am out of it cleverly for the present; and now for enjoyment."

So she took especial pains with her toilet, and went down stairs, quite prepared to work her poor young lover into a still greater state of infatuation, if that were possible.

"Miss Mabel is a queer young lady, surely," soliloquized the Abigail, as she tidied up her young mistress's room; "she is carrying on now with his lordship and this young gentleman, and which it's to be I'm blest if I know—perhaps she couldn't tell herself—but it is my belief they are both a sight too good for her, for she is the artfullest piece ever stepped; not to say but she is good-natured, and gives her maid lots of good dresses."

I was some time at home before I saw Claude more than once or twice; he was so fully occupied with Miss Prendergast that he had no time to come and look me up, and whenever I went there he was sure to be out. I gave him up after one or two attempts to meet him, contenting myself by observing that I should see enough of him when I went back.

But though I did not see him I heard quite enough about his goings on to convince me, if Gwendoline Bambridge was not forgotten, it was at least something very like it. With me it was not so: I did not mope; that would have been useless and foolish. I did what I had to do, and amused myself to the best of my ability; but I suppose I must have been graver and more serious than my wont, for one day my mother asked me what was the matter with me.

"You are not at all like what you used to be, Vivian. All your gay spirits seem gone, and sometimes you give me the idea of a sober, middle-aged man, instead of a boy not yet nineteen."

I need not say I was fond of my mother; she was beautiful, and had spoiled me with a kind of judicious spoiling, if there is such a thing, ever since I could remember. She never refused me any thing it was possible I could have, and it now struck me I would tell her my troubles and sorrows, and see what help she could give me. If she disapproved of my love, at any rate I should be no worse placed than I was before, and if she was inclined to help me, I had such unbounded confidence in her powers, that it almost seemed as if every thing would then come round. I answered, "You are right, mother dear; I am not

very happy just at present, but I think you will hardly guess the cause."

"Do you think I am so blind, my boy, as not to know the symptoms?" she replied, passing her white hand through my arm. "Come into the conservatory—we shall be more comfortable there—and I will tell you my guess at the cause of the change in you. You can tell me if I am right. The fact is, my son found he had a heart just as he lost it; is it not so?"

"You are right, dearest," I answered; "but she will not have me; you know that too, I suppose; but very likely you do not know her reason for refusing me."

"Refusing you!" she repeated after me, with a slight inflection of pride in her voice, as though she would say, who has dared to do this to my son? "What were her motives?" she questioned, anxiously.

"She liked Claude Feversham, I think, mother, though she refused him too. He was desperately in love with her then, and I never could make out why she would not have him; but now they say all over the county that he is after Miss Prendergast."

"I have heard that report," answered my mother, "and I am sure Lady Feversham would like such a match, Miss Prendergast being a great friend of hers; but whether he is false to his first love or not at present has little bearing on your case, as you say she refused you. Now, my dear boy, listen to me. Many mothers would be greatly alarmed and distressed by what you have just told me, and would do all in their power to prevent it; it is not so with me, and I know your father thinks as I do. Your happiness has always been our great object, and if you truly love this girl, far from throwing obstacles in your way, we would give you every assistance in our power, always supposing she is a lady. Indeed I feel sure you would not love one who was not such; but you are too young, my child, to think of such things at present, and she, it appears, will not have you. Wait a little, and then urge your suit again if you see a prospect of success; if not, turn away from the vain pursuit, and devote yourself to duty and work. It will be hard at first, but we will help you, and occupation will take the sting out of the disappointment before very long. You are so young still," she added, with tears in her eyes, "it can not be that your life is blighted."

I kissed her for her pitying words, and thought how happy I was to have such a mother. There was that poor fellow Claude—he might have been happy now had Lady Feversham acted thus. As to her advice, it pointed out the only course I could pursue; and one thing at least was certain, that if I could win over Gwendoline I would have no opposition from the powers at home.

CHAPTER XVII.

ON THE ICE.

I DID not spend all my leave at home, but, after a week or two there, returned to Belmurphy, determined, now the field was clear, to do the most I could quietly to obtain Gwendoline's favor, or at least find out for certain who my rival was.

It was a sparkling, frosty winter's day when I

again stood on the steps of the hotel at Belmurphy, and strolling, as of old, into the billiard-room, found there several officers of the 144th, who had replaced us in the little country town.

They took no notice of me when I entered, and I, while waiting for the car I had ordered to go and call on the Bambridges, lounged about watching their play, and criticising their manners and appearance.

They were fine-looking men, two of them very handsome, and, I could not help thinking, must present a great contrast, in the eyes of the inhabitants, to the rather shady appearance of our lot. To be sure, Feversham was as fine a looking man as you would see anywhere, but Ussher was insignificant and married, and all the rest of us were more or less juvenile and unmanly looking.

Suddenly I heard one of them, whom the others called Fortescue, exclaim,

"I say, I wonder who will be at the Bambridges' to-morrow? The entertainment is to be skating on the lake, and dancing in the evening. Awfully jolly I am sure it will be; and those girls are such fun, though they say here the eldest has fallen off in her looks."

"Never was as good-looking as her sister," cried another. "I will back Clarissa against the county. You will see there will be nothing there to-morrow to beat her."

"Awfully slow, this frost," went on Fortescue; "just as one had got one's hunters into order. Skating is all very well, but give me hunting—and by Jove! this is the place to do it in. Did you ever see ladies ride so straight before, and so many of them?"

"Yes, they certainly seem to know how to do it," answered another; "but I think skating and dancing at the Bambridges' will not be a bad substitute."

Just then my car was ready, and I walked off, hearing Fortescue say as I went out:

"Nice-looking little chap, that; I do not know who he is. Waiter, who is that?"

"The Hon. Vivian Darrell, your honor," replied that functionary, with a grin. "He was one of the officers of the last regiment that was quartered here, and he is going to Endley now, sir."

How this intelligence was received I do not know, and did not care either; I congratulated myself as I drove along on having been so very fortunate as to drop in just when some little gayety was going on.

The frost had been very severe for some time; the roads were white and hard as iron, and the tramp of the horses' feet and the jingling of the harness rang out merrily on the still air as we trotted along. My spirits rose as each well-remembered mile-stone flew by, and before we got to Endley I had almost forgotten all my sorrows and disappointment in the thought that I was once more near her, and should soon gaze on her sweet face again.

They were all in, and delighted to see me, but I could not help, even in my joy, noticing how altered Gwendoline had become. It was not that she was less beautiful—in fact I do not think she ever could have appeared so to me—but the gay *insouciance* of her expression was gone, her eyes were deeper and more mournful, while round the mouth a dejected look was visible at times that I never remembered remarking there before.

As I noticed this, I thought indignantly of Claude as I had last seen him, flushed with the excitement of the hunt, and pleased with his beautiful companion. People tell you it is always so with us men : when the object of our affections is not by, we content ourselves with whatever in the shape of amusement is near at hand. It may be so with some—of that I can not judge—only I know it was not thus with me. Of course I do not mean to say that the rush and skurry of a clipping run would not put all thoughts of heaven and earth out of my mind except the one business before me, or that a hot corner at a battue would not occupy me to the entire exclusion of every other idea; but once these moments of breathless excitement were over, the remembrance of all I had hoped for and lost would rush upon me, and sober even the brilliant recollections of my late achievements.

On this poor girl the trial had told severely ; she had no thrilling pursuits to divert her mind from mental grief by exposing her to bodily peril ; all she could do was to sit and brood over her troubles, perhaps rendering them far greater than they really were by the power of imagination.

Clarissa was lively as ever, and paid me great attention, desiring me to be sure and come early to their party next day. Then she cried, after a minute's pause,

"Have you seen our new defenders?"

"I saw them in the billiard-room an hour or two ago," I answered, "but I know none of them. I heard the names of two as they talked to each other—Fortescue and Beresford. Very fine-looking men they seem to be."

"Yes," she cried, laughing; "do not you think so? But you have not heard the story connected with them. It appears some young lady from Belmurphy wrote to their colonel, as soon as it was known they were under orders for this place, requesting him to send fine, tall, handsome fellows—men, in fact. (Complimentary to you who had just left, was it not?) However, he was good-natured, and sent us down these good-looking specimens. The flower of the flock, I call them, as no doubt they are picked men."

I laughed.

"That is a good story, Miss Clarissa. Where did you hear it?"

"Oh! it is true, I assure you," she replied, nodding her head, gravely; "and don't you go Miss Clarissaing me, or I shall call you Mr. Darrell. Such old chums as we are need not stand on ceremony."

So she rattled away until it was time for me to leave, when she rushed to the window and watched me off with an intense appearance of interest; but no sooner was I out of sight than she turned to her sister with a comical half-sigh.

"Dear me! how foolish I was ever to fancy myself in love with that little pet, Vivian! He is as nice as can be, and my especial darling; but at the same time, I would rather have Captain Fortescue's little finger than Madcap's whole body. And the darling is just as madly in love with you as ever, Gwen. That is what brought him here to-day. I wish you could reward his constancy. But there—I will not say any thing more about it if it pains you. Come out and have a little skating; it is not too late for a turn."

Next day I drove out rather early, as I had been requested, and helped to get the dancing-room into order, under Miss Clarissa's directions, who, I suspect, gave me infinitely more trouble than was necessary, while Gwendoline interposed now and then to save me from my lively tormentor.

"Now then, Gwen," she cried at last, "I am going to play you a waltz, and do you try the floor with Vivian. If you pass it, I may be pretty sure it is perfection."

So saying she dashed off into a swinging measure, and, before I had time almost to know what I was doing, I was gliding down the room with her I loved, in long, easy steps that seemed to realize one's idea of floating upon air.

Round and round we went, when suddenly the door opened, and General Bambridge came in, followed by the 144th men, who laughed at the expression of our faces as we stopped, breathless with the pace, and intensely surprised at the interruption.

In a few minutes I had made their acquaintance. We were soon good friends, and set out toward the lake, where a space had been prepared for skating, and where many people had already assembled. It was a beautiful day, clear, cold, and crisp. The sun was bright in the cloudless heavens, but it was freezing bitterly still in the shade. The dark shadows of the mountains lay on the smooth, glassy surface of the frozen lake, and they themselves, wild, rugged, and stern, towered over our heads, exhibiting every variety of light and shade on their craggy sides.

In the foreground the bright dresses of the ladies, their fur coats, and dainty hats drawn low over arch, smiling faces, heightened the effect of the picture, and caused us to pause once or twice on our way down the hill leading to the spot, in order that we might the better contemplate the scene.

Soon we joined them, and then all was hustle, confusion, and laughter: gentlemen buckling on ladies' skates; ladies essaying to balance themselves for the first time, and nearly pulling down their assistant swains; chairs, occupied and unoccupied, being pushed over the ice—every thing was merry and full of life, and I was honored with the office of assisting Gwendoline to buckle on her skates. They must have been more than usually troublesome, I think, for I remember kneeling before her, and holding a long and pleasant conversation in that devotional position, looking up into her deep, sad eyes, that had brightened a little for me.

At last they were on, and away we glided among the busy throng, in which we presently got separated, and I amused myself watching her as she glided gracefully through the crowd. After a time she left the place where the ice had been swept and prepared, gliding off among the rougher ground, and gradually getting clear of the other skaters. I had just noticed this, and had determined to follow her as soon as I could shake off the young lady with whom I was talking, when a loud crack was heard, Gwendoline's figure seemed to totter and waver for a minute, and the next moment sank from sight. A cry, shrill and terrible in its agony, burst from her as the broken fragments floated over the spot where she had been, and active skaters from every part glided with marvelous rapidity toward the place.

But love lent me wings, and I was first there. How I got in I know not, nor how I found her or brought her to the edge, and supported her till she was taken from me. Then I believe I fell back into the water, and was only rescued myself with difficulty. But all this is a blank to me, and the next thing I remember is lying on a bed in a strange room, with anxious faces bending over me, and such painful sensations overpowering me that I longed to call out, "Let me alone, to die quietly!"

But I could not have spoken if I would; and, almost as soon as I had seen them, the grave faces faded away from before my eyes, and I was once more unconscious. Next time I came to myself I was considerably easier, and smiled at Clarissa, whose eager face I discerned peeping in at the door.

"You are better!" she cried, seeing me look at her. "I will go and tell Gwendoline; she is so very anxious."

I was tired then, and slept for many hours; I think it was next day before I became thoroughly conscious of every thing around me. Then Gwendoline came in to see me, thanked me with tears and smiles for having saved her life, and told me she had recovered very soon, not having been long under water; but as she was being drawn out I sank, got under the ice, and was not recovered for so long that they had almost despaired of my ever being brought to life again. Fortunately Dr. Brown was there, and under his care, after an hour of anxious watching, I began to give signs of vitality. After this I was very weak, and unable to move for a day or two, during which time Gwendoline devoted all her energies to amuse and beguile the weary hours I had to pass as an invalid.

One day she asked me where Lord Feversham was now; then some evil spirit tempted me to try and advance my cause at his expense, and I answered:

"He was at home until quite lately, but his place is a good way from ours, and I only saw him one day, when he was escorting Miss Prendergast, the heiress, out hunting."

Gwendoline started, and her color came and went fitfully as she replied,

"What is she like, this Miss Prendergast?"

"Very pretty," I answered; "some people admire her immensely, and she certainly is a splendid rider. They say in our county her people intend her to marry Claude, and he seems to pay her a good deal of attention."

I could have killed myself the next minute for having uttered those words, when I saw what an effect they produced on her. Her whole face, even to her lips, turned pale, and she turned away; then, before I had time to think or speak, the color mounted again hotly to cheek and brow, while, looking at me, she said, decidedly,

"I do not believe it; you do not know what you are talking of. Claude Feversham is farther above those who slander him in constancy, truth, and patience than they can even dream of. You do not know the man you malign, or you would surely refrain from speaking against him, and laying to his charge things of which he is incapable. Do not talk to me again like this; you have almost made me forget what you did for me, and why you are now lying there ill. Forgive me," she went on, holding out her hand; "you tried me too far, and I fear I have been hard on you."

I kissed the hand she held to me passionately,

yet wearily, for I felt the barrier was as great as ever between us, and I could not yet hope for success, even if I ever could dare to do so.

As for Gwendoline, it was evident she did not believe one word of the report I told her, and was inclined to consider I had caught up some stray remark and exaggerated it thus, through my earnest desire to see her separated entirely from him, and my wish to put myself in his place. She forgave me because I was ill, and had just saved her life; but it was evident she was not only pained, but disappointed in me, and became mistrustful.

Her suspicion of me grieved me deeply, and I determined that, as soon as I was able to move, I would return home for the remainder of my leave; but it was several days before I could do this, as I had caught cold in consequence of my ducking, and there was a good deal of low fever hanging about me, rendering it imperative I should keep quiet until I was stronger. During the time I remained, Gwendoline seemed to keep a constant watch over every thing I said, as though she feared I might pain her by a repetition of what I had before mentioned; but I was on my guard, and kept clear of all dangerous topics, so that shortly before I went she seemed to have reinstated me in the position I used to occupy in her favor.

At parting, the tears stood in her eyes as she said, "Farewell, Vivian! I shall never forget I owe my life to you." In another moment she was gone, and I was slowly saying good-bye to the rest of the family, in the hope she might return before I left. After dawdling some time, I was obliged to get on my car without seeing her, and drive off in a hurry, for fear of being late for the train.

CHAPTER XVIII.

MISUNDERSTANDINGS.

I HAVE said that when Claude was out hunting that day with Cecil Egerton and Miss Prendergast, his leave was nearly up, and that he went to Dublin next day. I was at Belmurphy for some time after, but when I did return to the regiment, of course the first thing I thought of doing was of going to see him. I had arrived at my quarters rather late in the evening, and when I went down to the anteroom I found Claude was out, though a good many of my other friends were there, among them, Mayleigh, looking as cunning and ferrety as ever. I was rather disappointed at not seeing Feversham, and asked Mayleigh, who was nearest to me, to tell me where he was.

"He has gone out to dinner somewhere," replied the little lieutenant; "Feversham has got quite lively, I can tell you, since his visit to England. I used to think he was very spooney about Miss Bambridge, but I suppose I must have been mistaken, for he goes about a good deal, and seems all right. Not that he is a fellow who would show it, if he was ever so hard hit. But there are reports that he is after some heiress in England. Is it true?"

"Indeed I can not tell," I replied; "I saw very little of him. Though we live in the same county, our places are so far apart, he might do any thing without our knowledge."

I said this, not because I did not think that in this instance report might be correct, but because I knew how annoyed Claude would be, and how angry he would feel with me, with very good reason, if I gave any information on the matter. So I evaded it, and something calling off Mayleigh's attention, I escaped any more questioning.

But his words had set me thinking of my cousin, and I began to remember how very anxious he had been to avoid me, whenever I had met him during our leave, and how very disagreeable his manner had invariably been. It was not like him, for even when most tried by the rivalry that had at one time existed between us, he had always—when not under the influence of jealous feeling—been most friendly with me: why he should be different now, I could not understand. I in no way interfered with his new fancy, and I had not even ventured to allude to it, when speaking to him, so I could not have annoyed him by any chance remark.

Of course I was sure a few minutes' explanation would dissipate any misunderstanding that could have sprung up between us, and would have been very grieved to think that he, my particular friend and ally, whom I loved for his strong, kind, upright character, should have learned to think badly of me, and to shun me. I fancied that perhaps, when he came back from the place at which he was dining, he would come up to my rooms to see me; it was what we had often done before, when either of us returned after an absence, and I knew that if this cloud that had been between us had passed away he would come and do so again. Being tired, therefore, I went up to my room, and sat down to dream before a blazing fire.

What pleasant things those dreams are, and what a pity it is that no reality ever comes up to them! They are dangerous too: they are so apt to make us discontented with life as it is, to make us long for a world much brighter and happier than this one can ever be. I wish I had a chance of being and doing all I can fancy myself being and doing; but I believe there is a fate follows me, and of late, in my low-spirited moods, I have begun to frame a theory to account for that which is sufficiently discouraging to those whom it concerns. It is this: there are in this world a great number of people who, without being very gay or high-spirited—though in many instances they are so—have a wonderful power of resistance to the depressing and overwhelming influences of life. They are the men who can never be entirely knocked down, or quelled by any blow, but who, as soon as it has fallen, gather themselves up again for the fight, and if forced to abandon one point turn to another; never yielding, and though knowing when and where they are beaten, not the less for that maintaining the struggle.

Napoleon praised us highly when he said that those Englishmen did not know when they were beaten; and yet I think the courage is higher that continues the battle, knowing it is defeated. The people of whom I have spoken, who will not give in, who turn from one standing-point to another, are precisely those on whom the heaviest trials are laid. "The back is fitted for the burden," we have all heard, and really in cases such as those of which I speak it appears as if the proverb was true. I thought, as I sat by the fire dreaming, that there was perhaps something of that tough power of resistance in me, and that thereby I was fated to the troubles I endured, and perhaps fitted to bear them; I hoped so. I had already experienced one very great sorrow, which I assured myself would be lasting, but I did not mean to let it crush me; on the contrary, I felt that it would perhaps stir me up to do more and better work than I should ever have effected without such a stimulant. But while thinking over Claude's late conduct, I seemed to feel some slight foreshadowing of sorrow in that quarter also, which I knew would add a little to the burden I already had to bear.

Unless your circumstances have been very prosperous, dreaming over the fire, though at first blissful, is almost sure in the end to give one the blues. I succeeded in working myself into that frame of mind very rapidly, though at intervals I used to laugh at myself, and call myself a fool for giving way to fancies.

Is there a great and wise man who can control his thoughts at all times, putting what is foolish and useless and bitter away at will; calling up pleasant, kindly, cheerful imaginations in their place? Certainly I am not such an individual; neither is Claude, I know. I doubt if such a mortal exists, though people often say to those who fret over "trifles light as air," "You should not think about them."

The evening passed on as I mused, and still I was alone, though I was sure when it got late that Feversham must have returned: there was no help for it, however; he was evidently not coming to see me that night. I wondered what could be the reason of his departure from our old kind custom while I prepared to turn in.

I did not see him till next morning on parade, and he was then so markedly and disagreeably distant in his manner, that I knew, whatever the cause of offense was between us, it had grown worse by thinking over, and not better. I was puzzled, and my mind was more occupied trying to discover what could be the matter than with the business on hand; so that I received two rebukes for stupid mistakes before I could concentrate my attention on my work. I was in Claude's company — he was my captain, as I have said several times — and it was he who now pulled me up for my blunders. I fancied he spoke with greater sharpness and bitterness than I had ever known him do about such matters before, and I am sure far more harshly than when he reprimanded Flower for something similar to what I had done. It seemed to me there was a cold, contemptuous tone in his voice, that if I had been conscious of wrong-doing would have cut me to the quick, that, as it was, nettled and chafed me, and almost made me determine I would make no efforts toward re-establishing the old friendship between us. But I had liked him so much, and I believed him to be so truly noble and upright in his character, that I could not bear he should think badly of me, and therefore was slow to relinquish the idea of finding out what it was that annoyed him.

When parade was over, Claude came to me, and said, in a sharp, business-like tone, "You are subaltern of the day, are you not, Darrell?"

"Yes," I replied; "is there any thing special to look after?"

"I only wanted to warn you," replied Feversh-
am, with severity, "that I find discipline has been a great deal too lax lately, and duty not properly attended to. When we were down in the country, I am afraid I was as careless as the rest of you, but I mean to be very strict in future; I thought it right to warn you that I shall expect you to attend to every thing that lies within your duty. If I find you have slurred over any thing, or hurried through any part of your work, I shall be seriously displeased, and shall find means for making you more careful in future. Have you been over the dormitories to-day?"

It so happened I had shirked that part of my duty that day. I had often done so before, as it was a task I particularly disliked; Porter, the battalion orderly-sergeant, had done it, and had reported on it to me. I hesitated, seeing by Claude's face that I was in for a row if I admitted the truth, yet of course never for a moment dreaming of not doing so. Such an idea as that of escaping from an awkward situation by equivocation would never have entered into my head; what held me silent was sheer vexation and wonder that, out of all the multifarious duties that fall to the lot of the subaltern of the day, he should have hit on the one which I had not only shirked on this particular morning, but which I was most frequently in the habit of shirking. Before I could reply he went on:

"You need not take the trouble of concocting an answer. I know that you have not been over the rooms, and will spare you inventing either a plausible tale to excuse your shortcomings, or an equivocation to deceive me."

His words were uttered in a tone of withering contempt, and he turned as if to walk away; but I was mad with passion, both at the words and at the tone in which they were uttered; and forgetting alike that he was my captain, and that he was a strong, full-grown man, while I was but a slight, active lad, I sprang at him, and seized him by the shoulder, shaking him in my anger, and saying,

"How dare you hint I do not speak the truth? How dare you insinuate I was about to invent any thing to deceive you?"

As soon as he recovered from the first shock of my attack, he pushed me back from him, calmly and firmly, with an irresistible strength I could not withstand, and answered,

"You ask me why I doubt your truth. Must I remind you of the French proverb, '*Qui a menti une fois mentira toujours?*' I should have thought you could understand, without my being obliged to bring by-gones to your memory."

I stood and gazed at him, too astonished, too dumfounded, to renew my assault, even had I wished to do so; but I had no means of chastising him, and my own strength was not adequate to the task. Still I could not allow this insult to pass unpunished, and I determined, the next time we were on leave together, he should render me an account for every dishonoring word he had uttered.

As this, my only means of retaliation, dawned on me, I said,

"I do not understand to what you allude, Lord Feversham — I think you must be mad; but this I do know, that no man, whether sane or insane, shall use such words to me without paying for it dearly. In the position we occupy now to each other, I can not treat you as you deserve, but when we are next on leave, you must meet the consequences of having so grossly insulted me."

"It is a pity you did not remember the difference in our positions a little sooner," he said, dryly. "Fortunately for you, there was no one by" (we were in a corridor leading up to my quarters) "when you flew at my throat just now. It is only on account of your father and mother, not for your own sake, that I refrain from reporting your conduct; but if you are not more cautious in future, I shall be driven to exposing you. As to your talk about my meeting the consequences when we go on leave, I decline to do so, if you mean by that that I am to fight a duel with you. There are many reasons why I should not do so. First, it is forbidden by the laws of the land and the regulations of the service; second, your relationship to me makes it impossible that I could run the risk of staining my hands with your blood; then your extreme youth, and many more reasons besides, all render it impossible. I could not listen to such a challenge from you, even if I did not consider that the crime of which I accuse you is quite sufficient to put you beyond all recognition as a gentleman, or one whom an honorable man could in any way be bound to meet. Do not make a fool of yourself again," he continued, as he saw that, stung by his last speech, I was about to strike him. "Remember, already I could have you brought before a court-martial; if I spare you, it is only because I know what sorrow your being turned out of the army would cause your poor mother."

"Pray do not spare me on that account," I cried; "my mother, if she knew what provoked me to act in the way I did, would be the very last person to wish I had taken it quietly. But I insist that you do not drag her name into our conversation, or try to shelter yourself from the results of your evil-speaking behind any allusion to her. After the unprovoked manner in which you have brought such charges against me, you are not fit to mention her, or to claim relationship with her."

"Say, rather, that you are not fit to do so," he replied, coldly. "What could have tempted you to be so base, Darrell? I do not understand it."

His tone changed as he uttered the latter part of the sentence, and he seemed to look at me wonderingly. At the change my anger abated—it was evident there was some mystery here; I was so totally ignorant of what wrong-doing he could be hinting at, that I thought I would make a trial to settle matters.

"I do not in the least know to what baseness you allude," I said. "I am not aware of having done any thing wrong, except this business of the dormitories, which, after all, is a trifle. But if you will tell me what has annoyed you, perhaps I can explain it. It strikes me as being both ridiculous and uncomfortable that we old friends should be quarreling with one another without an attempt to come to an understanding."

"I will hear no explanation from you," he replied, coldly. "You must be well aware, from what I have said, that I have found out your double-dealing. It is not likely that, knowing what I do know, I would listen to your plausible account of how the thing happened, or perhaps your denial of what I know to be the truth."

—"By Heaven! you shall pay for this!" I cried, springing toward him, quite beside myself. I believe that if I had had a knife, or any deadly weapon with me then except my sword, I should have killed him in my rage; but I had not been accustomed to use my sword as a weapon of offense, and except that I found it in my way as I tried to close with him, I did not think about it. He kept his temper, and leaning his back against the wall, held me motionless, in spite of my violent efforts to free myself. While holding me so, he spoke again.

"Don't be a fool, Darrell!" he said, with icy distinctness; "you will force me to report you, and take steps against you, if you behave in this insane fashion. It would be much wiser and better for you to make a resolution to correct yourself of such debasing tendencies; you ought to be thankful that it was I, and not another man, whom you were tempted to treat in such a manner. Had this occurred to any one else, you would soon have been known for what you are, and public opinion in the regiment would have compelled you to leave, even had you not made yourself amenable to its legal jurisdiction by some overt act of violence and insubordination, as you have done this day. Go. As I told you before, I am willing to spare you for your parents' sake, but I am not willing to have any thing more to do with you than I can help."

He let me go as he spoke, and moved off to his quarters, but I followed him.

"I will be revenged for this!" I cried, as I came up with him again. "You may not be willing to meet me in an honorable and gentlemanly manner; but if you will not, I will take my satisfaction some other way. You have refused to explain the gross insults you have offered me—insults such as no Darrell has ever received tamely, and you shall pay for them."

"No Darrell so far forgot what was due to his honor and his name before as to lay himself open to such words being used of him truly," replied Feversham. "I grieve for the fall of the old chivalrous code of your family, even while I tell you what I consider you: a traitor—and worse."

"A traitor!" I cried, a vague conception that this misunderstanding might in some way be connected with Gwendoline Bambridge rising within me. "Surely you do not mean to say that you think I should not have continued true to my old allegiance, merely because you were not successful?—that I should not try to win her when I found your suit was in vain?"

"How dare you speak of that to me?" cried Claude, turning almost livid with passion. "You ought to be ashamed to mention her name; you ought to shrink from speaking about the ill success of my love, knowing what you do about it. I will not listen to you any more; and I warn you to keep well out of my sight in future; for if you speak to me again as you have spoken this morning, I think I might almost be mad enough to take your punishment into my own hands."

Then, while I shrank back in dismay at the terrible hatred shown in his flashing eyes and set features, he turned from me, and going into his own rooms, which were near, shut the door with a bang. I heard him turn the key in the lock, as if he would say that by that action he locked me forever out of his sight and from his mind.

I stood where he left me, feeling dazed and bewildered, which was partly the effect of the height to which my own passions had been raised, and partly the result of the intense mystery that hung over all this. I seemed like a man groping in the dark, and ever getting farther and farther away from the light, losing myself in a labyrinth of confusing conjecture. Was Claude mad? or had some one been inventing wicked stories of me? and if so, who could that person be? Supposing any one had done so, why had he not come to me and asked me about it, and listened to my explanations, instead of persistently refusing to hear any thing I had to say? And he had hinted that I was that most vile and cowardly of all vile and cowardly things —a liar; for that, in plain unvarnished English, was the meaning of what he had said; he had declared that I had sullied our noble and honorable name by so contemptible a vice that in me the family had been disgraced. When I came to remember all that he had said, my thoughts were maddening, and set all the blood in my body boiling, till my head was dizzy with the tumultuous throbbing caused by the violence of my passion.

And I had no redress for it, no hope of revenge, at least for some time. It was true, as he had said, that I had put myself in his power by my attack on him; he could no doubt have brought me up before a court-martial, and my violent acts would then have told terribly against me, perhaps caused my dismissal from the service. I was not quite sure about that. I had interest, and my ideas were still hazy as to how far interest would go hand in hand with military usage; moreover, I had never had any experience in a case like this one of mine. I really did not want to leave the army yet. I had been such a short time in it, that it would seem something very like disgrace were I to be turned out so summarily, just at the commencement of my career, even if the offense with which I was charged was not considered a very heinous one.

But the insults my cousin had heaped upon me could not be passed over and submitted to; the time would come when I should have it in my power to show him that the man he despised had not forgotten his words. I began to feel for the first time the full strength of a Corsican proverb I but dimly remembered, which was something to the effect that if one kept an injury seven years, and then seven years more, in the end the day of retaliation would come.

I had never felt inclined to look upon revenge as a duty before; now it seemed to me the honor of the family would be tarnished if I did not resent those words of Feversham's.

I had leaned thus motionless against the wall, where Claude left me, for a good while, taking no heed of the flight of time, so deeply was I absorbed in considering what had just happened, when Feversham came out of his room, and passed by me on his way along the corridor, without looking at me, or appearing to see me. I knew he did see me, by the fixed expression of his eyes, but it was evident he did not wish to renew the discussion between us, and hoped by pretending not to observe me he might be allowed to pass in peace.

And I did let him pass; first because there could be no possible good in repeating what had been already said, which would be the probable result of any attempt on my part to make a change in our relations, whether with a view to resenting the insults I had received, or to establishing a better understanding. Then it suddenly struck me that no doubt he believed I had remained there on purpose to besiege him in his rooms, and either to prevent his leaving them, or to attack him when he did leave them. In spite of this idea, for which I had certainly given him some cause, he had come boldly forth, braving the probabilities of a scene. I had not considered, until I saw him, in what light my presence there might be viewed, but when I did recognize the aspect it must bear to others I left him alone; and when he had passed I went on to my own room.

I was very much put out by the whole affair, and grieved and desperately angry. My mental state resembled the bodily state of a man who has had a severe beating. My mind was sore all over; there was hardly a thought that could come into it that did not press more or less heavily on some aching part. All former associations, all present pleasures, all future anticipations had been trampled on and injured, because he had been my best friend all my life, and since I had joined we had been so much together that I could not look forward to enjoyment of a life in which henceforth he was to have no part.

He was ungrateful too, for in my small way I had done much for him, and had always been willing to do more, even to the furthest limit of my ability. I had even pleaded his cause with Gwendoline Bambridge (my conscience told me that of that service at least he was not aware), and this was the way in which he rewarded me.

My idol was shattered, at least in a great measure, but it was not entirely dethroned, and for that I ought to have been more thankful than I was. It was evident he had heard something very bad against me, which he believed. A man such as I had imagined him should in justice have given me a chance of defending myself; but it was his keen appreciation and worship of honor that caused his over-severity, and it rose in part from his old affection for me. We are always hardest on the faults of those we love best.

Long afterward I knew what Claude had felt and endured on that day; how he had been torn by conflicting feelings; by disgust and anger at what he believed to be my baseness—for he had taken his mother's equivocation as a full acknowledgment of my guilt—and by the old tender liking for one who had been his little companion and pupil in all the manly sports in which he excelled. He remembered how we had been accustomed to spend his holiday time together, when I was still too young to go in for many lessons; and afterward, when I was under a tutor, how he used to stir me up to greater exertions than I should have cared to make but for his influence, or than my tutor would have expected of me. I was always at the Castle when he was there, and he had felt for me the protecting love of an elder for a younger brother.

Now it was all changed. He wondered how it was that I could have fallen so low as I must have done to act such a part, either toward him or toward any other man. I had had no such example, either in my own home or among those

I had met since I had been out in the world. He could only account for it by supposing that I had by nature some miserable degeneracy of character, which showed itself thus. He thought me a fellow with a black drop in his heart, that neither kindness, nor precept, nor example had been able to eradicate, and that would break forth again and again, during my course through life, when it was least expected to show itself.

But whatever passed through his mind, and in whatever light he viewed my supposed conduct, the results of his thoughts on that subject were soon apparent; he was harsh to me in a manner that was unusual from him to any body, and still more extraordinary in the eyes of our comrades as coming from him to me, for they were all well aware that I used to be a favorite with him—in fact that in his eyes, if every thing that Madcap did was not altogether and absolutely right, it was certainly pardonable, and must be overlooked accordingly. Now he seemed to be perpetually on the watch for some wrong-doing on my part, and any neglect of duty, or even the foolish pranks in which I sometimes indulged, always provoked from him either punishment or censure. I was irritated almost beyond all bearing constantly. I had not been accustomed to command my temper, and had great difficulty in restraining my tongue when I was chidden in no measured terms for some oversight so slight that I knew any body else would not have remarked it.

"What is up between you and Feversham?" asked Mayleigh one day, after a very curious scene between us.

Something had occurred which did not please Claude, and he as usual had blamed me for it. I answered rather hotly that I had had nothing to do with the matter in question; whereupon Feversham looked at me hard, with a reproachful, contemptuous expression, opened his mouth as if to speak, and then, controlling himself with a visible effort, turned away and left the room. I knew what all this meant well enough — he simply did not believe what I said, but did not choose to show his opinion of me before the others. So far it was considerate, for the old proverb says if you throw mud enough some of it is sure to stick; if Feversham had loudly announced his opinion of me—or rather if, for fear of consequences, he had said what he thought of me quietly—he would have found plenty of fellows willing to take his view of my character and side with him, notwithstanding the fact that I was generally liked.

However, Mayleigh had asked me what was up, and I had put him off as best I might, telling him that Feversham had been down on me of late, for some cause I could not fathom or understand.

"It is very odd," replied Mayleigh, "for he used to be so fond of you, and I believe that is what makes him so savage now. I will ask him, and find out what it is."

"You had better mind what you are about," I said, warningly.

I had an idea that Mayleigh would get a rap over the knuckles if he attempted to meddle with Feversham in his present mood; and though I did not like Mayleigh, I thought I might as well spare him the snubbing he was sure to get. Mayleigh, however, was one of those fellows who always know better than every body else, so he laughed at me, thinking, I really believe, that Claude would feel quite flattered at his impertinent questions.

Next time they were alone, he accordingly opened the subject.

"What is wrong between you and Madcap?" he said. "You used to be such friends, and now you never speak; and you are dreadfully down on the poor little beggar besides."

"Any quarrel I have with Darrell is entirely of a private nature, and not at all connected with the regiment," answered Feversham, stiffly.

If Mayleigh had not had such a very good opinion of himself, he might have seen he was approaching dangerous ground, from the dark frown that gathered on his captain's brow.

"Ah! then there is a quarrel between you and the little fellow. I thought so, though he said he did not know why you were so savage to him. Tell me what it is, and perhaps I can put matters straight," he continued, with what I believe was a kind intention.

"I thank you, Mayleigh," replied Claude, dryly, "but I have a fancy I can manage my own affairs better than other people can do it for me. I will trouble you not to interfere between Darrell and me in future." With that Claude laid down his paper and walked out of the room, thinking as he went, "So that young ruffian said he did not know why I was annoyed with him. Just what I should have expected him to say, after all that has occurred; but it is very dreadful. What would his parents say if they knew how he was turning out? I must hide it as long as I can. Whenever it does come to light, as those things always do, they will suffer quite enough misery, without my letting the knowledge poison their lives so soon."

Sometimes when I had been given a number of irritating and aggravating things to attend to, or had been worried about minutiæ which I did not understand, and which I considered it was the duty of the non-commissioned officers to attend to, I would be ready to break into open revolt — to take a horsewhip and thrash my cousin, or do some other mad and foolish act that should be a revenge for the insults I had received, and would insure my dismissal from the service. I could have left it any day peaceably and quietly, but that was not what I wanted. I was goaded almost to madness, and I felt as if some desperate, insane act would relieve my mind, and that its attendant consequences would, by the mere fact of their increasing the magnitude of the evil, calm the wild turbulence of my passion.

I do not know how it was that I did not break out into some terrible act of insubordination at that time. I was constantly on the point of doing so; I think it was only the companionship of Cecil Egerton, who had by that time returned from leave, that prevented me, and made me, day by day, submit myself without complaint to the contemptuous looks and constant severity of my cousin.

CHAPTER XIX.

AN ACCIDENT.

It was getting near the end of winter by this time, or rather it was the beginning of spring, being near the end of March. The ground was being plowed and sown, and many packs of hounds had given up hunting. That was a matter of great regret to many of us. We had had plenty of good hunting during the winter; but it is one of those things for which one's liking increases the more opportunity one has for gratifying that liking.

We had, many of us, very good hunters, and they were now in tiptop condition. It would be a shame not to turn them to account, in the way of a steeple-chase or something of that kind, when they were in such good training. So we all thought, and talked the matter over, to see when, where, and how it was to be managed.

I had old Blackfoot over with me, and I was pleased to think he had never been fitter in his life. There were good horses, as I have said, in the regiment, but I thought his science, experience, and cool courage ought to be worth something in the matter; considering also that he was up to weight, and as sound in wind and limb as a hunter need be. I was inclined to be confidential with him, as one often is with a horse that one has long known and valued, and used to talk to him about the matter when I went down to see him every day. He was of opinion that he might do the trick, though both he and I were obliged to confess we were a little afraid of James's mare Brunette, a beautiful creature, with a fiery temper, and the speed of an antelope. As for Thunderbolt, Claude Feversham's horse, we entertained a kind of contempt for him, which was greatly heightened by my bitter feelings against his master, in which of course I supposed Blackfoot shared.

I have a tendency to theorize about horses, and to endue them with a great deal more, not only of individual character themselves, but also of perception of individual character; and I never could ride a horse for a quarter of an hour without fancying I understood its thoughts and feelings, almost as plainly as if it had been endowed with powers of speech. It was no wonder, therefore, that, in the case of my old friend Blackfoot, I imagined he really sympathized with me, and that I persuaded myself I could understand and sympathize with him.

Every thing was arranged; our course was chosen, our day fixed, and we were all on the tiptoe of excitement. We had got up a very good card, and expected to have a large attendance—that is to say, if the day was fine, which I fervently prayed it might be, as I hate riding in rain, with the reins slipping through your fingers at every jump. Old Blackfoot was steady enough, as a rule, but I knew that in the first rush and skurry of a steeple-chase he would require a good deal of holding, being inclined to be ambitious, and having some fine notions about taking a lead, and keeping it, which, though doubtless glorious, were too high-flown in style for him to be quite sure of carrying them out successfully. Any one who has tried to ride a pulling horse in wet weather will understand why I hoped it would be dry, and why I really experienced a feeling of relief when the day dawned bright and sunny; not too bright, however, because the sun was frequently obscured by light passing clouds, but sufficiently so to make the landscape look its best, and to give us the certainty of a fine day, and of a good attendance of spectators.

It was a glorious spring morning, when we assembled on the course to see the race run; gay indeed was the scene as our drag drove up, and halted near the winning-post. Our stewards had arranged every thing with an eye to appearance as well as comfort, a forethought which resulted in a very pretty *coup-d'œil*, and called forth several exclamations of admiration from the carriage loads of ladies that now began to appear from all directions.

Claude was going to ride, of course, and underneath his light gray overcoat concealed a very smart and jockey-like turn-out, of green and white, colors that were sure to win him the applause of the populace, no matter whether he was successful or not. But I do not suppose he had remembered that fact in choosing his colors; more probably it was because green had been a favorite with Gwendoline Bambridge, for which reason I would also have worn it, but that he had taken it. Finding the colors I wished for appropriated, I had contented myself with a dark blue and white, a mixture that I believed suited my dingy complexion. The other riders divided among them all the colors of the rainbow, and many more besides, no doubt, but at present all their gay trappings were concealed from observation under their overcoats.

We were weighed after some delay, without which no amateur races could ever come off, and as soon as the bell rang for mounting we sprang into our seats. Claude, on his chestnut hunter, Thunderbolt, was the first to canter past the grand stand; it is unnecessary to say that, wearing green, the crowd cheered him to the echo. Being in Ireland, that was but natural, and whether he lost or won, the rider of Thunderbolt might make sure of applause. But independently of that, his handsome face and graceful seat would have earned him all the ladies' good wishes, but that he was followed closely by a still more good-looking man, dressed all in scarlet, a color that well became his dark complexion, and that set off the deep rich tints of the brown-black mare he rode. This was James, our adjutant, and the beautiful animal that carried him, and that danced along the ground with impatience as it walked, was Brunette, the only thing in the race that Blackfoot and I had agreed to fear.

As for me, I came in for a great deal more praise than I had ever expected, or than I deserved; but part of this, no doubt, was owing to the beauty of my horse (Blackfoot was a very handsome, steel-gray thorough-bred, with black points), and my own youthful appearance.

"As handsome as a picture, bless his pretty face!" I heard one old woman say to another; and I felt almost as much indignation as pleasure, for I knew that if they had not thought me a small boy they would not have considered me so good-looking.

"Thunderbolt is in a worse temper than usual," said the colonel to Captain Carruthers. "Don't you notice it? He is a headstrong, mischievous brute, and I would rather Feversham rode him in a steeple-chase than that I did."

"Oh! he is all safe, with such a man as he has on him," replied Carruthers, carelessly. "I think he has as good a chance of winning as any of the others."

That chestnut brute's temper put us all out dreadfully at the start, but at last, after several failures, we got away well together, and then I noticed that Thunderbolt was really more unmanageable than usual. He had an unpleasant habit, when he was galloping, of throwing himself forward into the air, coming down with a downward swing of his head and powerful forehand, enough almost to pull his rider out of the saddle; every time he did this, he seemed to do it more violently. When we were nearing the first fence, I wondered how he would ever get over it, if he continued to go wild like that. Claude was trying to wait on Brunette, who was leading, but I fancied he would have to give way to the impetuosity of his steed presently, and go to the front whether he liked it or not. In any case, Brunette, speedy and hot-tempered, was making the pace a cracker, and I was content to keep up quietly a little in the rear, trusting to the gray's staying powers to bring him to the right place when he was wanted.

In this order we passed the first fence, Brunette leading, Thunderbolt, who very nearly tumbled head over heels over the wall, from overhaste, next, and I along with four or five others, all in a clump together behind. So we went on over several fences, the headstrong chestnut having now got the head, and becoming apparently more impracticable every minute; it was not the least good letting him out, in the hopes of calming him; the sound of the hoof-strokes behind him added to his fury; the faster he was allowed to go the faster he wanted to go. There is a limit to pace in every thing, even in steeple-chasing, and Feversham was evidently in difficulties, trying to keep his unmanageable quadruped within the limits that would admit of his getting safely over the obstacles before him. It must have been severe work, and it was likely he would get blown before the horse.

We were coming now to the leap of the day— the water jump—and we went down at it like a flight of gayly-tinted autumnal leaves blown before the wind. Over we went, one after the other, Brunette clearing it in magnificent style, though she was evidently fretting at Thunderbolt's presence in front of her, and was rather annoyed at an awkward scramble he made on landing. Blackfoot was not to be beat at water; besides, the old fox was beginning to creep up, and consequently, better pleased with the position I allowed him to maintain, was not taking so much out of himself by impatience. It seemed to me that Thunderbolt was showing signs of distress, but his violent temper made him struggle on long after another horse would have given in. We were nearing the last fence, and my gray was coming up gallantly; Brunette had again taken the lead, though I could tell that even on her the pace at which Thunderbolt had forced us to ride was beginning to tell, and the chestnut himself was decidedly very nearly pumped, though, if he got over the next fence, he might struggle on to the winning-post.

Still I knew now that I could pass him, and I hoped to distance Brunette also, but I did not intend to make my effort until we were over this last fence, which was a formidable double ditch —one that would severely tax the energies of all the horses now in the race. We had left a number in the brook, or on the other side of it. Brunette topped the ditch cleverly, but I could see her knees tremble, and she was near coming to grief as she landed on the other side. The chestnut followed her almost instantaneously; and then, I know not how it happened, I remember finding myself on top of the bank, with a confused mass, horse and rider, lying on the ground in front of me. The only thing I could distinguish was Claude's face, looking ghastly and death-like, with fixed, glassy eyes turned up to the blue spring sky.

The next minute old Blackfoot had taken his jump from the top of the bank, snorting loudly his indignation that such an obstacle should lie exactly in the place where he ought to alight. With the instinct of his kindly species, however, the brave old beast turned in the air, landing sideways beside the two prostrate forms; then, with a sudden spring, he leaped clear over them, and taking the matter in his own hands—for I was too horror-struck to know or feel any thing but a keen desire to return to Claude and ascertain what had happened—he flew after Brunette, regularly running away with me, in spite of my frantic efforts to stop him and get back. My efforts were useless; the old fellow knew where he was now and what he was about, and I, feeling myself powerless, let myself be borne onward toward the lane that opened for our passage in that shouting, cheering mass, from which I heard a cry rising, "The gray wins! The gray wins!"

I could not see any thing for the remembrance of that white, death-like face, and was hardly conscious that we passed Brunette and her rider apparently without an effort, and flashed onward toward the winning-post, the good gray, who had been steeple-chased before, straining every nerve to do his best, as he saw the waving of caps and hats, and heard the tumultuous shouting of the crowd—sights and sounds that betokened to him a speedy termination to his exertions.

I hardly know how it was we stopped after passing the winning-post. I only know that I could not wait to give my staunch old friend the caresses he deserved, but throwing the reins to my groom, I snatched the overcoat he offered me, and hurried back to where I had left Feversham lying.

There was a small crowd round the spot when I got near, which confirmed the dreadful fears that had taken possession of my mind. Several of the riders, seeing that the race was over, had dismounted, and were very conspicuous among the more sober coverings of the other people that composed the motley group.

"What has happened?" I asked, as I ran up. "Is he hurt?"

"Badly, I fear," replied Preston, who was one of those near.

Without waiting to hear any more, I pushed my way through the crowd of curious, unhelpful by-standers, and found that he had been extricated from his horse, which did not seem much hurt, and which stood near, trembling and dejected. He was still unconscious—or was he dead? I asked myself, as I looked at his ghastly white face. There did not seem to be any bones broken; whatever injury he received it must have been internal, as there was no outward disfigurement—nothing to mar the cold, terrible beauty of that death-like swoon.

I pushed away the man who was supporting

his head, and, kneeling down, held it myself tenderly. We had not been friends lately; he had been hard and unkind to me, and had said cruel, insulting things of me; and we had been rivals; but the remembrance of all that vanished when I saw him lying before me as one dead—believing him, indeed, to be dead. I remembered only the love we had once had for each other—a friendship as dear and as true as that of Jonathan and David, as we had often jokingly been called—a friendship the remembrance of which could never be totally effaced from the minds of either of us, no matter what differences or estrangements the circumstances of life might call up between us.

How long I knelt thus I do not know. I was conscious of nothing going on around, did not recognize the familiar faces of our comrades as they hurried up to see what was the matter, did not hear the muttered lamentations that passed among the crowd for the fine fellow whose life they believed to be so suddenly cut short. I believed it myself, and heard and saw nothing but the dingy, down-trodden grass, seamed and scarred with hoof-prints, on which he lay, and the white, still face that I supported on my knee. A vague thought of his mother, and of her terrible grief when she should come to hear this, did rouse me a little now and then, but the overwhelming pain of dreadful uncertainty drove it away again. The doctor had been sent for. Until he came, and I knew for certain what had happened, I could think of nothing but that my friend lay there dying, and I was powerless to help him; and with this thought came the added bitterness of knowing that we had been estranged of late, and that he might go without learning that he had wronged me—without hearing that I forgave him.

At length, after minutes that seemed to me interminable, the doctor arrived. He was a small, bustling, sharp-looking man, rather youthful in appearance; indeed, if he had been an older man, in a good practice, it is not likely he would have been on the course. I was intensely glad to see him, however, no matter who or what he was; and I think the whole crowd, which had now swelled to large dimensions, was relieved when he announced that Claude still lived. He thought the poor fellow was suffering from concussion of the brain, and deemed it probable that there were also some internal injuries, judging from the position in which his horse had been found lying over him. But it was not possible to ascertain that there; and finding that all efforts to restore consciousness failed, he gave directions for removing my poor cousin's insensible body to a comfortable farm-house that we could see two or three fields away.

A door having been taken off a hovel near at hand, he was laid on it, and a very melancholy procession set out toward the farm-house. As we approached it, I saw it was one of those comfortable dwellings that are much more rarely met with in Ireland than in England. They are seen occasionally, and are then almost invariably a guarantee that the people who reside in them are of a better class than the ordinary population, and have received a better education. The house was only a one-storied, thatched cottage, but the thatch was fastened on with ornamental woodwork, painted white, the whitewashed walls were

dazzlingly clean, and a number of creepers were carefully trained up the front and round the doorway and windows. The door was adorned with a brass knocker, that sparkled in the cold spring sunlight as we approached, and the windows had large panes, and were scrupulously clean. In front of the house was a neat flower-garden, which even at that time of year looked almost gay with hepaticas and snow-drops. My eye took all this in mechanically; it told something about the people from whom we were about to beg the favor of their receiving Claude, and it seemed to promise that, if they would receive him, he would be well cared for and comfortable.

As our ominous-looking procession drew near, a man came hurrying after us from the racecourse. He was short, thick-set, and dark, with a frank, good face, and a respectful manner. Coming up to us before we reached the cottage, he touched his hat, and addressed me, I suppose because I was carrying the door on the side next him.

"Is the gentleman badly hurted, yer honor?" he asked.

"Indeed he is," I replied sadly.

"Will yez be plazed to bring him into the farm here," he said, indicating the cottage to which we were bound with his hand. "We'll make him as comfortable as we can, and may be yerself would stay along with him, and see how he gets on, till ye can move him."

"We were just going to ask leave to bring him to this house, until we know how far he is hurt, and when he can be moved," I answered. "You are the master, I suppose; it is very kind of you to be so good-natured to a stranger. I am afraid we shall give you a great deal of trouble."

"Not at all, sir," he answered, briskly. "I am sorry for the gentleman, for he was a beautiful rider, and managed that troublesome baste of his well. I love a bit of good riding, and would do any thing for a man as can go well across country. Sure it was just to see the sport that I came out to-day, when I should have been thrashing."

By this time we had arrived at the door of the snug cottage, and looking in through the windows, one could see that one room was arranged as a kind of compromise between drawing-room and parlor; a sort of state-room, in which visitors were received. It contained a fine Yankee clock, that stood on the chimney-piece, over against the window, and that was so obtrusively brilliant in its coloring it seemed to fill and pervade the whole room. That was the only thing I could see, in my first hurried glance, as my friend the farmer ran round to the back that he might get in to open the front door, and to prepare his wife for our arrival. The room on the other side of the door-way, as far as I could catch a glimpse of it, for the window was a good deal shaded by white muslin curtains, was the bedroom of the house; they might have had more than that one, but it is not usual in an Irish farm, no matter how comfortable and respectable the people may be. I had hardly made these observations, when the door was opened and the farmer invited us to enter, throwing open the door of the before-described parlor, to indicate that we were to turn in there. We did so, and found one of the principal pieces of furniture in the room was a large horse-hair sofa, which our host proceeded to assure us would make a most comfortable bed for the gentleman, with the addition of a few chairs added to it on one side, to enlarge its width and prevent the occupant falling out. His wife, a very pretty young woman, now entered, and proceeded to improvise a bed in the manner described, while we laid our burden down on the floor and waited.

Very swiftly and dexterously the hard horsehair sofa was transformed in a soft luxurious bed, the foundation being one of those enormous feather-beds which all well-to-do Irish housewives pride themselves upon. The sheets were of homespun linen, spotlessly clean, but very coarse, as might have been expected; and over all was spread a counterpane of particularly gaudy patchwork.

All this while Claude had never recovered consciousness, nor did he after he had been laid on the bed thus hastily improvised; but after some hours anxious watching he opened his eyes for a few seconds, without however appearing to know where he was, or who those gathered around him were; then closing them again, he seemed presently to fall into a kind of lethargic sleep.

The doctor seemed anxious to get the case off his hands; and as of course we had sent for Wilson, our surgeon, we did not try to keep him, when, on Feversham appearing to sleep, he said he must be going. I do not myself believe he knew much about the matter, and that the cleverness and intelligence he undoubtedly possessed were directed into quite a different channel from his profession, which is much too slow up-hill work to suit a man who has a taste for dissipation and expensive pleasures, such as had our friend Dr. Brown.

He had not long left when Wilson appeared. His first step was to send away all the curious people, who still hung about the room and the door-way, quite preventing the free passage of air. He looked at Feversham thoughtfully and intently for some time, felt his pulse and head, and otherwise ascertained his state as well as he could, without disturbing him, and then said there was nothing he could do at present; that Claude seemed quiet and not feverish, and was to all appearance doing well. He said he would run back to town, where he had some business, and would be down again in the evening. In the mean time I, having constituted myself nurse, was to remain so, until Wilson should send down a woman from town. This I refused to hear of, however; I felt in some way as if Claude belonged to me, and I was bound to bring him through this. I fancy I had a vague idea in my mind that, when he came to himself, and knew that I had nursed him through his illness, he would explain this unhappy misunderstanding that existed between us, and we should be friends once more.

I did not exactly know that this was my reason for insisting on keeping the attendance on my cousin entirely to myself, but I believe now that was the motive which actuated me, judging by my feelings afterward, when the moment for which I waited came. So I told Wilson, if I wanted help in watching I would get the farmer's wife to relieve me; but in my own opinion I considered myself able to sit up in such a cause for an indefinite period.

Then Wilson left, after ordering the most perfect quiet in the house. Kavanagh (our host) and his wife retired into the back premises, and a profound stillness settled down on the little room, where I sat beside Feversham's bedside. Only his quick, hurried breathing disturbed the silence, and after a time that became painful to listen to, I found myself counting the respirations in a mechanical way, and when, owing to the irregularity of his breathing, one was delayed longer than the others, I waited to hear it anxiously and nervously.

I could not stand that kind of thing. I knew I should get frightened, and begin imagining he was worse. I must make myself think of something that should give my mind occupation. I was sorry I had not a book, and determined to make Wilson send me some down, so that, if this state of things lasted any time, I might have something to keep up my spirits and courage.

Then I began to think, ought one to write to Lady Feversham? She was my aunt, but I did not know as much of her as I did of many of my mother's friends who were not related to me. I did not care for her much, she was so different from her sister (my mother). I fancied she would worry Claude, and that perhaps the best thing I could do would be to wait until the doctor saw him again; then I could consult Wilson as to whether I ought to send for his mother or not.

All this time I had never remembered that I had won the race in which this dreadful accident had occurred. It was certainly not with my own will and intent that it was won, and I am almost ashamed to think that, since I had left my gallant gray in the hands of his groom, I had not once remembered him, nor his determination to have matters his own way, until the evening had closed in, and the room in which I was sitting was in darkness, but for the flickering light of a coal fire in the small, neatly-kept grate.

By-and-by the door opened noiselessly, and Kavanagh put in his head.

"How's the gentleman doing, your honor?" he asked.

"He is sleeping," I replied, moving toward the door, that our conversation might not disturb him. "I think he will do. Mr. Wilson seemed to say that sleep was good."

"Ay, surely," replied the man, his honest, sunburned face brightening up as soon as he saw there was no present prospect of a death in the house.

Like all Irish peasants, he and his wife, though of a better class than most of their neighbors, entertained a superstitious dread of a death in their house, and it was only intense kindness of disposition that had induced Kavanagh to allow our bringing Claude into his cottage when he was in such a critical state. I knew something of this —had heard the Bambridges talking of it once —so I was able to interpret the sudden lighting up of his countenance, and the almost joyous tone in which he asked me if he might bring me something to eat.

"I will go and join you and Mrs. Kavanagh," I answered. "I suppose you have your supper now; I confess I am hungry. I have eaten nothing since breakfast. I think I may leave him for a while. The medicine the doctor said he would send has not come yet, so I suppose he will bring it himself."

Kavanagh looked rather confused, I thought,

for a minute, at the idea of having a person whom he evidently regarded as a swell to sit down to supper with him; but the gentlemanly instinct of the rural classes in Ireland prevented him from showing any awkwardness, and he took me with him to the kitchen.

It was a long, low room, with a hearth-stone instead of a grate, or range, and this hearth-stone was heaped with turf, which was blazing and roaring, and sending showers of sparks up the chimney.

The immense glowing surface of a good turf fire always seems to me to send out a much greater amount of heat than an ordinary coal fire. I know many people are quite of the opposite opinion, but I generally find those are people who have never found themselves face to face with a large, well-kindled turf fire.

For one thing, there is always a larger surface to radiate heat in a good well-built up fire of turf sods; and then they are, if the fire has been well kindled, all in a glow of white heat at the same time, instead of having a dead black top, with little gas jets here and there to enliven it, which is generally the case with coal, no matter how fierce the fire may be underneath.

But to return to the Kavanaghs' kitchen. They had no candles lighted when I came in; the brilliant leaping flame of the turf gave them light enough, and in that ruddy glow, reflected from plates and tins, glistening in endless rows in the white deal plate-rack, I could perceive Mrs. Kavanagh seated on a low stool by the fire, frying bacon, and burning her pretty face most uncomfortably, I should think, in the task. A little girl of about five years old was playing with a cat and a baby alternately; and another child, who I afterward found was a boy, and who was evidently intermediate between the girl and the baby, was building houses with sods of turf in a corner. From the ceiling hung a goodly supply of bacon, and a pot of potatoes, that might have contained food for a regiment, was standing by Mrs. Kavanagh, having just been lifted from the fire.

I do not think pretty little Mrs. Kavanagh had expected a visitor, but she seemed in no way put out or disconcerted when I appeared, looking up from her cooking with a smile, telling me I was welcome, and asking me to be seated, while her husband brought a chair for me quite close to the blazing turf fire, and the children noiselessly and quietly slunk into the background.

We began to talk. She was anxious to know how the accident had happened, and I described it, as it had seemed to me; and then Kavanagh repeated his version of it, though no doubt she had heard that two or three times already. But she appeared to listen with interest, and finally, when that side of the matter was exhausted, she inquired if I was any kin to him.

I told her our relationship, and she pitied me for the anxiety she saw I was in. By this time, however, the bacon was fried, and a supplement of poached eggs added. The table was laid, and candles having been lighted, we drew round it. Certainly the table equipments were primitive, but they were clean; even the coarse linen cloth was clean and spotless, and the awkward two-pronged forks shone again. Of course I knew this was an exception to the ordinary state of things in Ireland, but I found out the reason of it all in the course of conversation. They had

both been in service; he as kind of butler and coachman, a factotum, in short, and she as a housemaid. They had met at a house where they were both living in their respective capacities, had married, and having some small savings, they had invested them in stock and set up a farm. At first it was very up-hill work, the man told me, but after three or four years he began to get his head above water, and they had since prospered very much. The neat and cleanly habits they had acquired in service remained with them, and made their cottage the admiration and envy of all the neighbors.

We were still enjoying our meal, when Wilson again drove up. He found Claude much as he had left him, except that his breathing was more regular and easy. He had brought the things necessary, as I had imagined he would, and after administering something that seemed to have a reviving effect, for Claude opened his eyes and looked at us for a minute or two, we left him, and went back to our supper, in which the doctor joined us. It was a homely meal, and the load of anxiety, though greatly lessened, was still heavy on my mind; yet in a quiet way we enjoyed ourselves very much. These people, who had been so generous and good-natured to us, had very little opportunity of hearing the news of the outer world, and their interest was greatly excited by the little bits of gossip from the city that we were able to tell them.

They were curious also about the Fenian disturbances, anxious to know what hope the movement had of success; not that they sympathized with it, but because they were afraid of it, as a great many of the well-to-do farmers were. They felt they had every thing to lose and nothing to gain by such a change. People like these have no sympathy with idleness or disorder; they do not idle themselves; they make their living by constant, intelligent hard work, and look with secret contempt on the lazy, thriftless drones who are the agitators, and who would be the only ones to profit by misrule. Those who pay their rent regularly, and who do so at the cost of very hard labor, are not the ones who talk of landlord tyranny, knowing that if they pay their way with him they are safe; but under the reign of disorder and violence, neither diligence, nor intelligence, nor paying their way, would avail them any thing, but only the right of the strong hand.

All this and more John Kavanagh expounded to us as we sat round the supper-table, evidently glad to have got an audience to whom he could open his mind, and with whom he could talk over the matter fully; for his pretty wife seemed unable to enter more into the matter than could be conveyed by unhesitating acquiescence in every thing he said, which she gave now and then in a low-toned "Ay, surely."

After a time Wilson and I returned to Feversham. He was sleeping again; but Wilson was satisfied with his appearance; and said he would do well. I asked him whether I should send for Lady Feversham, but that he would not hear of.

"There is no danger now," he said; "he will be all right in time. I have examined him carefully, and I do not believe he has any internal injuries; the damage done to his head will right itself if he is kept perfectly quiet. I do not know Lady Feversham, and you do, so you are a better judge than I am of whether she would be quiet; but, at any rate, I do not think it worth while bringing her over. After I have seen him to-morrow you may write and report; but I think you will be able to tell her it is unnecessary she should undertake the journey."

I had my own opinion about Lady Feversham, and was inclined to think he would get on better without her, and therefore agreed heartily in the doctor's plan. When I had said so, he continued:

"You had better make up some kind of bed on the floor here and lie down. You will have to get up every two hours to give him this mixture, and he must have some nourishment also."

As he thought of this, Wilson went out to the kitchen to consult with Mrs. Kavanagh what she could get for the invalid. When he returned he said,

"I have settled it all. You will have a shake-down got up for you here, and the little woman will bring you in presently some mess I have ordered for him. I am off now. I shall be down the first thing in the morning, and expect to find him doing well. He has a splendid constitution, and is in first-rate health, which is all in his favor. It will not be as long a job as I feared at first. Good-night. I think you will get tired of this freak of minding your cousin before long, and will be glad to get a professional."

I did not think so; however, I laughed and shook hands, and he went out. A few minutes after I heard the hoof-strokes of his horses ringing out on the hard road as he trotted merrily away.

Then Claude's stuff was brought, and while I administered it with some difficulty, for I was not experienced in such matters, Mrs. Kavanagh brought in the bedding, and proceeded to make up my couch on the floor. But I could not succeed in feeding Claude, and presently said:

"Mrs. Kavanagh, will you give this stuff to my cousin? I will make the bed. I understand that beautifully."

"Of course, sir, I'll do it for you," she replied, advancing to the bedside, and raising his head by putting her arm behind the pillows before she attempted to give him any thing. (I had been trying to feed him with his head lying flat back.) "Why, sir," she cried, "you have nearly choked him! You should have lifted him this way. How would you swallow with your head back like that?"

She spoke almost sharply, evidently hardly believing in an ignorance so great as to render one unable to spoon-feed a sick person.

"Go and make the bed," she added, with a little, quick, decisive manner, that seemed to say, "Let me see that you are good for something."

But here I met with an unforeseen difficulty. You all know that I could make an apple-pie bed, when the foundation of the real thing had been properly laid, but how to set about making a real bed puzzled me—and here all the bedding was tumbled pell-mell together. I had not the least idea how to begin, except that I thought I ought to spread the feather-bed on the floor first—and this I did.

I had just accomplished that feat satisfactorily, and was contemplating the result achieved with considerable pride—for, you know, it is not an easy thing to get a great, soft, flobby feather-bed to lie even and plump and straight—when Mrs. Kavanagh looked up from her task with Claude.

"That is right," she said, with more approval than she had shown before. "Now go on."

It was very easy to say go on, but how was I to do it? I took up first blankets, and then sheets, and tossed them about in confusion; but what I was to do with them, or with which I was to begin, I could not think. However, the bed was for myself, so it did not much matter, and I put them on somehow, covering them with another gorgeous patchwork counterpane. It was easy to know that ought to go on top.

I had just finished, when Mrs. Kavanagh spoke again.

"You had better come here, yer honor, and learn how to tend the gentleman here. Sure, it's a nurse he ought to have had—for it is not to be expected that the likes of you could care for him. If you let me, I'll sit up with him, and I'll give you the other room forninst ye."

"Oh, no!" I cried, eagerly. "I want to mind him myself. I see how you do with him now, and I shall be able to get on splendidly. Thanks to you for teaching me."

"You're welcome, sir," she answered, turning to leave the room—for she had succeeded in getting Claude to take a good deal of the broth, or whatever the stuff was she had brought him.

As she was leaving the room, something about the look of my bed-making attracted her. She went over to examine it, I watching her ruefully, as I had a conviction there was something very wrong about it. No sooner had she looked at it a little closely than I saw a smile that threatened to become a laugh, overspread her face.

"Oh, sir," she said, "you told me you could make a bed beautifully, or I wouldn't have troubled you to do it. But is this what you call doing it beautifully? Why, you've got all the blankets on top, and not a thing between the sheet and the mattress; and you've never put on the pillow-cover at all, but just laid it where your feet would come. Sure, you should have told me, and I'd have made it for you, and thought no trouble of it."

"Oh, never mind," I cried; "I shall sleep just as well that way. What difference does it make?"

"It makes just this difference—I wouldn't sleep the night if I thought a stranger in my house was on a bed like that. Be aisy, now, and I'll settle it in a minute."

I was silent, and watched her as she undid, in one minute, the structure it had taken me so long to build up. And then I continued looking, in a kind of fascinated amazement, while she dexterously re-settled the clothes, and made a very different-looking couch, in two or three minutes, from that which had resulted from my long and patient labor. Then, with a smile and a courtesy, she left the room, after depositing a small bowl with some more stuff for Claude on the hob by the fire.

A few minutes after I could hear faint, muffled sounds of laughter proceeding from the room opposite, which convinced me she was amusing her husband by detailing to him my experiments in the way of nursing and bed-making.

Soon the house was sunk in profound silence, so that a coal dropping out of the grate, or even a long-drawn sigh from the sleeper, appeared a loud, startling noise. The farmer and his family had gone to rest early, as these people, who rise very early, generally do. I was beginning to feel sleepy myself, and was only waiting to administer Claude's next dose before I turned in also. Indeed I was almost afraid to get into that comfortable-looking bed, for fear that, once there, I should not wake as I ought to do. But I was a light sleeper always, and in the end did very well in my capacity of nurse, catching Claude's slightest movement, and being with him almost before he was awake.

Next morning he was decidedly better. The doctor, when he came, was quite satisfied with his progress—a great deal more satisfied than I was, in fact, for this reason:

He had awaked after his night's rest to all appearance quite sensible, recognizing Wilson and me—at least we thought he recognized us from the calm, clear look in his eyes; but he made no attempt to speak, which was a good thing, as he would not have been permitted to do so had he tried. But the thing that made me uneasy was that he seemed to regard me with just as much pleasure as he did the doctor. He looked at me as he might have looked at me under similar circumstances in old times, before any thing had arisen between us. I was sure he did not remember the matter, or else he would have betrayed some awkwardness, some unwillingness to meet my eye; for even if he believed me again, and if my conduct toward him showed him that he had in some way judged me falsely, still he would then have felt ashamed of his conduct, and for that reason would have exhibited embarrassment. To me it seemed a serious thing that he should have forgotten the quarrel between us: it was a cause of so much pain and annoyance to me that I was sure if I were dying I should still remember it and grieve over it. But it might not be the same to Claude; I did not, and never had, occupied the same place in his affection and regard as he had occupied in mine.

I could not keep my anxiety on this subject to myself, but when Wilson was going away I followed him.

"Do you think," I asked, "that he is all right—that he remembers us, and all about us?"

"Yes, certainly," he replied; "I see it in his eye. No doubt he has thought over a good many things he is too weak to talk about, though of course he can not think much at present either."

"But suppose, now, one of us two was an enemy of his—some one to whom he had a special dislike; if he did not show aversion to them, but received them just as he does you and me, what would that mean?"

"Oh! that is different," replied Wilson, "and I do not see how it bears on the case in point. In such a position as you describe, I should say his memory had been affected—whether temporarily or permanently, time alone would tell. But we are neither of us enemies of his, and consequently his appearing equally pleased with both of us shows nothing wrong."

I was puzzled. I did not know whether I ought to confide all I knew to Wilson, or whether I ought not; but finally I said,

"Well, you know, doctor, I am no enemy of his, but lately something has gone wrong between us, and he has taken a terrible aversion to me. You must have noticed some of its results, even if you did not perceive the fact itself. And now he does not remember it—I know by the way in which he looks at me."

Wilson appeared thoughtful for a minute, and then replied,

"I think you will find that is nothing. This late row between you has not been of long duration, and of course the original state of affairs comes back to his mind first; you will probably think he will remember his grievance soon enough. Besides, you must remember he is not strong enough yet to think connectedly; unless any thing comes back to his mind spontaneously, he can not exert himself to bring it back."

It was a comfort to me that Wilson took the matter in this light, and what he said seemed very probable; I went back to my charge with a much more satisfied mind than I had possessed since I found out that Claude had ceased to hate me, glad as I was that such should be the case.

A few days passed this way, and very dull and monotonous they were, in spite of the kindness and attention of the Kavanaghs, and though a number of our fellows dropped in perpetually to see how the invalid was getting on. He had manifested a desire to talk once or twice, but any such tendency had been rigorously nipped in the bud by the doctor's orders, and he passed his time in a half-dozing state, with his eyes closed, only rousing up a little now and then when he had to take his food or medicine.

He was going on well, Wilson decided; and though I saw no signs as yet that he remembered the difference between us, still I could not but acknowledge that he was getting stronger, and that he evidently recognized all of our fellows who were admitted to see him. James and Flower, and some of the others, were good enough to remember that it must be dull work for me. James had got me leave for a time as soon as the accident occurred, and after I had expressed a wish to be with my cousin; he now brought me books and papers and things of that kind, to beguile my weary hours.

But in the whole business I think the people most to be pitied were our good entertainers, whose neat little house was overrun at all hours by strangers, and who were called upon to put up horses, or have them held, or otherwise exert themselves for the benefit of the said strangers perpetually. In spite of the annoyance it must have been, they were always kind and obliging, and never seemed to look forward to the day when they would be able to get rid of us again. Of course, we intended they should be well remunerated for all this, but I don't think they ever counted on such a reward, and I am sure it would have been impossible to repay, by any amount of money, all the good-will and real kindness they lavished upon us.

————◆————

CHAPTER XX.

STRANGERS YET.

DAYS passed on, and Feversham began to get decidedly better and stronger; he was allowed to talk, and then to sit up, and finally he was taken off his sofa and allowed to go into the great warm kitchen, and lie on an improvised couch there, watching pretty Mrs. Kavanagh at her housekeeping with interested, curious eyes. I fancy, after so long a period of weakness and seeming unconsciousness, it must have been like returning to a new life to be once more able to look at people, and to take account of their actions; then the sphere on which his newly awakened consciousness opened was one widely different from any he had formerly known, and between him and that past life my familiar face furnished the only connecting link. As he himself expressed it, he felt as if he had transmigrated, during his illness, into another phase of existence, where every thing around was new and strange, and where all the memories of his former life had grown dim and indistinct. This expression of his feelings relieved my mind somewhat; it was evident that all that had happened before his illness required too great an effort of the mind to be brought up before him just yet; consequently he did not seek to recall it, but amused himself like a child with the passing incidents that came under his eyes and claimed his attention. Sometimes, after he had been watching for a while Mrs. Kavanagh's busy, tidy figure flitting about her kitchen, he would turn and look at me fixedly, as I sat reading near him. I knew he was looking at me, and I knew he was trying to recall something about me; a vague impression was beginning to rise in his mind that there was something that he ought to remember. At such times I felt his eyes on me, and knew very well what it was he desired to recollect, but of course I did not tell him. It would all come back to him in time; then, if he still persisted in the assertions he had made before, I should be obliged to leave him; and in that case I was sure my liking for a man who could treat me so badly would not long survive.

But I hoped that all that he had gone through would soften his mind, and that at least he would consent to let me know definitely of what he accused me, and would listen to my defense, if defense there was to make.

One day he had sat watching me thus for some time; I had felt that the crisis was very near, that soon he would remember, and speak; presently, getting nervous from his continued silent scrutiny, I jumped up and said I would go out for a walk.

"Wait a minute," pleaded Claude, earnestly; "I want to ask you something."

"What is it?" I replied boldly, thinking that the time had come, and I should be able to vindicate my conduct, and convince him that I had done nothing of which I need be ashamed.

He pressed his hand to his forehead for a minute, and seemed as if he was forcing himself to think; then he said, "Why are you here minding me, Vivian? I have a kind of idea there was something wrong between us, I can not think what it was, but I don't imagine you would have remained here all this time to mind me if it had been true. And you know Wilson could have hired a woman at one of those places to look after me. I should then, perhaps, have had an opportunity of judging whether Sairey Gamp is overdrawn."

"Do you think I would have left you to Sairey Gamp, if she had come in person," I replied, laughing. It was evident as yet he remembered nothing distinctly about our differences, and I at least was not going to tell him.

"You are a good fellow, Vivian," he said, holding out his hand to me, and seeming pleased by my answer. "I can not think what can

have put this queer notion about you into my head, and yet I know I had it, for I remember the day of the race, when you were coming up so close behind me on old Blackfoot, and I felt my horse was done, I was mad with rage at the thought that you should win. I had some kind of an idea, I know, that you did not deserve it, that you were an impostor and a cheat, moving about among the rest as if you were as good as they; I had some extraordinary idea you were not, though it seemed to me I was the only person who knew any thing against you. It is very strange how such an impression can have got into my head, and there is a feeling of reality about it that annoys me."

"You will make yourself ill again, if you go on talking about it, and fretting yourself," I answered. "Try to have more cheerful thoughts when I come back. Here is Flower coming in at the gate; he will talk to you while I am away."

"Flower is not amusing," replied Claude, languidly and ungratefully; "I find it much pleasanter to keep quiet and watch Mrs. Kavanagh's pretty figure moving about, than to listen to his twaddle. However, as he is here, I must make the best of it; but come back soon."

I went out, leaving Flower telling his small chitchat, with a ready good-nature that I fear was not half appreciated. It is the nature of convalescents to be querulous and exacting, and to most people Claude was no exception to the rule. The odd thing was that with me he was always patient and gentle, and had, besides, an extraordinary fancy for keeping me always near him. He never seemed happy unless I was with him, and manifested much more affection for me than he had ever shown in the old days when I had worshiped him as the hero of my boyish imagination. Of course this fancy of his for me was the result of his weakness and dependence, acting on his former friendship, and I knew very well that much of it would probably disappear when he became strong and was going about again. Still it would probably influence him to listen to what I had to say, and then to retract his words and beg my pardon for having uttered them. This was what I wished, and as I trudged merrily along the road leading toward the sea, my fancy assured me this was what would ultimately happen.

When I returned, Flower had gone, but apparently his presence and conversation had aroused some recollections in Claude's mind, for, as soon as I appeared, he turned to me again.

"I know," he said, "Vivian, that I have not been good to you; the thing is getting clearer to me. I do not understand why I behaved ill to you yet, or what it is that is between us, but I know there is something, and I want to make it up."

He looked excited and eager, but I could tell his head was troubling him, from the expression of his eyes, and from his passing his hand across his forehead perpetually, as if to draw away something that oppressed him.

"You will be ill again," I said, "if you go on like this. What does any thing matter that was between us before? It is past now, and I don't think of it, neither must you: let by-gones be by-gones."

"You ought to tell me," he replied; "I am sure I should feel better if I knew."

"That is exactly what I can not do," I said, laughing, "as you never told me yourself what was the cause of it all. You were very angry with me, and I asked you several times for an explanation; then at other times I should have liked to have called you out and made you fight with me, but that you wisely would not hear of. However, it is all right now between us, I am sure; we shall neither of us think of the matter again, and you may as well dismiss it from your mind; you will get well all the faster."

He shook his head.

"I seem to have faint glimmerings of light on the matter now and then," he said; "but I can not catch them or collect them. I must wait. As soon as I remember we will talk it all over: will not that do?"

Satisfied with this resolution, he became more composed, and, I was pleased to see, evidently put the matter off his mind. I should have liked very much to know what it had been that had made my best friend turn so suddenly and bitterly against me, but of course, if he was content to let it rest, it was better for me it should be so than that old grievances should be raked up; besides, in his present state it really injured him to think of it.

Time passed on, and three weeks after his accident Claude came up to Dublin again. He was still far from well, but he thought he was inconveniencing the Kavanaghs by remaining there longer, and it was just as good for him to occupy his rooms in barracks as to be incurring expense elsewhere. The good people we had been with seemed quite sorry to lose us, and were inclined to be very indignant when I offered them payment. I insisted on their taking something, however, as I knew they had been at great expense with us, in many ways, and neither Claude nor I could have permitted ourselves to return their kindness so badly as to allow them to suffer on our account. We gave them just what we would have paid for board and lodging anywhere else, explaining to them that such was the usual custom in a case of this kind; but we sent them presents afterward, in the way of clothing, which I know they appreciated much more than they did the money.

The evening we returned to barracks, as I was sitting in Claude's room, I noticed the puzzled expression return to his face, and I knew that the subject which by common consent we had dropped the last few days was again troubling him.

Before he could make up his mind to say any thing about it, the late post came, and his letters were brought up to him. There was one from Lady Feversham, I could see, for I knew my aunt Anna's handwriting; she had been told of her son's illness, and had written both to him and to me constantly, thanking me for what she called my devotion to him, and begging him to come home as soon as he could travel. I had a long letter from my mother, and while I was reading it I could see that Claude had gone over his letter, which was much shorter, twice. When I had finished mine I looked up, and a change in his expression struck me at once. He was gazing at me with a sad, stern look, like that which had always come over his face when addressing me during the time of our estrangement.

I think he knew by my eyes that I understood his look, and saw that he remembered. I know I felt my heart beat rapidly, with the intensity of my expectation that he was about to say something which would explain the mystery of his conduct toward me. After a pause that I thought very long, but during which I would not speak, for fear of putting his mind off the clue that he seemed to have got hold of, he said,

"I remember now, Darrell, why you and I were not good friends before the accident. It is a pity you took so much trouble about me. I wish you had left me to a hired nurse, for I know I shall seem ungrateful to you if I do not treat you in the same way as I have done lately; and now that I remember all about you, it is impossible I should so treat you. In fact, the farther we keep from each other the better, I think. I wish I had continued to forget it—that I could have continued to believe in you; but that is impossible."

"Why is it impossible?" I cried. "I demand to know of what you accuse me, before you again dare to treat me as you did before. It was bad enough of you then; it will be worse now, and you are quite right in saying it will be thought ungrateful."

"Yes, I see that plainly," he replied. "You were clever enough to put me in that most odious position, for there is nothing worse than ingratitude, and that, too, for such kindness as you have shown me. But, under the circumstances, it is evident you did it for an object, in order to force me to countenance you when I recovered. I wish I could bring myself to do so, but this last ruse only increases my abhorrence of your character. It was ungenerous of you to take advantage of my unconsciousness, and do what you knew I would not wish."

"I swear I do not understand what you are always talking about," I cried, passionately, "and that nothing but our old friendship influenced me to watch over you. You might give me credit for so much, knowing how I always liked you. I was a fool for doing so, I see now; but the liking began in my childhood, therefore I am not so much to blame for feeling it as I should be if I had been older and known better when I first met you."

Claude sighed, and looked at me wistfully and reproachfully. "Why do you deny it?" he said; "you almost make me think at times that you are speaking the truth; but even if I could doubt the evidence of the person who knew all from you, I could not think where else to lay the blame. You are the only one who could have done it. It was not necessary; you need not have soiled your conscience. Are you not sorry, knowing that?"

"I tell you I do not understand you," I answered; "you pain both yourself and me by hinting at things that I know nothing of, and can not therefore deny. Why do you not speak them out boldly?"

"Because," he answered with sudden sternness, "I would spare myself the sorrow, and you the disgrace, of hearing you spoken of as you really are; because I can not bear to name such things in connection with you, even though I know the charges to be true. Vivian, you have been very good to me lately, whatever the motive may be that prompted you to be so, and that I can not forget; I can not be so ungrateful, even if I would. Have you ever thought," he added, in his curious, sudden way of digressing, in pursuit of an idea, "that man, called the noblest work of the creation, is more wanting in the noble virtue of gratitude than most of the lower animals? They all remember kindness, and cherish the memory of a friend who is good to them, while we, in spite of our superiority, are often prone to look upon a benefactor with dislike and aversion. We will not do that, Darrell, however. I owe you much; I am afraid lately you have owed me nothing but hatred, for in my anger at your wrong-doing I have been very bad to you. But let us remember the old times only. I will try to forget your miserable fault, and you will endeavor earnestly to give way to no such temptation again. Promise me that, Vivian, and we will be friends."

I looked in his eager face with fierce anger rising in my heart. It was too bad he should treat me thus, and I would not bear it; I would never be friends with a man who doubted my honor, and who, besides doubting it, would not give me the means of clearing myself from the imputation cast upon it. I answered scornfully, "Keep your friendship; I will not take it on those terms. You must either believe in me and trust me, in all and through all my life, or you are not worth having for a friend. Do you think I would have listened to any thing—believed any thing against you? Never! I should have gone to you, and asked you the truth of the matter; only from your own lips would I have condemned you—only from mine should you have judged me. Do you not see all this?" I continued, growing vehement. "Do you not know that we must be strangers while you treat me thus? Your doubt of me is an insult that only a full and complete explanation and apology can ever efface from my mind; and to one of my race, learning to bear insult is a new lesson. You have been kind enough to teach me a good deal about it lately, but remember, though I say nothing, it is not forgotten; there is a day of reckoning coming, when you will have to answer to me for this."

Feversham had listened quietly and sadly to my vehement outburst. When I had done speaking, he replied, slowly:

"I do not understand the matter. I could almost believe you, and yet I dare not; I should only be again deceived. If at any future time I find I have misjudged you, I shall be so glad, in spite of the pain and sorrow it has caused me, and you shall have full and ample apologies. In the mean time let us be strangers as much as we can be, living in the same regiment, and related as we are; it will hurt us both less. But, my boy, promise me you will try to do better in future."

I felt inclined to strike him, I was so enraged at his returning to the old theme. I had thought, when we agreed to be strangers, we should have done with that; but it seemed to have become a perfect monomania with him. In order to restrain myself, and to prevent myself saying or doing something that might make matters worse between us, I dashed out of the room and went out into the city.

It was late in the evening, and dark. The lamps had been lighted, and the few passers-by that were hurrying rapidly to their homes had a kind of air as if they were staying out beyond hours, and would catch it for doing so when they got in. I have no doubt I looked as wild and preoccupied as the rest, as I tore along at my best speed, pressing out in the Kingstown direction.

This last conversation with Feversham had quite upset me. It was really too preposterous that he should go on in that way; and it was so terribly insulting to me, and, through me, to an ancient and honored name. If I could only retaliate, could revenge myself in some way, and teach him to spare my character in word, even if he did not do so in thought! But there was no way open to me in which I could compel him to treat me with respect, except the law, and that was a resource only to be fallen back upon in the last extremity, for it would make public all his insinuations and innuendoes, that at present were known only to ourselves. I began to think those were the good old days indeed, when duelling was lawful and honorable, and when, for one tithe of what my cousin had said to me, either he or I would have settled the matter with our lives. It really was too hard, viewed in this light, that one could only protect one's character by the law—which remedy, in many cases, is worse than the disease, as it permits of throwing such an infinite quantity of mud.

My mind, when I started on my walk, strongly resembled the crater of a volcano, in which various minerals, and stones of every description, are fused up into the molten mass of lava, and seethe there, till their original state is no longer recognizable. So it was with my thoughts. Passion had risen to such a boiling heat that they had been melted and mixed together, till there was not one thought I could separate from another; and, like the overwhelming mass of lava that rushes forth, devouring and destroying in its course, the dominant idea of revenge, overshadowed and took possession of my whole being, rendering me capable of any madness that circumstances, or the influence of my companions, would give me opportunity to commit. For, finally, this idea of retaliation took definite shape and form, and I seemed at last to see that I might have some satisfaction, and perhaps without incurring risk.

I knew Feversham would be going on leave shortly. He was to meet his mother in London in the season, and I had been making interest to get away for a while at that time also. I thought I should succeed in doing so, and if I did I would go to London, and there horsewhip my cousin and quondam friend, as opportunity offered for me to do it. I would have done it at once, but for two reasons. The first of these was, that he was not yet strong, and it seemed to me cowardly to strike a sick man; the other was, that when we were both away on leave the matter would perhaps not be noticed by the authorities, who would regard it as an affair between one gentleman and another, and would not interfere; whereas at present it would cost me my commission, and, as I said before, I did not want to leave the army just then.

I became a great deal calmer, once this plan had arranged itself in my mind, and when I had walked till I was thoroughly tired I returned to barracks, very much more composed than when I had set out.

As for Claude, poor fellow, he had, I afterward found, grieved very much over what had happened, and what he had considered it his duty to say to me. He was really attached to me: as he told me long afterward, it nearly broke his heart to think that I could have behaved so badly as he had persuaded himself I had done.

He could not imagine who but I could have told his mother about Gwendoline Bambridge, and I had a reason for doing so also, being his rival. Though he had believed me at first, his mother's equivocation, when he taxed her with having heard it from me, was taken by him as a tacit admission of my guilt. My assertions that I did not understand him he took to be an equivocation on my part, got up to save myself from telling actual falsehood, and he despised me, and wondered at me accordingly.

He would gladly have been friends with me, he would even have forgiven me this grievous fault, if I had only confessed it, and shown some sorrow and wish for amendment; but my hardness and continued denial aggravated him, and prevented him showing the tenderness and affection he really felt for me.

And so we, who had been such dear and true friends all our lives, became estranged, and drifted gradually more apart, as one has seen two boats that have got into opposing currents float quietly and slowly away from each other, while those on shore are unable to perceive what it is draws them asunder.

There was great joy in the regiment at Feversham's return. He was a popular fellow—one of the most popular men we had; besides, the cause of his accident made more people to take an interest in him than might otherwise have been the case. He had ridden his unmanageable brute so pluckily and well, the ladies said he ought to have won; the men thought he might have done so, or at least come in second, but for the fall, and they pitied him accordingly. He got well rapidly, and wrote to his mother that he would not take his leave till the beginning of May, when he would meet her in London. No doubt that satisfied her, as she had laid her plans well for settling the matter between Claude and Mabel Prendergast that season.

She had asked and obtained permission to take Mabel out with her, the old people at The Poplars being thus spared the trouble of chaperoning their daughter, at which Mrs. Prendergast rejoiced greatly. She was a great deal too quiet and easy-going a woman to enjoy sitting up to unearthly hours at balls, or undergoing the slow torture of drums and crushes; and since Lady Feversham liked it, and intended Mabel for her son, why, she was welcome to take her whenever and wherever she chose. I think Claude knew that Mabel Prendergast was to be with his mother in London, and his feelings on the matter were curiously mixed. He hated himself whenever he was away from her for yielding to her fascination; he told himself again and again she was neither so good nor so true a woman as Gwendoline Bambridge, nor so dear to him either. He felt that, were he engaged to Mabel, even about to marry her, and that Gwendoline sent him a slip of paper with the one word "come" on it, he would leave his promised bride and go; yet, whenever he met her, he could not help following her and admiring her, and wishing to monopolize her attention, and discover whether she really cared for him or not.

In truth, it was the uncertainty that held him to her. He was inclined to be a little exacting, and he did not like to think that this girl with whom he had been thrown so much together, and for whom he felt a strange admiration that resembled love, but was not love, should not care for him a little also. I am sure Mabel Prendergast understood this far more clearly than he did; she played her cards accordingly, often laughing, no doubt, at the folly of her admirer, who had not wit enough to see it was curiosity and pique that held him captive, and not love. But Lady Feversham really believed that her son was beginning to care for this fascinating girl, and she was intensely pleased that it should be so. She wrote him long affectionate letters in the fullness of her joy, telling him so much about what Mabel said and did in them, that Claude would have been wearied had any of these reported sayings and doings been less enigmatical than the fair originator of them.

But that was the mystery: they were all just as sphinx-like as Mabel's pretty, faint smile, and the little friendly confidences with which she sometimes favored Claude, and that always had the effect of making him think, after every one of them, that he knew rather less of her than he had done before. Now, as formerly, Mabel's head dictated and governed the correspondence, and she knew her man so well that she could tell to a word how much to say, and how much to leave unsaid, to insure the effect on his feelings she desired.

At this time I used to wonder, when I saw how calm, and tranquil, and even happy Claude appeared, whether he ever thought of Gwendoline Bambridge. Among all my other business and pleasures, and even, what is more, among my vexations, I never forgot her for long; she was always coming into my mind, as she had looked that day when she had defended Claude against what she considered my unjust aspersions. I used to wonder what she would say could she see him now, and know that he looked forward with pleasure to being constantly with another woman during the London season.

She had really cared for him, but I had got to doubt his affection for her, as I had begun to doubt many things about him lately. Even if I met her, I should not dare to tell her so, nor even to let her know that we were no longer friends; she would be sure to think it was my fault, and perhaps would not care to talk to me when she knew I was no longer Claude's chief companion.

All this time Cecil Egerton was my great friend. I turned to him for sympathy and society when my cousin threw me over, and I got every day to like him more and more. It was as evident to me as to every one else, that he never would do any thing out of the ordinary way in his profession. His genius lay in quite a different direction from soldiering, and both he and I used to agree that it was very hard he had not been allowed to follow the bent of his inclination.

"I should have done something by this time, had I been an artist," he would say, regretfully, "and the woman I love might be proud when she heard my name mentioned. Now it will never say any thing to any ears but hers, and will consequently lose half its charm; for women are ambitious, are they not?"

"So I have heard," I replied, a little flattered

that one so much older than I should ask my advice on the subject. "But I did not know you cared about any one; you never told me you loved before. Who is it, if I may know?"

"Perhaps I was speaking of something in the future," he answered, with a happy smile; "perhaps I have not yet seen her, and only know that she will come some day. If I said that, you would not believe me," he added, correcting himself in his quick, irresolute way. "We all see three or four women we think we love before we get to the age of three-and-twenty, but rarely the right one, and I am speaking of the right one now."

"Then she does not yet exist?" I questioned, laughing. "She is a work of fiction until you meet her? Well, I hope she will be 'all your fancy painted her,' when you do come across her; for, do you know, I believe that fabricating of ideals is a most costly and disappointing process, and no wise woman would take a man that she knew indulged in it."

"But suppose she is not a fiction?—suppose she is very real, and very lovely, and much more than all my fancy painted her—what would you say then?"

"Then I should wish you joy, and I should ask you to tell me her name, that I may drink her health next time I indulge in 'the glorious vintage of Champagne.'"

"No, no," answered Cecil, with a smile, "you may drink her health as much as you like, but you will not know her name. At present she must have no name to you; remember, you are the only one of all my comrades to whom I have confided even this, so do not mention it."

And Cecil stuck to this resolution. Nothing I could say to him would induce him to tell me who she was, where he had met her, or what she was like, though I was sure he had her photograph somewhere about him. This time, at least, he displayed a decision of character for which I had never given him credit, and for which I honored him, though it balked my curiosity, which was strong on the subject, as I wanted to see what kind of woman Cecil admired.

I used to look at him enviously, after such a conversation, believing every fellow I met was happier in these matters than I; and I knew, or thought I knew, that this was the penalty of my abominable and disgusting youth.

"I know women are ambitious," Cecil would continue, "and she is more so than most women; she told me so herself, and said I must make haste and get on; as if one could get on by working at drill and routine work, like this we have so much of, in time of peace."

"I am sure I can't see why they should be ambitious," I replied; "there is nothing open to them to be ambitious about—or at least they can only get an opening after an amount of agitation, and toil, and trouble that must certainly frighten off any but very determined people. We have got the best of life, certainly, and I often think they must trust a great deal too much to the proverbial saying that women have the power of getting their own way, when they attempt to alter the existing state of things. Therefore, though some few may be ambitious—must be, to effect what they do—still the large majority can, merely from the dull monotony of their lives, have very little idea what the word means."

"It is forbidden fruit, and, in right of that, desirable," laughed Cecil. "I know from her lips that it is a fact, and she, if she has it more strongly developed in her mental system, is by so much wiser and more clever than the ordinary run of women."

I laughed a little, and answered mischievously, "Do you know, Cecil, I do not like the character you give of your future wife; I think she must be a caution, and that we shall see you by-and-by, when you are married, not daring to call your soul your own, out of respect to the superior capacities of Mrs. Egerton, who would doubtless be offended at any such self-assertion on your part."

"That is very fine," answered Egerton, a little nettled; and perhaps I had gone rather too far, for, owing to his weakness of character, the sketch I had drawn was not improbable, and no man likes to be told his wife will be master. "If you were to see her," he went on, "you would change your opinion; but I will not talk of the matter any more, or I shall be letting out secrets which I am bound not to disclose."

Saying this, he betook himself to whistling as a relief to his mind, and sat there going over the same tune, looking intensely happy, till he had roused me to a state of intense irritation, only to be soothed by immediate and violent action. It was quite bad enough that he should sit there with a dreamy, pleased smile on his face. When another fellow's prospects are not of the brightest, it is rather provoking to see a man so serenely and entirely pleased with his; but when, in addition to this, he will persist in whistling "Pop goes the weasel," or some equally charming and popular air, the matter becomes unbearable; and it was exactly these two things that Egerton was doing.

I got up and took him by the collar of the coat, and tried to lift him out of his chair; he was sitting by the fire in my room. This succeeded pretty well for a time, but then an unexpected difficulty presented itself; his legs were too long, and when I had raised him a certain height, he merely stood up, looked round the room, and asked me what I wanted of him.

"I want you to stop that abominable row," I said, crossly; "talk about something else, if you will not talk about her, but for goodness sake don't grin and whistle! One alone is aggravating, but the two combined are maddening."

"Is that all?" he said. "Oh! I will leave the room." And so saying, he made a few steps toward the door; then he came back, and sitting down again where he had been before, he went on: "By-the-bye, I want to speak to you. My uncle keeps bothering me to get my promotion, as if I could do it by an effort of my own will. Goodness knows I would have done it long ago if I could, but you see there's no chance of a vacancy, and so it is no good old Vansittart firing letters at me, telling me to offer fabulous sums, and get promotion at once. None of our fellows want to go out, or would do it for any thing I can offer. Then he wants me to exchange out of this regiment into some other, where I should have a better chance of getting steps, and so on. I do not want to leave, and I do not see that it is necessary. What do you advise?"

Of course I advised him to hang on with us and bide his time. There was certainly no present prospect of any steps going, but a few months might produce a change; besides, he was young and well off, and there was no reason he should be in a hurry.

He did not know, nor did I, that Mabel Prendergast was constantly at the Castle, and that she was to go out with Lady Feversham; but Mr. Vansittart knew all this, though he wisely kept it to himself, fearing that if Egerton heard it there might be a quarrel between them, and that, of all things, he wished to avoid. It was for this reason that he pressed on Cecil the importance of getting his promotion quickly, for then he would at once marry. Only when they were married would Mr. Vansittart feel sure that he had secured for his nephew the beautiful and fascinating heiress.

In spite of her beauty and her fascination, her mind was one made after the pattern of Mr. Vansittart's, and was of the kind with which he credited all the world. He had gauged it very accurately, and he was not far wrong in imagining that if Cecil did not make haste, she would slip through his fingers. She had begun to see that promotion in the army was not always rapid, or at least not sufficiently rapid for her impatience. She calculated that, under the most favorable circumstances, she should be a middle-aged woman before Egerton was made a colonel, and a very old woman before he gained the dignity of a general; even the K.C.B., which, she told herself, he ought to earn by that time, would not enable her to enjoy these honors when she had lost her youth and beauty. And he might never get any of these things she wished for. From all she could hear about him, she had horrible misgivings that he might be without any particular vocation for the army, with an incapacity for winning notice in it. If that were so, she feared he would retire in disgust, and relinquish all chances of the brilliant future she had dreamed for him.

Thus, all unknown by Cecil, she was turning her mind more and more away from him, fixing her thoughts on Lord Feversham's position and known talents, and stopping her ears to the pleading of her own heart, that at times protested vehemently against her mercenary schemes. At the same time, she wrote him long, affectionate letters, speaking of the pleasure she should have in seeing him again, and full of eagerness to know how much nearer he was to the promotion they both so much desired.

He believed in and trusted her implicitly, and took these letters to be the exponents of her entire heart and mind. He was as anxious as she, or more so, for his advancement; but he liked his regiment, and there was no necessity for him to leave it, as she would wait for years, if necessary, until he got the required rank. Besides, he had formed a scheme, which he did not tell even to her, for fear of weakening its power when it came to be put into action. He would get leave in the summer, go over to The Poplars, and then make another effort to persuade her to marry at once. Loving him as she did, it was natural to suppose that, when she saw how long it was likely they would have to wait, her resolutions would give way, and she would yield to his entreaties.

It was for this reason that he seemed so happy now—it was because of this hope that he smiled and whistled as he sat in my room that night, and it was in order that he might be confirmed in his decision that he appealed to me on the subject of his uncle's letters. He was such a good fellow! I liked him very much, and had even begun to think the weakness and indecision of character I had at first deplored was rather pleasant, as it led to his appealing to me and taking my advice on every possible subject. I find that is a kind of flattery no man is capable of resisting; in fact, one who could show such prodigious virtue as to do so would be a moral monster, whose acquaintance I should not care to cultivate.

<hr>

CHAPTER XXI.

GOSSIP.

ABOUT this time we had among us a fellow of the name of Morton, who had exchanged into the —th from another regiment. He was insignificant-looking—not from being a small man, as he was rather over, than under, the middle height —but because he was one of that class of people whose appearance is best described by the epithet, "washed out;" to add to that, he was of a quiet, unobtrusive nature. His close-cropped hair was of the color of tow, with none of the sheen and gloss on it that is generally seen on fair hair. One would fancy, to look at it, that it so far partook of the peculiarities of the man on whose head it grew as to avoid reflecting the sunlight, for fear of attracting observation. His face had been sunburned till it was a bad imitation of the color of his hair; his eyes were of a pale, watery blue, and his small, firmly shut mouth was shaded by a little tow-colored mustache. The whole face of this man, in spite of its insipid coloring, had a compressed, concentrated look that led me often to wonder what was concealed under such an insignificant exterior. With my usual habit of theorizing, I at once came to the conclusion it was a nature formed for great and secret evil, since so great a power of concealment as was expressed by the countenance had been bestowed upon it. Of course it was unfair and wrong of me so to prejudge the man, but I am rather subject to taking prejudices, both for and against, at first sight, and I had taken a very violent prejudice against this man.

I had often noticed his light-blue eyes slowly traveling round the table from one to another of us, as we sat chatting after mess, and at such times there would be a look of intense but carefully concealed cunning in his usually impassible face. I used to wonder of what he thought then, as he did not often join in our conversation, or, when he did join, his remarks were only of the average dull, commonplace type.

Though I disliked him, most of the others thought him a good fellow, but stupid; Egerton, who was inclined to be chums with him, used sometimes to scold me for my ill-nature and unbelief concerning him.

After he had been with us for a little time, some changes took place, resulting in his being appointed pay-master, temporarily, pending the arrival of some other man who was to have that post. He was a kind of man admirably fitted for such a charge, and he was much better liked in the place than his predecessor had been. In fact, he was much more appreciated and more thought of in that capacity than he had been before.

Time passed on, and he still held the appointment, some hitch having occurred with regard to the appointment of his successor.

A short time after Claude's accident, and when he had returned to Dublin and resumed his duties, I noticed that Captain Morton seemed very much put out about something: if one can use such an expression with regard to a man of his temperament, he seemed in low spirits. I saw him talking a good deal once or twice with Feversham and one or two of the senior officers, alone; but whenever any one to whom his conversation was not particularly addressed approached, he used to change the subject. However, after this had been going on for a few days, a rumor spread itself among us—how arising, I know not—that some of the regimental money in Captain Morton's hands had been stolen from him—or, rather, stolen out of a strong-box which he had in his room.

Egerton was the first person who told me, and I said immediately,

"It can not be true, you know. In the first place, I suppose the man never keeps it there but just the night or so before pay-day, and whoever stole it would have to understand that; in the second place, that box has a most formidable lock—I was looking at it a few days ago, when I went into his room to ask for something while he was talking to Feversham. I was greatly interested in the mechanism of it, for I thought it one of the best locks I had seen. It is some stupid, got-up story—one of the innumerable tales that spring up, no one knows how, without any apparent foundation. The famous teeth sown by Cadmus never produced such a prolific crop as the smallest fraction of reason for a report; more often gossip is like a fungus, shooting up in a night, without any visible seed whatever."

"Well, I don't know whether it is true or not," said Egerton. "I will ask him; some fellows told me, but they may have made a mistake, and taken up the matter wrongly."

"Very likely," I answered; "fellows who talk a great deal often do make mistakes of that kind; only then they generally make worse ones, for they fasten the misdemeanor on some particular individual. The beauty of what you have been telling me is its vagueness; no one in particular can feel injured, and every one in general may feel that for the honor of the regiment he would like to punch the particular head that originated this delightful bit of scandal."

"You are quite hot about it," said Egerton, looking at me with a little surprise in the expression of his handsome, melancholy eyes. "After all, no harm was meant; it is what any one might have said, without meaning to create scandal—if they had any foundation for it, that is to say."

"Of course if there is truth in it, that alters the matter; but I say it is absurd, and that there can be no truth in it. Ask Morton, next time you see him; I never talk to him, so I will not inquire: he always reminds me of an adder, with his curious, compressed, secretive expression. You have no such dislike to him, so you can find out all about it."

Cecil laughed. "What a queer, prejudiced, impulsive boy you are!" he said; "and what an immensity of unnecessary decision you waste on things of that kind! Once you have decided you don't like a person, you never change, but stick to it at all hazards: I must do you the justice to say, it is the same with your likings; they are quite as strong and as constant. But, you know, if I was to take up a prejudice I should reconsider it, and change my mind twenty times a day, and finally end by avoiding the person, in order to avoid the worry of having to decide about him. Not a very good way of getting on, is it? but it suits me; however, I am not as fickle in my likings—there I can be as true as you. I think the reason why I can not dislike heartily, is because it always seems unkind; then too, perhaps, just when I am most provoked, I remember I myself am as aggravating or distasteful to the person with whom I am irritated as he is to me. Now in liking there is never any fear of doing wrong; it must be right; even if you are deceived, and the person you liked turns out badly, I think it is better for you that you should have cared for him than that you should have judged him harshly without cause."

"That is a hit at my prejudices, on the Dr. Fell principle. I am sure you are right, and your kind nature enables you to do as you say; but a fellow like me would explode some day if he went about smothering impulses, and trying to turn them into what they ought to be, instead of what they are."

"For goodness sake, Madcap, don't get any more explosive than you are naturally, or it will be fearfully dangerous for us quiet fellows! Even with all your safety-valves open, you are rather a touch-me-not person at times; but you have one good quality—it is over in a minute, as the passionate husband in one of Leech's pictures says to his wife, after he has smashed every article of furniture in their sitting-room."

"You always make fun of a fellow," I answered, trying not to laugh; "but I am sure you can not say I smash the furniture of the rooms. I never go beyond words, do I?"

"What do you say about that business in James's rooms the other day?—wasn't it something like what I have been describing?"

I held my tongue. I do not think he should have brought the matter up, but as he did speak about it, I may as well tell what it was. A few days before there had been a whole lot of us sitting in James's room: we were smoking and talking, as it was a wet day, and we did not care about going out. After a time Mayleigh got at me, chaffing me, and making fun of me in a manner I could not stand. I bore it for a while tolerably, though becoming gradually more savage; but at length I got into such a passion that I seized a book lying near me and shied it at his head. He ducked just in time, or he would have got a knock that would have taught him not to chaff me for a while; and the book, passing over him, just caught a handsome bronze statuette on the chimney-piece, a thing James set great store by, and knocking it down, it was broken into several pieces on the fender.

I was dreadfully sorry when I saw what I had done, for James is a good fellow, and I knew he was distressed at the loss of his favorite ornament, though he laughed and tried to turn the matter off. I was sobered, and Mayleigh, I think, was a little taken aback, for he left me alone for the rest of the evening.

Since then I have been very careful, and have not been in as bad a temper again, though Mayleigh, knowing I am watching myself, delights in being fearfully aggravating. When he gets too bad I turn round quickly and look at him: I think he has got now to know by my eye when I am dangerous, for he gives over then; but it is very hard keeping quiet when one has a fellow like that always at one, and Cecil, knowing how I am tried, should not have alluded to the affair.

I told him so after I had thought over the matter for a few minutes, and then he said I had a good deal to put up with, and he ought not to have mentioned it, only the likeness to the passionate husband overcame him, and he could not help pointing it out.

I mention all this to show that I did take a good deal of chaff from them, and was not nearly such a fire-eater as they wished to make out. But there are some things I will not allow myself to be laughed at about.

"Have you not got a horse to sell?" asked Egerton suddenly. "I heard you wanted to part with that pretty brown mare, Twilight. I have not got a mount now, and I have taken a fancy to her. She seemed such a clever huntress the day I saw her out with you at the Wards'; though the hunting season is over, I should like to get her; she will come in useful next season, and do my quiet summer work besides."

"Yes, I will sell her," I replied. "I am sending Blackfoot home to Longhurst for the summer; we have splendid stabling there, and the most delightful boxes for summering horses. He deserves a rest, after winning that race so pluckily. I never thought he would have done it so easily, though I knew he would not be far behind at the finish. But I do not want to keep Twilight; she is a very good little mare, and I can recommend her, but I only bought her for the season, and always intended to sell her as soon as it was over. You can have her for eighty guineas, which I think very reasonable for an animal of her class."

"I need not ask you if she is all right," said Cecil; "or, rather, I suppose I ought to do so. But the fact is, you are the only man I know whose word I would take about a horse, and I do believe yours implicitly."

"Well, I think you may," I replied, laughing. "The only point on which I would mislead any one is whether the animal is gentle or not; for it is a fact that I have sold a horse that I considered as gentle and as kind as a horse could be, and that I was told afterward was a most dangerous and unmanageable brute. Of course I found out the people who had got him were afraid of him, and he bullied them, that was all. Now as to this mare Twilight, she is sound, and a perfectly trained, safe fencer, but, what is curious in a horse that does jump well, she can not bear to do it, and, unless you watch her when you are coming to your first fence she will balk. Give her a touch of the spur as you come near it, and she will take it, and go well for the rest of the day; let her balk, and it will take you a great deal of trouble to get her right again."

"Very well," answered Cecil, "I think I shall be able to manage her. And we may as well conclude the purchase: come up to my rooms presently and we will do the business part of the transaction, and then I shall take possession of her. I think her such a pretty creature, and up to a good deal of weight."

"Yes, indeed," I said. "That is one reason that I am parting with her. I ride ten stone twelve, and she is up to between fourteen and fifteen stone. If she was quite thorough-bred, you would not get her for double the money I am giving her to you for now."

A few hours after, going up to Cecil's room, he gave me the money, a good deal of it being in gold, with some silver and notes.

"I have been lately paid some money that was owing to me," he said, laughing, when I looked astonished at his producing all this out of an old battered leather desk that any evil-minded person might have opened easily. "I am not accustomed to keep money in this way, but having got it, and intending to buy the horse, I kept it by me."

"As I shall do," I answered. "I always like to have something ready to my hand in case I want it; to tell you the truth, though my father always gives me a very liberal allowance, I sometimes overdraw my account. I have done so just now; but I do not intend to put it straight with this. I just write and tell the governor that he must pay in some more to my account, and he does so, though I get a lecture now and then if I am supposed to have been too extravagant. Really, you know, this will go a very little way. Talk of money making itself wings—I say wings are nothing to it. I believe it first invented the electric telegraph."

Cecil was pleased with his purchase, which I was glad of, because people so rarely are satisfied with horses, that it is a very disagreeable thing, as a rule, selling one to a friend. But I knew, when he bought her, that if he could manage her she would please him; and as it happened, they got on very well together.

It was now the early part of May, and consequently beginning to get woefully stupid in Dublin. All who were worth knowing had taken themselves off to London for the season, and we were left pacing the pavement in Grafton Street, or looking out of the windows of the club in Stephen's Green, without a chance of catching a glimpse of the pretty faces we used to admire, and with whose owners we had so often danced at the Viceregal and elsewhere, earlier in the year.

It was very stupid work, and I think it was as a relief from the prevailing dullness that about this time we took to giving card-parties among ourselves. Nearly every evening some of us would assemble in the rooms belonging to one of the party (we took the duty of entertaining in turns), and would then pass the time at play. Sometimes it was loo, sometimes *trente et un*, and so on, but it was always a game that admitted of a good deal of gambling.

I am sure I do not know why I attended these affairs; cards were always antipathetic to me, and if the dullness of the town bored me, the evening game would have bored me still more, but for the companionship it gave me. All our merriest and most amusing fellows would be assembled there, and by not going I should miss so much mirth and laughter, so much gossip and scandal, which, when it did not affect the regiment, I am ashamed to confess, amused me as much as it did the others.

I had nearly forgotten to say that Cecil Egerton had inquired of Captain Morton the truth of the strange rumor which was steadily gaining ground. On his first alluding to the subject, Morton shut his mouth with a snap that reminded one of a steel-trap; but presently, thinking better of it, he went on to say that it was quite true—that several small sums of money had been missing, and quite lately a larger amount. But, he added, he had his eyes open, and would soon catch the offender. He did not wish the matter spoken of, as it might render the culprit cautious, but if matters were left as they were, he would lay his hand on him before long.

"Darrell says," continued Egerton, "that it is a most intricate lock. He was examining it one day when he was in the room with you and Feversham, and he says he can not understand how any one who has not the key can open it."

"I do not think Darrell knows much about the matter," replied Morton, coolly, "and he has no business giving his opinion when it was not asked."

Morton spoke sharply, for, as is often the case, my dislike of him recoiled on my own head.

"He did not mean any harm," resumed Egerton, apologetically. "He and I were talking together, and he merely mentioned that. Do you suspect any one? Have you any clue?"

"I may have my suspicions," replied Morton, almost rudely; "but it is better not to tell them. Things get talked of, and they go round, and every body hears them, and finally the man who has been doing it all would get to know I was on the watch, and would take care of himself. No, I shall keep my own counsel."

"Keep it by all means," answered Egerton, rather nettled by the other's tone; "but perhaps you will not mind telling me whether you suspect any of the men of the regiment. I hope not; it would be so unpleasant."

"The men of the regiment," laughed Morton, satirically; "so you think that would be unpleasant, do you? What should you say if it went higher than that?" and without waiting for an answer he moved away, leaving poor Egerton standing quite bewildered, thinking over those concluding words.

It was not possible, he thought, that Morton could really suspect any among themselves; he must have said it for a joke, but if so, it was a dreadfully bad joke, and in his quiet, uncertain way Egerton felt indignant. At first he thought he would come and tell me; I would sympathize in his indignation, and I would also tell him whether there could possibly be any chance of such a dreadful thing being true. But then, before he had made half a dozen steps in the direction in which he expected to find me, he changed his mind. It was quite possible, he thought, that I might get into a passion, and tell Morton, next time I saw him, that he was slandering us; that would be sure to create an unpleasantness, and make matters worse between Morton and me than they already were. It was very provoking that people would be quarrelsome and passionate, and it was very annoying to hear hints of the nature of this last one, without being able to find out if there was any foundation for them or not.

If the world, and the people in it, were not quite up to Mr. Vansittart's standard of badness, still they were sufficiently aggravating and incomprehensible at times, and very worrying to a man like Cecil, who was straightforward both from principle and a laziness of character that made it too great a trouble to go roundabout when he could go straight.

The end of his perplexity was the usual end of every thing that annoyed him—he left it to chance to direct his actions, and decide whether he should tell me or not.

Chance decided that he should tell me, as any one might have betted, with perfect certainty of winning. On all subjects but the one Cecil's nature demanded a confidant, and even on that one he had told me all but the name. I was extremely angry at Morton's having suggested that any of us could be implicated in such an affair. "A common theft—why, he is quite as likely to have done it as any of the others!" I cried, angrily. "I wonder how he dare give such liberty to his tongue, even if he thought it. You should have pitched into him, Cecil. I can tell you he would have had had cause to remember it if he said such a thing to me."

"I have no doubt he would," answered Cecil, a smile dawning on his troubled face; "but you see I have not your energy of character; besides, you know, though I believe he meant that as a bit at us, still he did not say any thing we could take hold of. What is the good of getting into rows unnecessarily? Promise me you will not say any thing to Morton, or he will pitch into me for having told you."

"Very well," I answered, feeling a little surly; "if you like to let that kind of thing pass, I can not help you; but you see the fellow will not speak so to me."

"Try him," Cecil replied, laughing. He had not repeated what Morton had said of me, not wishing to make mischief; indeed, in his good-nature, and wish to see us all friends, he often tried to persuade me that Morton was well disposed toward me, if I would let him show it. I used not to mind him; I knew it was a result of his overamiable disposition, that he took every thing at its best, and that, if by any chance Morton made a civil remark about me, he at once concluded the man was anxious to be on good terms with me, but was frightened off by my very apparent dislike.

We dropped the subject then, and I attended card-parties in Morton's room, just as I did in Egerton's, or James's, or in any of the other fellows' rooms; and all the time I did so, I used to grumble at their stupidity, and think I had much rather be whirling down St. Patrick's hall, with a good partner, than sitting there with a handful of stupid spotted pasteboard before me.

The money on the game was the only thing that redeemed it from perfect insipidity in my eyes—and, let me confess, I liked to win. Not that I cared one bit more about the money, I fancy, than any other fellow there; but because, in any thing I undertook, I could not bear to be beaten. Thinking cards dull, as I did, the ungovernable desire to be first in any pursuit I took up made me learn to play them well; whenever there was any head-work or skill in the matter, that would, in a measure, make me take an interest in what I was doing; but those horrid games of chance were my abomination: even winning at them gave me no satisfaction, because there was nothing but blind chance to thank for it when you did win.

Claude used to join us too. He had not yet gone on leave, though he was going very shortly. I fancy he had more of the gambler in him than I, for he appeared to enjoy the thing, and played rather high occasionally.

We were all in Morton's rooms one evening, for an entertainment of this kind. The business of the evening had not yet commenced: we were standing about talking, and Morton, who, I think, was rather excited, and was speaking more than usual, suddenly led of his own accord to the subject of the stolen money, about which he had before avoided talking.

"I have my eye on the culprit," he said, "and I intend to make an example of him. I have set a trap for him, and he has fallen into it. Very shortly he will be discovered before all eyes."

"Some poor beggar of a servant, I suppose?" said Claude, carelessly. "Of course, if he is discovered and brought to trial, the authorities will make an example of him without asking your advice. I suppose it is wrong, and soft-hearted of me, but I often feel sorry for people of that kind when they get into trouble. We have no conception, can form very little idea of what their temptations may be, and often are. And then one fall, if it is discovered, gets them looked upon as black sheep for the rest of their lives; whereas, if one of us were capable of doing such a thing, we should probably not make the case public, but only force him to sell out quietly; and he would then be at liberty to make a fresh beginning, with no heavier punishment for his sin than that. The burdens of this world are very unequally divided, and, I do believe, often weigh heaviest on those who have least courage to bear them."

"How do you make that out?" asked Cecil. "'The back is fitted to the burden,' we know is a proverb; but your theory does not agree with the crystallized essence of the wisdom of all ages, as it is thus handed down to us. Where would the weak ones of the world be, if it were they who were obliged to carry the heaviest burdens?"

Claude laughed.

"You think you have got me into a corner, Egerton, and you are right, in a kind of way. I can not explain what I mean, though I feel it. The ones who are most likely to give way under trouble are often sent the heaviest trials to bear. Perhaps it is their own disposition that makes it heavier to them than to other people—and yet that can not be the cause altogether. Let me be personal, and I will illustrate my meaning. Of the two of us, I should be, by most people, considered the strongest in will and character—indeed, I fancy I am very strong that way. But I may venture to predict that through life you will meet with greater misfortunes than I shall. Whether you will succumb under them, or whether you will fight against them boldly and bravely, remains to be proved; but that will be your fate, I am sure."

"Your opinion on those matters differs entirely from mine," I said boldly; while Cecil answered gloomily,

"You are rather of the character of Job's comforters. That is a cheerful prediction with which to begin the evening; and I am not even particularly fortunate at cards, to make up for the ill-luck I am destined to have in other things. Rather hard lines, is it not?"

"Never mind that," cried Morton; "let us get to business. But you never asked me how I intended to catch the culprit. It is rather an old trick, but if it serves my turn that will do. I had marked the money that was left in my box after I first found that some was gone. The marked money is missing now, and I shall be sure to trace it in a day or two."

Feversham laughed heartily.

"What an idea!" he said. "You will have to get a search-warrant, and examine the contents of the pockets of all the men in the regiment. It will be an arduous undertaking, and I would rather you did it than I."

"A search-warrant is not needed," replied Morton; "I shall find it out without doing that. Besides, I never said the culprit was among our men; indeed, Egerton can tell you I expressed a different opinion to him. 'You must look higher,' I said; didn't I, Egerton?"

As he appealed thus to Cecil, he laughed a most harsh, unmusical laugh, full of meaning and irony. Cecil looked at him rather contemptuously, and I put my hands into my pocket, to keep them off him. I had no need to champion us now, for Feversham came a step nearer to Morton, and, fixing his handsome dark eyes sternly on the pale cunning ones of Captain Morton, said,

"An allusion such as you have made can not be taken in jest. Do you wish me to take it in earnest?"

Morton seemed a little cowed, for he shrunk back, saying,

"I meant no offense to you, Captain Feversham. Wait a while, and you will see I never make mistakes, or say things rashly, as you know."

"If you spoke of any of us, you might just as well have spoken of me. Until one of them is proved to be wrong, any slur passed upon them is passed upon me also. Please remember this, Captain Morton, as my temper is short at times."

"There are many short tempers here, I can tell you," interrupted James. "Do not let us have any of your joking again; we will none of us take it, any more than Feversham."

Morton looked round at all of us, with a cynical sneer.

"I did not mean to offend the honorable company," he said. "Will that explanation do? Because, if so, we had better get to work, and not remain bickering here the whole evening."

A good many of us looked at each other in doubt. Morton's apology, if it was meant for such, was not of the most civil kind, and did not seem either as if meant. We all felt ourselves outraged by the suspicions he had hinted at, and all were sure that none of their comrades could be guilty of such a deed as this theft of money; perhaps I alone of all present, when mentally exonerating my companions, put in a proviso—except the man who accuses them. Not that I really for one minute believed him capable of any thing of the kind; but I was actuated to some such sentiment by my dislike for him, and my remembrance of an old belief among us in our school-days, that he who accused others of any thing very bad must be capable of such an act himself.

But, though there were many black looks, it

seemed to be decided by common consent that no more notice should be taken of Morton's innuendo, and we sat down together, in no very pleasant humor with our host, though he was exerting himself to the utmost to try to do away with the bad impression he had created.

CHAPTER XXII.

AT A CARD-TABLE.

WE sat down and began to play. I remember well our game that night was loo. It was a game which I disliked rather more than most others, and the rest of our set liked it, so we had it very often. I was always unfortunate in the cards I got, and, as we played moderately high, I sometimes lost a good deal. Then I would be provoked with myself for having been beguiled into joining in what I really did not care about; not that I cared much for the loss of the money, but that I would rather have spent it on something else. Money lost at cards is so clean gone, seems so deliberately wasted—or, rather, it is utterly, but not at all deliberately wasted, for more people lose by getting too excited to know what they are about than by any thing else.

Whether I was excited or not on that particular evening, I do not know; I think it is more likely I was obstinate. I used to take an obstinate fit sometimes, and determine to go on playing until I should win, and I made it a kind of point of honor not to be daunted by ill-luck. On this occasion I lost more than I had ever done before, and what annoyed me more than the losing was that Morton won all that I had to pay up. Of course it was fortune of war, and I could not blame him, but I scowled at him angrily, as I handed over gold and silver to him perpetually. I was aggravated, too, to notice that he examined the money he received carefully, though slyly, as if afraid of being observed, and all he received from me he placed on one side, and the rest of his winnings on the other. I had brought down a good deal of money with me for the evening, knowing that I should probably lose : it was some of what Egerton had paid me for the horse. But I soon came to an end of my stock of ready money, and in the end had to borrow, in order to finish the evening.

I saw Claude look at me once or twice, as if he was rather surprised at my recklessness, but we hardly ever spoke now, and so he said nothing. We sat up late, till between one and two, I think, and I was beginning to get too sleepy for any thing to keep me awake, when we rose from the table and prepared to leave. Before we had finished talking and putting up our money, however, Morton went to the door, opened it, looked out, and finally shutting it and putting his back against it, said, " I am sorry to be obliged to return to a subject that seemed so disagreeable to all when I mentioned it just now; but since I spoke to you before, it has become my duty, my painful duty, to allude to the matter again, and to point out the culprit to you. It is for you then to decide what shall be done to him."

" Really this is too bad !" I exclaimed, my anger awakening me thoroughly. " We all told you before we would not have you hinting that one of our number was a thief. If you have any thing to say, say it plainly, but mind you will have to prove it."

" You crow very loud, Darrell, for a fellow who has lost so much as you have this evening," answered Morton, pointing to the pile of my losings, which he had carefully set on one side. " See, he has lost this, as you all know, and yet he is not sobered enough to keep quiet and not speak till he is spoken to, which will, I have no doubt, be soon enough."

His tone was insufferably impertinent and supercilious, and I felt an insane desire to give him a good pommeling. I restrained myself, however, and replied, " If I can afford to lose, what is it to you whether I do it or not, and why should I be down-hearted ? If I can not afford it, it is still no business of yours, so long as you are paid."

" What is it you have to say, Morton ?" asked Feversham, coldly ; " we can not all stand here to watch you and Darrell sparring. But mind, as the boy said, you had better bring forward no charge unless you can prove it."

" What do you consider proof ? If the marked money is found on him, will that do ?"

" Unless he can explain how he got it, and prove that he received it from some other person, it will naturally go far toward condemning him : indeed you will then have ground for your assertions, and I suppose we might have to believe him. But why put such a case ?" continued Feversham, impatiently. " I do not believe you will be able to find your marked money on any one here."

" Do not be so sure," sneered Morton, getting defiant, as he began to feel sure of his ground ; " it may come nearer home to you than you think."

" What do you mean, you scoundrel !" cried Feversham, seizing Morton by the collar of the coat. " Do you dare to insinuate that I could do such a thing ?" and in his passion Claude shook Morton as though he had been a rat in the jaws of a terrier, while I grinned with delight at seeing him so treated.

" Take your hands off me !" cried Morton, angrily ; " I said nothing about you, and unless the cap fitted, there was not the least necessity for you to wear it. But though it is not you, it is a relation of yours. That is the fellow !" he continued, pointing to me.

This time I did not pause or think—I sprang at him, and struck him a blow with the back of my hand across the mouth, saying, " Take that, liar !"

I struck him hard, and for a minute, between pain and bewilderment, he was unable to speak, while all the others stood round looking at us in amazement. Claude alone retained his presence of mind, and seizing me by the arms, as I was about to renew the attack, drew me back, saying, in a low voice, " Keep quiet ; violence will make your case worse ; I will see that you have fair play."

" Then you do not believe that of me, Claude ?" I cried, almost pleadingly. I knew he had thought badly of me, and it seemed to me that, if he did not believe this of me, neither would any one else ; besides, his kind voice, his speaking soothingly to me, now that I was in trouble and wanted help—all this brought up to my mind my old boyish adoration for him, and I felt again as I used to do in the times so long past, that I could go through fire and water, to use an expressive saying among the country people, for his sake.

Before Claude could answer, Morton, boiling with rage, had caught up my words, and answered them. "Not believe you did it, you young miscreant!" he said; "whether he wishes to do so or not, he will have to believe it, for I can prove it. Come here, all of you, and look at this money; do you see all round the rim inside a deep scratch, as if it had been cut with a knife? That is exactly what has been done, and I was the person who did it. You yourselves saw Darrell give me this money; you all see how it has been marked. He has had the audacity to pay me back a good deal of it, you may observe, by way of settling his debts at cards; but there is more to be found yet. I must insist on searching his rooms."

"Really, Morton, you are acting a great deal too hastily," said Claude, coming forward and speaking in a strange, stiff manner, very unlike his usual way of talking. I could not tell whether he was angry with Morton, and grieved for me, or whether he was inclined to believe there was truth in the accusation and be down upon me. After an instant's pause, during which Morton looked at him defiantly, imagining he was going to take my part, he continued: "I do not wonder Darrell was annoyed at your insulting words. You must know that it is extremely probable he received it from some one else. At any rate you should first have pointed out to him that it was some of the stolen money, and then have asked him how it came into his possession."

"I shall act in whatever way I think fit in such a case as this," answered Morton, "and shall take any measures I may see to be right."

"Then you are extremely likely to get yourself into trouble some of these days," said Claude haughtily, drawing off from Morton, with a contemptuous expression, and placing himself by me, in a manner that seemed to say, "At least I will see fair play."

There was a short pause, during which several fellows took up the money and examined it. I experienced a curious sensation as I stood there by Feversham waiting for what should come next. I felt as if I was far away, at an immense distance in space, removed from this troubled scene, and that down the incalculable length of vista I saw dimly the eager, curious faces that crowded round the table, and glanced alternately from me to Morton, and the pile of coin that had caused this uproar. Low and distant, yet clear and distinct, I could hear their voices interrupted by a kind of throbbing in my head, that was caused by the quick pulsations of my passionate youthful blood: what struck me most of all was one figure, that seemed nearer to me than the others, and in whose eyes there was a hesitating, uncertain, and yet anxious look.

This figure was Egerton's; he had come nearer to me, after he had heard me accused of such a pitiful crime, as though he wished to show me by that action that he did not believe it; and all the time he looked at me with such troubled eyes, that seemed to be asking some question he would not put into words. His look haunted me; it contained a petition I felt sure, but— what petition? The money that I had paid down to Morton, and that was marked, I had received from Egerton, in payment for the mare Twilight. I had told him, laughing, that I intended to keep it by me for any emergency; and he must have known pretty well that it was this money which was causing the present disturbance.

Yet he did not come forward to say what he knew of it, and the questioning gaze he turned on me seemed to plead with me not to reveal that he had any thing to do in the matter. I could not, and would not, think ill of him; yet I wondered he did not avow the coin had come to me from him. At any rate, he wished to keep that fact a secret, and by me, at least it would not be divulged. I met his gaze openly and steadily, smiling to him to encourage him, and show him that he had nothing to fear from my telling how I came by the money. My look seemed to re-assure him, for after meeting it he turned away and examined the mark on one of the sovereigns.

Then Morton spoke.

"Notwithstanding your championing your cousin, Feversham, I shall think it my duty to search his room. But first we will hear what account he has to give of the way in which he became possessed of the money."

"I have no account to give," I answered stoutly, looking him boldly in the face. The charge was absurd, and I did not feel in the least frightened, and so I showed by my manner.

"It came to me through other hands, of course, or else I should not have it; but I am not in the habit of keeping a memorandum of every sum of money I receive, and who pays it to me. I deny your charge emphatically, and think you are a fool for having entertained such an idea for a minute. That is all. Now come and search the room if you like."

Here Claude put his hand on my shoulder.

"If you know who gave you that money, tell him," he said, in a low tone. "It is better to prove him in the wrong if you can. He is determined to give you trouble, and you may save yourself a great deal of annoyance if you are able to show at once how you came by it."

"That it is not possible for me to do, Claude," I answered. "I got it some way in change, I know; but at any rate, my denial is enough, or ought to be enough, and I will not attempt any other defense."

Claude shook his head as if he did not agree with me, and Morton looked at me with a fiendish exultation in his eye: he had me in his power, he fancied, and I could see he thought so by the triumphant malignity of his expression. He waited for a minute, as though giving me time for my defense; then, seeing I remained silent, he said,

"Let us come now to his room. We shall soon see if he has got any more of such ill-gotten gains in hiding."

Again I would have struck him could I have got at him, and this time I should have stuck to him and not let him off so easily; but Claude, fearing what might happen, put his arm within mine and held me back.

"The innocent are patient," he whispered. "Wait till he has committed himself to some course against which you can protest when your innocence is proved. Let him search; it will be all the better for you that he should do so, and will, when nothing is found, produce a good impression on those who would condemn you if you were to resist."

"But suppose he does find something?" I said; "it is quite probable he may. I keep a lot of cash about me always, and wherever I got that I may have got more. I can not say for certain that he may not find plenty more marked coin."

I could feel Claude's hand that rested on my arm tremble a little as I spoke, and I continued:

"If you begin to think badly of me, if you doubt my word and regret the course you have taken, leave me. I have courage to face this, I hope, and will stand or fall alone, as a brave man should."

"I won't leave you," he answered, "unless matters turn out worse than I expect. Only proof could make me believe you guilty, and proof you could not expect me to disbelieve."

"I think, in that case, you had better leave me now," I said. "This man is determined the theft shall be brought home to me, and has, no doubt, taken his measures accordingly. You would believe any case he has trumped up; unless you have an implicit and unswerving confidence in me that nothing can shake, you had better avoid the disgrace of having championed a losing cause."

I spoke bitterly and shook off his arm with sudden passion as I spoke. I had been too hasty in believing him to be the true friend I had expected, and the revulsion of feeling at finding him doubtful and lukewarm drove me to cast him off altogether.

He looked at me very reproachfully, very sadly. "You have none of the confidence of innocence," he said, "and yet I can not believe it of you."

"Do you expect me to be confident, when I know that man has laid his plans to convict me? Such things have been done before as proving an innocent man guilty, and may be done again; therefore I can not have any feeling of security. In this case innocence can not save me: only proving guilt in another would give me a chance."

"Is there any other, then, whom you think guilty?—who is it?"

"Ask Morton," I answered, shortly; "he seems to know so much about it, perhaps he knows that too, if he would only tell it."

We had by this time arrived at my rooms, and forthwith the search was to commence.

"There is no need for your doing that kind of thing," I cried indignantly, as I saw Morton looking into a box in which I kept a little leather case containing two photographs of Gwendoline Bambridge — how obtained it is unnecessary to state.

"Only a woman's portrait," said Morton, throwing it on the table with a coarse laugh. "Mr. Darrell has taste, it seems, for she is uncommonly good-looking. Will you introduce me to her, if I let you off free from this scrape?"

He had thrown the case open on the table, and Claude, standing nearer to it than I was, saw of whom it was the photograph. I could notice his hand clench, and the stern expression of his face grow sterner, as he listened to Morton's mocking words. Then, before I, choked and overcome by passion, could speak or step forward, he put out his hand and shut the case, saying,

"If duty gives you the right to search Darrell's rooms, it does not give you the right to be insulting, remember that; remember, too, I am your senior. Do not force me to show you that I will not allow you to outstep the limits of your duty."

"Here are my keys," I said, handing them to Feversham when I could speak. "In my desk you will find all my money, and you are at liberty to examine it. As for Captain Morton, our day of reckoning will come, of that I feel certain, and then, I hope, he will have occasion to remember the way in which he has treated me to-night."

I spoke coldly and proudly; I looked calmly and quietly at the faces around me, but it was by an effort I did it. I began to see that this was not an ebullition of rage and malice, working on a vague surmise, without plan or premeditation, but a deep-laid, long-concocted scheme; and I had no hope of escape from so cunning and crafty an enemy as this. I had not yet had time to realize what would be the consequences to me if this crime was brought home to me; I was too much occupied with the degradation it was to me that any one should think it possible he could, with any chance of proving it, accuse me of such a deed. There was the improbability. In the first place, I was rich; in the second place, I had never had any fondness for money, as money, that should lead me to try to accumulate it. Surely my comrades, knowing me, would laugh at the matter as absurd—would detect the spite that actuated the charge.

I looked at them as I thought thus. They were all grouped around my desk, busy examining the money that had been found there, and most of their faces wore a grave, constrained expression, as numerous marked pieces were discovered. Only Egerton did not join them—did not seem to care to take part in the search. He appeared to be in deep thought, but now and then fixed his eyes on me with that earnest, questioning gaze I could by no means comprehend. Then I heard Morton's harsh voice say,

"There must be more somewhere. Of course this is enough to criminate him—in my eyes, at least—but we had better search the room thoroughly, before we leave, for the thirty pounds that has not yet been discovered."

I thought he did it with a desire to prolong the annoyance he knew I experienced at seeing him handling my treasures, and so I sat down and pretended not to notice him; but I knew afterward he had other motives prompting him to continue the search.

He displayed marvelous ingenuity in this kind of domiciliary visit, so much so that at length, thoroughly aggravated, I called out: "I should say Captain Morton had been in the French police before he entered our army; he seems intended by nature as a spy. Only I think if he had ever made acquaintance with the police at all, it must have been in not quite so pleasant a manner as if he had been one of them."

Morton glared at me for a minute, and then answered: "I shall have the pleasure of seeing you in the position you allude to, some day, I hope. I shall not drop this, you may be sure, but will work it out to the uttermost."

"So I see," I replied, leaning back carelessly on the sofa. There was a good deal of bravado in my manner and attitude, but I could not help it in speaking to this man; he used to irritate me beyond all endurance. But as I answered him now, I could perceive that already several of my old companions looked coldly on me, and regarded my attempt at cheerfulness as a proof of hardened guilt.

I ceased speaking suddenly when I saw this, for among the number of those who so looked at me was Claude. For a moment the full magnitude of the danger, the enormity and depth of the disgrace that menaced me, flashed upon me, and I felt overwhelmed. Something seemed to rise in my throat and choke me, and the blood surged upward to my head in a blinding, tumultuous wave that rendered me dizzy and confused, and prevented me for a time from seeing what was going on around me.

I lost consciousness that any one was in the room with me; friends or foes might have seen my anguish then—it was all one to me; but they were too busy looking for more proofs of my guilt, and I was alone with my agony, though in a room full of people.

Can you understand what it was to me, that the man I had loved and reverenced above all others, the man who knew every thought of my heart, every impulse of my mind, "mine own familiar friend," should have turned his back on me and left me in my direst need? That he should have known me so little, cared for me so lightly, as to believe this terrible charge? No words can tell the bitterness of that moment; it was one of those that fortunately seldom occur even once in a lifetime. Alas for the boasted courage of a brave man, it would not long endure such trials as that! it endures them but poorly at any time, I think. I know that in my case, though I recovered sufficiently in a few minutes to meet the eyes that I expected every minute turned on me, I had no longer at heart any courage at all, and told myself it had been better for me I had never been born than that I should have lived for such an hour as this.

It seemed to me then as if all the coming years flashed before me, and I saw myself lonely and miserable, living always a blighted man, under the shadow of a great disgrace, branded with a tarnished name. I who had been so proud of our noble name—who had exulted in the honor and good report of many gallant ancestors—who, protected by the shadow of their fame, had made my way fearlessly so far in the world, dreaming that no act or word of mine should ever sully an unspotted shield, that no disgrace through deed of mine should darken the glorious renown of other days.

And now how was it? I could have groaned, but that there were malicious ears near to hear and glory in my misery. I could have wept bitter tears of outraged feeling, but that there were cruel eyes turned on me, that would have taken this as a cowardly shrinking from the consequences of sin. I tried to bear up; if every thing went against me, there would be time enough for grief and anguish by-and-by—all life, in fact; if I escaped, if the innocence that I knew to be mine was proclaimed openly, sorrow would be wasted; I would be strong, I would be patient, though it was hard to find either strength or patience under the circumstances.

But in this, at least, I would be master—I would govern my own thoughts, if I could control nothing else; and, full of this determination, I set myself to think of other things. But of what could I think? Of course my mind turned naturally to Gwendoline, but the only idea connected with her that presented itself was, What would she think of this? Would she believe my innocence, or would she be tempted, by her love for Claude, to take his side in the matter? I was torturing myself with these questions, to which I could return no possible answer, when a bustle at the other end of the room attracted my attention.

I heard exclamations of pained surprise, and looking toward the others, saw that they were all gathered round Captain Morton, examining some money he was showing them. He was standing near my easy-chair; he had taken up the cushion of the seat, and, as well as I could see, had ripped it open.

"Halloo!" I cried, seeing this, "I don't believe your powers give you the right of tearing up my furniture, and I object. Put down that cushion, if you please."

"We will, with pleasure," replied Captain Morton, in an ironically polite manner. "We have found out all we want from it. The covering of it was a little torn, which led me to examine it, and there I found the missing thirty pounds. It was an ingenious hiding-place, and if you had sat down in it, instead of on the sofa, you might have saved yourself, perhaps. What made you be such a fool?"

"Because I did not know as much about it as you did," I answered; "that money was put there, and you were the person who did it!"

"The money was put there, no doubt, or else it would not be there now," sneered Morton; "but I should like to know how, if it was I put it there, you came to be spending it. There is another fifty pounds, that was taken little by little at first, before I was aware there was a thief among us: your people will have to pay that up. I made it good, and took my time to catch the culprit; but for that I should not have found you out now. Your people, I imagine, will be willing to pay higher than that to keep it dark. I should have thought your allowance was sufficiently good to remove all temptation to theft."

The words were hardly out of his mouth before he measured his length on the ground. "Now," I said, looking round on all the stern, condemning faces around me, "that man is a liar, and I have treated him as he deserves; I will do the same by any man who addresses such words to me, or whom I hear of as having used such words in regard to me."

No one spoke; but this time, as I stood looking defiantly at my some-time comrades, so suddenly transformed into prejudiced judges, no friendly words from Claude's voice exercised their soothing influence over me, no kind pressure of his hand soothed the turbulence of my troubled spirit. I was all alone, I thought, and the bitterness of that feeling almost unmanned me. Not one of all my old friends to stand up for me! not one of them to clasp my hand in his, in token of frank and hearty belief!—nothing but cold, stern, frowning faces, whichever way I turned my eyes.

No, I made a mistake—there was one faithful and true, there was one who understood my sorrow and pitied me, and who, coming up to me boldly before them all, said clearly and distinctly, "Keep up your heart, Darrell. A great case has been made out against you; but I know you, as many here ought to know you, and I declare I would sooner mistrust myself than you. Have no fear, the guilty will be discovered some day, and you will come out of your trial with untarnished honor." He took my hand as he spoke, and grasping it warmly, said in a low tone in German: "There is a flaw in this; I see it—and I think I can trace it out; but give me a day or two, and say nothing."

The man who spoke thus boldly and bravely for me was Egerton. He looked as if he had wakened up out of dream-land; there was a fire in his eye, a decision in his tone, most unusual to him. Whatever had occupied his mind when I saw him musing had apparently resolved itself into some definite resolution, and that resolution, he fancied, would have good results for me.

But I had no such hope. I thought I knew very well what he was going to do. He intended to declare his share in the matter — to announce that it was he had given me the marked money (for he knew that the money found in my desk was part of what he had given me for Twilight), and perhaps state from whom he had obtained it; but he quite forgot that this would in no way account for the money found in the chair-cushion; or perhaps, in his absent-minded way, he may have thought I hid it there for safety. I could see his plea would avail me little; therefore, though I grasped his hand warmly in return, I did not feel as much cheered as I ought to have done.

Then they all left the room, and I was alone. I was placed under arrest, and told that next day some one would be sent to me to tell me what decision they had arrived at after considering the facts brought before them. They would then determine whether I should be brought before a court-martial, or in what manner they should deem it advisable to act toward me.

"And," said Morton, turning as he was about to leave the room, "you had better write to the old fellow to stump up; for whatever leniency we might be inclined to show you in letting you sell out quietly, would be prevented if I had to report the manner in which this money has been lost; and I must do so soon, if it is not at once made good."

Before I could answer he had left the room, and the door was shut.

◆

CHAPTER XXIII

A MIDNIGHT COUNCIL.

ALL my old friends—most of whom, at least, were now friends of mine no longer—went back to Morton's room to talk over the terrible discovery they had just made, and to deliberate what course they should pursue. Egerton went with them, to hear what they had to say, and to raise his voice against the general belief that I was in any way connected with the theft.

Morton was fiendishly exultant, and exclaimed:

"This explains the length of time that young villain took examining the lock of that box one day he was in my room when you were there, Feversham. Don't you remember how he looked at it, and he said it was the most complicated lock he had ever seen? We were not minding him; probably he took the impression of the key then. I always suspected him. People who make a loud talk and profession of their uprightness and principle are nearly always scoundrels."

"Why, what a bad character you are giving yourself, Captain Morton!" said Egerton, in a sly, quiet tone; and every one, in spite of the general concern and annoyance, laughed, for of all the men in the regiment perhaps Morton was the only one who did make much talk about, and a loud profession of, his high principles. We had often been inclined to think they were not more visible than those of most men who said less, but we heard about them all the same.

Morton bit his lip, and glared at Egerton as if he would like to eat him.

"You are a friend of that fellow's," he said, "and, I suppose, go in for standing up for him. 'Birds of a feather flock together' is an old saying, and you might as well look out for yourself before you champion him. Are you sure you have none of that money on you?"

Morton's manner was fearfully insulting, and I suppose every one looked at Egerton to see how he would take it—thinking, too, that if Morton did come in for another blow, he would richly deserve it, and Cecil's conduct would be excusable. Imagine their surprise when Cecil, with a lazy smile, said somewhat irrelevantly,

"If you give a rogue rope enough, he is sure to hang himself; but you are mistaken about my having any of that money, Captain Morton. Fortunately for myself, I paid it all away a few days ago."

He had been leaning up against the door in a languid attitude, looking very tired and worn out, for he had never thoroughly recovered since his accident, and the excitement of the evening had exhausted him. But when he spoke he stood up, and looked at Morton in a peculiar, meaning manner: what the meaning of his look might be no one knew, but its effect on Morton was apparent. For a few seconds he gazed at Cecil as if fascinated, and turned, not white, but a ghastly greenish hue; then recovering himself, apparently by a powerful effort, he turned away his head, laughed nervously, and said,

"That is a good joke, Egerton, but you may carry a joke too far, you know; and your words can be used against yourself."

"I never said I was joking," replied Cecil, falling back languidly into his former position, and taking no notice of the many curious looks directed at him. "Now, gentlemen, please decide on something. I want to turn in, and I can not do so until I hear the result of this. Do you know that it is three o'clock, and we shall soon be having day here again?"

He spoke in a pleased, cheerful manner, and had altogether lost the depression that had taken possession of him when I was first accused. Feversham looked up at him in surprise.

"You don't seem very sorry for your friend," he said.

"No," replied Cecil, "because I don't doubt him; because I know him to be innocent, and believe his innocence will yet be proved; because I have not turned my back on him in his trouble, and have therefore nothing wherewith to reproach myself."

Feversham's grave, sad eyes looked straight up at Cecil with a little admiration as he said this.

"Indeed you are right," he answered. "Though you may wonder at my acknowledging you are so, and not being of your opinion myself. But I know more of Darrell than you do: I know that he is not what I once thought him—he has disappointed me greatly; I *know* that it is possible for him to be grossly dishonorable—I have known it for some time, but I did not choose to mention my knowledge, fearing that if every one knew him for what he is, he would lose the incentive to good behavior furnished in a wish to appear well before the world. I only mention it now to show to you that I have good and just reason for doubting him: knowing, as from antecedent circumstances I think I do know, that this charge is true, there is no longer any object in trying to keep up his character before the world, for this theft can not remain hidden."

"You talk about justice," replied Egerton—"there is not much justice in you when you condemn a man before he is tried. You are too hard, Lord Feversham; you will not see that circumstances are often against people, and that they sometimes appear to have committed deeds that they have never had any hand in; some of the best qualities of human nature may prevent them clearing themselves from the charge brought against them. Such I believe to be the case with Darrell now. I am convinced he knows from whom he received the money; that he believes that person to be innocent, and that he prefers rather to bear the blame himself than to shift it on to other shoulders less able than his to bear the burden, unless that other comes forward and claims the matter as his own. After all, though the notes found in the chair were the ones missing, perhaps some one may yet be found to tell us how they got there. And out of all the money Captain Morton claims as stolen property, only four or five pieces were found with Darrell."

"Of course I did not mark it all," growled Morton. "I only scratched about a dozen pieces, between gold and silver."

"Yes, I can quite understand that," replied Egerton; "a few coins like that soon pass through a good many hands, and are less easily traced to their original source. But, you see, if Darrell has even half of it—that is all—where is the rest?"

"I suggested it might be with you."

"You did, Captain Morton — thanks for the suggestion; I shall remember it next time I have dealings with you. But, as I told you before, I have already passed it on. Shall I mention who gave it to me?"

"Can't you be serious, Egerton?" said Captain Morton, harshly; "you know very well you would not talk that way if you really ever had any of it."

"You don't seem to wish to believe me," said Egerton, sarcastically. "I am sure my words are quite suspicious enough to warrant my being searched and put under arrest; why don't you do it?"

Morton looked greatly distressed and agitated; his expression was that of a hunted wild animal. Every one noticed it, and wondered as he glanced from Feversham to Cecil, as though appealing to Feversham to interfere between them and make Egerton keep silence. Feversham noticed this at last, and looking up, said: "Really, Egerton, you had much better be quiet, and let us proceed to business. We shall have taken no definite resolution to-night if you interrupt the proceedings again in this way. If you interfere, I shall request you to leave the room."

Egerton did not answer; and then Morton, having recovered his self-possession, recapitulated the facts already related, alluding to Darrell's apparent implication in them with great virulence and malignity.

There was a good deal of talking over the matter, but Claude's words a few minutes before had greatly biased all minds, and it was the opinion of all who had heard him that if Darrell's own cousin believed he was guilty of this act it was as good as proof that he must be guilty. Men are so like a flock of sheep, with all their individual independence of judgment. Where one will step boldly forward and lead, the mass are sure to follow, and will ask no better reason for the course they are pursuing than that so-and-so does it. And in this case of mine it was the same. Claude had taken the lead against me, and his opinions carried more weight than was attached to that of any other man in the regiment; he was very deservedly popular, and was known to be a just and honorable man. He would not have condemned me without cause; he must know more about me than others, therefore I was guilty.

Yes, all those there assembled, with the exception of Egerton, were agreed on that point. It was decided that next morning those of our number who had not been in Morton's rooms that night should be told what had there passed, and should be asked to give their opinion on the matter also. If a majority agreed in thinking me guilty, I was to be given my choice, whether I would sell out at once quietly, paying Morton up the losses to avoid scandal, or whether I would prefer to remain and run my chance at a court-martial. This was the substance of their decision that evening, and certainly it was treating me very leniently, owing, I believe, to Claude's influence. He had done what he thought was right in declaring me guilty, but he put in his voice on the side of mercy, when it came to be a matter of discussing the punishment. Strange to say, also, Morton did not urge bringing me before a court-martial; he suggested it once, as a matter of form, but seemed relieved when no one took it up; and thus matters were settled before any of the party separated.

When they were all going off to their own rooms, Cecil followed James, saying, "Will you let me speak to you for a minute; it is about something important, and I will not keep you long."

"Don't, that's a good fellow," said James. "I am upset about this business, and I want to think it over. Of course, if Feversham says Darrell is guilty, I suppose he is so; and you see he says he caught him, some time ago, in something dishonorable; that is the reason they have not been good friends lately. But I should have held out stoutly against the idea of poor little Madcap being concerned in such a thing, but for his cousin saying he was so."

"Do not believe Feversham," cried Cecil eagerly. "I do not mean to say for one minute he would say what was not true, for any one; but do you not see there has been some misunderstanding between them, and Feversham is prejudiced."

They had arrived in James's rooms by this time, and Cecil looked round, as he always did on entering them, with an overpowering feeling of wonder at the orderly nature of this man. You could see it in his dress and all over him, even in the curl of his mustache, but above all in his rooms. They would have been a lesson to an old maid; and though he was a young fellow—five or six and twenty—his fate was already regarded as sealed. It was not possible that a man so preternaturally and punctiliously neat and orderly would ever consent to unite his lot with that of another person who would probably be unlike him in every respect, and who would ceaselessly vex his precise soul by untidy, reckless habits. For in his eyes every body was reckless and untidy except himself and his man Martin, whom he had picked up after constant and diligent search, and whom he had drilled in the way he should go, until he as nearly approached perfection as was possible.

Cecil had always been inclined to be vexed whenever he had entered James's room before. It is human nature to feel a little nettled at seeing any one in any way indisputably superior to one's self, especially when that person is rather fond of alluding to it; and this, it must be allowed, was a failing with James. Now, however, Egerton looked round with a certain sense of satisfaction. A man so very orderly in his mode of living must naturally be orderly about his money and expenses.

"Do you remember my paying you a small debt of two or three pounds I owed you, a week or two ago?" asked Egerton.

"Yes, certainly," replied James; "I have got it entered here"—taking out a small pocketbook. "It was—let me see—just ten days ago."

"Have you the money, or have you spent it?" demanded Cecil, eagerly.

"I have it. I have not been spending much lately, and it happens I have not used that. Do you want it again?"

"I want it to look at. Will you let me see it now?"

In a few minutes more Cecil was standing by the lamp, turning the money over eagerly in his hand. There were three sovereigns, and several pieces of silver money. Out of all this Cecil picked four pieces, and handing them to James, said,

"Examine those, and see if they are not marked, like the money we were looking at this evening."

"So they are!" cried James. "Why, I might have been taken up for having stolen money too, if they had only known. But I got them from you, Egerton. What does it all mean?"

Egerton laughed.

"You heard me tell Morton I had passed on all I had, and, you see, I spoke truly; but I will tell you more. I was the person who gave poor Darrell the money that has got him into trouble. I gave it to him in payment for a horse. He,

poor fellow! did not like to do me mischief, I could see, and therefore declined to tell how he came by it."

"But I do not understand this," said James, in a bewildered manner. "Why did you not at once clear him? Of course, as you acknowledge so coolly having the money, you can account for how you came by it? You really should not let that poor boy pass the night under such an imputation."

"I set it all right with him when I bade him good-night. You must promise not to breathe a word of this to any one until I ask you. I am going to catch a thief now, and secrecy is necessary."

"Very well," said James. "I must say I think this a rum start—and amateur thief-taking is not an occupation that seems by any means infallible, or that I should like to take to, from what I have seen of it. But you know your own business best, and, I must say, I think you will behave better, generally, to those whom you suspect than Morton does."

"Yes," answered Egerton, laughing; "I shall give them time for repentance and confession. But in the case of the man who did this, I know it will only be giving himself rope to hang himself with, as I said before."

"Will you keep the money, or shall I?" asked James, handling it doubtfully, and looking as if he would like to throw it behind the fire, only there was no fire lighted at the time.

"Yes, keep it, by all means. It shall not get you into trouble. But now mind, not a word of this to any one. I have not quite finished collecting my evidence, and a single premature hint of what was coming might prevent the matter being ever cleared up. And now good-night. Be quite easy about the issue of this, and remember that Darrell is not the culprit."

Egerton went away then, and left James in a perplexed frame of mind that made the idea of sleep seem a mockery. At any rate, he reflected, after he had lain some time thinking it over, it was some comfort to find that one person at least firmly believed in Darrell's innocence, though it might be a question whether that person was not implicated in the affair himself, if his own testimony was taken against him. This brought James to a very complicated point in the matter. He could not quite remember whether a man's words would or would not be used as evidence against him in a court of justice. It was either the one or the other, but which was it? And while considering this intricate problem he fell asleep.

Cecil had retired to his rooms, pleased and confident of ultimate success in what he had decided on undertaking, now that he had ascertained James had the money he had expected to find with him. If James had not kept it the matter would have been different, and the case perhaps more difficult to prove. He had one point now in his favor; he had an idea he might obtain a point more, in securing a witness that he believed had been present at a transaction that had not yet been laid before Darrell's judges. He did not even to himself specify what his case was, or what he intended to do, though there was a vague foreshadowing of what might happen if such and such preliminaries turned out as he expected and desired.

Feeling particularly pleased with himself, and having for once in his life a definite purpose that must be wrought out, and that would brook no delay, he kept himself awake also for a time, wondering how he should get hold of Darrell's servant, in order that he might put a few questions to him without exciting suspicion. He could not settle the point that night, however, and was finally obliged to leave it to chance to decide next morning.

Claude was perhaps the one who was most unhappy at the fate that had befallen me; all the more because, though he had acted, as he thought, according to the right, he felt that he had abandoned me when I most stood in need of a friend. It was not less bitter to him to remember that I had found one to stand by me, and that one was not himself. He would never have believed it possible that I could have been guilty of such a crime, but that the evidence seemed so conclusive; besides, there was my conduct toward him, which proved that I had, as he thought, neither honor nor principle in me. But what was the temptation in this case? In that other, he knew that I had an inducement which I had been unable to resist, that had lured many a man before me into the lowest depths of dishonor. But about this money—he could not understand it. I had a very liberal allowance; I was never limited in any way if I wanted to spend beyond that allowance. There was no supposition by which he could account for it, except by putting it down to the innate evil of my disposition.

It was strange, too, he continued musing, that the evil disposition had not shown itself many years before. Could it be possible that in all this there had been some hideous mistake, and that he had been a recreant in friendship, and believed the slanders of malicious tongues too hastily? He grew hot at the thought. Was this to be the end of all his fine theories about staunch, true-hearted confidence between those who cared for each other?—the end of his oft-proclaimed belief in a loyalty that would stand firm in the face of an army of facts and proofs? He had latterly got to fancy these theories of the foolish, by-gone days when he had first loved Gwendoline Bambridge were childish and Quixotic; but now, in his distress at what had happened, his old belief in them began to return, and he was harassed by doubt and perplexities as to how far his real conduct differed from the conduct he would have adopted had he adhered to his first faith in regard to friendship.

It is a painful thing to a person of firm, determined character, and strong, high principle, to find he has been acting in a weak, uncertain manner, trying to achieve good by siding first with one party, then with another, and too doubtful of where right lies to stand fast by either. He had earnestly desired to do what he believed he ought to do, and now it seemed to him he had not only failed in doing what he had wished, but he had also given opportunity for evil of some kind, which he should have been able to prevent by his influence and example; for if Darrell was not the culprit, if Feversham had continued his friend, this odious attempt to fix the guilt on him would never have taken place; and if he was guilty, Feversham's friendship and counsel might have kept him from falling into so evil a way.

No matter how things went, Claude thought he must blame himself for much of the mischief; and he sat up, staring moodily before him, for nearly an hour after the others had all gone to sleep, trying to settle in what particulars he had been to blame, and wondering sadly whether it was now too late to make amends, and whether he and the boy would ever be again the friends they had once been. He had an uncomfortable feeling that, having rejected my friendship at the time of his illness, I would never be willing to renew my intimacy with him; that the love then offered and rejected would never be won back to him by a tardy repentance and desire for forgiveness.

I do not know whether I ever felt as bitter against him as he supposed; I am sure I was very grieved at his conduct toward me, but I always had the feeling that there was some great reason for his change, all unknown though it was to me, or he would never have behaved to me as he had done.

Egerton's words had not been the comfort to me he had intended they should be, because I did not in the least understand them, or I understood them in a sense that made them seem very futile to me. It would not please me one bit that my sensitive, gentle-minded friend should have to change places with me, bear all the dreadful overwhelming shame and disgrace of such a charge, and be given over to the decision of a court-martial, which I doubted not would be my fate if he did not step in and rescue me. How he obtained the money was a mystery to me, but one which I knew he would explain when he next saw me. There was one other point which puzzled me more than all the rest, and which, as far as I could judge from his countenance, had actuated him to the course he had taken. This point was the finding of the notes in my chair. Until then I had noticed that his face wore a depressed, anxious expression; then he seemed to relapse into deep thought, out of which he presently aroused himself, looking cheerful, and, for him, very determined. Then his whole voice and bearing had been confident and fearless when he had muttered those German words into my ear: he would hardly have looked and spoken so, if the only means of escape for me was to be provided by his taking my place.

Never mind what he meant, he had been a true friend, when every eye had looked coldly on me; when malice had gloated over my pitiful plight, no friendly hand but his was outstretched to grasp mine, as I looked round for comfort and support. Do you know what it is to feel yourself an outcast and an alien?—to know that your enemies triumph and scorn you, that your friends hide their faces and turn away their heads in shame and sorrow, when your name is mentioned?—to feel that for you, as long as life lasts, while the seasons take their varying course and the old year wastes away and gives place to the new, there is no longer any hope of restoration to the position you once occupied in the honorable esteem of your fellow-men?—to feel that no repentance can avail to wipe away the stain that rests on your honor, in the sight of those once your equals and your friends, though it may be accepted by One higher far and more pitiful than they, and by Him received as a plea for His mercy and succor? Do you know what it is to feel that you have lost something lighter than down, more impalpable than air, and yet more powerful than the decree of an emperor to raise you in the minds of your fellow-creatures, to win their trust and homage? Do you know what it is to feel that, young though you may be, your future is blasted; that for you there are no more gallant achievements and noble deeds, because with them comes observation, and scandal follows hard upon renown, as the jackal follows the lion, to prey upon the offal the noble beast leaves untouched? If you know all this, you know that even the youthful heart will turn sick and faint under the pressure of that heavy chain which the joint opinion of men can lay upon their fellow-men. You know how that galling yoke can take from the summer sky its beauty, from the green earth its dewy freshness; how it can steal the enjoyment from health, the pleasure from youth, the strength from a noble heart and an active brain, and even rob beauty of its enchantment, and the excitements of life's spring-time of their ecstasy.

All this I knew and felt then, and it seemed to me as if the great shadow that had fallen upon me could never be lifted—as if under its baleful darkness I must live a dreary, blighted life. Never for me again would friends come gayly and gladly forth to meet me; the dear people at home would fret sorely and sadly over the blighted prospects and disgraced name of their loved and only son. They would not believe it of me; not the less would it break their hearts to know that others believed it. And as I thought of the mother of whom I was so proud shunning the world she had graced, that she might not have to blush for her boy, my feelings were indescribably bitter. I was young, and did not know how to suffer; and struggling against the yoke put upon me, the iron entered deeper into my soul, and wounded me more and more with every effort of resistance.

CHAPTER XXIV.

THE CULPRIT DETECTED.

NEXT day my case was laid before those among the officers of the regiment who had not been present the night before. They would never have suspected me of such a crime, but the proofs brought forward were startling, and quite strong enough to make these men agree in an opinion that had been expressed by those who were formerly among my best friends. Egerton was absent when this consultation was being held, and James had gone with him: their presence was not needed, however; they had seen how this affair originated, and had heard the decision arrived at the night before. It was known Egerton had maintained my innocence, in the face of the facts brought against me; though James had sided with the others at first, it was deemed probable he might have gone over to Egerton's opinion, as they had gone out together.

Claude was there, looking wretchedly pale and haggard; he had passed a sleepless night, upbraiding himself as having had a helping hand in his young cousin's ruin, and he was worn out accordingly. After he had listened to the recapitulation of the evidence, and seen the manner in which it impressed every body, he began to think that at least he had not erred in his opinion of me, and while he still blamed himself for not having kept a stricter watch over me, he reverted to his first idea that all this was due to something evil in my disposition.

Thus he had again hardened himself against any kindly feeling, when he was called upon to be the bearer of a message from the officers there assembled with him to me. James, who would probably have been sent on this errand, was out of the way, and it was wished to get the affair over as soon as possible. On consideration of my youth, my old friends wished to behave as kindly to me as possible, and they had an idea that in sending my cousin Claude to break their decision to me they were acting with great consideration.

Claude was startled and very much taken aback when he was told what was expected of him; it was about the very last thing he would have wished to do. He still blamed himself for much of this, and the sight of me stirred up his self-accusing conscience to greater activity: the old affection for his young cousin was not yet extinguished, which made it all the more difficult for him to show to me a proper amount of disapproval and reprobation. He felt much more inclined to implore my forgiveness for his having neglected me, and allowed me to be led astray by temptation; he was very much under the influence of an idea not uncommon in the world, that a man will not go wrong as long as he is strictly watched: he quite forgot that if evil is in a man, it will come out, if all the eyes of Argus were constantly upon him.

Under these circumstances, it was with great unwillingness that Claude accepted the duty laid upon him, and went off to my room to lay before me the decision they had arrived at, which was the same as that agreed upon the night before; namely, that I should be given my choice, whether I would make restitution to Morton of all the losses he had lately sustained, of money stolen from his strong-box, and sell out immediately; or whether I would prefer to remain and take my chance at a court-martial. Of course they never doubted for a minute but that I would catch gladly at the first offer, and there were some who thought I was far too leniently treated; but by acting thus toward me, it would be possible to keep the scandal in the regiment, and not have it published abroad in all the newspapers in the country, as would be the case if they were obliged to pursue the other course.

I was sitting alone in my room, feeling very dejected. It may be imagined my meditations were not lively, for I saw very clearly I was the victim of a cleverly concocted scheme which was not likely to miscarry, and the originator of which was my greatest enemy, a man who hated me as much as I despised him. On both sides these feelings were spontaneous natural antipathies; he had done nothing to me, I most certainly had never contaminated myself by having any thing to do with him; but from the first moment we saw one another we had been like fire and ice, antagonistic to the last degree, in every phase and particular of daily life and character.

When Claude entered I looked up, and was very much surprised to see him, of all people, come to visit me, for I did not guess his errand, imagining that he would in any case have declined to be the channel through which the officers' decision would be sent to me. Was it possible that Claude had discovered he had wronged me, and had come to ask my pardon for his cruel doubts, or, what was more probable, had come to reproach me with the ignominy my disgrace would bring, not only on my family, but on his also? I would not ask him to sit down as long as I remained in ignorance of his intentions, so I stood up and waited in silence for him to speak. He seemed to find some difficulty in opening the subject, for there was a pause, during which interval I had time to perceive that his face was worn and haggard, and there were lines of grief and thought about his mouth and on his broad, open brow. It was evident that if he condemned me it pained him to do so, and I felt more kindly toward him as I noticed this.

Presently he spoke, and in a low, hurried voice told me my comrades' decision.

"What answer shall I bring them from you?" he asked, when he had laid before me the choice presented to me.

"Tell them," I said firmly, "I will remain and run my chance at a court-martial. I am innocent, and by adopting the other course I should make it appear to every one that I was guilty, and was trying to avoid the punishment justly due to me."

"You are foolish, Vivian," replied Claude. "What is the use of trying to brazen it out? Your guilt will certainly be brought home to you, and you will fare worse than if you accepted the chance of escape now offered to you. Vivian, how could you have acted thus?—what tempted you? I knew before that you were not honorable in your dealings toward others, but I never believed you could have been a thief."

My blood boiled at that word; besides, an idea flashed into my head that the time for reckoning between Claude and me had come. I sprang to the door and placed my back against it, determined that he should not leave my room until he had explained to me what it was that he was always hinting as having been done by me, and which had first set him against me.

"Now," I cried, when I had cut off his chance of escape, "tell me what this wrong and dishonorable act of mine is to which you are eternally alluding. All is lost to me now—honor, and name, and fame. A man stripped of every thing becomes reckless, and I swear to you, you shall not leave this place until you have told me what it is you know against me. It matters nothing to me now if insubordination, or mutiny, or any thing else is added to the list of my offenses, but this unknown crime at which you hint must and shall be told to me plainly and openly. Do you think you have acted kindly and honestly by me, as one friend should act toward another, as man should act toward man even were they strangers, when you have believed evil against me, and have given me no chance of clearing myself in your eyes, leaving me in the dark as to what you deem wrong in my conduct, and yet visiting that wrong-doing upon me? Tell me at once what it is of which you accuse me."

"Of what avail is it your having things recapitulated that you know as well as I do? One can not be concerned in an affair of that kind and forget it; but since you will have it so, let me ask you if you remember my saying to you one day that I was disappointed in you for writing to my mother and telling her of my love for Miss Bambridge?"

"Yes, and I denied it," I answered. "It was false. I denied it then, and I deny it now."

"Yes, I knew you would," replied Claude, coldly. "The evil has gone deep indeed when you will not confess your guilt, even though you know it is discovered. When I went home after that, I asked my mother whether you had told her. Something had occurred again to raise my suspicions, or else, like a fool, I should have believed and trusted you still. She did not say in so many words you had told her, but she declined to deny it, and equivocated in a manner that it was painful to me to witness. After that there was no longer any room for doubt, and all your denials and pretenses of not understanding me could not produce any impression on my mind, except in deepening the bad opinion I was forced to entertain of you."

For some minutes after he had finished speaking I stood looking at him, almost stupefied at what he had told me. That he should have suspected me of such baseness was terrible. The idea should never have entered his head; but at the time he had told me of it before, I excused it on the plea of jealousy. That he should question his mother to ascertain if I was speaking the truth, and that she should so miserably deceive him and malign me, I could not understand. And now what was I to do? It was no good denying all this; it had obtained too firm a hold of his mind, and I had nothing but my own tarnished word to bring against it. No wonder he thought me a thief, or any thing else any body liked to call me. I only wonder that, with his character, he could bring himself to speak to me at all. I really pitied him as I saw the change sorrow had wrought in his face, and at last I spoke, more quietly than I had done before.

"If all this is as you say, if your mother led you to believe that I had spoken falsely to you, I do not wonder that you should think this other charge against me true. It is of very little use my telling you that every word of it is false; you would not believe me now. But I have a strong confidence that some day you will see how grossly you have been deceived, and in anticipation of that day, which will surely come, I entreat you to remember that I deny it all. I deny having told your mother, I deny having spoken falsely to you, and, more than all, and above all, I deny this charge for which I am about to suffer. Remember this when the time comes, and I know you will be sorry for your hardness to me. Then there will be no place for you to show your repentance to me, if the day is far distant, for I will not bear a dishonored name in the country where it was always held in reverence and esteem. You may go now; I will not make you longer endure what I know must be very painful to you. The heart takes a long time to harden thoroughly to those it has once loved. Tell them I will run my chance at the court-martial; and," I added, as he was about to leave the room, "would you ask Egerton to come and see me? I thought he would have been here before this."

"He has gone out with James, but I will tell him you want to see him, when he comes in." And so saying, Claude went off and left me.

So Cecil had gone out, and had not come to see his friend, though he knew I must be waiting anxiously for his arrival. It was cruel. I had trusted him, and he seemed no kinder to me than the others. A few scalding tears forced their way into my eyes as I thought thus, for I was broken down and worn out with trouble, and it seemed to me, besides, that I was utterly deserted and alone. I kept back the tears with a kind of savage pride. For none of those who had used me so badly would I shed them, nor for the manner in which they had used me. They should not have it in their power to say that they had broken my spirit and triumphed over my manhood. There would be time enough for tears in the years that were to come, that the golden sun of happiness should never lighten, nor the brightness of pleasure illumine.

As I was thinking thus, and trying to occupy myself in some way that would make it easier for me to endure my grief, the door opened, and Egerton entered.

"My poor fellow!" he said, "it must have seemed unkind of me not to come and see you before, but I have been working hard for you, and I have arranged a triumph on a grand scale. But first—do you remember that it was I gave you the marked money?"

"Yes, certainly," I replied; "I did not happen to have any other at hand."

"Then why did not you say so last night, and save yourself all this?"

"It might have saved me at first," I answered, "but not after my room was searched and the money found in that chair. How did it get there, I wonder? To me it is quite incomprehensible."

"It is not so to me, then," replied Egerton, "any more than your bearing the blame of the other money in silence. I can not tell you what I think of you, Vivian, but I can and do mean to show it, in as far as I am able, by working to save you. And now listen to me till I tell you what it is you must do. Send a message by me, saying that you wish to see all of us together, as you have something important to communicate concerning this business."

"But I have nothing important to say," I objected.

"Yes, you have. You have to say you got those notes from me. Do that, and leave me to manage the rest."

Egerton's manner was confident, though rather excited. As we all knew, he could never act unless he was excited, but then he could act promptly and well. It seemed to me now he had some plan in his head which would have good results; I therefore acquiesced in his demand, and sent a message by him, entreating that I might be allowed to communicate something bearing on the case to the officers who had sat in judgment on me.

When he had left me, I began to feel that, although Egerton might be put into the same scrape with me, yet I was not likely to get off, for I could not see how Egerton would explain the presence of the notes in the cushion of my chair, and until that was satisfactorily accounted for I was not likely to be set at liberty. But I had promised to act as Egerton desired, and I must do so.

Shortly after, James came to tell me that I was to go with him to Major Harvey's rooms, Colonel Dropmore being at that time away on leave. I followed him silently, and he never at-

tempted to address me, nor showed by his manner what view of the case he took, till just as we were going in at the door, when he said in a low tone,

"Keep up your courage. All is not lost yet."

These were encouraging words, coming, as they did, from one who had not been inclined to look favorably on me the night before; but I had not time to think about it when Egerton came forward and took my hand before them all; then he placed himself as near me as he could, and Major Harvey asked what it was I wished to communicate, and for what purpose I had called them together.

"I wish to account for the manner in which I became possessed of the marked money found on my person and in my desk," I answered. "I said last night I had got it in change, but I declined to give the name of the person by whom it had been paid to me, fearing to get him into trouble. It is at his special request that I mention him now. I received that money from Mr. Egerton, in payment for a mare I sold him about ten days ago."

"Egerton!" cried several men in astonishment, looking at him, as he stood calm and unconcerned near me.

"I thought that fellow had some hand in the matter," said Morton; "he was Darrell's accomplice. A nice pair, truly!"

"You remember, Captain Morton, that I told you last night I had had some of the money, but had passed it on," answered Egerton. "It is true I gave Darrell the money in payment for his mare Twilight."

"This is very extraordinary indeed," murmured Major Harvey. "I don't know that I ever remember to have met with so extraordinary a case. Your statement, Mr. Egerton, explains how Mr. Darrell became possessed of some of the stolen money, but it does not show how he became possessed of that part which was hidden in the cushions of his chair, nor how any of it got into your hands, either. Can you tell us now, Mr. Darrell, how those notes got into the cushion?"

"About that I know nothing," I answered, sadly. "It must have been the work of some one who had a spite against me, I think, and wished to get me out of the regiment."

Major Harvey shook his head; that did not seem to him at all probable. Then he turned to Egerton.

"Can you explain the matter?" he said.

"I think I can," answered Egerton, with flashing eyes, that told his spirit was up, and that the man who had planned this would not escape if it lay in Egerton's power to unearth him. "But first let me bring in a witness I have outside; it will not do in a case like this to have one's own unsupported word."

He was given leave to fetch his witness, and presently returned, to my surprise followed by my servant, who seemed rather bewildered at being brought before such an assemblage of officers.

"Remember," said Cecil, when he had again taken up his position near me, "this man knows nothing of the case; you may as well question him, to see that he has in no way been prepared, or put up to what is going on. When the right time comes, I shall ask him to tell you what he saw in a certain place, on a certain day. From what he says you may draw your own conclusions."

Morton had been fidgeting about, looking very white and anxious, ever since Egerton had come forward and avowed himself a participator in the business. He now interrupted Cecil, saying,

"Major Harvey, this is very irregular. That man, who is himself an accomplice in the crime, has no right to be addressing us, and bringing in witnesses for his friend; and the witness is the culprit's own servant. I move that Egerton be included in the judgment we have passed on the other."

"Without hearing if I can account for the way in which I became possessed of that money, I suppose," said Egerton. "No; you must allow me to give my explanation, and you can then take steps to verify it. But before I speak and disclose all, Major Harvey—before I show to what a base and cowardly plot my poor friend was about to fall a victim, let me pause a moment, and give the real culprit time for repentance and confession, if he will confess. If he were to do so, it might move us to punish him less severely than we shall assuredly do if he persists in the desperate course he has chosen."

There was a silence, and I could see that Egerton kept his eyes steadily fixed on the ground, for fear he might be tempted by the direction of his glance to point the address of his words. I looked round on the faces of those about me: they were very grave, and on all but one there was a concentrated look of intense expectation. On one face alone could be read deadly, sickening, overwhelming apprehension. I was not surprised to see that look there, but I wondered greatly—not that Cecil had divined the guilty one—I had all along suspected him myself—but that he should have obtained proofs of his guilt, and proofs he must have, or he would never speak and act as he was speaking and acting now.

After a few minutes' pause, Major Harvey spoke.

"Say what you have to say now, Mr. Egerton; it is evident that no one here will acknowledge having had any thing to do with this crime. If the culprit is present, as you say, name him, and let the matter be settled at once."

Then Egerton began.

"I have confessed," he said, "that I gave Darrell that money; in support of this assertion, you may question James, to whom I paid some money at the same time, among which you will find four marked pieces. You will want to know how I came by that money: my answer is, it was given to me by Captain Morton, in payment of a debt he owed me."

"It is false!—absolutely and entirely false!" shouted Captain Morton, and every one present noticed his ghastly paleness, and that his hands, and even his lips, trembled. "Nothing that he says is true. Why listen to him?"

"Pardon me," said James, in his quiet, straightforward manner, "I can vouch for the truth of one small part of his statement."

He threw the four coins on the table as he spoke: they spun round a moment and then were motionless.

"Go on, Mr. Egerton," said Major Harvey; "we will hear what you have to say, Captain Morton, when he has finished."

"It is perfectly true," continued Egerton,

"that I can not prove Captain Morton gave me that money, but I can prove something else that bears very strongly on the case. I was just turning the far corner of the corridor in which Darrell's room is situated yesterday, when I saw Captain Morton coming out of Darrell's room. He turned the other way when he came out, and therefore did not see me; but I, who had thought Darrell was out, now imagined he must be in, and went to seek him. He was not there, and I went into the inner room, where I found this man, his servant, who was doing something about the room. I asked him if he knew where his master was; he said he did not, but that Captain Morton had just been in, he supposed, looking for him. I thought nothing more of the matter until the affair last night, when the notes were found in the chair-cushion; then I began to suspect something, and to-day, taking James with me, we went to this man, and asked him if Captain Morton had seen him or spoken to him when he was in Mr. Darrell's room yesterday. He said no; we then asked him if he had any idea what Captain Morton wanted; he said he had not, but confessed to having watched the captain, and then related what he had seen. You can ask him about it yourselves."

The man, on being questioned, said that Captain Morton had walked round the room several times, and then taken the cushion out of the easy-chair and carried it to the window, where, to use the man's expression, he had been fumbling with it for some time. He in the next room, peeping through a crack in the door, could not see distinctly what the captain was doing. He might have looked afterward, but that Mr. Egerton coming in put the matter out of his head; indeed Mr. Egerton stopped a little while in the inner room with him, looking at an old sword that was one of his master's curiosities, and before he had done examining it Mr. Darrell returned.

"Now," said Egerton, when Jenkins had finished giving his evidence, "I assert that I got the marked money that I acknowledge was in my possession from Captain Morton; and Jenkins saw the same man yesterday afternoon doing something with the cushion in which the notes were found. You may draw your own conclusions from that; at any rate, this is all the light I can throw upon the matter."

When he had finished speaking, and before any one else could utter a word, Captain Morton, in a harsh, constrained voice, as though it was a great exertion to him to speak, demanded permission to go and fetch some memoranda that he thought would disprove the charges brought against him. James volunteered to go and fetch them, but he said they were in a secret drawer, and it would be necessary for him to go himself. Harvey, a good-natured, easy-going man, gave him permission, as this meeting was not an official affair, and we need not stand on etiquette. Morton accordingly went.

We waited for about a half an hour, and then James was sent to hurry him. In a few minutes James returned, saying he had absconded, that there was no trace of him to be seen, and the sentry at the gates said he had gone out nearly half an hour before.

It was true: he had fled from what he saw was before him, and had carried off with him all the money that had been taken out of my room the night before. What his object had been in acting as he had done was never rightly understood; perhaps he wanted the money badly when he first took it, and intended to pay. it back; failing that, he had been obliged to declare it stolen, had persuaded Egerton to lend him money to supply the deficit, and had made a great talk about his catching the thief immediately, and getting all that had been stolen refunded. It is probable that when Egerton asked him if it would be convenient to him to pay the money he owed, the idea first came into his head that he might make Cecil the victim, and he accordingly marked the money; afterward, finding Egerton had paid it over to me, he altered his plans and acted accordingly.

It was over, and my innocence was proved. I was very glad, very thankful, but I was still more glad and proud and thankful when Claude came over to me, saying, "I can not ask you to forgive me, or to let us be the friends we once were. I have wronged you too deeply for that, but I will ask you to let me tell you how ashamed of myself I am for ever having believed it possible you could have fallen so low from what you once were. I do not understand that matter about my mother, but I no longer believe you were guilty of deceit and treachery; my eyes have been opened, and I see that it is I who have behaved basely, not you."

He was about to turn away, looking very sorrowful, very unlike the dignified, irreproachable, proud man he once was, and I was moved at the sight of his self-accusation. I caught his hand, saying,

"Don't think of this any more; let all be as it once was, when we were at home together, and let nothing again ever come between us."

He did not answer, but nothing has ever come between us since then, and we are faster friends than even in the old days.

———◆———

CHAPTER XXV.

AT A BALL.

April came, and the Bambridges, as had before been determined, went to London, to spend a month or two there during the season. They had a good many friends in town, and were persuaded Lord Fevershnm's military duties would prevent him from putting in an appearance; they were therefore a little surprised, a day or two after their arrival, to see his name down at various fashionable entertainments, and were rather put out to think that Gwendoline's recovery might be retarded by the presence of the man for whom they were sure she still sorrowed, though her refusal of him remained as impenetrable a mystery as ever. Besides, there were rumors going about which before long reached their ears, that Lord Feversham was about to be married to Miss Prendergast, the heiress. Gwendoline shivered when she heard this confirmation of the story I had hinted to her before, but quickly recovering, she spoke out boldly, and asserted the report to be a calumny.

Nevertheless, Miss Prendergast was in London, and her name was also mentioned at every entertainment at which he appeared: that was not wonderful, if the Bambridges had known she was staying with Lady Feversham, and going out under her chaperonage. A knowledge of that fact would, however, have confirmed the truth of the rumor in Gwendoline's eyes, and at present, at least, she was happy enough to be able to disbelieve it, or at least to say that she did so, though at times her faith waxed very low indeed.

As yet they had not met even in the ride, for horses and various other arrangements were not looked after until they arrived in town; but Gwendoline knew it could not be long thus, and that probably their first night out, or first day in the Park, would bring them face to face once more.

After all, there was more truth in this rumor than is generally the case in such things. Mabel Prendergast had heard from her lover himself that there was no present prospect of his advancement, but he did not tell her how very little aptitude he had for his profession, nor that such was the opinion of his seniors. This, however, she learned from Feversham, whom she questioned closely, and who expressed great pity that the young man had so mistaken his vocation in life.

She listened calmly to this verdict on the future of the man she had promised to marry, the only sign of emotion she gave being that she loosened the ribbon round her white throat, as though the pressure choked her.

Could she do it? she wondered. Could she throw over this man she felt she loved so dearly, even though she now determined he and she must part. Her reason told her she could and would do it; her heart cried indignantly, "Never! You have enough; be happy, and leave every other consideration for the future."

Her brain was in a whirl whenever she thought about it, and she would often invent an excuse for leaving the room and going to brood over the matter in secret. One day she had thought over it in every light, and had almost resolved to be true, when her maid coming in to lay out her dress for Lady Longwreath's ball that night, put all idea of self-sacrifice out of her head. Yes, if she was true to her love, and married him, a subaltern in a marching regiment, then farewell to all the petting, courting, and caressing to which she had been accustomed lately. Then she must give up the balls she had been accustomed to grace, and where her presence was eagerly sought after; not but that she might no doubt have society as his wife too, but it would be many degrees lower than that in which she at present moved; for, being a woman of the world herself, she could quite understand she must hope for no support or sympathy from her present friends, once she had so far derogated from her position as to marry a subaltern in a line regiment.

She pushed the hair back from her aching brow, and tossed her head with her most defiant air, as she decided thus, and determined that at all costs the sacrifice must be made. Claude only wants a little encouragement from me to propose at once, she mused, and I think he likes me a little, though I fear I have not quite eclipsed Miss Bambridge yet; but that will come in time. He shall ask me this very night, and then it will be all right. Poor Cecil! he will feel it dreadfully at first, but I hope he will not insist on seeing me and asking me about it; I could not bear that. How will he take it, I wonder? "Oh! my love," she exclaimed, feeling really sorry for what she chose to consider the necessity for her falseness, "if I could but spare you this, but I dare not; I could not take your lot when a brighter and better lies ready to my hand. Is it wonderful I should choose it, and avoid a life of insignificance with you? Pity me! forgive me! but do not hate me though I wrong you."

The maid had left the room, and leaning her head on the pillow, she shed a few tears. For a minute or two she wept, and better feelings might have taken possession of her heart, when a warning knock announced the maid's return, and the next minute she entered, carrying in her hand a magnificent bouquet. Along with it she brought a note from Lord Feversham, explaining that he should not meet them before the ball, but he hoped then to have the pleasure of seeing her with his flowers.

"He shall speak out to-night," she murmured, as she glanced over his note. "Better have it over at once, and my fate decided in some way; then I shall no doubt be able to put aside these foolish regrets, and banish Cecil's image from my heart."

She dressed herself with more than ordinary care that evening, and looked, indeed, lovely and fairy-like in her gauzy green and white dress. No wonder Claude's eyes lighted up when he beheld her, for beauty commands admiration, even where the heart is not touched: he was at least bewitched by her, though still true, in a kind of way, to his former love.

Mabel saw his glance, and hardly restrained a smile of triumph as she thought of the victory within her grasp. His mother saw, too, that her plans were nearly realized, and looked commendingly on the girl who had overcome so many difficulties, and so nearly brought the matter to a successful conclusion.

Curiously enough, this night on which Mabel Prendergast proposed to make her own of Lord Feversham was the first evening for which the Bambridges had accepted any invitation since they came to London. They were going to Lady Longwreath's, quite unconscious that the Feversham party would be there also, though, of course, that was a thing to be expected. Clarissa asked Gwendoline, while they were dressing, what she should do if she met him there.

"Do," replied Gwendoline, rather sharply for her; "why will you all persist in thinking I care for him? He proposed for me, and I refused him, that is all. He is not the first man such a fate has happened to, and I do not feel bound to make a scene because of it. I shall bow to him, and pass on. At the same time, I should be better pleased if we did not meet him."

The Bambridges gained the ball-room, and were some time in it without seeing any thing of the Fevershams; the feeling of nervousness that had attacked Gwendoline, though she was a great deal too proud to own it, at length began to wear off.

She had just finished one dance, and had returned to her mother, waiting for her next partner to come and fetch her, when, feeling tired, and seeing the door of a room that appeared to be a boudoir open near her, she said to Mrs. Bambridge,

"Mamma, I am going in here to sit down and rest for a minute or two: if my partner comes for me, tell him where to find me." So saying, Gwendoline passed quietly into the room by herself.

It was not very light, and for a moment she almost thought she was alone; then she became aware there was a gentleman standing in the window recess. He was talking earnestly, in a low voice, when she first perceived him, but as she looked again, and discovered it was Lord Feversham, he ceased speaking, and bent forward for an answer to some one sitting near him, whom Gwendoline could not see. Her first impulse was to run away, but on reflection, being convinced she would be discovered before she reached the door, she walked quietly up the room, thinking her movements would acquaint them with her presence at once; but they were too much absorbed in themselves to heed her quiet, graceful approach. Just as she was about to seat herself in an easy-chair, and to take up a book in order that she might not observe their movements, Claude—her Claude, as she had till then persisted in thinking him—bent forward, and taking both the hands of a young and very beautiful girl in his, drew her toward him and kissed her hastily. At this sight Gwendoline felt her heart give one wild bound, and then stand still; the room seemed to turn round with her; she made a feeble effort to rise and get away before she could be recognized, but failed, and stood holding on by the table, trembling violently, and gazing at the lovers with scared, amazed eyes.

Her movement attracted Mabel's attention, and drawing back from Claude's embrace, she murmured,

"Let me go now; some one is watching us. We will go back to the dancers," she added aloud, taking his arm and leading him toward the door.

As yet Claude had not seen who the intruder was. As he passed her, with a pleased, excited look on his handsome face, he glanced carelessly toward the interloper, whose intrusion had been discovered just too late to prevent Mabel's answer to the question he had often before longed to put.

But as his indifferent, laughing eyes met the mute, agonized gaze in those once so dear to him, all color, and mirth, and light seemed to fade out of his face, and left it fixed and rigid as that of a corpse. He gave no sign of recognition, however, but hurried on with his lately won prize, thinking no more of her gay chatter, thinking no more of her peerless loveliness, that drew all men's looks toward them; only thinking how soon he could get rid of her, how soon he should see that dear—yes, still most dear—grief-struck face again.

"And yet," he thought to himself angrily, "she would not have me. Am I never to marry for her sake, never to beguile my loneliness by words and looks of love from others? Had she chosen even to wait for me till I should have earned enough for both to live on, I could have been faithful till death; but I had no hope, and my mother wished this other match so much, I could not refuse her. I must see her again," he went on thinking; "surely she does love me, or she would never have looked like that. What is the mystery? Let me but find it out, and all may yet be well."

He left Mabel with his mother, and hurried back to the place where he had seen Gwendoline Bambridge sitting. She was there still, but had recovered her self-possession, and bowed calmly in answer to his salutation. "I am to congratulate you, I see," she said, coldly. Any who had seen her a few minutes previously would hardly have believed the haughty beauty, with head erect and unmoved expression, to be the same pale, despairing girl of a short time before. "I had heard rumors," she went on, "but I scarcely believed them to be true; now, however, that I see they are so, allow me to wish you all happiness."

"Gwendoline," he cried, wildly, driven half beside himself at the chilling hauteur of her look and manner, "do not speak like that; every word of yours pierces me like a sword, and yet how have I been to blame? You refused me—said you never loved me, and told me there was no hope; then, when I went home sad and heavy with my disappointment, my mother pressed me to marry Miss Prendergast, and, all women being the same to me now, I consented. Have I sinned so much in all this that you can not forgive me?"

"I never accused you of any sin," she answered, coldly; "I only wished you happiness in the change of life before you. Why should you excuse yourself to me for what you have done? You only acted as all other men act, and therefore I suppose it is natural that you should forget one love and seek another, as soon as you imagined the first hopeless. I do not blame you for it, and wish you joy sincerely."

The tone of her voice was chill and cold, the words dropped slowly one by one with icy distinctness; every thing showed to Feversham's eager eye that, despite her refusal in the past and her freezing coldness in the present, she was wounded deeply by his having so quickly found some one to take her place. She loved him, he was certain; and with that conviction, every remembrance of Mabel Prendergast, and the duty he now owed her, vanished, and he cried, passionately, "Gwendoline, I love you as well, nay, better than ever; take me now, before it is too late. I know you care for me," he went on, taking her hands and turning her face toward him. "You can not look at me and tell me now you never loved me; you know you can not, and you turn away; but I will have an answer, and surely you will not repeat your refusal." She raised her head slowly and proudly, looking him full in the face: "I did right when I would not yield to your prayers," she answered; "you are now rich, honored, and powerful, with every prospect of a noble and useful life before you; how would it have been had I accepted you, and you were now a poor and struggling man, without any greater help on your path through the world than the affection of the woman who would have brought all that trouble on you?"

"I care not for a career or high prospects in life, so long as I have your love. Did I not tell you so before? Every thing is valueless to me without you, every thing golden and beautiful with you by my side. I am young and strong, I have brains also; but even wanting them, perseverance always succeeds in the end. Trust me, think no more of the future, and I will slave life away before want shall come near you."

She looked up, about to answer—and who knows what that answer might have been?—when she perceived two ladies advancing toward them. One was the young girl she had before seen with Claude, and whom she knew to be Miss Prendergast; the other she had also seen before. How well she remembered the day when that haughty old lady called at their lodgings in Dublin, to beg her son's refusal from Gwendoline Bambridge!

"You here, Claude!" cried Mabel, as they approached, though Gwendoline knew well she had not only seen and recognized him before, but had also heard the conclusion of the last sentence. It was not her cue, however, to pretend she had heard any thing, so she went on: "You have found an old acquaintance, I suppose? Will you introduce us? Your mother and I came in to rest here for a little; it is so hot in the ball-room."

Feversham was startled, and turned very white as his betrothed came up to him in so friendly a manner, standing by his side, too, as though she was determined he should introduce her to the lady with him. This, however, he did not care to do, but offering his arm to Gwendoline, said:

"Miss Bambridge, can I take you back to your mother? I think you said you wished to find her. Mother, I will return to you presently;" so saying, he moved off with Gwendoline, who, as soon as she entered the ball-room, and saw her mother in the distance, said,

"Good-bye, Lord Feversham. I will not detain you any longer from Miss Prendergast; and in future, if we meet, remember you have no longer a right to speak to me as you spoke to-night."

He would willingly have gone farther with her, and would have tried hard to persuade her to allow him at least to see her with her mother before he left her, but she quietly withdrew her hand from his arm, and moved off to her mother, threading the crowd with her peculiar ease and grace.

None of those who turned to watch her light step and graceful carriage guessed what a heavy heart she carried under that proud demeanor; even her mother, tenderly as she loved her daughter, and anxiously as she watched her, knowing that her old lover was somewhere at the ball, was deceived, and imagined she could not have seen him, or that, if she had, all remembrance of the old folly had passed away— if indeed Gwendoline had ever cared for him, which Mrs. Bambridge had not been able to prove quite to her satisfaction; though she was very certain, if she had not cared for him, she had cared for some one else much about that time, and that love of hers had left its mark on her life, as such things will do now and then, when the sufferer is young and impressionable.

But Gwendoline was not a girl to let the world smile over her misery, so she laughed and flirted through the rest of that long evening, which she thought would never come to an end, as gayly, to all appearance, as the merry, light-hearted Clarissa, who exclaimed, as they drove home,

"Is not Mr. De Veaux delightful? I wonder how I ever could have thought little Madcap so pleasant. He is not to be compared with Gerald de Veaux."

"Poor Darrell!" Gwendoline answered, pityingly. "So he is really cut out? You don't care for him now?"

"Why, no," answered Clarissa. "You see it was very foolish of me ever to think of him; he was so wrapped up in you no one else had a chance. It was much better I should transfer my affections than allow them to be blighted, as it seems to me his will be."

Gwendoline sighed. Perhaps those foolish words of Clarissa's awoke in her mind the idea which she afterward carried out; perhaps she had been thinking of it before she questioned her sister—who knows? At any rate, she spoke no more then, but lay back in the carriage, leaning her head against the cushions wearily, and wishing she was at home again.

As for Clarissa, she was too full of her conquests, and the fun she had had that evening, to be very quiet; but her chatter could not divert the thoughts of at least one of the party, and after a few attempts to get up a laugh, she ceased trying to do so, and went off into a pleasant reverie, in which Gerald de Veaux's handsome face, and the marked attentions he had paid her, formed the principal subject for reflection.

It was late that morning before Gwendoline's eyes closed in a restless, broken sleep, in which she passed through all the experiences of the night over again, and imagined herself face to face with Miss Prendergast, defying her to take her lover from her, now that she knew he still cared for her. But when she awoke, and the real events of the evening flashed back on her mind, she felt that, however hard it had been, she had acted wisely; she was sure, despite his ardent protestations to her, he had spoken with warmth and earnestness to Miss Prendergast before he had recognized her, and she was certain his caresses had been more those of a lover than of one acting in obedience to orders.

After all, her experience of men had told her that it was very possible for a man to love one girl, and yet to flirt with another till he almost fancied himself in love with her also; but such a character had always seemed to her despicable and unworthy, and was one of the very last she would have ascribed to Lord Feversham. Now her idol was shattered; he had proved himself before her eyes to be no better than the common clay out of which all her friends' treasured images were formed; but though she recognized the fact, and hated herself for ever having been deceived, she found to her astonishment that she cared for him as much as ever. She had thought that scorn of his weak fickleness would have rooted up affection in her heart, but it was not so; on the contrary, the cry of her inmost soul now was, "If I could but have him again I would forgive him all, and show him how much better my love is than hers.

"And she is beautiful," Gwendoline went on thinking; "it was not for her money only he took her; she pleased his fancy as well, yet many would think I could rival her, and I will too; I will show him that, though he may have scorned me, yet there are many others would be glad to gain one of those smiles he has rejected. Poor Darrell! he loves me; though I have refused him twice, he has not gone after new faces. I wonder would he take me now: if he asks me again I will accept him, and some day I shall have

the precedence of Lord Feversham's wife, and will show him that, though a penniless Irish girl, I am no disgrace to a high position. Yet stay," she added, pressing her hands to her brow, "it is not his fault that we are not now married; it is mine. I thought such a union would be ruin to him, and I said I never loved him. Truly I am punished for my sin: I did evil that good might come, and it only brings more evil. I think I remember his saying once only truth could prosper; while poor little Madcap agreed with me, and said for the good of a friend he would say what was false and stand by it. Oh, what a fool I have been!" she sobbed; "my punishment is greater than I can bear!"

After that evening the Bambridges went out everywhere in London, meeting the Feversham party constantly, and everywhere Gwendoline maintained a calm composure by force of will and stern determination. She carried out her resolve that she should be admired, and that Lord Feversham should see that she was. Her smile was the brightest, her wit the most sparkling, her dancing the most perfect, of all the beauties then crowding the hot London ball-rooms, and she had soon quite a little court, that followed her about in all places. *La belle Irlandaise* was the fashion; she was a queen of beauty, wielding her sceptre gracefully, skillfully, yet very firmly, drawing men round her by the magic of a smile, yet keeping them always respectful and devoted, by a certain latent dignity that was more felt than seen, and that would have deterred the boldest from saying a word that could displease her.

She might have married over and over again, wealth and title too, for men got infatuated about her. Perhaps the one who worshiped her most madly, though always at a distance, was Claude Feversham, whom Mabel found it almost impossible to keep in her train any longer, now that Gwendoline's beauty and Gwendoline's triumph were so constantly before his eyes.

If Gwendoline had known this, she would perhaps have been satisfied, and not hurried on to another step, which, while it left little mark on her life, fatally injured that of another.

I came up to London for a few days about this time. My father and mother were there, and I, knowing nothing of what was going on, thought I might get a little amusement and distraction from sad thoughts in the busy life of the metropolis. Of course the first thing my mother asked me was whether this beautiful Miss Bambridge, that everybody was running after, was the same lady I had met in Ireland. A little description sufficed to assure me it was the same; besides, I knew they had intended to be in London in the spring.

At the account of the manner in which she was followed and run after, my heart beat very quickly, and jealous fears began to rise. It was impossible that she should not accept one of the many brilliant offers she had received; and even if she did not, all this flattery and adulation would naturally incline her to look indifferently on so small a fish as myself. However, next day at the proper time I was in the Park, mounted of course, on the chance of fate's favoring me and giving me an opportunity of riding beside her.

Presently she came along, receiving salutations on all sides with her sweet sunny smile, in which

lurked a shade of sadness I did not remember to
have noticed there before. Two gentlemen, whom
I recognized as two of the most eligible matches
at that time in London, rode on either side of her;
while behind came Clarissa, the colonel, and another gentleman, who seemed to find that gay
young lady's smiles no bad substitute for those
of her sister.

As they came near, and I was about to lift my
hat, Gwendoline perceived me, and immediately
pulled her horse into a walk.

"I am so glad to see you!" she cried; "it is
long since we have met. How did you get over
the cold you had when you left us?"

Thus speaking, she reined in sufficiently to
place her horse beside mine, throwing one of her
escort out of his position, a manœuvre he did not
seem to relish, for, after riding a few steps farther, he raised his hat abruptly and left us.

There was a change in Gwendoline's manner
that I, knowing nothing of what had happened,
could not account for; it seemed to me so strange
that she whom I had seen sad and broken-hearted should now blaze out the gayest of the gay,
the queen of beauty, and the admired of all admirers. But such she appeared to be, and for a
few minutes I almost feared that the Gwendoline
I had known and loved was gone forever, driven
out by the beautiful worldly spirit now before me.

But when we were alone for a few minutes together that night at a ball, as we stood talking by
an open window, a change passed over her, and
from the gay queen of fashion I had just seen she
faded quietly into her old sweet girlishness, and
spoke of her home under the mountains, and the
happy days we had spent there, her glorious eyes
gleaming with unshed tears in the soft starlight.

"But every thing is changed since then," she
went on; "even I am. Do you remember, Vivian, what you have twice asked me, and twice I
have refused?"

I was about to speak and ask her if there was
yet hope, but she signed to me to be silent.

"I must tell you why I refused you then—
why I would accept you now, if you still cared
for me. Do not think me very bad and bold for
speaking thus, but I am very unhappy, Vivian,
and I feel as if you who are unhappy also would
sympathize more with me who have caused your
misery, than any one else would be likely to do.
I liked some one else better than you when you
asked me before to marry you, though circumstances prevented my having any hope, at least
at that time; yet as long as he remained true to
me, I should have been faithful to him. Now,
however, he cares for me no longer; he is about
to marry another, and therefore if you still care
for me, knowing that my heart is dead in that
other love, I will have you; I would willingly
show him others value me, though he does not.
I would not say this to you, but that you seem
so changed and saddened since our last meeting:
if the sisterly affection I feel for you seems to
you a fitting return for your love, I will give myself to you gladly."

"Gwendoline," I murmured, with a mixture
of doubt and rapture, "you have made me too
happy. I do not fear the dead love—it was not
worthy of you; and soon you will teach your
heart to care for me more than you once cared
for him."

I pressed her hand to my lips as I spoke, for
we were quite alone, but I dared not yet take her
to my heart as I longed to do. She shuddered
a little as my hot lips touched her hand, and drew
back, saying,

"I am cold here; let us join the dancers."

So we went back among them, and whirled
along as merrily as the rest, I with every pulse
in my body bounding with delight; she, I knew
long afterward, with so heavy a heart she might
well have envied the poorest beggar in the streets.

How happy I was! I never cared that she
loved another, and that other Claude Feversham.
It was quite enough for me that she was mine
now: I believed firmly she would, in time, care
more for me than she had ever done for Claude.
I knew that she liked me very warmly already,
and I felt that my passionate adoration must win
more affection in return. Yes, my heart knew
no fear at the dangerous contract, and beat high
with rapture when I thought with what pride I
should present her to my mother.

Neither my father nor my mother were at the
ball that night, so I knew I must wait at least
till next day before I could introduce her to my
family; besides, I should have to talk over the
matter with General Bambridge before it could
be finally settled; though that, I knew, was a
mere matter of form, as of course he would not
refuse his consent. I dare say Gwendoline told
them all about it that night, however, for it was
evident Clarissa suspected something; and, her
suspicions once aroused, there was never rest for
any one till her curiosity was satisfied.

"What has happened to Vivian?" she cried,
as I brought Gwendoline back to her mother.
"I think I never saw him looking so radiant.
And you were very doleful when you came in
this evening," she continued, turning to me.
"There is something up. Tell me, what is it?"

"Miss Bambridge has been with me all the
time," I answered; "she knows every thing I
know—ask her about it. And now, I think,
this is our dance," I continued, putting my arm
round Clarissa's slender waist and whirling her
off amidst the dancers.

Somehow, I can not quite tell how it was, before we had gone many times round the room
Clarissa had found out my secret, and was so
evidently delighted that I felt quite pleased, as
though I had done some great thing.

"I am so glad!" she cried. "Gwendoline, I
know, will be happy with you, and we all like you
so much that nothing could give us more pleasure."

In what a fool's paradise I passed that evening! I seemed to move on air, and to be carried
along far above mortal pains and sorrows; my
head was turned with happiness, and even the
knowledge that her heart was not mine, but perhaps still another's, could not chill my ecstasy.
She would love me soon, I fondly hoped and believed; she liked me well now. I had only a few
more steps to make in her affections, and the
battle would be won—she would be mine entirely. So I told myself joyfully, as I walked home
through the cool night air, after putting my beloved, carefully cloaked by my hands, into her
carriage.

The streets were quiet, and the faint gray of
the summer twilight made them look ghostly and
peaceful as I wended my way onward, thinking
of my happiness, and vowing to deserve it by
such devotion as no woman ever won before.

How is it that at some moments of intense joy a shadow passes before you, and dims your visions of the bright future?—a shadow for which you can not account in any way, that you can not describe, except that it turns the golden dreams dead and dull, all the life and glitter fading out of them, till, bewildered and alarmed, you seek vainly for the cause of this sudden change.

Such a gloom passed over me as I neared our house. It seemed as if suddenly, and without any warning, a voice in my heart called loudly: "This happiness, that seems within your grasp, is not for you. She whom you love will never be yours."

As these words passed through me and rang in my ears, I staggered against the railings and leaned there for a minute or two, stunned by the sudden revulsion of feeling. Not a footstep rang along the quiet street, the lamps were looking pale and sickly in the increasing light of day, and the cool, soft summer air, blowing gently over my brow, calmed me after a time.

"It is the reaction after being so happy," I muttered. "It seems like a dream, too good to be true. But it is true, I know, and to-morrow I will speak to the general."

As I decided thus I recovered my spirits again, and, raising my head, stepped gayly on, gained our door, let myself in, and was soon dreaming blissfully about the events of the evening. My first business, next day, was to tell my mother all about it, and get her on my side; I therefore sent her a message, a little before her usual breakfast hour, to say if she had no objection I would take that meal with her. This was rather an unusual step on my part, as generally I was up too late the night before to appear when she did, and my father and she usually took breakfast alone together. This was only when we were in London, however; in the country we were as regular and domestic as our neighbors, but in town that is out of the question.

Of course my mother was delighted to have me for a companion, and sent word to that effect. In a short time I was seated opposite to her at table, feeling too nervous to do justice to the meal before me. Certainly I had talked the matter over with my mother before, and she had been most kind and sympathizing about it, in spite of which I could not but feel she might not like so speedy an arrangement of the matter as I desired. I did not broach the subject therefore for some time, but sat in an abstracted manner, wondering how I should begin, when she settled that difficulty for me by saying, "What was it you wanted to consult me about, my boy? I suppose it must be something important, to have aroused you so early."

Then I told her all, and, when I had finished, waited impatiently for an answer. She mused thoughtfully for some time over my story, and then said: "We would not have a word to say against it, my son, if you were a little older, but you are too young to take so important a step in life. This is your first love, and no doubt very dear to you now, but it is in the nature of most men's hearts that the first love is never the last; in a year, or at most two, you will have seen some other face you will consider for a time fairer and dearer; or if you marry her, and she has tact and attractions enough to keep you true, and remain in your eyes the one woman in the world for you, you will still see everywhere that a young married man like you is at a great disadvantage in society, and you will perhaps feel inclined to exclaim, 'Why did not my parents make me wait a year or two, till I had seen a little more of life, and was more sobered and steadied down?'"

"Never, mother, never!" I cried, earnestly; "believe me, she only can make me happy. I tell you, mother, I know my own heart, and I feel that for me at least the first love will be the last. I have her promise now; don't let any worldly scruples spoil my happiness."

My mother smiled gently down on me as I came and knelt beside her, passing my arm round her waist coaxingly. "My child," she said, "if you are sure of your own heart, and if her people consent, I will answer for your father and myself. I will call on Mrs. Bambridge to-day and see the young lady. It will be very pleasant to have a daughter as well as a son, and I know you could not love any one who was not good; therefore I look forward to her being a great comfort to me, now I am getting old."

"Getting old, darling mother!" I cried; "why, you look younger than most of the belles in their second season here. My mother is the most beautiful and youngest-looking matron in London," I added, proudly, as I thought what a sensation her appearance always created, and how men's eyes followed her admiringly wherever she moved. "Did I tell you," I went on, brimming over with happiness, "what young Montague of the Guards said to me: 'By Jove, Darrell, you're the luckiest fellow alive to have such a mother. A man need never desire to leave his own fireside when he has such an angel as that always beside it.' And I agree with him, mother, only you will be, if possible, more charming when my Gwendoline is your daughter."

It was easy to arrange matters with General Bambridge, once my father's consent was guaranteed, so you may imagine my delight when, preliminaries being settled, and settlements talked over, it was decided we should be married within two or three months. I was very much against a long engagement, in which all the elder people agreed with me; for, as my mother said, such an ordeal is generally very trying to young affections.

As to Gwendoline herself, it struck me sometimes that she was afraid of the step she had taken; but this was more from the manner in which she avoided being left alone with me, or turned off my passionate protestations of affection, than from any avowal on her part that such was the case. Indeed, once or twice, when, stung by this fear, I said, "Gwendoline, darling, I am afraid you regret having made me so happy," she answered, "Do not think so, Vivian. I like you better than ever, but I can not be quite as gay yet as you would wish me to be, and as I hope to be some day."

At the same time that the news of our approaching marriage startled sleepy chaperons out of their propriety, and caused them to launch into severe condemnation of Lady Traverscourt's folly in permitting that foolish boy to settle so early in life, and, moreover, in allowing him to choose, not a well-trained bird out of their fashionable nests, but a wild dove out of an Irish dove-cote —before they had got over this shock, I say, they received another, less violent certainly, because more correct and conventional, but still severe enough to anxious young men on their preferment, and to the mothers of damsels in the same case—viz., that Lord Feversham was about to be married to Miss Prendergast.

It was very hard, two such prizes being united, and rendered useless, but still it was natural and proper: they could be forgiven, while my scheme for my own happiness was utterly preposterous and absurd.

I knew by Gwendoline's face when she heard the news about Lord Feversham, and I almost felt pleased as I thought that, now all hope was over, she would soon forget him. Certainly successful love is a selfish passion, let who will say nay. Unsuccessful, one may be self-denying, and think of the happiness of the beloved more than of one's own; but once fear and doubt are banished, then one takes it for granted that one's own pleasure pleases also the one loved, and, I fear, her wishes are often but little consulted.

While I dreaded to lose her, I could see how much happier she would be with Feversham; I could urge his claims and try to advance his cause. Now, though I knew she still loved him, I was rejoiced at a circumstance that I knew must pain her, and part them forever.

I think I had a half-ashamed consciousness of this as I looked at her pale face and sad, soft eyes, the day the announcement first reached her ears; yet, though I pitied her, I triumphed, and would not for worlds have had it otherwise.

And now my leave was drawing to a close, as was Claude's also; in fact, we determined to join on the same day, and journey back to Dublin together; then in about two months' time I hoped to obtain leave again and be married, and I had a kind of idea Feversham's plans were the same as mine, though I had no opportunity of asking him of late. I should hear all about it in the train, I knew, and in the mean time I was a great deal too much taken up with my own happiness to care about him, or to hunt him up now and then for a chat, as I should have done had not my own time been so pleasantly occupied.

CHAPTER XXVI.

A SCENE IN BARRACKS.

AFTER all it is a very pleasant thing, finding one's self back with the regiment after an absence, no matter how one has enjoyed one's self on leave, not because of the regimental work, certainly, for to all except a select few that always remains rather a bore than otherwise; but because one meets again the old cheery, familiar faces, hears all the familiar sounds, and finds one's self once more in an atmosphere of *camaraderie* never found quite in perfection out of the service, I fancy. One likes to listen to what so-and-so has been doing with himself during one's absence, and he, in his turn, takes an interest in one's exploits, and participates in the pride with which we tell how we cut down such a one in that tremendous run with the Blankshire hounds, or made the largest bag at Lord Bluestocking's battue; for being done by one of "ours," does it not reflect credit on all?

Something of this pleasant feeling of return among old friends and familiar scenes soothed away the loneliness that began to settle on my spirit when I parted from Gwendoline. I was very young, and it was my first experience of separation, so that, with all my buoyancy of spirit and hopefulness, I had been rather downcast, and a poor companion for Claude, who seemed himself in low spirits, and I fancied was inclined almost to avoid me.

I had not seen him to speak to since his engagement became public, so when we were alone in the mail, having a carriage to ourselves, I thought I ought to congratulate him on his approaching happiness, being sure that, if his feelings in any way resembled mine, he would be only too pleased to talk about it.

"You are a lucky fellow," I said, "to have won that beautiful girl, Miss Prendergast, whom I saw riding with you last winter. You are one of the most fortunate people I know."

"Do you think so?" he answered, dryly. "I do not." Then, seeing my expression of astonishment, he went on: "My dear Darrell, do not talk about things you do not understand. I dare say I shall do very well; but I am older and more experienced than you, and can not be expected to fall into the same ecstasies over the common lot of all men as you do."

He was very silent after this during the whole journey, but told me the wedding was to take place in two months' time—in fact, just about a week after the time fixed for my own; but of this I did not remind him, as he seemed in no mood to sympathize with my joyful feelings.

I do not think I had been back long before every fellow in barracks knew all about my fate, and a great deal of condolence I got from them, they having made up their minds that the marriage of a young man was an unmitigated evil, and I was to be pitied accordingly. In vain I assured them of my happiness, and represented that only my own wishes impelled me to the step; it was all the same to them—they shook their heads gravely, and only replied by some wise old saw, as "A young man married is a man that's marred," or something of that sort. Indeed, Mayleigh said, "Only we know you so well, and you are already in the regiment and liked, we would not have a married ensign. As it is, it is a bad example to the youngsters, and I fear will cause us some trouble."

What is the origin of the popular prejudice against a young man's marrying, even when he has plenty of money, and can maintain his wife in proper comfort? Of course, if the woman only marries him for his money, or is a coquette, or ill-tempered, no doubt he would do better without her; but if she loves him, and he loves her, how much trouble and evil-doing does her gentle influence guard him from; how much fewer scrapes he gets into, and how much happier, even if less boisterously gay, is his life, than when roaming about with several choice spirits, if possible wilder than himself, as it is usual for our young men to do. As for me, I was too happy to mind these expressions of commiseration, which indeed would have been better suited to Claude than to me, judging by his countenance.

As I said, every one knew every thing about my engagement just half an hour after I arrived in the barracks; but I do not think Claude told any one of his, and I certainly was not going to do so, as I knew he would not take such interference well.

Next morning, however, Cecil Egerton came into my room, having promised to breakfast with me, and then drive over to Belrush with me, to look at a stream where we had been offered some good fishing. I was not quite ready, so, tossing him the paper, I told him to look at that until I was able to sit down. He did so, and all was quiet for a minute or two, when suddenly I was startled by a smothered exclamation, and, glancing round, saw Egerton sitting straight up in his chair, the newspaper held up before him, showing by its trembling the agitation of his nerves. As I looked he crushed the paper in his hand, and seemed as though he was about to tear it to pieces. I had not read it, however, so I called out, "Halloo! I say, Egerton, do not destroy that before I have seen it."

He started at the sound of my voice, and the blood came back with a rush into his face, as, smoothing out the crumpled sheet slowly and deliberately, he got up as if with an effort, and held it toward me, saying, "Read that. I did not know Feversham was going to be married."

I glanced at the place he pointed out, and saw it was an announcement of the approaching marriage of Lord Feversham with Miss Prendergast. It was all plain enough, and quite true, though why it should affect Egerton in so violent a manner I was at first at a loss to determine. Then I remembered he had been staying with the Prendergasts in the winter, and no doubt had fallen under the spell of Mabel's fascination. Poor fellow! it was evident he was desperately hard hit, and I hardly liked to answer his remark, when I saw the pain he was suffering.

"Tell me," he asked again, in a changed, hoarse voice, "is it true? What is the foundation for such a report?"

"It is true," I replied, briefly. "It is all settled, though I don't think Feversham has told any of our fellows yet."

As these words, confirming the newspaper report, fell slowly and reluctantly from my lips, Egerton turned so white I feared he would have fallen, but he controlled himself, and grasped the back of a chair for support, as he answered,

"I do not believe it. It is a vile fabrication, got up either by Lord Feversham or his mother, with a view to increasing his importance in the eyes of the world; they think perhaps by doing this they may cause her to see the desirability of the step. But their pains are in vain," he went on, with a wild, excited laugh. "I know she is true; I could not believe her false, if she told me herself she was so. No, she is mine, only mine! Darrell, you must have made a mistake, or Lord Feversham has deceived you."

I looked at him with astonishment, and began to think he must certainly be a little touched in the brain, for though he had spent a month or two in the winter at The Poplars, yet it was absurd to imagine that any thing more than an ordinary flirtation existed between him and Miss Prendergast. True, I could quite believe any such intimacy with her would be very fatal, but this young fellow seemed to allude to something more; he spoke of her as his, as though he had told his love and been accepted. It was nonsense, of course; still I could not help feeling that very likely he had been led on and badly treated,

and I pitied him accordingly. Not so very long ago, under such circumstances, I should have abused all women unmercifully, and thanked my stars I was above such weakness. Now, I felt for him deeply, and thought thankfully, "Gwendoline would not have acted so."

"I suppose Feversham will be in the anteroom after breakfast," went on Egerton. "I must speak to him about this, and get him to contradict it. She would not like it a bit more than I do, but if it is denied at once it does not so much matter."

I was surprised at the tone of proprietorship he assumed when speaking of Miss Prendergast, and began really to think he must be mad, the more so as, though he sat down to breakfast, he continued talking in a flighty, excited manner, and kept helping himself to one dish after another, and then pushing away his plate without touching what was on it.

"Feversham is sure to be about," I answered. "I hope you and he will be able to make it all right with each other. But don't you intend to come with me, then?"

"Oh! yes," he replied, "if you do not mind waiting two or three minutes for me. Feversham is a good fellow, after all, and, whatever his motive for this can be, I think, when I tell him I object, he will write at once to have it contradicted. You do not mind waiting, do you?"

"Certainly not," I answered, thinking at the same time the matter promised to be a little more difficult of settlement than Cecil seemed to anticipate, at least by words; but his trembling hands and hurried, nervous manner told a different tale.

I do not fancy we either of us enjoyed our breakfast much that morning. To me there seemed to be a shadow of coming trouble, or, as I mentally expressed it, of a jolly good row, hanging over our heads; as for Egerton, I understood well afterward why his face had changed so sadly and suddenly, why such a strained, anxious look had come into the deep, soft eyes, usually so placid and indolent in their beauty. It was inevitable that a man with his intensely, womanishly affectionate nature should suffer deep and bitter pain through the keenness of his feelings, but it is rare indeed that even those weak as he, where those they love are concerned, are so mercilessly and cruelly betrayed, so shamefully deceived; as yet, though he did not know, though he dared not guess the extent of the calamity that had befallen him, the sensitive nerves of his mind had been jarred, and a thousand vague, wild ideas floated through his brain, like the throbbing pulsations of pain that succeed a heavy blow.

"I'll go with you, old fellow," I cried, as Cecil, after hastily swallowing a cup of coffee, rose to seek Feversham. "I want to speak to Mayleigh, and will no doubt find him in the anteroom; then, after you have settled this matter, we can go off on our expedition."

I spoke thus confidently and cheerfully, though I was far from feeling so. I knew for certain Claude was engaged to Mabel Prendergast, and that he would not for a moment think of denying his engagement; but what course Egerton would take, when he found his worst suspicions confirmed, I was at a loss to imagine; besides, above all, what right had he to demand this explanation, and to go on in the violent manner in which he seemed inclined to act?

To tell the truth, my business with Mayleigh was purely fictitious. I wanted to be somewhere about, so that I might know if there was any row, and perhaps get Claude to explain it all to me afterward. Gwendoline used to say I was the most curious person—man, woman, or child—she had ever met; and though I do not at all see the truth in that assertion, yet I acknowledge on this occasion I was very anxious to know how matters would end.

Egerton took my paper with him, carrying it so folded as to show the obnoxious paragraph uppermost. He glanced at it once or twice on the way, and I noticed, as he did so, his very lips grew white with the intensity of his emotion, and though it was a chilly day, large drops stood upon his brow. His eyes, too, as he turned them on me now and then while listening to my chatter, had a sad, pitiful, pleading expression in them, like that you see sometimes in the eyes of a spaniel.

At last we reached the anteroom: there were several fellows there besides Claude, and I fully expected Egerton would have asked him to leave the room for a minute, that their explanation might be settled in private. No idea of this kind, however, entered Cecil's head; he was too disturbed, and too terribly in earnest, to heed for one moment the inquisitive eyes around. Once he found himself in Feversham's presence, he seemed to forget every thing but that the man was before him whom report placed between him and his love. Stepping up to Claude, he laid the paper on the table, and pointing out the place, said,

"Do you see that? Of course you will deny it!"

With a quiet, cool gravity that must have been infinitely torturing to the man whose heart was beating so madly with suspense as to cause every thing in the room to grow dim before him, Claude took up the paper, and read the passage slowly and deliberately before he answered, looking Egerton calmly in the face with curious, questioning eyes,

"Why should I deny it? I did not put it in the papers, but it is true."

"By heaven, it is false!—false as hell!" cried Egerton, starting into furious, active, passionate life from his late despondency and depression. "Take that!" he went on, striking Claude a blow on the mouth, that caused a deep flush to spring to his brow, not from the pain of the blow, but from the outrage, the insult from his subaltern, a man whom he had always befriended. He sprang to his feet, and for a moment, in his indignation and anger, looked as though he could crush Egerton with one grasp of the strong white fingers he laid on the young man's shoulder. But his nature was a brave and true one. As he faced his foe, a glance at the pale, heart-broken face convinced him something was wrong, and quelling his passion by a powerful effort, he said, gravely,

"You must be mad, Egerton. Don't you know that in striking me you have laid yourself open to a trial by court-martial, and such a trial can only result in your being dismissed the service? What you can possibly mean by speaking in that way to me, I am at a loss to understand;

there has been some misconception here. Will you be good enough to explain?"

The young man drew back from Claude's retaining hand, and raised his head till his flashing eyes met those of his opponent haughtily and firmly. I had never seen him look so splendidly handsome: the weak look that generally spoiled his face had vanished, his slight form had dilated with the force of his passionate anger, and although his expression was pained and grief-stricken, there was a grandeur of despair in it; it was an expression such as one might imagine would rest on the countenances of those who fall overpowered by countless numbers, yet fighting bravely to the last.

He drew back from Claude, and answered coldly and sneeringly, "Did not that blow show you my meaning? I did not think you were a coward, as well as a liar and a sneak! If you wish to know why I call you so, I will tell you. The lady whose engagement with you is here announced, and whose engagement you maintain, is not so bound to you—she is mine, we are betrothed, and only wait for my lieutenancy to be married. If it be true—which I can never believe till I hear it from her own lips—then you have supplanted me, drawn her away from me, bribed her by your superior worldly advantages; in either case the answer to my blow remains the same. Shall I be obliged to refresh your memory with another?"

He stepped forward as he spoke, laughing bitterly and scornfully. But Claude drew back, saying,

"This is unnecessary. I comprehend you. But," he added, with a glance round at our surprised and anxious faces, "I should have thought more of your love if you had kept this scene private."

Egerton started, and flushed blood-red over cheek and brow as he perceived us all looking on.

"I did not know," he murmured; then recovering himself, he went on: "You need not teach me what my love requires to make it perfect. If I have erred, it was from intensity, not from want of feeling. I shall be in my room whenever you have any communication to make to me." And so saying, he turned to leave. As he came near me he staggered, and passed his hand over his eyes with a hurried, nervous motion, then tried to move on, but stumbled, and would have fallen, only I caught him, and helped him into the cool air outside. There he leaned against the wall, and after the breeze had fanned his cheek for a minute or two, he asked, "What did I say just now, Darrell? I do not remember. I seem bewildered! I know something has happened about Mabel, but I hardly can understand it yet. I thought some one said she had jilted me, but that is false!"

He would have gone on wildly, but just then the orderly entered the square with the letter-bag —the English letters were always a late post, and this day they were rather later than usual.

"Wait here for a minute," I cried; "or go back to your quarters, while I go in to see if there are any letters. I will bring yours, if there are any, for you."

"Very well," he answered absently, and went off, while I followed the orderly in and returned to the anteroom, where I found every one in a great state of excitement about the scene they had just witnessed.

"What is the meaning of it all?" cried several voices as I entered the room; while Claude's quiet sentence could be heard above all the confusion, "I think the fellow is mad!"

"I do not know the rights of the case," I replied, "but, from all I can make out, he seems to fancy himself badly treated by some lady, and thinks that Feversham is the cause of it." I did not explain more fully, because I thought most probably Claude would not care to have the name of his future wife mixed up in this affair. "Here are the letters," I went on, seizing mine, and glancing rapidly over the outsides to know from whom they came; "and here is one for Egerton. I suppose I had better take it in to him. And I dare say he can wait a minute or two for that, while I look over mine."

Claude had also received one or two letters by that post, and I noticed, as he finished reading the one he first opened, he uttered an impatient exclamation, and his face clouded over, as though something had happened to annoy him, then, turning to me, he said,

"You are going to Egerton's quarters now, are you not? Let me walk so far with you—I have something to tell you."

I assented, and as soon as we were outside, and crossing the square, Feversham said to me,

"I am afraid Egerton has cause for complaint, though I did not think it could be true at first. Here is a letter from her, which I have just received, confessing that she had, through pity for Egerton when he was ill, consented to engage herself to him, but now that a happier fate" (she calls it that, poor child! he muttered aside) "has been presented to her, she has not the courage to sacrifice herself, and has written to tell him so. She seems very penitent for the mischief she may have caused, and begs me not to let Egerton quarrel with me. She appears also to think he will soon get over it, when he finds there is no possible chance of his winning her."

"So do not I," I replied. "He is awfully cut up, and I am convinced feels himself deeply wronged. It is a bad thing for a girl to do, and I must say I think her conduct heartless."

"Remember, Darrell, my good boy, she is to be my wife, so I must trouble you not to comment on her conduct, at least before me. However, I was about to say I think that letter to Egerton may be from her, as she told me she was going to write to him."

"Very likely," I answered, coolly. "A girl (though she is to be your wife, I will say it) who could treat a man as she seems to have treated this poor fellow, would also be just the one to write him a calm, cold letter, telling him she had mistaken her feelings, that she never had felt the love for him she had imagined, and now, having found some one on whom her affections really were fixed, he must excuse her breaking off with him, and favoring this other more happy mortal with her hand."

This I said in spite of Claude's frowning looks, for I felt sure Egerton had been ill-used by the lovely, fair-faced girl I remembered; moreover, it seemed to me he was not the man to bear up against such a calamity. I could not but pity him, as I recalled the despair of his handsome face when he first began to realize the truth of the dreadful news, and I was too young, and too happy in my love, not to sympathize profoundly

with one whose dream of joy was thus rudely shattered.

When he reached his quarters, Claude, who had been silent since my last speech, said suddenly,

"I had better not go near him now. If, when he sees I have spoken the truth, he is willing to withdraw the insulting speeches made to me, and to let the matter rest, I will assuredly not resent his action. His state of mind was too painful for me to think more of his insult than as an outburst of blind passion, for which he is sure to be sorry when he comes to his senses. I do not fancy you will see much more of him to-day. Shall I wait here for you?"

I assented, and running nimbly up stairs, knocked at his door. He opened it slightly, but still standing behind it, so that I could not see his face, and took the letter I held to him, saying as he did so,

"I fear I can not accompany you to-day, Darrell. And I say, old fellow," he added, with an attempt at easy cheerfulness in his voice, "will you see me through this affair—be my second, I mean?"

"Do not talk about that now," I answered, thinking that the perusal of the letter he held would change his mind. "Think over it till evening. Then, if you are still of the same mind, I will do what you want, but do not do any thing of this kind in a hurry. You will never repent it but once, you know."

"You have got an old head on young shoulders, Darrell," he answered, closing his door slowly, "or you would not talk to me like that. Come and see me when you return." And so saying, he shut the door, while I went back to Claude.

"Well, have you heard any thing?" asked Feversham, anxiously, as I rejoined him.

"No," I replied. "I can not make him out. He is evidently trying to bear up and hide what he suffers, but you can see all his misery in the way he shuts himself up, in the very tone of his voice as he answers your most careless speech. I am very sorry for him; he was a good fellow, and a clever one too, but far too sensitive for this hard workaday world, where every one must take his knocks as they come, and smile at the pain they cause him."

"Poor fellow, I am very sorry for him!" murmured Claude. "But I can not blame Mabel. It was natural, poor child, that she should engage herself to him, and fancy she loved him, after taking care of him through a long illness, and it is natural now that, finding some one she likes better, she should wish to free herself from the chain with which she is bound. Doubtless she forms no idea to herself of the misery and hopeless despair it is to him, and perhaps would feel the same herself, if she was obliged to hold to her engagement and throw me over. But at least I will not challenge him, as he wishes. I will pass over his insult, if he will allow me, and some day, when he has got over the shock, I am sure he will thank me for not yielding to his mad desire for revenge."

How easy it is to deceive a man, if he thinks himself beloved! with what dexterity a pair of small white hands can throw a veil over the most clear-sighted eyes, or a few words spoken by a soft voice confuse the clearest judgment!

Here was Claude, without doubt a clever, sensible man of the world, up to any trick or plant of the sharpers and blacklegs, both in society and out of it—a man impossible to outmanœuvre and get round in the general course of events, yet now as completely beguiled and bamboozled as was ever the greenest subaltern in a marching regiment. It seemed quite natural to him that Mabel should love him better than Egerton, and throw that youngster over for his sake, even though he knew himself he did not bring her his heart, and he had a shrewd suspicion she was aware of that fact also. Never mind that, however; it was clear the girl loved him, he thought; and then, what an innocent, childish thing she was, with her sweet half-smile, and the sudden uplifting of her grave eyes to his! It was a pretty trick, and at times, as she did it, he was almost angry with himself that he did not love her as he believed she deserved. Had he seen her practice that half-shy, half-tender look before her glass, and then smile a triumphant smile at the result, he perhaps would not have admired it quite so much.

As it was, he walked across the square with me, and on our way took out her letter, glancing over it with fond eyes, no doubt, but not with that rapturous expression that a love-letter is supposed to call forth — indeed, after a moment a troubled look crossed his face.

"I hope nothing will come of this between Egerton and me," he said slowly; "it would pain and alarm her so, and, after all, she was not much to blame; it was like her pitying, child-like character to engage herself to the man when he was ill, hoping thereby to please him, and recall him to life and happiness; and it is equally like an impatient petulance I have sometimes observed in her character when annoyed, that she should refuse to bear the portion she had chosen for herself in life when she finds it too irksome, and when a better one is presented to her. These are faults, no doubt, but she is always the more charming for her faults. A perfect woman could never be so wayward, and yet beguiling, as she is, and one other also whom I have known."

He sighed as he spoke the last words, and I knew his thoughts were wandering back to the one woman I believe he had ever really loved as a man should love his bride—the woman that, before many weeks passed, was to be my wife; and I, knowing well her value and her noble true-heartedness, felt somehow a chill run through me at that sigh. It seemed to speak of things that might yet be, of old feelings revived, of old memories awaked — nay, if that were possible, old associations, old affections renewed. What if they were to meet now ?—would the ties that bound them be strong enough to keep off unavailing regrets, painful, yet sweet retrospections, hopes and vows for a future to which they could no longer have the right to look forward? Yes, I could answer that; with her, at least, though the troubled heart might throb and beat with visions of by-gone days, no disloyal thought to me would be allowed to harbor there; and if a struggle there was betwixt the old love, vainly given, and the new love that was to come, she would be the conqueror over the forbidden feeling, and I should be more secure in her heart afterward than before.

———•———

CHAPTER XXVII.

FOR THE LAST TIME.

If Feversham could have seen Mabel Prendergast, as she sat down to write that letter to Egerton which was to blight his hopes and crush all the young vigorous life out of his heart, he might perhaps have thought her less child-like than he did. . It was a hard task that she had set herself, and she felt it to be so, even while she determined it should be done; but the pale, sad face told its own tale of grief, however sternly repressed, as she locked herself into her sunny boudoir and sat down to her self-imposed trial.

She placed her elbows on the table, with her open desk before her, and, leaning her head on her hands, meditated long and deeply. The white, soft fingers, buried in the waves of her dark hair, clasped and unclasped themselves nervously; the glorious eyes, usually so brilliant and full of light, were sombre and deep, with a gloomy pain in their expression; and tears she was too proud to shed over the love to which she was herself about to deal the death-blow hung glistening in her long thick lashes. Now and then the sensitive, finely-cut lips quivered, but that expression of pain would pass away quickly, and a resolute, stern look, strange to that fresh young face, would take its place, and the set, pale features would grow so hard that, had Claude Feversham seen her then, he would almost have feared the woman he had chosen for his wife.

Sitting thus, she thought over the young dream of love in which for a short time she had reveled, as one basks in the sunshine, and which she was now about to destroy with her own hand and of her own free-will. She lingered over her memories of the past before writing the fatal words that would efface and blot them out forever. She thought of the day she found him, of the evening when she first knew him to be handsome, beautiful as the sun-god of the Greek mythology, and to her the king of men ; she heard again the voice in which he first uttered words of love to her ear; she remembered the time when he had almost found strength to leave her, and how she had lured him back, and stolen his strength from him by the false promise she was now about to reclaim.

All these things passed through her mind as she sat there, holding absently his last letter crumpled in her hand. She dared not look at it now; it was so tender, so true, so trustful, that every word cried out against her meditated treachery, and contrasted strangely with Claude Feversham's kind but never impassioned epistle. lying close by. She felt the difference, and shrugged her shoulders with a scornful gesture, as her eye fell on the favored lover's letter, while she muttered slowly,

"And for him! Stupid fool that he is, his heart is so little mine that he never perceives I have none to give him. Oh, my love, my love! you are worth ten thousand such as he ; and yet he wins the day—or rather," she added, with sudden energy, "not he, but his gold, his influence, his position—these are the foes you had to fight against. They were too many and too strong, and I too weak, for you to prevail against them."

As she finished this strange soliloquy she seized her pen and began to write with a feverish deter-

mination strangely at variance with the cool resolution of her ordinary character. Often she
paused as she wrote, gazing fixedly into vacancy,
till some new idea would strike her, and her pen
would again glide over the paper with frantic
haste; she sighed often and deeply, like one in
pain, as her rapid hand traced hard, irrevocable
words; but when it was ended, the long-drawn
breath had as much relief as of sorrow in its
sound, and she whispered to herself:

"It is all over now, that mad, foolish dream.
I wonder will he grieve much? But I need not
wonder. He told me once if he lost me he should
die, and I fear it will be so."

She paused and clasped her hands tightly,
looking irresolutely at the letter lying before her,
as though half determined to destroy it; then
she recovered herself, and shaking her head with
an impatient gesture, she folded, sealed, and directed the letter, musing as she did so over its
contents. It was all false for the most part, false
as her own fair, sweet face, and the tender, loving words she had so lately written to Claude
Feversham.

She told him how pity for him in his state of
weakness had misled her, and now she had mistaken her feelings for something deeper and more
tender than they were; that now she had discovered herself capable of a stronger, purer affection, and threw herself on his generosity to
release her from the promise given in her foolish,
childish days, before she knew what true love
was. She feared he would think she had used
him badly, and very prettily she expressed her
contrition for the pain she was about to cause
him, reverting always to her childishness and
folly, her ignorance until now of what love really
was, and the sin of betraying both him and herself by concealing the real state of her heart, once
she had discovered it.

It was a letter such as might have been written by a child without a heart, a mortal Undine,
in fact, but never surely by a woman who loved
and had been loved, as she had been. And this
was the missive I handed in to Egerton that
morning through his half-open door, and that he
held unopened in his hand till I had left. Then
he tore it open with eager, trembling fingers, and
glanced hurriedly over its contents. The events
of the morning should have prepared him in some
way for what was about to happen, yet now the
blow seemed to fall with as much force as though
it came unexpectedly. He fell back against the
window-sash, catching blindly at a chair to steady
himself, and moaned the dismal, inarticulate
moan of a soul in agony. In that first bitter
hour he found no words to express his anguish;
he only hid his face from the light and groaned in his cruel sorrow. He uttered no word
or sound as he lay through the weary hours,
crouched up in a heap in the window. His face
was hidden from sight, had there been any one
near to see, by the arm on which his head rested; he moved not, stirred not; like one dead he
lay; none could know what passed through his
mind during that terrible time. The sunlight
streamed in through the window, and wandered
along the walls, and over the table and floor,
resting brightly on every object in the room, but
longest and most gayly on his bowed and strick-
en head. But he saw and heeded not; before
his mental eyes the sun should shine never more,

to him all the beauty and gladsome light of nature were dead and gone forever.

At length he rose, but tottered as he stood upright, and moved through the room with the feeble, uncertain steps of one walking in a strange
place in the twilight. After a time he seemed
to recover a little, and stepped more certainly,
while his handsome face wore an expression never seen there before: it was pale, calm, and determined; but the calm was that of despair, the
determination that of a man whom nothing in
heaven or earth could alter in his resolution.
He wrote a note or two, put a few things into
a portmanteau, made preparations for a hurried
journey, all in the same unmoved way, and then
paused for a moment, as though uncertain what
next to do.

Just at this moment I appeared, according to
promise, having returned empty-handed from my
excursion. The alteration in Egerton's manner
and appearance in those few short hours was so
great that I hardly recognized him, and could
not refrain from uttering an exclamation of astonishment. But the strange, calm sternness
of his pale face awed me; I felt instinctively
that grief must indeed be terrible which could so
remove all trace of his former self in the expression of a man's countenance. He looked absently at me for a minute or two after he had admitted me, and then, as if remembering suddenly the
events of the morning, said,

"I have heard nothing from him as yet; I
expected I should have before now. Do you
think he will not take up the matter?"

"What matter?—what is it you expect?" I
asked, hardly recollecting what had happened,
and not sure either that he meant to follow up
his insult, now he knew all, if Claude declined to
take notice of what had already passed.

"Did you not see? Do you not understand
that I want him—the villain who has supplanted
me—to meet me in fair fight; that I may revenge
myself for the wrong he has wrought me? If he
does not take the blow I gave him this morning
as a sufficiently marked insult, and challenge me,
I will send him a message; and if he will not receive that, I will horsewhip his cowardly carcass
till he shall wish he had fought with the weapons of a brave and honorable man."

"That will not be necessary, I assure you,"
I replied, thinking that in courage and strength
few men could surpass Claude; "but if you are
determined to fight, you had better send him a
challenge, for I know that, considering the painful circumstances of the case, he had intended
to pass over your insults this morning, fancying
that, after you had thought the matter over a little, you would see he had not been to blame, and
that you had acted hastily."

"No, no," he cried angrily, "I was right, and
he shall at least give me this satisfaction. Stay,
I will write him a line, which I beg you will take
to him; I must also ask you to be my second in
the affair when it comes off."

I promised to do as he wished, though in truth
I did not care to be mixed up in the affair. In
old days it was a feather in a young man's cap
to have even assisted at a thing of this sort, while
to have been a principal covered one with glory;
but now it is all different. People look coldly
on the practice, and it is flat against the rules
and regulations of the service. So altogether I

should have been just as well pleased had he asked some one else to stand by him on this occasion, and I waited, while he wrote his note, in rather a disturbed frame of mind.

"There," he said, when it was finished, handing it to me, "I have asked him to meet me at A——, a small sea-port in Brittany, four days hence. You will join me there also: and now I shall apply for a week's leave. Do not let me keep you," he added, seeing me linger, uncertain whether I should again try to dissuade him or not; "only let me have an answer as soon as possible."

I knew by the expression of his face that all efforts to turn him from his purpose would fail, so I took the note silently and proceeded with it to Feversham's quarters.

"It is a bad affair altogether!" he exclaimed, after glancing over the missive I brought him. "In these days it is hardly possible to hush up a matter of this kind; and if it once reaches the authorities, we are done for—he at least is; as for you and me, Darrell, we might by interest escape, but we run the risk of losing our profession also. However, what must be must, I suppose, so I shall have to agree to this meeting, and will hope it may pass off without injury to any one. I at least will not fire at him. He is much to be pitied, and I greatly fear Mabel has not made a wise choice in preferring my affection at second-hand to his passionate, undivided heart."

So it was settled that Feversham and Egerton were to meet at A—— next Friday, I being Egerton's second, and Mayleigh acting in the same capacity for Claude.

When I went back to tell Egerton all these preliminaries had been arranged, and the weapons were to be pistols, I found he had already obtained the leave he was about to apply for when I last saw him, and that he was thinking of crossing by the early boat next morning. He was calm and collected, with the intense, impenetrable calm of despair: it seemed almost as though all human thoughts and passions had left him—as though no wild throbs of hope or fear should ever again cause his pulse to leap madly—as though no danger should ever again call forth a flash of the during spirit he had once shown. He listened to my words with the same immovable countenance, and nodded without speaking, in token that he was satisfied with the arrangements, when I had done detailing them. Then, after a pause, he spoke slowly, and with visible effort:

"I shall not see you before I go to-morrow, Darrell, and I have a few things to settle in England before I go on, which is what obliges me to leave at once. On Friday we will meet at A——; till then, farewell. Pray that your cousin's aim be straight and his hand steady—it is the only favor he can do me now." And saying this, with a short and bitter laugh, he turned into the inner room and left me alone.

I went away, and joined the mess-table in rather low spirits. The man's changed face and manner haunted me, and I seemed to feel that such a nature as his would not only never forget the wound it had received, but that also he would never outlive it—never more be the same sweet-tempered, gay companion, the forward rider when the hounds threw their heads to a burning

scent, the graceful valseur in the gay ball-room, that he once had been: even to me, careless and happy, thinking little of others' joys or sorrows, it seemed a pity that so promising a life should thus be blighted for the sake of a fair face that I greatly feared was false as fair, and for the memory of honeyed words that carried a sting in their sweetness.

And now he was going off in a hurry, though the meeting was not to take place till Friday, and this was Monday. What business could he have to do? He had no friends or relations that I knew of: then suddenly the conviction flashed into my mind, he has gone to bid her good-bye, gone to craze his brain yet more by a sight of her bewitching beauty, gone to try to strike some spark of feeling from that flinty heart, and gone, as I feared, without the very faintest chance of success. Much as I pitied him, I could not wish him to succeed, for was not the fair, false-faced girl Claude's promised bride, and was it not better he should suffer than Feversham, who had once before been so unfortunate? As I thought this, it flashed through my mind that Claude would not feel this misfortune so deeply; moreover, he had more strength of character to fall back on in distress than the handsome, weak young man over whom I was lamenting.

Next morning, early, Egerton was up and away, leaving no word or message to me or Claude, all arrangements having been settled the night before. He was gone on his way to The Poplars, whither the Prendergasts had now returned, and where he hoped to get a farewell glimpse of the girl that had beguiled and betrayed him.

He had no definite idea in his head when he set out toward the place where he had spent so many happy hours; it was merely a half-formed hope or wish that he might see her once more before his death that urged him onward. He had no thought of speaking to her in his mind, did not even intend to approach near enough to the house to render a meeting probable; yet, when he found himself on the familiar ground, wandering along the well-known shady paths, an irresistible impulse drew him farther and farther on, till he approached Mabel's favorite haunt, a seat under a wide-spreading chestnut that drooped its heavy masses of foliage into the still surface of the pond, a large and beautiful sheet of artificial water. She was not there, and he knew, at that hour of day, was most probably at dinner. There was, therefore, no fear of an interruption from her, and thus thinking, he sat down to dream, and gaze into the still water, which seemed to offer such a peaceful haven to his weary heart, and under the glassy surface of which he would so gladly have buried his sorrows, had such a course seemed to him honorable.

But though he had not courage to fight the battle of life bravely, now the prize he had hitherto struggled for was withdrawn, still he preferred the fictitious appearance of honor and bravery offered by a duel with the man who had supplanted and robbed him. It never struck him that, with the intentions he cherished, a duel was as cowardly a way of shirking the pain of living as if he had followed the promptings of his weary heart and thrown himself into the still, peaceful waters, there to rest safe from all misery and trouble, near in death to the false love that had deceived him in life.

Such vague thoughts, half of peace and dreamless rest, half of bitter sorrow and painful action yet to be gone through, haunted him as he sat there under the broad, leafy boughs, watching with listless, unobservant eyes the dragon-flies hovering over the water, the lazy cattle standing knee-deep in the shady pond, the water-fowl gliding in and out among the islets—seeing them all without heeding, and the sounds of the hot summer day falling just as unnoticed on his ear. The buzzing of the myriad flies, the chirp of the hidden birds, the grasshopper's loud whirring, the gentle footfall of some one approaching through the long grass—all these he might have heard, but did not, only sat there dreaming a cruel, agonizing dream, but one from which he could not tear himself away.

Suddenly through his whole frame he seemed to feel her presence, and raised his head hurriedly, dreading to encounter the glance of those eyes that were, of all things in the world, most dear to him, and yet most to be avoided. His instinct had not deceived him. She was standing by the water's edge, her face half turned toward him, yet not seeing him, so completely was he hidden by the overhanging boughs. Silently he gazed, the wildest hopes and fears rising in his mind as he watched her, while she, all unconscious of his presence, remained looking at the wild fowl at play, with a strange wistful glance, as though she gazed at something beyond them that was invisible to all but her. She did not seem very happy, he thought, and certainly she sighed once or twice heavily. After all, he reasoned with himself, it was possible, nay, it was probable, that the breaking of his engagement was not her doing, but that of her parents; perhaps her heart was as sore at what she had been forced to do as even his had been, when he read the cruel words that blasted his life and ruined his hopes.

Quick as the idea flashed through his mind, new hope sprang up, and he resolved to make one effort more to secure the love that was to him all in all, and without which he was determined not to live. Quietly he stepped from his hiding-place and came toward her: as he drew near, the sound of his footfall caught her ear for the first time, and she turned hurriedly to meet the intruder. As she recognized him, a terrified expression came into her calm, unfathomable eyes, like the piteous gaze of a hunted deer, and she looked eagerly from one side to the other, as though searching for a means of escape. He was too near for her to get away, so she stood motionless, and cried in a frightened, trembling voice,

"Leave me, I beg of you! I can not speak to you now, and you must come here no more."

For the first time in her life, perhaps, the cool, proud-spirited girl felt a sensation of fear, and the feeling was so new to her that for a minute it mastered and overcame her. Her alarm and agitation strengthened in the young man's mind the belief that it was not by her will that all this misery had come to pass. As for her, his seeking her, after the letter she had written, seemed to her cold mind, which was still incapable of comprehending all the depth of feeling in his, as if revenge alone could be the motive for which he sought her presence: the wild, excited look in his face as he came toward her confirmed her in this impression.

She had heard of men who had gone mad under such cruel treatment as Egerton had received at her hands—men who had killed the woman they loved, when she proved false to them, sooner than see her smile on another man as she had once smiled on them; and her blood ran cold as she thought that here, alone and defenceless, there was nothing between her and him she had wronged—nothing that could prevent his wreaking his vengeance on her, as he had doubtless come with the intention of doing. She trembled at the thought, and glanced round wildly to see if there was any way of escape open; but unless she had been endowed with the fleetness of a deer, he was too close for flight to avail her, and no help could she discern far or near.

He whom she wronged thus—for her very suspicions were yet another wrong done to the generous, tender heart she had betrayed—noticed the terror in her looks, and ascribed it to a fear that her parents should discover with whom she was speaking, which confirmed him in his idea that their wishes, and theirs alone, had dictated the letter that had almost broken his heart, and was about to plunge him into a dangerous quarrel.

As he thought thus, he stood close before her, and, impelled by the strong hope that had sprung up in his heart, he drew her trembling, shrinking form to him, murmuring,

"Mabel, dearest, I know you are true. They made you write that heartless letter. But I do not believe it; and we will be happy in spite of them, if you will but wait a little longer."

He stroked her soft, wavy hair fondly, but she shivered at his touch, and, her confidence returning as she felt he would never harm her, she drew herself from him, and with a sigh that was almost a sob, steeled herself for the struggle between love and ambition that lay before her.

"For Heaven's sake, Mabel," he cried, as she with returning courage drew herself from his embrace, "tell me that you had no part in this cruel business—that you were forced against your will to write that dreadful letter? You love me still, do you not? Time and absence can not change you any more than they can me."

Then she answered, determined to shelter herself behind her parents' names, and replied,

"But how, Cecil, would you have me act against the wishes of my father and mother? I must obey them, and they do not like our marriage."

"They will cease to object," he answered, eagerly, "if they find you reject the alliance they had designed for you; and if you are willing to wait till I have a home to offer you, they will soon get tired of keeping us apart. I will work for your sake as I have never worked before, and with the hope I have of your love, success, I know, will attend me."

He tried again to draw her toward him, but she stepped back angrily.

"I will not oppose my parents," she cried; "and after their kindness to you, you should be the last to ask me to do so. It is true I am engaged to marry Lord Feversham, as I told you in my letter; knowing that, you should never have come here to speak to me as you have done; but as I was in the wrong to give you hopes that can never be realized, I forgive you fully, and hope, when we next meet, all this may be forgotten, and that we may be the fast friends I should wish us to be."

As she spoke she held out her hand with a calm smile, though her voice was hardly steady, and one less stunned and blinded than Cecil Egerton was could have seen her face pale and her lip quiver as she stepped toward him, about to pass on. But her words had stung him to the soul, and somewhere about this young man, gentle and forbearing as he seemed, there lurked a hidden fire that could on occasion blaze up, and burn as fiercely as that which rages in the hearts of other and outwardly more passionate men.

"You shall not go!" he cried fiercely, taking both her hands in his, and holding her full before him—"you shall not go until you have told me plainly and clearly, is this all your doing? Your parents, I know, never denied your wishes, and from what you said now, I begin to believe at last that you alone have framed this accursed villainy—that your hand alone has wounded the heart that loved you."

She was frightened again now, as he held her with a force that hurt her hands, and caused the rings to cut into her tender flesh; but she was brave, in spite of her bad heart—perhaps, indeed, it was the only quality about her that deserved real admiration, for it was not the blind bravery of ignorance that knows nothing, and therefore fears nothing; it was a loftier courage, that, fully comprehending danger, could rise superior to natural terror and trample it underfoot. When the first shock of this unexpected meeting had worn off, her old dauntless spirit had returned, and she resolved to put an end to this scene at once, let the consequences to herself be what they might. Looking calmly up into Egerton's excited eyes, she answered,

"Could you not have told from my letter that such an interview as this would be disagreeable to me? It is my wish, as I told you in writing, that every thing should be at an end between us. You would not be content without hearing the avowal from my lips; if it has pained you, I am not to blame."

She tried to wrest herself from his grasp and move off as she spoke, but he still held her, gazing with eager eyes at the loveliness he had prized so much, worshiped so blindly. At length he spoke, and his voice was so harsh and bitter she hardly recognized the tones.

"You are right," he said. "I was to blame in coming here, but I believed your mind to be as lovely as your face, and never dreamed so much outward beauty could cover so base a heart. Go," he added, pushing her from him; "I could curse you for having ruined my life, but henceforth I have no place among men, and the evil wishes of one who will soon be nameless and forgotten shall never cloud the happy future of the woman he loved too well."

Finding herself free to move, Mabel hardly listened to his words, but turned quickly away, walking with a dignified though rapid step, like that of one who, while disdaining to flee, longs to be out of the way as soon as possible. As for Cecil Egerton, he remained where she left him, looking after her retreating form, all life and light fading out of his eyes as he watched, and a set, rigid look of overwhelming despair creeping over his noble face. When she disappeared under the overhanging boughs, he sighed and turned to leave, but it seemed as though the shock had bewildered and weakened him, for, gazing blindly around, he turned first in one direction, then in another, unable to remember which path led out of the domain and back to the village. Several times he set out, as he supposed, in the right way, but always returned to the point from which he had started, and at length sat down again by the water-side, saying,

"I must wait a little; let me think calmly, and then I shall recollect every thing."

But calm thoughts would not come to his overtaxed brain, only the remembrance of Mabel's cold, unconcerned face when she told him she had written the letter, only her cruel parting words; while now and then a thought of the duel that lay before him at A——, on Friday, darted through his mind, and every time it flashed on his memory he would make an effort to rise, exclaiming, "I must be going," and would then sink down again, trembling and confused, on the grassy bank.

Poor fellow! he had not the determination or energy to keep down his sorrow with a strong hand, and turn himself to his work in the world, as a relief from agonizing thought. No, he was by nature too much of a dreamer to turn to active exertion as a distraction from his grief; and now his golden visions were so shattered, his fond hopes so destroyed, that no dreams of a happier future could find place in his heart. Satisfied that the world no longer contained any thing worth living for, he let sorrow take possession of him, and sought only for some corner in which he might lie down and die, apart from human observation and sympathy. But first he must have his revenge—the man who had supplanted and cheated him must suffer, although he had once been friendly and kind; yet all that must now be forgotten—no remembrance of any friend must hold back his hand when vengeance lay before him, for this injury Claude Feversham had wrought him was too great, too maddening to pass unpunished.

It was possible, too, that his rival might escape unscathed, and that he might be the one to suffer. It was not only possible, it was probable. All through life he had been unfortunate, struggling to exist, while others no better fitted by nature to enjoy prosperity than he were living in happiness and comfort. His genius (for he had genius, certainly) had been unrecognized and unprotected, and the short, brief episode of ecstasy he had enjoyed seemed only to have been granted him that he might feel more keenly his utter misery when hope and love were snatched from him. Therefore it seemed to him, as he sat there thinking, that the punishment he designed to inflict on Lord Feversham might very probably recoil on his own head; but this thought pleased far more than it terrified him; for, after all, death was now what he desired most, and, if he failed in killing his rival, it would be far happier that that fate should await him. One or other it must be—which he hardly cared; for if he was victor, life had still no attraction for him, was only indeed, to his imagination, a dreary, pain-stricken waste, and he felt, without actually framing any fixed plan in his mind, that he should not long endure the misery that lay before him.

When his thoughts reverted to Mabel, his brain seemed to whirl, and his very heart felt on fire; that she whom he had loved as perhaps few men had loved before—that she should have proved so false, was maddening. Had he been made of sterner and stronger stuff, as a man should be, he might no doubt have felt as keenly; but after the first shock was over he would have braced up the nerves of his mind, and turned resolutely away from all thoughts of the love that had deceived and betrayed him. The wound would open and smart again and again, no doubt, and the stronger and truer-hearted the man, the longer would the scar throb and burn; but the old physician, Time, and the work of the busy, bustling world, would at last heal the pain and the aching, even though the man should be destined to carry the mark to his grave.

But Cecil Egerton was not a brave soldier in the field of life, as such silent, struggling heroes are. The great fault of his character was his womanish weakness and tenderness, a fault which caused him at once to give up the battle when the stress and heat of the fight for life threatened to overwhelm him; the man who loses heart in this strife is as surely lost as though he were dead already, for the crowds behind rush onward madly, not heeding the figure stricken and kneeling in their path; or, if they notice him at all, they only exclaim, "The goal is before us, we can not wait for him." Then, planting their cruel feet on the weary shoulders, they trample him under the moving mass, never caring that the stepping-stone helping them onward is the prostrate form of one that once felt, and dared, and struggled as they; that perhaps even yet breathes and groans in his agony, but whose breath in a few short moments will be quenched, whose groans will die away in silence, his life beaten and crushed out by the mighty human tide that sweeps so unpityingly over the fallen.

So he sat in his misery through the long hours of the summer's day, only able to realize his pain, only feeling the anguish of love slighted and betrayed, only exclaiming bitterly in his inmost heart, "God help me! I loved her too well!"

It was all he said and all he thought. In the ever-recurring murmur there was a monotonous pathos, corresponding lamentably to the bewildered state of his once brilliant mind. Could any have seen and heard, it would have affected them more than the wildest, maddest ejaculations uttered by sorrowing humanity.

At last, as the evening shadows began to fall, he rose slowly, and, after one or two efforts to collect his scattered thoughts, seemed to remember the road by which he had come. Several times he wandered out of the right path, but at last reached the village, and learning, in answer to his confused though eager questions, that the last train to London for the night had not passed through, betook himself to the station, there to await its arrival.

CHAPTER XXVIII.

THE DUEL.

It was a still, gray morning, and the woods around the little village of A—— were stirred by the faint breeze that announced the approach of dawn, when Feversham, Mayleigh, and I drove up to the spot appointed for our meeting with Egerton. I was to be his second, Mayleigh was Claude's; not perhaps because he was a greater friend of my cousin than any of the others, indeed he was far less so, but because Mayleigh was on leave, and Claude had feared that so many of us asking for a few days' leave together might excite suspicion if any talk arose about the duel; besides, Mayleigh, though of a most pertinacious and inquisitive disposition, could keep a secret better than most men. We brought with us a French doctor, a quiet, self-absorbed-looking man, who expressed no curiosity or surprise about our quarrel, or the cause of it, but brought what he considered necessary without asking questions, a characteristic which raised him greatly in our estimation.

The spot we had appointed for our place of meeting was a beautiful glade in the large wood that lies to the south of A——. A stream ran through it, keeping up constant verdure even during the fierce heats of summer; now as we entered it in the still gray morning light, the deep repose that rested on every thing, the utter silence, broken only by the tinkling of the brook, seemed an unspoken protest against the design with which we had invaded that peaceful spot, and some at least among us felt that it would be almost sacrilege to mar with this outbreak of man's worst passions the holy quietude that brooded around.

At first sight Egerton did not appear to be there, and Feversham, speaking in a low tone to me, said,

"Darrell, can we not manage to settle this affair somehow if he turns up?—though I would rather he did not keep his appointment, so grieved am I at what has happened. I liked the young fellow, and I can not bear the idea of shooting at him, as if he were a mark set up for practice. Besides, I feel as if I were to blame in the matter, for certainly it was through my instrumentality he was jilted, though of course I was ignorant of his engagement, or I should have taken care to avoid Mabel, instead of seeking her company as I did."

So spoke Claude, generously trying to take the blame of her false conduct off his *fiancée* and transfer it to his own shoulders; but I had seen a little of the young lady's manœuvres, and had heard more, therefore I could not help thinking that, if the whole truth were known, it would be found she had sought him a great deal more than he had sought her.

I fancy Claude was unhappy and uneasy whenever he thought of Mabel's conduct in this affair. Even though he was fairly bewitched by her beauty and pretty ways, and mistook his passionate admiration for genuine love, he could not but see that her behavior had been heartless and cruel; though he excused it to himself on the plea of her childishness and youth, and her ardent affection for himself, yet it made him desire earnestly to avoid a duel with the young fellow who, he felt, had been cruelly wronged through his means.

"I shall try and make it up, at all events," he

said, turning from me, as a slight figure stepped into the glade, and by the now increasing light we recognized Cecil Egerton. But what misery and despair were visible in his countenance!—how changed it was, even since I last saw him, when the blow had only just fallen. He was only the ghost of a man, worn, meagre, hungry-looking, with great hollow, wild eyes, that roamed restlessly from one to the other of our party, never remaining steady for an instant, with quivering, eager lips, that opened to speak several times, and then closed without uttering a sound. Truly he was a pitiable object, for no brave man has a right to give way so to despair while life and work lie before him.

As he stood thus before us, I saw a change come over Claude Feversham's face—a change expressing sorrow, pity, and a kind of pained surprise, like that a man might be expected to feel at the sight of one whom he had known and liked, so utterly and irretrievably broken down, and for such a cause. However, after all, it is for such causes that men in all ages, even the best and wisest, have committed the maddest follies, the blackest crimes—have even allowed the light of fame illumining their works to fade away into darkness, to let their names grow silent on the lips of their brother men—all because a woman's smile has been withdrawn, a woman's voice grown cold, a woman's heart proved false. Though such is the case, and the history of the world shows us that in all ages it was so, it seemed to me, as I looked at Egerton standing there dull and immovable in his despair, that those men are more noble and worthy by far who, after receiving such a blow, have strength to draw the mantle of their pride over the wound, to look the world boldly in the face, to seek their work and do it, not stopping to seek for pity and sympathy from the crowd, ever more ready to ridicule than to sympathize, but determined to conquer the pain at last, though utter oblivion of what was once suffered may never be theirs.

But this was no time for moralizing, and I was just about to settle the preliminaries with Mayleigh, when Claude, stepping up to Cecil, said,

"Can we not avoid this, Egerton? I admit I have done you a grievous wrong, but it was unintentional, and now I can not bear to add to that injury yet this other, of fighting a duel with you. Remember, if discovered, it will cost both of us our commissions; and while that is a matter of little moment to me, it may perhaps be more important to you. Besides," he added, showing a little awkwardness in his manner, as men are apt to do when speaking to another on a subject dear to their heart, "she would be pained to hear of it, and that ought to have some weight, both with you and me."

Egerton had hardly seemed to listen to these few words, spoken gently, in Claude's grave, sweet voice; but no sooner had his captain ceased speaking than a rush of color overspread his pale face, and a light seemed to flash from his eye as he raised his head and looked round haughtily.

"You seem very anxious on my account, Lord Feversham, to avoid the scandal of this duel. Of course I can not attribute your backwardness to want of courage, because I believe you do not consider yourself at all wanting in that quality, whatever others may think: only I do not feel inclined to deprive you of this opportunity of displaying it—unless, indeed, you might prefer to receive a lesson of a rather more disagreeable nature from my hands."

As the young man said this, with the most insulting sneer on his handsome features, Claude's face became white with passion, and for a minute he looked as if he could have taken Egerton by the throat and choked back the taunting words ere they came forth; but with a violent effort he commanded himself, and answered, in a hurried, trembling voice, very unlike his usual sweet tones,

"Egerton, since you have been under my command you have never observed any thing in me that authorizes your addressing such language to me; for the sake of the friendship I felt for you, I am sorry to think you have used words which I know you believed to be untrue, even while you uttered them. But after this, unless you retract what you have said, no course remains open to me but to carry out the object of this meeting. Will you still have it so?"

"You know my wishes," answered the young man sternly. "Darrell, pray settle it all as soon as possible."

While he spoke, a remembrance of Feversham's unvarying kindness, and of the utter injustice of his aspersions, flashed across his mind; but he was too bent on vengeance for the wrong that had been done him to allow better feelings to turn him back from the course he had chosen. Besides, in it lay his chief hope of oblivion and rest from trouble. Feversham, if roused, was perhaps as blindly passionate as himself, only he was not easily excited to anger. If, however, Egerton could so raise his ire as to make him desirous of injuring his antagonist, his eye was keen, his aim steady, and there would be little doubt the young man's rest from the pain of living would not be long delayed. Indeed Egerton desired this far more than to harm Claude—that would avail him nothing; besides, his captain had been kind to him, and stood by him at all times; above all, any mischief done to Lord Feversham would trouble her most, the girl whom he had loved so well, who had loved him so little, and wronged him so cruelly.

For all these reasons, therefore, it was but a form Cecil desired to go through—the form of fighting a duel; his real intent was merely to stand as a mark for Feversham's fire, and himself discharge his pistol in the air. By this time all preliminaries had been settled, the ground had been stepped, the principals placed, and only the signal remained to be given. Egerton, who by his looks seemed to have been several days without sleep or food, appeared by this time perfectly exhausted with all the excitement he had gone through. As he took the pistol I placed in his hands, I could see that he trembled excessively; as it seemed to me, more from weakness than from any sentiment of fear.

The signal was given at last, after a final appeal on my part to Egerton that the matter might be made up without proceeding further; but all was in vain—he was obdurate, and reluctantly I signed to Mayleigh that it must go on. Egerton, near whom I was standing, fired in the air—that I could see distinctly. I also saw, or seemed to see him start, and press his hand to his side, directly after Feversham's fire, but he gave no other sign of having been hurt; and it was impossible to tell by his countenance if he was wounded, for it had been before as white and pain-stricken as mortal face could be.

Turning toward me, without noticing either Feversham or Mayleigh, he said, "Farewell, Darrell, we shall never meet again. Do not ask me to speak to Captain Feversham—I can not do it. Say good-bye for me to all who cared for me in 'ours.' And now I must be gone. Farewell."

So saying, and just as Claude and Mayleigh approached, he turned away, and pushing into the surrounding woods vanished from sight. Once, as he walked hurriedly away, it seemed to me as if he stumbled and almost fell, but quickly recovering he went on, and I thought no more about it for the time.

"Well, this is curious," began Mayleigh, when he came up to me. "Your principal has ske-daddled, without ever stopping to ask mine if he is satisfied, or to make it up, in case they have both had enough. What does it all mean?"

"Don't ask me, indeed," I answered rather crossly, for the whole affair had distressed and annoyed me. "Egerton is an unaccountable fellow at the best of times, and since he heard this bad news I do believe he has been a little touched. He did not fire at you at all, Claude, after his insisting so strenuously on fighting."

"Did he not?" answered Claude, sadly. "Well, I took no aim at all—I fired straight before me. I was afraid if I fired in the air he might make that an excuse for having another round, he seemed so determined about it. I do not know whether my ball went near him or not; do you?"

"I almost fancied he was hit at first," I replied; "but I think I must have been mistaken, for he said nothing, and walked off quite briskly. I am very sorry all this has occurred, for it seems he does not intend to return to the regiment, and he was always a good kind of fellow. We shall miss him, I am sure."

"Very likely at our steeple-chases," put in Mayleigh, with a cynical smile. "After all, he was a softy, not good for much; besides, he is all right—got off better than he deserves, I think. Let us go back to A—— now and get some break-fast."

This was Mayleigh's way of dismissing the subject, and I have no doubt many of the others would have indorsed his opinion, for Egerton, though greatly liked by those who knew him well, was somehow too retiring and gentle in his disposition to make friends among the more bois-terous youngsters, of whom there were a good many in the regiment. As for me, I had liked him very well, yet, though I confess I had no right to feel it, there was a dash of contempt in my affection for him, which was not at all of the same kind as that I entertained for my cousin Claude. As I said before, I had hardly any right to think of him in this contemptuous manner, for it was only a difference of disposition, and greater youth, that prevented me from losing my-self as utterly as he had done, when Gwendoline Bambridge first showed me she loved my cousin, and not myself.

Claude was silent and grave enough on our way back to A——; one would almost have thought, from the expression of his countenance, that the duel had had a fatal ending, or that he

would have been better pleased had the termina-tion been more serious. Such was not the case, however; for calling me to him, as soon as our breakfast was over, he said,

"I am very uneasy, Vivian, about that poor fellow Egerton. I noticed he appeared hardly able to stand from weakness this morning, and I should say, from the look of his face, he was ill. I fear, indeed, from his conduct altogether, that his brain must be affected, and, having had so much share in causing his misery, I can not be satisfied till I hear of his safety. Let us make a few inquiries through the town, and find out whether he has been here since, and if he has, whether he has yet left."

We did so accordingly, and succeeded in dis-covering that a young man answering to his de-scription had left A—— by the earliest train, passing through to Calais. Very ill he seemed, the porter said who gave us this information. He kept his hand pressed to his side, and appear-ed to walk with difficulty.

"Can it be possible he was wounded?" I ask-ed of Claude, when we were alone again; and I then related what I had seen, or fancied I had seen, at the time of the duel; but Claude insist-ed I must have been mistaken.

"I know very well the poor fellow is ill," he said, "but it is not the result of a wound. I took no aim, and I don't think it possible, under those circumstances, that I could have hurt him."

"Perhaps you are right," I answered, and we thought no more about the matter, only deter-mined to seek him out the moment we returned to England. We did not imagine we should have to look far for him, as we both fancied he must have rejoined, at least until he should have sold out; for, from his last words to me, I had a kind of idea he did not intend remaining with us.

But when we got back to Dublin we were rather astonished to find that Cecil had not been heard of by any of our fellows since the day he left; and a day or two more passed without our being able to obtain any clue to his whereabouts. Two or three days after our return, when I lounged into the mess-room shortly after post-hour, Claude was just opening out the *Times*, with an indifferent, uninterested expression, like that of a man who looked at the news be-cause it was the correct thing to know what was going on, but who did not feel any personal anx-iety about the state of affairs. I had a letter from home, and took it over to the window to read it in peace, for there were a lot of other fellows in the room, talking and laughing, and I wanted to be quiet while looking at the news from home.

Suddenly an exclamation from Claude caused me to look up. He had sprung to his feet, and stood with horror-stricken face, gazing at the paper that trembled visibly in his hands.

"What is the matter?" I asked, coming to him, and looking over his shoulder.

"Look at that!" he answered, pointing to a paragraph in the paper. "He is dead! Wretch-ed boy, can he have killed himself?"

By this time every one in the room had crowded round, eager to hear what was up, and it was soon known among them all that their comrade, Cecil Egerton, was dead. How and why was not yet known, but no doubt all partic-ulars would come out in time, and in the mean while every variety of report was circulated as to the possible manner in which he had come by his death—this much being, at least, known to us, that his body had been found in the grounds of Mr. Prendergast's place, The Poplars.

CHAPTER XXIX.

UNDER THE GREENWOOD-TREE.

It was a lovely morning early in the summer when Mabel Prendergast sauntered out of the low French window in the drawing room, on to the green, well-kept lawn, and thence wandered slowly onward through the shady glades, with which the domain abounded. It was a beautiful day, and the sun shone down fiercely on the heavy woods by which her home was encircled; the fresh green of early summer was assuming a bronzed, burnished look that told how, before long, they would don the gorgeous tints of autumn. The ferns among the long grass emitted a faint aromatic fragrance as she crushed them in passing; the hum of flies among the scented fir boughs sounded like a low, monotonous song; the air seemed thrilling with heat, and life, and sweet odors, as she wandered on, pausing now and then to draw in her breath, with a keen appreciation of the delicious feeling of the air, and yet she did not seem particularly happy. To tell the truth, she had never felt so since the day when she wrote that cruel letter to her whilom lover, Cecil Egerton: if it had troubled her before she met him that day at the pond, it had certainly not grieved her less since.

As she roamed onward quietly in the balmy morning air, it seemed to her that she might very well have been contented to live with him on what she possessed, without desiring more fame and power than would in that position fall to her lot. He had loved her so truly—she felt and knew it; and she—well, she had loved him quite as well as it was in her nature to love—nay, more than she would have thought it possible she could love; for though ambition had for a while hardened her heart and led her astray, yet now she began to repent, and she felt that if he were to stand before her again and ask her once more to join her fate to his, she could not refuse him. Was it too late even yet? What if she broke off with Lord Feversham, would he come to her again? The world, she knew, would be against her; it was a very small crime that she had jilted a nameless ensign in a marching regiment—indeed, most of the dowagers who sat in conclave over that misdemeanor, when it became known, had agreed she had done very right, when they found she had by the same stroke succeeded in catching one of the best matches going. But it would be a very different matter, she knew, throwing over Lord Feversham. All their circle—and it was a pretty extensive one—would be down on her: after all, what did that matter, with the object she had in view, though every friend she had should turn against her? He would still be true—nay more, the greater the blame thrown on her, the more censure she received, the more would he cherish and protect her, if she would grant him the right to do so.

But then her long-planned scheme, soon to be fulfilled—could she bear to abandon it now, when so near its completion? It would be a struggle, and she might repent the sacrifice afterward; at any rate, she would do nothing hastily; she would wander onward, and leave her decision to accident. She would look out for omens, after the manner of the ancient Romans, as perhaps many around us do at the present day, only we are ashamed of ourselves, and hide our superstitions, while they believed in theirs openly, and admitted them as part of their religion.

So it happened as Mabel Prendergast went slowly on under the shade of the stately trees, pushing her way, sometimes with difficulty, through the under-wood, she came suddenly on a man, lying apparently asleep under a wide-spreading beech. The long grass and bracken nodded over him, half concealing him from sight. His face was turned from her, but the attitude was that of a man who had lain down in utter weariness, and had so fallen asleep. For a minute or two she was frightened by the intense silence and stillness of the place—the very birds seemed to have fled the presence of the intruder, and she dreaded to step backward or forward lest an unguarded footstep should arouse the slumberer, which, little timid though she was, Mabel Prendergast did not desire, now she was alone, a good way from her father's house.

After pausing for a minute, however, her self-possession returned to her. As well as she could see, he did not look like a vagrant, and something in the faint outline she caught, through waving grass and feathery ferns, reminded her strangely of the man on whom her thoughts had been so lately dwelling.

Quietly, therefore, she walked round the sleeper, intending to obtain a view of his face. If it was the person she guessed, her self-questioning was answered at once. She would awake him, ask his pardon and forgiveness, which she never for one minute doubted he would accord her, and then they would be happier together than they ever yet had been—for she had learned now to know her own heart, and albeit her suffering had not been great, as hers was not a sensitive nature, still it had taught her that affection may be a torment as well as a blessing; she had made up her mind that for her henceforth it should be the latter. If, however, it was a stranger whom she had discovered lying there, she would retire as quietly as she had come, trusting her noiseless movements would not disturb him.

As she came round in front of him she perceived that his hat had been placed or had fallen over his face, so as to conceal it almost entirely—yet, from the little she did see, she could no longer doubt that it was Cecil. But how deathly white, how thin, how wretched! And he slept so calmly, the deep sleep of exhausted nature, she thought; though, as she stood watching, this intensity of repose seemed unnatural, and she would fain have awaked him.

But now that she was beside him, and knew for certain it was none other than he, she felt a kind of shyness about what she should say were she to awake him; she remained standing and hesitating for nearly a quarter of an hour before she could make up her mind to act. Then she bent down beside him, and called gently, "Cecil, Cecil;" but he neither stirred nor answered—only the long grass cast flickering shadows over his quiet form, and a ray of sunlight, darting through the overhanging boughs, lighted up his half-hidden face, making it seem even more white and wan than before. Again she called, and again silence only answered her. Her heart began to beat quicker, she hardly knew why, as, impatient and eager, she put out her hand and touched him on the shoulder. But even at her touch, that should have thrilled him through and through, he stirred not; she paused, clasping her hands over her heart to still its beating, and looking eagerly round as though seeking some companion to assist her, and to chase away the horrible feeling that was creeping over her.

But no one was in sight, and after a minute's pause, during which period of suspense her breath came in quick, panting sobs, she raised the hat from his face, and as her eyes fell on it, the terrible truth against which she had been fighting for the last few minutes forced its way to her heart. She had never seen death in any human form before, but her heart told her that the dead now lay before her. Dead! and through her, conscience whispered to her; and yet she had loved him well, in her fashion. As she knelt beside the cold form, and gazed with dry, aching eyes on the marble face, she felt she had never known till now how much she cared for him; and now it was too late!

Too late to bring life back to him; too late for repentance and love to avail; too late for any thing but despair, remorse, and anguish — that was all that was left her; and, alas! the dead could never know that she had sorrowed, that she had repented; that the burden of her life would be her conduct toward him, her grief for his loss.

Calm and self-controlled as she was by nature, she was now so no longer; she threw herself on her knees beside him, kissed his cold brow and the lips that were now rigid and colorless: kissed them with a passionate love she had never felt in the happy days that were passed, that she was destined never again to feel in the future. It seemed as if her very nature had been changed by the suddenness and magnitude of the blow, for she cried as she knelt beside him,

"Oh! Cecil, my love! would I had died instead of you! Would to God I lay here, and you were alive and happy!"

Thus she cried, half heart-broken by the consequences of her own wrong-doing; and the minutes slipped on silently while still she lingered, weeping burning, bitter tears that gave no relief as they fell.

She thought no more of the world now, nor of home and parents either; all she desired was to rest by him, if that might be. Life had nothing more that seemed desirable to her. She sat with her arms supporting the dear head, that was ten thousand times dearer then than it had ever been before, while the summer day crept on, and the birds, encouraged by the stillness, flitted about, twittering, and the squirrels sprang from branch to branch, eying the sad group inquisitively, and sometimes venturing so near that the girl might almost have touched them. But she never raised her eyes from the pallid face before her, never changed her position from the spot where she had first sat down, heeded not the pattering drops on the leaves overhead, that betokened a passing shower; she saw only, as through a mist, the eyes

now glazed and lifeless looking on her with love from afar; she only seemed to see the cold, motionless lips smiling tenderly, as they used to do in happy days gone by. Then at length every thing around grew dark and swam before her eyes, and, exhausted by the anguish of her now awakened heart, she fell forward across the dead, almost as lifeless as the body on which she lay.

It was merciful, perhaps, that oblivion had come thus to her, else her remorse would have driven her mad; for perhaps never had any woman sinned more daringly against the dictates of her own heart than she, and perhaps on none had so cruel and sudden a punishment fallen. For a time she lay there insensible, almost lifeless, across the heart that had throbbed so wildly for love of her, but that could never more feel rapture at her tenderness or despair at her displeasure.

She was found thus by her father, who had gone out in search of her, her prolonged absence having alarmed her family. When she came to herself she was lying on her own bed, and for a few short minutes flattered herself that the terrible truth which had been discovered by her among the luxuriant under-wood and waving ferns in the park was a dream that would vanish before her waking thoughts. But the faces around her were grave and sad, and the first question she put was answered by a pained silence that spoke more than words could have done. Then a kind of madness seized on her. She must know where he was lying; she must see the dear face, so still and marble-white, once more—this she would do, and none should prevent her.

She sprang from her bed as she thought thus, and, shaking off those who sought to detain her, hurried to where the corpse was laid. She seemed to know by instinct it was lying in the room which he had inhabited when alive. There, having found it, she threw herself on her knees beside the bed, and remained long in that attitude, speechless, because her feelings lay too deep for words.

At length, yielding to her mother's entreaties, she rose, and passing those around her, made her way, with tottering, feeble steps, to her own room, where she sat down almost unconscious and sullenly despairing, refusing either food or comfort, even from those dearest to her. She remained for two days thus, differing little in outward appearance from the dead for whom she grieved. But suddenly a change seemed to come over her —it was as though some recollection of the world had aroused her. Being left alone for a few minutes, she astonished her mother by appearing dressed in the drawing-room, where Mrs. Prendergast was writing to a celebrated London physician for advice on her daughter's case. But the change, though outwardly an improvement, did not seem to benefit her mind. All her former pursuits were abandoned, and she spent her days roaming restlessly through the house, with dull, unobservant looks, and no apparent cause for her restlessness.

It had been discovered at the inquest that Cecil Egerton had been very recently wounded in the left side, and though the doctor gave it as his opinion that the wound would not have been fatal if properly attended to, yet exposure to cold, damp, and hunger, while so weakened, had caused his death. Thus Claude found himself, at least in part, guilty of his young comrade's fate, though he had, as he thought, made sure of letting him off without any injury. Of course he came forward and stated his share in the unhappy event, but his family having great interest, and he himself being considered a rising man, the matter was hushed up, and few knew that he had been mixed up in it at all.

Mr. Vansittart bore the loss of his intended heir with the equanimity that might have been expected from him. Cecil had not lately been as strong as the heir to Beaumanoir should have been; an invalid was not the sort of person who should inherit a fine property, and people who would be more willing than he had ever been to enter into Mr. Vansittart's views, and who were more likely to get on in the world, if given the position of his heir presumptive, were as plentiful as blackberries. So the old man soon consoled himself for his poor nephew's untimely death.

When some weeks had passed away, and Mabel had regained her calmness, though only in the strange, unnatural manner described, her mother found her busy writing one morning. On asking her daughter with whom she was corresponding, she observed a little hesitation and unwillingness to answer.

"Never mind, dear," Mrs. Prendergast said kindly; she was so glad to see her daughter resume any of her old occupations, or employ herself at all, that she would have allowed her to correspond privately with any one; besides which, she had implicit faith in the girl's discretion. But Mabel, after a moment's pause, held the letter toward her mother, saying,

"You may read it. You would know all about it soon enough, and I am sure you will think I am right."

It was a letter to Claude Feversham—a penitent, self-reproachful letter, accusing herself of being the cause of all the evil that had happened, and begging Claude to release her from her engagement.

"I can not marry you," she said, "for I have never cared for you. It was ambition led me to accept you, and now that my conduct has caused the death of the only man I ever loved, ambition has lost its charms for me. A quiet, lonely life is all I now desire or hope for. You will, I am sure, not refuse me this request, the first and last I shall ever make to you. I know," the letter went on, "that I have wronged you deeply, I have persuaded you I loved you, and perhaps have won love from you in return. If this bo so, I pray you to pardon me, but also have pity on me. You will find many others to take my place with you; your wound can never go as deep as mine, for it is not your own evil-doing that has caused it."

So the letter went on, begging forgiveness, and declaring how utterly impossible it was she could ever be more to him than she was then; in her remorse and anguish, she also confessed that it was she who had found out Claude's love for Miss Bambridge, and had told his mother.

Her mother read it slowly through, and when she had finished, said gently,

"Have you considered this step well, Mabel? At some future time you may regret having given up Lord Feversham in the first bitterness of your grief; for you can not feel always as you do now. Your sorrow will wear away, and you will perhaps wish you had not acted so hastily."

She held the letter in her hand as she spoke, looking irresolutely at her daughter, who hardly appeared to hear what was said; but as her mother ceased speaking, she roused herself with a kind of effort, and in a wondering tone repeated:

"Wish I had not acted so hastily! This is not a hasty action; it is the one I have been meditating all these days; only I did not feel myself strong enough to carry out my resolution till to-day. I shall never repent having given up Lord Feversham. My great sorrow is that I ever accepted him. And, mother, you need never more fear your daughter's leaving you. If I were a Roman Catholic, I should go into a convent, and seek peace in penance and fasting; as it is, our home here must be my retreat, and whatever happiness or content the future has in store for me, must be in loving you and my father as you deserve for all your goodness to me, and in trying to do my duty by you, as I fear I have never done it before."

Mrs. Prendergast said nothing; she felt that Mabel had sinned, and been grievously punished for that sin, and she had sorrowed both over the fault and its chastisement, as only a fond mother can sorrow over her child's misfortunes. But she knew words of hers could not comfort now; whatever peace her daughter would ever feel in the future, could only be the work of time; so returning the letter with the simple remark, "It shall be as you please, my dearest," she took up a book and pretended to read, though all the while her eyes were scanning her child's white, wan face, from which all the old laughing looks, the sudden indefinable smiles had fled.

Claude, when he received Mabel's letter, suffered keenly for a few hours, for he had admired her beauty passionately, and had even loved her, in a different way from that in which he had loved Gwendoline Bambridge. And this cleared up all the mystery about the way in which his mother had heard of his attachment, and for her discovery of which he had so long blamed me. But in a short time he began to think that she had acted rightly, after what had passed, in severing herself from him. He could also see plainly now that, true and high-minded as he had fancied her, she had been deceiving him all along; for in the time of her greatest grief, when the heart speaks its most secret thoughts openly, she assured him the only man she had ever loved was his old comrade, Cecil Egerton, whose death clearly lay between him and her. Therefore, if this was so, she had done the right thing at last in giving him up. After a while, when the first shock had passed over, he expressed himself thus to me, and wrote a short note to her, agreeing in her decision as being the best for them both under the circumstances. So this second romance of my handsome cousin's life passed off, without resulting either in much misery or happiness, as far as he was concerned; in fact, he never should have taken up with Mabel Prendergast until he was quite sure he had outlived his love for Gwendoline Bambridge; and as he had not done so, it was almost fortunate for him that Mabel threw him off; otherwise he would only have endured a life-long misery with a girl so utterly heartless and unimpressionable as she had always been, except in the one instance, when even her cold nature had been stirred into real feeling.

The affair was a nine days' wonder among us all, for of course it got about, and was much talked of; but in a short time it was forgotten, as even the most stirring incidents are, and some among us no doubt hardly remembered that poor Egerton had ever lived.

Such is the way of the world, however, and I think we should be thankful that it is so. Had we not this power of forgetfulness, did not time carry healing as well as destruction with him, life would be one long period of mourning, from its commencement to its close; for who has not sustained some grievous blow, even in early life, that, if not mercifully deadened, would have clouded his whole future?

CHAPTER XXX.

TROUBLES FOR VIVIAN DARNELL.

ABOUT this time I ran over to Belmurphy. I had three months' leave, and intended spending the fortnight or so that must elapse before my marriage at the Bambridges' house. It was a fine day late in autumn when I arrived at Endley, and as it was early in the afternoon, I fully expected the young ladies would be out walking, as I had not written to announce my coming. However, my car had hardly drawn up before the door, when Clarissa came flying down in breathless haste to meet me.

"Why, Madcap!" she cried—she would still adhere to the title of former days, though I often assured her it was quite a misnomer now—"I am so glad to see you, though we were not expecting you. Why did you not write and let us know? We would have driven to Belmurphy to meet you."

"Well, you see," I replied, "I did not get leave till yesterday morning, so I thought you would take me without expecting a formal announcement, as I should have had to wait a day, that you might get my letter before I could arrive. Where's Gwendoline?"

"She has a headache, poor thing," answered Clarissa, compassionately. "You will see a great change in her, Vivian, I think; she seems to me looking very ill, and she is always in low spirits now. You remember how different she used to be."

"What is the matter, Clarissa?" I cried in alarm, for the girl's face was serious, and her voice low—in fact, she looked as unlike her usual laughing self as possible. "Do tell me, quick! there's a dear. And why didn't you write and let me know before, if she was ill?"

"Oh! it is nothing serious," she said, though I noticed that her face belied her words, and her manner was nervous and disturbed. "Come and take a walk with me," she went on, after a pause. "Gwen is lying down just now, so you would not see her even if you staid in the house. Come down to the river, and let us see what the falls are like after the rain last night; we can have a good quiet talk on the way."

I assented, as may be imagined. I was anxious and alarmed about Gwendoline, and knew I could hear all about it from Clarissa during the walk, so in a minute or two more we were trudging away briskly in the direction of the falls.

"Now, then," I exclaimed, after a short si-lence, "tell me what is the matter. I know you have something to say, and about Gwen, too."

"It is only what you knew before, Vivian, as far as regards the cause of her illness—or, at least, you did not know all before, no doubt, though you knew part. But I am almost afraid to tell you, and I know you will not thank me, though for her sake, perhaps, I ought to do it."

She stopped and looked at me nervously, a most unusual thing with Clarissa Bambridge, and I, seeing she expected me to speak, replied,

"If it is for her good, tell me, and don't spare my feelings. I can bear any thing necessary for me to know. Is she, then, so very ill?" and as I spoke I felt a pang shoot through my heart at the bare idea of danger to her whom I so loved.

"No, she is not in danger at present," was the answer; "but her health is not good, and she is unhappy, which makes us fear sometimes that her illness may increase. The doctor tells us to keep her cheerful and lively, but that is rather a hard thing, let me tell you, when a girl is determined to mope."

"But what is the cause of this moping?" I inquired, anxiously. "Does she think I should have been more with her? Indeed, I assure you I could not get away one minute sooner, and I did not wait to write to you as it is."

"Poor fellow! I wish I had not to tell him," sighed Clarissa, half unconsciously; and then, turning to me, she said, "No, Vivian, it is not that; but do you remember when your cousin, Claude Feversham, was here, how he admired Gwen, and she liked him too, although she refused him? Why she did so, I could never make out, as I knew she loved him dearly—yes, and loves him still," she continued; "and now you know all I have to tell you. You can find the explanation of her moping in that, can you not?"

"I could have found an explanation for her refusing me in that, had she done so," I answered; "but why she should mope about it now, when every thing is settled, and our marriage is so near, I can not imagine."

"It is precisely because your marriage is drawing near," Clarissa replied, "that she feels so wretched. When it seemed a long way off in the future, she persuaded herself she could live down her love, and be an affectionate and faithful wife to you, if not a passionately attached one. But now that the time of trial draws near, I suppose she feels herself unequal to the task, and is wearing herself to death between the natural impulses of her heart and her desire to do her duty by you."

Clarissa ceased speaking, and I walked on silently beside her, feeling as if I could neither talk nor think; my brain was in a whirl, and even the girl walking along with me seemed blurred and indistinct, as though a long way off, while the landscape around was hidden in a dark mist, which did not quite disperse even when, after several efforts, I had sufficiently mastered myself to speak again.

"If this be as you say, Clarissa," I answered, trying hard to steady my voice, and for the honor of my boasted manhood to force back the hot tears that rushed to my eyes, "I must speak to Gwendoline, and if she desire it, I suppose I must release her from her engagement. It is very hard," I went on, all my fortitude giving way; "I love her, and none but her, and yet have not gained a place in her heart, while he who can take up another love a month after he leaves her obtains all her affection almost without seeking for it. I can not help grieving, Clarissa; she is more to me than the world besides; and I had built so on our marriage, and her learning to love me! God help me! I must learn to bear my sorrow, if it is to be so. Let us go home and ask her to see me—I can not live in this suspense; and when I know the worst, I will go or stay—as fate decides."

"I am so very sorry to have grieved you, Vivian!" murmured Clarissa, sorrowfully; "but what could I do? Gwendoline was getting more and more wretched every day, till really I almost feared she would fret herself to death. I do not know that she will break off with you—I almost think not, as she considers herself in honor bound; but I hope, when she sees you know the cause of her grief, she will make an effort to conquer it."

"Don't talk any more to me just now, Clarissa," I said, rather crossly.

My heart was very sore; it was she who had dealt the blow, and though I really believed she had done it with the best intentions, I could not bear to hear her calm chatter on the subject just yet a while. My cross tone surprised her for a moment, for she looked up at me anxiously, and then, comprehending perhaps that I was suffering, she ceased speaking, and walked home with me very silently.

Gwendoline, who had heard of my arrival, was in the drawing-room when we returned, but when Clarissa turned to go away and leave us together, she called her back nervously, and seemed afraid of being alone with me. But Clarissa disregarded her entreaties, and, saying she had business to do, vanished, leaving me an opportunity for finding out the real feelings of my betrothed.

I could see at a glance that part of Clarissa's statement was correct, and that Gwendoline had been fretting greatly of late, but it was very hard for me to believe just at first that it was on account of her engagement to me.

I loved her so entirely and devotedly, was so determined to make her happy, it never struck me that very devotion might be the cause of misery to her. My love, no doubt, was selfish at that time—not intentionally, surely, but selfish without design, as it is, in fact, the nature of man's love to be till tried and purified by suffering. A little of this I was beginning to understand as I gazed on my darling's face, made thin and pale by anxiety and grief, and felt that, loving her as I did, I could endure almost any thing so that I might once more behold her bright and radiant as formerly.

But no thought of giving her up as yet entered my head—indeed, I did not suppose she could wish it—and felt unhappy and anxious on her account solely, not on my own. She did not talk much, but after the first few sentences of greeting, remained silent and abstracted, with her hands lying listlessly on her lap, and her deep, sad eyes, fixed on the wild mountain scenery visible from the window. So we sat for a little while, I endeavoring to summon up courage to speak on what lay next my heart—this communication of Clarissa's relative to her. At length I opened the matter with a jerk, and hurried over the little speech I had made up, as though I feared the words would stop in my throat and choke me.

"Gwendoline," I said—and I remember still my voice trembled so that I could hardly speak distinctly—"Clarissa tells me your illness is occasioned by fretting about our approaching marriage. Tell me, dearest, you are not afraid that my love will ever weary—that I will ever cease trying to win yours, though I know it is not mine at present."

"Oh, no!" she cried. "I know you too well, Vivian, to dread that; but I had rather you should hate me, and hold me as your worst enemy, than that you should view me thus, and cloud your young, hopeful life by trying to win a heart that has died to all such feelings forever."

"I can not—I will not believe that!" I exclaimed, passionately. "And if I am not afraid of such a fate, why do you fret and worry yourself about it? You consented to take me if, after hearing what you had to tell me, I should still wish to marry you. I did so; we are engaged, and shall be united very shortly; you must have known all this would be so from the moment you submitted to my decision. Why do you grieve over it now, and make me, as well as yourself, miserable?"

She answered impatiently:

"How can I tell why I do so? My heart rebels against this marriage, though I have fought against my feelings, and tried to make them submit. Vivian Darrell, I like you too well to wish to bring upon you all the misery that must be yours if you take me as I now am."

There were tears in her hot, aching eyes, and she turned away angrily, as though in contempt of her own weakness. My thoughts flying back to the days passed there long ago, I spoke in sheer desperation.

"If you loved him, Gwendoline, so that you can not forget him, and so that no other man can take his place in your heart, why in Heaven's name did you refuse him when he proposed to you, a year ago? It would have saved us all much misery had you known your own mind then."

I spoke bitterly, for I was stung with a sense of having been unfairly treated; and I seemed to see vaguely before me that perhaps I should feel myself bound to release her, and lose thus the hopes on which my future happiness was built.

She turned and looked at me in a frightened manner, and exclaimed hurriedly:

"Do not blame me for that, Vivian; I had to do it. If you find fault with me, it must be because I consented to marry you, knowing I loved another, and that I never could care for you as a wife should do. That is all my sin to you; and you knew all I thought and felt when you consented to take me as I was."

"But what is the meaning of your conduct to Feversham?" I continued, still sternly. "You say you had to do it; tell me every thing—it is but right I should know—and we shall understand each other better afterward."

For a minute or two she made no answer, then she turned toward me, and said,

"I will tell you; and when you know all, you will not speak as harshly to me as you have done just now. His mother came to me one day when we were in Dublin; she told me, if he married me his prospects in life would be ruined, and besought me, if not for my own sake, at least for his, to refuse him. I fought against this, for I loved him dearly, as you, Vivian, guessed even at that time; but when I heard that his mother would disown him, and his friends look down on him—that prosperity and fortune would be swept from him by such a step as that, it seemed to me I should be showing him a truer affection by seeking his interest rather than my own happiness; I promised Lady Feversham her son should never know from me that I cared for him otherwise than as a friend. It was just as well for him, I am convinced now," she added, "because in a short time he found some one more suited to him in every way than I could ever have been. But that does not make me feel it the less—knowing that I was right, and that he is reconciled and will be happy."

"But that engagement is broken off," I said; and I then wished I had bitten my tongue out before I had spoken.

What business had I to point out to her that the man she loved was still free, and might return to his old allegiance? But she evinced no surprise on hearing it, merely answered, "I believe so," and relapsed again into silence.

After a pause of a few minutes, during which time I was too busy with bitter, confusing thoughts to speak, she went on:

"I did wrong, I know, in telling him I did not love him. It was untrue; and a falsehood will bring its punishment, though told with a good motive. How could I expect to be happy, when I denied the very existence of all that made life pleasant to me, and hurried into an engagement that sometimes seems worse than death to me?"

She seemed to have forgotten my presence as she spoke, and gazed fixedly toward the distant mountains, clasping and unclasping her white, thin fingers with a restless action that showed how keenly she was suffering. I sat and looked at her, feeling hope and joy ebbing away from me as I watched; feeling powerless to prevent all I loved from eluding my grasp, and seeing a lonely, forsaken future stretching out before me. Yet I could not at first summon up courage to go and meet it like a man, but cowered before it, looking at its approach, seeing it was inevitable, yet shrinking from it every minute, as I saw more and more surely that it must be; the sacrifice was called for, and I must make it, no matter what pain the effort might cost me.

At last, as she never moved or spoke, I looked up, and seeing her eyes still fixed vacantly on the distant landscape, I rose, and stood before her, taking her hands and holding her, so as to compel her attention.

"Gwendoline," I said, as steadily as I could force myself to speak, "it seems to me one of us must suffer in this matter. I am the strongest, and I think (do not be offended with me, dearest) that I love better than perhaps you can form any idea of; therefore it is for me to make the sacrifice which I trust will insure your happiness. You want your liberty again, though you will not ask me for it; and I am glad you do not—it would make the pain I must bear something greater; but for the love I bear you, Gwendoline, I give you back your promise. It is better to say nothing more about it; but accept my offer, if you feel it right. Do not spare me. I

was born, I know, for suffering, and will not shrink from it, if you are made happier by it."

I turned away as I finished speaking, yet, though not looking at her, I paused anxiously for her answer. I did not dare to hope she would refuse to take back her promise, and still I could not believe all hope was over for me until I should hear it from her own lips. I waited therefore in breathless expectation, every minute seeming hours of dull aching pain, and no sound disturbed the silence but the shrill autumnal song of a robin from the old beech-tree outside the window. Even in the midst of my suspense that song struck my ear and imprinted itself on my brain; I never hear that little red-breasted warbler nowadays without a vivid image rising before me of that cozy room, with its long window open to the lawn, before which she sat, and her sad, abstracted face as she turned it toward me, after some minutes' silent thought, and answered,

"You are too good, too generous, dear Vivian, and I would so gladly be all to you that you desire; but that is not possible, and therefore I will accept your sacrifice, feeling sure that it would be worse pain for you in the end if I fulfilled the letter of the promise and failed in keeping the spirit. But I will not pretend it is for you only I do it. I fear my own selfish feelings have the most influence over me. Happy I never expect to be again—at least, not happy as I once was, for Lord Feversham and I can never be as we were to each other; but contented and cheerful I may now be, when not weighed down by the load of a duty I should never have heart to fulfill. All that makes me sorry now, dear, is what you feel. I wish I could have spared you this pain; but believe me it will be better in the end."

"Oh! Gwendoline," I cried passionately, pressing her hand to my lips again and again, "why could you not learn to love me? What is there about me that I can not hope to win your affection by mine? It may be best, as you say, that we should part, since that can not be; and, once parted, we shall not soon meet again; but think of me kindly sometimes, as one who loved you well, and pray for me always, that I may not lose heart and sink into evil, because my love was hopeless."

I took her in my arms for the last time, and held all I loved best, all that I was forever renouncing, to my heart for a few short moments. In the tumult of despair, love, and jealousy that then rose within me, I could almost have killed her, as I held her to my breast. At least she would have died in my arms, and none other could ever have claimed her; but I put the temptation from me, and loosing her with lingering regret, I bounded out of the window and hurried away, without ever glancing behind me for an instant.

After I had gone a little way, I turned aside into the woody glades that covered the mountain, and, sitting down in a solitary shady spot, leaned my face on my hands and wept. It was a childish relief from overwhelming sorrow, no doubt, and many men would have scorned it; but the tears seemed to scorch my eyes as they rose, and would force their way, no matter how I tried to keep them back. Besides, I was not much more than a child in years, and had never suffered such sorrow; so I yielded to my weakness for a while, and then remembering that I had a long way to walk, and must get away from the country as soon as possible, I rose, and gulping down my emotion as best I might, set out on my return back to town.

This was the end of my sweet, short dream of love; a hard, cruel ending, that darkened my life, and almost imbittered me with every thing for some time, causing even my gentle mother to exclaim harshly against the girl who was the cause of the change. But this I could not allow. It may have been that I had not been well treated, but of this I was sure, Gwendoline had fought to do right, and it was only when I opened the way that her strength yielded and she gave up the struggle. No doubt it was right and good for me to go through this trial, and most men earlier or later pass through some such sorrow, either having set their affections on what is unattainable, or else failing to win the love they crave.

I was more cut up about it than perhaps a young fellow with life before him should have been; but in such troubles as these, my friends, we seldom know reason; and though I strove hard against depression before the eyes of the world, it gained on me, and made me feel as if life had nothing more in store for me, now I had lost her love.

After I had built so long on the certainty of winning her, after our wedding-day had been fixed, after all the fond hopes and aspirations centred in her, it was indeed a cruel shock to find these visions passing away like a morning dream. I returned home, after that day when I found my fond love and devotion was of no avail, and remained there during the rest of my leave, trying, by hard bodily exercise, and at times by severe study, to lessen the dull, aching pain of unsatisfied longing that tormented me.

After my leave was out I returned to the regiment, where, of course, every one knew by this time what had befallen me, but where little allusion was made to it, all guessing too well that I had rather the matter were passed over in silence, than that any attempt were made to condole with me. As for Claude, whom at first I almost hated, regarding him as the cause of all my sorrow, he was so gentle and forbearing, whenever he met, and took so little notice of my petulant and offensive manner, that I soon began to excuse him in my heart for his share in my misery; for, after all, it was not his fault, and, besides, he was in sorrow also, not for the loss of Mabel—that it never seemed to me he could regret—but because the woman whom both he and I loved, and who had told me she loved him, was lost to him for the present at least, and, as he thought, forever; but that I did not myself believe: I knew they would come across each other again some day, and then, I hoped, with a happier result. In the mean time Claude was almost as much to be pitied as myself; and though I several times determined to let him know his case was not hopeless, and he was beloved, yet whenever I approached the subject he shut me up so sternly that after a while I began to imagine there was more in the matter than I had at first thought, and I left interference for some future time.

Mayleigh was the only man among us who made any jesting allusion to my misfortune, and he, with his usual good taste and feeling, observed,

"So you are not going to be a Benedick yet, Master Madcap. A good thing for you, I should say, as I suppose you know the old proverb, 'A young man married is a man that's marred?'"

"I'll thank you, Mayleigh, to keep your opinions to yourself till you are asked for them," I answered, haughtily. Something in my tone and look so overawed the impudent fellow that I never had any trouble with his impertinent observations from that time forth.

CHAPTER XXXI.

CLAUDE FEVERSHAM'S SUCCESS.

"I AM going on leave next week, Darrell," said Claude Feversham to me one evening, a few months after the events related in the last chapter. "What do you say to coming with me? We shall have plenty of hunting, and I think, if we get a little frost between times, we may have a chance at the woodcock."

"I have been on leave lately," I replied; "I don't think I could get off so soon again. And then the hunting here is just as good as any we could get elsewhere, so I think I shall remain where I am for a little longer. Thanks all the same for thinking of me."

"The fact is, Vivian," pursued Feversham, after a pause, "I am sick of this kind of thing. I do not know that I ever intended going in for any thing else when I first joined the army; but too much of it gets wearisome, and I think of selling out, and going on some exploring expedition, either into Africa after Livingstone, or to the north in search of Sir John Franklin, or on some other stirring and adventurous route, which it will require all a man's wits and all a man's daring to get over safely. Perhaps, in danger and excitement, longing, and hope, and disappointment may all be forgotten; at any rate, I shall try them, and see whether the Lethe of the ancients was all a fable."

"I would not, if I were you, Claude," I answered, earnestly; "it would be different if I were to think of such a thing. For me there is no hope; but were I in your position, I would remain at home, and prefer happiness to peril."

"I do not see how your position differs from mine," he answered, gloomily; "we have both been deceived and jilted by the same woman; and then, again, I was misled by another. Of her, however, I will not speak harshly, as she has suffered for it; but there is no excuse, no extenuating circumstances, to make me think gently of that most accomplished coquette, Gwendoline Bambridge."

He spoke very bitterly, and frowned darkly, looking straight before him, as though fearing to meet my eye while uttering these words; but I cared little for his black looks on such a subject, and interrupted him, saying,

"Hush! you know nothing about the matter. You will repent when you know how cruel are the words you have spoken. Gwendoline Bambridge loves you, has always loved you, is true to you now, and yet you speak thus of her. Not knowing this, could you not have dealt more gently with the name of the woman you once said you loved?—or has your affection turned to something more bitter and lasting?"

I hardly know what gave me strength to make this confession of Gwendoline's love for him, knowing, as I did, that it would complete the ruin of my hopes; but, stung by his harshness to her, I blurted it all out before I had time to think of what I said, and almost before I had finished speaking he turned on me sternly.

"Boy," he said, "do you know what you are saying, what mad hopes and wishes you are stirring up anew in my heart? Do you know that she told me with her own lips she had never loved me, and though I could have sworn that she had, and that she denied it when she knew me poor, yet I was obliged to be satisfied with that answer; indeed, seeing and knowing the reason of her refusal, I would not have altered it if I could."

"You wrong her cruelly," I replied, and then I paused. Should I tell him all I knew, and finish the work I had begun? or should I leave him to work out his fate his own way, and make or mar it as he chose? A thought decided me: she was unhappy; she might, by my means, be made happy, and she should be so. It was but a continuation of the struggle against my natural feelings for a little longer, and then all would be over; my misery might be lessened also by knowing her well-being secured; arming myself with this thought, I again addressed Feversham, in spite of his lowering brow and threatening glances.

"Don't you know," I continued hurriedly, and with an effort, "why she refused you? As you rightly guessed, she loved you, and having divined so much, you might at least have known her better than to believe your poverty would ever have influenced her to reject you. I am a boy, you say, and you do not think much of my power of loving, but I tell you I could not so insult the woman I cared for as to believe, without certain and positive proof, that she was mercenary enough to throw aside her affection for riches. If I found such a thing to be true, my love for her would die out at once, like the ashes I knock off this cigar; but until it was clearly proved to me, the mere suspicion should never be allowed to enter my mind."

Claude remained silent, looking at me with a troubled expression for a minute or two; then he answered,

"Well, but what other meaning could there be for her conduct? If you know the reason of it, why don't you tell me, instead of talking in such a confoundedly mysterious manner that you make me feel quite uncomfortable—in fact, as if I had behaved badly to her, when at present I can't help thinking she behaved badly to me."

"It was your mother's doing, Claude," I replied. "Do not be angry; you wish me to speak out, and I will do so. Excuse me if any thing I say pains you. Lady Feversham went over to Dublin when the Bambridges were staying there the spring before last, and when there had a private interview with Gwendoline. In the conversation that took place, she so worked upon the girl's feelings for you, persuading her that, if she accepted you, you would be ruined both in fortune and career, that she wrung from her a promise to refuse you if you should ask her to become your wife; this Gwendoline promised, fearing that, though she was willing to bear poverty and

trial for your sake, you in time might come to regret the sacrifice you would have to make in marrying her. Believe me, Claude, it was a greater proof of affection, her studying your happiness at the expense of her own, than if she had resisted your mother's arguments and accept your love as freely as it was offered."

"Why do you tell me this now?" cried Claude greatly excited. "Do you not know all chance for me is over? I have behaved so badly. I had hardly been refused by her when I allowed my mother to cajole me into engaging myself to that poor girl, Mabel Prendergast. Do you think any woman would forgive one after such a thing? No, indeed! Any thing else seems more pardonable in their eyes than finding comfort in another love for their cruelty—and Gwendoline will be the same as the others in that respect."

"I am sure she will not," I answered, eagerly; "only try her, and see how readily you will be forgiven! Besides, you know that she can not blame you for being unfaithful, because, though true to you in heart always, she was not one who more constant in appearance."

I stopped with a sigh, and Claude, turning quickly to me, asked,

"Why do you tell me all this, Vivian? It is against your own interest, you know."

"I believe it is only with you that she can be happy," I answered, slowly; "and I wish her happiness above all things. I have now done what I could toward setting things straight; act as you see best, but do not talk to me any more about it."

So saying, I left the room. Feversham told me no more about his plans just then, but the day before he left he met me going out for a walk, and passing his arm through mine, accompanied me, talking at first on indifferent subjects. After a while, however, he began:

"I am going home to-morrow, Vivian, as I told you, and I intend to ask my mother about that which you mentioned to me the other day. It would make the happiness of my life if this matter could all be settled as I wished long ago; but I fear I can not hope for such good fortune, as I know I do not deserve it. Whether I am successful or not, old fellow, I can not be too thankful to you for telling what has at least raised my opinion of Gwendoline, and has shown me how unjust I was when I accused her mentally of mean and mercenary motives."

"That is right, Claude," I answered: "you were unjust, and I am glad you see that you were. As to your success, I know that if you make a stand with your mother and get her consent, you have nothing to fear from Gwendoline, who, I do not doubt, accuses herself of all the wrong-doing in the matter."

So Claude went off next day, looking happier than I had seen him look for a long time; and I remained behind, feeling sad and lonely enough, in spite of Flower's company: he, though amiable and sympathizing, was not very bright, and little calculated to cheer up a fellow who had come such a cropper as I had. Of course I heard all that happened between Claude and his mother afterward. It came to pass in this way:

He had not long been home—about a few hours, perhaps—when, standing near the fire in the twilight before dinner, he asked suddenly,

"Mother, what is this I hear about your having gone over to Dublin last spring? You never told me of it."

"I was there such a short time, Claude," she answered, rather nervously—"only two days, I 'hink; and I hardly thought it worth while to 'l you I had been in Ireland, as I could not ' down and see you."

"Perhaps you thought your errand did not concern me," he replied, sternly, looking at her as he had never looked at her before. "All this trouble through which I have passed is of your making, and I am not the only one who has suffered through your means. Had you no pity for a woman like yourself that you hunted her out, and bound her over by a promise to sacrifice her heart to your ambition? Tell me all that passed between you, for I will know it."

"Oh! Claude," she cried, "don't look at me and speak to me like that. I did it all for your good, and she knows I did. She ought to tell you so, if she has any truth in her. Have you met her again? Have you and she been talking about it, and arranging how to get round your mother? The artful creature! I knew she would never keep her promise!"

"Hush!" he said, holding up his hand warningly. "Not another word against her, if you please. I have never seen her since, and have heard nothing from her. Are you satisfied now?"

"Well, I was stupid to think you had heard it from her," Lady Feversham admitted, more calmly. "Of course she would not look at you now, as she has made a better catch in Vivian Darrell. Poor child! I wonder what his parents are about, to allow him to make such a match at his age. When does the wedding take place?"

"Never, I believe," answered Claude, growing sterner and more stern, as his mother's manner roused all the passionate temper of his race. "But that is not what I wish to talk about. I shall be sorry to speak to you in any way unbecoming a son to his mother, but in this matter I will not be trifled with. Tell me fully and truly what passed between Miss Bambridge and you that day in Dublin."

"Well, if you will hear all about it, I suppose you must, though I do not see what good it can do you now. I imagine, however, from your answer about Vivian, the girl has jilted him. The world has come to a pretty pass, when a girl like Miss Bambridge thinks she can reject noblemen with as little consideration as though they were plow-boys; but, as you must know, all I said to her was that it would be ruin and destruction to your career and prospects marrying her; I may say I laid this view of the case very strongly before her, for, to tell the truth, at first she seemed disposed to give me a great deal of trouble, and talked about love, and hearts, and all that sentimental kind of nonsense. She said something about loving you, and that, if you asked her, she would never be so false to you, and to her own heart, as to reject you; but I put a stop to that quickly enough, and at length got her to hear reason, and promise you should never know that she regarded you with any warmer feelings than those of mere friendship. Who can have told you the contrary, as you say she did not, I can not think; but I fancy she is a sensible girl, and saw so clearly the force of my arguments that she would never take you now

without my consent, which you will certainly never obtain."

Lady Feversham drew herself up as she finished speaking, and pulled out the lace border of her handkerchief, as though the subject was finally disposed of, and she intended to occupy her mind with something else.

"I have no doubt," Claude answered, coldly, "that your estimate, in one way, of Miss Bambridge is correct, and that, after what has passed between you, she would not consent to enter your family unless you yourself begged her to do so. Now that is exactly what I wish you to do; in fact, I shall not renew my proposals until you signify to her that you are willing to receive her as my wife. I wish the matter settled as soon as possible, and shall be greatly obliged by your writing as soon as possible to intimate to her the change in your feelings."

"Are you mad, Claude?" cried his mother, looking up at him with wide-open eyes of amazement. "I have not the smallest intention of doing any such thing, and if you wait to marry until I do so, you will have to wait a good while, I warn you."

"There is one thing I forgot to mention," went on Claude, calmly, as though he had not heard her speak. "In case you refuse my very reasonable request, I intend to sell out, leave England, and seek a better fortune and kinder friends in a strange land. You can choose between your child and your pride."

He ceased speaking, and, as the dinner was just then announced, offered his mother his arm and led her to the dining-room. This opportune diversion enabled Lady Feversham to defer making any reply to her son's last speech for the present, for which she was thankful, as it was very far from her wishes to drive him from her, though she would not yet consent, even in thought, to acknowledge Gwendoline as her daughter. Claude saw that his words were producing an effect in his mother's mind, by the abstracted manner in which she lingered over her dinner, speaking little, and avoiding his eye whenever he looked in her direction.

She was a stubborn old lady, although as much attached to her son as it was possible for her to be to any one; but she had taken this idea of furthering his well-being by a rich alliance into her head, and one failure, along with his determined opposition, was not enough to make her relinquish the scheme. There are as good matches as Mabel Prendergast going, she thought, and I am sorry now I wasted so much time endeavoring to secure her; but as for this Miss Bambridge, that is not to be thought of for a minute. I will wait a day or two, and see what his next move will be. Of course that threat of leaving the army is all nonsense.

Claude did not mean it so, however, for two days afterward, when his mother had begun to hope he had forgotten the conversation between them, and that matters would go on as they then were for a while, she was taken completely by surprise by his entering the room one morning with a letter in his hand, which he showed to her as he said,

"I am writing to my colonel, mother, and perhaps you may guess the reason why. It is to tell him I am going to sell out, and that I shall send in my papers in a day or two."

"Oh! Claude, dear, do not be so rash!" cried Lady Feversham, imploringly, and half crying; "you surely can never be so foolish as to do such a thing all because of that chit of a girl, whom I wish you had never seen. Just wait a little longer, before taking such an imprudent step. Wait, and see if something will turn up."

"What do you mean by something turning up, mother?" he demanded, fixing his grave dark eyes on hers.

"You might see some one else you would like better," she answered faintly, "and so forget this girl. Indeed," she went on, with a little hesitation, "Miss Vavasour is coming here next week. I have just written to ask her. I hear she is very handsome, and—"

"Say no more, mother," he replied, sternly. "I should be a fool indeed if, knowing what I know, I should allow you to bend me a second time to your wishes. No; you have heard the only terms on which I will consent to remain. You have had two days in which to think the matter over, and I insist on getting an answer at once, that I may know what course to pursue without further delay."

"But tell me, dear," again began Lady Feversham, "if you sell out and leave the country, you are not one whit nearer gaining Miss Bambridge than if you remained in the army, and I continued to withhold my consent."

"That remains for her to decide," he answered calmly. "Of course I should tell her that I had nothing to offer her but a strong arm and a loving heart, but that I hoped the means of earning a livelihood would be open to me, wherever stout hearts and willing hands were needed; that she could not spoil my prospects in life now, seeing that no prospect is left to me; and if she be what I take her to be, I should not have to experience a second refusal, when she saw that her love was all I had to look to for comfort and encouragement in the new life I was beginning."

"Well, please yourself; marry her, and remain in the army," replied Lady Feversham, crossly. "I am sure I will not say any thing against it, since you are so set on it; but mind, you will live to wish you had followed my advice."

"That will not do, mother," he answered. "If Miss Bambridge remains in this country as my wife, it must be made apparent, not only to herself, but to every one else, that she is so with your approbation. I wish you now to write her a few lines signifying your consent to our marriage, and inviting her to come and pay you a visit here before it takes place. Make your letter as kind as possible, to do away with any disagreeable impression she may have preserved of your last interview."

"Upon my word, Claude, you take matters with too high a hand. Fancy telling me to do away with any impression she may have received of me last time. I hardly know whether I shall write at all; but if I do you can hardly expect a letter written under compulsion to be cordial, and I by no means promise to make it so."

"I dare say it sounds badly from me to you, mother," he answered; "but remember, I am a man now, and however much I honor and love you as my mother—and believe me I do, though we differ sometimes—still I can not submit my man's will and judgment to yours, as I used to do when I was a little boy. Dearest mother, the thing I ask of you is not so much, after all, and it will make me very happy, and you too, when you have got over your prejudice against her. I know you will do it for my sake, and I won't send this letter."

So saying, he stooped, kissed his mother, and left the room, confident that what he had said would produce a good effect, and that in a short time he might hope to see the letter he had asked for written. He was not mistaken in his conjecture, for about two hours afterward his mother entered the library, where he was reading, and holding an open envelope toward him, said,

"It is done, my dear boy, for your sake; you can see what I have said."

"Indeed I will not," he answered, rising gayly. "I think I can trust my mother to do a thing thoroughly, when she makes up her mind to do it; but sometimes she takes a good deal of persuasion."

He kissed his mother fondly, and she smiled, though something very like a tear glittered in each eye as she said, tremulously,

"And now, what are you going to do, Claude? It is no good your sending that, unless you write or go yourself to renew your offer."

"I will run over myself," he answered, "taking this with me; and, not to lose a day, I will set off this afternoon. I shall not be long before I return, dear, and perhaps Gwendoline will come with me; but you shall hear from me before then, and know what success I have had."

"Oh! I have no doubt of your success," she murmured, half in bitterness, half in admiration, as she gazed on her stalwart, handsome son, with his frank, honest eyes and his sweet smile, thinking the while, "No girl could refuse him, if she were free to choose."

Claude set off on his journey that afternoon, and arrived next day at Endley, just as it was falling dusk in the evening. As he walked up the avenue, he caught sight of a figure before him that seemed strangely familiar and dear to him: he stepped out more quickly, and presently overtaking Gwendoline, for it was she, stopped beside her and held out his hand.

It was rather dark, and Gwendoline, a little nervous about being out so late, was hurrying home when this happened. She started, gave one quick glance at his face, and failing to recognize him, set off homeward with more speed than before.

"Are you so angry with me, then, that you won't speak to me, Gwendoline?" pleaded the intruder, keeping up with her, and bending forward to catch a glimpse of her face.

She knew the voice, and her heart beat high with joy, for she felt assured he would never have returned thus unless all difficulties in their way had been removed. Half laughing, half crying, she turned, and holding out both hands, exclaimed,

"Is it you, indeed? I did not know you at first, it is so dark."

Not a word more did she say, but there was more welcome and love in those sentences than many people could have imagined possible. They were quite satisfactory to Claude, and he answered them in a very conclusive manner as he murmured,

"You are not going to treat me so badly again, darling?"

What answer she gave him might have been guessed from their faces as they entered the drawing-room about a quarter of an hour after.

"Mamma, here is a truant come back to us," cried Gwendoline gayly, drawing Claude out of the shadow, in which he was standing, into the full light of a blazing fire.

"Claude Feversham, I declare!" cried Clarissa, springing up, and throwing a book, over which she had been dozing, to the other end of the room. "You are all right, I can see, Claude," she went on, "so I shall not make the usual polite inquiries; and as to Gwendoline, she must have been in Fairy-land this afternoon, for she is looking at least twenty years younger than when she went out."

Gwendoline blushed, but was too happy to call her younger sister to order; and Mrs. Bambridge, divining the state of affairs at a glance, made room for the new-comer by the fire, ordered his room to be prepared, and otherwise occupied herself about his comfort, while he, the first buzz of greeting over, drew his mother's letter from his pocket and handed it to Gwendoline, who forthwith retired to her own room with it, whence she emerged half an hour afterward radiantly handsome, but with a slight tendency to redness about the eyes that looked suspicious of tears.

After this there is not much to tell; for of course Gwendoline accepted Lady Feversham's invitation, which had indeed been expressed very graciously, though she told Claude in confidence she only did it for his sake. Now they are, I believe, the best of friends, and I am quite sure the Dowager Lady Feversham regrets nothing so much as that hurried visit she paid to Dublin; a visit Gwendoline playfully reminded her of after her marriage, when they were all good friends, by showing her the dark-red rose the elder lady dropped that day from her bonnet, and that Gwendoline had picked up after she was gone.

They were married about two months after Lady Feversham's consent had been obtained, and Claude remained in the army; but I, not having sufficient courage to see my lost love day by day before me, exchanged into another regiment and went out to India.

I am a good many years older now, and have accustomed myself to think of her as the wife of another man, and that man my cousin and chosen friend; but still I never think of the time when I fondly dreamed she was my own, and worshiped her with a boy's blind adoration, without a dull, aching, regretful pain. And though I have seen many women that my eye unwillingly acknowledged as fairer, and my mind approved as more clever and witty, yet—let people call me romantic and absurd as they will—I have never seen one with power to win my heart from its allegiance to her.

Clarissa—pretty, merry Clarissa—made a very good match a few months after her sister's marriage. I have seen her since, and she has sometimes asked me if I intend to become an old bachelor for Gwen's sake; adding, sometimes, with a half sigh,

"Ah, Vivian! people don't know what they are talking of when they say sometimes with a laugh, 'He will get over it.' I used to think so too, but I know now it is not always true."

So ends the story of my life, as far as it goes: its interest to me seems already gone. And though I am not miserable—as who can be while work remains to be done, and while one puts forth one's strength to do it?—still my best happiness all passed away long ago, in that brief dream, though it was only a boy's love.

THE END.

OR,

JEALOUSY.

BY

CHARLES READE,

AUTHOR OF "PEG WOFFINGTON," "CHRISTIE JOHNSTONE," "NEVER TOO LATE
TO MEND," "WHITE LIES," ETC.

WITH ILLUSTRATIONS.

BOSTON:
JAMES R. OSGOOD AND COMPANY,
LATE TICKNOR & FIELDS, AND FIELDS, OSGOOD, & CO.
1875.

GRIFFITH GAUNT;

JEALOUSY.

CHAPTER I.

"THEN I say, once for all, that priest shall never darken my doors again."

"Then I say they are my doors, and not yours, and that holy man shall brighten them whenever he will."

The gentleman and lady who faced each other pale and furious, and interchanged this bitter defiance, were man and wife, and had loved each other well.

Miss Catharine Peyton was a young lady of ancient family in Cumberland, and the most striking, but least popular, beauty in the county. She was very tall and straight, and carried herself a little too imperiously; yet she would sometimes relax and all but dissolve that haughty figure, and hang sweetly drooping over her favorites; then the contrast was delicious, and the woman fascinating.

Her hair was golden and glossy, her eyes a lovely gray; and she had a way of turning them on slowly and full, so that their victim could not fail to observe two things: first, that they were grand and beautiful orbs; secondly, that they were thoughtfully overlooking him, instead of looking at him.

So contemplated by glorious eyes, a man feels small and bitter.

Catharine was apt to receive the blunt compliments of the Cumberland squires with this sweet, celestial, superior gaze, and for this and other imperial charms was more admired than liked.

The family estate was entailed on her brother; her father spent every farthing he could; so she had no money, and no expectations, except from a distant cousin, — Mr. Charlton, of Hernshaw Castle and Bolton Hall.

Even these soon dwindled. Mr. Charlton took a fancy to his late wife's relation, Griffith Gaunt, and had him into his house, and treated him as his heir. This disheartened two admirers who had hitherto sustained Catharine Peyton's gaze, and they retired. Comely girls, girls long-nosed, but rich, girls snub-nosed, but winning, married on all sides of her; but the imperial beauty remained Miss Peyton at two-and-twenty.

She was rather kind to the poor; would give them money out of her slender purse, and would even make clothes for the women, and sometimes read to them: very few of them could read to themselves in that day. All she required in return was, that they should be Roman Catholics, like herself, or at least pretend they might be brought to that faith by little and little.

She was a high-minded girl, and could be a womanly one, — whenever she chose.

She hunted about twice a week in the season, and was at home in the saddle, for she had ridden from a child; but so ingrained was her character, that this sport, which more or less unsexes most women, had no perceptible effect on her mind, nor even on her manners. The scarlet riding-habit and little purple cap, and the great, white, bony horse she rode, were often seen in a good place at the end of a long run ; but, for all that, the lady was a most ungenial fox-huntress. She never spoke a word but to her acquaintances, and wore a settled air of dreamy indifference, except when the hounds happened to be in full cry, and she galloping at their heels. Worse than that, when the dogs were running into the fox, and his fate certain, she had been known to rein in her struggling horse, and pace thoughtfully home, instead of coming in at the death, and claiming the brush.

One day, being complimented at the end of a hard run by the gentleman who kept the hounds, she turned her celestial orbs on him, and said, —

"Nay, Sir Ralph, I love to gallop ; and this sorry business gives me an excuse."

It was full a hundred years ago. The country teemed with foxes ; but it abounded in stiff coverts, and a knowing fox was sure to run from one to another ; and then came wearisome efforts to dislodge him ; and then Miss Peyton's gray eyes used to explore vacancy, and ignore her companions, biped and quadruped.

But one day they drew Yewtree Brow, and found a stray fox. At Gaylad's first note he broke cover, and went away for home across the open country. A hedger saw him steal out, and gave a view halloo ; the riders came round helter-skelter ; the dogs in cover one by one threw up their noses and voices ; the horns blew, the canine music swelled to a strong chorus, and away they swept across country, — dogs, horses, men ; and the Deuse take the hindmost !

It was a gallant chase, and our dreamy virgin's blood got up. Erect, but lithe and vigorous, and one with her great white gelding, she came flying behind the foremost riders, and took leap for leap with them. One glossy, golden curl streamed back in the rushing air ; her gray eyes glowed with earthly fire ; and two red spots on the upper part of her cheeks showed she was much excited, without a grain of fear. Yet in the first ten minutes one gentleman was unhorsed before her eyes, and one came to grief along with his animal, and a thorough-bred chestnut was galloping and snorting beside her with empty saddle. Presently young Featherstone, who led her by about fifteen yards, crashed through a high hedge, and was seen no more, but heard wallowing in the deep, unsuspected ditch beyond. There was no time to draw bridle. "Lie still, Sir, if you please," said Catharine, with cool civility ; then up rein, in spur, and she cleared the ditch and its muddy contents, alive and dead, and away without looking behind her.

On, on, on, till all the pinks and buckskins, erst so smart, were splashed with clay and dirt of every hue, and all the horses' late glossy coats were bathed with sweat and lathered with foam, and their gaping nostrils blowing and glowing red ; and then it was that Harrowden Brook, swollen wide and deep by the late rains, came right between the fox and Dogmore Underwood, for which he was making.

The hunt sweeping down a hillside caught sight of Reynard running for the brook. They made sure of him now. But he lapped a drop, and then slipped in, and soon crawled out on the other side, and made feebly for the covert, weighted with wet fur.

At sight of him, the hunt hallooed and trumpeted, and came tearing on with fresh vigor.

But when they came near the brook, lo, it was twenty feet wide, and running fast and brown. Some riders skirted it, looking for a narrow part. Two horses, being spurred at it, came to the bank, and then went rearing round on their heels, depositing one hat and another rider in the current. One gallant steed planted his feet like a tower, and snorted down at the water. One flopped gravely in, and had to swim, and be dragged out. Another leaped, and landed with his feet on the other bank, his haunches in the water, and his rider curled round his neck, and glaring out between his retroverted ears.

But Miss Peyton encouraged her horse with spur and voice, set her teeth, turned rather pale this time, and went at the brook with a rush, and cleared it like a deer. She and the huntsman were almost alone together on the other side, and were as close to the dogs as the dogs were to poor Pug, when he slipped through a run in a quickset hedge, and, reducing the dogs to single file, glided into Dogmore Underwood, a stiff hazel coppice of five years' growth.

The other riders soon straggled up, and then the thing was to get him out again. There were a few narrow roads cut in the underwood ; and up and down these the huntsman and whipper-in went trotting, and encouraged the stanch hounds, and whipped the skulkers back into covert. Others galloped uselessly about, pounding the earth, for daisy-cutters were few in those days ; and Miss Peyton relapsed into the transcendental. She sat in one place, with her elbow on her knee, and her fair chin supported by two fingers, as undisturbed by the fracas of horns and voices as an equestrian statue of Diana.

She sat so still and so long at a corner of the underwood that at last the harassed fox stole out close to her with lolling tongue and eye askant, and took the open field again. She thrilled at first sight of him, and her cheeks burned ; but her quick eye took in all the signs of his distress, and she sat quiet, and watched him coolly. Not so her horse. He plunged, and then trembled all over, and planted his fore-feet together at this angle \, and parted his hind-legs a little, and so stood quivering, with cocked ears, and peeped over a low paling at the retiring quadruped, and fretted and sweated in anticipation of the gallop his long head told him was to follow. He looked a deal more statuesque than any three statues in England, and all about a creature not up to his knee. — And by the bye : the gentlemen who carve horses in our native isle, did they ever see one — out of an omnibus ? — The whipper-in came by,

and found him in this gallant attitude, and suspected the truth, but, observing the rider's tranquil position, thought the fox had only popped out and then in again. However, he fell in with the huntsman, and told him Miss Peyton's gray had seen something. The hounds appeared puzzled ; and so the huntsman rode round to Miss Peyton, and, touching his cap, asked her if she had seen nothing of the fox.

She looked him dreamily in the face. " The fox ? " said she ; " he broke cover ten minutes ago."

The man blew his horn lustily, and then asked her reproachfully why she had not tally-hoed him, or winded her horn : with that he blew his own again impatiently.

Miss Peyton replied, very slowly and pensively, that the fox had come out soiled and fatigued, and trailing his brush. " I looked at him," said she, " and I pitied him. He was one, and we are many ; he was so little, and we are so big ; *he had given us a good gallop;* and so I made up my mind he should live to run another day."

The huntsman stared stupidly at her for a moment, then burst into a torrent of oaths, then blew his horn till it was hoarse, then cursed and swore till he was hoarse himself, then to his horn again, and dogs and men came rushing to the sound.

" Couple up, and go home to supper," said Miss Peyton, quietly. " The fox is half-way to Gallowstree Gorse ; and you won't get him out of that this afternoon, I promise you."

As she said this, she just touched her horse with the spur, leaped the low hedge in front of her, and cantered slowly home across country. She was one that seldom troubled the hard road, go where she would.

She had ridden about a mile, when she heard a horse's feet behind her. She smiled, and her color rose a little ; but she cantered on.

" Halt, in the king's name ! " shouted a mellow voice ; and a gentleman galloped up to her side, and reined in his mare.

"What! have they killed?" inquired Catharine, demurely.

"Not they; he is in the middle of Gallowstree Gorse by now."

"And is this the way to Gallowstree Gorse?"

"Nay, Mistress," said the young man; "but when the fox heads one way and the deer another, what is a poor hunter to do?"

"Follow the slower, it seems."

"Say the lovelier and the dearer, sweet Kate."

"Now, Griffith, you know I hate flattery," said Kate; and the next moment came a soft smile, and belied this unsocial sentiment.

"Flattery?" said the lover. "I have no tongue to speak half your praises. I think the people in this country are as blind as bats, or they 'd —— "

"All except Mr. Griffith Gaunt; *he* has found a paragon, where wiser people see a wayward, capricious girl."

"Then *he* is the man for you. Don't you see that, Mistress?"

"No, I don't quite see that," said the lady, dryly.

This cavalier reply caused a dismay the speaker never intended. The fact is, Mr. George Neville, young, handsome, and rich, had lately settled in the neighborhood, and had been greatly smitten with Kate. The county was talking about it, and Griffith had been secretly on thorns for some days past. And now he could hide his uneasiness no longer; he cried out, in a sharp, trembling voice, —

"Why, Kate, my dear Kate! what! could you love any man but me? Could you be so cruel? could you? There, let me get off my horse, and lie down on this stubble, and you ride over me, and trample me to death. I would rather have you trample on my ribs than on my heart, with loving any one but me."

"Why, what now?" said Catharine, drawing herself up; "I must scold you handsomely"; and she drew rein and turned full upon him; but by this means she saw his face was full of real distress; so, instead of reprimanding him,

she said, gently, "Why, Griffith, what is to do? Are you not my servant? Do not I send you word, whenever I dine from home?"

"Yes, dearest; and then I call at that house, and stick there till they guess what I would be at, and ask me, too."

Catharine smiled, and proceeded to remind him that thrice a week she permitted him to ride over from Bolton, (a distance of fifteen miles,) to see her.

"Yes," replied Griffith, "and I must say you always come, wet or dry, to the shrubbery-gate, and put your hand in mine a minute. And, Kate," said he, piteously, "at the bare thought of your putting that same dear hand in another man's my heart turns sick within me, and my skin burns and trembles on me."

"But you have no cause," said Catharine, soothingly. "Nobody, except yourself, doubts my affection for you. You are often thrown in my teeth, Griffith, — and" (clenching her own) "I like you all the better, of course."

Griffith replied with a burst of gratitude; and then, as men will, proceeded to encroach.

"Ah," said he, "if you would but pluck up courage, and take the matrimonial fence with me at once."

Miss Peyton sighed at that, and drooped a little upon her saddle. After a pause, she enumerated the "just impediments." She reminded him that neither of them had means to marry on.

He made light of that; he should soon have plenty; Mr. Charlton has as good as told him he was to have Bolton Hall and Grange: "Six hundred acres, Kate, besides the park and paddocks."

In his warmth he forgot that Catharine was to have been Mr. Charlton's heir. Catharine was too high-minded to bear Griffith any grudge; but she colored a little, and said she was averse to come to him a penniless bride.

"Why, what matters it which of us has the dross, so that there is enough for both?" said Griffith, with an air of astonishment.

Catharine smiled approbation, and

tacitly yielded that point. But then she objected the difference in their faith.

"Oh, · honest folk get to heaven by different roads," said Griffith, carelessly.

"I have been taught otherwise," replied Catharine, gravely.

"Then give me your hand and I 'll give you my soul," said Griffith Gaunt, impetuously. "I 'll go to heaven your way, if you can't go mine. Anything sooner than be parted in this world or the next."

She looked at him in silence ; and it was in a faint, half apologetic tone she objected, that all her kinsfolk were set against it.

"It is not their business ; it is ours," was the prompt reply.

"Well, then," said Catharine, sadly, "I suppose I must tell you the true reason : I feel I should not make you happy ; I do not love you quite as you want to be loved, as you deserve to be loved. You need not look so ; nothing in flesh and blood is your rival. But my heart bleeds for the Church ; I think of her ancient glory in this kingdom, and, when I see her present condition, I long to devote myself to her service. I am very fit to be an abbess or a nun, — most unfit to be a wife. No, no, — I must not, ought not, dare not, marry a Protestant. Take the advice of one who esteems you dearly ; leave me, — fly from me, — forget me, — do everything but hate me. Nay, do not hate me ; you little know the struggle in my mind. Farewell ; the saints, whom you scorn, watch over and protect you ! Farewell !"

And with this she sighed, and struck her spur into the gray, and he darted off at a gallop.

Griffith, little able to cope with such a character as this, sat petrified, and would have been rooted to the spot, if he had happened to be on foot. But his mare set off after her companion, and a chase of a novel kind commenced. Catharine's horse was fresher than Griffith's mare, and the latter, not being urged by her petrified master, lost ground.

But when she drew near to her father's gate, Catharine relaxed her speed, and Griffith rejoined her.

She had already half relented, and only wanted a warm and resolute wooer to bring her round. But Griffith was too sore, and too little versed in woman. Full of suspicion and bitterness, he paced gloomy and silent by her side, till they reached the great avenue that led to her father's house.

And while he rides alongside the capricious creature in sulky silence, I may as well reveal a certain foible in his own character.

This Griffith Gaunt was by no means deficient in physical courage ; but he was instinctively disposed to run away from mental pain the moment he lost hope of driving it away from him. For instance, if Catharine had been ill and her life in danger, he would have ridden day and night to save her, — would have beggared himself to save her ; but if she had died, he would either have killed himself, or else fled the country, and so escaped the sight of every object that was associated with her and could agonize him. I do not think he could have attended the funeral of one he loved.

The mind, as well as the body, has its self-protecting instincts. This of Griffith's was, after all, an instinct of that class, and, under certain circumstances, is true wisdom. But Griffith, I think, carried the instinct to excess ; and that is why I call it his foible.

"Catharine," said he, resolutely, "let me ride by your side to the house for once ; for I read your advice my own way, and I mean to follow it : after today you will be troubled with me no more. I have loved you these three years, I have courted you these two years, and I am none the nearer ; I see I am not the man you mean to marry : so I shall do as my father did, ride down to the coast, and sell my horse, and ship for foreign parts."

"Oh, as you will," said Catharine, haughtily : she quite forgot she had just recommended him to do something of this very kind.

Presently she stole a look. His fine ruddy cheek was pale ; his manly brown eyes were moist ; yet a gloomy and resolute expression on his tight-drawn lips. She looked at him sidelong, and thought how often he had ridden thirty miles on that very mare to get a word with her at the shrubbery-gate. And now the mare to be sold ! The man to go broken-hearted to sea, — perhaps to his death ! Her good heart began to yearn.

"Griffith," said she, softly, "it is not as if I were going to wed anybody else. Is it nothing to be preferred by her you say you love ? If I were you, I would do nothing rash. Why not give me a little time ? In truth, I hardly know my own mind about it two days together."

"Kate," said the young man, firmly, "I am courting you this two years. If I wait two years more, it will be but to see the right man come and carry you in a month ; for so girls are won, when they are won at all. Your sister that is married and dead, she held Josh Pitt in hand for years ; and what is the upshot ? Why, he wears the willow for her to this day ; and her husband married again, before her grave was green. Nay, I have done all an honest man can to woo you ; so take me now, or let me go."

At this, Kate began to waver secretly, and ask herself whether it would not be better to yield, since he was so abominably resolute.

But the unlucky fellow did not leave well alone. He went on to say, —

"Once out of sight of this place, I may cure myself of my fancy. Here I never could."

"Oh," said Catharine, directly, "if you are so bent on being cured, it would not become me to say nay."

Griffith Gaunt bit his lip and hung his head, and made no reply.

The patience with which he received her hard speech was more apparent than real ; but it told. Catharine, receiving no fresh positive provocation, relented again of her own accord, and, after a considerable silence, whispered, softly, —

"Think how we should all miss you."

Here was an overture to reconciliation. But, unfortunately, it brought out what had long been rankling in Griffith's mind, and was in fact the real cause of the misunderstanding.

"Oh," said he, "those I care for will soon find another to take my place ! Soon ? quotha. They have not waited till I was gone for that."

"Ah, indeed !" said Catharine, with some surprise ; then, like the quick-witted girl she was, "so this is what all the coil is about."

She then, with a charming smile, begged him to inform her who was his destined successor in her esteem. Griffith colored purple at her cool hypocrisy, (for such he considered it,) and replied, almost fiercely, —

"Who but that young black-a-viséd George Neville, that you have been coquetting with this month past, — and danced all night with him at Lady Munster's ball, you did."

Catharine blushed, and said, deprecatingly, —

"*You* were not there, Griffith, or to be sure I had not danced with *him.*"

"And he toasts you by name, wherever he goes."

"Can I help that ? Wait till I toast him, before you make yourself ridiculous, and me very angry — about nothing."

Griffith, sticking to his one idea, replied, doggedly, —

"Mistress Alice Peyton shilly-shallied with her true lover for years, till Richard Hilton came, that was not fit to tie his shoes ; and then " ——

Catharine cut him short, —

"Affront me, if nothing less will serve ; but spare my sister in her grave."

She began the sentence angrily, but concluded it in a broken voice. Griffith was half disarmed ; but only half. He answered, sullenly, —

"She did not die till she had jilted an honest gentleman and broken his heart, and married a sot, to her cost. And you are of her breed, when all is done ; and now that young coxcomb has come, like Dick Hilton, between you and me."

"But I do not encourage him."

"You do not *dis*courage him," retorted Griffith, "or he would not be so hot after you. Were you ever the woman to say, 'I have a servant already that loves me dear' ? That one frank word had sent him packing."

Miss Peyton colored, and the water came into her eyes.

"I may have been imprudent," she murmured. "The young gentleman made me smile with his extravagance. I never thought to be misunderstood by him, far less by you." Then, suddenly, as bold as brass, — "It 's all your fault ; if he had the power to make you uneasy, why did you not check me before ?"

"Ay, forsooth, and have it cast in my teeth I was a jealous monster, and played the tyrant before my time. A poor fellow scarce knows what to be at that loves a coquette."

"Coquette I am none," replied the lady, bridling magnificently.

Griffith took no notice of this interruption. He proceeded to say that he had hitherto endured this intrusion of a rival in silence, though with a sore heart, hoping his patience might touch her, or the fire go out of itself. But at last, unable to bear it any longer in silence, he had shown his wound to one he knew could feel for him, his poor friend Pitt. Pitt had then let him know that his own mistake had been overconfidence in Alice Peyton's constancy.

"He said to me, 'Watch your Kate close, and, at the first blush of a rival, say you to her, Part with him, or part with me.' "

Catharine pinned him directly.

"And this is how you take Joshua Pitt's advice, — by offering to run away from this sorry rival."

The shrewd reply, and a curl of the lip, half arch, half contemptuous, that accompanied the thrust, staggered the less ready Griffith. He got puzzled, and showed it.

"Well, but," stammered he at last, "your spirit is high ; I was mostly afeard to put it so plump to you. So I thought I would go about a bit. However, it comes to the same thing ; for this I do know, — that, if you refuse me your hand this day, it is to give it to a new acquaintance, as your Alice did before you. And if it is to be so, 't is best for me to be gone : best for *him*, and best for you. You don't know me, Kate ; for, as clever as you are, at the thought of your playing me false, after all these years, and marrying that George Neville, my heart turns to ice, and then to fire, and my head seems ready to burst, and my hands to do mad and bloody acts. Ay, I feel I should kill him, or you, or both, at the church-porch. Ah ! "

He suddenly griped her arm, and at the same time involuntarily checked his mare.

Both horses stopped.

She raised her head with an inquiring look, and saw her lover's face discolored with passion, and so strangely convulsed that she feared at first he was in a fit, or stricken with death or palsy.

She uttered a cry of alarm, and stretched forth her hand towards him.

But the next moment she drew it back from him ; for, following his eye, she discerned the cause of this ghastly look. Her father's house stood at the end of the avenue they had just entered ; but there was another approach to it, namely, by a bridle-road at right angles to the avenue or main entrance ; and up that bridle-road a gentleman was walking his horse, and bid fair to meet them at the hall-door.

It was young Neville. There was no mistaking his piebald charger for any other animal in that county.

Kate Peyton glanced from lover to lover, and shuddered at Griffith. She was familiar with petty jealousy ; she had even detected it pinching or coloring many a pretty face that tried very hard to hide it all the time. But that was nothing to what she saw now : hitherto she had but beheld the feeling of jealousy ; but now she witnessed the livid passion of jealousy writhing in every lineament of a human face. That terrible passion had transfigured its victim in a moment: the ruddy, genial, kindly Griffith, with his soft brown eye, was gone; and in his place lowered a face older, and discolored, and convulsed, and almost demoniacal.

Women (wiser, perhaps, in this than men) take their strongest impressions by the eye, not ear. Catharine, I say, looked at him she had hitherto thought she knew, — looked and feared him. And even while she looked and shuddered, Griffith spurred his mare sharply, and then drew her head across the gray gelding's path. It was an instinctive impulse to bar the lady he loved from taking another step towards the place where his rival awaited her.

"I cannot bear it," he gasped. "Choose you now, once for all, between that puppy there and me": and he pointed with his riding-whip at his rival, and waited with his teeth clenched for her decision.

The movement was rapid, the gesture large and commanding, and the words manly: for what says the fighting poet? —

> "He either fears his fate too much,
> Or his deserts are small,
> Who fears to put it to the touch,
> To win or lose it all."

CHAPTER IL

MISS PEYTON drew herself up and back by one motion, like a queen at bay; but still she eyed him with a certain respect, and was careful now not to provoke nor pain him needlessly.

"I prefer *you*, — though you speak harshly to me, sir," said she, with gentle dignity.

"Then give me your hand, with *that man* in sight, and end my torments; promise to marry me this very week. Ah, Kate, have pity on your poor, faithful servant, who has loved you so long!"

"I do, Griffith, I do," said she, sweetly; "but I shall never marry now. Only set your mind at rest about Mr. Neville there. He has never asked me, for one thing."

"He soon will, then."

"No, no; I declare I will be very cool to him, after what you have said to me. But I cannot marry you, neither. I dare not. Listen to me, and do, pray, govern your temper, as I am doing mine. I have often read of men with a passion for jealousy, — I mean, men whose jealousy feeds upon air, and defies reason. I know you now for such a man. Marriage would not cure this madness; for wives do not escape admiration any more than maids. Something tells me you would be jealous of every fool that paid me some stale compliment, jealous of my female friends, and jealous of my relations, and perhaps jealous of your own children, and of that holy, persecuted Church which must still have a large share of *my* heart. No, no; your face and your words have shown me a precipice. I tremble and draw back, and now I never *will* marry at all: from this day I give myself to the Church."

Griffith did not believe one word of all this.

"That is your answer to me," said he, bitterly. "When the right man puts the question (and he is not far off) you will tell another tale. You take me for a fool, and you mock me; you are not the lass to die an old maid: and men are not the fools to let you. With faces like yours, the new servant comes before the old one is gone. Well, I have got my answer. County Cumberland, you are no place for me! The ways and the fields we two have ridden together, — oh, how could I bear their sight without my dear? Why, what a poor-spirited fool I am to stay and whine! Come, Mistress, your lover waits you there, and your discarded servant knows good-breeding: he leaves the country not to spoil your sport."

Catharine panted heavily.

"Well, sir," said she, "then it is your doing, not mine. Will you not even shake hands with me, Griffith?"

"I were a brute else," sighed the jealous one, with a sudden revulsion of feeling. "I have spent the happiest hours of my life beside you. If I loved thee less, I had never left thee."

He clung a little while to her hands, more like a drowning man than anything else, then let them go, and suddenly shook his clenched fist in the direction of George Neville, and cried out with a savage yell, —

"My curse on him that parts us twain! And you, Kate, may God bless you single, and curse you married! and that is my last word in Cumberland."

"Amen!" said Catharine, resignedly.

And even with this they wheeled their horses apart, and rode away from each other: she very pale, but erect with wounded pride; he reeling in his saddle like a drunken man.

And so Griffith Gaunt, stung mad by jealousy, affronted his sweetheart, the proudest girl in Cumberland, and, yielding to his foible, fled from his pain.

Our foibles are our manias.

CHAPTER III.

MISS PEYTON was shocked and grieved; but she was also affronted and wounded. Now anger seems to have some fine buoyant quality, which makes it rise and come uppermost in an agitated mind. She rode proudly into the court-yard of her father's house, and would not look once behind to see the. last of her perverse lover.

The old groom, Joe, who had taught her to ride when she was six years old, saw her coming, and hobbled out to hold her horse, while she alighted.

"Mistress Kate," said he, "have you seen Master Griffith Gaunt anywheres?"

The young lady colored at this question.

"Why?" said she.

"Why?" repeated Old Joe, a little contemptuously. "Why, where have *you* been not to know the country is out after un? First comed Jock Dennet, with his horse all in a lather, to say old Mr. Charlton was took ill, and had asked for Master Griffith. I told him to go to Dogmore Copse: 'Our Kate is

a-hunting to-day,' says I; 'and your Griffith, he is sure not to be far from her gelding's tail'; a sticks in his spurs and away a goes. What, ha'n't you seen Jock, neither?"

"No, no," replied Miss Peyton, impatiently. "What, is there anything the matter?"

"The matter, quo' she! Why, Jock had n't been gone an hour when in rides the new footman all in a lather, and brings a letter for Master Griffith from the old gentleman's housekeeper. 'You leave the letter with me, in case,' says I, and I sends him a-field after t' other. Here be the letter."

He took off his cap and produced the letter.

Catharine started at the sight of it.

"Alack!" said she, "this is a heavy day. Look, Joe; sealed with black. Poor Cousin Charlton! I doubt he is no more."

Joe shook his head expressively, and told her the butcher had come from that part not ten minutes ago, with word that the blinds were all down at Bolton Hall.

Poor human nature! A gleam of joy shot through Catharine's heart; this sad news would compel Griffith to stay at home and bury his benefactor; and that delay would give him time to reflect; and, somehow or other, she felt sure it would end in his not going at all.

But these thoughts had no sooner passed through her than she was ashamed of them and of herself. What! welcome that poor old man's death because it would keep her cross-grained lover at home? Her cheeks burned with shame; and, with a superfluous exercise of self-defence, she retired from Old Joe, lest he should divine what was passing in her mind.

But she was so wrapt in thought that she carried the letter away with her unconsciously.

As she passed through the hall, she heard George Neville and her father in animated conversation. She mounted the stairs softly, and went into a little boudoir of her own on the first floor, and sat down. The house stood high, and there was a very expansive and beautiful view of the country from this window. She sat down by it and drooped, and looked wistfully through the window, and thought of the past, and fell into a sad reverie. Pity began to soften her pride and anger, and presently two gentle tears dimmed her glorious eyes a moment, then stole down her delicate cheeks.

While she sat thus lost in the past, jovial voices and creaking boots broke suddenly upon her ear, and came up the stairs; they jarred upon her; so she cast one last glance out of the window, and rose to get out of their way, if possible. But it was too late; a heavy step came to the door, and a ruddy, Port-drinking face peeped in. It was her father.

"See-ho!" roared the jovial Squire. "I've found the hare on her form; bide thou outside a moment."

And he entered the room; but he had no sooner closed the door than his whole manner changed from loud and jovial to agitated and subdued.

"Kate, my girl," said he, piteously, "I have been a bad father to thee. I have spent all the money that should have been thine; thy poor father can scarce look thee in the face. So now I bring thee a good husband; be a good child now, and a dutiful. Neville's Court is his, and Neville's Cross will be, by the entail; and so will the baronetcy. I shall see my girl Lady Neville."

"Never, papa, never!" cried Kate.

"Hush! hush!" said the Squire, and put up his hand to her in great agitation and alarm; "hush, or he will hear ye. Kate," he whispered, "are you mad? Little I thought, when he asked to see me, it was to offer marriage. Be a good girl now; don't you quarrel with good luck. You are not fit to be poor; and you have made enemies: do but think how they will flout you when I die, and Bill's jade of a wife puts you to the door, as she will. And now you can triumph over them all, my Lady Neville, — and make your poor father happy, my Lady Neville. Enough said, for I promised you; so don't go and make a

fool of me, and yourself into the bargain. And — and — a word in your ear: he hath lent me a hundred pounds."

At this climax, the father hung his head; the daughter winced and moaned out, —

"Papa, how *could* you ?"

Mr. Peyton had gradually descended to that intermediate stage of degradation, when the substance of dignity is all gone, but its shadow, shame, remains. He stamped impatiently on the ground, and cut his humiliation short by rushing out of the room.

"Here, try your own luck, youngster," he cried at the door. "She knows my mind."

He trampled down the stairs, and young George Neville knocked respectfully at the door, though it was half open, and came in with youth's light foot, and a handsome face flushed into beauty by love and hope.

Miss Peyton's eye just swept him as he entered, and with the same movement she turned away her fair head and blushing cheek towards the window; yet — must I own it? — she quietly moulded the letter that lay in her lap, so that the address was no longer visible to the new-comer.

(Small secrecy, verging on deceit, you are bred in woman's bones!)

This blushing and averted cheek is one of those equivocal receptions that have puzzled many a sensible man. It is a sign of coy love; it is a sign of gentle aversion; *our* mode of interpreting it is simple and judicious: whichever it happens to be, we go and take it for the other.

The brisk, bold wooer that now engaged Kate Peyton was not the man to be dashed by a woman's coyness. Handsome, daring, good-humored, and vain, he had everything in his favor but his novelty.

Look at Kate! her eye lingers wistfully on that disconsolate horseman whose every step takes him farther from her; but George has her ear, and draws closer and closer to it, and pours love's mellow murmurs into it.

He told her he had made the grand tour, and seen the beauties of every land, but none like her; other ladies had certainly pleased his eye for a moment, but she alone had conquered his heart. He said many charming things to her, such as Griffith Gaunt had never said. Amongst the rest, he assured her the beauty of her person would not alone have fascinated him so deeply; but he had seen the beauty of her mind in those eyes of hers, that seemed not eyes, but souls; and begging her pardon for his presumption, he aspired to wed her mind.

Such ideas had often risen in Kate's own mind; but to hear them from a man was new. She looked askant through the window at the lessening Griffith, and thought "how the grand tour improves a man!" and said, as coldly as she could, —

"I esteem you, sir, and cannot but be flattered by sentiments so superior to those I am used to hear; but let this go no farther. I shall never marry now."

Instead of being angry at this, or telling her she wanted to marry somebody else, as the injudicious Griffith had done, young Neville had the address to treat it as an excellent jest, and drew such comical pictures of all the old maids in the neighborhood that she could not help smiling.

But the moment she smiled, the inflammable George made hot love to her again. Then she besought him to leave her, piteously. Then he said, cheerfully, he would leave her as soon as ever she had promised to be his. At that she turned sullen and haughty, and looked through the window and took no notice of him whatever. Then, instead of being discouraged or mortified, he showed imperturbable confidence and good-humor, and begged archly to know what interesting object was in sight from that window. On this she blushed and withdrew her eyes from the window, and so they met his. On that he threw himself on his knees (custom of the day), and wooed her with such a burst of passionate and tearful

eloquence that she began to pity him, and said, lifting her lovely eyes, —

"Alas! I was born to make all those I esteem unhappy!" and she sighed deeply.

"Not a bit of it," said he; "you were born, like the sun, to bless all you shine upon. Sweet Mistress Kate, I love you as these country boors can never be taught to love. I lay my heart, my name, my substance, at your feet; you shall not be loved, — you shall be worshipped. Ah! turn those eyes, brimful of soul, on me again, and let me try and read in them that one day, no matter how distant, the delight of my eyes, the joy of all my senses, the pride of Cumberland, the pearl of England, the flower of womankind, the rival of the angels, the darling of George Neville's heart, will be George Neville's wife."

Fire and water were in his eyes, passion in every tone; his manly hand grasped hers and trembled, and drew her gently towards him.

Her bosom heaved; his passionate male voice and touch electrified her, and made her flutter.

"Spare me this pain," she faltered; and she looked through the window and thought, "Poor Griffith was right, after all, and I was wrong. He had cause for jealousy, and CAUSE FOR FEAR."

And then she pitied him who panted at her side, and then she was sorry for him who rode away disconsolate, still lessening to her eye; and what with this conflict and the emotion her quarrel with Griffith had already caused her, she leaned her head back against the shutter, and began to sob low, but almost hysterically.

Now Mr. George Neville was neither a fool nor a novice; if he had never been downright in love before (which I crave permission to doubt), he had gone far enough on that road to make one Italian lady, two French, one Austrian, and one Creole, in love with him; and each of these love-affairs had given him fresh insight into the ways of woman. Enlightened by so many bitter - sweet experiences, he saw at once that there was something more going on inside Kate's heaving bosom than he could have caused by offering her his hand. He rose from his knees and leaned against the opposite shutter, and fixed his eyes a little sadly, but very observantly, on her, as she leaned back against the shutter, sobbing low, but hysterically, and quivering all over.

"There 's some other man at the bottom of this," thought George Neville.

"Mistress Kate," said he, gently, "I do not come here to make you weep. I love you like a gentleman. If you love another, take courage, tell me so, and don't let your father constrain your inclinations. Dearly as I love you, I would not wed your person, and your heart another's : that would be too cruel to you, and " (drawing himself up with sudden majesty) "too unjust to myself."

Kate looked up at him through her tears, and admired this man, who could love ardently, yet be proud and just. And if this appeal to her candor had been made yesterday, she would have said, frankly, "There is one I — esteem." But, since the quarrel, she would not own to herself, far less to another, that she loved a man who had turned his back upon her. So she *parried*.

"There is no one I love enough to wed," said she. "I am a cold-hearted girl, born to give pain to my betters. But I shall do something desperate to end all this."

"All what?" said he, keenly.

"The whole thing : my unprofitable life."

"Mistress Kate," said Neville, "I asked you, was there another man. If you had answered me, ' In truth there is, but he is poor and my father is averse or the like,' then I would have secretly sought that man, and, as I am very rich, you should have been happy."

"O, Mr. Neville, that is very generous, but how meanly you must think of me !"

"And what a bungler you must think

me ! I tell you, you should never have known. But let that pass ; you have answered my question ; and you say there is no man you love. Then I say you shall be Dame Neville."

"What, whether I will or no ? "

"Yes ; whether you *think* you will or no."

Catharine turned her dreamy eyes on him.

"You have had a good master. Why did you not come to me sooner ? "

She was thinking more of him than of herself, and, in fact, paying too little heed to her words. But she had no sooner uttered this inadvertent speech than she felt she had said too much. She blushed rosy red, and hid her face in her hands in the most charming confusion.

"Sweetest, it is not an hour too late, as you do not love another," was stout George Neville's reply.

But nevertheless the cunning rogue thought it safest to temporize, and put his coy mistress off her guard. So he ceased to alarm her by pressing the question of marriage, but seduced her into a charming talk, where the topics were not so personal, and only the tones of his voice and the glances of his expressive eyes were caressing. He was on his mettle to please her by hook or by crook, and was delightful, irresistible. He set her at ease, and she began to listen more, and even to smile faintly, and to look through the window a little less perseveringly.

Suddenly the spell was broken for a while.

And by whom ?

By the other.

Ay, you may well stare. It sounds strange, but it is true, that the poor forlorn horseman, hanging like a broken man, as he was, over his tired horse, and wending his solitary way from her he loved, and resigning the field, like a goose, to the very rival he feared, did yet (like the retiring Parthian) shoot an arrow right into that pretty boudoir and hit both his sweetheart and his rival, — hit them hard enough to spoil their sport, and make a little mischief between them — for that afternoon, at all events.

The arrow came into the room after this fashion.

Kate was sitting in a very feminine attitude. When a man wants to look in any direction, he turns his body and his eye the same way, and does it; but women love to cast oblique regards; and this their instinct is a fruitful source of their graceful and characteristic postures.

Kate Peyton was at this moment a statue of her sex. Her fair head leaned gently back against the corner of the window-shutter; her pretty feet and fair person in general were opposite George Neville, who sat facing the window, but in the middle of the room; her arms, half pendent, half extended, went listlessly aslant her, and somewhat to the right of her knees, yet, by an exquisite turn of the neck, her gray eyes contrived to be looking dreamily out of the window to her left. Still in this figure, that pointed one way and looked another, there was no distortion; all was easy, and full of that subtile grace we artists call repose.

But suddenly she dissolved this feminine attitude, rose to her feet, and interrupted her wooer civilly.

"Excuse me," said she, "but can you tell me which way that road on the hill leads to?"

Her companion stared a little at so sudden a turn in the conversation, but replied by asking her, with perfect good-humor, what road she meant.

"The one *that gentleman on horse-back has just taken.* Surely," she continued, "that road does not take to Bolton Hall."

"Certainly not," said George, following the direction of her finger. "Bolton lies to the right. That road takes to the sea-coast by Otterbury and Stanhope."

"I thought so," said Kate. "How unfortunate! He cannot know; but, indeed, how should he?"

"Who cannot know? and what? You speak in riddles, Mistress. And how pale you are! Are you ill?"

"No, not ill, sir," faltered Kate; "but you see me much discomposed. My cousin Charlton died this day; and the news met me at the very door." She could say no more.

Mr. Neville, on hearing this news, began to make many excuses for having inadvertently intruded himself upon her on such a day; but, in the midst of his apologies, she suddenly looked him full in the face, and said, with nervous abruptness, —

"You *talk* like a *preux chevalier.* I wonder whether you would ride five or six miles to do me a service."

"Ay, a thousand!" said the young man, glowing with pleasure. "What is to do?"

Kate pointed through the window.

"You see that gentleman on horseback. Well, I happen to know that he is leaving the country; he thinks that he — that I — that Mr. Charlton has many years to live. He must be told Mr. Charlton is dead, and his presence is required at Bolton Hall. I *should* like somebody to gallop after him, and give him this letter; but my own horse is tired, and I am tired; and, to be frank, there is a little coolness between the gentleman himself and me. O, I wish him no ill, but really I am not upon terms — I do not feel complaisant enough to carry a letter after him; yet I do feel that he *must* have it. Do not *you* think it would be malicious and unworthy in me to keep the news from him, when I know it is so?"

Young Neville smiled.

"Nay, Mistress, why so many words? Give me your letter, and I will soon overtake the gentleman: he seems in no great hurry."

Kate thanked him, and made a polite apology for giving him so much trouble, and handed him the letter. When it came to that, she held it out to him rather irresolutely; but he took it promptly, and bowed low, after the fashion of the day. She curtsied; he marched off with alacrity. She sat down again, and put her head in her hand to think it all over, and a chill thought ran through her. Was her conduct wise? What would Griffith think at her employing his rival? Would he not infer Neville had entered her service in more senses than one? Perhaps he would throw the letter in the dirt in a rage, and never read it.

Steps came rapidly, the door opened, and there was George Neville again, but not the same George Neville that went out but thirty seconds before. He stood in the door looking very black, and with a sardonic smile on his lips.

"An excellent jest, Mistress!" said he, ironically.

"Why, what is the matter?" said the lady, stoutly; but her red cheeks belied her assumption of innocence.

"O, not much," said George, with a bitter sneer. "It is an old story; only I thought you were nobler than the rest of your sex. This letter is to Mr. Griffith Gaunt."

"Well, sir!" said Kate with a face of serene and candid innocence.

"And Mr. Griffith Gaunt is a suitor of yours."

"Say, *was*. He is so no longer. He and I are out. But for that, think you I had even listened to — what you have been saying to me this ever so long?"

"O, that alters the case," said George. "But stay!" and he knitted his brows and reflected.

Up to a moment ago, the loftiness of Catharine Peyton's demeanor, and the celestial something in her soul-like, dreamy eyes, had convinced him she was a creature free from the small dishonesty and lubricity he had noted in so many women otherwise amiable and good. But this business of the letter had shaken the illusion.

"Stay!" said he, stiffly. "You say Mr. Gaunt and you are out?"

Catharine assented by a movement of her fair head.

"And he is leaving the country. Perhaps this letter is to keep him from leaving the country."

"Only until he has buried his benefactor," murmured Kate, in deprecating accents.

George wore a bitter sneer at this.

"Mistress Kate," said he, after a significant pause, "do you read Molière?"

She bridled a little, and would not reply. She knew Molière quite well enough not to want his wit levelled at her head.

"Do you admire the character of Célimène?"

No reply.

"You do not. How can you? She was too much your inferior. She never sent one of her lovers with a letter to the other to stop his flight. Well, you may eclipse Célimène; but permit me to remind you that I am George Neville, and not Georges Dandin."

Miss Peyton rose from her seat with eyes that literally flashed fire; and — the horrible truth must be told — her first wild impulse was to reply to all this Molière with one cut of her little riding-whip. But she had a swift mind, and two reflections entered it together: first, that this would be unlike a gentlewoman; secondly, that, if she whipped Mr. Neville, however inefficaciously, he would not lend her his piebald horse. So she took stronger measures; she just sank down again, and faltered, —

"I do not understand these bitter words. I have no lover at all; I never will have one again. But it is hard to think I cannot make a friend nor keep a friend," — and so lifted up her hands, and began to cry piteously.

Then the stout George was taken aback, and made to think himself a ruffian.

"Nay, do not weep so, Mistress Kate," said he, hurriedly. "Come, take courage. I am not jealous of Mr. Gaunt, — a man that hath been two years dangling after you, and could not win you. I look but to my own self-respect in the matter. I know your sex better than you know yourselves. Were I to carry that letter, you would thank me now, but by and by despise me. Now, as I mean you to be my wife, I will not risk your contempt. Why not take my horse, put whom you like on him, and so convey the letter to Mr. Gaunt?"

Now this was all the fair mourner wanted; so she said, —

"No, no, she would not be beholden to him for anything; he had spoken harshly to her, and misjudged her cruelly, cruelly, — oh! oh! oh!"

Then he implored her to grant him this small favor; then she cleared up, and said, Well, sooner than bear malice, she would. He thanked her for granting him that favor. She went off with the letter, saying, —

"I will be back anon."

But once she got clear, she opened the door again, and peeped in at him gayly, and said she, —

"Why not ask me who *wrote* the letter, before you compared me to that French coquette?"—and, with this, made him an arch curtsy and tripped away.

Mr. George Neville opened his eyes with astonishment. This arch question, and Kate's manner of putting it, convinced him the obnoxious missive was not a love-letter at all. He was sorry now, and vexed with himself, for having called her a coquette, and made her cry. After all, what was the mighty favor she had asked of him? To carry a sealed letter from somebody or other to a person who, to be sure, had been her lover, but was so no longer, — a simple act of charity and civility; and he had refused it in injurious terms.

He was glad he had lent his horse, and almost sorry he had not taken the letter himself.

To these chivalrous self-reproaches succeeded an uneasy feeling that perhaps the lady might retaliate somehow. It struck him, on reflection, that the arch query she had let fly at him was accompanied with a certain sparkle of the laughing eye, such as ere now had, in his experience, preceded a stroke of the feminine claw.

As he walked up and down, uneasy, awaiting the fair one's return, her father came up, and asked him to dine and sleep. What made the invitation more welcome was, that it in reality came from Kate.

"She tells me she has borrowed your horse," said the Squire; "so, says she, I am bound to take care of you till day-light; and, indeed, our ways are perilous at night."

"She is an angel!" cried the lover, all his ardor revived by this unexpected trait. "My horse, my house, my hand, and my heart are all at her service, by night and day."

Mr. Peyton, to wile away the time before dinner, invited him to walk out and see — a hog, deadly fat, as times went. But Neville denied himself that satisfaction, on the plea that he had his orders to await Miss Peyton's return where he was. The Squire was amused at his excessive docility, and winked, as much as to say, "I have been once upon a time in your plight," and so went and gloried in his hog alone.

The lover fell into a delicious reverie. He enjoyed, by anticipation, the novel pleasure of an evening passed all alone with this charming girl. The father, being friendly to his suit, would go to sleep after dinner; and then, by the subdued light of a wood fire, he would murmur his love into that sweet ear for hours, until the averted head should come round by degrees, and the delicious lips yield a coy assent. He resolved the night should not close till he had surprised, overpowered, and secured his lovely bride.

These soft meditations reconciled him for a while to the prolonged absence of their object.

In the midst of them, he happened to glance through the window; and he saw a sight that took his very breath away, and rooted him in amazement to the spot. About a mile from the house, a lady in a scarlet habit was galloping across country as the crow flies. Hedge, ditch, or brook, nothing stopped her an instant; and as for the pace, —

"She seemed in running to devour the way."

It was Kate Peyton on his piebald horse.

CHAPTER IV.

GRIFFITH GAUNT, unknown to himself, had lost temper as well as heart before he took the desperate step of leaving the country. Now his temper was naturally good ; and ere he had ridden two miles, he recovered it. To his cost ; for the sustaining force of anger being gone, he was alone with his grief. He drew the rein half mechanically, and from a spirited canter declined to a walk.

And the slower he went, the chillier grew his heart, till it lay half ice, half lead, in his bosom.

Parted ! oh, word pregnant with misery !

Never to see those heavenly eyes again, nor hear that silver voice ! Never again to watch that peerless form walk the minuet ; nor see it lift the gray horse over a fence with the grace and spirit that seemed inseparable from it !

Desolation streamed over him at the thought. And next his forlorn mind began to cling even to the inanimate objects that were dotted about the place which held her. He passed a little farm - house into which Kate and he had once been driven by a storm, and had sat together by the kitchen fire ; and the farmer's wife had smiled on them for sweethearts, and made them drink rum and milk and stay till the sun was fairly out.

"Ah ! good by, little farm !" he sighed ; "when shall I ever see you again ? "

He passed a brook where they had often stopped together and given their panting horses just a mouthful after a run with the harriers.

"Good by, little brook !" said he ; "you will ripple on as before, and warble as you go ; but I shall never drink at your water more, nor hear your pleasant murmur with her I love."

He sighed and crept away, still making for the sea.

In the icy depression of his heart his body and his senses were half paralyzed, and none would have known the accomplished huntsman in this broken man, who hung anyhow over his mare's neck and went to and fro in the saddle.

When he had gone about five miles, he came to the crest of a hill ; he re-membered, that, once past that brow, he could see Peyton Hall no more. He turned slowly and cast a sorrowful look at it.

It was winter, but the afternoon sun had come out bright. The horizontal beams struck full upon the house, and all the western panes shone like burnished gold. Her very abode, how glorious it looked ! And he was to see it no more.

He gazed and gazed at the bright house till love and sorrow dimmed his eyes, and he could see the beloved place no more. Then his dogged will prevailed and carried him away towards the sea, but crying like a woman now, and hanging all dislocated over his horse's mane.

Now about half a mile farther on, as he crept along on a vile and narrow road, all woebegone and broken, he heard a mighty scurry of horse's feet in the field to his left ; he looked languidly up ; and the first thing he saw was a great piebald horse's head and neck in the act of rising in the air, and doubling his fore-legs under him, to leap the low hedge a yard or two in front of him.

He did leap, and landed just in front of Griffith ; his rider curbed him so keenly that he went back almost on his haunches, and then stood motionless all across the road, with quivering tail. A lady in a scarlet riding - habit and purple cap sat him as if he had been a throne instead of a horse, and, without moving her body, turned her head swift as a snake, and fixed her great gray eyes full and searching upon Griffith Gaunt.

He uttered a little shout of joy and amazement ; his mare reared and plunged, and then was quiet. And thus Kate Peyton and he met, — at right angles, — and so close that it looked as if she had meant to ride him down.

How he stared at her ! How more than mortal fair she shone, returning to those bereaved eyes of his, as if she had really dropt from heaven !

His clasped hands, his haggard face channelled by tears, showed the keen girl she was strong where she had thought herself weak, and she comported herself accordingly, and in one moment took a much higher tone than she had intended as she came along.

"I am afraid," said she, very coldly, "you will have to postpone your journey a day or two. I am grieved to tell you that poor Mr. Charlton is dead."

Griffith uttered an exclamation.

"He asked for you; and messengers are out after you on every side. You must go to Bolton at once."

"Well-a-day!" said Griffith, "has he left me, too? Good, kind old man, on any other day I had found tears for thee! But now, methinks, happy are the dead. Alas! sweet mistress, I hoped you came to tell me you had — I might — what signifies what I hoped? — when I saw you had deigned to ride after me. Why should I go to Bolton, after all?"

"Because you will be an ungrateful wretch else. What! leave others to carry your kinsman and your benefactor to his grave, while you turn your back on him, and inherit his estate? For shame, sir! for shame!"

Griffith expostulated, humbly.

"How hardly you judge me! What are Bolton Hall and Park to me now? They were to have been yours, you know. And yours they shall be. I came between and robbed you. To be sure, the old man knew my mind. He said to himself, — 'Griffith or Kate, what matters it who has the land? They will live together on it.' But all that is changed now; you will never share it with me; and so I do feel I have no right to the place. Kate, my own Kate, I have heard them sneer at you for being poor, and it made my heart ache. I 'll stop that, any way. Go you in my place to the funeral; he that is dead will forgive me; his spirit knows now what I endure; and I 'll send you a writing, all sealed and signed, shall make Bolton Hall and Park yours; and when you are happy with some one you *can* love, as well as I love you, think sometimes of poor jealous Grif-

fith, that loved you dear and grudged you nothing; but," grinding his teeth and turning white, "I *can't* live in Cumberland, and see you in another man's arms."

Then Catharine trembled, and could not speak awhile; but at last she faltered out, —

"You will make me *hate* you."

"God forbid!" said simple Griffith.

"Well, then, don't thwart me, and provoke me so, but just turn your horse's head and go quietly home to Bolton Hall, and do your duty to the dead and the living. You can't go *this* way, for me and my horse." Then, seeing him waver, this virago faltered out, "And I have been so tried to-day, first by one, then by another, surely *you* might have some pity on me. Oh! oh! oh! oh!"

"Nay, nay," cried Griffith, all in a flutter, "I 'll go without more words; as I am a gentleman, I will sleep at Bolton this night, and will do my duty to the dead and the living. Don't you cry, sweetest; I give in. I find I have no will but yours."

The next moment they were cantering side by side, and never drew rein till they reached the cross-roads.

"Now tell me one thing," stammered Griffith, with a most ghastly attempt at cheerful indifference. "How — do you — happen to be — on George Neville's horse?"

Kate had been expecting this question for some time; yet she colored high when it did come. However, she had her answer pat. The horse was in the stable-yard, and fresh; her own was tired.

"What was I to do, Griffith? And now," added she, hastily, "the sun will soon set, and the roads are bad; be careful. I wish I could ask you to sleep at our house; but — there are reasons —— "

She hesitated; she could not well tell him George Neville was to dine and sleep there.

Griffith assured her there was no danger; his mare knew every foot of the way.

They parted : Griffith rode to Bolton, and Kate rode home.

It was past dinner-time. She ran up stairs, and hurried on her best gown and her diamond comb. For she began to quake now at the prank she had played with her guest's horse; and Nature taught her that the best way to soften censure is — to be beautiful.

"On pardonne tout aux belles."

And certainly she was passing fair, and queenly with her diamond comb.

She came down stairs and was received by her father. He grumbled at being kept waiting for dinner.

Kate easily appeased the good-natured Squire, and then asked what had become of Mr. Neville.

"O, he is gone long ago! Remembered, all of a sudden, he had promised to dine with a neighbor."

Kate shook her head sceptically, but said nothing. But a good minute after, she inquired, —

"How did he go? on foot?"

The Squire did not know.

After dinner old Joe sought an interview, and was admitted into the dining-room.

"Be it all right about the gray horse, Master?"

"What of him?" asked Kate.

"He be gone to Neville Court, Mistress. But I suppose" (with a horrid leer) "it is all right. Muster Neville told me all about it. He said, says he, —

"'Some do break a kine or the likes on these here j'yful occasions; other some do exchange goold rings. Your young mistress and me, *we* exchange nags. She takes my pieball, I take her gray,' says he. 'Saddle him for me, Joe,' says he, 'and wish me j'y.'

"So I clapped Muster Neville's saddle on the gray, and a gave me a goolden guinea, a did; and I was so struck of a heap I let un go without wishing on him j'y; but I hollered it arter un, as hard as I could. How you looks! It be all right, bain't it?"

Squire Peyton laughed heartily, and said he concluded it was all right.

"The piebald," said he, "is rising five, and *I've* had the gray ten years. We have got the sunny side of that bargain, Joe."

He gave Joe a glass of wine and sent him off, inflated with having done a good stroke in horseflesh.

As for Kate, she was red as fire, and kept her lips close as wax; not a word could be got out of her. The less she said, the more she thought. She was thoroughly vexed, and sore perplexed how to get her gray horse back from such a man as George Neville; and yet she could not help laughing at the trick, and secretly admiring this chevalier, who had kept his mortification to himself, and parried an affront so gallantly.

"The good-humored wretch!" said she to herself. "If Griffith ever goes away again, he will have me, whether I like or no. No lady could resist the monster long without some other man close at hand to help her."

CHAPTER V.

As, when a camel drops in the desert, vultures, hitherto unseen, come flying from the horizon, so Mr. Charlton had no sooner succumbed than the air darkened with undertakers flocking to Bolton for a lugubrious job. They rode up on black steeds, they crunched the gravel in grave gigs, and sent in black-edged cards to Griffith, and lowered their voices, and bridled their briskness, and tried hard, poor souls! to be sad; and were horribly complacent beneath that thin japan of venal sympathy.

Griffith selected his Raven, and then sat down to issue numerous invitations.

The idea of eschewing funereal pomp had not yet arisen. A gentleman of that day liked his very remains to make a stir, and did not see the fun of stealing into his grave like a rabbit slipping aground. Mr. Charlton had even left behind him a sealed letter containing a list of the persons he wished to follow him to the grave and attend the reading of his will. These were thirty-four, and amongst them three known to fame: namely, George Neville, Esq., Edward Peyton, Esq., and Miss Catharine Peyton.

To all and each of the thirty-four young Gaunt wrote a formal letter, inviting them to pay respect to their deceased friend, and to honor himself, by coming to Bolton Hall at nigh noon on Saturday next. These letters, in compliance with another custom of the time and place, were all sent by mounted messengers, and the answers came on horseback, too; so there was much clattering of hoofs coming and going, and much roasting, baking, drinking of ale, and bustling, all along of him who lay so still in an upper chamber.

And every man and woman came to Mr. Gaunt to ask his will and advice, however simple the matter; and the servants turned very obsequious, and laid themselves out to please the new master, and retain their old places.

And, what with the sense of authority, and the occupation, and growing ambition, love-sick Griffith grew another man, and began to forget that two days ago he was leaving the country and going to give up the whole game.

He found time to send Kate a loving letter, but no talk of marriage in it. He remembered she had asked him to give her time. Well, he would take her advice.

It wanted just three days to the funeral, when Mr. Charlton's own carriage, long unused, was found to be out of repair. Griffith had it sent to the nearest town, and followed it on that and other business. Now it happened to be what the country folk called "justicing day"; and who should ride into the yard of the "Roebuck" but the new magistrate, Mr. Neville? He alighted off a great bony gray horse before Griffith's very nose, and sauntered into a private room.

Griffith looked, and looked, and, scarcely able to believe his senses, followed Neville's horse to the stable, and examined him all round.

Griffith was sore perplexed, and stood at the stable-door glaring at the horse; and sick misgivings troubled him. He forgot the business he came about, and went and hung about the bar, and tried to pick up a clew to this mystery. The poor wretch put on a miserable assumption of indifference, and asked one or two of the magistrates if that was not Mr. Peyton's gray horse young Neville had ridden in upon.

Now amongst these gentlemen was a young squire Miss Peyton had refused, and galled him. He had long owed Gaunt a grudge for seeming to succeed where he had notably failed, and now, hearing him talk so much about the gray, he smelt a rat. He stepped into the parlor and told Neville Gaunt was fuming about the gray horse, and questioning everybody. Neville, though he put so bold a face on his recent adventure at Peyton Hall, was secretly smarting, and quite disposed to sting Gaunt in return. He saw a tool in this treacherous young squire, — his name was Galton, — and used him accordingly.

Galton, thoroughly primed by Neville, slipped back, and choosing his opportunity, poisoned Griffith Gaunt.

And this is how he poisoned him.

"Oh," said he, "Neville has bought the gray nag; and cost him dear, it did."

Griffith gave a sigh of relief; for he at once concluded old Peyton had sold his daughter's very horse. He resolved to buy her a better one next week with Mr. Charlton's money.

But Galton, who was only playing with him, went on to explain that Neville had paid a double price for the nag: he had given Miss Peyton his piebald horse in exchange, and his troth into the bargain. In short, he lent the matter so adroit a turn, that the exchange of horses seemed to be Kate's act as much as Neville's, and the inference inevitable.

"It is a falsehood!" gasped Griffith.

"Nay," said Galton, "I had it on the best authority: but you shall not quarrel with me about it; the lady is nought to me, and I but tell the tale as 't was told to me."

"Then who told it you?" said Gaunt, sternly.

"Why, it is all over the country, for that matter."

"No subterfuges, sir! I am the lady's servant, and you know it: this report, it slanders her, and insults me: give me the author, or I 'll lay my hunting-whip on your bones."

"Two can play at that game," said Galton; but he turned pale at the prospect of the pastime.

Griffith strode towards him, black with ire.

Then Galton stammered out, —

"It was Neville himself told me."

"Ah!" said Griffith; "I thought so. He is a liar, and a coward."

"I would not advise you to tell *him* so," said the other, maliciously. "He has killed his man in France: spitted him like a lark."

Griffith replied by a smile of contempt.

"Where is the man?" said he, after a pause.

"How should I know?" asked Galton, innocently.

"Where did you leave him five minutes ago?"

Galton was dumfoundered at this stroke, and could find nothing to say.

And now, as often happens, the matter took a turn not in the least anticipated by the conspirators.

"You must come with me, sir, if you please," said Griffith, quietly: and he took Galton's arm.

"Oh, with all my heart," said the other. "But, Mr. Gaunt, do not you take these idle reports to heart: *I* never do. What the Devil, where are you carrying me to? For Heaven's sake, let this foolish business go no farther."

For he found Griffith was taking him to the very room where Neville was.

Griffith deigned no reply; he just opened the door of the room in question, and walked the tale-bearer into the presence of the tale-maker. George Neville rose and confronted the pair

with a vast appearance of civility; but under it a sneer was just discernible.

The rivals measured each other from head to foot, and then Neville inquired to what he owed the honor of this visit.

Griffith replied, —

"He tells me you told him Miss Peyton has exchanged horses with you."

"Oh, you indiscreet person!" said George, shaking his finger playfully at Galton.

"And, by the same token, has plighted her troth to you."

"Worse and worse," said George. "Galton, I 'll never trust you with any secrets again. Besides, you exaggerate."

"Come, sir," said Griffith, sternly, "this Ned Galton was but your tool, and your mouth-piece; and therefore I bring him in here to witness my reply to *you*: Mr. George Neville, you are a liar and a scoundrel."

George Neville bounded to his feet like a tiger.

"I 'll have your life for those two words," he cried.

Then he suddenly governed himself by a great effort.

"It is not for me to bandy foul terms with a Cumberland savage," said he. "Name your time and place."

"I will. Ned Galton, you may go. I wish to say a few words in private to Mr. Neville."

Galton hesitated.

"No violence, Gentlemen: consider."

"Nonsense!" said Neville. "Mr. Gaunt and I are going to fight: we are not going to brawl. Be so good as to leave us."

"Ay," said Griffith; "and if you repeat a word of all this, woe be to your skin!"

As soon as he was gone, Griffith Gaunt turned very grave and calm, and said to George Neville, —

"The Cumberland savage has been better taught than to expose the lady he loves to gossiping tongues."

Neville colored up to the eyes at this thrust.

Griffith continued, —

"The least you can do is to avoid fresh scandal."

" I shall be happy to co-operate with you so far," said Neville, stiffly. " I undertake to keep Galton silent ; and for the rest, we have only to name an early hour for meeting, and confide it to but one discreet friend apiece who will attend us to the field. Then there will be no gossip, and no bumpkins nor constables breaking in : such things have happened in this country, I hear."

It was Wednesday. They settled to meet on Friday at noon on a hillside between Bolton and Neville's Court. The spot was exposed, but so wild and unfrequented that no interruption was to be feared. Mr. Neville being a practised swordsman, Gaunt chose pistols, — a weapon at which the combatants were supposed to be pretty equal. To this Neville very handsomely consented.

By this time a stiff and elaborate civility had taken the place of their heat, and at parting they bowed both long and low to each other.

Griffith left the inn and went into the street ; and as soon as he got there, he began to realize what he had done, and that in a day or two he might very probably be a dead man. The first thing he did was to go with sorrowful face and heavy step to Mr. Houseman's office.

Mr. Houseman was a highly respectable solicitor. His late father and he had long enjoyed the confidence of the gentry, and this enabled him to avoid litigious business, and confine himself pretty much to the more agreeable and lucrative occupation of drawing wills, settlements, and conveyances, and effecting loans, sales, and transfers. He visited the landed proprietors, and dined with them, and was a great favorite in the country.

" Justicing day " brought him many visits : so on that day he was always at his place of business. Indeed, a client was with him when Griffith called, and the young gentleman had to wait in the outer office for full ten minutes.

Then a door opened and the client in question came out, looking mortified and anxious. It was Squire Peyton.

At sight of Gaunt, who had risen to take his vacant place, Kate's father gave him a stiff nod, and an unfriendly glance, then hurried away.

Griffith was hurt at his manner. He knew very well Mr. Peyton looked higher for his daughter than Griffith Gaunt : but for all that the old gentleman had never shown him any personal dislike or incivility until this moment.

So Griffith could not but fear that Neville was somehow at the bottom of this, and that the combination was very strong against him. Now in thus interpreting Mr. Peyton's manner he fell into a very common error and fruitful cause of misunderstanding. We go and fancy that Everybody is thinking of *us*. But he is not : he is like us ; he is thinking of himself.

" Well, well," thought Griffith, " if I am not to have her, what better place for me than the grave ? "

He entered Mr. Houseman's private room and opened his business at once.

But a singular concurrence of circumstances induced Lawyer Houseman to confide to a third party the substance of what passed between this young gentleman and himself. So, to avoid repetition, the best way will be to let Houseman tell this part of my tale, instead of me ; and I only hope his communication, when it comes, may be half as interesting to my reader as it was to his hearer.

Suffice it for me to say that lawyer and client were closeted a good hour, and were still conversing together when a card was handed in to Mr. Houseman that seemed to cause him both surprise and pleasure.

" In five minutes," said he to the clerk. Griffith took the hint, and bade him good by directly.

As he went out, the gentleman who had sent in his card rose from a seat in the outer office to go in.

It was Mr. George Neville.

Griffith Gaunt and he saluted and scanned each other curiously. They little thought to meet again so soon. The clerks saw nothing more than two polite gentlemen passing each other.

The more Griffith thought of the approaching duel, the less he liked it. He was an impulsive man, for one thing; and with such, a cold fit naturally succeeds a hot one. And besides, as his heat abated, Reason and Reflection made themselves heard, and told him that in a contest with a formidable rival he was throwing away an advantage. After all, Kate had shown him great favor; she had ridden Neville's horse after him, and made him resign his purpose of leaving her; surely, then, she preferred him on the whole to Neville; yet he must go and risk his chance of possessing her upon a personal encounter, in which Neville was at least as likely to kill him as he to kill Neville. He saw too late that he was playing his rival's game. He felt cold and despondent, and more and more convinced that he should never marry Kate, but that she would very likely bury him.

With all this he was too game to recoil, and indeed he hated his rival too deeply. So, like many a man before him, he was going doggedly to the field against his judgment, with little to win and all to lose.

His deeper and more solemn anxieties were diversified by a lighter one. A few days ago he had invited half the county to bury Mr. Charlton on Saturday, the 19th of February. But now he had gone and fixed Friday the 18th for a duel. A fine thing if he should be himself a corpse on Friday afternoon! Who was to receive the guests? who conduct the funeral?

The man, with all his faults, had a grateful heart; and Mr. Charlton was his benefactor, and he felt he had no right to go and get himself killed until he had paid the last rites to his best friend.

The difficulty admits of course of a comic view, and smells Hibernian; but these things seem anything but droll to those whose lives and feelings are at stake; and, indeed, there was something chivalrous and touching in Griffith's vexation at the possibility of his benefactor being buried without due honors, ow-

ing to his own intemperate haste to be killed. He resolved to provide against that contingency: so, on the Thursday, he wrote an urgent letter to Mr. Houseman, telling him he must come early to the funeral, and be prepared to conduct it.

This letter was carried to Mr. Houseman's office at three o'clock on Thursday afternoon.

Mr. Houseman was not at home. He was gone to a country-house nine miles distant. But Griffith's servant was well mounted, and had peremptory orders; so he rode after Mr. Houseman, and found him at Mr. Peyton's house, — whither, if you please, we, too, will follow him.

In the first place, you must know that the real reason why Mr. Peyton looked so savage, coming out of Mr. Houseman's office, was this: Neville had said no more about the hundred pounds, and, indeed, had not visited the house since; so Peyton, who had now begun to reckon on this sum, went to Houseman to borrow it. But Houseman politely declined to lend it him, and gave excellent reasons. All this was natural enough, common enough; but the real reason why Houseman declined was a truly singular one. The fact is, Catharine Peyton had made him promise to refuse.

Between that young lady and the Housemans, husband and wife, there was a sincere friendship, founded on mutual esteem; and Catharine could do almost what she liked with either of them. Now, whatever might have been her faults, she was a proud girl, and an intelligent one: it mortified her pride to see her father borrowing here, and borrowing there, and unable to repay; and she had also observed that he always celebrated a new loan by a new extravagance, and so was never a penny the richer for borrowed money. He had inadvertently let fall that he should apply to Houseman. She raised no open objection, but just mounted Piebald, and rode off to Houseman, and made him solemnly promise her not to lend her father a shilling.

Houseman kept his word; but his refusal cost him more pain than he had calculated on when he made the promise. Squire Peyton had paid him thousands, first and last; and when he left Houseman's room, with disappointment, mortification, and humiliation deeply marked on his features, usually so handsome and jolly, the lawyer felt sorry and ashamed, — and did *not* show it.

But it rankled in him; and the very next day he took advantage of a little business he had to do in Mr. Peyton's neighborhood, and drove to Peyton Hall, and asked for Mistress Kate.

His was a curious errand. Indeed, I think it would not be easy to find a parallel to it.

For here was an attorney calling upon a beautiful girl, — to do what?

To soften her.

On a daughter, — to do what?

To persuade her to permit him to lend her father £100 on insufficient security.

Well, he reminded her of his ancient obligations to her family, and assured her he could well afford to risk a hundred or even a thousand pounds. He then told her that her father had shown great pain at his refusal, and that he himself was human, and could not divest himself of gratitude and pity and good-nature, — all for £100.

"In a word," said he, "I have brought the money; and you must give in for this once, and let me lend it him without more ado."

Miss Peyton was gratified and affected, and a tear trembled a moment in her eye, but went in-doors again, and left her firm as a rock sprinkled with dew. She told him she could quite understand his feeling, and thanked him for it; but she had long and seriously weighed the matter, and could not release him from his promise.

"No more of this base borrowing," said she, and clenched her white teeth indomitably.

He attacked her with a good many weapons; but she parried them all so gently, yet so nobly, and so successfully, that he admired her more than ever.

Still, lawyers fight hard, and die very hard. Houseman got warm in his cause, and cross-examined this defendant, and asked her whether *she* would refuse to lend her father £100 out of a full purse.

This question was answered only by a flash of her glorious eyes, and a magnificent look of disdain at the doubt implied.

"Well, then," said Houseman, "be your father's surety for repayment, with interest at six per centum, and then there will be nothing in the business to wound your dignity. I have many hundreds out at six per centum."

"Excuse me: that would be dishonest," said Kate; "I have no money to repay you with."

"But you have expectations."

"Nay, not I."

"I beg your pardon."

"Methinks I should know, sir. What expectations have I? and from whom?"

Houseman fidgeted on his seat, and then, with some hesitation, replied, —

"Well, from two that I know of."

"You are jesting, methinks, good Mr. Houseman," said she, reproachfully.

"Nay, dear Mistress Kate, I wish you too well to jest on such a theme."

The lawyer then fidgeted again on his seat in silence, —sign of an inward struggle, —during which Kate's eye watched him with some curiosity. At last his wavering balance inclined towards revealing something or other.

"Mistress Kate," said he, "my wife and I are both your faithful friends and humble admirers. We often say you would grace a coronet, and wish you were as rich as you are good and beautiful."

Kate turned her lovely head away, and gave him her hand. That incongruous movement, so full of womanly grace and feeling, and the soft pressure of her white hand, completed her victory, and the remains of Houseman's reserve melted away.

"Yes, my dear young lady," said he, warmly, "I have good news for you; only mind, not a living soul must ever know it from your lips. Why, I am going to do for you what I never did in my life before, — going to tell you something that passed yesterday in my office. But then I know you; you are a young lady out of a thousand; I can trust you to be discreet and silent, — can I not?"

"As the grave."

"Well, then, my young mistress, — in truth it was like a play, though the scene was but a lawyer's office " ——

"Was it?" cried Kate. "Then you set me all of a flutter; you must sup here, and sleep here. Nay, nay," said she, her eyes sparkling with animation, "I'll take no denial. My father dines abroad: we shall have the house to ourselves."

Her interest was keenly excited: but she was a true woman, and must coquette with her very curiosity; so she ran off to see with her own eyes that sheets were aired, and a roasting fire lighted in the blue bedroom for her guest.

While she was away, a servant brought in Griffith Gaunt's letter, and a sheet of paper had to be borrowed to answer it.

The answer was hardly written and sent out to Griffith's servant, when supper and the fair hostess came in almost together.

After supper fresh logs were heaped on the fire, and the lawyer sat in a cosey arm-chair, and took out his diary, and several papers, as methodically as if he was going to lay the case by counsel before a judge of assize.

Kate sat opposite him with her gray eyes beaming on him all the time, and searching for the hidden meaning of everything he told her. During the recital which follows, her color often came and went, but those wonderful eyes never left the narrator's face a moment.

They put the attorney on his mettle, and he elaborated the matter more than I should have done: he articulated his topics; marked each salient fact by a long pause. In short, he told his story like an attorney, and not like a romancist. I cannot help that, you know; I'm not Procrustes.

MR. HOUSEMAN'S LITTLE NARRATIVE.

"WEDNESDAY, the seventeenth day of February, at about one of the clock, called on me at my place of business Mr. Griffith Gaunt, whom I need not here describe, inasmuch as his person and place of residence are well known to the court — what am I saying? — I mean, well known to yourself, Mistress Kate.

"The said Griffith, on entering my room, seemed moved, and I might say distempered, and did not give himself time to salute me and receive my obeisance, but addressed me abruptly and said as follows: 'Mr. Houseman, I am come to make my will.'"

("Dear me!" said Kate: then blushed, and was more on her guard.)

"I seated the young gentleman, and then replied, that his resolution aforesaid did him credit, the young being as mortal as the old. I said further, that many disasters had happened, in my experience, owing to the obstinacy with which men, in the days of their strength, shut their eyes to the precarious tenure under which all sons of Adam hold existence; and so, many a worthy gentleman dies in his sins, — and, what is worse, dies intestate.

"But the said Griffith interrupted me with some signs of impatience, and asked me bluntly, would I draw his will, and have it executed on the spot.

"I assented, generally; but I requested him, by way of needful preliminary, to obtain for me a copy of Mr. Charlton's will, under which, as I have always understood, the said Griffith inherits whatever real estate he hath to bequeath.

"Mr. Griffith Gaunt then replied to me, that Mr. Charlton's will was in London, and the exact terms of it could not be known until after the funeral, — that is to say, upon the nineteenth instant.

"Thereupon I explained to Mr. Gaunt that I must see and know what properties were devised in the will aforesaid, by the said Charlton, to Gaunt aforesaid, and how devised and described. Without this, I said, I could not correctly and sufficiently describe the same in the instrument I was now requested to prepare.

"Mr. Gaunt did not directly reply to this objection. But he pondered a little while, and then asked me if it were not possible for him, by means of general terms, to convey to a sole legatee whatever lands, goods, chattels, etc., Mr. Charlton might hereafter prove to have devised to him, the said Griffith Gaunt.

"I admitted this was possible, but objected that it was dangerous. I let him know that in matters of law general terms are a fruitful source of dispute, and I said I was one of those who hold it a duty to avert litigation from our clients.

"Thereupon Mr. Gaunt drew out of his bosom a pocket-book.

"The said pocket-book was shown to me by the said Gaunt, and I say it contained a paragraph from a newspaper, which I believe to have been cut out of the said newspaper with a knife, or a pair of scissors, or some trenchant instrument; and the said paragraph purported to contain an exact copy of a certain will and testament under which (as is, indeed, matter of public notoriety) one Dame Butcher hath inherited and now enjoys the lands, goods, and chattels of a certain merry parson late deceased in these parts, and, *I believe,* little missed.

"Mr. Gaunt would have me read the will and testament aforesaid, and I read it accordingly : and inasmuch as bad things are best remembered, the said will and testament did, by its singularity and profaneness, fix itself forthwith in my memory ; so that I can by no means dislodge it thence, do what I may.

"The said document, to the best of my memory and belief, runneth after this fashion.

"'I, John Raymond, clerk, at present residing at Whitbeck, in the County of Cumberland, being a man sound in body, mind, and judgment, do deliver this as my last will and testament.

"'I give and bequeath all my real property, and all my personal property, and all the property, whether real or personal, I may hereafter possess or become entitled to, to my housekeeper, Janet Butcher.

"'And I appoint Janet Butcher my sole executrix, and I make Janet Butcher my sole residuary legatee ; save and except that I leave my solemn curse to any knave who hereafter shall at any time pretend that he does not understand the meaning of this my will and testament.'"

(Catharine smiled a little at this last bequest.)

"Mr. Gaunt then solemnly appealed to me as an honest man to tell him whether the aforesaid document was bad, or good, in law.

"I was fain to admit that it was sufficient in law; but I qualified, and said I thought it might be attacked on the score of the hussy's undue influence, and the testator's apparent insanity. Nevertheless, I concluded candidly that neither objection would prevail in our courts, owing to the sturdy prejudice in the breasts of English jurymen, whose ground of faith it is that every man has a right to do what he will with his own, and even to do it how he likes.

"Mr. Gaunt did speedily abuse this my candor. He urged me to lose no time, but to draw his will according to the form and precedent in that case made and provided by this mad parson ; and my clerks, forsooth, were to be the witnesses thereof.

"I refused, with some heat, to sully

my office by allowing such an instrument to issue therefrom ; and I asked the said Gaunt, in high dudgeon, for what he took me.

"Mr. Gaunt then offered, in reply, two suggestions that shook me. *Imprimis*, he told me the person to whom he now desired to leave his all was Mistress Catharine Peyton." (An ejaculation from Kate.) "*Secundo*, he said he would go straight from me to that coxcomb Harrison, were I to refuse to serve him in the matter.

"On this, having regard to your interest and my own, I temporized : I offered to let him draw a will after his parson's precedent, and I agreed it should be witnessed in my office ; only I stipulated that next week a proper document should be drawn by myself, with due particulars, on two sheets of paper, and afterwards engrossed and witnessed : and to this Mr. Gaunt assented, and immediately drew his will according to newspaper precedent.

"But when I came to examine his masterpiece, I found he had taken advantage of my pliability to attach an unreasonable condition, to wit : that the said Catharine should forfeit all interest under this will, in case she should ever marry a certain party therein nominated, specified, and described."

("Now that was Griffith all over," cried Catharine, merrily.)

"I objected stoutly to this. I took leave to remind the young gentleman, that, when a Christian man makes his last will and testament, he should think of the grave and of the place beyond, whither we may carry our affections, but must leave the bundle of our hates behind, the gate being narrow. I even went so far as to doubt whether such a proviso could stand in *law ;* and I also put a practical query : what was to hinder the legatee from selling the property and diverting the funds, and then marrying whom she liked ?

"Mr. Gaunt was deaf to reason. He bade me remember that he was neither saint nor apostle, but a poor gentleman of Cumberland, who saw a stranger come between him and his lover dear : with that he was much moved, and did not conclude his argument at all, but broke off, and was fain to hide his face with both hands awhile. In truth, this touched me ; and I looked another way, and began to ask myself, why should I interfere, who, after all, know not your heart in the matter ; and, to be brief, I withstood him and Parson's law no more, but sent his draught will to the clerks, the which they copied fair in a trice, and the duplicates were signed and witnessed in red-hot haste, — as most of men's follies are done, for that matter.

"The paper writing now produced and shown to me — tush ! what am I saying ? — I mean the paper writing I now produce and show to you is the draught of the will aforesaid, in the handwriting of the testator."

And with this he handed Kate Peyton Griffith Gaunt's will, and took a long and satirical pinch of snuff while she examined it.

Miss Peyton took the will in her white hands and read it. But, in reading it, she held it up and turned it so that her friend could not see her face while she read it, but only her white hands, in which the document rustled a little.

It ran thus : —

"I, Griffith Gaunt, late of the Eyrie, and now residing at Bolton Hall, in the County of Cumberland, being sound in body and mind, do deliver this as my last will and testament. I give and bequeath all the property, real or personal, which I now possess or may hereafter become entitled to, to my dear friend and mistress, Catharine Peyton, daughter of Edward Peyton, Esquire, of Peyton Hall : provided always that the said Catharine Peyton shall at no time within the next ten years marry George Neville of Neville's Court in this county. But should the said Catharine marry the said George within ten years of this day, then I leave all my said property, in possession, remainder, or reversion, to my heir-at-law."

The fair legatee read this extraordinary testament more than once. At last she handed it back to Mr. Houseman without a word. But her cheek was red, and her eyes glistening.

Mr. Houseman was surprised at her silence ; and as he was curious to know her heart, he sounded her, asked her what she thought of that part of his story. But she evaded him with all the tact of her sex.

"What! that is not all, then ?" said she, quickly.

Houseman replied, that it was barely half.

"Then tell me all, pray tell me all," said Kate, earnestly.

"I am here to that end," said Houseman, and recommenced his narrative.

The business being done to Mr. Gaunt's satisfaction, though not to mine, we fell into some friendly talk ; but in the midst of it my clerk Thomas brought me in the card of a gentleman whom I was very desirous to secure as a client.

"Mr. Gaunt, I think, read my mind ; for he took leave of me forthwith. I attended him to the door, and then welcomed the gentleman aforesaid. It was no other than Mr. George Neville.

"Mr. Neville, after such gracious civilities as his native breeding and foreign travel have taught him, came to business, and requested me — to draw his will."

("La !" said Kate.)

"I was a little startled, but hid it and took his instructions. This done, I requested to see the title-deeds of his estates, with a view to describing them, and he went himself to his banker's for them and placed them in my hands.

"I then promised to have the will ready in a week or ten days. But Mr. Neville, with many polite regrets for hurrying me, told me upon his honor he could give me but twenty-four hours. 'After that,' said he, 'it might be too late.' "

("Ah !" said Miss Peyton.)

"Determined to retain my new client, I set my clerks to work, and this very day was engrossed, signed, and witnessed, the last will and testament of George Neville, Esquire, of Neville's Court, in the County of Cumberland, and Leicester Square, London, where he hath a noble mansion.

"Now as to the general disposition of his lands, manorial rights, messuages, tenements, goods, chattels, etc., and his special legacies to divers ladies and gentlemen and domestic servants, these I will not reveal even to you.

"The paper I now produce is a copy of that particular bequest which I have decided to communicate to you in strict and sacred confidence."

And he handed her an extract from George Neville's will.

Miss Peyton then read what follows : —

"And I give and bequeath to Mistress Catharine Peyton, of Peyton Hall, in the said County of Cumberland, in token of my respect and regard, all that my freehold estate called Moniton Grange, with the messuage or tenement standing and being thereon, and the farm-yard buildings and appurtenances belonging thereto, containing by estimation three hundred and seventy-six acres three roods and five perches, be the same little more or less, to hold to her the said Catharine Peyton, her heirs and assigns, forever."

The legatee laid down the paper, and leaned her head softly on her fair hand, and her eyes explored vacancy.

"What means all this ?" said she, aloud, but to herself.

Mr. Houseman undertook the office of interpreter.

"Means? Why, that he has left you one of the snuggest estates in the county. 'T is not quite so large as Bolton; but lies sunnier, and the land richer. Well, Mistress, was I right? Are you not good for a thousand pounds?"

Kate, still manifestly thinking of something else, let fall, as it were, out of her mouth, that Mr. Gaunt and Mr. Neville were both men in the flower of their youth, and how was she the richer for their folly?

"Why," said Houseman, "you will not have to wait for the death of these testators,—Heaven forbid! But what does all this making of wills show me? That both these gentlemen are deep in love with you, and you can pick and choose; I say, you can wed with Bolton Hall or Neville's Court to-morrow; so, prithee, let the Squire have his hundred pounds, and do you repay me at your leisure."

Miss Peyton made no reply, but leaned her exquisite head upon her hand and pondered.

She did not knit her brows, nor labor visibly at the mental oar; yet a certain reposeful gravity and a fixity of the thoughtful eye showed she was applying all the powers of her mind.

Mr. Houseman was not surprised at that: his own wife had but little intellect: yet had he seen her weigh two rival bonnets in mortal silence, and with all the seeming profundity of a judge on the bench. And now this young lady was doubtless weighing farms with similar gravity, care, and intelligence.

But as this continued, and still she did not communicate her decision, he asked her point-blank which of the two she settled to wed: Neville's Court or Bolton Grange.

Thus appealed to, Miss Peyton turned her great eye on him, without really looking at him, and replied,—

"You have made me very uneasy."

He stared. She relapsed into thought a moment, and then, turning to Houseman, asked him how *he* accounted for those two gentlemen making their wills. They were very young to make their wills all of a sudden.

"Why," said Houseman, "Mr. Neville is a man of sense, and every man of sense makes his will; and as for Mr. Gaunt, he has just come into prospect of an estate; that 's why."

"Ah, but why could not Griffith wait till after the funeral?"

"Oh, clients are always in a hurry."

"So you see nothing in it? nothing alarming, I mean?"

"Nothing very alarming. Two landed proprietors in love with you; that is all."

"But, dear Mr. Houseman, that is what makes me uneasy; at this rate, they must look on one another as—as—rivals; and you know rivals are sometimes enemies."

"Oh, I see now," said Houseman: "you apprehend a quarrel between the gentlemen. Of course there is no love lost between them: but they met in my office and saluted each other with perfect civility. I saw them with my own eyes."

"Indeed! I am glad to hear that,—very glad. I hope it was only a coincidence then, their both making their wills."

"Nothing more, you may depend: neither of them knows from me what the other has done, nor ever will."

"That is true," said Kate, and seemed considerably relieved.

To ease her mind entirely, Houseman went on to say, that, as to the report that high words had passed between the clients in question at the "Roebuck," he had no doubt it was exaggerated.

"Besides," said he, "that was not about a lady: I 'm told it was about a horse,—some bet belike."

Catharine uttered a faint cry.

"About a horse?" said she. "Not about a gray horse?"

"Nay, that is more than I know."

"High words about a horse," said Catharine,—"and they are making their wills. Oh! my mind misgave me from the first." And she turned pale. Presently she clasped her hands together,—"Mr. Houseman!" she cried, "what shall I do? What! do you not see that both their lives are in danger, and that is why they make their wills? And how should *both* their lives be in danger, but from each other? Madmen! they have quarrelled; they are going to fight,—fight to the death; and I fear it is about me,—me, who love neither of them, you know."

"In that case, *let* them fight," said her legal adviser, dispassionately. "Whichever fool gets killed, you will be none the poorer." And the dog wore a sober complacency.

Catharine turned her large eyes on him with horror and amazement, but said nothing.

As for the lawyer, he was more struck with her sagacity than with anything. He somewhat overrated it,—not being aware of the private reasons she had for thinking that her two testators were enemies to the death.

"I almost think you are right," said he; "for I got a curious missive from Mr. Gaunt scarce an hour agone, and he says—let me see what he says——"

"Nay, let *me* see," said Kate.

On that he handed her Griffith's note. It ran thus:—

"It is possible I may not be able to conduct the funeral. Should this be so, I appoint you to act for me. So, then, good Mr. Houseman, let me count on you to be here at nine of the clock. For Heaven's sake fail me not.

"Your humble servant,

"G. G."

This note left no doubt in Kate's mind.

"Now, first of all," said she, "what answer made you to this?"

"What answer should I make? I pledged my word to be at Bolton at nine of the clock."

"Oh, blind!" sighed Kate. "And I must be out of the room! What shall I do? My dear friend, forgive me: I am a wretched girl. I am to blame. I ought to have dismissed them both, or else decided between them. But who would have thought it would go this length? I did not think Griffith was brave enough. Have pity on me, and help me. Stop this fearful fighting." And now the young creature clung to the man-of-

business, and prayed and prayed him earnestly to avert bloodshed.

Mr. Houseman was staggered by this passionate appeal from one who so rarely lost her self-command. He soothed her as well as he could, and said he would do his best,—but added, which was very true, that he thought her interference would be more effective than his own.

"What care these young bloods for an old attorney? I should fare ill, came I between their rapiers. To be sure, I might bind them over to keep the peace. But, Mistress Kate, now be frank with me; then I can serve you better. You love one of these two: that is clear. Which is the man?—that I may know what I am about."

For all her agitation, Kate was on her guard in some things.

"Nay," she faltered, "I love neither, —not to say love them: but I pity him so!"

"Which?"

"Both."

"Ay, Mistress; but which do you pity most?" asked the shrewd lawyer.

"Whichever shall come to harm for my sake," replied the simple girl.

"You could not go to them to-night, and bring them to reason?" asked she, piteously.

She went to the window to see what sort of a night it was. She drew the heavy crimson curtains and opened the window. In rushed a bitter blast laden with flying snow. The window-ledges, too, were clogged with snow, and all the ground was white.

Houseman shuddered, and drew nearer to the blazing logs. Kate closed the window with a groan.

"It is not to be thought of," said she, "at your age, and not a road to be seen for snow. What shall I do?"

"Wait till to-morrow," said Mr. Houseman.

(Procrastination was his daily work, being an attorney.)

"To-morrow!" cried Catharine. "Perhaps to-morrow will be too late. Perhaps even now they have met, and he lies a corpse."

"Who?"

"Whichever it is, I shall end my days in a convent praying for his soul."

She wrung her hands while she said this, and still there was no catching her.

Little did the lawyer think to rouse such a storm with his good news. And now he made a feeble and vain attempt to soothe her, and ended by promising to start the first thing in the morning and get both her testators bound over to keep the peace by noon. With this resolution he went to bed early.

She was glad to be alone, at all events.

Now, mind you, there were plenty of vain and vulgar, yet respectable girls, in Cumberland, who would have been delighted to be fought about, even though bloodshed were to be the result. But this young lady was not vain, but proud. She was sensitive, too, and troubled with a conscience. It reproached her bitterly: it told her she had permitted the addresses of two gentlemen, and so mischief had somehow arisen — out of her levity. Now her life had been uneventful and innocent: this was the very first time she had been connected with anything like a crime, and her remorse was great; so was her grief; but her fears were greater still. The terrible look Griffith had cast at his rival flashed on her: so did his sinister words. She felt, that, if he and Neville met, nothing less than Neville's death or his own would separate them. Suppose that even now one of them lay a corpse, cold and ghastly as the snow that now covered Nature's face!

The agitation of her mind was such that her body could not be still. Now she walked the room in violent distress, wringing her hands; now she kneeled and prayed fervently for both those lives she had endangered; often she flew to the window and looked eagerly out, writhing and rebelling against the network of female custom that entangled her and would not let her fly out of her cage even to do a good action, — to avert a catastrophe by her prayers, or her tears, or her good sense.

And all ended in her realizing that she was a woman, a poor, impotent being, born to lie quiet and let things go: at that she wept helplessly.

So wore away the first night of agony this young creature ever knew.

Towards morning, exhausted by her inward struggles, she fell asleep upon a sofa.

But her trouble followed her. She dreamed she was on a horse, hurried along with prodigious rapidity, in a darkened atmosphere, a sort of dry fog: she knew somehow she was being taken to see some awful, mysterious thing. By and by the haze cleared and she came out upon pleasant, open, sunny fields, that almost dazzled her. She passed gates, and hedges too, all clear, distinct, and individual. Presently a voice by her side said, "This way!" and her horse seemed to turn of his own accord through a gap, and in one moment she came on a group of gentlemen. It was Griffith Gaunt, and two strangers. Then she spoke, and said, —

"But Mr. Neville?"

No answer was made her; but the group opened in solemn silence, and there lay George Neville on the snow, stark and stiff, with blood issuing from his temple, and trickling along the snow.

She saw distinctly all his well-known features: but they were pinched and sharpened now. And his dark olive skin was turned to bluish white. It was his corpse. And now her horse thrust out his nose and snorted like a demon. She looked down, and ah! the blood was running at her preternaturally fast along the snow. She screamed, her horse reared high, and she was falling on the blood-stained snow. She awoke, screaming; and the sunlight seemed to rush in at the window.

Her joy that it was only a dream overpowered every other feeling at first. She kneeled and thanked God for that.

The next thing was, she thought it might be a revelation of what had actually occurred.

But this chilling fear did not affect her long. Nothing could shake her conviction that a duel was on foot, — and, indeed, the intelligent of her sex do sometimes put this and that together, and spring to a just, but obvious inference, in a way that looks to a slower and safer reasoner like divination, — but then she knew that yesterday evening both parties were alive. Coupling this with Griffith's broad hint that after the funeral might be too late to make his will, she felt sure that it was this very day the combatants were to meet. Yes, and this very morning : for she knew that gentlemen always fought in the morning.

If her dream was false as to the past, it might be true as to what was at hand. Was it not a supernatural warning, sent to her in mercy? The history of her Church abounded in such dreams and visions ; and, indeed, the time and place she lived in were rife with stories of the kind, — one, in particular, of recent date.

This thought took hold of her, and grew on her, till it overpowered even the diffidence of her sex ; and then up started her individual character ; and now nothing could hold her. For, languid and dreamy in the common things of life, this Catharine Peyton was one of those who rise into rare ardor and activity in such great crises as seem to benumb the habitually brisk, and they turn tame and passive.

She had seen at a glance that Houseman was too slow and apathetic for such an emergency. She resolved to act herself. She washed her face and neck and arms and hands in cold water, and was refreshed and invigorated. She put on her riding-habit and her little gold spur, (Griffith Gaunt had given it her,) and hurried into the stable-yard.

Old Joe and his boy had gone away to breakfast : he lived in the village.

This was unlucky : Catharine must wait his return and lose time, or else saddle the horse herself. She chose the latter. The piebald was a good horse, but a fidgetty one ; so she saddled and bridled him at his stall. She then led him out to the stone steps in the stable-yard, and tried to mount him. But he sidled away ; she had nobody to square him ; and she could get nothing to mount but his head. She coaxed him, she tickled him on the other side with her whip. It was all in vain.

It was absurd, but heart-sickening. She stared at him with wonder that he could be so cruel as to play the fool when every minute might be life or death. She spoke to him, she implored him piteously, she patted him. All was in vain.

As a last resource, she walked him back to the stable and gave him a sieveful of oats, and set it down by the corn-bin for him, and took an opportunity to mount the bin softly.

He ate the oats, but with retroverted eye watched her. She kept quiet and affected *nonchalance* till he became less cautious,—then suddenly sprang on him, and taught him to set his wit against a woman's. My Lord wheeled round directly, ere she could get her leg over the pommel, and made for the stable-door. She lowered her head to his mane and just scraped out without injury, — not an inch to spare. He set off at once, but luckily for her she had often ridden a bare-backed horse. She sat him for the first few yards by balance, then reined him in quietly, and soon whipped her left foot into the stirrup and her right leg over the pommel ; and then the piebald nag had to pay for his pranks : the roads were clogged with snow, but she fanned him along without mercy, and never drew bridle till she pulled him up, drenched and steaming like a washtub, at Netley Cross-Roads.

Here she halted irresolute. The road to the right led to Bolton, distant two miles and a half. The road in front led to Neville's Court, distant three miles. Which should she take? She had asked herself this a dozen times upon the road, yet could never decide until she got to the place and *must.* The question was, With which of them had she most influence? She hardly knew. But Griffith Gaunt was her old sweetheart ; it seemed somewhat less strange and indelicate to go to him than to the new one. So she turned her horse's head towards Bolton ; but she no longer went quite so fast as she had gone before she felt going to either in particular. Such is the female mind.

She reached Bolton at half past eleven, and, now she was there, put a bold face on it, rode up to the door, and, leaning forward on her horse, rang the hall-bell.

A footman came to the door.

With composed visage, though beating heart, she told him she desired to speak for a moment to Mr. Griffith Gaunt. He asked her would she be pleased to alight; and it was clear by his manner no calamity had yet fallen.

"No, no," said Kate; "let me speak to him here."

The servant went in to tell his master. Kate sat quiet, with her heart still beating, but glowing now with joy. She was in time, then, thanks to her good horse. She patted him, and made the prettiest excuses aloud to him for riding him so hard through the snow.

The footman came back to say that Mr. Gaunt had gone out.

"Gone out? Whither? On horseback?"

The footman did not know, but would ask within.

While he was gone to inquire, Catharine lost patience, and rode into the stable-yard and asked a young lout, who was lounging there, whether his master was gone out on horseback.

The lounging youth took the trouble to call out the groom, and asked him.

The groom said, "No," and that Mr. Gaunt was somewhere about the grounds, he thought.

But in the midst of this colloquy, one of the maids, curious to see the lady, came out by the kitchen-door, and curtsied to Kate, and told her Mr. Gaunt was gone out walking with two other gentlemen. In the midst of her discourse, she recognized the visitor, and, having somehow imbibed the notion that Miss Peyton was likely to be Mrs. Gaunt, and govern Bolton Hall, decided to curry favor with her; so she called her "My Lady," and was very communicative. She said one of the gentlemen was strange to her; but the other was Doctor Islip, from Stanhope town.

She knew him well: he had taken off her own brother's leg in a jiffy.

"But, dear heart, Mistress," said she, "how pale you be! Do come in, and have a morsel of meat and a horn of ale."

"Nay, my good girl," said Kate; "I could not eat; but bring me a mug of new milk, if you will. I have not broken my fast this day."

The maid bustled in, and Catharine asked the groom if there were no means of knowing where Mr. Gaunt was. The groom and the boy scratched their heads, and looked puzzled. The lounging lout looked at their perplexity, and grinned satirically.

This youth was Tom Leicester, born in wedlock, and therefore, in the law's eye, son of old Simon Leicester; but gossips said his true father was the late Captain Gaunt. Tom ran with the hounds for his own sport, — went out shooting with gentlemen, and belabored the briers for them at twopence per day and his dinner, — and abhorred all that sober men call work.

By trade, a Beater; profession, a Scamp.

Two maids came out together now, — one with the milk and a roll, the other with a letter. Catharine drank the milk, but could not eat. Then says the other maid, —

"If so be you are Mistress Peyton, why, this letter is for you. Master left it on his table in his bedroom."

Kate took the letter and opened it all in a flutter. It ran thus : —

"SWEET MISTRESS, — When this reaches you, I shall be no more here to trouble you with my jealousy. This Neville set it abroad that you had changed horses with him, as much as to say you had plighted troth with him. He is a liar, and I told him so to his teeth. We are to meet at noon this day, and one must die. Methinks I shall be the one. But come what may, I have taken care of thee; ask Jack Houseman else. But, O dear Kate, think of all that hath passed between us, and do not wed this Neville, or I could not rest in my grave. Sweetheart, many a letter have I written thee, but none so sad as this. Let the grave hide my faults from thy memory; think only that I loved thee well. I leave thee my substance — would it were ten times more ! — and the last thought of my heart.

"So no more in this world
　"From him that is thy true lover
　　'} And humble servant till death,
　　　"GRIFFITH GAUNT."

There seems to be room in the mind for only one violent emotion at one instant of time. This touching letter did not just then draw a tear from her, who now received it some hours sooner than the writer intended. Its first effect was to paralyze her. She sat white and trembling, and her great eyes filled with horror. Then she began to scream wildly for help. The men and women came round her.

"Murder! murder!" she shrieked. "Tell me where to find him, ye wretches, or may his blood be on your heads !"

The Scamp bounded from his lounging position, and stood before her straight as an arrow.

"Follow me !" he shouted.

Her gray eyes and the Scamp's black ones flashed into one another directly. He dashed out of the yard without another word.

And she spurred her horse, and clattered out after him.

He ran as fast as her horse could canter, and soon took her all round the house ; and while he ran, his black gypsy eyes were glancing in every direction.

When they got to the lawn at the back of the house, he halted a moment, and said quietly, —

"Here they be."

He pointed to some enormous footsteps in the snow, and bade her notice that they commenced at a certain glass door belonging to the house, and that they all pointed outwards. The lawn was covered with such marks, but the Scamp followed those his intelligence had selected, and they took him through a gate, and down a long walk, and into

3

the park. Here no other feet had trodden that morning except those Tom Leicester was following.

"This is our game," said he. "See, there be six footsteps ; and, now I look, this here track is Squire Gaunt's. I know his foot in the snow among a hundred. Bless your heart, I 've often been out shooting with Squire Gaunt, and lost him in the woods, and found him again by tracking him on dead leaves, let alone snow. I say, was n't they useless idiots ? Could n't tell ye how to run into a man, and snow on the ground ! Why, you can track a hare to her form, and a rat to his hole, — let alone such big game as this, with a hoof like a frying-pan, — in the snow."

"Oh, do not talk ; let us make haste," panted Kate.

"Canter away !" replied the Scamp.

She cantered on, and he ran by her side.

"Shall I not tire you ?" said she.

The *mauvais sujet* laughed at her.

"Tire *me ?* Not over this ground. Why, I run with the hounds, and mostly always in at the death ; but that is not altogether speed; ye see I know Pug's mind. What ! don't you know *me ?* I 'm Tom Leicester. Why, I know you : I say, you are a good-hearted one, you are."

"Oh, no ! no !" sighed Kate.

"Nay, but you are," said Tom. "I saw you take Harrowden Brook that day, when the rest turned tail ; and that is what I call having a good heart. Gently, Mistress, here, — this is full of rabbit-holes. I seen Sir Ralph's sorrel mare break her leg in a moment in one of these. Shot her dead that afternoon, a did, and then b'iled her for the hounds. She 'd often follow at their tails ; next hunting-day she ran inside their bellies. Ha ! ha ! ha !"

"Oh, don't laugh ! I am in agony !"

"Why, what is up, Mistress ?" asked the young savage, lowering his voice. 'Murder,' says you ; but that means *nought.* The lasses they cry murder, if you do but kiss 'em."

"Oh, Tom Leicester, it *is* murder! It 's a duel, a fight to the death, unless we are in time to prevent them."

"A jewel!" cried Master Leicester, his eyes glittering with delight. "I never saw a jewel. Don't you hold him in for me, Mistress: gallop down this slope as hard as you can pelt; it is grass under foot, and ye can't lose the tracks, and I shall be sure to catch ye in the next field."

The young savage was now as anxious to be in at the death as Kate was to save life. As he spoke, he gave her horse a whack on the quarter with his stick, and away she went full gallop, and soon put a hundred yards between her and Tom.

The next field was a deep fallow, and the hard furrows reduced her to a trot; and before she got out of it Tom was by her side.

"Did n't I tell you?" said he. "I 'd run you to Peyton Hall for a pot o' beer."

"Oh, you good, brave, clever boy!" said Kate, "how fortunate I am to have you! I think we shall be in time."

Tom was flattered.

"Why, you see, I am none of Daddy Leicester's breed," said he. "I 'm a gentleman's by-blow, if you know what that is."

"I can't say I do," said Kate; "but I know you are very bold and handsome, and swift of foot; and I know my patron saint has sent you to me in my misery. And, oh, my lad, if we are in time, — what can I do for you? Are you fond of money, Tom?"

"That I be, — when I can get it."

"Then you shall have all I have got in the world if you get me there in time to hinder mischief."

"Come on!" shouted Tom, excited in his turn, and took the lead; and not a word more passed till they came to the foot of a long hill. Then said Tom, —

"Once we are at top of this, they can't fight without our seeing 'em. That is Scutchemsee Nob: you can see ten miles all round from there."

At this information Kate uttered an ejaculation, and urged her horse forward.

The first part of this hill, which stood

between her and those whose tracks she followed, was grass; then came a strip of turnips; then on the bleak top a broad piece of heather. She soon cantered over the grass, and left Tom so far behind he could not quite catch her in the turnips. She entered the heather, but here she was much retarded by the snow-drifts and the ups and downs of the rough place. But she struggled on bravely, still leading.

She fixed her eyes earnestly on the ridge, whence she could cry to the combatants, however distant, and stop the combat.

Now as she struggled on, and Tom came after, panting a little for the first time, suddenly there rose from the crest of the hill two columns of smoke, and the next moment two sharp reports ran through the frosty air.

Kate stopped, and looked round to Tom with a scared, inquiring air.

"Pistols!" yelled Tom behind her.

At that the woman overpowered the heroine, and Kate hid her face and fell to trembling and wailing. Her wearied horse came down to a walk.

Presently up comes Tom.

"Don't lose your stomach for that," he panted out. "Gentlefolks do pop at one another all day sometimes, and no harm done."

"Oh, bless you!" cried Kate; "I may yet be in time."

She spurred her horse on. He did his best, but ere he had gone twenty yards he plunged into a cavity hidden by the snow.

While he was floundering there, crack went a single pistol, and the smoke rose and drifted over the hill-top.

"Who—op!" muttered Tom, with horrible *sang-froid*. "There 's one done for this time. Could n't shoot back, ye see."

At this horrible explanation Kate sank forward on her horse's mane as if she herself had been killed; and the smoke from the pistol came floating thinner and thinner, and eddied high over her head.

Tom spoke rude words of encouragement to her. She did not even seem to hear them. Then he lost all patience at her, and clutched her arm to make her hear him. But at that it seemed as if some of his nature passed into her down his arm; for she turned wild directly, and urged her horse fiercely up the crest. Her progress was slow at first; but the sun had melted the snow on the Nob or extreme summit. She tore her way through the last of the snow on to the clear piece, — then, white as ashes, spurred and lashed her horse over the ridge, and dashed in amongst them on the other side. For there they were.

What was the sight that met her eyes?

That belongs to the male branch of my story, and shall be told forthwith, but in its proper sequence.

CHAPTER VI.

THE two combatants came to the field in a very different spirit. Neville had already fought two duels, and been successful in both. He had confidence in his skill and in his luck. His conscience, too, was tolerably clear; for he was the insulted person; and if a bullet should remove this dangerous rival from his path, why, all the better for him, and all the worse for the fool who had brought the matter to a bloody issue, though the balance of the lady's heart inclined his way.

He came in high spirits, and rode upon Kate Peyton's gray, to sting his adversary, and show his contempt of him.

Not so Griffith Gaunt. His heart was heavy, and foreboded ill. It was his first duel, and he expected to be killed. He had played a fool's game, and he saw it.

The night before the duel he tried hard to sleep; he knew it was not giving his nerves fair play to lie thinking all night. But coy sleep, as usual when most wanted, refused to come. At daybreak the restless man gave it up in despair, and rose and dressed himself. He wrote that letter to Catharine, little

thinking it would fall into her hands while he lived. He ate a little toast, and drank a pint of Burgundy, and then wandered listlessly about till Major Rickards, his second, arrived.

That experienced gentleman brought a surgeon with him, — Mr. Islip.

Major Rickards deposited a shallow wooden box in the hall; and the two gentlemen sat down to a hearty breakfast.

Griffith took care of his guests, but beyond that spoke scarcely a word; and the surgeon, after a ghastly attempt at commonplaces, was silent too. Major Rickards satisfied his appetite first, and then, finding his companions dumb, set to work to keep up their spirits. He entertained them with a narrative of the personal encounters he had witnessed, and especially of one in which his principal had fallen on his face at the first fire, and the antagonist had sprung into the air, and both had lain dead as doornails, and never moved, nor even winked, after that single discharge.

Griffith sat under this chilling talk for more than an hour.

At last he rose gloomily, and said it was time to go.

"Got your tools, Doctor?" inquired the Major.

The surgeon nodded slightly. He was more discreet than his friend.

When they had walked nearly a mile in the snow, the Major began to complain.

"The Devil!" said he; "this is queer walking. My boots are full of water. I shall catch my death."

The surgeon smiled satirically, comparing silent Griffith's peril with his second's.

Griffith took no notice. He went like Fortitude plodding to Execution.

Major Rickards fell behind, and whispered Mr. Islip, —

"Don't like his looks; does n't march like a winner. A job for you or the sexton, you mark my words."

They toiled up Scutchemsee Nob, and when they reached the top, they saw Neville and his second, Mr. Hammersley, riding towards them. The pair had halters as well as bridles, and, dismounting, made their nags fast to a large blackthorn that grew there. The seconds then stepped forward, and saluted each other with formal civility.

Griffith looked at the gray horse, and ground his teeth. The sight of the animal in Neville's possession stirred up his hate, and helped to steel his heart. He stood apart, still, pale, and gloomy.

The seconds stepped out fifteen paces, and placed the men. Then they loaded two pair of pistols, and put a pistol in each man's hand.

Major Rickards took that opportunity to advise his principal.

"Stand sharp. Keep your arm close to your side. Don't fire too high. How do you feel?"

"Like a man who must die, but will try to die in company."

The seconds now withdrew to their places; and the rivals held their pistols lowered, but fixed their deadly eyes on each other.

The eye, in such a circumstance, is a terrible thing: it is literally a weapon of destruction; for it directs the deadly hand that guides the deadly bullet. Moreover, the longer and the more steadily the duellist fixes his eye on his adversary, the less likely he is to miss.

Griffith was very pale, but dogged. Neville was serious, but firm. Both eyed each other unflinchingly.

"Gentlemen, are you ready?" asked Neville's second.

 { "Yes."
 { "Yes."

"Then," said Major Rickards, "you will fire when I let fall this handkerchief, and not before. Mark me, Gentlemen: to prevent mistakes, I shall say, 'One, — two, — three!' and then drop the handkerchief. Now, then, once more, are you quite ready?"

 { "Yes."
 { "Yes."

".One, ——— two, ——— three!"

He dropped the handkerchief, and both gentlemen fired simultaneously. Mr. Neville's hat spun into the air; Griffith stood untouched.

The bullet had passed through Neville's hat, and had actually cut a lane through his magnificent hair.

The seconds now consulted, and it was intimated to Griffith that a word of apology would be accepted by his antagonist. Griffith declined to utter a syllable of apology.

Two more pistols were given to the men.

"Aim lower," said Rickards.

"I mean to," said Griffith.

The seconds withdrew, and the men eyed each other, — Griffith dogged and pale, as before, Neville not nearly so self-assured: Griffith's bullet, in grazing him, had produced the effect of a sharp, cold current of air no wider than a knife. It was like Death's icy forefinger laid on his head, to mark him for the next shot, — as men mark a tree, then come again and fell it.

"One, ——— two, ——— three!"

And Griffith's pistol missed fire; but Neville's went off, and Griffith's arm sank powerless, and his pistol rolled out of his hand. He felt a sharp twinge, and then something trickled down his arm.

The surgeon and both seconds ran to him.

"Nay, it is nothing," said he; "I shoot far better with my left hand than my right. Give me another pistol, and let me have fair play. He has hit me; and now I'll hit him."

Both seconds agreed this was impossible.

"It is the chance of war," said Major Rickards; "you cannot be allowed to take a cool shot at Mr. Neville. If you fire again, so must he."

"The affair may very well end here," said Mr. Hammersley. "I understand there was some provocation on our side; and on behalf of the party insulted I am content to let the matter end, Mr. Gaunt being wounded."

"I demand my second shot to his third," said Griffith, sternly; "he will not decline, unless he is a poltroon, as well as — what I called him."

The nature of this reply was com-

" She drew up in the middle, right between the levelled pistols." — Page 37.

municated to Neville, and the seconds, with considerable reluctance, loaded two more pistols ; and during the process Major Rickards glanced at the combatants.

Griffith, exasperated by his wound and his jealousy, was wearing out the chivalrous courage of his adversary ; and the Major saw it. His keen eye noticed that Neville was getting restless, and looking confounded at his despised rival's pertinacity, and that Gaunt was more dogged and more deadly.

"My man will kill yours this time," said he, quietly, to Neville's second ; "I can see it in his eye. He is hungry: t' other has had his bellyful."

Once more the men were armed, and the seconds withdrew to their places, intimating that this was the last shot they would allow under any circumstances whatever.

"Are you both ready ? "

{ "Yes."
{ "Yes."

A faint wail seemed to echo the response.

All heard it, and in that superstitious age believed it to be some mysterious herald of death.

It suspended even Major Rickards's voice a minute. He recovered himself, however, and once more his soldier-like tones rang in the keen air : —

"One, ——— "

There was a great rushing, and a pounding of the hard ground, and a scarlet Amazon galloped in, and drew up in the middle, right between the levelled pistols.

Every eye had been so bent on the combatants, that Kate Peyton and her horse seemed to have sprung out of the very earth. And there she sat, pale as ashes, on the steaming piebald, and glanced from pistol to pistol.

The duellists stared in utter amazement, and instinctively lowered their weapons ; for she had put herself right in their line of fire with a recklessness that contrasted nobly with her fear for others. In short, this apparition literally petrified them all, seconds as well as combatants.

And while they stood open-mouthed, yet dumb, in came the Scamp, and, with a brisk assumption of delegated authority, took Griffith's weapon out of his now unresisting hand, then marched to Neville. He instantly saluted Catharine, and then handed his pistol to her seeming agent, with a high-bred and inimitable air of utter nonchalance.

Kate, seeing them, to her surprise, so easily disarmed, raised her hands and her lovely eyes to heaven, and, in a feeble voice, thanked God and Saint Nescioquis.

But very soon that faint voice quavered away to nothing, and her fair head was seen to droop, and her eyes to close ; then her body sank slowly forward like a broken lily, and in another moment she lay fainting on the snow beside her steaming horse.

He never moved, he was so dead beat too.

O, lame and impotent conclusion of a vigorous exploit ! Masculine up to the crowning point, and then to go and spoil all with "woman's weakness " !

"N. B. This is rote sarcasticul," as Artemus the Delicious says. Woman's weakness ! If Solomon had planned and Samson executed, they could not have served her turn better than this most seasonable swooning did ; for, lo. at her fall, the doughty combatants uttered a yell of dismay, and there was an indiscriminate rush towards the fair sufferer.

But the surgeon claimed his rights.

"This is my business," said he, authoritatively. "Do not crowd on her, gentlemen : give her air."

Whereupon the duellists and seconds stood respectfully aloof, in a mixed group, and watched with eager interest and pity.

The surgeon made a hole in the snow, and laid his fair patient's head low.

"Don't be alarmed," said he ; "she has swooned ; that is all."

It was all mighty fine to say, "Don't be alarmed." But her face was ashy, and her lips the color of lead ; and she was so like death, they could not help being terribly alarmed; and now, for the first time, the duellists felt culprits; and as for fighting, every idea of such a thing went out of their heads. The rivals now were but rival nurses; and never did a lot of women make more fuss over a child than all these blood-thirsty men did over this Amazon *manquée*. They produced their legendary lore. One's grandmother had told him burnt feathers were the thing; another, from an equally venerable source, had gathered that those pink palms must be profanely slapped by the horny hand of man, — for at no less a price could resuscitation be obtained. The surgeon scorning all their legends, Griffith and Neville made hasty rushes with brandy and usquebaugh; but whether to be taken internally or externally they did not say, nor, indeed, know, but only thrust their flasks wildly on the doctor; and he declined them loftily. He melted snow in his hand, and dashed it hard in her face, and put salts close to her pretty little nostrils. And this he repeated many times without effect.

But at last her lips began to turn from lead color to white, and then from white to pink, and her heavenly eyes to open again, and her mouth to murmur things pitiably small and not bearing on the matter in hand.

Her cheek was still colorless, when her consciousness came back, and she found she was lying on the ground with ever so many gentlemen looking at her.

At that, Modesty alarmed sent the blood at once rushing to her pale cheek.

A lovely lily seemed turning to a lovely rose before their eyes.

The next thing was, she hid that blushing face in her hands, and began to whimper.

The surgeon encouraged her: " Nay, we are all friends," he whispered, paternally.

She half parted her fingers and peered through them at Neville and Gaunt. Then she remembered all, and began to cry hysterically.

New dismay of the unprofessionals!

" *Now*, gentlemen, if you will lend me your flasks," said Mr. Islip, mighty calmly.

Griffith and Neville were instantly at his side, each with a flask.

The surgeon administered snow and brandy. Kate sipped these, and gulped down her sobs, and at last cried composedly.

But when it came to sipping brandied snow and crying comfortably, Major Rickards's anxiety gave place to curiosity. Without taking his eye off her, he beckoned Mr. Hammersley apart, and whispered, —

" Who the Deuse is it ? "

" Don't you know ? " whispered the other in return. " Why, Mistress Peyton herself."

" What ! the girl it is all about ? Well, I never heard of such a thing: the *causa belli* to come *galloping* and *swooning* on the field of battle, and so stop the fighting ! What will our ladies do next ? By Heaven ! she is worth fighting for, though. Which is the happy man, I wonder ? She does n't look at either of them."

" Ah ! " said the gentleman, " that is more than I know, more than Neville knows, more than anybody knows."

" Bet you a guinea *she* knows, — and lets it out before she leaves the field," said Major Rickards.

Mr. Hammersley objected to an even bet; but said he would venture one to three she did not. It was an age of bets."

" Done ! " said the Major.

By this time Kate had risen, with Mr. Islip's assistance, and was now standing with her hand upon the piebald's mane. She saw Rickards and Hammersley were whispering about her, and she felt very uneasy; so she told Mr. Islip, timidly, she desired to explain her conduct to *all* the gentlemen present, and avert false reports.

They were soon all about her, and she began, with the most engaging embarrassment, by making excuses for her weakness. She said she had ridden all the way from home, fasting; that was what had upset her. The gentlemen took the cue directly, and vowed eagerly and unanimously it was enough to upset a porter.

"But, indeed," resumed Kate, blushing, "I did not come here to make a fuss, and be troublesome, but to prevent mischief, and clear up the strangest misunderstanding between two worthy gentlemen, that are, both of them, my good friends.

She paused, and there was a chilling silence : everybody felt she was getting on ticklish ground now. She knew that well enough herself. But she had a good rudder to steer by, called Mother-Wit.

Says she, with inimitable coolness, —

" Mr. Gaunt is an old friend of mine, and a little too sensitive where I am concerned. Some chatterbox has been and told him Mr. Neville should say I have changed horses with him ; and on that the gossips put their own construction. Mr. Gaunt hears all this, and applies insulting terms to Mr. Neville. Nay, do not deny it, Mr. Gaunt, for I have it here in your own handwriting.

" As for Mr. Neville, he merely defends his honor, and is little to blame. But now I shall tell the true story about these horses, and make you all ashamed of this sorry quarrel.

" Gentlemen, thus it is. A few days ago Mr. Gaunt bade me farewell, and started for foreign parts. He had not been long gone, when word came from Bolton that Mr. Charlton was no more. You know how sudden it was. Consider, gentlemen : him dead, and his heir riding off to the Continent in ignorance. So I thought, ' O, what shall I do ?' just then Mr. Neville visited me, and I told him : on that he offered me his piebald horse to carry the news after Mr. Gaunt, because my gray was too tired : it was the day we drew Yew-tree Brow, and crossed Harrowden Brook, you know," ——

Griffith interrupted her.

" Stay a bit," said he : " this is news to me. You never told me he had lent you the piebald nag to do me a good turn."

" Did I not ? " said Kate, mighty innocently. " Well, but I tell you now.

Ask him : he cannot deny it. As for the rest, it was all done in a hurry : Mr. Neville had no horse now to ride home with ; he did me the justice to think I should be very ill pleased, were he to trudge home afoot and suffer for his courtesy ; so he borrowed my gray to keep him out of the mire ; and, indeed, the ways were fouler than usual, with the rains. Was there any ill in all this ? HONI SOIT QUI MAL Y PENSE ! say I."

The gentlemen all sided loudly with her on this appeal,—except Neville, who held his tongue, and smiled at her plausibility, and Griffith, who hung his head at her siding with Neville.

At last he spoke, and said, sorrowfully, —

" If you did exchange horses with him, of course I have only to ask his pardon — and go."

Catharine reflected a moment before she replied.

" Well," said she, " I did exchange, and I did not. Why quarrel about a word ? Certainly he took my horse, and I took his ; but it was only for the nonce. Mr. Neville is foreign bred, and an example to us all : he knows his piebald is worth two of my gray, and so he was too fine a gentleman to send me back my old hunter and ask for his young charger. He waited for me to do that ; and if anybody deserves to be shot, it must be Me. But, dear heart, I did not foresee all this fuss ; I said to myself, ' La, Mr. Neville will be sure to call on my father or me some day, or else I shall be out on the piebald and meet him on the gray, and then we can each take our own again.' Was I so far out in my reckoning ? Is not that my Rosinante yonder ? Here, Tom Leicester, you put my side - saddle on that gray horse, and the man's saddle on the piebald there. And now, Griffith Gaunt, it is your turn : you must withdraw your injurious terms, and end this superlative folly."

Griffith hesitated.

" Come," said Kate, " consider : Mr. Neville is esteemed by all the county : you are the only gentleman in it who has ever uttered a disparaging word against him. Are you sure you are more free from passion and prejudice and wiser than all the county? Oblige *me* and do what is right. Come, Griffith Gaunt, let your reason unsay the barbarous words your passion hath uttered against a worthy gentleman whom we all esteem."

Her habitual influence, and these last words, spoken with gentle and persuasive dignity, turned the scale. Griffith turned to Neville, and said in a low voice that he began to fear he had been hasty, and used harsher words than the occasion justified: he was going to stammer out something more, but Neville interrupted him with a noble gesture.

"That is enough, Mr. Gaunt," said he. "I do not feel quite blameless in the matter, and have no wish to mortify an honorable adversary unnecessarily."

"Very handsomely said," put in Major Rickards; "and now let me have a word. I say that both gentlemen have conducted themselves like men — under fire; and that honor is satisfied, and the misunderstanding at an end. As for my principal here, he has shown he can fight, and now he has shown he can hear reason against himself, when the lips of beauty utter it. I approve his conduct from first to last, and am ready to defend it in all companies, and in the field, should it ever be impugned."

Kate colored with pleasure, and gave her hand eloquently to the Major. He bowed over it, and kissed the tips of her fingers.

"Oh, sir," she said, looking on him now as a friend, "I dreamed I saw Mr. Neville lying dead upon the snow, with the blood trickling from his temple."

At this Neville's dark cheek glowed with pleasure. So! it was her anxiety on *his* account had brought her here.

Griffith heard too, and sighed patiently.

Assured by Major Rickards that there neither could nor should be any more fighting, Kate made her adieus, mounted her gray horse, and rode off, discreetly declining all attendance. She beckoned

Tom Leicester, however. But he pretended not to see the signal, and let her go alone. His motive for lingering behind was characteristic, and will transpire shortly.

As soon as she was gone, Griffith Gaunt quietly reminded the surgeon that there was a bullet in his arm all this time.

"Bless my soul!" said Mr. Islip, "I forgot that, I was so taken up with the lady.

Griffith's coat was now taken off, and the bullet searched for: it had entered the fleshy part of his arm below the elbow, and, passing round the bone, projected just under the skin. The surgeon made a slight incision, and then, pressing with his finger and thumb, out it rolled. Griffith put it in his pocket.

Neville had remained out of civility, and now congratulated his late antagonist, and himself, that it was no worse.

The last words that passed between the rivals, on this occasion, were worth recording, and characteristic of the time.

Neville addressed Gaunt with elaborate courtesy, and to this effect: —

"I find myself in a difficulty, sir. You did me the honor to invite me to Mr. Charlton's funeral, and I accepted; but now I fear to intrude a guest, the sight of whom may be disagreeable to you. And, on the other hand, my absence might be misconstrued as a mark of disrespect, or of a petty hostility I am far from feeling. Be pleased, therefore, to dispose of me entirely in this matter."

Griffith reflected.

"Sir," said he, "there is an old saying, 'Let every tub stand on its own bottom.' The deceased wished you to follow him to the grave, and therefore I would on no account have you absent. Besides, now I think of it, there will be less gossip about this unfortunate business, if our neighbors see you under my roof, and treated with due consideration there, as you will be."

"I do not doubt that, sir, from so manly an adversary; and I shall do myself the honor to come."

Such was Neville's reply. The rivals then saluted each other profoundly, and parted.

Hammersley and Rickards lingered behind their principals to settle their little bet about Kate's affections : and, by the by, they were indiscreet enough to discuss this delicate matter within a dozen yards of Tom Leicester : they forgot that "little pitchers have long ears."

Catharine Peyton rode slowly home, and thought it all over as she went, and worried herself finely. She was one that winced at notoriety ; and she could not hope to escape it now. How the gossips would talk about her ! they would say the gentlemen had fought about *her;* and she had parted them for love of one of them. And then the gentlemen themselves ! The strict neutrality she had endeavored to maintain on Scutchemsee Nob, in order to make peace, would it not keep them both her suitors ? She foresaw she should be pulled to pieces, and live in hot water, and be " the talk of the county."

There were but two ways out : she must marry one of them, and petition the other not to shoot him ; or else she must take the veil, and so escape them both.

She preferred the latter alternative. She was more enthusiastic in religion than in any earthly thing ; and now the angry passions of men thrust her the same road that her own devout mind had always drawn her.

As soon as she got home, she sent a message to Father Francis, who drove her conscience, and begged him to come and advise her.

After that she did the wisest thing, perhaps, she had done all day, — went to bed.

CHAPTER VII.

THE sun was just setting when Catharine's maid came into her room and told her Father Francis was below. She sent down to say she counted on his

sleeping at Peyton Hall, and she would come down to him in half an hour. She then ordered a refection to be prepared for him in her boudoir ; and made her toilet with all reasonable speed, not to keep him waiting. Her face beamed with quiet complacency now, for the holy man's very presence in the house was a comfort to her.

Father Francis was a very stout, muscular man, with a ruddy countenance ; he never wore gloves, and you saw at once he was not a gentleman by birth. He had a fine voice : it was deep, mellow, and, when he chose, sonorous. This, and his person, ample, but not obese, gave him great weight, especially with his female pupils. If he was not quite so much reverenced by the men, yet he was both respected and liked ; in fact, he had qualities that make men welcome in every situation, — good humor, good sense, and tact. A good son of his Church, and early trained to let' no occasion slip of advancing her interests.

I wish my readers could have seen the meeting between Catharine Peyton and this burly ecclesiastic. She came into the drawing - room with that imperious air and carriage which had made her so unpopular with her own sex ; and at the bare sight of Father Francis, drooped and bent in a moment as she walked ; and her whole body indicated a submissiveness, graceful, but rather abject : it was as if a young poplar should turn to a weeping willow in half a moment. Thus metamorphosed, the Beauty of Cumberland glided up to Francis, and sank slowly on her knees before him, crossed her hands on her bosom, lowered her lovely head, and awaited his benediction.

The father laid two big, coarse hands, with enormous fingers, on that thorough-bred head and golden hair, and blessed her business-like.

"The hand of less employment hath the daintier sense." — *Shakespeare.*

Father Francis blessed so many of these pretty creatures every week, that he had long outgrown your fine, romantic way of blessing a body. (We manage these things better in the theatre.) Then he lent her his hand to rise, and asked her in what she required his direction at present.

"In that which shall decide my whole life," said she.

Francis responded by a look of paternal interest.

"But first," murmured she, "let me confess to you, and obtain absolution, if I may. Ah, Father, my sins have been many since last confession!"

"Be it so," said Father Francis, resignedly. "Confession is the best preface to Direction." And he seated himself with a certain change of manner, an easy assumption of authority.

"Nay, Father," suggested the lady, "we shall be more private in my room."

"As you will, Mistress Catharine Peyton," said the priest, returning to his usual manner.

So then the fair penitent led her spiritual judge captive up another flight of stairs, and into her little boudoir. A cheerful wood fire crackled and flamed up the chimney, and a cloth had been laid on a side table: cold turkey and chine graced the board, and a huge glass magnum of purple Burgundy glowed and shone in the rays of the cheery fire.

Father Francis felt cosey at the sight; and at once accepted Kate's invitation to take some nourishment before entering on the labor of listening to the catalogue of her crimes. "I fasted yesterday," he muttered; and the zeal with which he attacked the viands rendered the statement highly credible.

He invited Kate to join him, but she declined.

He returned more than once to the succulent meats, and washed all down with a pint of the fine old Burgundy, perfumed and purple. Meantime she of the laïty sat looking into the fire with heavenly-minded eyes.

At last, with a gentle sigh of content, the ghostly father installed himself in an arm-chair by the fire, and invited his penitent to begin.

She took a footstool and brought it to his side, so that, in confessing her blacker vices, she might be able to whisper them in his very ear. She kneeled on her little footstool, put her hands across her breast, and in this lowly attitude murmured softly after this fashion, with a contrite voice : —

"I have to accuse myself of many vices. Alas! in one short fortnight I have accumulated the wickedness of a life. I have committed the seven deadly sins. I have been guilty of Pride, Wrath, Envy, Disobedience, Immodesty, Vanity, Concupiscence, Fibs,"——

"Gently, daughter," said the priest, quietly; "these terms are too general : give me instances. Let us begin with Wrath : ah! we are all prone to that."

The fair penitent sighed and said, —

"Especially me. Example: I was angry beyond reason with my maid, Ruth. (She does comb my hair so uncouthly!) So, then, the other night, when I was in trouble, and most needed soothing by being combed womanly, she gets thinking of Harry, that helps in the stable, and she tears away at my hair. I started up and screamed out, 'Oh, you clumsy thing! go curry-comb my horse, and send that oaf your head is running on to handle my hair.' And I told her my grandam would have whipped her well for it, but now-a-days mistresses were the only sufferers : we had lost the use of our hands, we are grown so squeamish. And I stamped like a fury, and said, 'Get you gone out of the room!' and 'I hated the sight of her!' And the poor girl went from me, crying, without a word, being a better Christian than her mistress. *Mea culpa! mea culpa!*"

"Did you slap her?"

"Nay, Father, not so bad as that."

"Are you quite sure you did not slap her?" asked Francis, quietly.

"Nay. But I had a mind to. My heart slapped her, if my hand forbore. Alas!"

"Had she hurt you?"

"That she did, — but only my head. I hurt her heart: for the poor wench loves me dear, — the Lord knows for what."

"Humph!—proceed to Pride."

"Yes, Father. I do confess that I was greatly puffed up with the praises of men. I was proud of the sorriest things: of jumping a brook, when 't was my horse jumped it, and had jumped it better with a fly on his back than the poor worm Me; of my good looks, forgetting that God gave them me; and besides, I am no beauty, when all is done; it is all their flattery. And at my Lady Munster's dinner I pridefully walked out before Mistress Davies, the rich cheesemonger's wife, that is as proud of her money as I of my old blood, (God forgive two fools!) which I had no right to do,—a maid to walk before a wife; and oh, Father, I whispered the gentleman who led me out—it was Mr. Neville "——

Here the penitent put one hand before her face, and hesitated.

"Well, daughter, half-confession is no confession. You said to Mr. Neville?"——

"I said,' Nothing comes after cheese.'"

This revelation was made most dolefully.

"It was pert and unbecoming," said Father Francis, gravely, though a twinkle in his eye showed that he was not so profoundly shocked as his penitent appeared to be. "But go to graver matters. Immodesty, said you? I shall be very sorry, if this is so. You did not use to be immodest."

"Well, Father, I hope I have not altogether laid aside modesty; otherwise it would be time for me to die, let alone to confess; but sure it cannot be modest of me to ride after a gentleman and take him a letter. And then that was not enough: I heard of a duel,—and what did I do but ride to Scutchemsee Nob, and interfere? What gentlewoman ever was so bold? I was not their wife, you know,—neither of them's."

"Humph!" said the priest, "I have already heard a whisper of this,—but told to your credit. *Beati pacifici:* Blessed are the peacemakers. You had better lay that matter before me by and by, as your director. As your confessor,

tell me why you accuse yourself of concupiscence."

"Alas!" said the young lady, "scarce a day passes that I do not offend in *that* respect. Example: last Friday, dining abroad, the cooks sent up a dish of collops. O, Father, they smelt so nice! and I had been a-hunting. First I smelt them, and that I could n't help. But then I forgot *custodia oculorum*, and I eyed them. And the next thing was, presently—somehow—two of 'em were on my plate."

"Very wrong," said Francis; "but that is a harsher term than I should have applied to this longing of a hungry woman for collops o' Friday. Pray, what do you understand by that big word?"

"Why, you explained it yourself, in your last sermon. It means 'unruly and inordinate desires.' Example: Edith Hammersley told me I was mad to ride in scarlet, and me so fair and my hair so light. 'Green or purple is your color,' says she; and soon after this did n't I see in Stanhope town the loveliest piece of purple broadcloth? O, Father, it had a gloss like velvet, and the sun did so shine on it as it lay in the shop-window; it was fit for a king or a bishop; and I stood and gloated on it, and pined for it, and died for it, and down went the Tenth Commandment."

"Ah," said Francis, "the hearts of women are set on vanity! But tell me, —these unruly affections of yours, are they ever fixed on persons of the other sex?"

The fair sinner reflected.

"On gentlemen?" said she. "Why, they come pestering one of their own accord. No, no,—I could do without *them* very well. What I sinfully pine for is meat on a Friday as sure as ever the day comes round, and high-couraged horses to ride, and fine clothes to wear every day in the week. *Mea culpa! mea culpa!*"

Such being the dismal state of things, Francis slyly requested her to leave the seven deadly sins in peace, and go to her small offences: for he argued, shrewdly enough, that, since her sins were peccadilloes, perhaps some of her peccadilloes might turn out to be sins.

"Small!" cried the culprit, turning red, — "they are none of them small."

I really think she was jealous of her reputation as a sinner of high degree.

However, she complied, and, putting up her mouth, murmured a miscellaneous confession without end. The accents were soft and musical, like a babbling brook; and the sins, such as they were, poor things, rippled on in endless rotation.

Now nothing tends more to repose than a purling brook; and erelong something sonorous let the fair culprit know she had lulled her confessor asleep.

She stopped, indignant. But at that he instantly awoke, (*sublatâ causâ, tollitur effectus,*) and addressed her thus, with sudden dignity, —

"My daughter, you will fast on Monday next, and say two Aves and a Credo. *Absolvo te.*"

"And now," said he, "as I am a practical man, let us get back from the imaginary world into the real. Speak to me at present as your director; and mind, you must be serious now, and call things by their right names."

Upon this Kate took a seat, and told her story, and showed him the difficulty she was in.

She then reminded him, that, notwithstanding her unfortunate itch for the seven deadly sins, she was a good Catholic, a zealous daughter of the Church; and she let him know her desire to retire from both lovers into a convent, and so, freed from the world and its temptations, yield up her soul entire to celestial peace and divine contemplation.

"Not so fast," said the priest. "Even zeal is naught without obedience. If you could serve the Church better than by going into a convent, would you be wilful?"

"O, no, Father! But how can I serve the Church better than by renouncing the world?"

"Perhaps by remaining in the world, as she herself does, — and by making converts to the faith. You could hard-

ly serve her worse than by going into a convent: for our convents are poor, and you have no means; you would be a charge. No, daughter, we want no poor nuns; we have enough of them. If you are, as I think, a true and zealous daughter of the Church, you must marry, and instil the true faith, with all a mother's art, a mother's tenderness, into your children. Then the heir to your husband's estates will be a Catholic, and so the true faith get rooted in the soil."

"Alas!" said Catharine, "are we to look but to the worldly interests of the Church?"

"They are inseparable from her spiritual interests here on earth: our souls are not more bound to our bodies."

Catharine was deeply mortified.

"So the Church rejects me because I am poor," said she, with a sigh.

"The Church rejects you not, but only the Convent. No place is less fit for you. You have a high spirit, and high religious sentiments: both would be mortified and shocked in a nunnery. Think you that convent-walls can shut out temptation? I know them better than you: they are strongholds of vanity, folly, tittle-tattle, and all the meanest vices of your sex. Nay, I forbid you to think of it: show me now your faith by your obedience."

"You are harsh to me, Father," said Catharine, piteously.

"I am firm. You are one that needs a tight hand, Mistress. Come, now, humility and obedience, these are the Christian graces that best become your youth. Say, can the Church, through me, its minister, count on these from you? or" (suddenly letting loose his diapason) "did you send for me to ask advice, and yet go your own way, hiding a high stomach and a wilful heart under a show of humility?"

Catharine looked at Father Francis with dismay. This was the first time that easy-going priest had shown her how impressive he could be. She was downright frightened, and said she hoped she knew better than to defy her director; she laid her will at his feet, and would obey him like a child, as was her duty.

"Now I know my daughter again," said he, and gave her his horrible paw, the which she kissed very humbly, and that matter was settled to her entire dissatisfaction.

Soon after that, they were both summoned to supper; but as they went down, Kate's maid drew her aside and told her a young man wanted to speak to her.

"A young man?" screamed Kate. "Hang young men! They have got me a fine scolding just now! Which is it, pray?"

"He is a stranger to me."

"Perhaps he comes with a message from some fool. You may bring him to me in the hall, and stay with us: it may be a thief, for aught I know."

The maid soon reappeared, followed by Mr. Thomas Leicester.

That young worthy had lingered on Scutchemsee Nob, to extract the last drop of enjoyment from the situation, by setting up his hat at ten paces, and firing the gentlemen's pistols at it. I despair of conveying to any rational reader the satisfaction, keen, though brief, this afforded him; it was a new sensation: gentlemen's guns he had fired many; but duelling-pistols, not one, till that bright hour.

He was now come to remind Catharine of his pecuniary claims. Luckily for him, she was one who did not need to be reminded of her promises.

"Oh, it is you, child!" said she. "Well, I 'll be as good as my word."

She then dismissed her maid, and went up stairs, and soon returned with two guineas, a crown piece, and three shillings in her hand.

"There," said she, smiling, "I am sorry for you, but that is all the money I have in the world."

The boy's eyes glittered at sight of the coin: he rammed the silver into his pocket with hungry rapidity; but he shook his head about the gold.

"I 'm afeard o' these," said he, and eyed them mistrustfully in his palm. "These be the friends that get you

your throat cut o' dark nights. Mistress, please you keep 'em for me, and let me have a shilling now and then when I 'm dry."

"Nay," said Kate, "but are you not afraid I shall spend your money, now I have none left of my own?"

Tom seemed quite struck with the reasonableness of this observation, and hesitated. However, he concluded to risk it.

"You don't look one of the sort to wrong a poor fellow," said he; "and besides, you 'll have brass to spare of your own before long, I know."

Kate opened her eyes.

"Oh, indeed!" said she; "and pray, how do you know that?"

Mr. Leicester favored her with a knowing wink. He gave her a moment to digest this, and then said, almost in a whisper,—

"Hearkened the gentlefolks on Scutchemsee Nob, after you was gone home, Mistress."

Kate was annoyed.

"What! they must be prating as soon as one's back is turned! Talk of women's tongues! Now what did they say, I should like to know?"

"It was about the bet, ye know."

"A bet? Oh, that is no affair of mine."

"Ay, but it is. Why, 't was you they were betting on. Seems that old soger and Squire Hammersley had laid three guineas to one that you should let out which was your fancy of them two."

Kate's cheeks were red as fire now; but her delicacy overpowered her curiosity, and she would not put any more questions. To be sure, young Hopeful needed none; he was naturally a chatterbox, and he proceeded to tell her, that, as soon as ever she was gone, Squire Hammersley took a guinea and offered it to the old soldier, and told him he had won, and the old soldier pocketed it. But after that, somehow, Squire Hammersley let drop that Mr. Neville was the favorite.

"Then," continued Mr. Leicester, "what does the old soger do, but pull out guinea again, and says he,—

" 'You must have this back; bet is not won: for you do think 't is Neville; now I do think 't is Gaunt.'

"So then they fell to argufying and talking a lot o' stuff."

"No doubt, the insolent meddlers! Can you remember any of their nonsense? — not that it is worth remembering, I 'll be bound."

"Let me see. Well, Squire Hammersley, he said you owned to dreaming of Squire Neville, — and that was a sign of love, said he; and, besides, you sided with him against t' other. But the old soger, he said you called Squire Gaunt 'Griffith'; and he built on that. Oh, and a said you changed the horses back to please our Squire. Says he, —

" 'You must look to what the lady did; never heed what she said. Why, their sweet lips was only made to kiss us, and deceive us,' says that there old soger."

"I 'll — I 'll —— And what did you say, Sir? — for I suppose your tongue was not idle."

"Oh, me? I never let 'em know I was hearkening, or they 'd have 'greed in a moment for to give me a hiding. Besides, I had no need to cudgel my brains; I 'd only to ask you plump. You 'll tell *me*, I know. Which is it, Mistress? I 'm for Gaunt, you know, in course. Alack, Mistress," gabbled this voluble youth, "sure you won't be so hard as sack my Squire, and him got a bullet in his carcass, for love of you, this day."

Kate started, and looked at him in surprise.

"Oh," said she, "a bullet! Did they fight again the moment they saw my back was turned? The cowards!"

And she began to tremble.

"No, no," said Tom; "that was done before ever you came up. Don't ye remember that single shot while we were climbing the Nob? Well, 't was Squire Gaunt got it in the arm that time."

"Oh!"

"But I say, was n't our man game? Never let out he was hit while you was there; but as soon as ever you was gone, they cut the bullet out of him, and I seen it."

"Ah! — ah!"

"Doctor takes out his knife, — precious sharp and shiny 't was! — cuts into his arm with no more ado than if he was carving a pullet, — out squirts the blood, a good un."

"Oh, no more! no more! You cruel boy! how could you bear to look?"

And Kate hid her own face with both hands.

"Why, 't was n't *my* skin as was cut into. Squire Gaunt, he never hollered; a winced, though, and ground his teeth; but 't was over in a minute, and the bullet in his hand.

" 'That is for my wife,' says he, 'if ever I have one,' — and puts it in his pocket.

"Why, Mistress, you be as white as your smock!"

"No, no! Did he faint, poor soul?"

"Not he! What was there to faint about?"

"Then why do I feel so sick, even to hear of it?"

"Because you ha'n't got no stomach," said the boy, contemptuously. "Your courage is skin-deep, I 'm thinking. However, I 'm glad you feel for our Squire, about the bullet; so now I hope you will wed with *him*, and sack Squire Neville. Then you and I shall be kind o' kin: Squire Gaunt's feyther was my feyther. That makes you stare, Mistress. Why, all the folk do know it. Look at this here little mole on my forehead. Squire Gaunt have got the fellow to that."

At this crisis of his argument he suddenly caught a glimpse of his personal interest; instantly he ceased his advocacy of Squire Gaunt, and became ludicrously impartial.

"Well, Mistress; wed whichever you like," said he, with sublime indifference; "only whichever you *do* wed, prithee speak a word to the gentleman, and get me to be his gamekeeper. I 'd liever be your goodman's gamekeeper than king of England."

He was proceeding with vast volubility to enumerate his qualifications for that confidential post, when the lady cut him short, and told him to go and get his supper in the kitchen, for she was wanted elsewhere. He made a scrape, and clattered away with his hobnailed shoes.

Kate went to the hall window and opened it, and let the cold air blow over her face.

Her heart was touched, and her bosom filled with pity for her old sweetheart.

How hard she had been! She had sided with Neville against the wounded man. And she thought how sadly and patiently he had submitted to her decision, — and a bullet in his poor arm all the time.

The gentle bosom heaved, and heaved, and the tears began to run.

She entered the dining-room timidly, expecting some comment on her discourteous absence. Instead of that, both her father and her director rose respectfully, and received her with kind and affectionate looks. They then pressed her to eat this and that, and were remarkably attentive and kind. She could see that she was deep in their good books. This pleased her ; but she watched quietly, after the manner of her sex, to learn what it was all about. Nor was she left long in the dark. Remarks were made that hit her, though they were none of them addressed to her.

Father Francis delivered quite a little homily on Obedience, and said how happy a thing it was, when zeal, a virtue none too common in these degenerate days, was found tempered by humility, and subservient to ghostly counsel and authority.

Mr. Peyton dealt in no general topics of that kind ; his discourse was secular : it ran upon Neville's Cross, Neville's Court, and the Baronetcy ; and he showed Francis how and why this title must sooner or later come to George Neville and the heirs of his body.

Francis joined in this topic for a while, but speedily diverged into what might be called a collateral theme. He described to Kate a delightful spot on the Neville estate, where a nunnery might be built and endowed by any good Catholic lady having zeal, and influence with the owner of the estate, and with the lord-lieutenant of the county.

" It is three parts an island, (for the river Wey curls round it lovingly,) but backed by wooded slopes that keep off the north and east winds : a hidden and balmy place, such as the forefathers of the Church did use to choose for their rustic abbeys, whose ruins still survive to remind us of the pious and glorious days gone by. Trout and salmon come swimming to the door ; hawthorn and woodbine are as rife there as weeds be in some parts ; two broad oaks stand on turf like velvet, and ring with songbirds. A spot by nature sweet, calm, and holy, — good for pious exercises and heavenly contemplation : there, methinks, if it be God's will I should see old age, I would love to end my own days, at peace with Heaven and with all mankind."

Kate was much moved by this picture, and her clasped hands and glistening eyes showed the glory and delight it would be to her to build a convent on so lovely a spot. But her words were vague. " How sweet! how sweet! " was all she committed herself to. For, after what Tom Leicester had just told her, she hardly knew what to say or what to think or what to do ; she felt she had become a mere puppet, first drawn one way, then another.

One thing appeared pretty clear to her now : Father Francis did not mean her to choose between her two lovers ; he was good enough to relieve her of that difficulty by choosing for her. She was to marry Neville.

She retired to rest directly after supper ; for she was thoroughly worn out. And the moment she rose to go, her father bounced up, and lighted the bedcandle for her with novel fervor, and kissed her on the cheek, and said in her ear, —

" Good night, my Lady Neville ! "

CHAPTER VIII.

WHAT with the day's excitement, and a sweet secluded convent in her soul, and a bullet in her bosom, and a ringing in her ear, that sounded mighty like "Lady Neville! Lady Neville! Lady Neville!" Kate spent a restless night, and woke with a bad headache.

She sent her maid to excuse her, on this score, from going to Bolton Hall. But she was informed, in reply, that the carriage had been got ready expressly for her; so she must be good enough to shake off disease and go; the air would do her a deal more good than lying abed.

Thereupon she dressed herself in her black silk gown, and came down, looking pale and languid, but still quite lovely enough to discharge what in this age of cant I suppose we should call "her mission": *videlicet*, to set honest men by the ears.

At half past eight o'clock the carriage came round to the front door. Its body all glorious with the Peyton armorials and with patches of rusty gilding, swung exceedingly loose on long leathern straps instead of springs; and the fore-wheels were a mile from the hind-wheels, more or less. A pretentious and horrible engine; drawn by four horses; only two of them being ponies impaired the symmetry and majestic beauty of the pageant. Old Joe drove the wheelers; his boy rode the leaders, and every now and then got off and kicked them in the pits of their stomachs, or pierced them with hedge-stakes, to rouse their mettle. Thus encouraged and stimulated, they effected an average of four miles and a half per hour, notwithstanding the snow, and reached Bolton just in time. At the lodge, Fráncis got out, and lay in ambush, — but only for a time. He did not think it orthodox to be present at a religious ceremony of his Protestant friends, — nor common-sense-o-dox to turn his back upon their dinner.

The carriage drew up at the hall-door. It was wide open, and the hall lined with servants, male and female, in black. In the midst, between these two rows, stood Griffith Gaunt, bareheaded, to welcome the guests. His arm was in a sling. He had received all the others in the middle of the hall; but he came to the threshold to meet Kate and her father. He bowed low and respectfully, then gave his left hand to Kate to conduct her, after the formal fashion of the day. The sight of his arm in a sling startled and affected her; and with him giving her his hand almost at the same moment, she pressed it, or indeed squeezed it nervously, and it was in her heart to say something kind and womanly: but her father was close behind, and she was afraid of saying something too kind, if she said anything at all; so Griffith only got a little gentle nervous pinch. But that was more than he expected, and sent a thrill of delight through him; his brown eyes replied with a volume, and holding her hand up in the air as high as her ear, and keeping at an incredible distance, he led her solemnly to a room where the other ladies were, and left her there with a profound bow.

The Peytons were nearly the last persons expected; and soon after their arrival the funeral procession formed. This part was entirely arranged by the undertaker. The monstrous custom of forbidding ladies to follow their dead had not yet occurred even to the idiots of the nation, and Mr. Peyton and his daughter were placed in the second carriage. The first contained Griffith Gaunt alone, as head mourner. But the Peytons were not alone: no other relation of the deceased being present, the undertaker put Mr. Neville with the Peytons, because he was heir to a baronetcy.

Kate was much startled, and astonished to see him come out into the hall. But when he entered the carriage, she welcomed him warmly.

"Oh, I am so glad to see you here!" said she.

"Guess by that what my delight at meeting you must be," said he.

She blushed and turned it off.

"I mean, that your coming here gives me good hopes there will be no more mischief."

She then lowered her voice, and begged him on no account to tell her papa of her ride to Scutchemsee Nob.

"Not a word," said George.

He knew the advantage of sharing a secret with a fair lady. He proceeded to whisper something very warm in her ear : she listened to some of it ; but then remonstrated, and said, —

"Are you not ashamed to go on so at a funeral ? Oh, do, pray, leave compliments a moment, and think of your latter end."

He took this suggestion, as indeed he did everything from her, in good part ; and composed his visage into a decent gravity.

Soon after this they reached the church, and buried the deceased in his family vault.

People who are not bereaved by the death are always inclined to chatter, coming home from a funeral. Kate now talked to Neville of her own accord, and asked him if he had spoken to his host. He said yes, and, more than that, had come to a clear understanding with him.

"We agreed that it was no use fighting for you. I said, if either of us two was to kill the other, it did not follow you would wed the survivor."

"Me wed the wretch !" said Kate. "I should abhor him, and go into a convent in spite of you all, and end my days praying for the murdered man's soul."

"Neither of us is worth all that," suggested Neville, with an accent of conviction.

"That is certain," replied the lady, dryly ; "so please not to do it."

He bade her set her mind at ease : they had both agreed to try and win her by peaceful arts.

"Then a pretty life mine will be ! "

"Well, I think it will, till you decide."

"I could easily decide, if it were not for giving pain to — somebody."

"Oh, you can't help that. My sweet mistress, you are not the first that has had to choose between two worthy men. For, in sooth, I have nothing to say against my rival, neither. I know him

better than I did : he is a very worthy gentleman, though he is damnably in my way."

"And you are a very noble one to say so."

"And you are one of those that make a man noble : I feel that petty arts are not the way to win you, and I scorn them. Sweet Mistress Kate, I adore you ! You are the best and noblest, as well as the loveliest of women ! "

"Oh, hush, Mr. Neville ! I am a creature of clay, — and you are another, — and both of us coming home from a funeral. Do think of *that.*"

Here they were interrupted by Mr. Peyton asking Kate to lend him a shilling for the groom. Kate replied aloud that she had left her purse at home, then whispered in his ear that she had not a shilling in the world : and this was strictly true ; for her little all was Tom Leicester's now. With this they reached the Hall, and the coy Kate gave both Neville and Gaunt the slip, and got amongst her mates. There her tongue went as fast as her neighbors', though she had just come back from a funeral.

But soon the ladies and gentlemen were all invited to the reading of the will.

And now chance, which had hitherto befriended Neville by throwing him into one carriage with Kate, gave Gaunt a turn. He found her a moment alone and near the embrasure of a window. He seized the opportunity, and asked her, might he say a word in her ear ?

"What a question ! " said she, gayly ; and the next moment they had the embrasure to themselves.

"Kate," said he, hurriedly, "in a few minutes, I suppose, I shall be master of this place. Now you told me once you would rather be an abbess or a nun than marry me."

"Did I ?" said Kate. "What a sensible speech ! But the worst of it is, I 'm never in the same mind long."

"Well," replied Griffith, "I think of all that falls from your lips, and your will is mine ; only for pity's sake do not wed any man but me. You have known me so long ; why, you know the worst of me by this time : and you have only seen the outside of *him*."

"Detraction ! is that what you wanted to say to me ?" asked Kate, freezing suddenly.

" Nay, nay ; it was about the abbey. I find you can be an abbess without going and shutting yourself up and breaking one's heart. The way is, you build a convent in Ireland, and endow it ; and then you send a nun over to govern it under you. Bless your heart, you can do anything with money; and I shall have money enough before the day is over. To be sure, I *did* intend to build a kennel and keep harriers, and you know that costs a good penny : but we could n't manage a kennel and an abbey too ; so now down goes the English kennel, and up goes the Irish abbey."

"But you are a Protestant gentleman. You could not found a nunnery."

" But my wife could. Whose business is it what she does with her money ?"

" With your money, you mean."

" Nay, with hers, when I give it her with all my heart."

" Well, you astonish me," said Kate, thoughtfully. " Tell me, now, who put it into your head to bribe a poor girl in this abominable way ? "

" Who put it in my head ? " said Griffith, looking rather puzzled; "why, I suppose my heart put it in my head."

Kate smiled very sweetly at this answer, and a wild hope thrilled through Griffith that perhaps she might be brought to terms.

But at this crisis the lawyer from London was announced, and Griffith, as master of the house, was obliged to seat the company. He looked bitterly disappointed at the interruption, but put a good face on it, and had more chairs in, and saw them all seated, beginning with Kate and the other ladies.

The room was spacious, and the entire company sat in the form of a horse-shoe.

The London solicitor was introduced by Griffith, and bowed in a short, business-like way, seated himself in the horse-shoe aforesaid, and began to read the will aloud.

It was a lengthy document, and there is nothing to be gained by repeating every line of it. I pick out a clause here and there.

" I, Septimus Charlton, of Hernshaw Castle and Bolton Grange, in the County of Cumberland, Esquire, being of sound mind, memory, and understanding, — thanks be to God, — do make this my last will and testament, as follows : —

" First, I commit my soul to God who gave it, and my body to the earth from which it came. I desire my executors to discharge my funeral and testamentary expenses, my just debts, and the legacies hereinafter bequeathed, out of my personal estate."

Then followed several legacies of fifty and one hundred guineas ; then several small legacies, such as the following : —

" To my friend Edward Peyton, of Peyton Hall, Esquire, ten guineas to buy a mourning ring.

" To the worshipful gentlemen and ladies who shall follow my body to the grave, ten guineas each, to buy a mourning ring."

" To my wife's cousin, Griffith Gaunt, I give and bequeath the sum of two thousand pounds, the same to be paid to him within one calender month from the date of my decease.

" And as to all my messuages, or tenements, farms, lands, hereditaments, and real estate, of what nature or what kind soever, and wheresoever situate, together with all my moneys, mortgages, chattels, furniture, plate, pictures, wine, liquors, horses, carriages, stock, and all the rest, residue, and remainder of my personal estate and effects whatsoever, (after the payment of the debts and legacies hereinbefore mentioned,) I give, devise, and bequeath the same to my cousin, Catharine Peyton, daughter of Edward Peyton, Esquire, of Peyton Hall, in the County of Cumberland, her heirs, executors, administrators, and assigns, forever."

When the lawyer read out this unexpected blow, the whole company turned in their seats and looked amazed at her who in a second and a sentence was turned before their eyes from the poorest girl in Cumberland to an heiress in her own right, and proprietor of the house they sat in, the chairs they sat on, and the lawn they looked out at.

Ay, we turn to the rising sun. Very few looked at Griffith Gaunt to see how he took his mistress's good fortune, that was his calamity; yet his face was a book full of strange matter. At first a flash of loving joy crossed his countenance; but this gave way immediately to a haggard look, and that to a glare of despair.

As for the lady, she cast one deprecating glance, swifter than lightning, at him she had disinherited, and then she turned her face to marble. In vain did curious looks explore her to detect the delight such a stroke of fortune would have given to themselves. Faulty, but, great of soul, and on her guard against the piercing eyes of her own sex, she sat sedate, and received her change of fortune with every appearance of cool composure and exalted indifference; and as for her dreamy eyes, they seemed thinking of heaven, or something almost as many miles away from money and land.

But the lawyer had not stopped a moment to see how people took it; he had gone steadily on through the usual formal clauses; and now he brought his monotonous voice to an end, and added, in the same breath, but in a natural and cheerful tone, —

"Madam, I wish you joy."

This operated like a signal. The company exploded in a body; and then they all came about the heiress, and congratulated her in turn. She curtsied politely, though somewhat coldly, but said not a word in reply, till the disappointed one spoke to her.

He hung back at first. To understand his feelings, it must be remembered, that in his view of things, Kate gained nothing by this bequest, compared with what he lost. As his wife, she would have been mistress of Bolton Hall, etc. But now she was placed too far above him. Sick at heart, he stood aloof while they all paid their court to her. But by and by he felt it would look base and hostile, if he alone said nothing; so he came forward, struggling visibly for composure and manly fortitude.

The situation was piquant; and the ladies' tongues stopped in a moment, and they were all eyes and ears.

CHAPTER IX.

GRIFFITH, with an effort he had not the skill to hide, stammered out, "Mistress Kate, I do wish you joy." Then, with sudden and touching earnestness, "Never did good fortune light on one so worthy of it."

"Thank you, Griffith," replied Kate, softly. (She had called him "Mr. Gaunt" in public till now.) "But money and lands do not always bring content. I think I was happier a minute ago than I feel now," said she, quietly.

The blood rushed into Griffith's face at this; for a minute ago might mean when he and she were talking almost like lovers about to wed. He was so overcome by this, he turned on his heel, and retreated hastily to hide his emotion, and regain, if possible, composure to play his part of host in the house that was his no longer.

Kate herself soon after retired, nominally to make her toilet before dinner; but really to escape the public and think it all over.

The news of her advancement had spread like wildfire; she was waylaid at the very door by the housekeeper, who insisted on showing her her house.

"Nay, never mind the house," said Kate; "just show me one room where I can wash my face and do my hair."

Mrs. Hill conducted her to the best bedroom; it was lined with tapestry, and all the colors flown; the curtains were a deadish yellow.

"Lud! here's a colored room to show *me* into," said the blonde Kate; "and a black grate, too. Why not take me out o' doors and bid me wash in the snow ?"

" Alack, mistress," said the woman, feeling very uneasy, "we had no orders from Mr. Gaunt to light fires *up* stairs."

"O, if you wait for gentlemen's orders to make your house fit to live in ! You knew there were a dozen ladies coming, yet you were not woman enough to light them fires. Come, take me to your own bedroom."

The woman turned red. " Mine is but a small room, my lady," she stammered.

" But there 's a fire in it," said Kate, spitefully. " You servants don't wait for gentlemen's orders, to take care of yourselves."

Mrs. Hill said to herself, " I 'm to leave ; that 's flat." However, she led the way down a passage, and opened the door of a pleasant little room in a square turret ; a large bay window occupied one whole side of the room, and made it inexpressibly bright and cheerful, though rather hot and stuffy ; a clear coal fire burned in the grate.

" Ah !" said Kate, " how nice ! Please open those little windows, every one. I suppose you have sworn never to let wholesome air into a room. Thank you : now go and forget every cross word I have said to you, — I am out of sorts, and nervous, and irritable. There, run away, my good soul, and light fires in every room ; and don't you let a creature come near me, or you and I shall quarrel downright."

Mrs. Hill beat a hasty retreat. Kate locked the door and threw herself backwards on the bed, with such a weary recklessness and *abandon* as if she was throwing herself into the sea, to end all her trouble, — and burst out crying.

It was one thing to refuse to marry her old sweetheart ; it was another to take his property and reduce him to poverty. But here was she doing both, and going to be persuaded to marry Neville, and swell his wealth with the very possessions she had taken from Griffith ; and him wounded into the bargain for love of her. It was really too

cruel. It was an accumulation of different cruelties. Her bosom revolted ; she was agitated, perplexed, irritated, unhappy, and all in a tumult ; and although she had but one fit of crying, — to the naked eye, — yet a person of her own sex would have seen that at one moment she was crying from agitated nerves, at another from worry, and at the next from pity, and then from grief.

In short, she had a good long, hearty, multiform cry ; and it relieved her swelling heart, so far that she felt able to go down now, and hide her feelings, one and all, from friend and foe ; to do which was unfortunately a part of her nature.

She rose and plunged her face into cold water, and then smoothed her hair.

Now, as she stood at the glass, two familiar voices came in through the open window, and arrested her attention directly. It was her father conversing with Griffith Gaunt. Kate pricked up her quick ears and listened, with her back hair in her hand. She caught the substance of their talk, only now and then she missed a word or two.

Mr. Peyton was speaking rather kindly to Griffith, and telling him he was as sorry for his disappointment as any father could be whose daughter had just come into a fortune. But then he went on and rather spoiled this by asking Griffith bluntly what on earth had ever made him think Mr. Charlton intended to leave him Bolton and Hernshaw.

Griffith replied, with manifest agitation, that Mr. Charlton had repeatedly told him he was to be his heir. "Not," said Griffith, "that he meant to wrong Mistress Kate, neither : poor old man, he always thought she and I should be one."

" Ah ! well," said Squire Peyton, coolly, " there is an end of all that now."

At this observation Kate glided to the window, and laid her cheek on the sill to listen more closely.

But Griffith made no reply.

Mr. Peyton seemed dissatisfied at his silence, and being a person who, notwithstanding a certain superficial goodnature, saw his own side of a question very big, and his neighbor's very little, he was harder than perhaps he intended to be.

"Why, Master Gaunt," said he, "surely you would not follow my daughter now, — to feed upon a woman's bread. Come, be a man ; and, if you are the girl's friend, don't stand in her light. You know she can wed your betters, and clap Bolton Hall on to Neville's Court. No doubt it is a disappointment to *you :* but what can't be cured must be endured ; pluck up a bit of courage, and turn your heart another way ; and then I shall always be a good friend to you, and my doors open to you come when you will."

Griffith made no reply. Kate strained her ears, but could not hear a syllable. A tremor ran through her. She was in distance farther from Griffith than her father was ; but superior intelligence provided her with a bridge from her window to her old servant's mind. And now she felt that this great silence was the silence of despair.

But the Squire pressed him for a definite answer, and finally insisted on one. "Come, don't be so sulky," said he ; "I 'm her father : give me an answer, ay or no."

Then Kate heard a violent sigh, and out rushed a torrent of words that each seemed tinged with blood from the unfortunate speaker's heart. "Old man," he almost shrieked, "what did I ever do to you, that you torment me so ? Sure you were born without bowels. Beggared but an hour agone, and now you must come and tell me I have lost *her* by losing house and lands ! D' ye think I need to be *told* it ? She was too far above me before, and now she is gone quite out of my reach. But why come and fling it in my face ? Can't you give a poor, undone man one hour to draw his breath in trouble ? And when you know I have got to play the host this bitter day, and smile, and smirk, and make you all merry, with my heart breaking ! O Christ, look down and pity me, for men are made of stone ! Well, then, no ; I will not, I cannot say the word to give her up. *She* will discharge *me*, and then I 'll fly the country and never trouble you more. And to think that one little hour ago she was so kind, and I was so happy ! Ah, sir, if you were born of a woman, have a little pity, and don't speak to me of her at all, one way or other. What are you afraid of ? I am a gentleman and a man, though sore my trouble : I shall not run after the lady of Bolton Hall. Why, sir, I have ordered the servants to set her chair in the middle of the table, where I shall not be able to speak to her, or even see her. Indeed I dare not look at her : for I must be merry. Merry ! My arm it worries me, my head it aches, my heart is sick to death. Man ! man ! show me some little grace, and do not torture me more than flesh and blood can bear."

"You are mad, young sir," said the Squire, sternly, "and want locking up on bread and water for a month."

"I *am* almost mad," said Griffith, humbly. "But if you would only let me alone, and not tear my heart out of my body, I could hide my agony from the whole pack of ye, and go through my part like a man. I wish I was lying where I laid my only friend this afternoon."

"O, I don't want to speak to you," said Peyton, angrily; "and, by the same token, don't you speak to my daughter no more."

"Well, sir, if she speaks to me, I shall be sure to speak to her, without asking your leave or any man's. But I will not force myself upon the lady of Bolton Hall ; don't you think it. Only for God's sake let me alone. I want to be by myself." And with this he hurried away, unable to bear it any more.

Peyton gave a hostile and contemptuous snort, and also turned on his heel, and went off in the opposite direction.

The effect of this dialogue on the

listener was not to melt, but exasperate her. Perhaps she had just cried away her stock of tenderness. At any rate, she rose from her ambush a very basilisk; her eyes, usually so languid, flashed fire, and her forehead was red with indignation. She bit her lip, and clenched her hands, and her little foot beat the ground swiftly.

She was still in this state when a timid tap came to the door, and Mrs. Hill asked her pardon, but dinner was ready, and the ladies and gentlemen all a waiting for her to sit down.

This reminded Kate she was the mistress of the house. She answered civilly she would be down immediately. She then took a last look in the glass; and her own face startled her.

"No," she thought, "they shall none of them know nor guess what I feel." And she stood before the glass and deliberately extracted all emotion from her countenance, and by way of preparation screwed on a spiteful smile.

When she had got her face to her mind, she went down stairs.

The gentlemen awaited her with impatience, the ladies with curiosity, to see how she would comport herself in her new situation. She entered, made a formal courtesy, and was conducted to her seat by Mr. Gaunt. He placed her in the middle of the table. "I play the host for this one day," said he, with some dignity; and took the bottom of the table himself.

Mr. Hammersley was to have sat on Kate's left, but the sly Neville persuaded him to change, and so got next to his inamorata: opposite to her sat her father, Major Rickards, and others unknown to fame.

Neville was in high spirits. He had the good taste to try and hide his satisfaction at the fatal blow his rival had received, and he entirely avoided the topic; but Kate saw at once, by his demure complacency, he was delighted at the turn things had taken, and he gained nothing by it: he found her a changed girl. Cold monosyllables were all he could extract from her. He returned to the charge a hundred times,

with indomitable gallantry, but it was no use. Cold, haughty, sullen!

Her other neighbor fared little better; and in short the lady of the house made a vile impression. She was an iceberg, — a beautiful kill-joy, — a wet blanket of charming texture.

And presently Nature began to coöperate with her: long before sunset it grew prodigiously dark; and the cause was soon revealed by a fall of snow in flakes as large as a biscuit. A shiver ran through the people; and old Peyton blurted out, "I shall not go home to-night." Then he bawled across the table to his daughter: "*You* are at home. We will stay and take possession."

"O papa!" said Kate, reddening with disgust.

But if dulness reigned around the lady of the house, it was not so everywhere. Loud bursts of merriment were heard at the bottom of the table. Kate glanced that way in some surprise, and found it was Griffith making the company merry, — Griffith of all people.

The laughter broke out at short intervals, and by and by became uproarious and constant. At last she looked at Neville inquiringly.

"Our worthy host is setting us an example of conviviality," said he. "He is getting drunk."

"O, I hope not," said Kate. "Has he no friend to tell him not to make a fool of himself?"

"You take a great interest in him," said Neville, bitterly.

"Of course I do. Pray, do you desert your friends when ill luck·falls on them?"

"Nay, Mistress Kate, I hope not."

"You only triumph over the misfortunes of your enemies, eh?" said the stinging beauty.

"Not even that. And as for Mr. Gaunt, I am not his enemy."

"O no, of course not. You are his best friend. Witness his arm at this moment."

"I am his rival, but not his enemy. I'll give you a proof." Then he lowered his voice, and said in her ear:

"You are grieved at his losing Bolton; and, as you are very generous and noble-minded, you are all the more grieved because his loss is your gain." (Kate blushed at this shrewd hit.) Neville went on: "You don't like him well enough to marry him; and since you cannot make him happy, it hurts your good heart to make him poor."

"It is you for reading a lady's heart," said Kate, ironically.

George proceeded steadily. "I 'll show you an easy way out of this dilemma."

"Thank you," said Kate, rather insolently.

"Give Mr. Gaunt Bolton and Hernshaw, and give me — your hand."

Kate turned and looked at him with surprise; she saw by his eye it was no jest. For all that, she affected to take it as one. "That would be long and short division," said she; but her voice faltered in saying it.

"So it would," replied George, coolly; "for Bolton and Hernshaw both are not worth one finger of that hand I ask of you. But the value of things lies in the mind that weighs 'em. Mr. Gaunt, you see, values Bolton and Hernshaw very highly; why, he is in despair at losing them. Look at him; he is getting rid of his reason before your very eyes, to drown his disappointment."

"Ah! oh! that is it, is it?" And, strange to say, she looked rather relieved.

"That is it, believe me: it is a way we men have. But, as I was saying, *I* don't care one straw for Bolton and Hernshaw. It is *you* I love, — not your land nor your house, but your sweet self; so give me that, and let the lawyers make over this famous house and lands to Mr. Gaunt. His antagonist I have been in the field, and his rival I am and must be, but not his enemy, you see, and not his ill-wisher."

Kate was softened a little. "This is all mighty romantic," said she, "and very like a *preux chevalier*, as you are; but you know very well he would fling land and house in your face, if you offered them him on these terms."

"Ay, in my face, if I offered them; but not in yours, if you."

"I am sure he would, all the same."

"Try him."

"What is the use?"

"Try him."

Kate showed symptoms of uneasiness. "Well, I will," said she, stoutly. "No, that I will not. You begin by bribing me; and then you would set me to bribe him."

"It is the only way to make two honest men happy."

"If I thought that — "

"You know it. Try him."

"And suppose he says nay?"

"Then we shall be no worse than we are."

"And suppose he says ay?"

"Then he will wed Bolton Hall and Hernshaw, and the pearl of England will wed me."

"I have a great mind to take you at your word," said Kate; "but no; it is really too indelicate."

George Neville fixed his eyes on her. "Are you not deceiving yourself?" said he. "Do you not like Mr. Gaunt better than you think? I begin to fear you dare not put him to this test: you fear his love would not stand it?"

Kate colored high, and tossed her head proudly. "How shrewd you gentlemen are!" she said. "Much you know of a lady's heart. Now the truth is, I don't know what might not happen were I to do what you bid me. Nay, I 'm wiser than you would have me; and I 'll pity Mr. Gaunt at a safe distance, if you please, sir."

Neville bowed gravely. He felt sure this was a plausible evasion, and that she really was afraid to apply his test to his rival's love.

So now, for the first time, he became silent and reserved by her side. The change was noticed by Father Francis, and he fixed a grave, remonstrating glance on Kate. She received it, understood it, affected not to notice it, and acted upon it.

Drive a donkey too hard, it kicks.

Drive a man too hard, it hits.

Drive a woman too hard, it cajoles.

Now amongst them they had driven Kate Peyton too hard ; so she secretly formed a bold resolution; and, this done, her whole manner changed for the better. She turned to Neville, and flattered and fascinated him. The most feline of her sex could scarcely equal her *calinerie* on this occasion. But she did not confine her fascination to him. She broke out, *pro bono publico*, like the sun in April, with quips and cranks and dimpled smiles, and made everybody near her quite forget her late hauteur and coldness, and bask in this sunny, sweet hostess. When the charm was at its height, the siren cast a seeming merry glance at Griffith, and said to a lady opposite, " Methinks some of the gentlemen will be glad to be rid of us," and so carried the ladies off to the drawing-room.

There her first act was to dismiss her smiles without ceremony ; and her second was to sit down and write four lines to the gentleman at the head of the dining-table.

And he was as drunk as a fiddler.

CHAPTER X.

GRIFFITH's friends laughed heartily with him while he was getting drunk ; and when he had got drunk, they laughed still louder, only at him.

They " knocked him down " for a song ; and he sang a rather Anacreontic one very melodiously, and so loud that certain of the servants, listening outside, derived great delectation from it ; and Neville applauded ironically.

Soon after, they " knocked him down " for a story ; and as it requires more brains to tell a story than to sing a song, the poor butt made an ass of himself. He maundered and wandered, and stopped, and went on, and lost one thread and took up another, and got into a perfect maze. And while he was thus entangled, a servant came in and brought him a note, and put it in his hand. The unhappy narrator received it with a sapient nod, but was too polite, or else too stupid, to open it, so closed his fingers on it, and went maundering on till his story trickled into the sand of the desert, and somehow ceased ; for it could not be said to end, being a thing without head or tail.

He sat down amidst derisive cheers. About five minutes afterwards, in some intermittent flash of reason, he found he had got hold of something. He opened his hand, and lo, a note ! On this he chuckled unreasonably, and distributed sage, cunning winks around, as if he, by special ingenuity, had caught a nightingale, or the like ; then, with sudden hauteur and gravity, proceeded to examine his prize.

But he knew the handwriting at once ; and it gave him a galvanic shock that half sobered him for the moment.

He opened the note, and spelled it with great difficulty. It was beautifully written, in long, clear letters ; but then those letters kept dancing so !

" I much desire to speak to you before 't is too late, but can think of no way save one. I lie in the turreted room : come under my window at nine of the clock ; and prithee come sober, if you respect yourself, or

" KATE."

Griffith put the note in his pocket, and tried to think ; but he could not think to much purpose. Then this made him suspect he was drunk. Then he tried to be sober ; but he found he could not. He sat in a sort of stupid agony, with Love and Drink battling for his brain. It was piteous to see the poor fool's struggles to regain the reason he had so madly parted with. He could not do it ; and when he found that, he took up a finger-glass, and gravely poured the contents upon his head.

At this there was a burst of laughter.

This irritated Mr. Gaunt ; and, with that rapid change of sentiments which marks the sober savage and the drunken European, he offered to fight a gentleman he had been hitherto holding up to the company as his best friend. But his best friend (a very distant acquaintance) was by this time as tipsy as himself, and offered a piteous disclaimer, mingled with tears ; and these maudlin drops so affected Griffith that he flung his one available arm round his best friend's head, and wept in turn ; and down went both their lachrymose, empty noddles on the table. Griffith's remained there ; but his best friend extricated himself, and, shaking his skull, said, dolefully, " He is very drunk." This notable discovery, coming from such a quarter, caused considerable merriment.

" Let him alone," said an old toper ; and Griffith remained a good hour with his head on the table. Meantime the other gentlemen soon put it out of their power to ridicule him on the score of intoxication.

Griffith, keeping quiet, got a little better, and suddenly started up with a notion he was to go to Kate this very moment. He muttered an excuse, and staggered to a glass door that led to the lawn. He opened this door, and rushed out into the open air. He thought it would set him all right ; but, instead of that, it made him so much worse that presently his legs came to a misunderstanding, and he measured his length on the ground, and could not get up again, but kept slipping down.

Upon this he groaned and lay quiet.

Now there was a foot of snow on the ground ; and it melted about Griffith's hot temples and flushed face, and mightily refreshed and revived him.

He sat up and kissed Kate's letter, and Love began to get the upper hand of Liquor a little.

Finally he got up and half strutted, half staggered, to the turret, and stood under Kate's window.

The turret was covered with luxuriant ivy, and that ivy with snow. So the glass of the window was set in a massive frame of winter ; but a bright fire burned inside the room, and this set the panes all aflame. It was cheery and glorious to see the window glow like a sheet of transparent fire in its deep frame of snow ; but Griffith could not appreciate all that. He stood there

a sorrowful man. The wine he had taken to drown his despair had lost its stimulating effect, and had given him a heavy head, but left him his sick heart.

He stood and puzzled his drowsy faculties why Kate had sent for him. Was it to bid him good by forever, or to lessen his misery by telling him she would not marry another ? He soon gave up cudgelling his enfeebled brains. Kate was a superior being to him, and often said things, and did things, that surprised him. She had sent for him, and that was enough. He should see her and speak to her once more, at all events. He stood, alternately nodding and looking up at her glowing room, and longing for its owner to appear. But as Bacchus had inspired him to mistake eight o'clock for nine, and as she was not a votary of Bacchus, she did not appear ; and he stood there till he began to shiver.

The shadow of a female passed along the wall ; and Griffith gave a great start. Then he heard the fire poked. Soon after he saw the shadow again ; but it had a large servant's cap on : so his heart had beaten high for Mary or Susan. He hung his head disappointed ; and, holding on by the ivy, fell a nodding again.

By and by one of the little casements was opened softly. He looked up, and there was the right face peering out.

O, what a picture she was in the moonlight and the firelight! They both fought for that fair head, and each got a share of it: the full moon's silvery beams shone on her rose-like cheeks and lilified them a shade, and lit her great gray eyes and made them gleam astoundingly ; but the ruby firelight rushed at her from behind, and flowed over her golden hair, and reddened and glorified it till it seemed more than mortal. And all this in a very picture-frame of snow.

Imagine, then, how sweet and glorious she glowed on him who loved her, and who looked at her perhaps for the last time.

The sight did wonders to clear his head ; he stood open-mouthed, with his heart beating. She looked him all over a moment. "Ah!" said she. Then, quietly, "I am so glad you are come." Then, kindly and regretfully, "How pale you look! you are unhappy."

This greeting, so gentle and kind, overpowered Griffith. His heart was too full to speak.

Kate waited a moment; and then, as he did not reply to her, she began to plead to him. "I hope you are not angry with *me*," she said. "*I* did not want him to leave me your estates. I would not rob you of them for the world, if I had my way."

"Angry with you!" said Griffith. "I 'm not such a villain. Mr. Charlton did the right thing, and —" He could say no more.

"I do not think so," said Kate. "But don't you fret: all shall be settled to your satisfaction. I cannot quite love you, but I have a sincere affection for you; and so I ought. Cheer up, dear Griffith; don't you be down-hearted about what has happened to-day."

Griffith smiled. "I don't feel unhappy," he said; "I did feel as if my heart was broken. But then you seemed parted from me. Now we are together, I feel as happy as ever. Mistress, don't you ever shut that window and leave me in the dark again. Let me stand and look at your sweet face all night, and I shall be the happiest man in Cumberland."

"Ay," said Kate, blushing at his ardor; "happy for a single night; but when I go away you will be in the dumps again, and perhaps get tipsy; as if that could mend matters! Nay, I must set your happiness on stronger legs than that. Do you know I have got permission to undo this cruel will, and let you have Bolton Hall and Hernshaw again?"

Griffith looked pleased, but rather puzzled.

Kate went on, but not so glibly now. "However," said she, a little nervously, "there is one condition to it that will cost us both some pain. If you consent to accept these two estates from me, who don't value them one straw, why then—"

"Well, what?" he gasped.

"Why, then, my poor Griffith, we shall be bound in honor — you and I — not to meet for some months, perhaps for a whole year: in one word, — do not hate me, — not till you can bear to see me — another — man's — wife."

The murder being out, she hid her face in her hands directly, and in that attitude awaited his reply.

Griffith stood petrified a moment; and I don't think his intellects were even yet quite clear enough to take it all in at once. But at last he did comprehend it, and when he did, he just uttered a loud cry of agony, and then turned his back on her without a word.

Man does not speak by words alone. A mute glance of reproach has ere now pierced the heart a tirade would have left untouched; and even an inarticulate cry may utter volumes.

Such an eloquent cry was that with which Griffith Gaunt turned his back upon the angelical face he adored, and the soft, persuasive tongue. There was agony, there was shame, there was wrath, all in that one ejaculation.

It frightened Kate. She called him back. "Don't leave me so," she said. "I know I have affronted you; but I meant all for the best. Do not let us part in anger."

At this Griffith returned in violent agitation. "It is your fault for making me speak," he cried. "I was going away without a word, as a man should, that is insulted by a woman. You heartless girl! What! you bid me sell you to that man for two dirty farms! O, well you know Bolton and Hernshaw were but the steps by which I hoped to climb to you: and now you tell me to part with you, and take those miserable acres instead of my darling. Ah, mistress, you have never loved, or you would hate yourself and despise yourself for what you have done. Love! if you had known what that word means, you could n't look in my face and stab me to the heart like this. God forgive you ! And sure I hope he will ; for, after all, it is not *your* fault that you were born without a heart. WHY, KATE, YOU ARE CRYING."

CHAPTER XI.

"CRYING !" said Kate. "I could cry my eyes out to think what I have done ; but it is not my fault : they egged me on. I knew you would fling those two miserable things in my face if I did, and I said so ; but they would be wiser than me, and insist on my putting you to the proof."

"They ? Who is they ?"

"No matter. Whoever it was, they will gain nothing by it, and you will lose nothing. Ah, Griffith, I am so ashamed of myself, — and so proud of you."

"They ?" repeated Griffith, suspiciously. "Who is this they ?"

"What does that matter, so long as it was not Me ? Are you going to be jealous again ? Let us talk of you and me, and never mind who *them* is. You have rejected my proposal with just scorn : so now let me hear yours ; for we must agree on something this very night. Tell me, now, what can I say or do to make you happy ?"

Griffith was sore puzzled. "Alas ! sweet Kate," said he, "I don't know what you can do for me now, except stay single for my sake."

"I should like nothing better," replied Kate warmly ; "but unfortunately they won't let me do that. Father Francis will be at me to-morrow, and insist on my marrying Mr. Neville."

"But you will refuse."

"I would, if I could but find a good excuse."

"Excuse ? why, say you don't love him."

"O, they won't allow that for a reason."

"Then I am undone," sighed Griffith.

"No, no, you are not ; if I could be brought to pretend I love somebody else. And really, if I don't quite love

you, I like you too well to let you be unhappy. Besides, I cannot bear to rob you of these unlucky farms : I think there is nothing I would not do rather than that. I think — I would rather — do — something very silly indeed. But I suppose you don't want me to do that now ? Why don't you answer me ? Why don't you say something ? Are you drunk, sir, as they pretend ? or are you asleep ? O, I can't speak any plainer : this is intolerable. Mr. Gaunt, I 'm going to shut the window."

Griffith got alarmed, and it sharpened his wits. "Kate, Kate !" he cried, "what do you mean ? am I in a dream ? would you marry poor me after all ?"

"How on earth can I tell, till I am asked ?" inquired Kate, with an air of childlike innocence, and inspecting the stars attentively.

"Kate, will you marry me ?" said Griffith, all in a flutter.

"Of course I will — if you will let me," replied Kate, coolly, but rather tenderly, too.

Griffith burst into raptures. Kate listened to them with a complacent smile, then delivered herself after this fashion : "You have very little to thank me for, dear Griffith. I don't exactly downright love you, but I could not rob you of those unlucky farms, and you refuse to take them back any way but this ; so what can I do ? And then, for all I don't love you, I find I am always unhappy if you are unhappy, and happy when you are happy ; so it comes pretty much to the same thing. I declare I am sick of giving you pain, and a little sick of crying in consequence. There, I have cried more in the last fortnight than in all my life before, and you know nothing spoils one's beauty like crying. And then you are so good, and kind, and true, and brave ; and everybody is so unjust and so unkind to you, papa and all. You were quite in the right about the duel, dear. He *is* an impudent puppy ; and I threw dust in your eyes, and made you own you were in the wrong, and it was a great shame of me, but it was because I liked you best. I could take liberties with *you*, dear. And you are wounded for me, and now I have disinherited you. O, I can't bear it, and I won't. My heart yearns for you, — bleeds for you. I would rather die than you should be unhappy; I would rather follow you in rags round the world than marry a prince and make you wretched. Yes, dear, I am yours. Make me your wife; and then some day I dare say I shall love you as I ought."

She had never showed her heart to him like this before; and now it overpowered him. So, being also a little under vinous influence, he stammered out something, and then fairly blubbered for joy. Then what does Kate do, but cry for company?

Presently, to her surprise, he was half-way up the turret, coming to her.

"O, take care! take care!" she cried. "You 'll break your neck."

"Nay," cried he; "I must come at you, if I die for it."

The turret was ornamented from top to bottom with short ledges consisting of half-bricks. This ledge, shallow as it was, gave a slight foothold, insufficient in itself; but he grasped the strong branches of the ivy with a powerful hand, and so between the two contrived to get up and hang himself out close to her.

"Sweet mistress," said he, "put out your hand to me; for I can't take it against your will this time. I have got but one arm."

But this she declined. "No, no," said she; "you do nothing but torment and terrify me, — there." And so gave it him; and he mumbled it.

This last feat won her quite. She thought no other man could have got to her there with two arms; and Griffith had done it with one. She said to herself, "How he loves me! — more than his own neck." And then she thought, "I shall be wife to a strong man; that is one comfort."

In this softened mood she asked him demurely, would he take a friend's advice.

"If that friend is you, ay."

"Then," said she, "I 'll do a downright brazen thing, now my hand is in. I declare I 'll tell you how to secure me. You make me plight my troth with you this minute, and exchange rings with you, *whether I like or not;* engage my honor in this foolish business, and if you do that, I really do think you will have me in spite of them all. But there, — la! — am I worth all this trouble?"

Griffith did not share this chilling doubt. He poured forth his gratitude, and then told her he had got his mother's ring in his pocket; I meant to ask you to wear it," said he.

"And why did n't you?"

"Because you became an heiress all of a sudden."

"Well, what signifies which of us has the dross, so that there is enough for both?"

"That is true," said Griffith, approving his own sentiment, but not recognizing his own words. "Here 's my mother's ring, on my little finger, sweet mistress. But I must ask you to draw it off, for I have but one hand."

Kate made a wry face, "Well, that is my fault," said she, "or I would not take it from you so."

She drew off his ring, and put it on her finger. Then she gave him her largest ring, and had to put it on his little finger for him.

"You are making a very forward girl of me," said she, pouting exquisitely.

He kissed her hand while she was doing it.

"Don't you be so silly," said she; "and, you horrid creature, how you smell of wine! The bullet, please."

"The bullet!" exclaimed Griffith. "What bullet?"

"*The* bullet. The one you were wounded with for my sake. I am told you put it in your pocket; and I see something bulge in your waistcoat. That bullet belongs to me now."

"I think you are a witch," said he. "I do carry it about next my heart. Take it out of my waistcoat, if you will be so good."

She blushed and declined, and, with the refusal on her very lips, fished it out with her taper fingers. She eyed it with a sort of tender horror. The sight of it made her feel faint a moment. She told him so, and that she would keep it to her dying day. Presently her delicate finger found something was written on it. She did not ask him what it was, but withdrew, and examined it by her candle. Griffith had engraved it with these words : —

"I LOVE KATE."

He looked through the window, and saw her examine it by the candle. As she read the inscription, her face, glorified by the light, assumed a celestial tenderness he had never seen it wear before.

She came back and leaned eloquently out as if she would fly to him. "O Griffith, Griffith !" she murmured, and somehow or other their lips met, in spite of all the difficulties, and grew together in a long and tender embrace.

It was the first time she had ever given him more than her hand to kiss, and the rapture repaid him for all.

But as soon as she had made this great advance, virginal instinct suggested a proportionate retreat.

"You must go to bed," she said, austerely; "you will catch your death of cold out here."

He remonstrated: she insisted. He held out : she smiled sweetly in his face, and shut the window in it pretty sharply, and disappeared. He went disconsolately down his ivy ladder. As soon as he was at the bottom, she opened the window again, and asked him, demurely, if he would do something to oblige her.

He replied like a lover; he was ready to be cut in pieces, drawn asunder with wild horses, and so on.

"O, I know you would do anything stupid for me," said she ; "but will you do something clever for a poor girl that is in a fright at what she is going to do for you ? "

"Give your orders, mistress," said Griffith, "and don't talk of me obliging you. I feel quite ashamed to hear you talk so, — to-night especially."

"Well, then," said Kate, "first and foremost, I want you to throw yourself on Father Francis's neck."

"I 'll throw myself on Father Francis's neck," said Griffith, stoutly. "Is that all ? "

"No, nor half. Once upon his neck you must say something. Then I had better settle the very words, or perhaps you will make a mess of it. Say after me now : O Father Francis, 't is to you I owe her."

"O Father Francis, 't is to you I owe her."

"You and I are friends for life."

"You and I are friends for life."

"And, mind, there is always a bed in our home for you, and a plate at our table, and a right welcome, come when you will."

Griffith repeated this line correctly, but, when requested to say the whole, broke down. Kate had to repeat the oration a dozen times ; and he said it after her, like a Sunday-school scholar, till he had it pat.

The task achieved, he inquired of her what Father Francis was to say in reply.

At this simple question Kate showed considerable alarm. "Gracious heavens !" she cried, "you must not stop talking to him ; he will turn you inside out, and I shall be undone. Nay, you must gabble these words out, and then run away as hard as you can gallop."

"But is it true ? " asked Griffith. "Is he so much my friend ? "

"Hum !" said Kate, "it is quite true, and he is not at all your friend. There, don't you puzzle yourself, and pester me ; but do as you are bid, or we are both undone."

Quelled by a menace so mysterious, Griffith promised blind obedience ; and Kate thanked him, and bade him good night, and ordered him peremptorily to bed.

He went.

She beckoned him back.

He came.

She leaned out, and inquired, in a soft, delicious whisper, as follows: "Are you happy, dearest?"

"Ay, Kate, the happiest of the happy."

"Then so am I," she murmured.

And now she slowly closed the window, and gradually retired from the eyes of her enraptured lover.

CHAPTER XII.

BUT while Griffith was thus sweetly employed, his neglected guests were dispersing, not without satirical comments on their truant host. Two or three, however, remained, and slept in the house, upon special invitation. And that invitation came from Squire Peyton. He chose to conclude that Griffith, disappointed by the will, had vacated the premises in disgust, and left him in charge of them; accordingly he assumed the master with alacrity, and ordered beds for Neville, and Father Francis, and Major Rickards, and another. The weather was inclement, and the roads heavy; so the gentlemen thus distinguished accepted Mr. Peyton's offer cordially.

There were a great many things sung and said at the festive board in the course of the evening, but very few of them would amuse or interest the reader as they did the hearers. One thing, however, must not be passed by, as it had its consequences. Major Rickards drank bumpers apiece to the King, the Prince, Church and State, the Army, the Navy, and Kate Peyton. By the time he got to her, two thirds of his discretion had oozed away in loyalty, *esprit du corps*, and port wine; so he sang the young lady's praises in vinous terms, and of course immortalized the very exploit she most desired to consign to oblivion: *Arma viraginemque canebat.* He sang the duel, and in a style which I could not, consistently with the interests of literature, reproduce on a large scale. Hasten we to the concluding versicles of his song.

"So then, sir, we placed our men for the third time, and, you may take my word for it, one or both of these heroes would have bit the dust at that discharge. But, by Jove, sir, just as they were going to pull trigger, in galloped your adorable daughter, and swooned off her foaming horse in the middle of us, — disarmed us, sir, in a moment, melted our valor, bewitched our senses, and the great god of war had to retreat before little Cupid and the charms of beauty in distress."

"Little idiot!" observed the tender parent; and was much distempered.

He said no more about it to Major Rickards; but when they all retired for the night, he undertook to show Father Francis his room, and sat in it with him a good half-hour talking about Kate.

"Here's a pretty scandal," said he. "I must marry the silly girl out of hand before this gets wind, and you must help me."

In a word, the result of the conference was that Kate should be publicly engaged to Neville to-morrow, and married to him as soon as her month's mourning should be over.

The conduct of the affair was confided to Father Francis, as having unbounded influence with her.

CHAPTER XIII.

NEXT morning Mr. Peyton was up betimes in his character of host, and ordered the servants about, and was in high spirits; only they gave place to amazement when Griffith Gaunt came down, and played the host, and was in high spirits.

Neville too watched his rival, and was puzzled at his radiancy.

So breakfast passed in general mystification. Kate, who could have thrown a light, did not come down to breakfast. She was on her defence.

She made her first appearance out of doors.

Very early in the morning, Mr. Peyton, in his quality of master, had ordered the gardener to cut and sweep the snow off the gravel walk that went round the lawn. And on this path

Miss Peyton was seen walking briskly to and fro in the frosty, but sunny air.

Griffith saw her first, and ran out to bid her good morning.

Her reception of him was a farce. She made him a stately courtesy for the benefit of the three faces glued against the panes, but her words were incongruous. "You wretch," said she, "don't come here. Hide about, dearest, till you see me with Father Francis. I'll raise my hand *so* when you are to cuddle him, and fib. There, make me a low bow, and retire."

He obeyed, and the whole thing looked mighty formal and ceremonious from the breakfast-room.

"With your good leave, gentlemen," said Father Francis, dryly, "I will be the next to pay my respects to her." With this he opened the window and stepped out.

Kate saw him, and felt very nervous. She met him with apparent delight.

He bestowed his morning benediction on her, and then they walked silently side by side on the gravel; and from the dining-room window it looked like anything but what it was, — a fencing match.

Father Francis was the first to break silence. He congratulated her on her good fortune, and on the advantage it might prove to the true Church.

Kate waited quietly till he had quite done, and then said, "What, I may go into a convent *now* that I can bribe the door open?"

The scratch was feline, feminine, sudden, and sharp. But, alas! Father Francis only smiled at it. Though not what we call spiritually-minded, he was a man of a Christian temper. "Not with my good-will, my daughter," said he; "I am of the same mind still, and more than ever. You must marry forthwith, and rear children in the true faith."

"What a hurry you are in."

"Your own conduct has made it necessary."

"Why, what have I done now?"

"No harm. It was a good and humane action to prevent bloodshed, but the world is not always worthy of good actions. People are beginning to make free with your name for your interfering in the duel."

Kate fired up. "Why can't people mind their own business?"

"I do not exactly know," said the priest, coolly, "nor is it worth inquiring. We must take human nature as it is, and do for the best. You must marry him, and stop their tongues."

Kate pretended to reflect. "I believe you are right," said she, at last; "and indeed I must do as you would have me; for, to tell the truth, in an unguarded moment, I pitied him so that I half promised I *would*."

"Indeed!" said Father Francis. "This is the first I have heard of it."

Kate replied that was no wonder, for it was only last night she had so committed herself.

"Last night!" said Father Francis; "how can that be? He was never out of my sight till we went to bed."

"O, there I beg to differ," said the lady. "While you were all tippling in the dining-room, he was better employed, — making love by moonlight. And O what a terrible thing opportunity is, and the moon another! There! what with the moonlight, and my pitying him so, and all he has suffered for me, and my being rich now, and having something to give him, we two are engaged. See, else: this was his mother's ring, and he has mine."

"Mr. Neville?"

"Mr. Neville? No. My old servant, to be sure. What, do you think I would go and marry for wealth, when I have enough and to spare of my own? O, what an opinion you must have of me!" ·

Father Francis was staggered by this adroit thrust. However, after a considerable silence he recovered himself, and inquired gravely why she had given him no hint of all this the other night, when he had diverted her from a convent, and advised her to marry Neville.

"That you never did, I'll be sworn," said Kate.

Father Francis reflected.

"Not in so many words, perhaps; but I said enough to show you."

"O!" said Kate, "such a matter was too serious for hints and innuendoes; if you wanted me to jilt my old servant and wed an acquaintance of yesterday, why not say so plainly? I dare say I should have obeyed you, and been unhappy for life; but now my honor is solemnly engaged; my faith is plighted; and were even you to urge me to break faith, and behave dishonorably, I should resist. I would liever take poison, and die."

Father Francis looked at her steadily, and she colored to the brow.

"You are a very apt young lady," said he; "you have outwitted your director. That may be my fault as much as yours; so I advise you to provide yourself with another director, whom you will be unable, or unwilling, to outwit."

Kate's high spirit fell before this: she turned her eyes, full of tears, on him. "O, do not desert me, now that I shall need you more than ever, to guide me in my new duties. Forgive me; I did not know my own heart — quite. I 'll go into a convent now, if I must; but I can't marry any man but poor Griffith. Ah, father, he is more generous than any of us! Would you believe it? when he thought Bolton and Hernshaw were coming to him, he said if I married him I should have the money to build a convent with. He knows how fond I am of a convent."

"He was jesting; his religion would not allow it."

"His religion!" cried Kate. Then, lifting her eyes to Heaven, and looking just like an angel, "Love is *his* religion!" said she, warmly.

"Then his religion is Heathenism," said the priest, grimly.

"Nay, there is too much charity in it for that," retorted Kate, keenly.

Then she looked down, like a cunning, guilty thing, and murmured: "One of the things I esteem him for is he always speaks well of *you*. To be sure, just now the poor soul thinks you are his best friend with me. But that is my fault; I as good as told him so: and it is true, after a fashion; for you kept me out of the convent that was his only real rival. Why, here he comes. O father, now don't you go and tell him you side with Mr. Neville."

At this crisis Griffith, who, to tell the truth, had received a signal from Kate, rushed at Father Francis and fell upon his neck, and said with great rapidity: "O Father Francis, 't is to you I owe her,—you and I are friends for life. So long as we have a house there is a bed in it for you, and whilst we have a table to sit down to there 's a plate at it for you, and a welcome, come when you will."

Having gabbled these words he winked at Kate, and fled swiftly.

Father Francis was taken aback a little by this sudden burst of affection. First he stared,—then he knitted his brows, — then he pondered.

Kate stole a look at him, and her eyes sought the ground.

"That is the gentleman you arranged matters with last night?" said he, drily.

"Yes," replied Kate, faintly.

"Was this scene part of the business?"

"O father!"

"Why I ask, he did it so unnatural. Mr. Gaunt is a worthy, hospitable gentleman; he and I are very good friends; and really I never doubted that I should be welcome in his house —— until this moment."

"And can you doubt it now?"

"Almost: his manner just now was so hollow, so forced; not a word of all that came from his heart, you know."

"Then his heart is changed very lately."

The priest shook his head. "Anything more like a puppet, and a parrot to boot, I never saw. 'T was done so timely, too. He ran in upon our discourse. Let me see your hand, mistress. Why, where is the string with which you pulled yonder machine in so pat upon the word?"

"Spare me!" muttered Kate, faintly.

"Then do you drop deceit and the silly cunning of your sex, and speak to me from your heart, or not at all." (Diapason.)

At this Kate began to whimper.

"Father," she said, "show me some mercy." Then, suddenly clasping her hands: "HAVE PITY ON HIM, AND ON ME."

This time Nature herself seemed to speak, and the eloquent cry went clean through the priest's heart.

"Ah!" said he; and his own voice trembled a little: "now you are as strong as your cunning was weak. Come, I see how it is with you; and I am human, and have been young, and a lover into the bargain, before I was a priest. There, dry thy eyes, child, and go to thy room; he thou couldst not trust shall bear the brunt for thee this once."

Then Kate bowed her fair head and kissed the horrid paw of him that had administered so severe but salutary a pat. She hurried away up stairs, right joyful at the unexpected turn things had taken.

Father Francis, thus converted to her side, lost no time; he walked into the dining-room and told Neville he had bad news for him.

"Summon all your courage, my young friend," said he, with feeling, "and remember that this world is full of disappointments."

Neville said nothing, but rose and stood rather pale, waiting like a man for the blow. Its nature he more than half guessed: he had been at the window.

It fell,

"She is engaged to Gaunt, since last night; and she loves him."

"The double-faced jade!" cried Peyton, with an oath

"The heartless coquette!" groaned Neville.

Father Francis made excuses for her: "Nay, nay, she is not the first of her sex that did not know her own mind all at once. Besides, we men are blind,

5

in matters of love; perhaps a woman would have read her from the first. After all, she was not bound to give us the eyes to read a female heart."

He next reminded Neville that Gaunt had been her servant for years. "You knew that," said he, "yet you came between them —— at your peril. Put yourself in his place: say you had succeeded: would not his wrong be greater than yours is now? Come, be brave; be generous; he is wounded, he is disinherited; only his love is left him: 't is the poor man's lamb; and would you take it?"

"O, I have not a word to say against the *man*," said George, with a mighty effort.

"And what use is your quarrelling with the woman?" suggested the practical priest.

"None whatever," said George, sullenly. After a moment's silence he rang the bell feverishly. "Order my horse round directly," said he. Then he sat down, and buried his face in his hands, and did not, and could not, listen to the voice of consolation.

Now the house was full of spies in petticoats, amateur spies, that ran and told the mistress everything of their own accord, to curry favor.

And this no doubt was the cause that, just as the groom walked the piebald out of the stable towards the hall door, a maid came to Father Francis with a little note: he opened it, and found these words written faintly, in a fine Italian hand: —

"I scarce knew my own heart till I saw him wounded and poor, and myself rich at his expense. Entreat Mr. Neville to forgive me."

He handed the note to Neville without a word.

Neville read it, and his lip trembled; but he said nothing, and presently went out into the hall, and put on his hat, for he saw his nag at the door.

Father Francis followed him, and said, sorrowfully, "What, not one word in reply to so humble a request?"

"Well, here's my reply," said George,

grinding his teeth. "She knows French, though she pretends not.

'Le bruit est pour le fat, la plainte est pour le sot,
L'honnête homme trompé s'eloigne et ne dit mot.'"

And with this he galloped furiously away.

He buried himself at Neville's Cross for several days, and would neither see nor speak to a soul. His heart was sick, his pride lacerated. He even shed some scalding tears in secret; though, to look at him, that seemed impossible.

So passed a bitter week: and in the course of it he bethought him of the tears he had made a true Italian lady shed, and never pitied her a grain till now.

He was going abroad: on his desk lay a little crumpled paper. It was Kate's entreaty for forgiveness. He had ground it in his hand, and ridden away with it.

Now he was going away, he resolved to answer her.

He wrote a letter full of bitter reproaches; read it over; and tore it up.

He wrote a satirical and cutting letter; read it; and tore it up.

He wrote her a mawkish letter; read it; and tore it up.

The priest's words, scorned at first, had sunk into him a little.

He walked about the room, and tried to see it all like a by-stander.

He examined her writing closely: the pen had scarcely marked the paper. They were the timidest strokes. The writer seemed to kneel to him. He summoned all his manhood, his fortitude, his generosity, and, above all, his high-breeding; and produced the following letter; and this one he sent : —

"MISTRESS KATE, — I leave England to-day for your sake; and shall never return unless the day shall come when I can look on you but as a friend. The love that ends in hate, that is too sorry a thing to come betwixt you and me.

"If you have used me ill, your punishment is this; you have given me

the right to say to you —— I forgive you.

"GEORGE NEVILLE."

And he went straight to Italy.

Kate laid his note upon her knee, and sighed deeply; and said, "Poor fellow! How noble of him! What *can* such men as this see in any woman to go and fall in love with her?"

Griffith found her with a tear in her eye. He took her out walking, and laid all his radiant plans of wedded life before her. She came back flushed, and beaming with complacency and beauty.

Old Peyton was brought to consent to the marriage. Only he attached one condition, that Bolton and Hernshaw should be settled on Kate for her separate use.

To this Griffith assented readily; but Kate refused plump. "What, give him *myself*, and then grudge him my *estates!*" said she, with a look of lofty and beautiful scorn at her male advisers.

But Father Francis, having regard to the temporal interests of his Church, exerted his strength and pertinacity, and tired her out; so those estates were put into trustees' hands, and tied up tight as wax.

This done, Griffith Gaunt and Kate Peyton were married, and made the finest pair that wedded in the county that year.

As the bells burst into a merry peal, and they walked out of church man and wife, their path across the churchyard was strewed thick with flowers, emblematic, no doubt, of the path of life that lay before so handsome a couple.

They spent the honeymoon in London, and tasted earthly felicity.

Yet did not quarrel after it; but subsided into the quiet complacency of wedded life.

CHAPTER XIV.

MR. and Mrs. Gaunt lived happily together — as times went.

A fine girl and boy were born to

them ; and need I say how their hearts expanded and exulted, and seemed to grow twice as large.

The little boy was taken from them at three years old ; and how can I convey to any but a parent the anguish of that first bereavement?

Well, they suffered it together, and that poignant grief was one tie more between them.

For many years they did not furnish any exciting or even interesting matter to this narrator. And all the better for them : without these happy periods of dulness our lives would be hell, and our hearts eternally bubbling and boiling in a huge pot made hot with thorns.

In the absence of striking incidents, it may be well to notice the progress of character, and note the tiny seeds of events to come.

Neither the intellectual nor the moral character of any person stands stock-still : a man improves, or he declines. Mrs. Gaunt had a great taste for reading ; Mr. Gaunt had not : what was the consequence ? At the end of seven years the lady's understanding had made great strides ; the gentleman's had apparently retrograded.

Now we all need a little excitement, and we all seek it, and get it by hook or by crook. The girl who satisfies that natural craving with what the canting dunces of the day call a "sensational" novel, and the girl who does it by waltzing till daybreak, are sisters ; only one obtains the result intellectually, and the other obtains it like a young animal, and a pain in her empty head next day.

Mrs. Gaunt could enjoy company, but was never dull with a good book. Mr. Gaunt was a pleasant companion, but dull out of company. So, rather than not have it, he would go to the parlor of the "Red Lion," and chat and sing with the yeomen and rollicking young squires that resorted thither : and this was matter of grief and astonishment to Mrs. Gaunt.

It was balanced by good qualities she knew how to appreciate. Morals were much looser then than now ; and more than one wife of her acquaintance had a rival in the village, or even among her own domestics ; but Griffith had no loose inclinations of that kind, and never gave her a moment's uneasiness. He was constancy and fidelity in person.

Sobriety had not yet been invented. But Griffith was not so intemperate as most squires ; he could always mount the stairs to tea, and generally without staggering.

He was uxorious, and it used to come out after his wine. This Mrs. Gaunt permitted at first, but by and by says she, expanding her delicate nostrils : "You may be as affectionate as you please, dear, and you may smell of wine, if you will ; but please not to smell of wine and be affectionate at the same moment. I value your affection too highly to let you disgust me with it."

And the model husband yielded to this severe restriction ; and, as it never occurred to him to give up his wine, he forbore to be affectionate in his cups.

One great fear Mrs. Gaunt had entertained before marriage ceased to haunt her. Now and then her quick eye saw Griffith writhe at the great influence her director had with her ; but he never spoke out to offend her, and she, like a good wife, saw, smiled, and adroitly, tenderly soothed : and this was nothing compared to what she had feared.

Griffith saw his wife admired by other men, yet never chid nor chafed. The merit of this belonged in a high degree to herself. The fact is, that Kate Peyton, even before marriage, was not a coquette at heart, though her conduct might easily bear that construction ; and she was now an experienced matron, and knew how to be as charming as ever, yet check or parry all approaches to gallantry on the part of her admirers. Then Griffith observed how delicate and prudent his lovely wife was, without ostentatious prudery ; and his heart was at peace.

He was the happier of the two, for he looked up to his wife, as well as loved her ; whereas she was troubled at times with a sense of superiority to her husband. She was amiable enough, and wise enough, to try and shut her eyes to it; and often succeeded, but not always.

Upon the whole, they were a contented couple; though the lady's dreamy eyes seemed still to be exploring earth and sky in search of something they had not yet found, even in wedded life.

They lived at Hernshaw. A letter had been found among Mr. Charlton's papers explaining his will. He counted on their marrying, and begged them to live at the castle. He had left it on his wife's death; it reminded him too keenly of happier days; but, as he drew near his end, and must leave all earthly things, he remembered the old house with tenderness, and put out his dying hand to save it from falling into decay.

Unfortunately, considerable repairs were needed; and, as Kate's property was tied up so tight, Griffith's two thousand pounds went in repairing the house, lawn, park palings, and walled gardens; went, every penny, and left the bridge over the lake still in a battered, rotten, and, in a word, picturesque condition.

This lake was by the older inhabitants sometimes called the " mere," and sometimes " the fish-pools "; it resembled an hour-glass in shape, only curved like a crescent.

In mediæval times it had no doubt been a main defence of the place. It was very deep in parts, especially at the waist or narrow that was spanned by the decayed bridge. There were hundreds of carp and tench in it older than any He in Cumberland, and also enormous pike and eels; and fish from one to five pounds' weight by the million. The water literally teemed from end to end; and this was a great comfort to so good a Catholic as Mrs. Gaunt. When she was seized with a desire to fast, and that was pretty often, the gardener just went down to the lake and flung a casting-net in some favorite hole, and drew out half a bushel the first cast; or planted a flue-net round a patch of weeds, then belabored the

weeds with a long pole, and a score of fine fish were sure to run out into the meshes.

The " mere " was clear as plate glass, and came to the edge of the shaven lawn, and reflected flowers, turf, and overhanging shrubs deliciously.

Yet an ill name brooded over its seductive waters; for two persons had been drowned in it during the last hundred years: and the last one was the parson of the parish, returning from the squire's dinner in the normal condition of a guest, A. D. 1740-50. But what most affected the popular mind was, not the jovial soul hurried into eternity, but the material circumstance that the greedy pike had cleared the flesh off his bones in a single night, so that little more than a skeleton, with here and there a black rag hanging to it, had been recovered next morning.

This ghastly detail being stoutly maintained and constantly repeated by two ancient eye-witnesses, whose one melodramatic incident and treasure it was, the rustic mind saw no beauty whatever in those pellucid and delicious waters, where flowers did glass themselves.

As for the women of the village, they looked on this sheet of water as a trap for their poor bodies and those of their children, and spoke of it as a singular hardship in their lot, that Hernshaw Mere had not been filled up threescore years agone.

The castle itself was no castle, nor had it been for centuries. It was just a house with battlements; but attached to the stable was an old square tower, that really had formed part of the mediæval castle.

However, that unsubstantial shadow, a name, is often more durable than the thing, especially in rural parts; but, indeed, what is there in a name for Time's teeth to catch hold of?

Though no castle, it was a delightful abode. The drawing-room and dining-room had both spacious bay-windows, opening on to the lawn that sloped very gradually down to the pellucid lake, and there was mirrored. On this sweet lawn the inmates and guests walked for sun and mellow air, and often played bowls at eventide.

On the other side was the drive up to the house-door, and a sweep, or small oval plot, of turf, surrounded by gravel ; and a gate at the corner of this sweep opened into a grove of the grandest old spruce-firs in the island.

This grove, dismal in winter and awful at night, was deliciously cool and sombre in the dog-days. The trees were spires ; and their great stems stood serried like infantry in column, and flung a grand canopy of sombre plumes overhead. A strange, antique, and classic grove, — *nulli penetrabilis astro.*

This retreat was enclosed on three sides by a wall, and on the east side came nearly to the house. A few laurel-bushes separated the two. At night it was shunned religiously, on account of the ghosts. Even by daylight it was little frequented, except by one person, — and she took to it amazingly. That person was Mrs. Gaunt. There seems to be, even in educated women, a singular, instinctive love of twilight ; and here was twilight at high noon. The place, too, suited her dreamy, meditative nature. Hither, then, she often retired for peace and religious contemplation, and moved slowly in and out among the tall stems, or sat still, with her thoughtful brow leaned on her white hand, — till the cool, umbrageous retreat got to be called, among the servants, " The Dame's Haunt."

This, I think, is all needs be told about the mere place, where the Gaunts lived comfortably many years, and little dreamed of the strange events in store for them ; little knew the passions that slumbered in their own bosoms, and, like other volcanoes, bided their time.

CHAPTER XV.

ONE day, at dinner, Father Francis let them know that he was ordered to another part of the county, and should no longer be able to enjoy their hospi-tality. " I am sorry for it," said Griffith, heartily ; and Mrs. Gaunt echoed him out of politeness ; but, when husband and wife came to talk it over in private, she let out all of a sudden, and for the first time, that the spiritual coldness of her governor had been a great misfortune to her all these years. " His mind," said she, " is set on earthly things. Instead of helping the angels to raise my thoughts to heaven and heavenly things, he drags me down to earth. O that man's soul was born without wings ! "

Griffith ventured to suggest that Francis was, nevertheless, an honest man, and no mischief-maker.

Mrs. Gaunt soon disposed of this. " O, there are plenty of honest men in the world," said she ; " but in one's spiritual director one needs something more than that, and I have pined for it like a thirsty soul in the desert all these years. Poor good man, I love him dearly ; but, thank Heaven, he is go-ing."

The next time Francis came, Mrs. Gaunt took an opportunity to inquire, but in the most delicate way, who was to be his successor.

" Well," said he, " I fear you will have no one for the present : I mean no one very fit to direct you in practical matters ; but in all that tends directly to the welfare of the soul you will have one young in years but old in good works, and very much my superior in piety."

" I think you do yourself injustice, Father," said Mrs. Gaunt, sweetly. She was always polite ; and, to be always polite, you must be sometimes insin-cere.

" No, my daughter," said Father Francis, quietly, " thank God, I know my own defects, and they teach me a little humility. I discharge my religious duties punctually, and find them wholesome and composing ; but I lack that holy unction, that spiritual imagination, by which more favored Christians have fitted themselves to converse with angels. I have too much body, I suppose, and too little soul. I own to you that

I cannot look forward to the hour of death as a happy release from the burden of the flesh. Life is pleasant to me; immortality tempts me not; the pure in heart delight me; but in the sentimental part of religion I feel myself dry and barren. I fear God, and desire to do his will; but I cannot love him as the saints have done; my spirit is too dull, too gross. I have often been unable to keep pace with you in your pious and lofty aspirations; and this softens my regret at quitting you; for you will be in better hands, my daughter."

Mrs. Gaunt was touched by her old friend's humility, and gave him both hands, with the tears in her eyes. But she said nothing; the subject was delicate; and really she could not honestly contradict him.

A day or two afterwards he brought his successor to the house; a man so remarkable that Mrs. Gaunt almost started at first sight of him. Born of an Italian mother, his skin was dark, and his eyes coal-black; yet his ample but symmetrical forehead was singularly white and delicate. Very tall and spare, and both face and figure were of that exalted kind which make ordinary beauty seem dross. In short, he was one of those ethereal priests the Roman Catholic Church produces every now and then by way of incredible contrast to the thickset peasants in black that form her staple. This Brother Leonard looked and moved like a being who had come down from some higher sphere to pay the world a very little visit, and be very kind and patient with it all the time.

He was presented to Mrs. Gaunt, and bowed calmly, coldly, and with a certain mixture of humility and superiority, and gave her but one tranquil glance, then turned his eyes inward as before.

Mrs. Gaunt, on the contrary, was almost fluttered at being presented so suddenly to one who seemed to her Religion embodied. She blushed, and looked timidly at him, and was anxious not to make an unfavorable impression.

She found it, however, very difficult to make any impression at all. Leonard had no small talk, and met her advances in that line with courteous monosyllables; and when she, upon this, turned and chatted with Father Francis, he did not wait for an opening to strike in, but sought a shelter from her commonplaces in his own thoughts.

Then Mrs. Gaunt yielded to her genuine impulse, and began to talk about the prospects of the Church, and what might be done to reconvert the British Isles to the true faith. Her cheek flushed, and her eye shone with the theme; and Francis smiled paternally; but the young priest drew back. Mrs. Gaunt saw in a moment that he disapproved of a woman meddling with so high a matter uninvited. If he had said so, she had spirit enough to have resisted; but the cold, lofty look of polite but grave disapproval dashed her courage and reduced her to silence.

She soon recovered so far as to be piqued. She gave her whole attention to Francis, and, on parting with her guests, she courtesied coldly to Leonard, and said to Francis, "Ah, my dear friend, I foresee I shall miss you terribly."

I am afraid this pretty speech was intended as a side cut at Leonard.

"But on the impassive ice the lightnings play."

Her new confessor retired, and left her with a sense of inferiority, which would have been pleasing to her woman's nature if Leonard himself had appeared less conscious of it, and had shown ever so little approval of herself; but, impressed upon her too sharply, it piqued and mortified her.

However, like a gallant champion, she awaited another encounter. She so rarely failed to please, she could not accept defeat.

Father Francis departed.

Mrs. Gaunt soon found that she really missed him. She had got into a habit of running to her confessor twice a week, and to her director nearly every day that he did not come of his own accord to her.

Her good sense showed her at once

she must not take up Brother Leonard's time in this way. She went a long time, for her, without confession; at last she sent a line to Leonard asking him when it would be convenient to him to confess her. Leonard wrote back to say that he received penitents in the chapel for two hours after matins every Monday, Tuesday, and Saturday.

This implied, first come, first served; and was rather galling to Mrs. Gaunt.

However, she rode one morning, with her groom behind her, and had to wait until an old woman in a red cloak and black bonnet was first disposed of. She confessed a heap. And presently the soft but chill tones of Brother Leonard broke in with these freezing words: "My daughter, excuse me; but confession is one thing, gossip about ourselves is another."

This distinction was fine, but fatal. The next minute the fair penitent was in her carriage, her eyes filled with tears of mortification.

"The man is a spiritual machine," said she; and her pride was mortified to the core.

In these happy days she used to open her heart to her husband; and she went so far as to say some bitter little feminine things of her new confessor before him.

He took no notice at first; but at last he said one day: "Well, I am of your mind; he is very poor company compared with that jovial old blade, Francis. But why so many words, Kate? You don't use to bite twice at a cherry; if the milk-sop is not to your taste, give him the sack and be d—d to him." And with this homely advice Squire Gaunt dismissed the matter and went to the stable to give his mare a ball.

So you see Mrs. Gaunt was discontented with Francis for not being an enthusiast, and nettled with Leonard for being one.

The very next Sunday morning she went and heard Leonard preach. His first sermon was an era in her life. After twenty years of pulpit prosers, there suddenly rose before her a sacred orator; an orator born; blest with that divine and thrilling eloquence that no heart can really resist. He prepared his great theme with art at first; but, once warm, it carried him away, and his hearers went with him like so many straws on the flood, and in the exercise of this great gift the whole man seemed transfigured; abroad, he was a languid, rather slouching priest, who crept about, a picture of delicate humility, but with a shade of meanness; for, religious prejudice apart, it is ignoble to sweep the wall in passing as he did, and eye the ground: but, once in the pulpit, his figure rose and swelled majestically, and seemed to fly over them all like a guardian angel's; his sallow cheek burned, his great Italian eye shot black lightning at the impenitent, and melted ineffably when he soothed the sorrowful.

Observe that great, mean, brown bird in the Zoölogical Gardens, which sits so tame on its perch, and droops and slouches like a drowsy duck! That is the great and soaring eagle. Who would believe it, to look at him? Yet all he wants is to be put in his right place instead of his wrong. He is not himself in man's cages, belonging to God's sky. Even so Leonard was abroad in the world, but at home in the pulpit; and so he somewhat crept and slouched about the parish, but soared like an eagle in his native air.

Mrs. Gaunt sat thrilled, enraptured, melted. She hung upon his words; and when they ceased, she still sat motionless, spell-bound; loath to believe that accents so divine could really come to an end.

Even whilst all the rest were dispersing, she sat quite still, and closed her eyes. For her soul was too high-strung now to endure the chit-chat she knew would attack her on the road home, — chit-chat that had been welcome enough coming home from other preachers.

And by this means she came hot and undiluted to her husband; she laid her white hand on his shoulder, and said, "O Griffith, I have heard the voice of God."

Griffith looked alarmed, and rather shocked than elated.

Mrs. Gaunt observed that, and tacked on, "Speaking by the lips of his servant." But she fired again the next moment, and said, "The grave hath given us back St. Paul in the Church's need; and I have heard him this day."

"Good heavens! where?"

"At St. Mary's Chapel."

Then Griffith looked very incredulous. Then she gushed out with, "What, because it is a small chapel, you think a great saint cannot be in it. Why, our Saviour was born in a stable, if you go to that."

"Well, but my dear, consider," said Griffith; "who ever heard of comparing a living man to St. Paul, for preaching? Why, he was an apostle, for one thing; and there are no apostles now-a-days. He made Felix tremble on his throne, and almost persuaded Whatsename, another heathen gentleman, to be a Christian."

"That is true," said the lady, thoughtfully; "but he sent one man that *we* know of to sleep. Catch Brother Leonard sending any man to sleep! And then nobody will ever say of *him* that he was long preaching."

"Why, I do say it," replied Griffith. "By the same token, I have been waiting dinner for you this half-hour, along of his preaching."

"Ah, that's because you did not hear him," retorted Mrs. Gaunt; "if you had, it would have seemed too short, and you would have forgotten all about your dinner for once."

Griffith made no reply. He even looked vexed at her enthusiastic admiration. She saw, and said no more. But after dinner she retired to the grove, and thought of the sermon and the preacher: thought of them all the more that she was discouraged from enlarging on them. And it would have been kinder, and also wiser, of Griffith, if he had encouraged her to let out her heart to him on this subject, although it did not happen to interest him. A husband should not chill an enthusiastic wife, and, above all, should never separate

himself from her favorite topic, when she loves him well enough to try and share it with him.

Mrs. Gaunt, however, though her feelings were quick, was not cursed with a sickly or irritable sensibility; nor, on the other hand, was she one of those lovely little bores who cannot keep their tongues off their favorite theme. She quietly let the subject drop for a whole week; but the next Sunday morning she asked her husband if he would do her a little favor.

"I'm more likely to say ay than nay," was the cheerful reply.

"It is just to go to chapel with me; and then you can judge for yourself."

Griffith looked rather sheepish at this proposal; and he said he could not very well do that.

"Why not, dearest, just for once?"

"Well, you see, parties run so high in this parish; and everything one does is noted. Why, if I was to go to chapel, they'd say directly, 'Look at Griffith Gaunt, he is so tied to his wife's apron he is going to give up the faith of his ancestors.'"

"The faith of your ancestors! That is a good jest. The faith of your grandfather at the outside: the faith of your ancestors was the faith of mine and me."

"Well, don't let us differ about a word," said Griffith; "you know what I mean. Did ever I ask you to go to church with me? and if I were to ask you, would you go?"

Mrs. Gaunt colored; but would not give in. "That is not the same thing," said she. "I do profess religion: you do not. You scarce think of God on week-days; and, indeed, never mention his name, except in the way of swearing; and on Sunday you go to church — for what? to doze before dinner, you know you do. Come now, with you 't is no question of religion, but just of nap or no nap: for Brother Leonard won't let you sleep, I warn you fairly."

Griffith shook his head. "You are too hard on me, wife. I know I am not so good as you are, and never shall be;

but that is not the fault of the Protestant faith, which hath reared so many holy men : and some of 'em our *ancestors* burnt alive, and will burn in hell themselves for the deed. But, look you, sweetheart, if I 'm not a saint I 'm a gentleman, and, say I wear my faith loose, I won't drag it in the dirt none the more for that. So you must excuse me."

Mrs. Gaunt was staggered ; and if Griffith had said no more, I think she would have withdrawn her request, and so the matter ended. But persons unversed in argument can seldom let well alone ; and this simple Squire must needs go on to say, " Besides, Kate, it would come to the parson's ears, and he is a friend of mine, you know. Why, I shall be sure to meet him tomorrow."

"Ay," retorted the lady, "by the cover-side. Well, when you do, tell him you refused your wife your company for fear of offending the religious views of a fox-hunting parson."

" Nay, Kate," said Griffith, " this is not to ask thy man to go with thee ; 't is to say go he must, willy nilly." With that he rose and rang the bell. " Order the chariot," said he, " I am to go with our dame."

Mrs. Gaunt's face beamed with gratified pride and affection.

The chariot came round, and Griffith handed his dame in. He then gave an involuntary sigh, and followed her with a hang-dog look.

She heard the sigh, and saw the look, and laid her hand quickly on his shoulder, and said, gently but coldly, " Stay you at home, my dear. We shall meet at dinner."

" As you will," said he, cheerfully : and they went their several ways. He congratulated himself on her clemency, and his own escape.

She went along, sorrowful at having to drink so great a bliss alone ; and thought it unkind and stupid of Griffith not to yield with a good grace if he could yield at all : and, indeed, women seem cleverer than men in this, that, when they resign their wills, they do it graciously and not by halves. Perhaps they are more accustomed to knock under ; and you know practice makes perfect.

But every smaller feeling was swept away by the preacher, and Mrs. Gaunt came home full of pious and lofty thoughts.

She found her husband seated at the dinner-table, with one turnip before him ; and even that was not comestible ; for it was his grandfather's watch, with a face about the size of a new-born child's. " Forty-five minutes past one, Kate," said he, ruefully.

" Well, why not bid them serve the dinner ? " said she with an air of consummate indifference.

" What, dine alone o' Sunday ? Why, you know I could n't eat a morsel without you, set opposite."

Mrs. Gaunt smiled affectionately. " Well then, my dear, we had better order dinner an hour later next Sunday."

" But that will upset the servants, and spoil their Sunday."

" And am I to be their slave ? " said Mrs. Gaunt, getting a little warm. " Dinner ! dinner ! What ? shall I starve my soul, by hurrying away from the oracles of God to a sirloin ? O these gross appetites ! how they deaden the immortal half, and wall out Heaven's music ! For my part, I wish there was no such thing as eating and drinking. 'T is like falling from Heaven down into the mud, to come back from such divine discourse and be greeted with ' Dinner ! dinner ! dinner ! ' "

The next Sunday, after waiting half an hour for her, Griffith began his dinner without her.

And this time, on her arrival, instead of remonstrating with her, he excused himself. " Nothing," said he, " upsets a man's temper like waiting for his dinner."

" Well, but you have not waited."

" Yes, I did, a good half-hour. Till I could wait no longer."

" Well, dear, if I were you I would not have waited at all, or else waited till your wife came home."

"Ah, dame, that is all very well for you to say. You could live on hearing of sermons and smelling to rosebuds. You don't know what 't is to be a hungry man."

The next Sunday he sat sadly down, and finished his dinner without her. And she came home and sat down to half-empty dishes; and ate much less than she used when she had him to keep her company in it.

Griffith, looking on disconsolate, told her she was more like a bird pecking than a Christian eating of a Sunday.

"No matter, child," said she; "so long as my soul is filled with the bread of Heaven."

Leonard's eloquence suffered no diminution, either in quantity or quality; and, after a while, Gaunt gave up his rule of never dining abroad on the Sunday. If his wife was not punctual, his stomach was; and he had not the same temptation to dine at home he used to have.

And indeed, by degrees, instead of quietly enjoying his wife's company on that sweet day, he got to see less of her than on the week-days.

CHAPTER XVI.

YOUR mechanical preacher flings his words out happy-go-lucky; but the pulpit orator, like every other orator, feels his people's pulse as he speaks, and vibrates with them, and they with him.

So Leonard soon discovered he had a great listener in Mrs. Gaunt: she was always there whenever he preached, and her rapt attention never flagged. Her gray eyes never left his face, and, being upturned, the full orbs came out in all their grandeur, and seemed an angel's, come down from heaven to hear him: for, indeed, to a very dark man, as Leonard was, the gentle radiance of a true Saxon beauty seems always more or less angelic.

By degrees this face became a help to the orator. In preaching he looked sometimes to it for sympathy, and lo, it was sure to be melting with sympathy. Was he led on to higher or deeper thoughts than most of his congregation could understand, he looked to this face to understand him; and lo, it had quite understood him, and was beaming with intelligence.

From a help and an encouragement it became a comfort and a delight to him.

On leaving the pulpit and cooling, he remembered its owner was no angel, but a woman of the world, and had put him frivolous questions.

The illusion, however, was so beautiful, that Leonard, being an imaginative man, was unwilling to dispel it by coming into familiar contact with Mrs. Gaunt. So he used to make his assistant visit her, and receive her when she came to confess, which was very rarely; for she was discouraged by her first reception.

Brother Leonard lived in a sort of dwarf monastery, consisting of two cottages, an oratory, and a sepulchre. The two latter were old, but the cottages had been built expressly for him and another seminary priest who had been invited from France. Inside, these cottages were little more than cells; only the bigger had a kitchen which was a glorious place compared with the parlor; for it was illuminated with bright pewter plates, copper vessels, brass candlesticks, and a nice clean woman, with a plain gown kilted over a quilted silk petticoat; Betty Scarf, an old servant of Mrs. Gaunt's, who had married, and was now the Widow Gough.

She stood at the gate one day, as Mrs. Gaunt drove by; and courtesied, all beaming.

Mrs. Gaunt stopped the carriage, and made some kind and patronizing inquiries about her; and it ended in Betty asking her to come in and see her place. Mrs. Gaunt looked a little shy at that, and did not move. "Nay, they are both abroad till supper time," said Betty, reading her in a moment by the light of sex. Then Mrs. Gaunt smiled, and got out of her carriage. Betty took her in and showed her everything in doors and out. Mrs. Gaunt looked mighty demure and dignified, but scanned everything closely, only without seeming too curious.

The cold gloom of the parlor struck her. She shuddered, and said, "This would give me the vapors. But, doubtless, angels come and brighten it for *him*."

"Not always," said Betty. "I do see him with his head in his hand by the hour, and hear him sigh ever so loud as I pass the door. Why, one day he was fain to have me and my spinning-wheel aside him. Says he, 'Let me hear thy busy wheel, and see thee ply it.' 'And welcome,' says I. So I sat in his room, and span, and he sat a gloating of me as if he had never seen a woman spin hemp afore (he is a very simple man): and presently says he — but what signifies what *he* said?"

"Nay, Betty; if you please! I am much interested in him. He preaches so divinely."

"Ay," said Betty, "that's his gift. But a poor trencher-man; and I declare I 'm ashamed to eat all the vittels that are eaten here, and me but a woman."

"But what did he say to you that time?" asked Mrs. Gaunt, a little impatiently.

Betty cudgelled her memory. "Well, says he, 'My daughter,' (the poor soul always calls me his daughter, and me old enough to be his mother mostly,) says he, 'how comes it that you are never wearied, nor cast down, and yet you but serve a sinner like yourself; but I do often droop in my Master's service, and He is the Lord of heaven and earth?' Says I, 'I ll tell ye, sir: because ye don't eat enough o' vittels.'"

"What an answer!"

"Why, 't is the truth, dame. And says I, 'If I was to be always fasting, like as you be, d' ye think I should have the heart to work from morn till night?' Now, wasn't I right?"

"I don't know till I hear what answer he made," said Mrs. Gaunt, with mean caution.

"O, he shook his head, and said he ate mortal food enow, (poor simple body!) but drank too little of grace divine. That were his word."

Mrs. Gaunt was a good deal struck and affected by this revelation, and astonished at the slighting tone Betty took in speaking of so remarkable a man. The saying that "No man is a hero to his valet" was not yet current, or perhaps she would have been less surprised at that.

"Alas! poor man," said she, "and is it so? To hear him, I thought his soul was borne up night and day by angels' pinions — "

The widow interrupted her. "Ay, you hear him preach, and it is like God's trumpet mostly, and so much I say for him in all companies. But I see him directly after; he totters in to this very room, and sits him down pale and panting, and one time like to swoon, and another all for crying, and then he is ever so dull and sad for the whole afternoon."

"And nobody knows this but you? You have got my old petticoat still, I see. I must look you up another."

"You are very good, dame, I am sure. 'T will not come amiss; I 've only this for Sundays and all. No, my lady, not a soul but me and you. I 'm not one as tells tales out of doors, but I don't mind you, dame; you are my old mistress, and a discreet woman. 'T will go no further than your ear."

Mrs. Gaunt told her she might rely on that. The widow then inquired after Mrs. Gaunt's little girl, and admired her dress, and described her own ailments, and poured out a continuous stream of topics bearing no affinity to each other except that they were all of them not worth mentioning. And all the while she thus discoursed, Mrs. Gaunt's thoughtful eyes looked straight over the chatterbox's white cap, and explored vacancy; and by and by she broke the current of twaddle with the majestic air of a camelopard marching across a running gutter.

"Betsy Gough," said she, "I am thinking."

Mrs. Gough was struck dumb by an announcement so singular.

"I have heard, and I have read, that great and pious and learned men are often to seek in little simple things, such as plain bodies have at their fingers' ends. So, now, if you and I could only teach him something for all he has taught us! And, to be sure, we ought to be kind to him if we can; for O Betty, my woman, 't is a poor vanity to go and despise the great, and the learned, and the sainted, because forsooth we find them out in some one little weakness, — we that are all made up of weaknesses and defects. So, now, I sit me down in his very chair, so. And sit you there. Now let us, you and me, look at his room quietly, all over, and see what is wanting."

"First and foremost methinks this window should be filled with geraniums and jessamine and so forth. With all his learning perhaps he has to be taught, the color of flowers and golden green leaves, with the sun shining through, how it soothes the eye and relieves the spirits; yet every woman born knows that. Then do but see this bare table! a purple cloth on that, I say."

"Which he will fling it out of the window, I say."

"Nay, for I 'll embroider a cross in the middle with gold braid. Then a rose-colored blind would not be amiss; and there must be a good mirror facing the window; but, indeed, if I had my way, I 'd paint these horrid walls the first thing."

"How you run on, dame! Bless your heart, you 'd turn his den into a palace; he won't suffer that. He is all for self-mortification, poor simple soul."

"O, not all at once, I did not mean," said Mrs. Gaunt; "but by little and little, you know. We must begin with the flowers: God made them; and so to be sure he will not spurn *them.*"

Betty began to enter into the plot. "Ay, ay," said she: "the flowers first; and so creep on. But naught will avail to make a man of him so long as he eats but of eggs and garden-stuff, like the beasts of the field, 'that to-day are, and to-morrow are cast into the oven.'"

Mrs. Gaunt smiled at this ambitious attempt of the widow to apply Scripture. Then she said, rather timidly, "Could you make his eggs into omelets? and so pound in a little meat with your small herbs; I dare say he would be none the wiser, and he so bent on high and heavenly things."

"You may take your oath of that."

"Well, then. And I shall send you some stock from the castle, and you can cook his vegetables in good strong gravy, unbeknown."

The Widow Gough chuckled aloud.

"But stay," said Mrs. Gaunt; "for us to play the woman so, and delude a saint for his mere bodily weal, will it not be a sin, and a sacrilege to boot?"

"Let that flea stick in the wall," said Betty, contemptuously. "Find you the meat, and I 'll find the deceit: for he is as poor as a rat into the bargain. Nay, nay, God Almighty will' never have the heart to burn us two for such a trifle. Why 't is no more than cheating a froward child into taking 's physic."

Mrs. Gaunt got into her carriage and went home, thinking all the way. What she had heard filled her with feelings strangely but sweetly composed of veneration and pity. In that Leonard was a great orator and a high-minded priest, she revered him; in that he was solitary and sad, she pitied him; in that he wanted common sense, she felt like a mother, and must take him under her wing. All true women love to protect; perhaps it is a part of the great maternal element: but to protect a man, and yet look up to him, this is delicious. It satisfies their double craving; it takes them by both breasts, as the saying is.

Leonard, in truth, was one of those high-strung men who pay for their periods of religious rapture by hours of melancholy. This oscillation of the spirits in extraordinary men appears to be more or less a law of nature;

and this the Widow Gough was not aware of.

The very next Sunday, while he was preaching, she and Mrs. Gaunt's gardener were filling his bow-window with flower-pots, the flowers in full bloom and leaf. The said window was large and had a broad sill outside, and inside, one of the old-fashioned high window-seats that follow the shape of the window. Mrs. Gaunt, who did nothing by halves, sent up a cart-load of flower-pots, and Betty and the gardener arranged at least eighty of them, small and great, inside and outside the window.

When Leonard returned from preaching, Betty was at the door to watch. He came past the window with his hands on his breast, and his eyes on the ground, and never saw the flowers in his own window. Betty was disgusted. However, she followed him stealthily as he went to his room, and she heard a profound "Ah!" burst from him.

She bustled in and found him standing in a rapture, with the blood mantling in his pale cheeks, and his dark eyes glowing.

"Now blessed be the heart that hath conceived this thing, and the hand that hath done it," said he. "My poor room, it is a bower of roses, all beauty and fragrance."

And he sat down, inhaling them and looking at them; and a dreamy, tender complacency crept over his heart, and softened his noble features exquisitely.

Widow Gough, red with gratified pride, stood watching him, and admiring him; but, indeed, she often admired him, though she had got into a way of decrying him.

But at last she lost patience at his want of curiosity; that being a defect she was free from herself.

"Ye don't ask me who sent them," said she, reproachfully.

"Nay, nay," said he; "prithee do not tell me: let me divine."

"Divine, then," said Betty, roughly. "Which I suppose you means 'guess.'"

"Nay, but let me be quiet awhile," said he, imploringly; "let me sit down and fancy that I am a holy man, and some angel hath turned my cave into a Paradise."

"No more an angel than I am," said the practical widow. "But, now I think on 't, y' are not to know who 't was. Them as sent them they bade me hold my tongue."

This was not true; but Betty, being herself given to unwise revelations and superfluous secrecy, chose suddenly to assume that this business was to be clandestine.

The priest turned his eye inwards and meditated.

"I see who it is," said he, with an air of absolute conviction. "It must be the lady who comes always when I preach, and her face like none other; it beams with divine intelligence. I will make her all the return we poor priests can make to our benefactors. I will pray for her soul here among the flowers God has made, and she has given his servant to glorify his dwelling. My daughter, you may retire."

This last with surprising, gentle dignity; so Betty went off rather abashed, and avenged herself by adulterating the holy man's innutritious food with Mrs. Gaunt's good gravy; while he prayed fervently for her eternal weal among the flowers she had given him.

Now Mrs. Gaunt, after eight years of married life, was too sensible and dignified a woman to make a romantic mystery out of nothing. She concealed the gravy, because there secrecy was necessary; but she never dreamed of hiding that she had sent her spiritual adviser a load of flowers. She did not tell her neighbors, for she was not ostentatious; but she told her husband, who grunted, but did not object.

But Betty's nonsense lent an air of romance and mystery that was well adapted to captivate the imagination of a young, ardent, and solitary spirit like Leonard.

He would have called on the lady he suspected, and thanked her for her kindness. But this, he feared, would be unwelcome, since she chose to be his unknown benefactress. It would be ill taste in him to tell her he had found her out: it might offend her sensibility, and then she would draw in.

He kept his gratitude, therefore, to himself, and did not cool it by utterance. He often sat among the flowers, in a sweet revery, enjoying their color and fragrance; and sometimes he would shut his eyes, and call up the angelical face, with great, celestial, upturned orbs, and fancy it among her own flowers, and the queen of them all.

These day-dreams did not at that time interfere with his religious duties. They only took the place of those occasional hours when, partly by the reaction consequent on great religious fervor, partly by exhaustion of the body weakened by fasts, partly by the natural delicacy of his fibre and the tenderness of his disposition, his soul used to be sad.

By and by these languid hours, sad no longer, became sweet and dear to him. He had something so interesting to think of, to dream about. He had a Madonna that cared for him in secret.

She was human; but good, beautiful, and wise. She came to his sermons, and understood every word.

"And she knows me better than I know myself," said he; "since I had these flowers from her hand, I am another man."

One day he came into his room and found two watering-pots there. One was large and had a rose to it, the other small and with a plain spout.

"Ah!" said he; and colored with delight. He called Betty, and asked her who had brought them.

"How should I know?" said she, roughly. "I dare say they dropped from heaven. See, there is a cross painted on 'em in gold letters."

"And so there is!" said Leonard, and crossed himself.

"That means nobody is to use them but you, I trow," said Betty, rather crossly.

The priest's cheek colored high. "I will use them this instant," said he. "I will revive my drooping children as they have revived me." And he caught up a watering-pot with ardor.

"What, with the sun hot upon 'em?" screamed Betty. "Well, saving your presence, you *are* a simple man."

"Why, good Betty, 't is the sun that makes them faint," objected the priest, timidly, and with the utmost humility of manner, though Betty's tone would have irritated a smaller mind.

"Well, well," said she, softening; "but ye see it never rains with a hot sun, and the flowers they know that; and look to be watered after Nature, or else they take it amiss. You, and all your sort, sir, you think to be stronger than Nature; you do fast and pray all day, and won't look at a woman like other men; and now you wants to water the very flowers at noon!"

"Betty," said Leonard smiling, "I yield to thy superior wisdom, and I will water them at morn and eve. In truth we have all much to learn: let us try and teach one another as kindly as we can."

"I wish you 'd teach me to be as humble as you be," blurted out Betty, with something very like a sob: "and more respectful to my betters," added she, angrily.

Watering the flowers she had given him became a solace and a delight to the solitary priest: he always watered them with his own hands, and felt quite paternal over them.

One evening Mrs. Gaunt rode by with Griffith, and saw him watering them. His tall figure, graceful, though inclined to stoop, bent over them with feminine delicacy; and the simple act, which would have been nothing in vulgar hands, seemed to Mrs. Gaunt so earnest, tender, and delicate in him, that her eyes filled, and she murmured, "Poor Brother Leonard!"

"Why, what 's wrong with him now?" asked Griffith, a little peevishly.

"That was him watering the flowers."

"O, is that all?" said Griffith, carelessly.

Leonard said to himself, "I go too little abroad among my people." He made a little round, and it ended in Hernshaw Castle.

Mrs. Gaunt was out.

He looked disappointed; so the servant suggested that perhaps she was in the Dame's Haunt: he pointed to the grove.

Leonard followed his direction, and soon found himself, for the first time, in that sombre, solemn retreat.

It was a hot summer day, and the grove was delicious. It was also a place well suited to the imaginative and religious mind of the Italian.

He walked slowly to and fro, in religious meditation. Indeed, he had nearly thought out his next sermon, when his meditative eye happened to fall on a terrestrial object that startled and thrilled him. Yet it was only a lady's glove. It lay at the foot of a rude wooden seat beneath a gigantic pine.

He stooped and picked it up. He opened the little fingers, and called up in fancy the white and tapering hand that glove could fit. He laid the glove softly on his own palm, and eyed it with dreamy tenderness. "So this is the hand that hath solaced my loneliness," said he : "a hand fair as that angelical face, and sweet as the kind heart that doeth good by stealth."

Then, forgetting for a moment, as lofty spirits will, the difference between *meum* and *tuum*, he put the little glove in his bosom, and paced thoughtfully home through the woods, that were separated from the grove only by one meadow : and so he missed the owner of the glove, for she had returned home while he was meditating in her favorite haunt.

Leonard, amongst his other accomplishments, could draw and paint with no mean skill. In one of those hours that used to be of melancholy, but now were hours of dreamy complacency, he took out his pencils and endeavored to sketch the inspired face that he had learned to preach to, and now to dwell on with gratitude.

Clearly as he saw it before him, he could not reproduce it to his own satisfaction. After many failures he got very near the mark : yet still something was wanting.

Then, as a last resource, he actually took his sketch to church with him, and in preaching made certain pauses, and, with a very few touches, perfected the likeness ; then, on his return home, threw himself on his knees and prayed forgiveness of God with many sighs and tears, and hid the sacrilegious drawing out of his own sight.

Two days after, he was at work coloring it ; and the hours flew by like minutes, as he laid the mellow, melting tints on with infinite care and delicacy. *Labor ipse voluptas.*

Mrs. Gaunt heard Leonard had called on her in person. She was pleased at that, and it encouraged her to carry out her whole design.

Accordingly, one afternoon, when she knew Leonard would be at vespers, she sent on a loaded pony-cart, and followed it on horseback.

Then it was all hurry-skurry with Betty and her, to get their dark deeds done before their victim's return.

These good creatures set the mirror opposite the flowery window, and so made the room a very bower. They fixed a magnificent crucifix of ivory and gold over the mantel-piece, and they took away his hassock of rushes and substituted a *prie-dieu* of rich crimson velvet. All that remained was to put their blue cover, with its golden cross, on the table. To do this, however, they had to remove the priest's papers and things : they were covered with a cloth. Mrs. Gaunt felt them under it.

"But perhaps he will be angry if we move his papers," said she.

"Not he," said Betty. "He has no secrets from God or man."

"Well, *I* won't take it on me," said Mrs. Gaunt, merrily. "I leave that to you." And she turned her back and settled the mirror, officiously, leaving all the other responsibilities to Betty.

The sturdy widow laughed at her

scruples, and whipped off the cloth without ceremony. But soon her laugh stopped mighty short, and she uttered an exclamation.

"What is the matter?" said Mrs. Gaunt, turning her head sharply round.

"A wench's glove, as I 'm a living sinner," groaned Betty.

A poor little glove lay on the table; and both women eyed it like basilisks a moment. Then Betty pounced on it and examined it with the fierce keenness of her sex in such conjunctures, searching for a name or a clew.

Owing to this rapidity, Mrs. Gaunt, who stood at some distance, had not time to observe the button on the glove, or she would have recognized her own property.

"He have had a hussy with him unbeknown," said Betty, "and she have left her glove. 'T is easy to get in by the window and out again. Only let me catch her! I 'll tear her eyes out, and give him my mind. I 'll have no young hussies creeping in an' out where I be."

Thus spoke the simple woman, venting her coarse domestic jealousy.

The gentlewoman said nothing, but a strange feeling traversed her heart for the first time in her life.

It was a little chill, it was a little ache, it was a little sense of sickness; none of these violent, yet all distinct. And all about what? After this curious, novel spasm at the heart, she began to be ashamed of herself for having had such a feeling.

Betty held her out the glove: and she recognized it directly, and turned as red as fire.

"You know whose 't is?" said Betty, keenly.

Mrs. Gaunt was on her guard in a moment. "Why, Betty," said she, "for shame! 't is some penitent hath left her glove after confession. Would you belie a good man for that? O, fie!"

"Humph!" said Betty, doubtfully. "Then why keep it under cover? Now you can read, dame; let us see if there is n't a letter or so writ by the hand as owns this very glove."

Mrs. Gaunt declined, with cold dignity, to pry into Brother Leonard's manuscripts.

Her eye, however, darted sidelong at them, and told another tale; and, if she had been there alone, perhaps the daughter of Eve would have predominated.

Betty, inflamed by the glove, rummaged the papers in search of female handwriting. She could tell that from a man's, though she could not read either.

But there is a handwriting that the most ignorant can read at sight; and so Betty's researches were not in vain: hidden under several sheets of paper, she found a picture. She gave but one glance at it, and screamed out: "There, did n't I tell you? Here she is! the brazen, red-haired — LAWK A DAISY! WHY, 'T IS YOURSELF."

CHAPTER XVII.

"ME!" cried Mrs. Gaunt, in amazement: then she ran to the picture, and at sight of it every other sentiment gave way for a moment to gratified vanity. "Nay," said she, beaming and blushing, "I was never half so beautiful. What heavenly eyes!"

"The fellows to 'em be in your own head, dame, this moment."

"Seeing is believing," said Mrs. Gaunt, gayly, and in a moment she was at the priest's mirror, and inspected her eyes minutely, cocking her head this way and that. She ended by shaking it, and saying, "No. He has flattered them prodigiously."

"Not a jot," said Betty. "If you could see yourself in chapel, you do turn 'em up just so, and the white shows all round." Then she tapped the picture with her finger: "O them eyes! they were never made for the good of his soul, — poor simple man!"

Betty said this with sudden gravity: and now Mrs. Gaunt began to feel very awkward. "Mr. Gaunt would give fifty pounds for this," said she, to gain time: and, while she uttered that sentence, she whipped on her armor.

"I 'll tell you what I think," said she,

calmly, "he wished to paint a Madonna ; and he must take some woman's face to aid his fancy. All the painters are driven to that. So he just took the best that came to hand, and that is not saying much, for this is a rare ill-favored parish : and he has made an angel of her, a very angel. There, hide Me away again, or . I shall long for Me — to show to my husband. I must be going ; I would n't be caught here *now* for a pension."

"Well, if ye must," said Betty ; "but when will ye come again ? " (She had n't got the petticoat yet.)

"Humph ! " said Mrs. Gaunt, " I have done all I can for him ; and perhaps more than I ought. But there 's nothing to hinder you from coming to me. I 'll be as good as my word ; and I have an old Paduasoy, besides ; you can perhaps do something with it."

"You are very good, dame," said Betty, courtesying.

Mrs. Gaunt then hurried away, and Betty looked after her very expressively, and shook her head. She had a female instinct that some mischief or other was brewing.

Mrs. Gaunt went home in a revery.

At the gate she found her husband, and asked him to take a turn in the garden with her.

He complied ; and she intended to tell him a portion, at least, of what had occurred. She began timidly, after this fashion : " My dear, Brother Leonard is *so* grateful for your flowers," and then hesitated.

" I 'm sure he is very welcome," said Griffith. " Why does n't he sup with us, and be sociable, as Father Francis used ? Invite him ; let him know he will be welcome."

Mrs. Gaunt blushed ; and objected. " He never calls on us."

" Well, well, every man to his taste," said Griffith, indifferently, and proceeded to talk to her about his farm, and a sorrel mare with a white mane and tail that he had seen, and thought it would suit her.

She humored him, and affected a great interest in all this, and had not the courage to force the other topic on.

Next Sunday morning, after a very silent breakfast, she burst out, almost violently, " Griffith, I shall go to the parish church with you, and then we will dine together afterwards."

" You don't mean it, Kate," said he, delighted.

" Ay, but I do. Although you refused to go to chapel with me."

They went to church together, and Mrs. Gaunt's appearance there created no small sensation. She was conscious of that, but hid it, and conducted herself admirably. Her mind seemed entirely given to the service, and to a dull sermon that followed.

But at dinner she broke out, " Well, give me your church for a sleeping draught. You all slumbered, more or less : those that survived the drowsy, droning prayers sank under the dry, dull, dreary discourse. You snored, for one."

" Nay, I hope not, my dear."

" You did then, as loud as your bass fiddle."

" And you sat there and let me ! " said Griffith, reproachfully.

" To be sure I did. I was too good a wife, and too good a Christian, to wake you. Sleep is good for the body, and twaddle is not good for the soul. I 'd have slept too, if I could ; but with me going to chapel, I 'm not used to sleep at that time o' day. You can't sleep, and Brother Leonard speaking."

In the afternoon came Mrs. Gough, all in her best. Mrs. Gaunt had her into her bedroom, and gave her the promised petticoat, and the old Paduasoy gown ; and then, as ladies will, when their hand is once in, added first one thing, then another, till there was quite a large bundle.

" But how is it you are here so soon ? " asked Mrs. Gaunt.

" O, we had next to no sermon today. He could n't make no hand of it : dawdled on a bit ; then gave us his blessing, and bundled us out."

" Then I 've lost nothing," said Mrs. Gaunt.

"Not you. Well, I don't know. Mayhap if you had been there he'd have preached his best. But la! we warn't worth it."

At this conjecture Mrs. Gaunt's face burned, but she said nothing: only she cut the interview short, and dismissed Betty with her bundle.

As Betty crossed the landing, Mrs. Gaunt's new lady's-maid, Caroline Ryder, stepped accidentally, on purpose, out of an adjoining room, in which she had been lurking, and lifted her black brows in affected surprise. "What, are you going to strip the house, my woman?" said she, quietly.

Betty put down the bundle, and set her arms akimbo. "There is none on 't stolen, any way," said she.

Caroline's black eyes flashed fire at this, and her cheek lost color; but she parried the innuendo skilfully. "Taking my perquisites on the sly, — that is not so very far from stealing."

"O, there 's plenty left for you, my fine lady. Besides, you don't want *her;* you can set your cap at the master, they say. I 'm too old for that, and too honest into the bargain."

"Too ill-favored, you mean, ye old harridan," said Ryder, contemptuously.

But, for reasons hereafter to be dealt with, Betty's thrust went home: and the pair were mortal enemies from that hour.

Mrs. Gaunt came down from her room discomposed: from that she became restless and irritable; so much so, indeed, that at last Mr. Gaunt told her, good-humoredly enough, if going to church made her ill (meaning peevish), she had better go to chapel. "You are right," said she, "and so I will."

The next Sunday she was at her post in good time.

The preacher cast an anxious glance around to see if she was there. Her quick eye saw that glance, and it gave her a demure pleasure.

This day he was more eloquent than ever: and he delivered a beautiful passage concerning those who do good in secret. In uttering these eloquent sen-

tences his cheek glowed, and he could not deny himself the pleasure of looking down at the lovely face that was turned up to him. Probably his look was more expressive than he intended: the celestial eyes sank under it, and were abashed, and the fair cheek burned: and then so did Leonard's at that.

Thus, subtly yet effectually, did these two minds communicate in a crowd that never noticed nor suspected the delicate interchange of sentiment that was going on under their very eyes.

In a general way compliments did not seduce Mrs. Gaunt: she was well used to them, for one thing. But to be praised in that sacred edifice, and from the pulpit, and by such an orator as Leonard, and to be praised in words so sacred and beautiful that the ears around her drank them with delight, — all this made her heart beat, and filled her with soft and sweet complacency.

And then to be thanked in public, yet, as it were, clandestinely, this gratified the furtive tendency of woman.

There was no irritability this afternoon; but a gentle radiance that diffused itself on all around, and made the whole household happy, — especially Griffith, whose pipe she filled, for once, with her own white hand, and talked dogs, horses, calves, hinds, cows, politics, markets, hay, to please him: and seemed interested in them all.

But the next day she changed: ill at ease, and out of spirits, and could settle to nothing.

It was very hot for one thing: and, altogether, a sort of lassitude and distaste for everything overpowered her, and she retired into the grove, and sat languidly on a seat with half-closed eyes.

But her meditations were no longer so calm and speculative as heretofore. She found her mind constantly recurring to one person, and, above all, to the discovery she had made of her portrait in his possession. She had turned it off to Betty Gough; but here, in her calm solitude and umbrageous twilight, her mind crept out of its cave, like wild and timid things at dusk, and whispered to her heart that Leonard perhaps admired her more than was safe or prudent.

Then this alarmed her, yet caused her a secret complacency: and that, her furtive satisfaction, alarmed her still more.

Now, while she sat thus absorbed, she heard a gentle footstep coming near. She looked up, and there was Leonard close to her; standing meekly, with his arms crossed upon his bosom.

His being there so pat upon her thoughts scared her out of her habitual self-command. She started up, with a faint cry, and stood panting, as if about to fly, with her beautiful eyes turned large upon him.

He put forth a deprecating hand, and soothed her. "Forgive me, madam," said he; "I have unawares intruded on your privacy; I will retire."

"Nay," said she, falteringly, "you are welcome. But no one comes here; so I was startled." Then, recovering herself, "Excuse my ill-manners. 'T is so strange that you should come to me here, of all places."

"Nay, my daughter," said the priest, "not so very strange: contemplative minds love such places. Calling one day to see you, I found this sweet and solemn grove; the like I never saw in England: and to-day I returned in hopes to profit by it. Do but look around at these tall columns; how calm, how reverend! 'T is God's own temple, not built with hands."

"Indeed it is," said Mrs. Gaunt, earnestly. Then, like a woman as she was, "So you came to see my trees, not me."

Leonard blushed. "I did not design to return without paying my respects to her who owns this temple, and is worthy of it; nay, I beg you not to think me ungrateful."

His humility and gentle but earnest voice made Mrs. Gaunt ashamed of her petulance. She smiled sweetly, and looked pleased. However, erelong, she attacked him again. "Father Francis used to visit us often," said she. "He made friends with my husband, too.

And I never lacked an adviser while he was here."

Leonard looked so confused at this second reproach that Mrs. Gaunt's heart began to yearn. However, he said humbly that Francis was a secular priest, whereas he was convent-bred. He added, that by his years and experience Francis was better fitted to advise persons of her age and sex, in matters secular, than he was. He concluded timidly that he was ready, nevertheless, to try and advise her; but could not, in such matters, assume the authority that belongs to age and knowledge of the world.

"Nay, nay," said she, earnestly, "guide and direct my soul, and I am content."

He said, yes! that was his duty and his right.

Then, after a certain hesitation, which at once let her know what was coming, he began to thank her, with infinite grace and sweetness, for her kindness to him.

She looked him full in the face, and said she was not aware of any kindness she had shown him worth speaking of.

"That but shows," said he, "how natural it is to you to do acts of goodness. My poor room is a very bower now, and I am happy in it. I used to feel very sad there at times; but your hand has cured me."

Mrs. Gaunt colored beautifully. "You make me ashamed," said she. "Things are come to a pass indeed, if a lady may not send a few flowers and things to her spiritual father without being thanked for it. And, O, sir, what are earthly flowers compared with those blossoms of the soul you have shed so liberally over us? Our immortal parts were all asleep when you came here and wakened them by the fire of your words. Eloquence! 't was a thing I had read of, but never heard, nor thought to hear. Methought the orators and poets of the Church were all in their graves this thousand years, and she must go all the way to heaven that would hear the soul's true music. But I know better now."

Leonard colored high with pleasure. "Such praise from you is too sweet," he muttered. "I must not court it. The heart is full of vanity." And he deprecated further eulogy, by a movement of the hand extremely refined, and, in fact, rather feminine.

Deferring to his wish Mrs. Gaunt glided to other matters, and was naturally led to speak of the prospects of their Church, and the possibility of re-converting these islands. This had been the dream of her young heart; but marriage and maternity, and the universal coldness with which the subject had been received, had chilled her so, that of late years she had almost ceased to speak of it. Even Leonard, on a former occasion, had listened coldly to her; but now his heart was open to her. He was, in fact, quite as enthusiastic on this point as ever she had been; and then he had digested his aspirations into clearer forms. Not only had he resolved that Great Britain must be reconverted, but had planned the way to do it. His cheek glowed, his eyes gleamed, and he poured out his hopes and his plans before her with an eloquence that few mortals could have resisted.

As for this, his hearer, she was quite carried away by it. She joined herself to his plans on the spot; she begged, with tears in her eyes, to be permitted to support him in this great cause. She devoted to it her substance, her influence, and every gift that God had given her: the hours passed like minutes in this high converse; and when the tinkling of the little bell at a distance summoned him to vespers, he left her with a gentle regret he scarcely tried to conceal, and she went slowly in like one in a dream, and the world seemed dead to her forever.

Nevertheless, when Mrs. Ryder, combing out her long hair, gave one inadvertent tug, the fair enthusiast came back to earth, and asked her, rather sharply, who her head was running on.

Ryder, a very handsome young woman, with fine black eyes, made no reply, but only drew her breath audibly hard.

I do not very much wonder at that, nor at my having to answer that question for Mrs. Ryder. For her head was at that moment running, like any other woman's, on the man she was in love with.

And the man she was in love with was the husband of the lady whose hair she was combing, and who put her that curious question — plump.

CHAPTER XVIII.

THIS Caroline Ryder was a character almost impossible to present so as to enable the reader to recognize her should she cross his path; so great was the contradiction between what she was and what she seemed, and so perfect was the imitation.

She looked a respectable young spinster, with a grace of manner beyond her station, and a decency and propriety of demeanor that inspired respect.

She was a married woman, separated from her husband by mutual consent; and she had had many lovers, each of whom she had loved ardently — for a little while. She was a woman that brought to bear upon foolish, culpable loves a mental power that would have adorned the woolsack.

The moment prudence or waning inclination made it advisable to break with the reigning favorite, she set to work to cool him down by deliberate coldness, sullenness, insolence; and generally succeeded. But if he was incurable, she never hesitated as to her course; she smiled again on him, and looked out for another place: being an invaluable servant, she got one directly; and was off to fresh pastures.

A female rake; but with the air of a very prude.

A woman, however cunning and resolute, always plays this game at one great disadvantage; for instance, one day, Caroline Ryder, finding herself unable to shake off a certain boyish lover, whom she had won and got terribly

"Mrs. Ryder, combing out her long hair, gave one inadvertent tug." — Page 84.

tired of, retired from her place, and went home, and left him blubbering. But by and by, in a retired village, she deposited an angelic babe of the female sex, with fair hair and blue eyes, the very image of her abandoned Cherubin. Let me add, as indicating the strange force of her character, that she concealed this episode from Cherubin and all the rest of the world ; and was soon lady's maid again in another county, as demure as ever, and ripe for fresh adventures.

But her secret maternity added a fresh trait to her character ; she became mercenary.

This wise, silly, prudent, coquettish demon was almost perfect in the family relations : an excellent daughter, a good sister, and a devoted mother. And so are tigresses, and wicked Jewesses.

Item — the decency and propriety of her demeanor were not all hypocrisy, but half hypocrisy, and half inborn and instinctive good taste and good sense.

As dangerous a creature to herself and others as ever tied on a bonnet.

On her arrival at Hernshaw Castle she cast her eyes round to see what there was to fall in love with ; and observed the gamekeeper, Tom Leicester. She gave him a smile or two that won his heart ; but there she stopped : for soon the ruddy cheek, brown eyes, manly proportions, and square shoulders of her master attracted this connoisseur in male beauty. And then his manner was so genial and hearty, with a smile for everybody. Mrs. Ryder eyed him demurely day by day, and often opened a window slyly to watch him unseen.

From that she got to throwing herself in his way ; and this with such art that he never discovered it, though he fell in with her about the house six times as often as he met his wife or any other inmate.

She had already studied his character, and, whether she arranged to meet him full or to cross him, it was always with a courtesy and a sunshiny smile ; he smiled on her in his turn, and felt a certain pleasure at sight of her : for he loved to see people bright and cheerful about him.

Then she did, of her own accord, what no other master on earth would have persuaded her to do : looked over his linen ; sewed on buttons for him ; and sometimes the artful jade deliberately cut a button off a clean shirt, and then came to him and sewed it on during wear. This brought about a contact none knew better than she how to manage to a man's undoing. The seeming timidity that fills the whole eloquent person, and tempts a man to attack by telling him he is powerful, — the drooping lashes that hint, "Ah, do not take advantage of this situation, or the consequences may be terrible, and will certainly be delicious," — the delicate and shy, yet lingering touch, — the twenty stitches where nine would be plenty, — the one coy, but tender glance at parting, — all this soft witchcraft beset Griffith Gaunt, and told on him ; but not as yet in the way his inamorata intended.

"Kate," said he one day, "that girl of yours is worth her weight in gold."

"Indeed!" said Mrs. Gaunt, frigidly ; "I have not discovered it."

When Caroline found that her master was single-hearted, and loved his wife too well to look elsewhere, instead of hating him, she began to love him more seriously, and to hate his wife, that haughty beauty, who took such a husband as a matter of course, and held him tight without troubling her head.

It was a coarse age, and in that very county more than one wife had suffered jealous agony from her own domestic. But here the parts were inverted : the lady was at her ease ; the servant paid a bitter penalty for her folly. She was now passionately in love, and had to do menial offices for her rival every hour of the day : she must sit with Mrs. Gaunt, and make her dresses, and consult with her how to set off her hateful beauty to the best advantage. She had to dress her, and look daggers at her satin skin and royal neck, and to sit behind her an hour at a time.

combing and brushing her long golden hair.

How she longed to tear a handful of it out, and then run away ! Instead of that, her happy rival expected her to be as tender and coaxing with it as Madame de Maintenon was with the Queen's of France.

Ryder called it "yellow stuff" down in the kitchen ; that was one comfort, but a feeble one ; the sun came in at the lady's window, and Ryder's shapely hand was overflowed, and her eyes offended, by waves of burnished gold : and one day Griffith came in and kissed it in her very hand. His lips felt nothing but his wife's glorious hair ; but, by that exquisite sensibility which the heart can convey in a moment to the very finger-nails, Caroline's hand, beneath, felt the soft touch through her mistress's hair ; and the enamored hypocrite thrilled, and then sickened.

The other servants knew, as a matter of domestic history, that Griffith and Kate lived together a happy couple ; but this ardent prude was compelled by her position to see it, and realize it, every day. She had to witness little conjugal caresses, and they turned her sick with jealousy. She was Nobody. They took no more account of her than of the furniture. The creature never flinched, but stood at her post and ground her white teeth in silence, and burned, and pined, and raged, and froze, and was a model of propriety.

On the day in question she was thinking of Griffith, as usual, and wondering whether he would always prefer yellow hair to black. This actually put her off her guard for once, and she gave the rival hair a little contemptuous tug ! and the reader knows what followed.

Staggered by her mistress's question, Caroline made no reply, but only panted a little, and proceeded more carefully.

But O the struggle it cost her not to slap both Mrs. Gaunt's fair cheeks impartially with the backs of the brushes ! And what with this struggle, and the reprimand, and the past agitations, by and by the comb ceased, and the silence was broken by faint sobs.

Mrs. Gaunt turned calmly round and looked full at her hysterical handmaid.

"What is to do ?" said she. "Is it because I chid you, child ? Nay, you need not take that to heart ; it is just my way : I can bear anything but my hair pulled." With this she rose and poured some drops of sal-volatile into water, and put it to her secret rival's lips : it was kindly done, but with that sort of half contemptuous and thoroughly cold pity women are apt to show to women, and especially when one of them is Mistress and the other is Servant.

Still it cooled the extreme hatred Caroline had nursed, and gave her a little twinge, and awakened her intelligence. Now her intelligence was truly remarkable when not blinded by passion. She was a woman with one or two other masculine traits besides her roving heart. For instance, she could sit and think hard and practically for hours together : and on these occasions her thoughts were never dreamy and vague ; it was no brown study, but good hard thinking. She would knit her coal-black brows, like Lord Thurlow himself, and realize the situation, and weigh the pros and cons with a steady judicial power rarely found in her sex ; and, *nota bene*, when once her mind had gone through this process, then she would act with almost monstrous resolution.

She now shut herself up in her own room for some hours, and weighed the matter carefully.

The conclusion she arrived at was this : that, if she stayed at Hernshaw Castle, there would be mischief ; and probably she herself would be the principal sufferer to the end of the chapter, as she was now.

She said to herself: "I shall go mad, or else expose myself, and be turned away with loss of character ; and then what will become of me, and my child ? Better lose life or reason than character. I know what I have to go through ; I have left a man ere now with my heart tugging at me to stay beside him. It is a terrible wrench ; and then all seems dead for a long while without *him*. But the world goes on and takes you round with it ; and by and by you find there are as good fish left in the sea. I 'll go, while I 've sense enough left to see I must."

The very next day she came to Mrs. Gaunt and said she wished to leave.

"Certainly," said Mrs. Gaunt, coldly. "May I ask the reason ?"

"O, I have no complaint to make, ma'am, none whatever ; but I am not happy here ; and I wish to go when my month 's up, or sooner, ma'am, if you could suit yourself.

Mrs. Gaunt considered a moment : then she said, "You came all the way from Gloucestershire to me ; had you not better give the place a fair trial ? I have had two or three good servants that felt uncomfortable at first ; but they soon found out my ways, and stayed with me till they married. As for leaving me before your month, that is out of the question."

To this Ryder said not a word, but merely vented a little sigh, half dogged, half submissive ; and went cat - like about, arranging her mistress's things with admirable precision and neatness. Mrs. Gaunt watched her, without seeming to do so, and observed that her discontent did not in the least affect her punctual discharge of her duties. Said Mrs. Gaunt to herself, " This servant is a treasure ; she shall not go." And Ryder to herself, " Well, 't is but for a month ; and then no power shall keep me here."

CHAPTER XIX.

NOT long after these events came the county ball. Griffith was there, but no Mrs. Gaunt. This excited surprise, and, among the gentlemen, disappointment. They asked Griffith if she was unwell ; he thanked them dryly, she was very well ; and that was all they could get out of him. But to the ladies he let out that she had given up balls, and, indeed, all reasonable pleasures. "She does nothing but fast, and pray, and visit the sick." He added, with rather a weak smile, " I see next to nothing of her." A minx stood by and put in her word. " You should take to your bed ; then, who knows ? she might look in upon *you*."

Griffith laughed, but not heartily. In truth, Mrs. Gaunt's religious fervor knew no bounds. Absorbed in pious schemes and religious duties, she had little time, and much distaste, for frivolous society ; invited none but the devout, and found polite excuses for not dining abroad. She sent her husband into the world alone, and laden with apologies. "My wife is turned saint. 'T is a sin to dance, a sin to hunt, a sin to enjoy ourselves. We are here to fast, and pray, and build schools, and go to church twice a day."

And so he went about publishing his household ill ; but, to tell the truth, a secret satisfaction peeped through his lugubrious accents. An ugly saint is an unmixed calamity to jolly fellows ; but to be lord and master, and possessor, of a beautiful saint, was not without its piquant charm. His jealousy was dormant, not extinct ; and Kate's piety tickled that foible, not wounded it. He found himself the rival of heaven, — and the successful rival ; for, let her be ever so strict, ever so devout, she must give her husband many delights she could not give to heaven.

This soft and piquant phase of the passion did not last long. All things are progressive.

Brother Leonard was director now, as well as confessor ; his visits became frequent ; and Mrs. Gaunt often quoted his authority for her acts or her sentiments. So Griffith began to suspect that the change in his wife was entirely due to Leonard ; and that, with all her eloquence and fervor, she was but a priest's echo. This galled him. To be sure Leonard was only an ecclesiastic ; but if he had been a woman, Griffith was the man to wince. His wife to lean so on another ; his wife to withdraw from the social pleasures she had hitherto shared with him; and all because another human creature disapproved them. He writhed in silence awhile, and then remonstrated.

He was met at first with ridicule: "Are you going to be jealous of my confessor?" and, on repeating the offence, with a kind, but grave admonition, that silenced him for the time, but did not cure him, nor even convince him.

The facts were too strong: Kate was no longer to him the genial companion she had been; gone was the ready sympathy with which she had listened to all his little earthly concerns; and as for his hay-making, he might as well talk about it to an iceberg as to the partner of his bosom.

He was genial by nature, and could not live without sympathy. He sought it in the parlor of the "Red Lion."

Mrs. Gaunt's high-bred nostrils told her where he haunted, and it caused her dismay. Woman-like, instead of opening her battery at once, she wore a gloomy and displeased air, which a few months ago would have served her turn and brought about an explanation at once; but Griffith took it for a stronger dose of religious sentiment, and trundled off to the "Red Lion" all the more.

So then at last she spoke her mind, and asked him how he could lower himself so, and afflict her.

"Oh!" said he, doggedly, "this house is too cold for me now. My mate is priest-rid. Plague on the knave that hath put coldness 'twixt thee and me."

Mrs. Gaunt froze visibly, and said no more at that time.

One bit of sunshine remained in the house, and shone brighter than ever on its chilled master, — shone through two black, seducing eyes.

Some three months before the date we have now reached, Caroline Ryder's two boxes were packed and corded ready to go next day. She had quietly persisted in her resolution to leave, and Mrs. Gaunt, though secretly angry, had been just and magnanimous enough to give her a good character.

Now female domestics are like the little birds; if that great hawk, their mistress, follows them about, it is a deadly grievance; but if she does not, they follow her about, and pester her with idle questions, and invite the beak and claws of petty tyranny and needless interference.

— So, the afternoon before she was to leave, Caroline Ryder came to her mistress's room on some imaginary business. She was not there. Ryder, forgetting that it did not matter a straw, proceeded to hunt her everywhere; and at last ran out, with only her cap on, to "the Dame's Haunt," and there she was; but not alone: she was walking up and down with Brother Leonard. Their backs were turned, and Ryder came up behind them. Leonard was pacing gravely, with his head gently drooping as usual. Mrs. Gaunt was walking elastically, and discoursing with great fire and animation.

Ryder glided after, noiseless as a serpent, more bent on wondering and watching now than on overtaking; for inside the house her mistress showed none of this charming vivacity.

Presently the keen black eyes observed a "trifle light as air" that made them shine again.

She turned and wound herself amongst the trees, and disappeared. Soon after she was in her own room, a changed woman. With glowing cheeks, sparkling eyes, and nimble fingers, she uncorded her boxes, unpacked her things, and placed them neatly in the drawers.

What more had she seen than I have indicated?

Only this: Mrs. Gaunt, in the warmth of discourse, laid her hand lightly for a moment on the priest's shoulder. That was nothing, she had laid the same hand on Ryder; for, in fact, it was a little womanly way she had, and a hand that settled like down. But this time, as she withdrew it again, that delicate hand seemed to speak; it did not leave Leonard's shoulder all at once, it glided slowly away, first the palm, then the fingers, and so parted lingeringly.

The other woman saw this subtile touch of womanhood, coupled it with Mrs. Gaunt's vivacity and the air of happiness that seemed to inspire her whole eloquent person, and formed an extreme conclusion on the spot, though she could not see the lady's face.

When Mrs. Gaunt came in she met her, and addressed her thus: "If you please, ma'am, have you any one coming in my place?"

Mrs. Gaunt looked her full in the face. "You know I have not," said she, haughtily.

"Then, if it is agreeable to you, ma'am, I will stay. To be sure the place is dull; but I have got a good mistress — and —"

"That will do, Ryder: a servant has always her own reasons, and never tells *them* to her mistress. You can stay this time; but the next, you go; and once for all. — I am not to be trifled with."

Ryder called up a look all submission, and retired with an obeisance. But, once out of sight, she threw off the mask and expanded with insolent triumph. "Yes, I have my own reasons," said she. "Keep you the priest, and I 'll take the man."

From that hour Caroline Ryder watched her mistress like a lynx, and hovered about her master, and poisoned him slowly with vague, insidious hints.

CHAPTER XX.

BROTHER LEONARD, like many holy men, was vain. Not vainer than St. Paul, perhaps; but then he had somewhat less to be vain of. Not but what he had his gusts of humility and diffidence; only they blew over.

At first, as you may perhaps remember, he doubted his ability to replace Father Francis as Mrs. Gaunt's director; but, after a slight disclaimer, he did replace him, and had no more misgivings as to his fitness. But his tolerance and good sense were by no means equal to his devotion and his persuasive powers; and so his advice in matters spiritual and secular somehow sowed the first seeds of conjugal coolness in Hernshaw Castle.

And now Ryder slyly insinuated into Griffith's ear that the mistress told the priest everything, and did nothing but by his advice. Thus the fire already kindled was fanned by an artful woman's breath.

Griffith began to hate Brother Leonard, and to show it so plainly and rudely that Leonard shrank from the encounter, and came less often, and stayed but a few minutes. Then Mrs. Gaunt remonstrated gently with Griffith, but received short, sullen replies. Then, as the servile element of her sex was comparatively small in her, she turned bitter and cold, and avenged Leonard indirectly, but openly, with those terrible pins and needles a' beloved woman has ever at command.

Then Griffith became moody, and downright unhappy, and went more and more to the "Red Lion," seeking comfort there now as well as company.

Mrs. Gaunt saw, and had fits of irritation, and fits of pity, and sore perplexity. She knew she had a good husband; and, instead of taking him to heaven with her, she found that each step she made with Leonard's help towards the angelic life seemed somehow to be bad for Griffith's soul and for his earthly happiness.

She blamed herself; she blamed Griffith; she blamed the Protestant heresy; she blamed everybody and everything — except Brother Leonard.

One Sunday afternoon Griffith sat on his own lawn, silently smoking his pipe. Mrs. Gaunt came to him, and saw an air of dejection on his genial face. Her heart yearned. She sat down beside him on the bench, and sighed; then he sighed too.

"My dear," said she, sweetly, "fetch out your *viol da gambo*, and we will sing a hymn or two together here this fine afternoon. We can praise God together, though we must pray apart; alas that it is so!"

"With all my heart," said Griffith. "Nay, I forgot; my *viol da gambo* is not here. 'T is at the 'Red Lion.' "

"At the 'Red Lion'!" said she, bitterly. "What, do you sing there as well as drink? O husband, how can you so demean yourself?"

"What is a poor man to do, whose wife is priest-ridden, and got to be no company — except for angels?"

"I did not come here to quarrel," said she, coldly and sadly. Then they were both silent a minute. Then she got up and left him.

Brother Leonard, like many earnest men, was rather intolerant. He urged on Mrs. Gaunt that she had too many Protestants in her household: her cook and her nursemaid ought, at all events, to be Catholics. Mrs. Gaunt on this was quite ready to turn them both off, and that without disguise. But Leonard dissuaded her from so violent a measure. She had better take occasion to part with one of them, and by and by with the other.

The nursemaid was the first to go, and her place was filled by a Roman Catholic. Then the cook received warning. But this did not pass off so quietly. Jane Bannister was a buxom, hearty woman, well liked by her fellow-servants. Her parents lived in the village, and she had been six years with the Gaunts, and her honest heart clung to them. She took to crying; used to burst out in the middle of her work, or while conversing with fitful cheerfulness on ordinary topics.

One day Griffith found her crying, and Ryder consoling her as carelessly and contemptuously as possible.

"Heyday, lasses!" said he; "what is your trouble?"

At this Jane's tears flowed in a stream, and Ryder made no reply, but waited.

At last, and not till the third or fourth time of asking, Jane blurted out that she had got the sack; such was her homely expression, dignified, however, by honest tears.

"What for?" asked Griffith kindly.

"Nay, sir," sobbed Jane, "that is what I want to know. Our dame ne'er found a fault in me; and now she does pack me off like a dog. Me that have been here this six years, and got to feel at home. What will father say? He'll give me a hiding. For two pins I'd drown myself in the mere."

"Come, you must not blame the mistress," said the sly Ryder. "She is a good mistress as ever breathed: 't is all the priest's doings. I'll tell you the truth, master, if you will pass me your word I sha'n't be sent away for it."

"I pledge you my word as a gentleman," said Griffith.

"Well then, sir, Jane's fault is yours and mine. She is not a Papist; and that is why she is to go. How I come to know, I listened in the next room, and heard the priest tell our dame she must send away two of us, and have Catholics. The priest's word it is law in this house. 'T was in March he gave the order: Harriet, she went in May, and now poor Jane is to go — for walking to church behind *you*, sir. But there, Jane, I believe he would get our very master out of the house if he could; and then what would become of us all?"

Griffith turned black, and then ashy pale, under this venomous tongue, and went away without a word, looking dangerous.

Ryder looked after him, and her black eye glittered with a kind of fiendish beauty.

Jane, having told her mind, now began to pluck up a little spirit. "Mrs. Ryder," said she, "I never thought to like you so well";—and, with that, gave her a great, hearty, smacking kiss; which Ryder, to judge by her countenance, relished, as epicures albumen. "I won't cry no more. After all, this house is no place for us that be women; 't is a fine roost to be sure! where the hen she crows and the cock do but cluck."

Town-bred Ryder laughed at the rustic maid's simile; and, not to be outdone in metaphor, told her there were dogs that barked, and dogs that bit.

"Our master is one of those that bite. I 've done the priest's business. He is as like to get the sack as you are."

Griffith found his wife seated on the lawn reading. He gulped down his ire as well as he could; but nevertheless his voice trembled a little with suppressed passion.

"So Jane is turned off now," said he.

"I don't know about being turned off," replied Mrs. Gaunt, calmly; "but she leaves me next month, and Cicely Davis comes back."

"And Cicely Davis is a useless slut that cannot boil a potato fit to eat; but then she is a Papist, and poor Jenny is a Protestant, and can cook a dinner."

"My dear," said Mrs. Gaunt, "do not you trouble about the servants; leave them to me."

"And welcome; but this is not your doing, it is that Leonard's: and I cannot allow a Popish priest to turn off all my servants that are worth their salt. Come, Kate, you used to be a sensible woman and a tender wife; now I ask you, is a young bachelor a fit person to govern a man's family?"

Mrs. Gaunt laughed in his face. "A young bachelor!" said she; "who ever heard of such a term applied to a priest, — and a saint upon earth?"

"Why, he is not married, so he must be a bachelor; and I say again it is monstrous for a young bachelor to come between old married folk, and hear all their secrets, and have a finger in every pie, and set up to be master of my house, and order my wife to turn away my servants for going to church behind me. Why not turn *me* away too? Their fault is mine."

"Griffith, you are in a passion, and I begin to think you want to put me in one."

"Well, perhaps I am. Job's patience went at last, and mine has been sore tried this many a month. 'T was bad enough when the man was only your confessor; you told him everything, and you don't tell me everything. He knew your very heart, better than I do, and that was a bitter thing for me to bear,

that love you and have no secrets from you. But every man who marries a Catholic must endure this; so I put a good face on it, though my heart was often sore; 't was the price I had to pay for my pearl of womankind. But since he set up your governor as well, you are a changed woman; you shun company abroad, you freeze my friends at home. You have made the house so cold that I am fain to seek the ' Red Lion' for a smile or a kindly word: and now, to please this fanatical priest, you would turn away the best servants I have, and put useless, dirty slatterns in their place, that happen to be Papists. You did not use to be so uncharitable, nor so unreasonable. 'T is the priest's doing. He is my secret, underhand enemy; I feel him undermining me, inch by inch, and I can bear it no longer. I must make a stand somewhere, and I may as well make it here; for Jenny is a good girl, and her folk live in the village, and she helps them. Think better of it, dame, and let the poor wench stay, though she does go to church behind your husband."

"Griffith," said Mrs. Gaunt, "I might retort and say that you are a changed man; for to be sure you did never use to interfere between me and my maids. Are you sure some mischief-making woman is not advising *you?* But there, do not let us chafe one another, for you know we are hot-tempered both of us. Well, leave it for the present, my dear; prithee let me think it over till to-morrow, at all events, and try if I can satisfy you."

The jealous husband saw through this proposal directly. He turned purple. "That is to say, you must ask your priest first for leave to show your husband one grain of respect and affection, and not make him quite a cipher in his own house. No, Kate, no man who respects himself will let another man come between himself and the wife of his bosom. This business is between you and me; I will brook no interference in it; and I tell you plainly, if you turn this poor lass off to please this d—d priest, I 'll turn the priest off to please her and her folk. They are as good as he is, any way."

The bitter contempt with which he spoke of Brother Leonard, and this astounding threat, imported a new and dangerous element into the discussion : it stung Mrs. Gaunt beyond bearing. She turned with flashing eyes upon Griffith.

"As good as he is ? The scum of my kitchen ! You will make me hate the mischief-making hussy. She shall pack out of the house to-morrow morning."

"Then I say that priest shall never darken my doors again."

"Then I say they are my doors, not yours ; and that holy man shall brighten them whenever he will."

If to strike an adversary dumb is the tongue's triumph, Mrs. Gaunt was victorious ; for Griffith gasped, but did not reply.

They faced each other, pale with fury ; but no more words.

No : an ominous silence succeeded this lamentable answer, like the silence that follows a thunder-clap.

Griffith stood still awhile, benumbed as it were by the cruel stroke ; then cast one speaking look of anguish and reproach upon her, drew himself haughtily up, and stalked away like a wounded lion.

Well said the ancients that anger is a short madness. When we reflect in cold blood on the things we have said in hot, how impossible they seem ! how out of character with our real selves ! And this is one of the recognized symptoms of mania.

There were few persons could compare with Mrs. Gaunt in native magnanimity ; yet how ungenerous a stab had she given.

And had he gone on, she would have gone on ; but when he turned silent at her bitter thrust, and stalked away from her, she came to herself almost directly.

She thought, " Good God ! what have I said to him ? "

And the flush of shame came to her cheek, and her eyes filled with tears.

He saw them not ; he had gone away, wounded to the heart.

You see it was true. The house was hers ; tied up as tight as wax. The very money (his own money) that had been spent on the place, had become hers by being expended on real property ; he could not reclaim it ; he was her lodger, a dependent on her bounty.

During all the years they had lived together she had never once assumed the proprietor. On the contrary, she put him forward as the Squire, and slipped quietly into the background. *Bene latuit.* But, lo ! let a hand be put out to offend her saintly favorite, and that moment she could waken her husband from his dream, and put him down into his true legal position with a word. The matrimonial throne for him till he resisted her priest ; and then, a stool at her feet, and his.

He was enraged as well as hurt ; but being a true lover, his fury was levelled, not at the woman who had hurt him, but at the man who stood out of sight and set her on.

By this time the reader knows his good qualities, and his defects ; superior to his wife in one or two things, he was by no means so thorough a gentleman as she was a lady. He had begun to make a party with his own servants against the common enemy ; and, in his wrath, he now took another step, or rather a stride, in the same direction. As he hurried away to the public-house, white with ire, he met his gamekeeper coming in with a bucketful of fish fresh caught. "What have ye got there ? " said Griffith, roughly ; not that he was angry with the man, but that his very skin was full of wrath, and it must exude.

Mr. Leicester did not relish the tone, and replied, bluntly and sulkily, " Pike for our Papists."

The answer, though rude, did not altogether displease Griffith ; it smacked of *odium theologicum*, a sentiment he was learning to understand. " Put 'em down, and listen to me, Thomas Leicester," said he.

And his manner was now so impressive that Leicester put down the bucket with ludicrous expedition, and gaped at him.

"Now, my man, why do I keep you here?"

"To take care of your game, Squire, I do suppose."

"What? when you are the worst gamekeeper in the county. How many poachers do you catch in the year? They have only to set one of their gang to treat you at the public-house on a moonshiny night, and the rest can have all my pheasants at roost while you are boosing and singing."

"Like my betters in the parlor," muttered Tom.

"But that is not all," continued Gaunt, pretending not to hear him. "You wire my rabbits, and sell them in the town. Don't go to deny it; for I've half a dozen to prove it." Mr. Leicester looked very uncomfortable. His master continued: "I have known it this ten months, yet you are none the worse for 't. Now, why do I keep you here, that any other gentleman in my place would send to Carlisle jail on a justice's warrant?"

Mr. Leicester, who had thought his master blind, and was so suddenly undeceived, hung his head and snivelled out, "'T is because you have a good heart, Squire, and would not ruin a poor fellow for an odd rabbit or two."

"Stuff and nonsense!" cried Gaunt. "Speak your mind, for once, or else begone for a liar as well as a knave."

Thus appealed to, Leicester's gypsy eyes roved to and fro as if he were looking for some loophole to escape by; but at last he faced the situation. He said, with a touch of genuine feeling, "D—n the rabbits! I wish my hand had withered ere I touched one on them." But after this preface he sunk his voice to a whisper, and said, "I see what you are driving at, Squire; and since there is nobody with us" (he took off his cap,) "why, sir, 't is this here mole I am in debt to, no doubt."

Then the gentleman and his servant looked one another silently in the face, and what with their standing in the same attitude and being both excited and earnest, the truth must be owned, a certain family likeness came out. Certainly their eyes were quite unlike. Leicester had his gypsy mother's: black, keen, and restless. Gaunt had his mother's: brown, calm, and steady. But the two men had the same stature, the same manly mould and square shoulders; and, though Leicester's cheek was brown as a berry, his forehead was singularly white for a man in his rank of life, and over his left temple, close to the roots of the hair, was an oblong mole as black as ink, that bore a close resemblance in appearance and position to his master's.

"Tom Leicester; I have been insulted."

"That won't pass, sir. Who is the man?"

"One that I cannot call out like a gentleman, and yet I must not lay on him with my cane, or I am like to get the sack, as well as my servants. 'T is the Popish priest, lad; Brother Leonard, own brother to Old Nick; he has got our Dame's ear, she cannot say him 'nay.' She is turning away all my people, and filling the house with Papists, to please him. And when I interfered, she as good as told me I should go next; and so I shall, I or else that priest."

This little piece of exaggeration fired Tom Leicester. "Say ye so, Squire? then just you whisper a word in my ear, and George and I will lay that priest by the heels, and drag him through the horse-pond. He won't come here to trouble you after that, *I* know."

Gaunt's eyes flashed triumph. "A friend in need is a friend indeed," said he. "Ay, you are right, lad. There must be no broken bones, and no bloodshed; the horse-pond is the very thing: and if she discharges you for it, take no heed of her. You shall never leave Hernshaw Castle for that good deed; or, if you do, I'll go with you; for the world it is wide, and I'll never live a servant in the house where I have been a master."

They then put their heads together and concerted the means by which the priest at his very next visit was to be decoyed into the neighborhood of the horse-pond.

And then they parted, and Griffith went to the "Red Lion." And a pair of black eyes that had slyly watched this singular interview from an upper window withdrew quietly; and soon after Tom Leicester found himself face to face with their owner, the sight of whom always made his heart beat a little faster.

Caroline Ryder had been rather cold to him of late; it was therefore a charming surprise when she met him, all wreathed in smiles, and, drawing him apart, began to treat him like a bosom friend, and tell him what had passed between the master and her and Jane. Confidence begets confidence; and so Tom told her in turn that the Squire and the Dame had come to words over it. "However," said he, "'t is all the priest's fault: but bide awhile, all of ye."

With this mysterious hint he meant to close his revelations. But Ryder intended nothing of the kind. Her keen eye had read the looks and gestures of Gaunt and Leicester, and these had shown her that something very strange and serious was going on. She had come out expressly to learn what it was, and Tom was no match for her arts. She so smiled on him, and agreed with him, and led him, and drew him, and pumped him, that she got it all out of him on a promise of secrecy. She then entered into it with spirit, and, being what they called a scholar, undertook to write a paper for Tom and his helper to pin on the priest's back. No sooner said than done. She left him, and speedily returned with the following document, written out in large and somewhat straggling letters : —

"Honest Folk, behold a

Mischievious Priest, which

For causing of strife.

'Twixt man and wyfe

Hath made acquaintance

With Squire's horse-pond."

And so a female conspirator was added to the plot.

Mrs. Gaunt co-operated too, but, need I say? unconsciously.

She was unhappy, and full of regret at what she had said. She took herself severely to task, and drew a very unfavorable comparison between herself and Brother Leonard. "How ill," she thought, "am I fitted to carry out that meek saint's view. See what my ungoverned temper has done." So then, having made so great a mistake, she thought the best thing she could do was to seek advice of Leonard at once. She was not without hopes he would tell her to postpone the projected change in her household, and so soothe her offended husband directly.

She wrote a line requesting Leonard to call on her as soon as possible, and advise her in a great difficulty; and she gave this note to Ryder, and told her to send the groom off with it at once.

Ryder squeezed the letter, and peered into it, and gathered its nature before she gave it to the groom to take to Leonard.

When he was gone, she went and told Tom Leicester, and he chuckled, and made his preparations accordingly.

Then she retired to her own room, and went through a certain process I have indicated before as one of her habits : knitted her great black brows, and pondered the whole situation with a mental power that was worthy of a nobler sphere and higher materials.

Her practical revery, so to speak, continued until she was rung for to dress her mistress for dinner.

Griffith was so upset, so agitated and restless, he could not stay long in any one place, not even in the "Red Lion." So he came home to dinner, though he had mighty little appetite for it. And this led to another little conjugal scene.

Mrs. Gaunt mounted the great oak staircase to dress for dinner, languidly, as ladies are apt to do, when reflection and regret come after excitement.

Presently she heard a quick foot behind her : she knew it directly for her husband's, and her heart yearned. She did not stop nor turn her head : womanly pride withheld her from direct submission ; but womanly tenderness and tact opened a way to reconciliation. She drew softly aside, almost to the wall, and went slower ; and her hand, her sidelong drooping head, and her whole eloquent person, whispered plainly enough, " If somebody would like to make friends, here is the door open."

Griffith saw, but was too deeply wounded : he passed her without stopping (the staircase was eight feet broad).

But as he passed he looked at her and sighed, for he saw she was sorry.

She heard, and sighed too. Poor things, they had lived so happy together for years.

He went on.

Her pride bent : " Griffith ! " said she, timidly.

He turned and stopped at that.

" Sweetheart," she murmured, " I was to blame. I was ungenerous. I forgot myself. Let me recall my words. You know they did not come from my heart."

" You need not tell me that," said Griffith, doggedly. " I have no quarrel with you, and never will. You but do what you are bidden, and say what you are bidden. I take the wound from you as best I may : the man that set you on, 't is him I 'll be revenged on."

" Alas that you will think so ! " said she. " Believe me, dearest, that holy man would be the first to rebuke me for rebelling against my husband and flouting him. O, how *could* I say such things ? I thank you, and love you dearly for being so blind to my faults ;

but I must not abuse your blindness. Father Leonard will put me to penance for the fault you forgive. *He* will hear no excuses. Prithee, now, be more just to that good man."

Griffith listened quietly, with a cold sneer upon his lip ; and this was his reply : " Till that mischief-making villain came between you and me, you never gave me a bitter word : we were the happiest pair in Cumberland. But now what are we ? And what shall we be in another year or two ? — RE-VENGE ! ! "

He had begun bravely enough, but suddenly burst into an ungovernable rage ; and as he yelled out that furious word his face was convulsed and ugly to look at ; very ugly.

Mrs. Gaunt started : she had not seen that vile expression in his face for many a year ; but she knew it again.

" Ay ! " he cried, " he has made me drink a bitter cup this many a day. But I 'll force as bitter a one down his throat, and you shall see it done."

Mrs. Gaunt turned pale at this violent threat ; but, being a high-spirited woman, she stiffened and hid her apprehensions loftily. " Madman that you are," said she. " I throw away excuses on *Jealousy*, and I waste reason upon frenzy. I 'll say no more things to provoke you ; but, to be sure, 't is I that am offended now, and deeply too, as you will find."

" So be it," said Griffith, sullenly ; then, grinding his teeth, " he shall pay for that too."

Then he went to his dressing-room, and she to her bedroom. Griffith hating Leonard, and Kate on the verge of hating Griffith.

And, ere her blood could cool, she was subjected to the keen, cold scrutiny of another female, and that female a secret rival.

CHAPTER XXI.

WOULD you learn what men gain by admitting a member of the fair sex into their conspiracies ? read the tragedy of "Venice Preserved"; and, by way of afterpiece, this little chapter.

Mrs. Gaunt sat pale and very silent, and Caroline Ryder stood behind, doing up her hair into a magnificent structure that added eight inches to the lady's height; and in this operation her own black hair and keen black eyes came close to the golden hair and deep blue eyes, now troubled, and made a picture striking by contrast.

As she was putting the finishing touches, she said, quietly, "If you please, Dame, I have somewhat to tell you."

Mrs. Gaunt sighed wearily, expecting some very minute communication.

"Well, Dame, I dare say I am risking my place, but I can't help it."

"Another time, Ryder," said Mrs. Gaunt. "I am in no humor to be worried with my servants' squabbles."

"Nay, madam, 't is not that at all: 't is about Father Leonard. Sure you would not like him to be drawn through the horse-pond ; and that is what they mean to do next time he comes here."

In saying these words, the jade contrived to be adjusting Mrs. Gaunt's dress. The lady's heart gave a leap, and the servant's cunning finger felt it, and then felt a shudder run all over that stately frame. But after that Mrs. Gaunt seemed to turn to steel. She distrusted Ryder, she could not tell why ; distrusted her, and was upon her guard.

"You must be mistaken," said she. "Who would dare to lay hands on a priest in my house ?"

"Well, Dame, you see they egg one another on : don't ask me to betray my fellow-servants ; but let us balk them. I don't deceive you, Dame : if the good priest shows his face here, he will be thrown into the horse-pond, and sent home with a ticket pinned to his back. Them that is to do it are on the watch now, and have got their orders ; and 't is a burning shame. To be sure I am not a Catholic ; but religion is religion, and a more heavenly face I never saw :

and for it to be dragged through a filthy horse-pond!"

Mrs. Gaunt clutched her inspector's arm and turned pale. "The villains ! the fiends !" she gasped. "Go ask your master to come to me this moment."

Ryder took a step or two, then stopped. "Alack, Dame," said she, "that is not the way to do. You may be sure the others would not dare, if my master had not shown them his mind."

Mrs. Gaunt stopped her ears. "Don't tell me that *he* has ordered this impious, cruel, cowardly act. He is a lion : and this comes from the heart of cowardly curs. What is to be done, woman ? tell me ; for you are cooler than I am."

"Well, Dame, if I were in your place, I 'd just send him a line, and bid him stay away till the storm blows over."

"You are right. But who is to carry it ? My own servants are traitors to me."

"I 'll carry it myself."

"You shall. Put on your hat, and run through the wood; that is the shortest way."

She wrote a few lines on a large sheet of paper, for note-paper there was none in those days ; sealed it, and gave it to Ryder.

Ryder retired to put on her hat, and pry into the letter with greedy eyes.

It ran thus : —

"DEAR FATHER AND FRIEND, — You must come hither no more at present. Ask the bearer why this is, for I am ashamed to put it on paper. Pray for them : for you can, but I cannot. Pray for me, too, bereft for a time of your counsels. I shall come and confess to you in a few days, when we are all cooler ; but you shall honor *his* house no more. Obey *me* in this one thing, who shall obey you in all things else, and am

"Your indignant and sorrowful daughter,

"CATHARINE GAUNT."

"No more than that ?" said Ryder. "Ay, she guessed as I should look."

She whipped on her hat and went out.

Who should she meet, or, I might say, run against, at the hall door, but Father Leonard.

He had come at once, in compliance with Mrs. Gaunt's request.

CHAPTER XXII.

MRS. RYDER uttered a little scream of dismay. The priest smiled, and said, sweetly, "Forgive me, mistress, I fear I startled you."

"Indeed you did, sir," said she. She looked furtively round, and saw Leicester and his underling on the watch.

Leicester, unaware of her treachery, made her a signal of intelligence.

She responded to it, to gain time.

It was a ticklish situation. Some would have lost their heads. Ryder was alarmed, but all the more able to defend her plans. Her first move, as usual with such women, was — a lie.

"Our Dame is in the Grove, sir," said she. "I am to bring you to her."

The priest bowed his head, gravely, and moved towards the Grove with downcast eyes. Ryder kept close to him for a few steps ; then she ran to Leicester, and whispered, hastily, "Go you to the stable-gate ; I 'll bring him round that way : hide now ; he suspects."

"Ay, ay," said Leicester ; and the confiding pair slipped away round a corner to wait for their victim.

Ryder hurried him into the Grove, and, as soon as she had got him out of hearing, told him the truth.

He turned pale ; for these delicate organizations do not generally excel in courage.

Ryder pitied him, and something of womanly feeling began to mingle with her plans. "They shall not lay a finger on you, sir," said she. "I 'll scratch and scream and bring the whole parish out sooner ; but the best way is not to give them a chance ; please you follow me." And she hurried him through the Grove, and then into an unfrequented path of the great wood.

When they were safe from pursuit she turned and looked at him. He was a good deal agitated ; but the uppermost sentiment was gratitude. It soon found words, and, as usual, happy ones. He thanked her with dignity and tenderness for the service she had done him, and asked her if she was a Catholic.

"No," said she.

At that his countenance fell, but only for a moment. "Ah ! would you were," he said, earnestly. He then added, sweetly, "To be sure I have all the more reason to be grateful to you."

"You are very welcome, reverend sir," said Ryder, graciously. "Religion is religion ; and 't is a barbarous thing that violence should be done to men of your cloth."

Having thus won his heart, the artful woman began at one and the same time to please and to probe him. " Sir," said she, "be of good heart ; they have done you no harm, and themselves no good ; my mistress will hate them for it, and love you all the more."

Father Leonard's pale cheek colored all over at these words, though he said nothing.

"Since they won't let you come to her, she will come to you."

"Do you think so ?" said he, faintly.

"Nay, I am sure of it, sir. So would any woman. We still follow our hearts, and get our way by hook or by crook."

Again the priest colored, either with pleasure or with shame, or with both ; and the keen feminine eye perused him with microscopic power. She waited, to give him an opportunity of talking to her and laying bare his feelings ; but he was either too delicate, too cautious, or too pure.

So then she suddenly affected to remember her mistress's letter. She produced it with an apology. He took it with unfeigned eagerness, and read it in silence ; and, having read it, he stood patient, with the tears in his eyes.

Ryder eyed him with much curiosity and a little pity. "Don't you take on for that," said she. "Why, she will be more at her ease when she visits you at your place than here ; and she won't give you up, I promise."

The priest trembled, and Ryder saw it.

"But, my daughter," said he, "I am perplexed and grieved. It seems that I make mischief in your house : that is an ill office ; I fear it is my duty to retire from this place altogether, rather than cause dissension between those whom the Church by holy sacrament hath bound together." So saying, he hung his head and sighed.

Ryder eyed him with a little pity, but more contempt. "Why take other people's faults on your back ?" said she. "My mistress is tied to a man she does not love ; but that is not your fault : and he is jealous of you, that never gave him cause. If I was a man he should not accuse me — for nothing ; nor set his man on to drag me through a horse-pond — for nothing. *I 'd have the sweet as well as the bitter.*"

Father Leonard turned and looked at her with a face full of terror. Some beautiful, honeyed fiend seemed to be entering his heart and tempting it. "O, hush ! my daughter, hush !" he said ; "what words are these for a virtuous woman to speak, and a priest to hear ?"

"There, I have offended you by my blunt way," said the cajoling hussy, in soft and timid tones.

"Nay, not so ; but O speak not so lightly of things that peril the immortal soul ! "

"Well, I have done," said Ryder. "You are out of danger now ; so give you good day."

He stopped her. "What, before I have thanked you for your goodness. Ah, Mistress Ryder, 't is on these occasions a priest sins by longing for riches to reward his benefactors. I have naught to offer you but this ring ; it was my mother's, — my dear mother's." He took it off his finger to give it her.

But the little bit of goodness that cleaves even to the heart of an *in-trigante* revolted against her avarice. "Nay, poor soul, I 'll not take it," said she ; and put her hands before her eyes not to see it, for she knew she could not look at it long and spare it.

With this she left him ; but, ere she had gone far, her cunning and curiosity gained the upper hand again, and she whipped behind a great tree and crouched, invisible all but her nose and one piercing eye.

She saw the priest make a few steps homewards, then look around, then take Mrs. Gaunt's letter out of his pocket, press it passionately to his lips, and hide it tenderly in his bosom.

This done, he went home, with his eyes on the ground as usual, and measured steps. And to all who met him he seemed a creature in whom religion had conquered all human frailty.

Caroline Ryder hurried home with cruel exultation in her black eyes. But she soon found that the first thing she had to do was to defend herself. Leicester and his man met her, and the former looked gloomy, and the latter reproached her bitterly, called her a double-faced jade, and said he would tell the Squire of the trick she had played them. But Ryder had a lie ready in a moment. · "'T is you I have saved, not him," said she. "He is something more than mortal : why, he told me of his own accord what you were there for ; but that, if you were so unlucky as to lay hands on him, you would rot alive. It seems that has been tried out Stanhope way ; a man did but give him a blow, and his arm was stiff next day, and he never used it again ; and next his hair fell off his head, and then his eyes they turned to water and ran all out of him, and he died within the twelvemonth."

Country folk were nearly, though not quite, as superstitious at that time as in the Middle Ages. " Murrain on him," said Leicester. "Catch me laying a finger on him. I 'm glad he is gone ; and I hope he won't never come back no more."

"Not likely, since he can read all our hearts. Why he told me something about you, Tom Leicester ; he says you are in love."

"No! did he really now?" — and Leicester opened his eyes very wide. "And did he tell you who the lass is?"

"He did so ; and surprised me properly." This with a haughty glance.

Leicester held his tongue and turned red.

"Who is it, mistress?" asked the helper.

"He did n't say I was to tell *you*, young man."

And with these two pricks of her needle she left them both more or less discomfited, and went to scrutinize and anatomize her mistress's heart with plenty of cunning, but no mercy. She related her own part in the affair very briefly, but dwelt with well-feigned sympathy on the priest's feelings. "He turned as white as a sheet, ma'am, when I told him, and offered me his very ring off his finger, he was so grateful ; poor man!"

"You did not take it, I hope?" said Mrs. Gaunt, quickly.

"La, no ma'am! I had n't the heart."

Mrs. Gaunt was silent awhile. When she spoke again it was to inquire whether Ryder had given him the letter.

"That I did : and it brought the tears into his poor eyes ; and such beautiful eyes as he has, to be sure. You would have pitied him if you had seen him read it, and cry over it, and then kiss it and put it in his bosom he did."

Mrs. Gaunt said nothing, but turned her head away.

The operator shot a sly glance into the looking-glass, and saw a pearly tear trickling down her subject's fair cheek. So she went on, all sympathy outside, and remorselessness within. "To think of that face, more like an angel's than a man's, to be dragged through a nasty horse-pond. 'T is a shame of master to set his men on a clergyman." And so was proceeding, with well-acted and catching warmth, to dig as dangerous a pit for Mrs. Gaunt as ever was dug for any lady ; for whatever Mrs. Gaunt had

been betrayed into saying, this Ryder would have used without mercy, and with diabolical skill.

Yes, it was a pit, and the lady's tender heart pushed her towards it, and her fiery temper drew her towards it.

Yet she escaped it this time. The dignity, delicacy, and pride, that is oftener found in these old families than out of them, saved her from that peril. She did not see the trap ; but she spurned the bait by native instinct.

She threw up her hand in a moment, with a queenly gesture, and stopped the tempter.

"Not — one — word — from my servant against my husband in *my* hearing!" said she, superbly.

And Ryder shrank back into herself directly.

"Child," said Mrs. Gaunt, "you have done me a great service, and my husband too ; for if this dastardly act had been done in his name, he would soon have been heartily ashamed of it, and deplored it. Such services can never be quite repaid ; but you will find a purse in that drawer with five guineas ; it is yours ; and my lavender silk dress, be pleased to wear that about me, to remind me of the good office you have done me. And now, all you can do for me is to leave me ; for I am very, very unhappy."

Ryder retired with the spoil, and Mrs. Gaunt leaned her head over her chair, and cried without stint.

After this, no angry words passed between Mr. and Mrs. Gaunt ; but something worse, a settled coolness, sprung up.

As for Griffith, his cook kept her place, and the priest came no more to the Castle ; so, having outwardly gained the day, he was ready to forget and forgive ; but Kate, though she would not let her servant speak ill of Griffith, was deeply indignant and disgusted with him. She met his advances with such a stern coldness, that he turned sulky and bitter in his turn.

Husband and wife saw little of each other, and hardly spoke.

Both were unhappy; but Kate was angriest, and Griffith saddest.

In an evil hour he let out his grief to Caroline Ryder. She seized the opportunity, and, by a show of affectionate sympathy and zeal, made herself almost necessary to him, and contrived to establish a very perilous relation between him and her. Matters went so far as this, that the poor man's eye used to brighten when he saw her coming.

Yet this victory cost her a sore heart and all the patient self-denial of her sex. To be welcome to Griffith she had to speak to him of her rival, and to speak well of her. She tried talking of herself and her attachment; he yawned in her face: she tried smooth detraction and innuendo; he fired up directly, and defended her of whose conduct he had been complaining the very moment before.

Then she saw that there was but one way to the man's heart. Sore, and sick, and smiling, she took that way: resolving to bide her time; to worm herself in any how, and wait patiently till she could venture to thrust her mistress out.

If any of my readers need to be told why this she Machiavel threw her fellow-conspirators over, the reason was simply this: on calm reflection she saw it was not her interest to get Father Leonard insulted. She looked on him as her mistress's lover, and her own best friend. "Was I mad?" said she to herself. "My business is to keep him sweet upon her, till they can't live without one another: and then I'll tell *him;* and take your place in this house, my lady."

And now it is time to visit that extraordinary man, who was the cause of all this mischief; whom Gaunt called a villain, and Mrs. Gaunt a saint; and, as usual, he was neither one nor the other.

Father Leonard was a pious, pure, and noble-minded man, who had undertaken to defy nature, with religion's aid; and, after years of successful warfare, now sustained one of those defeats to which such warriors have been liable in every age. If his heart was pure, it was tender; and nature never intended him to live all his days alone. After years of prudent coldness to the other sex, he fell in with a creature that put him off his guard at first, she seemed so angelic. "At Wisdom's gate suspicion slept": and, by degrees, which have been already indicated in this narrative, she whom the Church had committed to his spiritual care became his idol. Could he have foreseen this, it would never have happened; he would have steeled himself, or left the country that contained this sweet temptation. But love stole on him, masked with religious zeal, and robed in a garment of light that seemed celestial.

When the mask fell, it was too late: the power to resist the soft and thrilling enchantment was gone. The solitary man was too deep in love.

Yet he clung still to that self-deception, without which he never could have been entrapped into an earthly passion; he never breathed a word of love to her. It would have alarmed her; it would have alarmed himself. Every syllable that passed between these two might have been published without scandal. But the heart does not speak by words alone: there are looks and there are tones of voice that belong to Love, and are his signs, his weapons; and it was in these very tones the priest murmured to his gentle listener about "the angelic life" between spirits still lingering on earth, but purged from earthly dross; and even about other topics less captivating to the religious imagination. He had persuaded her to found a school in this dark parish, and in it he taught the poor with exemplary and touching patience. Well, when he spoke to her about this school, it was in words of practical good sense, but in tones of love; and she, being one of those feminine women who catch the tone they are addressed in, and instinctively answer in tune, and, moreover, seeing no ill, but good, in the *subject* of their conversation, replied sometimes, unguardedly enough, in accents almost as tender.

In truth, if Love was really a personage, as the heathens feigned, he must have often perched on a tree in that quiet grove, and chuckled and mocked, when this man and woman sat and murmured together, in the soft seducing twilight, about the love of God.

And now things had come to a crisis. Husband and wife went about the house silent and gloomy, the ghosts of their former selves; and the priest sat solitary, benighted, bereaved of the one human creature he cared for. Day succeeded to day, and still she never came. Every morning he said, "She will come to-day," and brightened with the hope. But the leaden hours crept by, and still she came not.

Three sorrowful weeks went by; and he fell into deep dejection. He used to wander out at night, and come and stand where he could see her windows with the moon shining on them: then go slowly home, cold in body, and with his heart aching, lonely, deserted, and perhaps forgotten. O, never till now had he known the utter aching sense of being quite alone in this weary world!

One day, as he sat drooping and listless, there came a light foot along the passage, a light tap at the door, and the next moment she stood before him, a little paler than usual, but lovelier than ever, for celestial joy softened her noble features.

The priest started up with a cry of joy that ought to have warned her; but it only brought a faint blush of pleasure to her cheek and the brimming tears to her eyes.

"Dear father and friend," said she. "What! have you missed me? Think, then, how I have missed *you*. But 't was best for us both to let their vile passions cool first."

Leonard could not immediately reply. The emotion of seeing her again so suddenly almost choked him.

He needed all the self-possession he had been years acquiring not to throw himself at her knees and declare his passion to her.

Mrs. Gaunt saw his agitation, but did not interpret to his disadvantage.

She came eagerly and sat on a stool beside him. "Dear father," she said, "do not let their insolence grieve you. They have smarted for it, and *shall* smart till they make their submission to you, and beg and entreat you to come to us again. Meantime, since you cannot visit me, I visit you. Confess me, father, and then direct me with your counsels. Ah! if you could but give me the Christian temper to carry them out firmly but meekly! 'T is my ungoverned spirit hath wrought all this mischief, — *mea culpa! mea culpa!*"

By this time Leonard had recovered his self-possession, and he spent an hour of strange intoxication, confessing his idol, sentencing his idol to light penances, directing and advising his idol, and all in the soft murmurs of a lover.

She left him, and the room seemed to darken.

Two days only elapsed, and she came again. Visit succeeded to visit: and her affection seemed boundless.

The insult he had received was to be avenged in one place, and healed in another, and, if possible, effaced with tender hand. So she kept all her sweetness for that little cottage, and all her acidity for Hernshaw Castle.

It was an evil hour when Griffith attacked her saint with violence. The woman was too high-spirited, and too sure of her own rectitude, to endure that: so, instead of crushing her, it drove her to retaliation,—and to imprudence.

These visits to console Father Leonard were quietly watched by Ryder, for one thing. But, worse than that, they placed Mrs. Gaunt in a new position with Leonard, and one that melts the female heart. She was now the protectress and the consoler of a man she admired and revered. I say if anything on earth can breed love in a grand female bosom, this will.

She had put her foot on a sunny slope clad with innocent-looking flowers; but more and more precipitous at every step, and perdition at the bottom.

CHAPTER XXIII.

FATHER LEONARD, visited, soothed, and petted by his idol, recovered his spirits, and, if he pined during her absence, he was always so joyful in her presence that she thought of course he was permanently happy; so then, being by nature magnanimous and placable, she began to smile on her husband again, and a tacit reconciliation came about by natural degrees.

But this produced a startling result.

Leonard, as her confessor, could learn everything that passed between them; he had only to follow established precedents, and ask questions his Church has printed for the use of confessors. He was mad enough to put such interrogatories.

The consequence was, that one day, being off his guard, or literally unable to contain his bursting heart any longer, he uttered a cry of jealous agony, and then, in a torrent of burning, melting words, appealed to her pity. He painted her husband's happiness, and his own misery, and barren desolation, with a fervid, passionate eloquence that paralyzed his hearer, and left her pale and trembling, and the tears of pity trickling down her cheek.

Those silent tears calmed him a little; and he begged her forgiveness, and awaited his doom.

"I pity you," said she, angelically. "What? *you* jealous of my husband! O, pray to Christ and Our Lady to cure you of this folly."

She rose, fluttering inwardly, but calm as a statue on the outside, gave him her hand, and went home very slowly; and the moment she was out of his sight she drooped her head like a crushed flower.

She was sad, ashamed, alarmed.

Her mind was in a whirl; and, were I to imitate those writers who undertake to dissect and analyze the heart at such moments, and put the exact result on paper, I should be apt to sacrifice truth to precision; I must stick to my old plan, and tell you what she did: that will surely be some index to her mind, especially with my female readers.

She went home straight to her husband; he was smoking his pipe after dinner. She drew her chair close to him, and laid her hand tenderly on his shoulder. "Griffith," she said, "will you grant your wife a favor? You once promised to take me abroad: I desire to go now; I long to see foreign countries; I am tired of this place. I want a change. Prithee,.prithee take me hence this very day."

Griffith looked aghast. "Why, sweetheart, it takes a deal of money to go abroad; we must get in our rents first."

"Nay, I have a hundred pounds laid by."

"Well, but what a fancy to take all of a sudden!"

"O Griffith, don't deny me what I ask you, with my arm round your neck, dearest. It is no fancy. I want to be alone with *you*, far from this place where coolness has come between us." And with this she fell to crying and sobbing, and straining him tight to her bosom, as if she feared to lose him, or be taken from him.

Griffith kissed her, and told her to cheer up, he was not the man to deny her anything. "Just let me get my hay in," said he, "and I 'll take you to Rome, if you like."

"No, no: to-day, or to-morrow at furthest, or you don't love me as I deserve to be loved by you this day."

"Now Kate, my darling, be reasonable. I *must* get my hay in; and then I am your man."

Mrs. Gaunt had gradually sunk almost to her knees. She now started up with nostrils expanding and her blue eyes glittering. "Your hay!" she cried, with bitter contempt; "your hay before your wife? That is how *you* love me!" And, the next moment, she seemed to turn from a fiery woman to a glacier.

Griffith smiled at all this, with that lordly superiority the male sometimes wears when he is behaving like a dull ass ; and smoked his pipe, and resolved to indulge her whim as soon as ever he had got his hay in.

CHAPTER XXIV.

SHOWERY weather set in, and the hay had to be turned twice, and left in cocks instead of carried.

Griffith spoke now and then about the foreign tour ; but Kate deigned no reply whatever ; and the chilled topic died out before the wet hay could be got in : and so much for Procrastination.

Meantime, Betty Gough was sent for to mend the house-linen. She came every other day after dinner, and sat working alone beside Mrs. Gaunt till dark.

Caroline Ryder put her own construction on this, and tried to make friends with Mrs. Gough, intending to pump her. But Mrs. Gough gave her short, dry answers. Ryder then felt sure that Gough was a go-between, and, woman-like, turned up her nose at her with marked contempt. For why ? This office of go-between was one she especially coveted for herself under the circumstances ; and, a little while ago, it had seemed within her grasp.

One fine afternoon the hay was all carried, and Griffith came home in good spirits to tell his wife he was ready to make the grand tour with her.

He was met at the gate by Mrs. Gough, with a face of great concern ; she begged him to come and see the Dame ; she had slipped on the oak stairs, poor soul, and hurt her back.

Griffith tore up the stairs, and found Kate in the drawing-room, lying on a sofa, and her doctor by her side. He came in, trembling like a leaf, and clasped her piteously in his arms. At this she uttered a little patient sigh of pain, and the doctor begged him to moderate himself : there was no immediate cause of alarm ; but she must be kept quiet ; she had strained her back, and her nerves were shaken by the fall.

"O my poor Kate !" cried Griffith ; and would let nobody else touch her. She was no longer a tall girl, but a statuesque woman ; yet he carried her in his herculean arms up to her bed. She turned her head towards him and shed a gentle tear at this proof of his love ; but the next moment she was cold again, and seemed weary of her life.

An invalid's bed was sent to her by the doctor at her own request, and placed on a small bedstead. She lay on this at night, and on a sofa by day.

Griffith was now as good as a widower ; and Caroline Ryder improved the opportunity. She threw herself constantly in his way, all smiles, small talk, and geniality.

Like many healthy men, your sickness wearied him if it lasted over two days ; and whenever he came out, chilled and discontented, from his invalid wife, there was a fine, buoyant, healthy young woman, ready to chat with him, and brimming over with undisguised admiration.

True, she was only a servant, — a servant to the core. But she had been always about ladies, and could wear their surface as readily as she could their gowns. Moreover, Griffith himself lacked dignity and reserve ; he would talk to anybody.

The two women began to fill the relative situations of clouds and sunshine.

But, ere this had lasted long, the enticing contact with the object of her lawless fancy inflamed Ryder, and made her so impatient that she struck her long meditated blow a little prematurely.

The passage outside Mrs. Gaunt's door had a large window ; and one day, while Griffith was with his wife, Ryder composed herself on the window-seat in a forlorn attitude, too striking and unlike her usual gay demeanor to pass unnoticed.

Griffith came out and saw this drooping, disconsolate figure. " Hallo !" said he, " what is wrong with *you ?* " a little fretfully.

A deep sigh was the only response.

"Had words with your sweetheart?"

"You know I have no sweetheart, sir."

The good-natured Squire made an attempt or two to console her and find out what was the matter; but he could get nothing out of her but monosyllables and sighs. At last the crocodile contrived to cry. And having thus secured his pity, she said: "There, never heed me. I 'm a foolish woman; I can't bear to see my dear master so abused."

"What d' ye mean?" said Griffith, sternly. Her very first shaft wounded his peace of mind.

"O, no matter! why should I be your friend and my own enemy? If I tell you, I shall lose my place."

"Nonsense, girl, you shall never lose your place while I am here."

"Well, I hope not, sir; for I am very happy here; too happy methinks, when *you* speak kindly to me. Take no notice of what I said. 'T is best to be blind at times."

The simple Squire did not see that this artful woman was playing the stale game of her sex; stimulating his curiosity under pretence of putting him off. He began to fret with suspicion and curiosity, and insisted on her speaking out.

"Ah! but I am so afraid you will hate me," said she; "and that will be worse than losing my place."

Griffith stamped on the ground. "What is it?" said he, fiercely.

Ryder seemed frightened. "It is nothing," said she. Then she paused, and added, "but my folly. I can't bear to see you waste your feelings. She is not so ill as you fancy."

"Do you mean to say that my wife is pretending?"

"How can I say that? I was n't there: *nobody saw her fall;* nor *heard her either;* and the house full of people. No doubt there is something the matter with her; but I do believe her heart is in more trouble than her back."

"And what troubles her heart? Tell me, and she shall not fret long."

"Well, sir; then just you send for Father Leonard; and she will get up, and walk as she used, and smile on you as she used. That man is the main of her sickness, you take my word."

Griffith turned sick at heart; and the strong man literally staggered at this envenomed thrust of a weak woman's tongue. But he struggled with the poison.

"What d' ye mean, woman?" said he. "The priest has n't been near her these two months."

"That is it, sir," replied Ryder quietly; "*he* is too wise to come here against your will; and *she* is bitter against you for frightening him away. Ask yourself, sir, did n't she change to you the moment that you threatened that Leonard with the horse-pond?"

"That is true!" gasped the wretched husband.

Yet he struggled again. "But she made it up with me after that. Why, 't was but the other day she begged me to go abroad with her, and take her away from this place."

"Ay? indeed!" said Ryder, bending her black brows, "did she so?"

"That she did," said Griffith joyfully; "so you see you are mistaken."

"You should have taken her at her word, sir," was all the woman's reply.

"Well, you see the hay was out; so I put it off; and then came the cursed rain, day after day; and so she cooled upon it."

"Of course she did, sir." Then, with a solemnity that appalled her miserable listener, "I 'd give all I 'm worth if you had taken her at her word that minute. But that is the way with you gentlemen; you let the occasion slip; and we that be women never forgive that: she won't give you the same chance again, *I* know. Now, if I was not afraid to make you unhappy, I 'd tell you why she asked you to go abroad. She felt herself weak and saw her danger; she found she could not resist that Leonard any longer; and she had the sense to see it was n't worth her while to ruin herself for him; so she asked you to save her from him: that is the plain English. And you did n't."

At this, Griffith's face wore an expression of agony so horrible that Ryder hesitated in her course. "There, there," said she, "pray don't look so, dear master! after all, there 's nothing certain; and perhaps I am too severe where I see you ill-treated: and to be sure no woman could be cold to *you* unless she was bewitched out of her seven senses by some other man. I could n't use you as mistress does; but then there 's nobody I care a straw for in these parts, except my dear master."

Griffith took no notice of this overture: the potent poison of jealousy was coursing through all his veins and distorting his ghastly face.

"O God!" he gasped, "can this thing be? My wife! the mother of my child! It is a lie! I can't believe it; I won't believe it. Have pity on me, woman, and think again, and unsay your words; for, if 't is so, there will be murder in this house."

Ryder was alarmed. "Don't talk so," said she hastily; "no woman born is worth that. Besides, as you say, what do we know against her? She is a gentlewoman, and well brought up. Now, dear master, you have got one friend in this house, and that is me: I know women better than you do. Will you be ruled by me?"

"Yes, I will: for I do believe you care a little for me."

"Then don't you believe anything against our Dame. Keep quiet till you know more. Don't you be so simple as to accuse her to her face, or you 'll never learn the truth. Just you watch her quietly, without seeming; and I 'll help you. Be a man, and know the truth."

"I will!" said Griffith, grinding his teeth. "And I believe she will come out pure as snow."

"Well, I hope so too," said Ryder, dryly. Then she added, "But don't you be seen speaking to me too much, sir, or she will suspect me, and then she will be on her guard with *me*.

When I have anything particular to tell you, I 'll cough, so; and then I 'll run out into the Grove: nobody goes there now."

Griffith did not see the hussy was arranging her own affair as well as his. He fell into the trap bodily.

The life this man led was now infernal.

He watched his wife night and day to detect her heart; he gave up hunting, he deserted the "Red Lion"; if he went out of doors, it was but a step; he hovered about the place to see if messages came or went; and he spent hours in his wife's bedroom, watching her, grim, silent, and sombre, to detect her inmost heart. His flesh wasted visibly, and his ruddy color paled. Hell was in his heart. Ay, two hells: jealousy and suspense.

Mrs. Gaunt saw directly that something was amiss, and erelong she divined what it was.

But, if he was jealous, she was proud as Lucifer. So she met his ever-watchful eye with the face of a marble statue.

Only in secret her heart quaked and yearned, and she shed many a furtive tear, and was sore, sore perplexed.

Meantime Ryder was playing with her husband's anguish like a cat with a mouse.

Upon the pretence of some petty discovery or other, she got him out day after day into the Grove, and, to make him believe in her candor and impartiality, would give him feeble reasons for thinking his wife loved him still; taking care to overpower these reasons with some little piece of strong good-sense and subtle observation.

It is the fate of moral poisoners to poison themselves as well as their victims. This is a just retribution, and it fell upon this female Iago. Her wretched master now loved his wife to distraction, yet hated her to the death: and Ryder loved her master passionately, yet hated him intensely, by fits and starts.

These secret meetings on which she

had counted so, what did she gain by them ? She saw that, with all her beauty, intelligence, and zeal for him, she was nothing to him still. He suspected, he sometimes hated his wife, but he was always full of her. There was no getting any other wedge into his heart.

This so embittered Ryder that one day she revenged herself on him.

He had been saying that no earthly torment could equal his : all his watching had shown him nothing for certain. " O," said he, " if I could only get proof of her innocence, or proof of her guilt ! Anything better than the misery of doubt. It gnaws my heart, it consumes my flesh. I can't sleep, I can't eat, I can't sit down. I envy the dead that lie at peace. O my heart ! my heart ! "

" And all for a woman that is not young, nor half so handsome as yourself. Well, sir, I 'll try and cure you of your *doubt*, if that is what torments you. When you threatened that Leonard, he got his orders to come here no more. But *she* visited him at his place again and again."

" 'T is false ! How know you that ? "

" As soon as your back was turned, she used to order her horse and ride to him."

" How do you know she went to *him* ? "

" I mounted the tower, and saw the way she took."

Griffith's face was a piteous sight. He stammered out, " Well, he is her confessor. She always visited him at times."

" Ay, sir ; but in those days her blood was cool, and his too ; but bethink you now, when you threatened the man with the horse-pond, he became your enemy. All revenge is sweet ; but what revenge so sweet to any man as that which came to his arms of its own accord ? I do notice that men can't read men, but any woman can read a woman. Maids they are reserved, because their mothers have told them that is the only way to get married. But what have a wife

and a priest to keep them distant ! Can they ever hope to come together lawfully ? That is why a priest's light-o'-love is always some honest man's wife. What had those two to keep them from folly ? Old Betty Gough ? Why, the mistress had bought her, body and soul, long ago. No, sir, you had no friend there ; and you had three enemies, — love, revenge, and opportunity. Why, what did the priest say to me ? I met him not ten yards from here. ' Ware the horse-pond ! ' says I. Says he, ' *Since I am to have the bitter, I 'll have the sweet as well.*' "

These infernal words were not spoken in vain. Griffith's features were horribly distorted, his eyes rolled fearfully, and he fell to the ground, grinding his teeth, and foaming at the mouth. An epileptic fit !

An epileptic fit is a terrible sight : the simple description of one in our medical books is appalling.

And in this case it was all the more fearful, the subject being so strong and active.

Caroline Ryder shrieked with terror, but no one heard her ; at all events, no one came ; to be sure the place had a bad name for ghosts, etc.

She tried to hold his head, but could not, for his body kept bounding from the earth with inconceivable elasticity and fury, and his arms flew in every direction ; and presently Ryder received a violent blow that almost stunned her.

She lay groaning and trembling beside the victim of her poisonous tongue and of his own passions.

When she recovered herself he was snorting rather than breathing, but lying still and pale enough, with his eyes set and glassy.

She got up, and went with uneven steps to a little rill hard by, and plunged her face in it : then filled her beaver hat, and came and dashed water repeatedly in his face.

He came to his senses by degrees ; but was weak as an infant. Then Ryder wiped the foam from his lips, and, kneeling on her knees, laid a soft hand upon his heavy head, shedding tears of pity and remorse, and sick at heart herself.

For what had she gained by blackening her rival? The sight of *his* bodily agony, and *his* ineradicable love.

Mrs. Gaunt sat out of shot, cold, calm, superior.

Yet, in the desperation of her passion, it was something to nurse his weak head an instant, and shed hot tears upon his brow; it was a positive joy, and soon proved a fresh and inevitable temptation.

"My poor master," said she, tenderly, "I never will say a word to you again. It is better to be blind. My God! how you cling to her that feigns a broken back to be rid of you, when there are others as well to look at, and ever so much younger, that adore every hair on your dear head, and would follow you round the world for one kind look."

"Let no one love me like that," said Griffith feebly, "to love so is to be miserable."

"Pity her then, at least," murmured Ryder; and, feeling she had quite committed herself now, her bosom panted under Griffith's ear, and told him the secret she had kept till now.

My female readers will sneer at this temptation: they cannot put themselves in a man's place. My male readers know that scarcely one man out of a dozen, sick, sore, and hating her he loved, would have turned away from the illicit consolation thus offered to him in his hour of weakness with soft, seducing tones, warm tears, and heart that panted at his ear.

CHAPTER XXV.

How did poor, faulty Griffith receive it?

He raised his head, and turned his brown eye gentle but full upon her. "My poor girl," said he, "I see what you are driving at. But that will not do. I have nothing to give you in exchange. I hate my wife that I loved

so dear: d—n her! d—n her! But I hate all womankind for her sake. Keep you clear of me. I would ruin no poor girl for heartless sport. I shall have blood on my hands erelong, and that is enough."

And, with these alarming words, he seemed suddenly to recover all his vigor; for he rose and stalked away at once, and never looked behind him.

Ryder made no further attempt. She sat down and shed bitter tears of sorrow and mortification.

After this cruel rebuff she must hate somebody; and, with the justice of her sex, she pitched on Mrs. Gaunt, and hated her like a demon, and watched to do her a mischief by hook or by crook.

Griffith's appearance and manner caused Mrs. Gaunt very serious anxiety. His clothes hung loose on his wasting frame; his face was of one uniform sallow tint, like a maniac's; and he sat silent for hours beside his wife, eying her askant from time to time like a surly mastiff guarding some treasure.

She divined what was passing in his mind, and tried to soothe him; but almost in vain. He was sometimes softened for the moment; but *hæret lateri lethalis arundo;* he still hovered about, watching her and tormenting himself; gnawed mad by three vultures of the mind, — doubt, jealousy, and suspense.

Mrs. Gaunt wrote letters to Father Leonard: hitherto she had only sent him short messages.

Betty Gough carried these letters, and brought the answers.

Griffith, thanks to the hint Ryder had given him, suspected this, and waylaid the old woman, and roughly demanded to see the letter she was carrying. She stoutly protested she had none. He seized her, turned her pockets inside out, and found a bunch of keys; item, a printed dialogue between Peter and Herod, omitted in the canonical books, but described by the modern discoverer as an infallible charm for the toothache ; item, a brass thimble ; item, half a nutmeg.

"Curse your cunning," said he ; and went off muttering.

The old woman tottered trembling to Mrs. Gaunt, related this outrage with an air of injured innocence, then removed her cap, undid her hair, and took out a letter from Leonard.

"This must end, and shall," said Mrs. Gaunt, firmly ; "else it will drive him mad and me too."

Bolton fair-day came. It was a great fair, and had attractions for all classes. There were cattle and horses of all kinds for sale, and also shows, games, wrestling, and dancing till daybreak.

All the servants had a prescriptive right to go to this fair ; and Griffith himself had never missed one. He told Kate over-night he would go, if it were not for leaving her alone.

The words were kinder than their meaning ; but Mrs. Gaunt had the tact, or the candor, to take them in their best sense. "And I would go with you, my dear," said she ; "but I should only be a drag. Never heed me ; give yourself a day's pleasure, for indeed you need it. I am in care about you : you are so dull of late."

"Well, I will," said Griffith. "I 'll not mope here when all the rest are merry-making."

Accordingly, next day, about eleven in the morning, he mounted his horse and rode to the fair, leaving the house empty ; for all the servants were gone except the old housekeeper ; she was tied to the fireside by rheumatics. Even Ryder started, with a new bonnet and red ribbons ; but that was only a blind. She slipped back and got unperceived into her own bedroom.

Griffith ran through the fair ; but could not enjoy it. *Hærebat lateri arundo.* He came galloping back to watch his wife, and see whether Betty Gough had come again or not.

As he rode into the stable-yard he caught sight of Ryder's face at an upper window. She looked pale and agitated, and her black eyes flashed with a strange

expression. /\She made him a signal which he did not understand ; but she joined him directly after in the stable-yard.

"Come quietly with me," said she, solemnly.

He hooked his horse's rein to the wall, and followed her, trembling.

She took him up the back stairs, and, when she got to the landing, turned and said, "Where did you leave her ? "

"In her own room."

"See if she is there now," said Ryder, pointing to the door.

Griffith tore the door open ; the room was empty.

"Nor is she to be found in the house," said Ryder ; "for I 've been in every room."

Griffith's face turned livid, and he staggered and leaned against the wall. "Where is she ? " said he, hoarsely.

"Humph !" said Ryder, fiendishly. "Find *him*, and you 'll find her."

"I 'll find them if they are above ground," cried Griffith, furiously ; and he rushed into his bedroom, and soon came out again, with a fearful purpose written on his ghastly features and in his bloodshot eyes, and a loaded pistol in his hand.

Ryder was terrified ; but instead of succumbing to terror, she flew at him like a cat, and wreathed her arms round him.

"What would you do ? " cried she. "Madman, would you hang for them ? and break my heart, — the only woman in the world that loves you ? Give me the pistol. Nay, I will have it." And, with that extraordinary power excitement lends her sex, she wrenched it out of his hands.

He gnashed his teeth with fury, and clutched her with a gripe of iron ; she screamed with pain : he relaxed his grasp a little at that ; she turned on him and defied him.

"I won't let you get into trouble for a priest and a 'wanton," she cried ; you shall kill me first. Leave me the pistol, and pledge me your sacred word to do them no harm, and then I 'll tell you where they are. Refuse me this, and you shall go to your grave and know nothing more than you know now."

" No, no ; if you are a woman, have pity on me ; let me come at them. There, I 'll use no weapon. I 'll tear them to atoms with these hands. Where are they ? "

" May I put the pistol away then ? "

" Yes, take it out of my sight ; so best. Where are they ? "

Ryder locked the pistol up in one of Mrs. Gaunt's boxes. Then she said, in a trembling voice, " Follow me."

He followed her in awful silence.

She went rather slowly to the door that opened on the lawn ; and then she hesitated. " If you are a man, and have any feeling for a poor girl who loves you, — if you are a gentleman, and respect your word, — no violence."

" I promise," said he. " Where are they ? "

" Nay, nay. I fear I shall rue the day I told you. Promise me once more : no bloodshed — upon your soul."

" I promise. Where are they ? "

" God forgive me ; they are in the Grove."

He bounded away from her like some beast of prey ; and she crouched and trembled on the steps of the door : and, now that she realized what she was doing, a sickening sense of dire misgiving came over her, and made her feel quite faint.

And so the weak, but dangerous creature sat crouching and quaking, and launched the strong one.

Griffith was soon in the Grove ; and the first thing he saw was Leonard and his wife walking together in earnest conversation. Their backs were towards him. Mrs. Gaunt, whom he had left lying on a sofa, and who professed herself scarce able to walk half a dozen times across the room, was now springing along, elastic as a young greyhound, and full of fire and animation. The miserable husband saw, and his heart died within him. He leaned against a tree and groaned.

The deadly sickness of his heart soon gave way to sombre fury. He came softly after them, with ghastly cheek, and bloodthirsty eyes, like red-hot coals.

They stopped ; and he heard his wife say, " 'T is a solemn promise, then : this very night." The priest bowed assent. Then they spoke in so low a voice, he could not hear ; but his wife pressed a purse upon Leonard, and Leonard hesitated, but ended by taking it.

Griffith uttered a yell like a tiger, and rushed between them with savage violence, driving the lady one way with his wrists, and the priest another. She screamed : he trembled in silence.

Griffith stood a moment between these two pale faces, silent and awful.

Then he faced his wife. " You vile wretch ! " he cried : " so you *buy* your own dishonor, and mine." He raised his hand high over her head ; she never winced. " O, but for my oath, I 'd lay you dead at my feet ! But no ; I 'll not hang for a priest and a wanton. So, this is the thing you love, and pay it to love you." And with all the mad inconsistency of rage, which mixes small things and great, he tore the purse out of Leonard's hand : then seized him felly by the throat.

At that the high spirit of Mrs. Gaunt gave way to abject terror. " O mercy ! mercy ! " she cried ; " it is all a mistake." And she clung to his knees.

He spurned her furiously away. " Don't touch me, woman," he cried, " or you are dead. Look at this ! " And in a moment, with gigantic strength and fury, he dashed the priest down at her feet. " I know ye, ye proud, wanton devil ! " he cried ; " love the thing you have seen me tread upon ! love it — if ye can." And he literally trampled upon the poor priest with both feet.

Leonard shrieked for mercy.

" None, in this world or the next," roared Griffith ; but the next moment he took fright at himself. " God ! " he cried, " I must go or kill. Live and be damned forever, the pair of ye." And with this he fled from them, grinding his teeth and beating the air with his clenched fists.

He darted to the stable-yard, sprang on his horse, and galloped away from Hernshaw Castle, with the face, the eyes, the gestures, the incoherent mutterings of a raving Bedlamite.

CHAPTER XXVI.

He was gone for good, this time.

At the fair the wrestling was ended, and the tongues going over it all again, and throwing the victors; the greasy pole, with leg of mutton attached by ribbons, was being hoisted, and the swings flying, and the lads and lasses footing it to the fife and tabor, and the people chattering in groups; when the clatter of a horse's feet was heard, and a horseman burst in and rode recklessly through the market-place; indeed, if his noble horse had been as rash as he was, some would have been trampled under foot. The rider's face was ghastly: such as were not exactly in his path had time to see it, and wonder how this terrible countenance came into that merry place. Thus, as he passed, shouts of dismay arose, and a space opened before him, and then closed behind him with a great murmur that followed at his heels.

Tom Leicester was listening, spellbound, on the outskirts of the throng, to the songs and humorous tirades of a pedler selling his wares; and was saying to himself, " I too will be a pedler." Hearing the row, he turned round, and saw his master just coming down with that stricken face.

Tom could not read his own name in print or manuscript; and these are the fellows that beat us all at reading countenances: he saw in a moment that some great calamity had fallen on Griffith's head; and nature stirred in him. He darted to his master's side, and seized the bridle. " What is up ? " he cried.

But Griffith did not answer nor notice. His ears were almost deaf, and his eyes, great and staring, were fixed right ahead; and, to all appearance, he did not see the people. He seemed to be making for the horizon.

" Master ! for the love of God, speak to me," cried Leicester. " What have they done to you ? Whither be you going, with the face of a ghost ? "

" Away, from the hangman," shrieked Griffith, still staring at the horizon. " Stay me not; my hands itch for their throats; my heart thirsts for their blood; but I 'll not hang for a priest and a wanton." Then he suddenly turned on Leicester, " Let thou go, or —" and he lifted his heavy riding-whip.

Then Leicester let go the rein, and the whip descended on the horse's flank. He went clattering furiously over the stones, and drove the thinner groups apart like chaff, and his galloping feet were soon heard, fainter and fainter till they died away in the distance. Leicester stood gaping.

Griffith's horse, a black hunter of singular power and beauty, carried his wretched master well that day. He went on till sunset, trotting, cantering, and walking, without intermission; the whip ceased to touch him, the rein never checked him. He found he was the master, and he went his own way. He took his broken rider back into the county where he had been foaled. But a few miles from his native place they came to the " Packhorse," a pretty little roadside inn, with farm-yard and buildings at the back. He had often baited here in his infancy; and now, stiff and stumbling with fatigue, the good horse could not pass the familiar place; he walked gravely into the stable-yard, and there fairly came to an end; craned out his drooping head, crooked his limbs, and seemed of wood. And no wonder. He was ninety-three miles from his last corn.

Paul Carrick, a young farrier, who frequented the " Packhorse," happened just then to be lounging at the kitchen door, and saw him come in. He turned directly, and shouted into the house, "Ho! Master Vint, come hither. Here 's Black Dick come home, and brought you a worshipful customer."

The landlord bustled out of the kitchen, crying, "They are welcome both." Then he came lowly louting to Griffith, cap in hand, and held the horse, poor immovable brute; and his wife courtesied perseveringly at the door.

Griffith dismounted, and stood there looking like one in a dream.

"Please you come in, sir," said the landlady, smiling professionally.

He followed her mechanically.

"Would your worship be private? We keep a parlor for gentles."

"Ay, let me be alone," he groaned.

Mercy Vint, the daughter, happened to be on the stairs and heard him: the voice startled her, and she turned round directly to look at the speaker; but she only saw his back going into the room, and then he flung himself like a sack into the arm-chair.

The landlady invited him to order supper: he declined. She pressed him. He flung a piece of money on the table, and told her savagely to score his supper, and leave him in peace.

She flounced out with a red face, and complained to her husband in the kitchen.

Harry Vint rung the crown-piece on the table before he committed himself to a reply. It rang like a bell. "Churl or not, his coin is good," said Harry Vint, philosophically. "I 'll eat his supper, dame, for that matter."

"Father," whispered Mercy, "I do think the gentleman is in trouble."

"And that is no business of mine, neither," said Harry Vint.

Presently the guest they were discussing called loudly for a quart of burnt wine.

When it was ready, Mercy offered to take it in to him. She was curious. The landlord looked up rather surprised; for his daughter attended to the farm, but fought shy of the inn and its business.

"Take it, lass, and welcome for me," said Mrs. Vint, pettishly.

Mercy took the wine in, and found Griffith with his head buried in his hands. ,

She stood awhile with the tray, not knowing what to do.

Then, as he did not move, she said softly, "The wine, sir, an if it please you."

Griffith lifted his head, and turned two eyes clouded with suffering upon her. He saw a buxom, blooming young woman, with remarkably dove-like eyes that dwelt with timid, kindly curiosity upon him. He looked at her in a half-distracted way, and then put his hand to the mug. "Here 's perdition to all false women!" said he, and tossed half the wine down at a single draught.

"'T is not to me you drink, sir," said Mercy, with gentle dignity. Then she courtesied modestly and retired, discouraged, not offended.

The wretched Griffith took no notice, —did not even see he had repulsed a friendly visitor. The wine, taken on an empty stomach, soon stupefied him, and he staggered to bed.

He awoke at daybreak: and O the agony of that waking!

He lay sighing awhile, with his hot skin quivering on his bones, and his heart like lead; then got up and flung his clothes on hastily, and asked how far to the nearest seaport.

Twenty miles.

He called for his horse. The poor brute was dead lame.

He cursed that good servant for going lame. He walked round and round like a wild beast, chafing and fuming awhile; then sank into a torpor of dejection, and sat with his head bowed on the table all day.

He ate scarcely any food; but drank wine freely, remarking, however, that it was false-hearted stuff, did him no good, and had no taste as wine used to have. "But nothing is what it was," said he. "Even I was happy once. But that seems years ago."

"Alas! poor gentleman; God comfort you," said Mercy Vint, and came, with the tears in her dove-like eyes, and said to her father, "To be sure his worship hath been crossed in love;

and what could she be thinking of? Such a handsome, well-made gentleman!"

"Now that is a wench's first thought," said Harry Vint; "more likely lost his money, gambling, or racing. But, indeed, I think 't is his head is disordered, not his heart. I wish the 'Packhorse' was quit of him, maugre his laced coat. We want no kill-joys here."

That night he was heard groaning, and talking, and did not come down at all.

So at noon Mrs. Vint knocked at his door. A weak voice bade her enter. She found him shivering, and he asked her for a fire.

She grumbled, out of hearing, but lighted a fire.

Presently his voice was heard hallooing. He wanted all the windows open, he was so burning hot.

The landlady looked at him, and saw his face was flushed and swollen; and he complained of pain in all his bones. She opened the windows, and asked him would he have a doctor sent for. He shook his head contemptuously.

However, towards evening, he became delirious, and raved and tossed, and rolled his head as if it was an intolerable weight he wanted to get rid of.

The females of the family were for sending at once for a doctor; but the prudent Harry demurred.

"Tell me, first, who is to pay the fee," said he. "I 've seen a fine coat with the pockets empty, before to-day."

The women set up their throats at him with one accord, each after her kind.

"Out, fie!" said Mercy; "are we to do naught for charity?"

"Why, there 's his horse, ye foolish man," said Mrs. Vint.

"Ay, ye are both wiser than me," said Harry Vint, ironically. And soon after that he went out softly.

The next minute he was in the sick man's room, examining his pockets. To his infinite surprise he found twenty gold pieces, a quantity of silver, and some trinkets.

He spread them all out on the table, and gloated on them with greedy eyes. They looked so inviting, that he said to himself they would be safer in his custody than in that of a delirious person, who was even now raving incoherently before him, and could not see what he was doing. He therefore proceeded to transfer them to his own care.

On the way to his pocket, his shaking hand was arrested by another hand, soft, but firm as iron.

He shuddered, and looked round in abject terror; and there was his daughter's face, pale as his own, but full of resolution. "Nay, father," said she; "*I* must take charge of these: and well do you know why."

These simple words cowed Harry Vint, so that he instantly resigned the money and jewels, and retired, muttering that "things were come to a pretty pass," — "a man was no longer master in his own house," etc., etc., etc.

While he inveighed against the degeneracy of the age, the women paid him no more attention than the age did, but just sent for the doctor. He came, and bled the patient. This gave him a momentary relief; but when, in the natural progress of the disease, sweating and weakness came on, the loss of the precious vital fluid was fatal, and the patient's pulse became scarce perceptible. There he lay, with wet hair, and gleaming eyes, and haggard face, at death's door.

An experienced old crone was got to nurse him, and she told Mrs. Vint he would live may be three days.

Paul Carrick used to come to the "Packhorse" after Mercy Vint, and, finding her sad, asked her what was the matter.

"What should it be," said she, "but the poor gentleman a-dying overhead; away from all his friends."

"Let me see him," said Paul.

Mercy took him softly into the room.

"Ay, he is booked," said the farrier. "Doctor has taken too much blood out of the man's body. They kill a many that way."

"Alack, Paul! must he die? Can naught be done?" said Mercy, clasping her hands.

"I don't say that, neither," said the farrier. "He is a well-made man: he is young. *I* might save him, perhaps, if I had not so many beasts to look to. I 'll tell you what you do. Make him soup as strong as strong; have him watched night and day, and let 'em put a spoonful of warm wine into him every hour, and then of soup; egg flip is a good thing, too; change his bed-linen, and keep the doctors from him: that is his only chance; he is fairly dying of weakness. But I must be off. Farmer Blake's cow is down for calving; I must give her an ounce of salts before 't is too late."

Mercy Vint scanned the patient closely, and saw that Paul Carrick was right. She followed his instructions to the letter, with one exception. Instead of trusting to the old woman, of whom she had no very good opinion, she had the great arm-chair brought into the sick-room, and watched the patient herself by night and day; a gentle hand cooled his temples; a gentle hand brought concentrated nourishment to his lips; and a mellow voice coaxed him to be good and swallow it. There are voices it is not natural to resist; and Griffith learned by degrees to obey this one, even when he was half unconscious.

At the end of three days this zealous young nurse thought she discerned a slight improvement, and told her mother so. Then the old lady came and examined the patient, and shook her head gravely. Her judgment, like her daughter's, was influenced by her wishes.

The fact is, both landlord and landlady were now calculating upon Griffith's decease. Harry had told her about the money and jewels, and the pair had put their heads together, and settled that Griffith was a gentleman highwayman, and his spoil would never be reclaimed after his decease, but fall to those good Samaritans, who were now nursing him, and intended to bury him respectably. The future being thus settled, this

worthy couple became a little impatient; for Griffith, like Charles the Second, was "an unconscionable time dying."

We order dinner to hasten a lingering guest; and, with equal force of logic, mine host of the "Packhorse" spoke to White, the village carpenter, about a full-sized coffin; and his wife set the old crone to make a linen shroud, unobtrusively, in the bake-house.

On the third afternoon of her nursing, Mercy left her patient, and called up the crone to tend him. She herself, worn out with fatigue, threw herself on a bed in her mother's room, hard by, and soon fell asleep.

She had slept about two hours when she was wakened by a strange noise in the sick-chamber. A man and a woman quarrelling.

She bounded off the bed, and was in the room directly.

Lo and behold, there were the nurse and the dying man abusing one another like pickpockets.

The cause of this little misunderstanding was not far to seek. The old crone had brought up her work: *videlicet*, a winding-sheet all but finished, and certain strips of glazed muslin about three inches deep. She soon completed the winding-sheet, and hung it over two chairs in the patient's sight; she then proceeded to double the slips in six, and nick them; then she unrolled them, and they were frills, and well adapted to make the coming corpse absurd, and divest it of any little dignity the King of Terrors might bestow on it.

She was so intent upon her congenial task that she did not observe the sick man had awakened, and was viewing her and her work with an intelligent but sinister eye.

"What is that you are making?" said he, grimly.

The voice was rather clear, and strong, and seemed so loud and strange in that still chamber, that it startled the woman mightily. She uttered a little shriek, and then was wroth. "Plague take the man!" said she; "how you scared me. Keep quiet, do; and mind your own business." [The business of going off the hooks.]

"I ask you what is that you are making," said Griffith, louder, and raising himself on his arm.

"Baby's frills," replied the woman, coolly, recovering that contempt for the understandings of the dying which marks the veritable crone.

"Ye lie," said Griffith. "And there is a shroud. Who is that for?"

"Who should it be for, thou simple body? Keep quiet, do, till the change comes. 'T won't be long now; art too well to last till sundown."

"So 't is for me, is it?" screamed Griffith. "I 'll disappoint ye yet. Give me my clothes. I 'll not lie here to be measured for my grave, ye old witch."

"Here 's manners!" cackled the indignant crone. "Ye foul - mouthed knave! is this how you thank a decent woman for making a comfortable corpse of ye, you that has no right to die in your shoes, let a be such dainties as muslin neck-ruff, and shroud of good Dutch flax."

At this Griffith discharged a volley in which "vulture," "hag," "bloodsucker," etc., blended with as many oaths: during which Mercy came in.

She glided to him, with her dove's eyes full of concern, and laid her hand gently on his shoulder. "You 'll work yourself a mischief," said she; "leave me to scold her. Why, my good Nelly, how could ye be so hare - brained? Prithee take all that trumpery away this minute: none here needeth it, nor shall not this many a year, please God."

"They want me dead," said Griffith to her, piteously, finding he had got one friend, and sunk back on his pillow exhausted.

"So it seems," said Mercy, cunningly. "But I 'd balk them finely. I 'd up and order a beef-steak this minute."

"And shall," said Griffith, with feeble spite. "Leastways, do you order it, and I 'll eat it: — d—n her!"

Sick men are like children; and women soon find that out, and manage them accordingly. In ten minutes Mercy brought a good rump-steak to the bedside, and said, "Now for 't. Marry come up, with her winding-sheets!"

Thus played upon, and encouraged, the great baby ate more than half the steak; and soon after perspired gently, and fell asleep.

Paul Carrick found him breathing gently, with a slight tint of red in his cheek, and told Mercy there was a change for the better. "We have brought him to a true intermission," said he; "so throw in the bark at once."

"What, drench his honor's worship!" said Mercy, innocently. "Nay, send thou the medicine, and I 'll find womanly ways to get it down him."

Next day came the doctor, and whispered softly to Mrs. Vint, "How are we all up stairs?"

"Why could n't you come afore?" replied Mrs. Vint, crossly. "Here 's Farrier Carrick stepped in, and curing him out of hand, — the meddlesome body."

"A farrier rob me of my patient!" cried the doctor, in high dudgeon.

"Nay, good sir, 't is no fault of mine. This Paul is a sort of a kind of a follower of our Mercy's: and she is mistress here, I trow."

"And what hath his farriership prescribed? Friar's balsam, belike."

"Nay, I know not; but you may soon learn, for he is above, physicking the gentleman (a pretty gentleman!) and suiting to our Mercy — after a manner."

The doctor declined to make one in so mixed a consultation.

"Give me my fee, dame," said he; "and as for this impertinent farrier, the patient's blood be on his head; and I 'd have him beware the law."

Mrs. Vint went to the stair-foot, and screamed, "Mercy, the good doctor wants his fee. Who is to pay it, I wonder?"

"I 'll bring it him anon," said a gentle voice; and Mercy soon came down and paid it with a willing air that half disarmed professional fury.

"'T is a good lass, dame," said the doctor, when she was gone; "and, by the same token, I wish her better mated than to a scrub of a farrier."

Griffith, still weak, but freed of fever, woke one glorious afternoon, and heard a bird-like voice humming a quaint old ditty, and saw a field of golden wheat through an open window, and seated at that window the mellow songstress, Mercy Vint, plying her needle, with lowered lashes but beaming face, a picture of health and quiet womanly happiness. Things were going to her mind in that sick-room.

He looked at her, and at the golden corn and summer haze beyond, and the tide of life seemed to rush back upon him.

"My good lass," said he, "tell me, where am I? for I know not."

Mercy started, and left off singing, then rose and came slowly towards him, with her work in her hand.

Innocent joy at this new symptom of convalescence flushed her comely features, but she spoke low.

"Good sir, at the 'Packhorse,'" said she, smiling.

"The 'Packhorse'? and where is that?"

"Hard by Allerton village."

"And where is that? not in Cumberland?"

"Nay, in Lancashire, your worship. Why, whence come you that know not the 'Packhorse,' nor yet Allerton township? Come you from Cumberland?"

"No matter whence I come. I 'm going on board ship, — like my father before me."

"Alas, sir, you are not fit; you have been very ill, and partly distraught."

She stopped; for Griffith turned his face to the wall, with a deep groan. It had all rushed over him in a moment.

Mercy stood still, and worked on, but the water gathered in her eyes at that eloquent groan.

By and by Griffith turned round again, with a face of anguish, and filmy eyes, and saw her in the same place, standing, working, and pitying.

"What, are *you* there still?" said he, roughly.

"Ay, sir; but I 'll go, sooner than be troublesome. Can I fetch you anything?"

"No. Ay, wine; bring me wine to drown it all."

She brought him a pint of wine.

"Pledge me," said he, with a miserable attempt at a smile.

She put the cup to her lips, and sipped a drop or two; but her dove's eyes were looking up at him over the liquor all the time. Griffith soon disposed of the rest, and asked for more.

"Nay," said she, "but I dare not: the doctor hath forbidden excess in drinking."

"The doctor! What doctor?"

"Doctor Paul," said she, demurely. "He hath saved your life, sir, I do think."

"Plague take him for that!"

"So say not I."

Here she left him with an excuse. "'T is milking time, sir; and you shall know that I am our dairymaid. I seldom trouble the inn."

Next day she was on the window-seat, working and beaming. The patient called to her in peevish accents to put his head higher. She laid down her work with a smile, and came and raised his head.

"There, now, that is too high," said he; "how awkward you are."

"I lack experience, sir, but not good will. There, now, is that a little better?"

"Ay, a little. I 'm sick of lying here. I want to get up. Dost hear what I say? I — want — to get up."

"And so you shall. As soon as ever you are fit. To-morrow, perhaps. To-day you must e'en be patient. Patience is a rare medicine."

Tic, tic, tic! "What a noise they are making down stairs. Go, lass, and bid them hold their peace."

Mercy shook her head. "Good lack-a-day! we might as well bid the river give over running; but, to be sure, this comes of keeping a hostelry, sir. When we had only the farm, we were quiet, and did no ill to no one."

"Well, sing me, to drown their eternal buzzing: it worries me dead."

"Me sing! alack, sir, I 'm no songster."

"That is false. You sing like a throstle. I dote on music ; and, when I was delirious, I heard one singing about my bed ; I thought it was an angel at that time, but 't was only you, my young mistress : and now I ask you, you say me nay. That is the way with you all. Plague take the girl, and all her d—d, unreasonable, hypocritical sex. I warrant me you 'd sing, if I wanted to sleep, and dance the Devil to a standstill."

Mercy, instead of flouncing out of the room, stood looking on him with maternal eyes, and chuckling like a bird. "That is right, sir: tax us all to your heart's content. O, but I 'm a joyful woman to hear you ; for 't is a sure sign of mending when the sick take to rating of their nurses."

"In sooth, I am too cross-grained," said Griffith, relenting.

"Not a whit, sir, for my taste. I 've been in care for you : and now you are a little cross, that maketh me easy."

"Thou art a good soul. Wilt sing me a stave after all ? "

"La, you now ; how you come back to that. Ay, and with a good heart : for, to be sure, 't is a sin to gainsay a sick man. But indeed I am the homeliest singer. Methinks 't is time I went down and bade them cook your worship's supper."

"Nay, I 'll not eat nor sup till I hear thee sing."

"Your will is my law, sir," said Mercy, dryly, and retired to the window-seat ; that was the first obvious preliminary. Then she fiddled with her apron, and hemmed, and waited in hopes a reprieve might come ; but a peevish, relentless voice demanded the song at intervals.

So then she turned her head carefully away from her hearer, lowered her eyes, and, looking the picture of guilt and shame all the time, sang an ancient ditty. The poltroon's voice was rich, mellow, clear, and sweet as honey ; and she sang the notes for the sake of the words, not the words for the sake of the notes, as all but Nature's singers do.

The air was grave as well as sweet ; for Mercy was of an old Puritan stock, and even her songs were not giddy-paced, but solid, quaint, and tender : all the more did they reach the soul.

In vain was the blushing cheek averted, and the honeyed lips. The ravishing tones set the birds chirping outside, yet filled the room within, and the glasses rang in harmony upon the shelf as the sweet singer poured out from her heart (so it seemed) the speaking song : —

> "In vain you tell your parting lover
> You wish fair winds may waft him over,
> Alas ! what winds can happy prove
> That bear me far from her I love !
> Alas ! what dangers on the main
> Can equal those that I sustain
> From stinted love and cold disdain ?" etc.

Griffith beat time with his hand awhile, and his face softened and beautified as the melody curled about his heart. But soon it was too much for him. He knew the song, — had sung it to Kate Peyton in their days of courtship. A thousand memories gushed in upon his soul and overpowered him. He burst out sobbing violently, and wept as if his heart must break.

"Alas ! what have I done ? " said Mercy ; and the tears ran from her eyes at the sight. Then, with native delicacy, she hurried from the room.

What Griffith Gaunt went through that night, in silence, was never known but to himself. But the next morning he was a changed man. He was all dogged resolution, — put on his clothes unaided, though he could hardly stand to do it, and borrowed the landlord's staff, and crawled out a smart distance into the sun. "It was kill or cure," said he. "I am to live, it seems. Well, then, the past is dead. My life begins again to-day."

Hen-like, Mercy soon learned this sally of her refractory duckling, and was uneasy. So, for an excuse to watch him, she brought him out his money and jewels, and told him she had thought it safest to take charge of them.

He thanked her cavalierly, and offered her a diamond ring.

She blushed scarlet, and declined it; and even turned a meekly reproachful glance on him with her dove's eyes.

He had a suit of russet made, and put away his fine coat, and forbade any one to call him "Your worship." "I am a farmer, like yourselves," said he; "and my name is — Thomas Leicester."

A brain fever either kills the unhappy lover, or else benumbs the very anguish that caused it.

And so it was with Griffith. His love got benumbed, and the sense of his wrongs vivid. He nursed a bitter hatred of his wife; only, as he could not punish her without going near her, and no punishment short of death seemed enough for her, he set to work to obliterate her from his very memory, if possible. He tried employment: he pottered about the little farm, advising and helping, — and that so zealously that the landlord retired altogether from that department, and Griffith, instead of he, became Mercy's ally, agricultural and bucolical. She was a shepherdess to the core, and hated the poor "Packhorse."

For all that, it was her fate to add to its attractions: for Griffith bought a *viol da gambo*, and taught her sweet songs, which he accompanied with such skill, sometimes, with his voice, that good company often looked in on the chance of a good song sweetly sung and played.

The sick, in body or mind, are egotistical. Griffith was no exception: bent on curing his own deep wound, he never troubled his head about the wound he might inflict.

He was grateful to his sweet nurse, and told her so. And his gratitude charmed her all the more that it had been rather long in coming.

He found this dove-like creature a wonderful soother: he applied her more and more to his sore heart.

As for Mercy, she had been too good and kind to her patient not to take a tender interest in his convalescence. Our hearts warm more to those we have been kind to, than to those who have been kind to us: and the female reader can easily imagine what delicious feelings stole into that womanly heart when she saw her pale nursling pick up health and strength under her wing, and become the finest, handsomest man in the parish.

Pity and admiration, — where these meet, love is not far behind.

And then this man, who had been cross and rough while he was weak, became gentler, kinder, and more deferential to her, the stronger he got.

Mrs. Vint saw they were both fond of each other's company, and disapproved it. She told Paul Carrick if he had any thought of Mercy he had better give over shilly-shallying, for there was another man after her.

Paul made light of it, at first. "She has known me too long to take up her head with a new-comer," said he. "To be sure I never asked her to name the day; but she knows my mind well enough, and I know hers."

"Then you know more than I do," said the mother, ironically.

He thought over this conversation, and very wisely determined not to run unnecessary risks. He came up one afternoon, and hunted about for Mercy, till he found her milking a cow in the adjoining paddock.

"Well, lass," said he, "I've good news for thee. My old dad says we may have his house to live in. So now you and I can yoke next month if ye will."

"Me turn the honest man out of his house!" said Mercy, mighty innocently.

"Who asks you? He nobbut bargains for the chimney-corner: and you are not the girl to begrudge the old man that."

"O no, Paul. But what would father do if I were to leave *his* house? Methinks the farm would go to rack and ruin; he is so wrapped up in his nasty public."

"Why, he has got a helper, by all accounts : and if you talk like that, you will never wed at all."

"Never is a big word. But I 'm too young to marry yet. Jenny, thou jade, stand still."

The attack and defence proceeded upon these terms for some time ; and the defendant had one base advantage ; and used it. Her forehead was wedged tight against Jenny's ribs, and Paul could not see her face. This, and the feminine evasiveness of her replies, irritated him at last.

"Take thy head out o' the coow," said he, roughly, "and answer straight. Is all our wooing to go for naught ?"

"Wooing ? You never said so much to me in all these years as you have to-day."

"O, ye knew my mind well enough. There 's a many ways of showing the heart."

"Speaking out is the best, I trow."

"Why, what do I come here for twice a week, this two years past, if not for thee ? "

"Ay, for me, and father's ale."

"And thou canst look at me, and tell me that ? Ye false, hard-hearted hussy. But nay, thou wast never so : 't is this Thomas Leicester hath bewitched thee, and set thee against thy true lover."

"Mr. Leicester pays no suit to me," said Mercy, blushing. "He is a right civil-spoken gentleman, and you know you saved his life."

"The more fool I. I wish I had known he was going to rob me of my lass's heart, I 'd have seen him die a hundred times ere I 'd have interfered. But they say if you save a man's life he 'll make you rue it. Mercy, my lass, you are well respected in the parish. Take a thought, now : better be a farrier's wife than a gentleman's mistress."

Mercy did take her head "out of the cow" at this, and, for once, her cheek burned with anger ; but the unwonted sentiment died before it could find words, and she said, quietly, "I need not be either, against my will."

Young Carrick made many such appeals to Mercy Vint ; but he could never bring her to confess to him that he and she had ever been more than friends, or were now anything less than friends. Still he forced her to own to herself, that, if she had never seen Thomas Leicester, her quiet affection and respect for Carrick would probably have carried her to the altar with him.

His remonstrances, sometimes angry, sometimes tearful, awoke her pity, which was the grand sentiment of her heart, and disturbed her peace.

Moreover, she studied the two men in her quiet, thoughtful way, and saw that Carrick loved her with all his honest, though hitherto tepid heart ; but Griffith had depths, and could love with more passion than ever he had shown for her. "He is not the man to have a fever by reason of me," said the poor girl to herself. But I am afraid even this attracted her to Griffith. It nettled a woman's soft ambition ; which is, to be as well loved as ever woman was.

And so things went on, and, as generally happens, the man who was losing ground went the very way to lose more. He spoke ill of Griffith behind his back : called him a highwayman, a gentleman, an ungrateful, undermining traitor. But Griffith never mentioned Carrick ; and so, when he and Mercy were together, her old follower was pleasingly obliterated, and affectionate good-humor reigned. Thus Griffith, *alias* Thomas, became her sunbeam, and Paul her cloud.

But he who had disturbed the peace of others, his own turn came.

One day he found Mercy crying. He sat down beside her, and said, kindly, " Why, sweetheart, what is amiss ?"

"No great matter," said she ; and turned her head away, but did not check her tears, for it was new and pleasant to be consoled by Thomas Leicester.

"Nay, but tell me, child."

"Well, then, Jessie Carrick has been at me ; that is all." .

"The vixen ! what did she say ?

"*Mercy was carrying the pail, brimful, and that oaf sauntered by her side.*" — Page 119.

"Nay, I 'm not pleased enow with it to repeat it. She did cast something in my teeth."

Griffith pressed her to be more explicit : she declined, with so many blushes, that his curiosity was awakened, and he told Mrs. Vint, with some heat, that Jess Carrick had been making Mercy cry.

" Like enow," said Mrs. Vint, coolly. " She 'll eat her victuals all one for that, please God."

" Else I 'll wring the cock-nosed jade's neck, next time she comes here," replied Griffith ; " but, Dame, I want to know what she can have to say to Mercy to make her cry.

Mrs. Vint looked him steadily in the face for some time, and then and there decided to come to an explanation. " Ten to one 't is about her brother," said she ; " you know this Paul is our Mercy's sweetheart."

At these simple words Griffith winced, and his countenance changed remarkably. Mrs. Vint observed it, and was all the more resolved to have it out with him.

" Her sweetheart ! " said Griffith. " Why, I have seen them together a dozen of times, and not a word of courtship."

" O, the young men don't make many speeches in these parts. They show their hearts by act."

" By act ? why, I met them coming home from milking t' other evening. Mercy was carrying the pail, brimful ; and that oaf sauntered by her side, with his hands in his pockets. Was that the act of a lover ? "

" I heard of it, sir," said Mrs. Vint, quietly ; " and as how you took the pail from her, willy nilly, and carried it home. Mercy was vexed about it. She told me you panted at the door, and she was a' deal fitter to carry the pail than you, that is just off a sick-bed, like. But lawk, sir, ye can't go by the likes of that. The bachelors here they 'd see their sweethearts carry the roof into next parish on their backs, like a snail, and never put out a hand ; 't is not the custom hereaway. But, as I

was saying, Paul and our Mercy kept company, after a manner : he never had the wit to flatter her as should he, nor the stomach to bid her name the day and he 'd buy the ring ; but he talked to her about his sick beasts more than he did to any other girl in the parish, and she 'd have ended by going to church with him ; only you came and put a coolness atween 'em."

" I ! How ? "

" Well, sir, our Mercy is a kind-hearted lass, though I say it, and you were sick, and she did nurse you ; and that was a beginning. And, to be sure, you are a fine personable man, and capital company ; and you are always about the girl ; and, bethink you, sir, she is flesh and blood like her neighbors ; and they say, once a body has tasted venison-steak, it spoils their stomach for oat-porridge. Now that is Mercy's case, I 'm thinking ; not that she ever said as much to me, — she is too reserved. But, bless your heart, I 'm forced to go about with eyes in my head, and watch 'em all a bit, — me that keeps an inn."

Griffith groaned. " I 'm a villain ! " said he.

" Nay, nay," said Mrs. Vint. " Gentlefolks must be amused, cost what it may ; but, hoping no offence, sir, the girl was a good friend to you in time of sickness ; and so was this Paul, for that matter."

" She was," cried Griffith ; " God bless her. How can I ever repay her ? "

" Well, sir," said Mrs. Vint, " if that comes from your heart, you might take our Mercy apart, and tell her you like her very well, but not enough to marry a farmer's daughter, — don't say an innkeeper's daughter, or you 'll be sure to offend her. She is bitter against the ' Packhorse.' Says you, ' This Paul is an honest lad, turn your heart back to him.' And, with that, mount your black horse and ride away, and God speed you, sir ; we shall often talk of you at the ' Packhorse,' and naught but good."

Griffith gave the woman his hand, and his breast labored visibly.

Jealousy was ingrained in the man. Mrs. Vint had pricked his conscience, but she had wounded his foible. He was not in love with Mercy, but he esteemed her, and liked her, and saw her value, and, above all, could not bear another man should have her.

Now this gave the matter a new turn. Mrs. Vint had overcome her dislike to him long ago : still he was not her favorite. But his giving her his hand with a gentle pressure, and his manifest agitation, rather won her; and, as uneducated women are your true weathercocks, she went about directly. "To be sure," said she, "our Mercy is too good for the likes of him. She is not like Harry and me. She has been well brought up by her Aunt Prudence, as was governess in a nobleman's house. She can read and write, and cast accounts ; good at her sampler, and can churn and make cheeses, and play of the viol, and lead the psalm in church, and dance a minuet, she can, with any lady in the land. As to her nursing in time of sickness, that I leave to you, sir."

"She is an angel," cried Griffith, "and my benefactress : no man living is good enough for her." And he went away, visibly discomposed.

Mrs. Vint repeated this conversation to Mercy, and told her Thomas Leicester was certainly in love with her. "Shouldst have seen his face, girl, when I told him Paul and you were sweethearts. 'T was as if I had run a knife in his heart."

Mercy murmured a few words of doubt; but she kissed her mother eloquently, and went about, rosy and beaming, all that afternoon.

As for Griffith, his gratitude and his jealousy were now at war, and caused him a severe mental struggle.

Carrick, too, was spurred by jealousy, and came every day to the house, and besieged Mercy ; and Griffith, who saw them together, and did not hear Mercy's replies, was excited, irritated, alarmed.

Mrs. Vint saw his agitation, and determined to bring matters to a climax.

She was always giving him a side thrust ; and, at last, she told him plainly that he was not behaving like a man. "If the girl is not good enough for you, why make a fool of her, and set her against a good husband ?" And when he replied she was good enough for any man in England, "Then," said she, "why not show your respect for her as Paul Carrick does ? He likes her well enough to go to church with her."

With the horns of this dilemma she so gored Kate Peyton's husband that, at last, she and Paul Carrick, between them, drove him out of his conscience.

So he watched his opportunity and got Mercy alone. He took her hand and told her he loved her, and that she was his only comfort in the world, and he found he could not live without her.

At this she blushed and trembled a little, and leaned her brow upon his shoulder, and was a happy creature for a few moments.

So far, fluently enough ; but then he began to falter and stammer, and say that for certain reasons he could not marry at all. But if she could be content with anything short of that, he would retire with her into a distant country, and there, where nobody could contradict him, would call her his wife, and treat her as his wife, and pay his debt of gratitude to her by a life of devotion.

As he spoke, her brow retired an inch or two from his shoulder ; but she heard him quietly out, and then drew back and confronted him, pale, and, to all appearance, calm.

"Call things by their right names," said she. "What you offer me this day, in my father's house, is, to be your mistress. Then — God forgive you, Thomas Leicester."

With this oblique and feminine reply, and one look of unfathomable reproach from her soft eyes, she turned her back on him ; but, remembering her manners, courtesied at the door ; and so retired ; and unpretending Virtue lent her such true dignity that he was struck dumb, and made no attempt to detain her.

I think her dignified composure did not last long when she was alone ; at least, the next time he saw her, her eyes were red ; his heart smote him, and he began to make excuses and beg her forgiveness. But she interrupted him. "Don't speak to me no more, if you please, sir," said she, civilly, but coldly.

Mercy, though so quiet and inoffensive, had depth and strength of character. She never told her mother what Thomas Leicester had proposed to her. Her honest pride kept her silent, for one thing. She would not have it known she had been insulted. And, besides that, she loved Thomas Leicester still, and could not expose or hurt him. Once there was an Israelite without guile, though you and I never saw him ; and once there was a Saxon without bile, and her name was Mercy Vint. In this heart of gold the affections were stronger than the passions. She was deeply wounded, and showed it in a patient way to him who had wounded her, but to none other. Her conduct to him in public and private was truly singular, and would alone have stamped her a remarkable character. She declined all communication with him in private, and avoided him steadily and adroitly ; but in public she spoke to him, sang with him when she was asked, and treated him much the same as before. He could see a subtle difference, but nobody else could.

This generosity, coupled with all she had done for him before, penetrated his heart and filled him with admiration and remorse. He yielded to Mrs. Vint's suggestions, and told her she was right ; he would tear himself away, and never see the dear "Packhorse" again. "But oh! Dame," said he, "'t is a sorrowful thing to be alone in the world again, and naught to do. If I had but a farm, and a sweet little inn like this to go to, perchance my heart would not be quite so heavy as 't is this day at thoughts of parting from thee and thine."

"Well, sir," said Mrs. Vint, "if that is all, there is the 'Vine' to let at this moment. 'T is a better place of business than this ; and some meadows go with it, and land to be had in the parish."

"I 'll ride and see it," said Griffith, eagerly : then, dejectedly, "but, alas ! I have no heart to keep an inn without somebody to help me, and say a kind word now and then. Ah! Mercy Vint, thou hast spoiled me for living alone."

This vacillation exhausted Mrs. Vint's patience. "What are ye sighing about, ye foolish man ?" said she, contemptuously ; "you have got it all your own way. If 't is a wife ye want, ask Mercy, and don't take a nay. If ye would have a housekeeper, you need not want one long. I 'll be bound there 's plenty of young women where you came from as would be glad to keep the 'Vine' under you. And, if you come to that, our Mercy is a treasure on the farm, but she is no help in the inn, no more than a wax figure. She never brought us a shilling, till you came and made her sing to your bass-viol. Nay, what you want is a smart, handsome girl, with a quick eye and a ready tongue, and one as can look a man in the face, and not given to love nor liquor. Don't you know never such a one ?"

"Not I. Humph, to be sure there is Caroline Ryder. She is handsome, and hath a good wit. She is a lady's maid."

"That 's your woman, if she 'll come. And to be sure she will ; for to be mistress of an inn, that 's a lady's maid's Paradise."

"She would have come a few months ago, and gladly. I 'll write to her."

"Better talk to her, and persuade her."

"I 'll do that, too ; but I must write to her first."

"So do then ; but whatever you do, don't shilly-shally no longer. If wrestling was shilly - shallying, methinks you 'd bear the bell, you or else Paul Carrick. Why, all his trouble comes on 't. He might have wed our Mercy a year agone for the asking. Shilly-shally belongs to us that be women. 'T is despicable in a man."

Thus driven on all sides, Griffith rode and inspected the " Vine " (it was only seven miles off); and, after the usual chaffering, came to terms with the proprietor.

He fixed the day for his departure, and told Mrs. Vint he must ride into Cumberland first to get some money, and also to see about a housekeeper.

He made no secret of all this ; and, indeed, was not without hopes Mercy would relent, or perhaps be jealous of this housekeeper. But the only visible effect was to make her look pale and sad. She avoided him in private as before.

Harry Vint was loud in his regrets, and Carrick openly exultant. Griffith wrote to Caroline Ryder, and addressed the letter in a feigned hand, and took it himself to the nearest post-town.

The letter came to hand, and will appear in that sequence of events on which I am now about to enter.

CHAPTER XXVII.

IF Griffith Gaunt suffered anguish, he inflicted agony. Mrs. Gaunt was a high-spirited, proud, and sensitive woman ; and he crushed her with foul words. Leonard was a delicate, vain, and sensitive man, accustomed to veneration. Imagine such a man hurled to the ground, and trampled upon.

Griffith should not have fled ; he should have stayed and enjoyed his vengeance on these two persons. It might have cooled him a little had he stopped and seen the immediate consequences of his savage act.

The priest rose from the ground, pale as ashes, and trembling with fear and hate.

The lady was leaning, white as a sheet, against a tree, and holding it with her very nails for a little support.

They looked round at one another, — a piteous glance of anguish and horror. Then Mrs. Gaunt turned and flung her arm round so that the palm of her hand, high raised, confronted Leonard. I am thus particular because it was a gesture grand and terrible as the occasion that called it forth, — a gesture that *spoke*, and said, " Put the whole earth and sea between us forever after this."

The next moment she bent her head and rushed away, cowering and wringing her hands. She made for her house as naturally as a scared animal for its lair ; but, ere she could reach it, she tottered under the shame, the distress, and the mere terror, and fell fainting, with her fair forehead on the grass.

Caroline Ryder was crouched in the doorway, and did not see her come out of the grove, but only heard a rustle, and then saw her proud mistress totter forward and lie, white, senseless, helpless, at her very feet.

Ryder uttered a scream, but did not lose her presence of mind. She instantly kneeled over Mrs. Gaunt, and loosened her stays with quick and dexterous hand.

It was very like the hawk perched over and clawing the ringdove she has struck down.

But people with brains are never quite inhuman : a drop of lukewarm pity entered even Ryder's heart as she assisted her victim. She called no one to help her; for she saw something very serious had happened, and she felt sure Mrs. Gaunt would say something imprudent in that dangerous period when the patient recovers consciousness but has not all her wits about her. Now Ryder was equally determined to know her mistress's secrets, and not to share the knowledge with any other person.

It was a long swoon ; and, when Mrs. Gaunt came to, the first thing she saw was Ryder leaning over her, with a face of much curiosity, and some concern.

In that moment of weakness the poor lady, who had been so roughly handled, saw a woman close to her, and being a little kind to her ; so what did she do but throw her arms round Ryder's neck and burst out sobbing as if her heart would break.

Then that unprincipled woman shed a tear or two with her, half crocodile, half impulse.

Mrs. Gaunt not only cried on her servant's neck; she justified Ryder's forecast by speaking unguardedly: " I 've been insulted — insulted — insulted ! "

But, even while uttering these words, she was recovering her pride: so the first " insulted " seemed to come from a broken-hearted child, the second from an indignant lady, the third from a wounded queen.

No more words than this; but she rose, with Ryder's assistance, and went, leaning on that faithful creature's shoulder, to her own bedroom. There she sank into a chair and said, in a voice to melt a stone, "My child ! Bring me my little Rose."

Ryder ran and fetched the little girl; and Mrs. Gaunt held out both arms to her, angelically, and clasped her so passionately and piteously to her bosom, that Rose cried for fear, and never forgot the scene all her days; and Mrs. Ryder, who was secretly a mother, felt a genuine twinge of pity and remorse. Curiosity, however, was the dominant sentiment. She was impatient to get all these convulsions over, and learn what had actually passed between Mr. and Mrs Gaunt.

She waited till her mistress appeared calmer; and then, in soft, caressing tones, asked her what had happened.

" Never ask me that question again," cried Mrs. Gaunt, wildly. Then, with inexpressible dignity, " My good girl, you have done all you could for me ; now you must leave me alone with my daughter, and my God, who knows the truth."

Ryder courtesied and retired, burning with baffled curiosity.

Towards dusk Thomas Leicester came into the kitchen, and brought her news with a vengeance. He told her and the other maids that the Squire had gone raving mad, and fled the country. " O lasses," said he, " if you had seen the poor soul's face, a-riding headlong through the fair, all one as if it was a ploughed field ; 't was white as your smocks ; and his eyes glowering on 't other world. We shall ne'er see that face alive again."

And this was her doing.

It surprised and overpowered Ryder. She threw her apron over her head, and went off in hysterics, and betrayed her lawless attachment to every woman in the kitchen, — she who was so clever at probing others.

This day of violent emotions was followed by a sullen and sorrowful gloom.

Mrs. Gaunt kept her bedroom, and admitted nobody; till, at last, the servants consulted together, and sent little Rose to knock at her door, with a basin of chocolate, while they watched on the stairs.

" It 's only me, mamma," said Rose.

" Come in, my precious," said a trembling voice ; and so Rose got in with her chocolate.

The next day she was sent for early ; and at noon Mrs. Gaunt and Rose came down stairs ; but their appearance startled the whole household.

The mother was dressed all in black, and so was her daughter, whom she led by the hand. Mrs. Gaunt's face was pale, and sad, and stern, — a monument of deep suffering and high-strung resolution.

It soon transpired that Griffith had left his home for good ; and friends called on Mrs. Gaunt to slake their curiosity under the mask of sympathy.

Not one of them was admitted. No false excuses were made. " My mistress sees no one for the present," was the reply.

Curiosity, thus baffled, took up the pen ; but was met with a short, unvarying formula : " There is an unhappy misunderstanding between my husband and me. But I shall neither accuse him behind his back, nor justify myself."

Thus the proud lady carried herself before the world ; but secretly she writhed. A wife abandoned is a woman insulted, and the wives — that are not abandoned — cluck.

Ryder was dejected for a time, and, though not honestly penitent, suffered some remorse at the miserable issue of her intrigues. But her elastic nature soon shook it off, and she felt a certain satisfaction at having reduced Mrs. Gaunt to her own level. This disarmed her hostility. She watched her as keenly as ever, but out of pure curiosity.

One thing puzzled her strangely. Leonard did not visit the house; nor could she even detect any communication between the parties.

At last, one day, her mistress told her to put on her hat, and go to Father Leonard.

Ryder's eyes sparkled; and she was soon equipped. Mrs. Gaunt put a parcel and a letter into her hands. Ryder no sooner got out of her sight than she proceeded to tamper with the letter. But to her just indignation she found it so ingeniously folded and sealed that she could not read a word.

The parcel, however, she easily undid, and it contained forty pounds in gold and small notes. "Oho! my lady," said Ryder.

She was received by Leonard with a tender emotion he in vain tried to conceal.

On reading the letter his features contracted sharply, and he seemed to suffer agony. He would not even open the parcel. "You will take that back," said he, bitterly.

"What, without a word?"

"Without a word. But I will write, when I am able."

"Don't be long, sir," suggested Ryder. "I am sure my mistress is wearying for you. Consider, sir, she is all alone now."

"Not so much alone as I am," said the priest, "nor half so unfortunate."

And with this he leaned his head despairingly on his hand, and motioned to Ryder to leave him.

"Here 's a couple of fools," said she to herself, as she went home.

That very evening Thomas Leicester caught her alone, and asked her to marry him.

She stared at first, and then treated it as a jest. "You come at the wrong time, young man," said she. "Marriage is put out of countenance. No, no, I will never marry after what I have seen in this house."

Leicester would not take this for an answer, and pressed her hard.

"Thomas," said this plausible jade, "I like you very well; but I could n't leave my mistress in her trouble. Time to talk of marrying when master comes here alive and well."

"Nay," said Leicester, "my only chance is while he is away. You care more for his little finger than for my whole body; that they all say."

"Who says?"

"Jane, and all the lasses."

"You simple man, they want you for themselves; that is why they belie me."

"Nay, nay; I saw how you carried on, when I brought word he was gone. You let your heart out for once. Don't take me for a fool. I see how 't is, but I 'll face it, for I worship the ground you walk on. Take a thought, my lass. What good can come of your setting your heart on *him?* I 'm young, I 'm healthy, and not ugly enough to set the dogs a-barking. I 've got a good place; I love you dear; I 'll cure you of that fancy, and make you as happy as the day is long. I 'll try and make you as happy as you will make me, my beauty."

He was so earnest, and so much in love, that Mrs. Ryder pitied him, and wished her husband was in heaven.

"I am very sorry, Tom," said she, softly; "dear me, I did not think you cared so much for me as this. I must just tell you the truth. I have got one in my own country, and I 've promised him. I don't care to break my word; and, if I did, he is such a man, I am sure he would kill me for it. Indeed he has told me as much, more than once or twice."

"Killing is a game that two can play at."

"Ah! but 't is an ugly game; and I 'll have no hand in it. And—don't you be angry with me, Tom—I 've known him longest, and—I love him best."

By pertinacity and vanity in lying, she hit the mark at last. Tom swallowed this figment whole.

"That is but reason," said he. "I take my answer, and I wish ye both many happy days together, and well spent." With this he retired, and blubbered a good hour in an outhouse.

Tom avoided the castle, and fell into low spirits. He told his mother all, and she advised him to change the air. "You have been too long in one place," said she; "I hate being too long in one place myself."

This fired Tom's gypsy blood, and he said he would travel to-morrow, if he could but scrape together money enough to ·fill a pedler's pack.

He applied for a loan in several quarters, but was denied in all.

At last the poor fellow summoned courage to lay his case before Mrs. Gaunt.

Ryder's influence procured him an interview. She took him into the drawing-room, and bade him wait there. By and by a pale lady, all in black, glided into the room.

He pulled his front hair, and began to stammer something or other.

She interrupted him. "Ryder has told me," said she, softly. "I am sorry for you; and I will do what you require. And, to be sure, we need no gamekeeper here now."

She then gave him some money, and said she would look him up a few trifles besides, to put in his pack.

Tom's mother helped him to lay out this money to advantage; and, one day, he called at Hernshaw, pack and all, to bid farewell.

The servants all laid out something with him for luck; and Mrs. Gaunt sent for him, and gave him a gold thimble, and a pound of tea, and several yards of gold lace, slightly tarnished, and a Queen Anne's guinea.

He thanked her heartily. "Ay, Dame," said he, "you had always an open hand, married or single. My heart is heavy at leaving you. But I miss the Squire's kindly face too. Hernshaw is not what it used to be."

Mrs. Gaunt turned her head aside, and the man could see his words had made her cry. "My good Thomas," said she, at last, "you are going to travel the country: you might fall in with him."

"I might," said Leicester, incredulously.

"God grant you may; and, if ever you should, think of your poor mistress and give him — this." She put her finger in her bosom and drew out a bullet wrapped in silver paper. "You will never lose this," said she. " I value it more than gold or silver. O, if ever you *should* see him, think of me and my daughter, and just put it in his hand without a word."

As he went out of the room Ryder intercepted him, and said, "Mayhap you will fall in with our master. If ever you do, tell him he is under a mistake, and the sooner he comes home the better."

Tom Leicester departed; and, for days and weeks, nothing occurred to break the sorrowful monotony of the place.

But the mourner had written to her old friend and confessor, Francis; and, after some delay, involuntary on his part, he came to see her.

They were often closeted together, and spoke so low that Ryder could not catch a word.

Francis also paid several visits to Leonard; and the final result of these visits was that the latter left England.

Francis remained at Hernshaw as long as he could; and it was Mrs. Gaunt's hourly prayer that Griffith might return while Francis was with her.

He did, at her earnest request, stay much longer than he had intended; but, at length, he was obliged to fix next Monday to return to his own place.

It was on Thursday he made this arrangement; but the very next day the postman brought a letter to the Castle, thus addressed: —

"To Mistress Caroline Ryder,
Living Servant with Griffith Gaunt, Esq.,
at his house, called Hernshaw Castle,
near Wigeonmoor,
in the county of Cumberland.
These with speed."

The address was in a feigned hand. Ryder opened it in the kitchen, and uttered a scream.

Instantly three female throats opened upon her with questions.

She looked them contemptuously in their faces, put the letter into her pocket, and, soon after, slipped away to her own room, and locked herself in while she read it. It ran thus: —

"GOOD MISTRESS RYDER, — I am alive yet, by the blessing; though somewhat battered; being now risen from a fever, wherein I lost my wits for a time. And, on coming to myself, I found them making of my shroud; whereby you shall learn how near I was to death. And all this I owe to that false, perjured woman that was my wife, and is your mistress.

"Know that I have donned russet, and doffed gentility; for I find a heavy heart's best cure is occupation. I have taken a wayside inn, and think of renting a small farm, which two things go well together. Now you are, of all those I know, most fitted to manage the inn, and I the farm. You were always my good friend; and, if you be so still, then I charge you most solemnly that you utter no word to any living soul about this letter; but meet me privately where we can talk fully of these matters; for I will not set foot in Hernshaw Castle. Moreover, she told me once 't was hers; and so be it. On Friday I shall lie at Stapleton, and the next day, by an easy journey, to the place where I once was so happy.

"So then at seven of the clock on Saturday evening, be the same wet or dry, prithee come to the gate of the grove unbeknown, and speak to

"Your faithful friend
and most unhappy master,
"GRIFFITH GAUNT.

"Be secret as the grave. Would I were in it."

This letter set Caroline Ryder in a tumult. Griffith alive and well, and set against his wife, and coming to her for assistance!

After the first agitation, she read it again, and weighed every syllable. There was one book she had studied more than most of us, — the Heart. And she soon read Griffith's in this letter. It was no love-letter; he really intended business; but, weak in health and broken in spirit, and alone in the world, he naturally turned to one who had confessed an affection for him, and would therefore be true to his interests, and study his happiness.

The proposal was every way satisfactory to Mrs. Ryder. To be mistress of an inn, and have servants under her instead of being one herself. And then, if Griffith and she began as allies in business, she felt very sure she could make herself, first necessary to him, and then dear to him.

She was so elated she could hardly contain herself; and all her fellow-servants remarked that Mrs. Ryder had heard good news.

Saturday came, and never did hours seem to creep so slowly.

But at last the sun set, and the stars came out. There was no moon. Ryder opened the window and looked out; it was an admirable night for an assignation.

She washed her face again, put on her gray silk gown, and purple petticoat, — *Mrs. Gaunt* had given them to her, —and, at the last moment, went and made up her mistress's fire, and put out everything she thought could be wanted, and, five minutes after seven o'clock, tied a scarlet handkerchief over her head, and stepped out at the back door.

What with her coal-black hair, so streaked with red, her black eyes, flashing in the starlight, and her glowing cheeks, she looked bewitching.

And, thus armed for conquest, wily, yet impassioned, she stole out, with noiseless foot and beating heart, to her appointment with her imprudent master.

CHAPTER XXVIII.

THE bill was paid; the black horse saddled and brought round to the door. Mr. and Mrs. Vint stood bare-headed to honor the parting guest; and the latter offered him the stirrup-cup.

Griffith looked round for Mercy. She was nowhere to be seen.

Then he said, piteously, to Mrs. Vint, "What, not even bid me good by?"

Mrs. Vint replied, in a very low voice, that there was no disrespect intended. "The truth is, sir, she could not trust herself to see you go; but she bade me give you a message. Says she, 'Mother, tell him I pray God to bless him, go where he will.'"

Something rose in Griffith's throat. "O Dame!" said he, "if she only knew the truth, she would think better of me than she does. God bless her!"

And he rode sorrowfully away, alone in the world once more.

At the first turn in the road, he wheeled his horse, and took a last lingering look.

There was nothing vulgar, nor inn-like, in the "Packhorse." It stood fifty yards from the road, on a little rural green, and was picturesque itself. The front was entirely clad with large-leaved ivy. Shutters there were none: the windows, with their diamond panes, were lustrous squares, set like great eyes in the green ivy. It looked a pretty, peaceful retreat, and in it Griffith had found peace and a dove-like friend.

He sighed, and rode away from the sight; not raging and convulsed, as when he rode from Hernshaw Castle, but somewhat sick at heart, and very heavy.

He paced so slowly that it took him a quarter of an hour to reach the "Woodman," — a wayside inn, not two miles distant. As he went by, a farmer hailed him from the porch, and insisted on drinking with him; for he was very popular in the neighborhood. Whilst they were thus employed, who should come out but Paul Carrick, booted and spurred, and flushed in the face, and rather the worse for liquor imbibed on the spot.

"So you are going, are ye?" said he. "A good job, too." Then, turning to the other, "Master Gutteridge, never you save a man's life, if you can anyways help it. I saved this one's; and what does he do but turn round and poison my sweetheart against me?"

"How can you say so?" remonstrated Griffith. "I never belied you. Your name scarce ever passed my lips."

"Don't tell me," said Carrick. "However, she has come to her senses, and given your worship the sack. Ride you into Cumberland, and I to the 'Packhorse,' and take my own again."

With this, he unhooked his nag from the wall, and clattered off to the "Packhorse."

Griffith sat a moment stupefied, and then his face was convulsed by his ruling passion. He wheeled his horse, gave him the spur, and galloped after Carrick.

He soon came up with him, and yelled in his ear, "I 'll teach you to spit your wormwood in my cup of sorrow."

Carrick shook his fist defiantly, and spurred his horse in turn.

It was an exciting race, and a novel one, but soon decided. The great black hunter went ahead, and still improved his advantage. Carrick, purple with rage, was full a quarter of a mile behind, when Griffith dashed furiously into the stable of the "Packhorse," and, leaving Black Dick panting and covered with foam, ran in search of Mercy.

The girl told him she was in the dairy. He looked in at the window, and there she was with her mother. With instinctive sense and fortitude she had fled to work. She was trying to churn; but it would not do: she had laid her shapely arm on the churn, and her head on it, and was crying.

Mrs. Vint was praising Carrick, and offering homely consolation.

"Ah, mother," sighed Mercy, "I could have made him happy. He does not know that; and he has turned his back on content. What will become of him?"

Griffith heard no more. He went round to the front door, and rushed in.

"Take your own way, Dame," said he, in great agitation. "Put up the banns when you like. Sweetheart, wilt wed with me? I 'll make thee the best husband I can."

Mercy screamed faintly, and lifted up her hands; then she blushed and trembled to her very finger ends; but it ended in smiles of joy and her brow upon his shoulder.

In which attitude, with Mrs. Vint patting him approvingly on the back, they were surprised by Paul Carrick. He came to the door, and there stood aghast.

The young man stared ruefully at the picture, and then said, very dryly, "I 'm too late, methinks."

"That you be, Paul," said Mrs. Vint, cheerfully. "She is meat for your master."

"Don't — you — never — come to me — to save your life — no more," blubbered Paul, breaking down all of a sudden.

He then retired, little heeded, and came no more to the "Packhorse" for several days.

CHAPTER XXIX.

IT is desirable that improper marriages should never be solemnized; and the Christian Church saw this, many hundred years ago, and ordained that, before a marriage, the banns should be cried in a church three Sundays, and any person there present might forbid the union of the parties, and allege the just impediment.

This precaution was feeble, but not wholly inadequate — in the Middle Ages; for we know by good evidence that the priest was often interrupted and the banns forbidden.

But in modern days the banns are never forbidden; in other words, the precautionary measure that has come down to us from the thirteenth century is out of date and useless. It rests, indeed, on an estimate of publicity that has become childish, and almost asinine. If persons about to marry were compelled to inscribe their names and descriptions in a Matrimonial Weekly Gazette, and a copy of this were placed on a desk in ten thousand churches, perhaps we might stop one lady per annum from marrying her husband's brother, and one gentleman from wedding his neighbor's wife. But the crying of banns in a single parish church is a waste of the people's time and the parson's breath.

And so it proved in Griffith Gaunt's case. The Rev. William Wentworth published, in the usual recitative, the banns of marriage between Thomas Leicester, of the parish of Marylebone in London, and Mercy Vint, spinster, of *this* parish; and creation, present *ex hypothesi mediævale*, but absent in fact, assented, by silence, to the union.

So Thomas Leicester wedded Mercy Vint, and took her home to the "Packhorse."

It would be well if those who stifle their consciences, and commit crimes, would set up a sort of medico-moral diary, and record their symptoms minutely day by day. Such records might help to clear away some vague conventional notions.

To tell the truth, our hero, and now malefactor, (the combination is of high antiquity,) enjoyed, for several months, the peace of mind that belongs of right to innocence; and his days passed in a state of smooth complacency. Mercy was a good, wise, and tender wife; she naturally looked up to him after marrfage more than she did before; she studied his happiness, as she had never studied her own ; she mastered his character, admired his good qualities, discerned his weaknesses, but did not view them as defects ; only as little traits to be watched, lest she should give pain to "her master," as she called him.

Affection, in her, took a more obsequious form than it could ever assume in Kate Peyton. And yet she had great influence, and softly governed "her master" for his good. She would come into the room and take away the bottle, if he was committing excess ; but she had a way of doing it, so like a good, but resolute mother, and so unlike a termagant, that he never resisted. Upon the whole, she nursed his mind, as in earlier days she had nursed his body.

And then she made him so comfortable : she observed him minutely to that end. As is the eye of a maid to the hand of her mistress, so Mercy Leicester's dove-like eye was ever watching "her master's" face, to learn the minutest features of his mind.

One evening he came in tired, and there was a black fire in the parlor. His countenance fell the sixteenth of an inch. You and I, sir, should never have noticed it. But Mercy did, and, ever after, there was a clear fire when he came in.

She noted, too, that he loved to play the *viol da gambo*, but disliked the trouble of tuning it. So then she tuned it for him.

When he came home at night, early or late, he was sure to find a dry pair of shoes on the rug, his six-stringed viol tuned to a hair, a bright fire, and a brighter wife, smiling and radiant at his coming, and always neat ; for, said she, "Shall I don my bravery for strangers, and not for my Thomas, that is the best of company ?"

They used to go to church, and come back together, hand in hand like lovers ; for the arm was rarely given in those days. And Griffith said to himself every Sunday, "What a comfort to have a Protestant wife !"

But one day he was off his guard, and called her "Kate, my dear."

"Who is Kate ?" said she softly, but with a degree of trouble and intelligence that made him tremble.

"No matter," said he, all in a flutter. Then, solemnly, "Whoever she was, she is dead, — dead."

"Ah !" said Mercy, very tenderly and solemnly, and under her breath. "You loved her ; yet she must die." She paused ; then, in a tone so exquisite I can only call it an angel's whisper, "Poor Kate !"

Griffith groaned aloud. "For God's sake, never mention that name to me again. Let me forget she ever lived. She was not the true friend to me that you have been."

Mercy replied, softly, "Say not so, Thomas. You loved her well. Her death had all but cost me thine. Ah, well ! we cannot all be the first. I am not very jealous, for my part ; and I thank God for 't. Thou art a dear good husband to me, and that is enow."

Paul Carrick, unable to break off his habits, came to the "Packhorse" now and then ; but· Mercy protected her husband's heart from pain. She was kind, and even pitiful ; but so discreet and resolute, and contrived to draw the line so clearly between her husband and her old sweetheart, that Griffith's foible could not burn him, for want of fuel.

And so passed several months, and the man's heart was at peace. He could not love Mercy passionately as he had loved Kate ; but he was full of real regard and esteem for her. It was one of those gentle, clinging attachments that outlast grand passions, and survive till death ; a tender, pure affection, though built upon a crime.

They had been married, and lived in sweet content, about three quarters of a year — when trouble came ; but in a vulgar form. A murrain carried off several of Harry Vint's cattle ; and it then came out that he had purchased six of them on credit, and had been induced to set his hand to bills of exchange for them. His rent was also behind, and, in fact, his affairs were in a desperate condition.

He hid it as long as he could from them all; but at last, being served with a process for debt, and threatened with a distress and an execution, he called a family council and exposed the real state of things.

Mrs. Vint rated him soundly for keeping all this secret so long.

He whom they called Thomas Leicester remonstrated with him. "Had you told me in time," said he, "I had not paid forfeit for ' The Vine,' but settled there, and given you a home."

Mercy said never a word but " Poor father ! "

As the peril drew nearer, the conversations became more animated and agitated, and soon the old people took to complaining of Thomas Leicester to his wife.

"Thou hast married a gentleman; and he hath not the heart to lift a hand to save thy folk from ruin."

"Say not so," pleaded Mercy : "to be sure he hath the heart, but not the means. 'T was but yestreen he bade me sell his jewels for you. But, mother, I think they belonged to some one he loved, — and she died. So, poor thing, how could I ? Then, if you love me, blame me, and not him."

"Jewels, quotha ! will they stop such a gap as ours ? " was the contemptuous reply.

From complaining of him behind his back, the old people soon came to launching innuendoes obliquely at him. Here is one specimen out of a dozen.

" Wife, if our Mercy had wedded one of her own sort, mayhap he 'd have helped us a bit."

" Ay, poor soul ; and she so near her time : if the bailiffs come down on us next month, 't is my belief we shall lose her, as well as house and home."

The false Thomas Leicester let them run on, in dogged silence ; but every word was a stab.

And one day, when he had been baited sore with hints, he turned round on them fiercely, and said : " Did I get you into this mess ? It 's all your own doing. Learn to see your own faults, and not be so hard on one that has been the best servant you ever had, gentleman or not."

Men can resist the remonstrances that wound them, and so irritate them, better than they can those gentle appeals that rouse no anger, but soften the whole heart. The old people stung him ; but Mercy, without design, took a surer way. She never said a word ; but sometimes, when the discussions were at their height, she turned her dove-like eyes on him, with a look so loving, so humbly inquiring, so timidly imploring, that his heart melted within him.

Ah, that is a true touch of nature and genuine observation of the sexes, in the old song, —

> " My feyther urged me sair;
> My mither didna speak ;
> But she looked me in the face,
> Till my hairt was like to break."

These silent, womanly, imploring looks of patient Mercy were mightier than argument or invective.

The man knew all along where to get money, and how to get it. He had only to go to Hernshaw Castle. But his very soul shuddered at the idea. However, for Mercy's sake, he took the first step; he compelled himself to look the thing in the face, and discuss it with himself. A few months ago he could not have done even this, — he loved his lawful wife too much; hated her too much. But now, Mercy and Time had blunted both those passions ; and he could ask himself whether he could not encounter Kate and her priest without any very violent emotion.

When they first set up house together, he had spent his whole fortune, a sum of two thousand pounds, on repairing and embellishing Hernshaw Castle and grounds. Since she had driven him out of the house, he had a clear right to have back the money; and he now resolved he would have it;

but what he wanted was to get it without going to the place in person.

And now Mercy's figure, as well as her imploring looks, moved him greatly. She was in that condition which appeals to a man's humanity and masculine pity, as well as to his affection. To use the homely words of Scripture, she was great with child, and in that condition moved slowly about him, filling his pipe, and laying his slippers, and ministering to all his little comforts; she would make no difference: and when he saw the poor dove move about him so heavily, and rather languidly, yet so zealously and tenderly, the man's very bowels yearned over her, and he felt as if he could die to do her a service.

So, one day, when she was standing by him, bending over his little round table, and filling his pipe with her neat hand, he took her by the other hand and drew her gently on his knee, her burden and all. "Child!" said he, "do not thou fret. I know how to get money; and I 'll do 't, for thy sake."

"I know that," said she, softly; "can I not read thy face by this time?" and so laid her cheek to his. "But, Thomas, for my sake, get it honestly,—or not at all," said she, still filling his pipe, with her cheek to his.

"I 'll but take back my own," said he; "fear naught."

But, after thus positively pledging himself to Mercy, he became thoughtful and rather fretful; for he was still most averse to go to Hernshaw, and yet could hit upon no other way; since to employ an agent would be to let out that he had committed bigamy, and so risk his own neck, and break Mercy's heart.

After all his scale was turned by his foible.

Mrs. Vint had been weak enough to confide her trouble to a friend: it was all over the parish in three days.

Well, one day, in the kitchen of the inn, Paul Carrick, having drunk two pints of good ale, said to Vint, "Landlord, you ought to have married her to me. I 've got two hundred pounds laid by. I 'd have pulled you out of the mire, and welcome."

"Would you, though, Paul?" said Harry Vint; "then, by G—, I wish I had."

Now Carrick bawled that out, and Griffith, who was at the door, heard it.

He walked into the kitchen, ghastly pale, and spoke to Harry Vint first.

"I take your inn, your farm, and your debts on me," said he; "not one without t' other."

"Spoke like a man!" cried the landlord, joyfully; "and so be it — before these witnesses."

Griffith turned on Carrick: "This house is mine. Get out on 't, ye *jealous*, mischief-making cur." And he took him by the collar and dragged him furiously out of the place, and sent him whirling into the middle of the road; then ran back for his hat and flung it out after him.

This done, he sat down boiling, and his eyes roved fiercely round the room in search of some other antagonist. But his strength was so great, and his face so altered with this sudden spasm of reviving jealousy, that nobody cared to provoke him further.

After a while, however, Harry Vint muttered dryly, "There goes one good customer."

Griffith took him up sternly: "If your debts are to be mine, your trade shall be mine too, that you had not the head to conduct."

"So be it, son-in-law," said the old man; "only you go so fast: you do take possession afore you pays the fee."

Griffith winced. "That shall be the last of your taunts, old man." He turned to the ostler: "Bill, give Black Dick his oats at sunrise; and in ten days at furthest I 'll pay every shilling this house and farm do owe. Now, Master White, you 'll put in hand a new sign-board for this inn; a fresh 'Packhorse,' and paint him jet black, with one white hoof (instead of chocolate), in honor of my nag Dick ; and in place of Harry Vint you 'll put in Thomas Leicester See that is done against I come back, or come *you* here no more."

Soon after this scene he retired to tell Mercy; and, on his departure, the suppressed tongues went like mill-clacks.

Dick came round saddled at peep of day; but Mercy had been up more than an hour, and prepared her man's breakfast. She clung to him at parting, and cried a little; and whispered something in his ear, for nobody else to hear: it was an entreaty that he would not be long gone, lest he should be far from her in the hour of her peril.

Thereupon he promised her, and kissed her tenderly, and bade her be of good heart; and so rode away northwards with dogged resolution.

As soon as he was gone, Mercy's tears flowed without restraint.

Her father set himself to console her. "Thy good man," he said, "is but gone back to the high road for a night or two, to follow his trade of 'stand and deliver.' Fear naught, child; his pistols are well primed: I saw to that myself; and his horse is the fleetest in the county. You 'll have him back in three days, and money in both pockets. I warrant you his is a better trade than mine; and he is a fool to change it."

Griffith was two days upon the road, and all that time he was turning over and discussing in his mind how he should conduct the disagreeable but necessary business he had undertaken.

He determined, at last, to make the visit one of business only: no heat, no reproaches. That lovely, hateful woman might continue to dishonor his name, for he had himself abandoned it. He would not deign to receive any money that was hers; but his own two thousand pounds he would have; and two or three hundred on the spot by way of instalment. And, with these hard views, he drew near to Hernshaw; but the nearer he got, the slower he went; for what at a distance had seemed tolerably easy began to get more and more difficult and repulsive.

Moreover, his heart, which he thought he had steeled, began now to flutter a little, and somehow to shudder at the approaching interview.

CHAPTER XXX.

CAROLINE RYDER went to the gate of the Grove, and stayed there two hours; but, of course, no Griffith came.

She returned the next night, and the next; and then she gave it up, and awaited an explanation. None came, and she was bitterly disappointed, and indignant.

She began to hate Griffith, and to conceive a certain respect, and even a tepid friendship, for the other woman he had insulted.

Another clew to this change of feeling is to be found in a word she let drop in talking to another servant. "My mistress," said she, "bears it *like a man.*"

In fact, Mrs. Gaunt's conduct at this period was truly noble.

She suffered months of torture, months of grief; but the high-spirited creature hid it from the world, and maintained a sad but high composure.

She wore her black, for she said, "How do I know he is alive?" She retrenched her establishment, reduced her expenses two thirds, and busied herself in works of charity and religion.

Her desolate condition attracted a gentleman who had once loved her, and now esteemed and pitied her profoundly, — Sir George Neville.

He was still unmarried, and she was the cause; so far at least as this: she had put him out of conceit with the other ladies at that period when he had serious thoughts of marriage: and the inclination to marry at all had not since returned.

If the Gaunts had settled at Boulton, Sir George would have been their near neighbor; but Neville's Court was nine miles from Hernshaw Castle: and when they met, which was not very often, Mrs. Gaunt was on her guard to give Griffith no shadow of uneasiness.

She was therefore rather more dignified and distant with Sir George than her ,own inclination and his merits would have prompted ; for he was a superior and very agreeable man.

When it became quite certain that her husband had left her, Sir George rode up to Hernshaw Castle, and called upon her.

She begged to be excused from seeing him.

Now Sir George was universally courted, and this rather nettled him ; however, he soon learned that she received nobody except a few religious friends of her own sex.

Sir George then wrote her a letter that did him credit : it was full of worthy sentiment and good sense. For instance, he said he desired to intrude his friendly offices and his sympathy upon her, but nothing more. Time had cured him of those warmer feelings which had once ruffled his peace ; but Time could not efface his tender esteem for the lady he had loved in his youth, nor his profound respect for her character.

Mrs. Gaunt wept over his gentle letter, and was on the verge of asking herself why she had chosen Griffith instead of this chevalier. She sent him a sweet, yet prudent reply ; she did not encourage him to visit her ; but said, that, if ever she should bring herself to receive visits from the gentlemen of the county during her husband's absence, he should be the first to know it. She signed herself his unhappy, but deeply grateful, servant and friend.

One day, as she came out of a poor woman's cottage, with a little basket on her arm, which she had emptied in the cottage, she met Sir George Neville full.

He took his hat off, and made her a profound bow. He was then about to ride on, but altered his mind, and dismounted to speak to her.

The interview was constrained at first ; but erelong he ventured to tell her she really ought to consult with some old friend and practical man like himself. He would undertake to scour the country, and find her husband, if he was above ground.

"Me go a-hunting the man," cried she, turning red ; "not if he was my king as well as my husband. He knows where to find *me;* and that is enough."

"Well, but madam, would you not like to learn where he is, and what he is doing ? "

"Why, yes, my good, kind friend, I *should* like to know that." And, having pronounced these words with apparent calmness, she burst out crying, and almost ran away from him.

Sir George looked sadly after her, and formed a worthy resolution. He saw there was but one road to her regard. He resolved to hunt her husband for her, without intruding on her, or giving her a voice in the matter. Sir George was a magistrate, and accustomed to organize inquiries ; spite of the length of time that had elapsed, he traced Griffith for a considerable distance. Pending further inquiries, he sent Mrs. Gaunt word that the truant had not made for the sea, but had gone due south.

Mrs. Gaunt returned him her warm thanks for this scrap of information. So long as Griffith remained in the island there was always a hope he might return to her. The money he had taken would soon be exhausted ; and poverty might drive him to her ; and she was so far humbled by grief, that she could welcome him even on those terms.

Affliction tempers the proud. Mrs. Gaunt was deeply injured as well as insulted ; but, for all that, in her many days and weeks of solitude and sorrow, she took herself to task, and saw her fault. She became more gentle, more considerate of her servants' feelings, more womanly.

For many months she could not enter "the Grove." The spirited woman's very flesh revolted at the sight of the place where she had been insulted and abandoned. But, as she went deeper in religion, she forced herself to go to the gate and look in, and say out loud, "I gave the first offence," and then she would go in-doors again, quivering with the internal conflict.

Finally, being a Catholic, and therefore attaching more value to self-torture than we do, the poor soul made this very grove her place of penance. Once a week she had the fortitude to drag herself to the very spot where Griffith had denounced her; and there she would kneel and pray for him and for herself. And certainly, if humility and self-abasement were qualities of the body, here was to be seen their picture; for her way was to set her crucifix up at the foot of a tree; then to bow herself all down, between kneeling and lying, and put her lips meekly to the foot of the crucifix, and so pray long and earnestly.

Now, one day, while she was thus crouching in prayer, a gentleman, booted and spurred and splashed, drew near, with hesitating steps. She was so absorbed, she did not hear those steps at all till they were very near; but then she trembled all over; for her delicate ear recognized a manly tread she had not heard for many a day. She dared not move nor look, for she thought it was a mere sound, sent to her by Heaven to comfort her.

But the next moment a well-known mellow voice came like a thunder-clap, it shook her so.

"Forgive me, my good dame, but I desire to know —"

The question went no further, for Kate Gaunt sprang to her feet, with a loud scream, and stood glaring at Griffith Gaunt, and he at her.

And thus husband and wife met again, — met, by some strange caprice of Destiny, on the very spot where they had parted so horribly.

CHAPTER XXXI.

THE gaze these two persons bent on one another may be half imagined: it can never be described.

Griffith spoke first. "In black!" said he, in a whisper.

His voice was low; his face, though pale and grim, had not the terrible aspect he wore at parting.

So she thought he had come back in an amicable spirit; and she flew to him, with a cry of love, and threw her arm round his neck, and panted on his shoulder.

At this reception, and the tremulous contact of one he had loved so dearly, a strange shudder ran through his frame, — a shudder that marked his present repugnance, yet indicated her latent power.

He himself felt he had betrayed some weakness; and it was all the worse for her. He caught her wrist and put her from him, not roughly, but with a look of horror. "The day is gone by for that, madam," he gasped. Then, sternly: "Think you I came here to play the credulous husband ?"

Mrs. Gaunt drew back in her turn, and faltered out, "What! come back here, and not sorry for what you have done? not the least sorry? O my heart! you have almost broken it."

"Prithee, no more of this," said Griffith, sternly. "You and I are naught to one another now, and forever. But there, you are but a woman, and I did not come to quarrel with you." And he fixed his eyes on the ground.

"Thank God for that," faltered Mrs. Gaunt. "O sir, the sight of you — the thought of what you were to me once — till jealousy blinded you. Lend me your arm, if you are a man; my limbs do fail me."

The shock had been too much; a pallor overspread her lovely features, her knees knocked together, and she was tottering like some tender tree cut down, when Griffith, who, with all his faults, was a man, put out his strong arm, and she clung to it, quivering all over, and weeping hysterically.

That little hand, with its little feminine clutch, trembling on his arm, raised a certain male compassion for her piteous condition; and he bestowed a few cold, sad words of encouragement on her. "Come, come," said he, gently; "I shall not trouble you long: I 'm cured ot my jealousy. 'T is gone, along with my love. You and your saintly sinner are safe from me. I am come hither for my own, my two thousand pounds, and for nothing more."

"Ah! you are come back for money, not for me?" she murmured, with forced calmness.

"For money, and not for you, of course," said he, coldly.

The words were hardly out of his mouth, when the proud lady flung his arm from her. "Then money shall you have, and not me; nor aught of me but my contempt."

But she could not carry it off as heretofore. She turned her back haughtily on him; but, at the first step, she burst out crying, "Come, and I 'll give you what you are come for," she sobbed. "Ungrateful! heartless! O, how little I knew this man!"

She crept away before him, drooping her head, and crying bitterly; and he followed her, hanging his head, and ill at ease; for there was such true passion in her voice, her streaming eyes, and indeed in her whole body, that he was moved, and the part he was playing revolted him. He felt confused and troubled, and asked himself how on earth it was that she, the guilty one, contrived to appear the injured one, and made him, the wronged one, feel almost remorseful.

Mrs. Gaunt took no more notice of him now than if he had been a dog following at her heels. She went into the drawing-room, and sank helplessly on the nearest couch, threw her head wearily back, and shut her eyes. Yet the tears trickled through the closed lids.

Griffith caught up a hand-bell, and rang it vigorously.

Quick, light steps were soon heard pattering; and in darted Caroline Ryder, with an anxious face; for of late she had conceived a certain sober regard for her mistress, who had ceased to be her successful rival, and who bore her grief *like a man.*

At sight of Griffith, Ryder screamed aloud, and stood panting.

Mrs. Gaunt opened her eyes. "Ay, child, he has come home," said she, bitterly; "his body, but not his heart."

She stretched her hand out feebly, and pointed to a bottle of salts that stood on the table. Ryder ran and put them to her nostrils. Mrs. Gaunt whispered in her ear, "Send a swift horse for Father Francis; tell him, life or death!"

Ryder gave her a very intelligent look, and presently slipped out, and ran into the stable-yard.

At the gate she caught sight of Griffith's horse. What does this quick-witted creature do but send the groom off on that horse, and not on Mrs. Gaunt's.

"Now, Dame," said Griffith, doggedly, "are you better?"

"Ay, I thank you."

"Then listen to me. When you and I set up house together, I had two thousand pounds. I spent it on this house. The house is yours. You told me so, one day, you know."

"Ah, you can remember my faults."

"I remember all, Kate."

"Thank you, at least, for calling me Kate. Well, Griffith, since you abandoned us, I thought, and thought, and thought, of all that might befall you; and I said, 'What will he do for money?' My jewels, that you did me the honor to take, would not last you long, I feared. So I reduced my expenses three fourths at least, and I put by some money for your need."

Griffith looked amazed. "For my need?" said he.

"For whose else? I 'll send for it, and place it in your hands — to-morrow."

"To-morrow? Why not to-day?"

"I have a favor to ask of you first."

"What is that?"

"Justice. If you are fond of money, I too have something I prize: my honor. You have belied and insulted me, sir; but I know you were under a delusion. I mean to remove that delusion, and make you see how little I am to blame; for, alas! I own I was imprudent. But, O Griffith, as I hope to be saved, it was the imprudence of innocence and over-confidence."

"Mistress," said Griffith, in a stern, yet agitated voice, "be advised, and leave all this : rouse not a man's sleeping wrath. Let bygones be bygones."

Mrs. Gaunt rose, and said, faintly, "So be it. I must go, sir, and give some orders for your entertainment."

"O, don't put yourself about for me," said Griffith : "I am not the master of this house."

Mrs. Gaunt's lip trembled, but she was a match for him. "Then are you my guest," said she ; "and my credit is concerned in your comfort."

She made him a courtesy, as if he were a stranger, and marched to the door, concealing, with great pride and art, a certain trembling of her knees.

At the door she found Ryder, and bade her follow, much to that lady's disappointment ; for she desired a *tête-à-tête* with Griffith, and an explanation.

As soon as the two women were out of Griffith's hearing, the mistress laid her hand on the servant's arm, and, giving way to her feelings, said, all in a flutter : "Child, if I have been a good mistress to thee, show it now. Help me keep him in the house till Father Francis comes."

"I undertake to do so much," said Ryder, firmly. "Leave it to me, mistress."

Mrs. Gaunt threw her arms round Ryder's neck and kissed her.

It was done so ardently, and by a woman hitherto so dignified and proud, that Ryder was taken by surprise, and almost affected.

As for the service Mrs. Gaunt had asked of her, it suited her own designs.

"Mistress," said she, "be ruled by me ; keep out of his way a bit, while I get Miss Rose ready. You understand."

"Ah ! I have one true friend in the house," said poor Mrs. Gaunt. She then confided in Ryder, and went away to give her own orders for Griffith's reception.

Ryder found little Rose, dressed her to perfection, and told her her dear papa was come home. She then worked upon the child's mind in that subtle way known to women, so that Rose went down stairs loaded and primed, though no distinct instructions had been given her.

As for Griffith, he walked up and down, uneasy ; and wished he had stayed at the "Packhorse." He had not bargained for all these emotions ; the peace of mind he had enjoyed for some months seemed trickling away.

"Mercy, my dear," said he to himself, "'t will be a dear penny to me, I doubt."

Then he went to the window, and looked at the lawn, and sighed. Then he sat down, and thought of the past.

Whilst he sat thus moody, the door opened very softly, and a little cherubic face, with blue eyes and golden hair, peeped in. Griffith started. "Ah !" cried Rose, with a joyful scream ; and out flew her little arms, and away she came, half running, half dancing, and was on his knee in a moment, with her arms round his neck.

"Papa ! papa !" she cried. "O my dear, dear, dear, darling papa !" And she kissed and patted his cheek again and again.

Her innocent endearments moved him to tears. "My pretty angel !" he sighed : "my lamb ! "

"How your heart beats ! Don't cry, dear papa. Nobody is dead : only we thought you were. I 'm so glad you are come home alive. Now we can take off this nasty black : I hate it."

"What, 't is for me you wear it, pretty one ? "

"Ay. Mamma made us. Poor mamma has been so unhappy. And that reminds me : you are a wicked man, papa. But I love you all one for that. It *tis* so dull when everybody is good like mamma ; and she makes me dreadfully good too ; but now you are come back, there will be a little, little wickedness again, it is to be hoped. Are n't you glad you are not dead, and are come home instead ? I am."

"I am glad I have seen thee. Come,

take my hand, and let us go look at the old place."

"Ay. But you must wait till I get on my new hat and feather."

"Nay, nay; art pretty enough bareheaded."

"O papa! but I must, for decency. You are company now; you know."

"Dull company, sweetheart, thou 'lt find me."

"I don't mean that: I mean, when you were here always, you were only papa; but now you come once in an age, you 're COMPANY. I won't budge without 'em; so there, now."

"Well, little one, I do submit to thy hat and feather; only be quick, or I shall go forth without thee."

"If you dare," said Rose impetuously; "for I won't be half a moment."

She ran and extorted from Ryder the new hat and feather, which by rights she was not to have worn until next month.

Griffith and his little girl went all over the well-known premises, he sad and moody, she excited and chattering, and nodding her head down, and cocking her eye up every now and then, to get a glimpse of her feather.

"And don't you go away again, dear papa. It *tis* so dull without you. Nobody comes here. Mamma won't let 'em."

"Nobody except Father Leonard," said Griffith, bitterly.

"Father Leonard? Why, he never comes here. Leonard! That is the beautiful priest that used to pat me on the head, and bid me love and honor my parents. And so I do. Only mamma is always crying, and you keep away; so how can I love and honor you, when I never see you, and they keep telling me you are good for nothing, and dead."

"My young mistress, when did you see Father Leonard last?" said Griffith, gnawing his lip.

"How can I tell? Why, it was miles ago; when I was a mere girl. You know he went away before you did."

"I know nothing of the kind. Tell me the truth now. He has visited here since I went away."

"Nay, papa."

"That is strange. She visits him, then?"

"What, mamma? She seldom stirs out; and never beyond the village. We keep no carriage now. Mamma is turned such a miser. She is afraid you will be poor; so she puts it all by for you. But now you are come, we shall have carriages and things again. O, by the by, Father Leonard! I heard them say he had left England, so I did."

"When was that?"

"Well, I think that was a little bit after you went away."

"That is strange," said Griffith, thoughtfully.

He led his little girl by the hand, but scarcely listened to her prattle; he was so surprised and puzzled by the information he had elicited from her.

Upon the whole, however, he concluded that his wife and the priest had perhaps been smitten with remorse, and had parted — when it was too late.

This, and the peace of mind he had found elsewhere, somewhat softened his feelings towards them. "So," thought he, "they were not hardened creatures after all. Poor Kate!"

As these milder feelings gained on him, Rose suddenly uttered a joyful cry; and, looking up, he saw Mrs. Gaunt coming towards him, and Ryder behind her. Both were in gay colors, which, in fact, was what had so delighted Rose.

They came up, and Mrs. Gaunt seemed a changed woman. She looked young and beautiful, and bent a look of angelic affection on her daughter; and said to Griffith, "Is she not grown? Is she not lovely? Sure you will never desert her again."

"'T was not her I deserted, but her mother; and she had played me false with her d—d priest," was Griffith's reply.

Mrs. Gaunt drew back with horror. "This, before my girl?" she cried. "GRIFFITH GAUNT, YOU LIE!"

And this time it was the woman who menaced the man. She rose to six feet high, and advanced on him with her great gray eyes flashing flames at him. "O that I were a man!" she cried: "this insult should be the last. I'd lay you dead at her feet and mine."

Griffith actually drew back a step; for the wrath of such a woman was terrible, — more terrible perhaps to a brave man than to a coward.

Then he put his hands in his pockets with a dogged air, and said, grinding his teeth, "But — as you are not a man, and I'm not a woman, we can't settle it that way. So I give you the last word, and good day. I'm sore in want of money; but I find I can't pay the price it is like to cost me. Farewell."

"Begone!" said Mrs. Gaunt: "and, this time, forever. Ruffian, and fool, I loathe the sight of you."

Rose ran weeping to her. "O mamma, don't quarrel with papa": then back to Griffith, "O papa, don't quarrel with mamma, — for my sake."

Griffith hung his head, and said, in a broken voice: "No, my lamb, we twain must not quarrel before thee. We will part in silence, as becomes those that once were dear, and have thee to show for 't. Madam, I wish you all health and happiness. Adieu."

He turned on his heel; and Mrs. Gaunt took Rose to her knees, and bent and wept over her. Niobe over her last was not more graceful, nor more sad.

As for Ryder, she stole quietly after her retiring master. She found him peering about, and asked him demurely what he was looking for.

"My good black horse, girl, to take me from this cursed place. Did I not tie him to yon gate?"

"The black horse? Why I sent him for Father Francis. Nay, listen to me, master; you know I was always your friend, and hard upon *her*. Well, since you went, things have come to pass that make me doubt. I do begin to fear you were too hasty."

"Do you tell me this now, woman?" cried Griffith, furiously.

"How could I tell you before? Why did you break your tryst with me? If you had come according to your letter, I'd have told you months ago what I tell you now; but, as I was saying, the priest never came near her after you left; and she never stirred abroad to meet him. More than that, he has left England."

"Remorse! Too late."

"Perhaps it may, sir. I could n't say; but there is one coming that knows the very truth."

"Who is that?"

"Father Francis. The moment you came, sir, I took it on me to send for him. You know the man: he won't tell a lie to please our dame. And he knows all; for Leonard has confessed to him. I listened, and heard him say as much. Then, master, be advised, and get the truth from Father Francis."

Griffith trembled. "Francis is an honest man," said he; "I'll wait till he comes. But O, my lass, I find money may be bought too dear."

"Your chamber is ready, sir, and your clothes put out. Supper is ordered. Let me show you your room. We are all so happy now."

"Well," said he, listlessly, "since my horse is gone, and Francis coming, and I'm wearied and sick of the world, do what you will with me for this one day."

He followed her mechanically to a bedroom, where was a bright fire, and a fine shirt, and his silver-laced suit of clothes airing.

A sense of luxurious comfort struck him at the sight.

"Ay," said he, "I'll dress, and so to supper; I'm main hungry. It seems a man must eat, let his heart be ever so sore."

Before she left him, Ryder asked him coldly why he had broken his appointment with her.

"That is too long a story to tell you now," said he, coolly.

"Another time then," said she; and went out smiling, but bitter at heart.

Griffith had a good wash, and enjoyed

certain little conveniences which he had not at the "Packhorse." He doffed his riding suit, and donned the magnificent dress Ryder had selected for him ; and with his fine clothes he somehow put on more ceremonious manners.

He came down to the dining-room. To his surprise he found it illuminated with wax candles, and the table and sideboard gorgeous with plate.

Supper soon smoked upon the board ; but, though it was set for three, nobody else appeared.

Griffith inquired of Ryder whether he was to sup alone.

She replied : "My mistress desires you not to wait for her. She has no stomach."

"Well, then, I have," said Griffith, and fell to with a will.

Ryder, who waited on this occasion, stood and eyed him with curiosity : his conduct was so unlike a woman's.

Just as he concluded, the door opened, and a burly form entered. Griffith rose, and embraced him with his arms and lips, after the fashion of the day. "Welcome, thou one honest priest !" said he.

"Welcome, thrice welcome, my long lost son !" said the cordial Francis.

"Sit down, man, and eat with me. I 'll begin again, for you."

"Presently, Squire ; I 've work to do first. Go thou and bid thy mistress come hither to me."

Ryder, to whom this was addressed, went out, and left the gentlemen together.

Father Francis drew out of his pocket two packets, carefully tied and sealed. He took a knife from the table and cut the strings, and broke the seals. Griffith eyed him with curiosity.

Father Francis looked at him. "These," said he, very gravely, "are the letters that Brother Leonard hath written, at sundry times, to Catharine Gaunt, and these are the letters Catharine Gaunt hath written to Brother Leonard."

Griffith trembled, and his face was convulsed.

"Let me read them at once," said he : and stretched out his hand, with eyes like a dog's in the dark.

Francis withdrew them, quietly. "Not till she is also present," said he.

At that Griffith's good-nature, multiplied by a good supper, took the alarm. "Come, come, sir," said he, "have a little mercy. I know you are a just man, and, though a boon companion, most severe in all matters of morality. But, I tell you plainly, if you are going to drag this poor woman in the dirt, I shall go out of the room. What is the use tormenting her ? I 've told her my mind before her own child : and now I wish I had not. When I caught them in the grove I lifted my hand to strike her, and she never winced ; I had better have left that alone too, methinks. D—n the women : you are always in the wrong if you treat 'em like men. They are not wicked : they are weak. And this one hath lain in my bosom, and borne me two children, and one he lieth in the churchyard, and t' other hath her hair and my very eyes : and the truth is, I can't bear any man on earth to miscall her, but myself. God help me ; I doubt I love her still too well to sit by and see her tortured. She was all in black for her fault, poor penitent wretch. Give me the letters ; but let her be."

Francis was moved by this appeal, but shook his head solemnly ; and, ere Griffith could renew his argument, the door was flung open by Ryder, and a stately figure sailed in, that took both the gentlemen by surprise.

It was Mrs. Gaunt, in full dress. Rich brocade that swept the ground ; magnificent bust, like Parian marble varnished ; and on her brow a diadem of emeralds and diamonds that gave her beauty an imperial stamp.

She swept into the room as only fine women can sweep, made Griffith a haughty courtesy, and suddenly lowered her head, and received Father Francis's blessing : then seated herself, and quietly awaited events.

"The brazen jade!" thought Griffith. "But how divinely beautiful!" And he became as agitated as she was calm — in appearance. For need I say her calmness was put on? Defensive armor made for her by her pride and her sex.

The voice of Father Francis now rose, solid, grave, and too impressive to be interrupted.

"My daughter, and you who are her husband and my friend, I am here to do justice between you both, with God's help; and to show you both your faults. Catharine Gaunt, you began the mischief, by encouraging another man to interfere between you and your husband in things secular."

"But, father, he was my director, my priest."

"My daughter, do you believe, with the Protestants, that marriage is a mere civil contract; or do you hold, with us, that it is one of the holy sacraments?"

"Can you ask me?" murmured Kate, reproachfully.

"Well, then, those whom God and the whole Church have in holy sacrament united, what right hath a single priest to disunite in heart, and make the wife false to any part whatever of that most holy vow? I hear, and not from you, that Leonard did set you against your husband's friends, withdrew you from society, and sent him abroad alone. In one word, he robbed your husband of his companion and his friend. The sin was Leonard's; but the fault was yours. You were five years older than Leonard, and a woman of sense and experience; he but a boy by comparison. What right had you to surrender your understanding, in a matter of this kind, to a poor silly priest, fresh from his seminary, and as manifestly without a grain of common sense as he was full of piety?"

This remonstrance produced rather a striking effect on both those who heard it. Mrs. Gaunt seemed much struck with it. She leaned back in her chair, and put her hand to her brow with a sort of despairing gesture that Griffith could not very well understand, it seemed to him so disproportionate.

It softened him, however, and he faltered out, "Ay, father, that is how it all began. Would to heaven it had stopped there."

Francis resumed. "This false step led to consequences you never dreamed of; for one of your romantic notions is, that a priest is an angel. I have known you, in former times, try to take me for an angel: then would I throw cold water on your folly by calling lustily for chines of beef and mugs of ale. But I suppose Leonard thought himself an angel too; and the upshot was, he fell in love with his neighbor's wife."

"And she with him," groaned Griffith.

"Not so," said Francis; "but perhaps she was nearer it than she thinks."

"Prove that," said Mrs. Gaunt, "and I'll fall on my knees to him before you."

Francis smiled, and proceeded. "To be sure, from the moment you discovered Leonard was in love with you, you drew back, and conducted yourself with prudence and propriety. Read these letters, sir, and tell me what you think of them."

He handed them to Griffith. Griffith's hand trembled visibly as he took them.

"Stay," said Father Francis; "your better way will be to read the whole correspondence according to the dates. Begin with this of Mrs. Gaunt's."

Griffith read the letter in an audible whisper.

Mrs. Gaunt listened with all her ears.

"DEAR FATHER AND FRIEND, — The words you spoke to me to-day admit but one meaning; you are jealous of my husband.

"Then you must be — how can I write it? — almost in love with me.

"So then my poor husband was wiser than I. He saw a rival in you: and he has one.

"I am deeply, deeply shocked. I ought to be very angry too; but, thinking of your solitary condition, and all the good you have done to my soul, my heart has no place for aught but pity. Only, as I am in my senses, and you are not, you must now obey me, as heretofore I have obeyed you. You must seek another sphere of duty, without delay.

"These seem harsh words from me to you. You will live to see they are kind ones.

"Write me one line, and no more, to say you will be ruled by me in this.

"God and the saints have you in their holy keeping. So prays your affectionate and

"Sorrowful daughter and true friend,
"CATHARINE GAUNT."

"Poor soul!" said Griffith. "Said I not that women are not wicked, but weak? Who would think that after this he could get the better of her good resolves, — the villain!"

"Now read his reply," said Father Francis.

"Ay," said Griffith. "So this is his one word of reply, is it? three pages closely writ, — the villain, O the villain!"

"Read the villain's letter," said Francis, calmly.

The letter was very humble and pathetic, — the reply of a good, though erring man, who owned that in a moment of weakness he had been betrayed into a feeling inconsistent with his holy profession. He begged his correspondent, however, not to judge him quite so hardly. He reminded her of his solitary life, his natural melancholy, and assured her that all men in his condition had moments when they envied those whose bosoms had partners. "Such a cry of anguish," said he, "was once wrung from a maiden queen, maugre all her pride. The Queen of Scots hath a son; and I am but a barren stock." He went on to say that prayer and vigilance united do much. "Do not despair so soon of me. Flight is not cure: let me rather

stay, and, with God's help and the saints', overcome this unhappy weakness. If I fail, it will indeed be time for me to go, and never again see the angelic face of my daughter and my benefactress."

Griffith laid down the letter. He was somewhat softened by it, and said, gently, "I cannot understand it. This is not the letter of a thorough bad man neither."

"No," said Father Francis, coldly, "'t is the letter of a self-deceiver; and there is no more dangerous man to himself and others than your self-deceiver. But now let us see whether he can throw dust in her eyes, as well as his own." And he handed him Kate's reply.

The first word of it was, "You deceive yourself." The writer then insisted, quietly, that he owed it to himself, to her, and to her husband, whose happiness he was destroying, to leave the place at her request.

"Either you must go, or I," said she: "and pray let it be you. Also, this place is unworthy of your high gifts: and I love you, in my way, the way I mean to love you when we meet again — in heaven; and I labor your advancement to a sphere more worthy of you."

I wish space permitted me to lay the whole correspondence before the reader; but I must confine myself to its general purport.

It proceeded in this way: the priest, humble, eloquent, pathetic; but gently, yet pertinaciously, clinging to the place: the lady, gentle, wise, and firm, detaching with her soft fingers, first one hand, then another, of the poor priest's, till at last he was driven to the sorry excuse that he had no money to travel with, nor place to go to.

"I can't understand it," said Griffith. "Are these letters all forged, or are there two Kate Gaunts? the one that wrote these prudent letters, and the one I caught upon this very priest's arm. Perdition!"

Mrs. Gaunt started to her feet.

"Methinks 't is time for me to leave the room," said she, scarlet.

"Gently, my good friends; one thing at a time," said Francis. "Sit thou down, impetuous. The letters, sir, — what think you of them?"

"I see no harm in them," said Griffith.

"No harm! Is that all? But I say these are very remarkable letters, sir: and they show us that a woman may be innocent and unsuspicious, and so seem foolish, yet may be wise for all that. In her early communication with Leonard,

> 'At Wisdom's gate Suspicion slept;
> And thought no ill where no ill seemed.'

But, you see, suspicion being once aroused, wisdom was not to be lulled nor blinded. But that is not all: these letters breathe a spirit of Christian charity; of true, and rare, and exalted piety. Tender are they, without passion; wise, yet not cold; full of conjugal love, and of filial pity for an erring father, whom she leads, for his good, with firm yet dutiful hand. Trust to my great experience: doubt the chastity of snow rather than hers who could write these pure and exquisite lines. My good friend, you heard me rebuke and sneer at this poor lady for being too innocent and unsuspicious of man's frailty: now hear me own to you that I could no more have written these angelic letters than a barn-door fowl could soar to the mansions of the saints in heaven."

This unexpected tribute took Mrs. Gaunt's heart by storm; she threw her arms round Father Francis's neck, and wept upon his shoulder.

"Ah!" she sobbed, "you are the only one left that loves me."

She could not understand justice praising her: it must be love.

"Ay," said Griffith, in a broken voice, "she writes like an angel: she speaks like an angel: she looks like an angel. My heart says she is an angel. But my eyes have shown me she is naught. I left her, unable to walk, by her way of it; I came back and found her on that priest's arm, springing along like a greyhound." He buried his head in his hands, and groaned aloud.

Francis turned to Mrs. Gaunt, and said, a little severely, "How do you account for that?"

"I 'll tell *you*, Father," said Kate, "because you love me. I do not speak to *you*, sir: for you never loved me."

"I could give thee the lie," said Griffith, in a trembling voice; "but 't is not worth while. Know, sir, that within twenty-four hours after I caught her with that villain, I lay a-dying for her sake; and lost my wits; and, when I came to, they were a-making my shroud in the very room where I lay. No matter; no matter; I never loved her."

"Alas! poor soul!" sighed Kate. "Would I had died ere I brought thee to that!" And, with this, they both began to cry at the same moment.

"Ay, poor fools," said Father Francis, softly; "neither of ye loved t' other; that is plain. So now sit you there, and let us have your explanation; for you must own appearances are strong against you."

Mrs. Gaunt drew her stool to Francis's knee; and addressing herself to him alone, explained as follows: —

"I saw Father Leonard was giving way, and only wanted one good push, after a manner. Well, you know I had got him, by my friends, a good place in Ireland: and I had money by me for his journey; so, when my husband talked of going to the fair, I thought, 'O, if I could but get this settled to his mind before he comes back!' So I wrote a line to Leonard. You can read it if you like. 'T is dated the 30th of September, I suppose."

"I will," said Francis, and read this out: —

"DEAR FATHER AND FRIEND, — You have fought the good fight, and conquered. Now, therefore, I *will* see you once more, and thank you for my husband (he is so unhappy), and put the money for your journey into your hand myself, — your journey to Ireland. You are the Duke of Leinster's chaplain ; for I have accepted that place for you. Let me see you to-morrow in the Grove, for a few minutes, at high noon. God bless you.

"CATHARINE GAUNT."

"Well, father," said Mrs. Gaunt, "'t is true that I could only walk two or three times across the room. But, alack, you know what women are : excitement gives us strength. With thinking that our unhappiness was at an end, — that, when he should come back from the fair, I should fling my arm round his neck, and tell him I had removed the cause of his misery, and so of mine, — I seemed to have wings ; and I did walk with Leonard, and talked with rapture of the good he was to do in Ireland, and how he was to be a mitred abbot one day (for he is a great man), and poor little me be proud of him ; and how we were all to be happy together in heaven, where is no marrying nor giving in marriage. This was our discourse ; and I was just putting the purse into his hands, and bidding him God-speed, when he — for whom I fought against my woman's nature, and took this trying task upon me — broke in upon us, with the face of a fiend ; trampled on the poor, good priest, that deserved veneration and consolation from him, of all men ; and raised his hand to me ; and was not man enough to kill me after all ; but called me — ask him what he called me — see if he dares to say it again before you ; and then ran away, like a coward as he is, from the lady he had defiled with his rude tongue, and the heart he had broken. Forgive him ? that I never will, — never, — never."

"Who asked you to forgive him ?" said the shrewd priest. "Your own heart. Come, look at him."

"Not I," said she, irresolutely. Then, still more feebly : "He is naught to me." And so stole a look at him.

Griffith, pale as ashes, had his hand on his brow, and his eyes were fixed with horror and remorse.

"Something tells me she has spoken the truth," he said, in a quavering voice. Then, with concentrated horror, "But if so — O God, what have I done ? — What shall I do ?"

Mrs. Gaunt extended her arms towards him across the priest.

"Why, fall at thy wife's knees and ask her to forgive thee."

Griffith obeyed : he fell on his knees, and Mrs. Gaunt leaned her head on Francis's shoulder, and gave her hand across him to her remorse-stricken husband.

Neither spoke, nor desired to speak ; and even Father Francis sat silent, and enjoyed that sweet glow which sometimes blesses the peacemaker, even in this world of wrangles and jars.

But the good soul had ridden hard, and the neglected meats emitted savory odors ; and by and by he said dryly, "I wonder whether that fat pullet tastes as well as it smells : can you tell me, Squire ?"

"O, inhospitable wretch that I am !" said Mrs. Gaunt : "I thought but of my own heart."

"And forgot the stomach of your unspiritual father. But, my dear, you are pale, you tremble."

"'T is nothing, sir : I shall soon be better. Sit you down and sup : I will return anon."

She retired, not to make a fuss ; but her heart palpitated violently, and she had to sit down on the stairs.

Ryder, who was prowling about, found her there, and fetched her hartshorn.

Mrs. Gaunt got better ; but felt so languid, and also hysterical, that she retired to her own room for the night, attended by the faithful Ryder, to whom she confided that a reconciliation had taken place, and, to celebrate it, gave her a dress she had only worn a year. This does not sound queenly to you ladies ; but know that a week's wear tells far more on the flimsy trash you wear now-a-days, than a year did on the glorious silks of Lyons Mrs. Gaunt put on; thick as broadcloth, and embroidered so cunningly by the loom, that it would pass for rarest needle-work. Besides, in those days, silk was silk.

As Ryder left her, she asked, "Where is master to lie to-night?"

Mrs. Gaunt was not pleased at this question being put to her. She would have preferred to leave that to Griffith. And, as she was a singular mixture of frankness and finesse, I believe she had retired to her own room partly to test Griffith's heart. If he was as sincere as she was, he would not be content with a public reconciliation.

But the question being put to her plump, and by one of her own sex, she colored faintly, and said, "Why, is there not a bed in his room?"

"O yes, madam."

"Then see it be well aired. Put down all the things before the fire; and then tell me: I'll come and see. The feather-bed, mind, as well as the sheets and blankets."

Ryder executed all this with zeal. She did more; though Griffith and Francis sat up very late, she sat up too; and, on the gentlemen leaving the supper-room, she met them both, with bed-candles, in a delightful cap, and undertook, with cordial smiles, to show them both their chambers.

"Tread softly on the landing, an if it please you, gentlemen. My mistress hath been unwell; but she is in a fine sleep now, by the blessing, and I would not have her disturbed."

Good, faithful, single-hearted Ryder!

Father Francis went to bed thoughtful. There was something about Griffith he did not like: the man every now and then broke out into boisterous raptures, and presently relapsed into moody thoughtfulness. Francis almost feared that his cure was only temporary.

In the morning, before he left, he drew Mrs. Gaunt aside, and told her his misgivings. She replied that she thought she knew what was amiss, and would soon set that right.

Griffith tossed and turned in his bed, and spent a stormy night. His mind was in a confused whirl, and his heart distracted. The wife he had loved so tenderly proved to be the very reverse of all he had lately thought her! She was pure as snow, and had always loved him; loved him now, and only wanted a good excuse to take him to her arms again. But Mercy Vint!—his wife, his benefactress! a woman as chaste as Kate, as strict in life and morals,—what was to become of her? How could he tell her she was not his wife? how reveal to her her own calamity, and his treason? And, on the other hand, desert her without a word! and leave her hoping, fearing, pining, all her life! Affection, humanity, gratitude, alike forbade it.

He came down in the morning, pale for him, and worn with the inward struggle.

Naturally there was a restraint between him and Mrs. Gaunt; and only short sentences passed between them.

He saw the peacemaker off, and then wandered all over the premises, and the past came nearer, and the present seemed to retire into the background.

He wandered about like one in a dream; and was so self-absorbed, that he did not see Mrs. Gaunt coming towards him, with observant eyes.

She met him full; he started like a guilty thing.

"Are you afraid of me?" said she, sweetly.

"No, my dear, not exactly; and yet I am: afraid, or ashamed, or both."

"You need not. I said I forgive you; and you know I am not one that does things by halves."

"You are an angel!" said he, warmly; "but" (suddenly relapsing into despondency) "we shall never be happy together again."

She sighed. "Say not so. Time and sweet recollections may heal even this wound by degrees."

"God grant it," said he, despairingly.

"And, though we can't be lovers

again all at once, we may be friends. To begin, tell me, what have you on your mind? Come, make a friend of me."

He looked at her in alarm.

She smiled. " Shall I guess?" said she.

"You will never guess," said he; "and I shall never have the heart to tell you."

"Let me try. Well, I think you have run in debt, and are afraid to ask me for the money."

Griffith was greatly relieved by this conjecture; he drew a long breath; and, after a pause, said cunningly, "What made you think that?"

"Because you came here for money, and not for happiness. You told me so in the Grove."

"That is true. What a sordid wretch you must think me!"

"No, because you were under a delusion. But I do believe you are just the man to turn reckless, when you thought me false, and go drinking and dicing." She added eagerly, "I do not suspect you of anything worse."

He assured her that was not the way of it.

"Then tell me the way of it. You must not think, because I pester you not with questions, I have no curiosity. O, how often I have longed to be a bird, and watch you day and night unseen! How would you have liked that? I wish you had been one, to watch me. Ah, you don't answer. Could you have borne so close an inspection, sir?"

Griffith shuddered at the idea; and his eyes fell before the full gray orbs of his wife.

"Well, never mind," said she. "Tell me your story."

"Well, then, when I left you, I was raving mad."

"That is true, I 'll be sworn."

"I let my horse go; and he took me near a hundred miles from here, and stopped at — at — a farm-house. The good people took me in."

"God bless them for it. I 'll ride and thank them."

"Nay, nay; 't is too far. There I

fell sick of a fever, a brain-fever: the doctor blooded me."

"Alas! would he had taken mine instead."

"And I lost my wits for several days; and when I came back, I was weak as water, and given up by the doctor; and the first thing I saw was an old hag set a-making of my shroud."

Here the narrative was interrupted a moment by Mrs. Gaunt seizing him convulsively; and then holding him tenderly, as if he was even now about to be taken from her.

"The good people nursed me, and so did their daughter, and I came back from the grave. I took an inn; but I gave up that, and had to pay forfeit; and so my money all went; but they kept me on. To be sure I helped on the farm: they kept a hostelry as well. By and by came that murrain among the cattle. Did you have it in these parts, too?"

"I know not; nor care. Prithee, leave cattle, and talk of thyself."

"Well, in a word, they were ruined, and going to be sold up. I could not bear that: I became bondsman for the old man. It was the least I could do. Kate, they had saved thy husband's life."

"Not a word more, Griffith. How much stand you pledged for?"

"A large sum."

"Would five hundred pounds be of any avail?"

"Five hundred pounds! Ay, that it would, and to spare; but where can I get so much money? And the time so short."

"Give me thy hand, and come with me," said Mrs. Gaunt, ardently.

She took his hand, and made a swift rush across the lawn. It was not exactly running, nor walking, but some grand motion she had when excited. She put him to his stride to keep up with her at all; and in two minutes she had him into her boudoir. She unlocked a bureau, all in a hurry, and took out a bag of gold. "There!" she cried, thrusting it into his hand, and blooming all over with joy and eagerness: "I thought you would want money ; so I saved it up. You shall not be in debt a day longer. Now mount thy horse, and carry it to those good souls ; only, for my sake, take the gardener with thee, — I have no groom now but he, — and both well armed."

"What ! go this very day ? "

"Ay, this very hour. I can bear thy absence for a day or two more, — I have borne it so long ; but I cannot bear thy plighted word to stand in doubt a day, no, not an hour. I am your wife, sir, your true and loving wife : your honor is mine, and is as dear to me now as it was when you saw me with Father Leonard in the Grove, and read me all awry. Don't wait a moment. Begone at once."

" Nay, nay, if I go to-morrow, I shall be in time."

" Ay, but," said Mrs. Gaunt, very softly, " I am afraid if I keep you another hour I shall not have the heart to let you go at all ; and the sooner gone, the sooner back for good, please God. There, give me one kiss, to live on, and begone this instant."

He covered her hands with kisses and tears. " I 'm not worthy to kiss any higher than thy hand," he said, and so ran sobbing from her.

He went straight to the stable, and saddled Black Dick.

CHAPTER XXXII.

HE went straight to the stable, and saddled Black Dick.

But, in the very act, his nature revolted. What, turn his back on her the moment he had got hold of her money, to take to the other. He could not do it.

He went back to her room, and came so suddenly that he caught her crying. He asked her what was the matter.

" Nothing," said she, with a sigh : " only a woman's foolish misgivings. I was afraid perhaps you would not come back. Forgive me."

" No fear of that," said he. " However, I have taken a resolve not to go to-day. If I go to-morrow, I shall be just in time ; and Dick wants a good day's rest."

Mrs. Gaunt said nothing ; but her expressive face was triumphant.

Griffith and she took a walk together ; and he, who used to be the more genial of the two, was dull, and she full of animation.

This whole day she laid herself out to bewitch her husband, and put him in high spirits.

It was up-hill work ; but when such a woman sets herself in earnest to delight a man, she reads our sex a lesson in the art, that shows us we are all babies at it.

However, it was at supper she finally conquered.

Here the lights, her beauty set off with art, her deepening eyes, her satin skin, her happy excitement, her wit and tenderness, and joyous sprightliness, enveloped Griffith in an atmosphere of delight, and drove everything out of his head but herself ; and with this, if the truth must be told, the sparkling wines co-operated.

Griffith plied the bottle a little too freely. But Mrs. Gaunt, on this one occasion, had not the heart to check him. The more he toasted her, the more uxorious he became, and she could not deny herself even this joy ; but, besides, she had less of the prudent wife in her just then than of the weak, indulgent mother. Anything rather than check his love : she was greedy of it.

At last, however, she said to him, " Sweetheart, I shall go to bed ; for, I see, if I stay longer, I shall lead thee into a debauch. Be good now ; drink no more when I am gone. Else I 'll say thou lovest thy bottle more than thy wife."

He promised faithfully. But, when she was gone, modified his pledge by drinking just one bumper to her health, which bumper let in another ; and, when at last he retired to rest, he was in that state of mental confusion wherein the limbs appear to have a memory independent of the mind.

In this condition do some men's hands wind up their watches, the mind taking no appreciable part in the ceremony.

By some such act of what physicians call "organic memory," Griffith's feet carried him to the chamber he had slept in a thousand times, and not into the one Mrs. Rider had taken him to the night before.

The next morning he came down rather late for him, and found himself treated with a great access of respect by the servants.

His position was no longer doubtful; he was the master of the house.

Mrs. Gaunt followed in due course, and sat at breakfast with him, looking young and blooming as Hebe, and her eye never off him long.

She had lived temperately, and had not yet passed the age when happiness can restore a woman's beauty and brightness in a single day.

As for him, he was like a man in a heavenly dream : he floated in the past and the present : the recent and the future seemed obscure and distant, and comparatively in a mist.

But that same afternoon, after a most affectionate farewell, and many promises to return as soon as ever he had discharged his obligations, Griffith Gaunt started for the "Packhorse," to carry to Mercy Leicester, alias Vint, the money Catharine Gaunt had saved by self-denial and economy.

And he went south a worse man than he came.

When he left Mercy Leicester, he was a bigamist in law, but not at heart. Kate was dead to him : he had given her up forever, and was constant and true to his new wife.

But now he was false to Mercy, yet not true to Kate ; and, curiously enough, it was a day or two passed with his lawful wife that had demoralized him. His unlawful wife had hitherto done nothing but improve his character.

A great fault once committed is often the first link in a chain of acts that look like crimes, but are, strictly speaking, consequences.

This man, blinded at first by his own foible, and after that the sport of circumstances, was single-hearted by nature ; and his conscience was not hardened. He desired earnestly to free himself and both his wives from the cruel situation ; but to do this, one of them, he saw, must be abandoned entirely ; and his heart bled for her.

A villain or a fool would have relished the situation ; many men would have dallied with it ; but, to do this erring man justice, he writhed and sorrowed under it, and sincerely desired to end it.

And this was why he prized Kate's money so. It enabled him to render a great service to her he had injured worse than he had the other, to her he saw he must abandon.

But this was feeble comfort, after all. He rode along a miserable man ; none the less wretched and remorseful, that, ere he got into Lancashire, he saw his way clear. This was his resolve : to pay old Vint's debts with Kate's money ; take the "Packhorse," get it made over to Mercy, give her the odd two hundred pounds and his jewels, and fly. He would never see her again ; but would return home, and get the rest of the two thousand pounds from Kate, and send it Mercy by a friend, who should tell her he was dead, and had left word with his relations to send her all his substance.

At last the "Packhorse" came in sight. He drew rein, and had half a mind to turn back ; but, instead of that, he crawled on, and very sick and cold he felt.

Many a man has marched to the scaffold with a less quaking heart than he to the "Packhorse."

His dejection contrasted strangely with the warm reception he met from everybody there. And the house was full of women ; and they seemed, somehow, all cock-a-hoop, and filled with admiration of *him*.

"Where is she ? " said he, faintly.

"Hark to the poor soul ! " said a

gossip. "Dame Vint, where's thy daughter? gone out a-walking belike?"

At this, the other women present chuckled and clucked.

"I'll bring you to her," said Mrs. Vint; "but prithee be quiet and reasonable; for to be sure she is none too strong."

There was some little preparation, and then Griffith was ushered into Mercy's room, and found her in bed, looking a little pale, but sweeter and comelier than ever. She had the bedclothes up to her chin.

"You look wan, my poor lass," said he; "what ails ye?"

"Naught ails me now thou art come," said she, lovingly.

Griffith put the bag on the table. "There," said he, "there's five hundred pounds in gold. I come not to thee empty-handed."

"Nor I to thee," said Mercy, with a heavenly smile. "See!"

And she drew down the bedclothes a little, and showed the face of a babe scarcely three days old,—a little boy.

She turned in the bed, and tried to hold him up to his father, and said, "Here's *my* treasure for thee!" And the effort, the flush on her cheek, and the deep light in her dove-like eyes, told plainly that the poor soul thought she had contributed to their domestic wealth something far richer than Griffith had with his bag of gold.

The father uttered an ejaculation, and came to her side, and, for a moment, Nature overpowered everything else. He kissed the child; he kissed Mercy again and again.

"Now God be praised for both," said he, passionately; "but most for thee, the best wife, the truest friend—" Here, thinking of her virtues, and the blow he had come to strike her, he broke down, and was almost choked with emotion; whereupon Mrs. Vint exerted female authority, and bundled him out of the room. "Is that the way to carry on at such an a time?" said she.

"'T was enow to upset her altogether. O, but you men have little sense in women's matters. I looked to you to give her courage, not to set her off into hysterics after a manner. Nay, keep up her heart, or keep your distance, say I, that am her mother."

Griffith took this hint, and ever after took pity on Mercy's weak condition; and, suspending the fatal blow, did all he could to restore her to health and spirits.

Of course, to do that, he must deceive her; and so his life became a lie.

For, hitherto, she had never looked forward much; but now her eyes were always diving into futurity; and she lay smiling and discussing the prospects of her boy; and Griffith had to sit by her side, and see her gnaw the boy's hand, and kiss his feet, and anticipate his brilliant career. He had to look and listen with an aching heart, and assent with feigned warmth, and an inward chill of horror and remorse.

One Drummond, a travelling artist, called; and Mercy, who had often refused to sit to him, consented now; "for," she said, "when he grows up, he shall know how his parents looked in their youth, the very year their darling was born." So Griffith had to sit with her, and excellent likenesses the man produced; but a horrible one of the child. And Griffith thought, "Poor soul! a little while and this picture will be all that shall be left to thee of me."

For all this time he was actually transacting the preliminaries of separation. He got a man of law to make all sure. The farm, the stock, the furniture and good-will of the "Packhorse," all these he got assigned to Mercy Leicester for her own use, in consideration of three hundred and fifty pounds, whereof three hundred were devoted to clearing the concern of its debts, the odd fifty was to sweeten the pill to Harry Vint.

When the deed came to be executed, Mercy was surprised, and uttered a gentle remonstrance. "What have I to do with it?" said she. "'T is thy money, not mine."

"No matter," said Griffith; "I choose to have it so."

"Your will is my law," said Mercy.

"Besides," said Griffith, "the old folk will not feel so sore, nor be afraid of being turned out, if it is in thy name."

"And that is true," said Mercy. "Now who had thought of that, but my good man?" And she threw her arms lovingly round his neck, and gazed on him adoringly.

But his lion-like eyes avoided her dove-like eyes; and an involuntary shudder ran through him.

The habit of deceiving Mercy led to a consequence he had not anticipated. It tightened the chain that held him. She opened his eyes more and more to her deep affection, and he began to fear she would die if he abandoned her.

And then her present situation was so touching. She had borne him a lovely boy;' that must be abandoned too, if he left her; and somehow the birth of this child had embellished the mother; a delicious pink had taken the place of her rustic bloom; and her beauty was more refined and delicate. So pure, so loving, so fair, so maternal, to wound her heart now, it seemed like stabbing an angel.

One day succeeded to another, and still Griffith had not the heart to carry out his resolve. He temporized; he wrote to Kate that he was detained by the business; and he stayed on and on, strengthening his gratitude and his affection, and weakening his love for the absent, and his resolution; till, at last, he became so distracted and divided in heart, and so demoralized, that he began to give up the idea of abandoning Mercy, and babbled to himself about fate and destiny, and decided that the most merciful course would be to deceive both women. Mercy was patient. Mercy was unsuspicious. She would content herself with occasional visits, if he could only feign some plausible tale to account for long absences.

Before he got into this mess, he was a singularly truthful person; but now a lie was nothing to him. But, for that matter, many a man has been first made a liar by his connection with two women; and by degrees has carried his mendacity into other things.

However, though now blessed with mendacity, he was cursed with a lack of invention; and sorely puzzled how to live at Hernshaw, yet visit the "Packhorse."

The best thing he could hit upon was to pretend to turn bagman; and so Mercy would believe he was travelling all over England, when all the time he was quietly living at Hernshaw.

And perhaps these long separations might prepare her heart for a final parting, and so let in his original plan a few years hence.

He prepared this manœuvre with some art; he told her, one day, he had been to Lancaster, and there fallen in with a friend, who had as good as promised him the place of a commercial traveller for a mercantile house there.

"A traveller!" said Mercy. "Heaven forbid! If you knew how I wearied for you when you went to Cumberland!"

"To Cumberland! How know you I went thither?"

"O, I but guessed that; but now I know it, by your face. But go where thou wilt, the house is dull directly. Thou art our sunshine. Is n't he, my poppet?"

"Well, well; if it kept me too long from thee, I could give it up. But, child, we must think of young master. You could manage the inn, and your mother the farm, without me; and I should be earning money on my side. I want to make a gentleman of him."

"Anything for *him*," said Mercy; "anything in the world." But the tears stood in her eyes.

In furtherance of this deceit, Griffith did one day actually ride to Lancaster, and slept there. He wrote to Kate from that town, to say he was detained by a slight illness, but hoped to be home in a week: and the next day brought Mercy home some ribbons, and told her he had seen the merchant, and his brother, and they had made him a very fair offer. "But I 've a week to think of it," said he; "so there 's no hurry."

Mercy fixed her eyes on him in a very peculiar way, and made no reply. You must know that something very curious had happened whilst Griffith was gone to Lancaster.

A travelling pedler, passing by, was struck with the name on the sign-board. "Hallo!" said he, "why here 's a namesake of mine; I 'll have a glass of his ale any way."

So he came into the public room, and called for a glass; taking care to open his pack, and display his inviting wares. Harry Vint served him. "Here 's your health," said the pedler. "You must drink with me, you must."

"And welcome," said the old man.

"Well," said the pedler, "I do travel five counties; but for all that, you are the first namesake I have found. I am Thomas Leicester, too, as sure as you are a living sinner."

The old man laughed, and said, "Then no namesake of mine are you; for they call me Harry Vint. Thomas Leicester, he that keeps this inn now, is my son-in-law; he is gone to Lancaster this morning."

The pedler said that was a pity, he should have liked to see his namesake, and drink a glass with him.

"Come again to-morrow," said Harry Vint, ironically. "Dame," he cried, "come hither. Here 's another Thomas Leicester for ye, wants to see our one."

Mrs. Vint turned her head, and inspected the pedler from afar, as if he was some natural curiosity.

"Where do you come from, young man?" said she.

"Well, I came from Kendal last; but I am Cumberland born."

"Why, that is where t' other comes from," suggested Paul Carrick, who was once more a frequenter of the house.

"Like enow," said Mrs. Vint.

With that she dropped the matter as one of no consequence, and retired. But she went straight to Mercy, in the parlor, and told her there was a man in the kitchen that called himself Thomas Leicester.

"Well, mother?" said Mercy, with high indifference, for she was trying new socks on King Baby.

"He comes from Cumberland."

"Well, to be sure, names do run in counties."

"That is true; but, seems to me, he favors your man: much of a height, and — There, do just step into the kitchen a moment."

"La, mother," said Mercy, "I don't desire to see any more Thomas Leicesters than my own: 't is the man, not the name. Is n't it, my lamb?"

Mrs. Vint went back to the kitchen discomfited; but, with quiet pertinacity, she brought Thomas Leicester into the parlor, pack and all.

"There, Mercy," said she, "lay out a penny with thy husband's namesake."

Mercy did not reply, for at that moment Thomas Leicester caught sight of Griffith's portrait, and gave a sudden start, and a most extraordinary look besides.

Both the women's eyes happened to be upon him, and they saw at once that he knew the original.

"You know my husband?" said Mercy Vint, after a while.

"Not I," said Leicester, looking askant at the picture.

"Don't tell no lies," said Mrs. Vint. "You do know him well." And she pointed her assertion by looking at the portrait.

"O, I know him whose picture hangs there, of course," said Leicester.

"Well, and that *is* her husband."

"O, that is her husband, is it?" And he was unaffectedly puzzled.

Mercy turned pale. "Yes, he is my husband," said she, "and this is our child. Can you tell me anything about him? for he came a stranger to these parts. Belike you are a kinsman of his?"

"So they say."

This reply puzzled both women.

"Any way," said the pedler, "you see we are marked alike." And he showed a long black mole on his forehead.

Mercy was now as curious as she had been indifferent. "Tell me all about him," said she : "how comes it that he is a gentleman and thou a pedler ? "

".Well, because my mother was a gypsy, and his a gentlewoman."

"What brought him to these parts ? "

"Trouble, they say."

"What trouble ? "

"Nay, I know not." This after a slight but visible hesitation.

"But you have heard say."

"Well, I am always on the foot, and don't bide long enough in one place to learn all the gossip. But I do remember hearing he was gone to sea : and that was a lie, for he had settled here and married you. I'fackins, he might have done worse. He has got a bonny buxom wife, and a rare fine boy, to be sure."

And now the pedler was on his guard, and determined he would not be the one to break up the household he saw before him, and afflict the dove-eyed wife and mother. He was a good - natured fellow, and averse to make mischief with his own hands. Besides, he took for granted Griffith loved his new wife better than the old one ; and, above all, the punishment of bigamy was severe, and was it for him to get the Squire indicted, and branded in the hand for a felon ?

So the women could get nothing more out of him ; he lied, evaded, shuffled, and feigned utter ignorance ; pleading, adroitly enough, his vagrant life.

All this, however, aroused vague suspicions in Mrs. Vint's mind, and she went and whispered them to her favorite, Paul Carrick. "And, Paul," said she, "call for what you like, and score it to me ; only treat this pedler till he leaks out summut : to be sure he 'll tell a man more than he will us."

Paul entered with zeal into this commission : treated the pedler to a chop, and plied him well with the best ale.

All this failed to loose the pedler's tongue at the time, but it muddled his judgment : on resuming his journey, he gave his entertainer a wink. Carrick rose and followed him out.

"You seem a decent lad," said the pedler, "and a good-hearted one. Wilt do me a favor ? "

Carrick said he would, if it lay in his power.

"O, it is easy enow," said the pedler. "'T is just to give young Thomas Leicester, into his own hand, this here trifle as soon as ever he comes home." And he handed Carrick a hard substance wrapped up in paper. Carrick promised.

"Ay, ay, lad," said the pedler, "but see you play fair, and give it him unbeknown. Now don't you be so simple as show it to any of the women-folk. D' ye understand ? "

"All right," said Carrick, knowingly. And so the boon companions for a day shook hands and parted.

And Carrick took the little parcel straight to Mrs. Vint, and told her every word the pedler had said.

And Mrs. Vint took the little parcel straight to Mercy, and told her what Carrick said the pedler had said.

And the pedler went off flushed with beer and self-complacency ; for he thought he had drawn the line precisely ; had faithfully discharged his promise to his lady and benefactress, but not so as to make mischief in another household.

Such was the power of Ale — in the last century.

Mercy undid the paper and found the bullet, on which was engraved

"I LOVE KATE."

As she read these words a knife seemed to enter her heart, the pang was so keen.

But she soon took herself to task. "Thou naughty woman," said she. "What ! jealous of the dead ? "

She wrapped the bullet up ; put it carefully away ; had a good cry ; and was herself again.

But all this set her watching Griffith, and reading his face. She had subtle, vague misgivings, and forbade her mother to mention the pedler's visit to Griffith yet awhile. Woman-like she preferred to worm out the truth.

On the evening of his return from Lancaster, as he was smoking his pipe, she quietly tested him. She fixed her eyes on him, and said, " One was here to-day that knows thee, and brought thee this." She then handed him the bullet, and watched his face.

Griffith undid the paper carelessly enough ; but, at sight of the bullet, uttered a loud cry, and his eyes seemed ready to start out of his head.

He turned as pale as ashes, and stammered piteously, " What ? what ? what d' ye mean ? In Heaven's name, what is this ? How ? Who ? "

Mercy was surprised, but also much concerned at his distress ; and tried to soothe him. She also asked him piteously, whether she had done wrong to give it him. " God knows," said she, " 't is no business of mine to go and remind thee of her thou hast loved better mayhap than thou lovest me. But to keep it from thee, and she in her grave, — O, I had not the heart."

But Griffith's agitation increased instead of diminishing ; and, even while she was trying to soothe him, he rushed wildly out of the room, and into the open air.

Mercy went, in perplexity and distress, and told her mother.

Mrs. Vint, not being blinded by affection, thought the whole thing had a very ugly look, and said as much. She gave it as her opinion that this Kate was alive, and had sent the token herself, to make mischief between man and wife."

" That shall she never," said Mercy, stoutly ; but now her suspicions were thoroughly excited, and her happiness disturbed.

The next day, Griffith found her in tears. He asked her what was the matter. She would not tell him.

" You have your secrets," said she ; " and so now I have mine."

Griffith became very uneasy.

For now Mercy was often in tears, and Mrs. Vint looked daggers at him.

All this was mysterious and unintelligible, and, to a guilty man, very alarming.

At last he implored Mercy to speak out. He wanted to know the worst.

Then Mercy did speak out. " You have deceived me," said she. " Kate is alive. This very morning, between sleeping and waking, you whispered her name ; ay, false man, whispered it like a lover. You told me she was dead. But she is alive, and has sent you a reminder, and the bare sight of it hath turned your heart her way again. What shall I do ? Why did you marry me, if you could not forget her ? I did not want you to desert any woman for me. The desire of my heart was always for your happiness. But O Thomas, deceit and falsehood will not bring you happiness, no more than they will me. What shall I do ? what shall I do ? "

Her tears flowed freely, and Griffith sat down, and groaned with horror and remorse, beside her.

He had not the courage to tell her the horrible truth, — that Kate was his wife, and she was not.

" Do not thou afflict thyself," he muttered. " Of course, with you putting that bullet in my hand so sudden, it set my fancy a wandering back to other days."

" Ah ! " said Mercy, " if it be no worse than that, there 's little harm. But why did thy namesake start so at sight of thy picture ? "

" My namesake ! " cried Griffith, all aghast.

" Ay, he that brought thee that love-token, — Thomas Leicester. Nay, for very shame, feign not ignorance of him. Why, he hath thy very mole on his temple, and knew thy picture in a moment. He is thy half-brother, is he not ? "

" I am a ruined man," cried Griffith, and sank into a chair without power of motion.

" God help me, what is all this ? "

cried Mercy. "O Thomas, Thomas, I could forgive thee aught but deceit: for both our sakes speak out, and tell me the worst. No harm shall come near thee while I live." •

"How can I tell thee? I am an unfortunate man. The world will call me a villain; yet I am not a villain at heart. But who will believe me? I have broken the law. Thee I could trust, but not thy folk; they never loved me. Mercy, for pity's sake, when was that Thomas Leicester here?"

"Four days ago."

"Which way went he?"

"I hear he told Paul he was going to Cumberland."

"If he gets there before me, I shall rot in gaol."

"Now God forbid! O Thomas, then mount and ride after him."

"I will, and this very moment."

He saddled Black Dick, and loaded his pistols for the journey; but, ere he went, a pale face looked out into the yard, and a finger beckoned. It was Mercy. She bade him follow her. She took him to her room, where their child was sleeping; and then she closed and even locked the door.

"No soul can hear us," said she; "now look me in the face, and tell me God's truth. Who and what are you?"

Griffith shuddered at this exordium; he made no reply.

Mercy went to a box and took out an old shirt of his, — the one he wore when he first came to the "Packhorse." She brought it to him and showed him "G. G." embroidered on it with a woman's hair. (Ryder's.)

"Here are your initials," said she; "now leave useless falsehoods; be a man, and tell me your real name."

"My name is Griffith Gaunt."

Mercy, sick at heart, turned her head away; but she had the resolution to urge him on. "Go on," said she, in an agonized whisper: "if you believe in God and a judgment to come, deceive me no more. The truth, I say! the truth!"

"So be it," said Griffith, desperately: "when I have told thee what a villain I am, I can die at thy feet, and then thou wilt forgive me.

"Who is Kate?" was all she replied.

"Kate is my wife."

"I thought her false; who could think any other? appearances were so strong against her: others thought so beside me. I raised my hand to kill her; but she never winced. I trampled on him I believed her paramour: I fled, and soon I lay a-dying in this house for her sake. I told thee she was dead. Alas! I thought her dead to me. I went back to our house (it is her house) sore against the grain, to get money for thee and thine. Then she cleared herself, bright as the sun, and pure as snow. She was all in black for me; she had put by money, against I should come to my senses and need it. I told her I owed a debt in Lancashire, a debt of gratitude as well as money: and so I did. How have I repaid it? The poor soul forced five hundred pounds on me. I had much ado to keep her from bringing it hither with her own hands. O, villain! villain! Then I thought to leave thee, and send thee word I was dead, and heap money on thee. Money! But how could I? thou wast my benefactress, my more than wife. All the riches of the world can make no return to thee. What, what shall I do? Shall I fly with thee and thy child across the seas? Shall I go back to her? No; the best thing I can do is to take this good pistol, and let the life out of my dishonorable carcass, and free two honest women from me by one resolute act."

In his despair he cocked the pistol; and, at a word from Mercy, this tale had ended.

But the poor woman, pale and trembling, tottered across the room, and took it out of his hand. "I would not harm thy body, nor thy soul," she gasped. "Let me draw my breath and think."

She rocked herself to and fro in silence.

Griffith stood trembling like a criminal before his judge.

It was long ere she could speak, for anguish. Yet when she did speak, it was with a sort of deadly calm.

"Go tell the truth to *her*, as you have done to me ; and, if she can forgive you, all the better for you. I can never forgive you, nor yet can harm you. My child ! my child ! Thy father is our ruin. O, begone, man, or the sight of you will kill us both."

Then he fell at her knees ; kissed, and wept over her cold hand ; and, in his pity and despair, offered to cross the seas with her and her child, and so repair the wrong he had done her.

"Tempt me not," she sobbed. "Go, leave me ! None here shall ever know thy crime, but she whose heart thou hast broken, and ruined her good name."

He took her in his arms, in spite of her resistance, and kissed her passionately ; but, for the first time, she shuddered at his embrace ; and that gave him the power to leave her.

He rushed from her, all but distracted, and rode away to Cumberland ; but not to tell the truth to Kate, if he could possibly help it.

CHAPTER XXXIII.

AT this particular time, no man's presence was more desired in that county than Griffith Gaunt's.

And this I need not now be telling the reader, if I had related this story on the plan of a miscellaneous chronicle. But the affairs of the heart are so absorbing, that, even in a narrative, they thrust aside important circumstances of a less moving kind.

I must therefore go back a step, before I advance further. You must know that forty years before our Griffith Gaunt saw the light, another Griffith Gaunt was born in Cumberland : a younger son, and the family estate entailed ; but a shrewd lad, who chose rather to hunt fortune elsewhere than to live in miserable dependence on his elder brother. His godfather, a city merchant, encouraged him, and he left Cumberland. He went into commerce, and in twenty years became a wealthy man, — so wealthy that he lived to look down on his brother's estate, which he had once thought opulence. His life was all prosperity, with a single exception ; but that a bitter one. He laid out some of his funds in a fashionable and beautiful wife. He loved her before marriage ; and, as she was always cold to him, he loved her more and more.

In the second year of their marriage she ran away from him ; and no beggar in the streets of London was so miserable as the wealthy merchant.

It blighted the man, and left him a sore heart all his days. He never married again ; and railed on all womankind for this one. He led a solitary life in London till he was sixty-nine ; and then, all of a sudden, Nature, or accident, or both, changed his whole habits. Word came to him that the family estate, already deeply mortgaged, was for sale, and a farmer who had rented a principal farm on it, and held a heavy mortgage, had made the highest offer.

Old Griffith sent down Mr. Atkins, his solicitor, post haste, and snapped the estate out of that purchaser's hands.

When the lands and house had been duly conveyed to him, he came down, and his heart seemed to bud again, in the scenes of his childhood.

Finding the house small, and built in a valley instead of on rising ground, he got an army of bricklayers, and began to build a mansion with a rapidity unheard of in those parts ; and he looked about for some one to inherit it.

The name of Gaunt had dwindled down to three, since he left Cumberland ; but a rich man never lacks relations. Featherstonhaughs, and Underhills, and even Smiths, poured in, with parish registers in their laps, and proved themselves Gauntesses, and flattered and carneyed the new head of the family.

Then the perverse old gentleman felt

inclined to look elsewhere. He knew he had a namesake at the other side of the county, but this namesake did not come near him.

This independent Gaunt excited his curiosity and interest. He made inquiries, and heard that young Griffith had just quarrelled with his wife, and gone away in despair.

Griffith senior took for granted that the fault lay with Mrs. Gaunt, and wasted some good sympathy on Griffith junior.

On further inquiry he learned that the truant was dependent on his wife. Then, argued the moneyed man, he would not run away from her but that his wound was deep.

The consequence of all this was, that he made a will very favorable to his absent and injured (?) namesake. He left numerous bequests; but made Griffith his residuary legatee; and, having settled this matter, urged on, and superintended his workmen.

Alas! just as the roof was going on, a narrower house claimed him, and he made good the saying of the wise bard, —

> "Tu secunda marmora
> Locas sub ipsum funus et sepulchri
> Immemor struis domos."

The heir of his own choosing could not be found to attend his funeral; and Mr. Atkins, his solicitor, a very worthy man, was really hurt at this. With the quiet bitterness of a displeased attorney, he merely sent Mrs. Gaunt word her husband inherited something under the will, and she would do well to produce him, or else furnish him (Atkins) with proof of his decease.

Mrs. Gaunt was offended by this cavalier note, and replied very like a woman, and very unlike Business.

"I do not know where he is," said she, "nor whether he is alive or dead. Nor do I feel disposed to raise the hue and cry after him. But favor me with your address, and I shall let you know should I hear anything about him."

Mr. Atkins was half annoyed, half amused, at this piece of indifference.

It never occurred to him that it might be all put on.

He wrote back to say that the estate was large, and, owing to the terms of the will, could not be administered without Mr. Griffith Gaunt; and, in the interest of the said Griffith Gaunt, and also of the other legatees, he really must advertise for him.

La Gaunt replied, that he was very welcome to advertise for whomsoever he pleased.

Mr. Atkins was a very worthy man; but human. To tell the truth, he was himself one of the other legatees. He inherited (and, to be just, had well deserved) four thousand guineas, under the will, and could not legally touch it without Griffith Gaunt. This little circumstance spurred his professional zeal.

Mr. Atkins advertised for Griffith Gaunt, in the London and Cumberland papers, and in the usual enticing form. He was to apply to Mr. Atkins, Solicitor, of Gray's Inn, and he would hear of something greatly to his advantage.

These advertisements had not been out a fortnight, when Griffith Gaunt came home, as I have related.

But Mr. Atkins had punished Mrs. Gaunt for her *insouciance*, by not informing her of the extent of her good fortune; so she merely told Griffith, casually, that old Griffith Gaunt had left him some money, and the solicitor, Mr. Atkins, could not get on without him. Even this information she did not vouchsafe until she had given him her £500, for she grudged Atkins the pleasure of supplying her husband with money.

However, as soon as Griffith left her, she wrote to Mr. Atkins to say that her husband had come home in perfect health, thank God; had only stayed two days, but was to return in a week.

When ten days had elapsed, Atkins wrote to inquire.

She replied he had not yet returned; and this went on till Mr. Atkins showed considerable impatience.

As for Mrs. Gaunt, she made l'g'

of the matter to Mr. Atkins; but, in truth, this new mystery irritated her and pained her deeply.

In one respect she was more unhappy than she had been before he came back at all. Then she was alone; her door was closed to commentators. But now, on the strength of so happy a reconciliation, she had re-entered the world, and received visits from Sir George Neville, and others; and, above all, had announced that Griffith would be back for good in a few days. So now his continued absence exposed her to sly questions from her own sex, to the interchange of glances between female visitors, as well as to the internal torture of doubt and suspense.

But what distracted her most was the view Mrs. Ryder took of the matter.

That experienced lady had begun to suspect some other woman was at the bottom of Griffith's conduct; and her own love for Griffith was now soured. Repeated disappointments and affronts, *spretæque injuria formæ*, had not quite extinguished it, but had mixed so much spite with it that she was equally ready to kiss or to stab him.

So she took every opportunity to instil into her mistress, whose confidence she had won at last, that Griffith was false to her.

"That is the way with these men that are so ready to suspect others. Take my word for it, Dame, he has carried your money to his leman. 'T is still the honest woman that must bleed for some nasty trollop or other."

She enforced this theory by examples drawn from her own observations in families, and gave the very names; and drove Mrs. Gaunt almost mad with fear, anger, jealousy, and cruel suspense. She could not sleep, she could not eat; she was in a constant fever.

Yet before the world she battled it out bravely, and indeed none but Ryder knew the anguish of her spirit, and her passionate wrath.

At last there came a most eventful day.

Mrs. Gaunt had summoned all her pride and fortitude, and invited certain ladies and gentlemen to dine and sup.

She was one of the true Spartan breed, and played the hostess as well as if her heart had been at ease. It was an age in which the host struggled fiercely to entertain the guests; and Mrs. Gaunt was taxing all her powers of pleasing in the dining-room, when an unexpected guest strolled into the kitchen: the pedler, Thomas Leicester.

Jane welcomed him cordially, and he was soon seated at a table eating his share of the feast.

Presently Mrs. Ryder came down, dressed in her best, and looking handsomer than ever.

At sight of her, Tom Leicester's affection revived; and he soon took occasion to whisper an inquiry whether she was still single.

"Ay," said she, "and like to be."

"Waiting for the master still? Mayhap I could cure you of that complaint. But least said is soonest mended."

This mysterious hint showed Ryder he had a secret burning his bosom. The sly hussy said nothing just then, but plied him with ale and flattery; and, when he whispered a request for a private meeting out of doors, she cast her eyes down, and assented.

And in that meeting she carried herself so adroitly, that he renewed his offer of marriage, and told her not to waste her fancy on a man who cared neither for her nor any other she in Cumberland.

"Prove that to me," said Ryder, cunningly, "and may be I 'll take you at your word."

The bribe was not to be resisted. Tom revealed to her, under a solemn promise of secrecy, that the Squire had got a wife and child in Lancashire; and had a farm and an inn, which latter he kept under the name of — Thomas Leicester.

In short, he told her, in his way, all the particulars I have told in mine.

Which told it the best will never be known in this world.

She led him on with a voice of very velvet. He did not see how her cheek paled and her eyes flashed jealous fury.

When she had sucked him dry, she suddenly turned on him, with a cold voice, and said, "I can't stay any longer with you just now. She will want me."

"You will meet me here again, lass?" said Tom, ruefully.

"Yes, for a minute, after supper."

She then left him, and went to Mrs. Gaunt's room, and sat crouching before the fire, all hate and bitterness.

What? he had left the wife he loved, and yet had not turned to her!

She sat there, waiting for Mrs. Gaunt, and nursing her vindictive fury, two mortal hours.

At last, just before supper, Mrs. Gaunt came up to her room, to cool her fevered hands and brow, and found this creature crouched by her fire, all in a heap, with pale cheek, and black eyes that glittered like basilisk's.

"What is the matter, child?" said Mrs. Gaunt. "Good heavens! what hath happened?"

"Dame!" said Ryder, sternly, "I have got news of him."

"News of *him?*" faltered Mrs. Gaunt. "Bad news?"

"I don't know whether to tell you or not," said Ryder, sulkily, but with a touch of human feeling.

"What cannot I bear? What have I not borne? Tell me the truth."

The words were stout, but she trembled all over in uttering them.

"Well, it is as I said, only worse. Dame, he has got a wife and child in another county; and no doubt been deceiving her, as he has *us.*"

"A wife!" gasped Mrs. Gaunt, and one white hand clutched her bosom, and the other the mantel-piece.

"Ay, Thomas Leicester, that is in the kitchen now, saw her, and saw his picture hanging aside hers on the wall. And he goes by the name of Thomas Leicester. That was what made Tom go into the inn, seeing his own name on the signboard. Nay, Dame, never give way like that. Lean on me,—so.

He is a villain,—a false, jealous, double-faced villain."

Mrs. Gaunt's head fell back on Ryder's shoulder, and she said no word; but only moaned and moaned, and her white teeth clicked convulsively together.

Ryder wept over her sad state: the tears were half impulse, half crocodile.

She applied hartshorn to the sufferer's nostrils, and tried to rouse her mind by exciting her anger. But all was in vain. There hung the betrayed wife, pale, crushed, and quivering under the cruel blow.

Ryder asked her if she should go down and excuse her to her guests.

She nodded a feeble assent.

Ryder then laid her down on the bed with her head low, and was just about to leave her on that errand, when hurried steps were heard outside the door; and one of the female servants knocked; and, not waiting to be invited, put her head in, and cried, "O, Dame, the Master is come home. He is in the kitchen."

CHAPTER XXXIV.

MRS. RYDER made an agitated motion with her hand, and gave the girl such a look withal, that she retired precipitately.

But Mrs. Gaunt had caught the words, and they literally transformed her. She sprang off the bed, and stood erect, and looked a Saxon Pythoness: golden hair streaming down her back, and gray eyes gleaming with fury.

She caught up a little ivory-handled knife, and held it above her head.

"I'll drive this into his heart before them all," she cried, "and tell them the reason *afterwards.*"

Ryder looked at her for a moment in utter terror. She saw a woman with grander passions than herself; a woman that looked quite capable of executing her sanguinary threat. Ryder made no more ado, but slipped ont directly to prevent a meeting that might be attended with terrible consequences.

She found her master in the kitchen, splashed with mud, drinking a horn of ale after his ride, and looking rather troubled and anxious; and, by the keen eye of her sex, she saw that the female servants were also in considerable anxiety. The fact is, they had just extemporized a lie.

Tom Leicester, being near the kitchen window, had seen Griffith ride into the court-yard.

At sight of that well-known figure, he drew back, and his heart quaked at his own imprudence, in confiding Griffith's secret to Caroline Ryder.

"Lasses," said he, hastily, "do me a kindness for old acquaintance. Here's the Squire. For Heaven's sake, don't let him know I am in the house, or there will be bloodshed between us. He is a hasty man, and I'm another. I'll tell ye more by and by."

The next moment Griffith's tread was heard approaching the very door, and Leicester darted into the housekeeper's room, and hid in a cupboard there.

Griffith opened the kitchen door, and stood upon the threshold.

The women courtesied to him, and were loud in welcome.

He returned their civilities briefly; and then his first word was, "Hath Thomas Leicester been here?"

You know how servants stick together against their master! The girls looked him in the face, like candid doves, and told him Leicester had not been that way for six months or more.

"Why, I have tracked him to within two miles," said Griffith, doubtfully.

"Then he is sure to come here," said Jane, adroitly. "He wouldn't ever think to go by us."

"The moment he enters the house, you let me know. He is a mischief-making loon."

He then asked for a horn of ale; and, as he finished it, Ryder came in, and he turned to her, and asked her after her mistress.

"She was well, just now," said Ryder; "but she has been took with a spasm: and it would be well, sir, if you could dress, and entertain the company in her place awhile. For I must tell you, your being so long away hath set their tongues going, and almost broken my lady's heart."

Griffith sighed, and said he could not help it, and now he was here, he would do all in his power to please her. "I'll go to her at once," said he.

"No, sir!" said Ryder, firmly. "Come with me. I want to speak to you."

She took him to his bachelor's room, and stayed a few minutes to talk to him.

"Master," said she, solemnly, "things are very serious here. Why did you stay so long away? Our dame says some woman is at the bottom of it, and she'll put a knife into you if you come a-nigh her."

This threat did not appall Griffith, as Ryder expected. Indeed, he seemed rather flattered.

"Poor Kate!" said he; "she is just the woman to do it. But I am afraid she does not love me enough for that. But indeed how should she?"

"Well, sir," replied Ryder, "oblige me by keeping clear of her for a little while. I have got orders to make your bed here. Now, dress, like a good soul, and then go down and show respect to the company that is in your house; for they know you are here."

"Why, that is the least I can do," said Griffith. "Put you out what I am to wear, and then run and say I'll be with them anon."

Griffith walked into the dining-room, and, somewhat to his surprise, after what Ryder had said, found Mrs. Gaunt seated at the head of her own table, and presiding like a radiant queen over a brilliant assembly.

He walked in, and made a low bow to his guests first: then he approached to greet his wife more freely; but she drew back decidedly, and made him a courtesy, the dignity and distance of which struck the whole company.

Sir George Neville, who was at the bottom of the table, proposed, with his usual courtesy, to resign his place to Griffith. But Mrs. Gaunt forbade the arrangement.

"No, Sir George," said she; "this is but an occasional visitor; you are my constant friend."

If this had been said pleasantly, well and good; but the guests looked in vain into their hostess's face for the smile that ought to have accompanied so strange a speech and disarmed it.

"Rarities are the more welcome," said a lady, coming to the rescue; and edged aside to make room for him.

"Madam," said Griffith, "I am in your debt for that explanation; but I hope you will be no rarity here, for all that."

Supper proceeded; but the mirth languished. Somehow or other, the chill fact that there was a grave quarrel between two at the table, and those two man and wife, insinuated itself into the spirits of the guests. There began to be lulls, — fatal lulls. And in one of these, some unlucky voice was heard to murmur, "Such a meeting of man and wife I never saw."

The hearers felt miserable at this personality, that fell upon the ear of silence like a thunderbolt.

Griffith was ill-advised enough to notice the remark, though clearly not intended for his ears. For one thing, his jealousy had actually revived at the cool preference Kate had shown his old rival, Neville.

"Oh!" said he, bitterly, "a man is not always his wife's favorite."

"He does not always deserve to be," said Mrs. Gaunt, sternly.

When matters had gone that length, one idea seemed to occur pretty simultaneously to all the well-bred guests; and that idea was, *Sauve qui peut.*

Mrs. Gaunt took leave of them, one by one, and husband and wife were left alone.

Mrs. Gaunt by this time was alarmed at the violence of her own passions, and wished to avoid Griffith for that night at all events. So she cast one terribly stern look upon him, and was about to retire in grim silence. But he, indignant at the public affront she had put on him, and not aware of the true cause, unfortunately detained her. He said, sulkily, "What sort of a reception was that you gave me?"

This was too much. She turned on him furiously. "Too good for thee, thou heartless creature! Thomas Leicester is here, and I know thee for a villain."

"You know nothing," cried Griffith. "Would you believe that mischief-making knave? What has he told you?"

"Go back to *her!*" cried Mrs. Gaunt furiously. "Me you can deceive and pillage no more. So, this was your jealousy! False and forsworn yourself, you dared to suspect and insult me. Ah! and you think I am the woman to endure this? I 'll have your life for it! I 'll have your life."

Griffith endeavored to soften her, — protested that, notwithstanding appearances, he had never loved but her.

"I 'll soon be rid of you, and your love," said the raging woman. "The constables shall come for you to-morrow. You have seen how I can love, you shall know how I can hate."

She then, in her fury, poured out a torrent of reproaches and threats that made his blood run cold. He could not answer her: he *had* suspected her wrongfully, and been false to her himself. He *had* abused her generosity, and taken her money for Mercy Vint.

After one or two vain efforts to check the torrent, he sank into a chair, and hid his face in his hands.

But this did not disarm her, at the time. Her raging voice and raging words were heard by the very servants, long after he had ceased to defend himself.

At last she came out, pale with fury, and, finding Ryder near the door, shrieked out, "Take that reptile to his den, if he is mean enough to lie in this house," — then, lowering her voice, "and bring Thomas Leicester to me."

Ryder went to Leicester, and told

him. But he objected to come. "You have betrayed me," said he. "Curse my weak heart and my loose tongue. I have done the poor Squire an ill turn. I can never look him in the face again. But 't is all thy fault, double-face. I hate the sight of thee."

At this Ryder shed some crocodile tears ; and very soon, by her blandishments, obtained forgiveness.

And Leicester, since the mischief was done, was persuaded to see the dame, who was his recent benefactor, you know. He bargained, however, that the Squire should be got to bed. first ; for he had a great dread of meeting him. "He 'll break every bone in my skin," said Tom ; "or else I shall do *him* a mischief in my defence."

Ryder herself saw the wisdom of this. She bade him stay quiet, and she went to look after Griffith.

She found him in the drawing-room, with his head on the table, in deep dejection.

She assumed authority, and said he must go to bed.

He rose humbly, and followed her like a submissive dog.

She took him to his room. There was no fire.

"That is where you are to sleep," said she, spitefully.

"It is better than I deserve," said he, humbly.

The absurd rule about not hitting a man when he is down has never obtained a place in the great female soul ; so Ryder lashed him without mercy.

"Well, sir," said she, "methinks you have gained little by breaking faith with me. Y' had better have set up your inn with me, than gone and sinned against the law."

"Much better : would to Heaven I had ! "

"What d' ye mean to do now ? You know the saying. Between two stools — "

"Child," said Griffith, faintly, "methinks I shall trouble neither long. I am not so ill a man as I seem ; but who will believe that ? I shall not live long. And I shall leave an ill

name behind me. *She* told me so just now. And oh ! her eye was so cruel ; I saw my death in it."

"Come, come," said Ryder, relenting a little ; "you must n't believe every word an angry woman says. There, take my advice ; go to bed ; and in the morning don't speak to her. Keep out of her way a day or two."

And with this piece of friendly advice she left him ; and waited about till she thought he was in bed and asleep.

Then she brought Thomas Leicester up to her mistress.

But Griffith was not in bed ; and he heard Leicester's heavy tread cross the landing. He waited and waited behind his door for more than half an hour, and then he heard the same heavy tread go away again.

By this time nearly all the inmates of the house were asleep.

About twenty-five minutes after Leicester left Mrs. Gaunt, Caroline Ryder stole quietly up stairs from the kitchen, and sat down to think it all over.

She then proceeded to undress ; but had only taken off her gown, when she started and listened ; for a cry of distress reached her from outside the house.

She darted to the window and threw it open.

Then she heard a cry more distinct, "Help ! help ! "

It was a clear starlight night, but no moon.

The mere shone before her, and the cries were on the bank.

Now came sbmething more alarming still. A flash, — a pistol shot, — and an agonized voice cried loudly, "Murder ! Help ! Murder ! "

That voice she knew directly. It was Griffith Gaunt's.

CHAPTER XXXV.

RYDER ran screaming, and alarmed the other servants.

All the windows that looked on the mere were flung open.

But no more sounds were heard. A

terrible silence brooded now over those clear waters.

The female servants huddled together, and quaked ; for who could doubt that a bloody deed had been done ?

It was some time before they mustered the presence of mind to go and tell Mrs. Gaunt. At last they opened her door. She was not in her room.

Ryder ran to Griffith's. It was locked. She called to him. He made no reply.

They burst the door open. He was not there ; and the window was open.

While their tongues were all going, in consternation, Mrs. Gaunt was suddenly among them, very pale.

They turned, and looked at her aghast.

"What means all this ? " said she. " Did not I hear cries outside ? "

"Ay," said Ryder. "Murder ! and a pistol fired. O, my poor master ! "

Mrs. Gaunt was white as death ; but self-possessed. "Light torches this moment, and search the place," said she.

There was only one man in the house ; and he declined to go out alone. So Ryder and Mrs. Gaunt went with him, all three bearing lighted links.

They searched the place where Ryder had heard the cries. They went up and down the whole bank of the mere, and cast their torches' red light over the placid waters themselves. But there was nothing to be seen, alive or dead, — no trace either of calamity or crime.

They roused the neighbors, and came back to the house with their clothes all draggled and dirty.

Mrs. Gaunt took Ryder apart, and asked her if she could guess at what time of the night Griffith had made his escape. "He is a villain," said she, "yet I would not have him come to harm, God knows. There are thieves abroad. But I hope he ran away as soon as your back was turned, and so fell not in with them."

"Humph ! " said Ryder. Then, looking Mrs. Gaunt in the face, she said,

quietly, "Where were you when you heard the cries ? "

" I was on the other side of the house."

"What, out o' doors, at that time of night ! "

"Ay ; I was in the grove, — praying."

" Did you hear any voice you knew ? "

"No : all was too indistinct. I heard a pistol, but no words. Did you ? "

" I heard no more than you, madam," said Ryder, trembling.

No one went to bed any more that night in Hernshaw Castle.

CHAPTER XXXVI.

THIS mysterious circumstance made a great talk in the village and in the kitchen of Hernshaw Castle ; but not in the drawing-room ; for Mrs. Gaunt instantly closed her door to visitors, and let it be known that it was her intention to retire to a convent ; and, in the mean time, she desired not to be disturbed.

Ryder made one or two attempts to draw her out upon the subject, but was sternly checked.

Pale, gloomy, and silent, the mistress of Hernshaw Castle moved about the place, like the ghost of her former self. She never mentioned Griffith ; forbade his name to be uttered in her hearing ; and, strange to say, gave Ryder strict orders not to tell any one what she had heard from Thomas Leicester.

" This last insult is known but to you and me. If it ever gets abroad, you leave my service that very hour."

This injunction set Ryder thinking. However, she obeyed it to the letter. Her place was getting better and better ; and she was a woman accustomed to keep secrets.

A pressing letter came from Mr. Atkins.

Mrs. Gaunt replied that her husband had come to Hernshaw, but had left again ; and the period of his ultimate return was now more uncertain than ever.

On this Mr. Atkins came down to Hernshaw Castle. But Mrs. Gaunt would not see him. He retired very angry, and renewed his advertisements, but in a more explicit form. He now published that Griffith Gaunt, of Hernshaw and Bolton, was executor and residuary legatee to the late Griffith Gaunt of Coggleswade ; and requested him to apply directly to James Atkins, Solicitor, of Gray's Inn, London.

In due course this advertisement was read by the servants at Hernshaw, and shown by Ryder to Mrs. Gaunt.

She made no comment whatever ; and contrived to render her pale face impenetrable.

Ryder became as silent and thoughtful as herself, and often sat bending her black judicial brows.

By and by dark mysterious words began to be thrown out in Hernshaw village.

"He will never come back at all."

"He will never come into that fortune."

"'Tis no use advertising for a man that is past reading."

These, and the like equivocal sayings, were followed by a vague buzz, which was traceable to no individual author, but seemed to rise on all sides, like a dark mist, and envelop that unhappy house.

And that dark mist of Rumor soon condensed itself into a palpable and terrible whisper, — "Griffith Gaunt hath met with foul play."

No one of the servants told Mrs. Gaunt this horrid rumor.

But the women used to look at her, and after her, with strange eyes.

She noticed this, and felt, somehow, that her people were falling away from her. It added one drop to her bitter cup. She began to droop into a sort of calm, despondent lethargy.

Then came fresh trouble to rouse her.

Two of the county magistrates called on her in their official capacity, and, with perfect politeness, but a very grave air, requested her to inform them of all the circumstances attending her husband's disappearance.

She replied, coldly and curtly, that she knew very little about it. Her husband had left in the middle of the night.

"He came to stay ?"

"I believe so."

"Came on horseback ?"

"Yes."

"Did he go away on horseback ?"

"No; for the horse is now in my stable."

"Is it true there was a quarrel between you and him that evening ?"

"Gentlemen," said Mrs. Gaunt, drawing herself back, haughtily, "did you come here to gratify your curiosity ?"

"No, madam," said the elder of the two; "but to discharge a very serious and painful duty, in which I earnestly request you, and even advise you, to aid us. Was there a quarrel ?"

"There was — a mortal quarrel."

The gentlemen exchanged glances, and the elder made a note.

"May we ask the subject of that quarrel ?"

Mrs. Gaunt declined, positively, to enter into a matter so delicate.

A note was taken of this refusal.

"Are you aware, madam, that your husband's voice was heard calling for help, and that a pistol-shot was fired ?"

Mrs. Gaunt trembled visibly.

"I heard the pistol-shot," said she; "but not the voice distinctly. O, I hope it was not his voice Ryder heard !"

"Ryder, who is he ?"

"Ryder is my lady's maid : her bedroom is on that side the house."

"Can we see Mrs. Ryder ?"

"Certainly," said Mrs. Gaunt, and rose and rang the bell.

Mrs. Ryder answered the bell, in person, very promptly ; for she was listening at the door.

Being questioned, she told the magistrates what she had heard down by "the mere"; and said she was sure it was her master's voice that cried "Help!" and "Murder!" And with this she began to cry.

Mrs. Gaunt trembled and turned pale.

The magistrates confined their questions to Ryder.

They elicited, however, very little more from her. She saw the drift of their questions, and had an impulse to defend her mistress there present. Behind her back it would have been otherwise.

That resolution once taken, two children might as well have tried to extract evidence from her as two justices of the peace.

And then Mrs. Gaunt's pale face and noble features touched them. The case was mysterious, but no more ; and they departed little the wiser, and with some apologies for the trouble they had given her.

The next week down came Mr. Atkins, out of all patience, and determined to find Griffith Gaunt, or else obtain some proof of his decease.

He obtained two interviews with Ryder, and bribed her to tell him all she knew. He prosecuted other inquiries with more method than had hitherto been used, and elicited an important fact, namely, that Griffith Gaunt had been seen walking in a certain direction at one o'clock in the morning, followed at a short distance by a tall man with a knapsack, or the like, on his back.

The person who gave this tardy information was the wife of a certain farmer's man, who wired hares upon the sly. The man himself, being assured that, in a case so serious as this, no particular inquiries should be made how he came to be out so late, confirmed what his wife had let out, and added, that both men had taken the way that would lead them to the bridge, meaning the bridge over the mere. More than that he could not say, for he had met them, and was full half a mile from the mere before those men could have reached it.

Following up this clew, Mr. Atkins learned so many ugly things, that he went to the Bench on justicing day, and demanded a full and searching inquiry on the premises.

Sir George Neville, after in vain opposing this, rode off straight from the Bench to Hernshaw, and, in feeling terms conveyed the bad news to Mrs. Gaunt ; and then, with the utmost delicacy, let her know that some suspicion rested upon herself, which she would do well to meet with the bold front of innocence.

" What suspicion, pray ? " said Mrs. Gaunt, haughtily.

Sir George shrugged his shoulders, and replied, " That you have done Gaunt the honor to put him out of the way."

Mrs. Gaunt took this very differently from what Sir George expected.

" What ! " she cried, " are they so sure he is dead, — murdered ? "

And with this she went into a passion of grief and remorse.

Even Sir George was puzzled, as well as affected, by her convulsive agitation.

CHAPTER XXXVII.

THOUGH it was known the proposed inquiry might result in the committal of Mrs. Gaunt on a charge of murder, yet the respect in which she had hitherto been held, and the influence of Sir George Neville, who, having been her lover, stoutly maintained her innocence, prevailed so far that even this inquiry was private, and at her own house. Only she was present in the character of a suspected person, and the witnesses were examined before her.

First, the poacher gave his evidence.

Then Jane, the cook, proved that a pedler called Thomas Leicester had been in the kitchen, and secreted about the premises till a late hour ; and this Thomas Leicester corresponded exactly to the description given by the poacher.

This threw suspicion on Thomas Leicester, but did not connect Mrs. Gaunt with the deed in any way.

But Ryder's evidence filled this gap. She revealed three serious facts : —

First, that, by her mistress's orders, she had introduced this very Leicester into her mistress's room about midnight, where he had remained nearly half an hour, and had then left the house.

Secondly, that Mrs. Gaunt herself had been out of doors after midnight.

And, thirdly, that she had listened at the door, and heard her threaten Griffith Gaunt's life.

This is a mere *précis* of the evidence, and altogether it looked so suspicious, that the magistrates, after telling Mrs. Gaunt she could ask the witnesses any question she chose, a suggestion she treated with marked contempt, put their heads together a moment and whispered. Then the eldest of them, Mr. Underhill, who lived at a considerable distance, told her gravely he must commit her to take her trial at the next assizes.

"Do what you conceive to be your duty, gentlemen," said Mrs. Gaunt, with marvellous dignity. "If I do not assert my innocence, it is because I disdain the accusation too much."

"I shall take no part in the committal of this innocent lady," said Sir George Neville, and was about to leave the room.

But Mrs. Gaunt begged him to stay. "To be guilty is one thing," said she, "to be accused is another. I shall go to prison as easy as to my dinner; and to the gallows as to my bed."

The presiding magistrate was staggered a moment by these words; and it was not without considerable hesitation he took the warrant and prepared to fill it up.

Then Mr. Houseman, who had watched the proceedings very keenly, put in his word. "I am here for the accused person, sir, and, with your good leave, object to her committal — on grounds of law."

"What may they be, Mr. Houseman?" said the magistrate, civilly; and laid his pen down to hear them.

"Briefly, sir, these. Where a murder is proven, you can commit a subject of this realm upon suspicion. But you cannot suspect the murder as well as the culprit, and so commit. The murder must be proved to the senses. Now in this case, the death of Mr. Gaunt by violence is not proved. Indeed, his very death rests but upon suspicion. I

admit that the law of England in this respect has once or twice been tampered with, and persons have even been executed where no *corpus delicti* was found; but what was the consequence? In each case the murdered man turned out to be alive, and justice was the only murderer. After Harrison's case, and ——'s, no Cumberland jury will ever commit for murder, unless the *corpus delicti* has been found, and with signs of violence upon it. Come, come, Mr. Atkins, you are too good a lawyer, and too humane a man, to send my client to prison on the suspicion of a suspicion, which you know the very breath of the judge will blow away, even if the grand jury let it go into court. I offer bail, ten thousand pounds in two sureties; Sir George Neville here present, and myself."

The magistrate looked to Mr. Atkins.

"I am not employed by the crown," said that gentleman, "but acting on mere civil grounds, and have no right nor wish to be severe. Bail by all means: but is the lady so sure of her innocence as to lend me her assistance to find the *corpus delicti?*"

The question was so shrewdly put, that any hesitation would have ruined Mrs. Gaunt.

Houseman, therefore, replied eagerly and promptly, "I answer for her, she will."

Mrs. Gaunt bowed her head in assent.

"Then," said Atkins, "I ask leave to drag, and, if need be, to drain that piece of water there, called 'the mere.'"

"Drag it or drain it, which you will," said Houseman.

Said Atkins, very impressively, "And, mark my words, at the bottom of that very sheet of water there, I shall find the remains of the late Griffith Gaunt."

At these solemn words, coming as they did, not from a loose unprofessional speaker, but from a lawyer, a man who measured all his words, a very keen observer might have seen a sort of tremor run all through Mr. Houseman's

" There rose to the surface a Thing to strike terror to the stoutest heart." —Page 165.

frame. The more admirable, I think, was the perfect coolness and seeming indifference with which he replied, "Find him, and I 'll admit suicide; find him, with signs of violence, and I 'll admit homicide — by some person or persons unknown."

All further remarks were interrupted by bustle and confusion.

Mrs. Gaunt had fainted dead away.

CHAPTER XXXVIII.

OF course pity was the first feeling; but, by the time Mrs. Gaunt revived, her fainting, so soon after Mr. Atkins's proposal, had produced a sinister effect on the minds of all present; and every face showed it, except the wary Houseman's.

On her retiring, it broke out first in murmurs, then in plain words.

As for Mr. Atkins, he now showed the moderation of an able man who feels he has a strong cause.

He merely said, " I think there should be constables about, in case of an escape being attempted; but I agree with Mr. Houseman that your worships will be quite justified in taking bail, provided the *corpus delicti* should not be found. Gentlemen, you were most of you neighbors and friends of the deceased, and are, I am sure, lovers of justice; I do entreat you to aid me in searching that piece of water, by the side of which the deceased gentleman was heard to cry for help; and, much I fear, he cried in vain."

The persons thus appealed to entered into the matter with all the ardor of just men, whose curiosity as well as justice is inflamed.

A set of old, rusty drags was found on the premises; and men went punting up and down the mere, and dragged it.

Rude hooks were made by the village blacksmith, and fitted to cart-ropes; another boat was brought to Hernshaw in a wagon; and all that afternoon the bottom of the mere was raked, and some curious things fished up. But no dead man.

The next day a score of amateur dragsmen were out; some throwing their drags from the bridge; some circulating in boats, and even in large tubs.

And, meantime, Mr. Atkins and his crew went steadily up and down, dragging every foot of those placid waters.

They worked till dinner-time, and brought up a good copper pot with two handles, a horse's head, and several decayed trunks of trees, which had become saturated, and sunk to the bottom.

At about three in the afternoon, two boys, who, for want of a boat, were dragging from the bridge, found something heavy but elastic at the end of their drag: they pulled up eagerly, and a thing like a huge turnip, half gnawed, came up, with a great bob, and blasted their sight.

They let go, drags and all, and stood shrieking, and shrieking.

Those who were nearest them called out, and asked what was the matter; but the boys did not reply, and their faces showed so white, that a woman, who saw them, hailed Mr. Atkins, and said she was sure those boys had seen something out of the common.

Mr. Atkins came up, and found the boys blubbering. He encouraged them, and they told him a fearful thing had come up; it was like a man's head and shoulders all scooped out and gnawed by the fishes, and had torn the drags out of their hands.

Mr. Atkins made them tell him the exact place; and he was soon upon it with his boat.

The water here was very deep; and though the boys kept pointing to the very spot, the drags found nothing for some time.

But at last they showed, by their resistance, that they had clawed hold of something.

"Draw slowly," said Mr. Atkins: "and, *if it is*, be men, and hold fast."

The men drew slowly, slowly, and presently there rose to the surface a Thing to strike terror and loathing into the stoutest heart.

The mutilated remains of a human face and body.

The greedy pike had cleared, not the features only, but the entire flesh off the face; but had left the hair, and the tight skin of the forehead, though their teeth had raked this last. The remnants they had left made what they had mutilated doubly horrible; since now it was not a skull, not a skeleton; but a face and a man gnawed down to the bones and hair and feet. These last were in stout shoes, that resisted even those voracious teeth; and a leathern stock had offered some little protection to the throat.

The men groaned, and hid their faces with one hand, and pulled softly to the shore with the other; and then, with half-averted faces, they drew the ghastly remains and fluttering rags gently and reverently to land.

Mr. Atkins yielded to nature, and was violently sick at the sight he had searched for so eagerly.

As soon as he recovered his powers, he bade the constables guard the body (it was a body, in law), and see that no one laid so much as a finger on it until some magistrate had taken a deposition. He also sent a messenger to Mr. Houseman, telling him the *corpus delicti* was found. He did this, partly to show that gentleman he was right in his judgment, and partly out of common humanity; since, after this discovery, Mr. Houseman's client was sure to be tried for her life.

A magistrate soon came, and viewed the remains, and took careful notes of the state in which they were found.

Houseman came, and was much affected both by the sight of his dead friend, so mutilated, and by the probable consequences to Mrs. Gaunt. However, as lawyers fight very hard, he recovered himself enough to remark that there were no marks of violence before death, and insisted on this being inserted in the magistrate's notes.

An inquest was ordered next day, and, meantime, Mrs. Gaunt was told she could not quit the upper apartments of her own house. Two constables were placed on the ground-floor night and day.

Next day the remains were removed to the little inn where Griffith had spent so many jovial hours; laid on a table, and covered with a white sheet.

The coroner's jury sat in the same room, and the evidence I have already noticed was gone into, and the finding of the body deposed to. The jury, without hesitation, returned a verdict of wilful murder.

Mrs. Gaunt was then brought in. She came, white as a ghost, leaning upon Houseman's shoulder.

Upon her entering, a juryman, by a humane impulse, drew the sheet over the remains again.

The coroner, according to the custom of the day, put a question to Mrs. Gaunt, with the view of eliciting her guilt. If I remember right, he asked her how she came to be out of doors so late on the night of the murder. Mrs. Gaunt, however, was in no condition to answer queries. I doubt if she even heard this one. Her lovely eyes, dilated with horror, were fixed on that terrible sheet, with a stony glance. "Show me," she gasped, "and let me die too."

The jurymen looked, with doubtful faces, at the coroner. He bowed a grave assent.

The nearest juryman withdrew the sheet. The belief was not yet extinct that the dead body shows some signs of its murderer's approach. So every eye glanced on her and on It by turns; as she, with dilated, horror-stricken eyes, looked on that awful Thing.

CHAPTER XXXIX.

SHE recoiled with a violent shudder at first; and hid her face with one hand. Then she gradually stole a horror-stricken side-glance.

She had not looked at it a moment, when she uttered a loud cry, and pointed at its feet with quivering hand.

"THE SHOES! THE SHOES!—IT IS NOT MY GRIFFITH."

With this she fell into violent hysterics, and was carried out of the room at Houseman's earnest entreaty.

As soon as she was gone, Mr. Houseman, being freed from his fear that his client would commit herself irretrievably, recovered a show of composure, and his wits went keenly to work.

"On behalf of the accused," said he, "I admit the suicide of some ·person unknown, wearing heavy hobnailed shoes ; probably one of the lower order of people."

This adroit remark produced some little effect, notwithstanding the strong feeling against the accused.

The coroner inquired if there were any bodily marks by which the remains could be identified.

"My master had a long black mole on his forehead," suggested Caroline Ryder.

"'T is here!" cried a juryman, bending over the remains.

And now they all gathered in great excitement round the *corpus delicti;* and there, sure enough, was a long black mole.

Then was there a buzz of pity for Griffith Gaunt, followed by a stern murmur of execration.

"Gentlemen," said the coroner solemnly, "behold in this the finger of Heaven. The poor gentleman may well have put off his boots, since, it seems, he left his horse; but he could not take from his forehead his natal sign; and that, by God's will, hath strangely escaped mutilation, and revealed a most foul deed. We must now do our duty, gentlemen, without respect of persons."

A warrant was then issued for the apprehension of Thomas Leicester. And, that same night, Mrs. Gaunt left Hernshaw in her own chariot between two constables, and escorted by armed yeomen.

Her proud head was bowed almost to her knees, and her streaming eyes hidden in her lovely hands. For why? A mob accompanied her for miles, shouting, "Murderess!—Bloody Papist!—Hast done to death the kindliest gentleman in Cumberland. We'll all come to see thee hanged.— Fair face but foul heart!"—and groaning, hissing, and cursing, and indeed only kept from violence by the escort.

And so they took that poor proud lady and lodged her in Carlisle jail.

She was *enceinte* into the bargain. By the man she was to be hanged for murdering.

CHAPTER XL.

THE county was against her, with some few exceptions. Sir George Neville and Mr. Houseman stood stoutly by her.

Sir George's influence and money obtained her certain comforts in jail ; and, in that day, the law of England was so far respected in a jail that untried prisoners were not thrown into cells, nor impeded, as they now are, in preparing their defence.

Her two stanch friends visited her every day, and tried to keep her heart up.

But they could not do it. She was in a state of dejection bordering upon lethargy.

"If he is dead," said she, "what matters it ? If, by God's mercy, he is alive still, he will not let me die for want of a word from him. Impatience hath been my bane. Now, I say, God's will be done. I am weary of the world."

Houseman tried every argument to rouse her out of this desperate frame of mind; but in vain.

It ran its course, and then, behold, it passed away like a' cloud, and there came a keen desire to live and defeat her accusers.

She made Houseman write out all the evidence against her ; and she studied it by day, and thought of it by night, and often surprised both her friends by the acuteness of her remarks.

Mr. Atkins discontinued his advertisements. It was Houseman, who now filled every paper with notices informing Griffith Gaunt of his accession to fortune, and entreating him for that, and other weighty reasons, to communicate in confidence with his old friend, John Houseman, attorney at law.

Houseman was too wary to invite him to appear and save his wife ; for, in that case, he feared the Crown would use his advertisements as evidence at the trial, should Griffith not appear.

The fact is, Houseman relied more upon certain *lacunæ* in the evidence, and the absence of all marks of violence, than upon any hope that Griffith might be alive.

The assizes drew near, and no fresh light broke in upon this mysterious case.

Mrs. Gaunt lay in her bed at night, and thought and thought.

Now the female understanding has sometimes remarkable power under such circumstances. By degrees Truth flashes across it, like lightning in the dark.

After many such nightly meditations, Mrs. Gaunt sent one day for Sir George Neville and Mr. Houseman, and addressed them as follows : — "I believe he is alive, and that I can guess where he is at this moment."

Both the gentlemen started, and looked amazed.

"Yes, sirs ; so sure as we sit here, he is now at a little inn in Lancashire, called the 'Packhorse,' with a woman he calls his wife." And, with this, her face was scarlet, and her eyes flashed their old fire.

She exacted a solemn promise of secrecy from them, and then she told them all she had learned from Thomas Leicester.

"And so now," said she, "I believe you can save my life, if you think it is worth saving." And with this, she began to cry bitterly.

But Houseman, the practical, had no patience with the pangs of love betrayed, and jealousy, and such small deer, in a client whose life was at stake. "Great Heaven ! madam," said he, roughly : "why did you not tell me this before ? "

"Because I am not a man — to go and tell everything, all at once," sobbed Mrs. Gaunt. Besides, I wanted to shield his good name, whose dear life they pretend I have taken."

As soon as she recovered her composure, she begged Sir George Neville to ride to the "Packhorse" for her. Sir George assented eagerly, but asked how he was to find it. "I have thought of that, too," said she. "His black horse has been to and fro. Ride that horse into Lancashire, and give him his head : ten to one but he takes you to the place, or where you may hear of it. If not, go to Lancaster, and ask about the 'Packhorse.' He wrote to me from Lancaster : see." And she showed him the letter.

Sir George embraced with ardor this opportunity of serving her. "I 'll be at Hernshaw in one hour," said he, "and ride the black horse south at once."

"Excuse me," said Houseman ; "but would it not be better for me to go ? As a lawyer, I may be more able to cope with her."

"Nay," said Mrs. Gaunt, "Sir George is young and handsome. If he manages well, she will tell him more than she will you. All I beg of him is to drop the chevalier for this once, and see women with a woman's eyes and not a man's,— see them as they are. Do not go telling a creature of this kind that she has had my money, as well as my husband, and ought to pity me lying here in prison. Keep me out of her sight as much as you can. Whether Griffith hath deceived her or not, you will never raise in her any feeling but love for him, and hatred for his lawful wife. Dress like a yeoman ; go quietly, and lodge in the house a day or two ; begin by flattering her ; and then get from her when she saw him last, or heard from him. But indeed I fear you will surprise him with her."

"Fear ? " exclaimed Sir George.

"Well, hope, then," said the lady ; and a tear trickled down her face in a moment. "But if you do, promise me, on your honor as a gentleman, not to affront him. For I know you think him a villain."

"A d—d villain, saving your presence."

"Well, sir, you have said it to me. Now promise me to say naught to *him*, but just this: 'Rose Gaunt's mother, she lies in Carlisle jail, to be tried for her life for murdering you. She begs of you not to let her die publicly upon the scaffold; but quietly at home, of her broken heart.'"

"Write it," said Sir George, with the tears in his eyes, "that I may just put it in his hand; for I can never utter your sweet words to such a monster as he is."

Armed with this appeal, and several minute instructions, which it is needless to particularize here, that stanch friend rode into Lancashire.

And next day the black horse justified his mistress's sagacity, and his own.

He seemed all along to know where he was going, and late in the afternoon he turned off the road on to a piece of green: and Sir George, with beating heart, saw right before him the sign of the "Packhorse," and, on coming nearer, the words

THOMAS LEICESTER.

He dismounted at the door, and asked if he could have a bed.

Mrs. Vint said yes; and supper into the bargain, if he liked.

He ordered a substantial supper directly.

Mrs. Vint saw at once it was a good customer, and showed him into the parlor.

He sat down by the fire. But the moment she retired, he got up and made a circuit of the house, looking quietly into every window, to see if he could catch a glance of Griffith Gaunt.

There were no signs of him; and Sir George returned to his parlor heavy-hearted. One hope, the greatest of all, had been defeated directly. Still, it was just possible that Griffith might be away on temporary business.

In this faint hope Sir George strolled about till his supper was ready for him.

When he had eaten his supper, he rang the bell, and, taking advantage of a common custom, insisted on the landlord, Thomas Leicester, taking a glass with him.

"Thomas Leicester!" said the girl. "He is not at home. But I 'll send Master Vint."

Old Vint came in, and readily accepted an invitation to drink his guest's health.

Sir George found him loquacious, and soon extracted from him that his daughter Mercy was Leicester's wife, that Leicester was gone on a journey, and that Mercy was in care for him. "Leastways," said he, "she is very dull, and cries at times when her mother speaks of him; but she is too close to say much."

All this puzzled Sir George Neville sorely.

But greater surprises were in store.

The next morning, after breakfast, the servant came and told him Dame Leicester desired to see him.

He started at that, but put on nonchalance, and said he was at her service.

He was ushered into another parlor, and there he found a grave, comely young woman, seated working, with a child on the floor beside her. She rose quietly; he bowed low and respectfully; she blushed faintly; but, with every appearance of self-possession, courtesied to him; then eyed him point-blank a single moment, and requested him to be seated.

"I hear, sir," said she, "you did ask my father many questions last·night. May I ask you one?"

Sir George colored, but bowed assent.

"From whom had you the black horse you ride?"

Now, if Sir George had not been a veracious man, he would have been caught directly. But, although he saw at once the oversight he had committed, he replied, "I had him of a lady in Cumberland, one Mistress Gaunt."

Mercy Vint trembled. "No doubt," said she, softly. "Excuse my question: you shall understand that the horse is well known here."

"Madam," said Sir George, "if you admire the horse, he is at your service for twenty pounds, though indeed he is worth more."

"I thank you, sir," said Mercy; "I have no desire for the horse whatever. And be pleased to excuse my curiosity: you must think me impertinent."

"Nay, madam," said Sir George, "I consider nothing impertinent that hath procured me the pleasure of an interview with you."

He then, as directed by Mrs. Gaunt, proceeded to flatter the mother and the child, and exerted those powers of pleasing which had made him irresistible in society.

Here, however, he found they went a very little way. Mercy did not even smile. She cast out of her dove-like eyes a gentle, humble, reproachful glance, as much as to say, "What! do I seem so vain a creature as to believe all this?"

Sir George himself had tact and sensibility; and by and by became discontented with the part he was playing, under those meek, honest eyes.

There was a pause; and, as her sex have a wonderful art of reading the face, Mercy looked at him steadily, and said, "*Yes*, sir, 't is best to be straightforward, especially with women-folk."

Before he could recover this little facer, she said, quietly, "What is your name?"

"George Neville."

"Well, George Neville," said Mercy, very slowly and softly, "when you have a mind to tell me what you came here for, and who sent you, you will find me in this little room. I seldom leave it now. I beg you to speak your errand to none but me." And she sighed deeply.

Sir George bowed low, and retired to collect his wits. He had come here strongly prepossessed against Mercy. But, instead of a vulgar, shallow woman, whom he was to surprise into confession, he encountered a soft-eyed Puritan, all unpretending dignity, grace, propriety, and sagacity.

"Flatter her!" said he, to himself. "I might as well flatter an iceberg.

Outwit her! I feel like a child beside her."

He strolled about in a brown study, not knowing what to do.

She had given him a fair opening. She had invited him to tell the truth. But he was afraid to take her at her word; and yet what was the use to persist in what his own eyes told him was the wrong course?

Whilst he hesitated, and debated within himself, a trifling incident turned the scale.

A poor woman came begging, with her child, and was received rather roughly by Harry Vint. "Pass on, good woman," said he, "we want no tramps here."

Then a window was opened on the ground-floor, and Mercy beckoned the woman. Sir George flattened himself against the wall, and listened to the two talking.

Mercy examined the woman gently, but shrewdly, and elicited a tale of genuine distress. Sir George then saw her hand out to the woman some warm flannel for herself, a piece of stuff for the child, a large piece of bread, and a sixpence.

He also caught sight of Mercy's dove-like eyes as she bestowed her alms, and they were lit with an inward lustre.

"She cannot be an ill woman," said Sir George. "I 'll e'en go by my own eyes and judgment. After all, Mrs. Gaunt has never seen her, and I have."

He went and knocked at Mercy's door.

"Come in," said a mild voice.

Neville entered, and said, abruptly, and with great emotion, "Madam, I see you can feel for the unhappy; so I take my own way now, and appeal to your pity. I *have* come to speak to you on the saddest business."

"You come from *him*," said Mercy, closing her lips tight; but her bosom heaved. Her heart and her judgment grappled like wrestlers that moment.

"Nay, madam," said Sir George, "I come from *her*."

Mercy knew in a moment who "her" must be.

She looked scared, and drew back with manifest signs of repulsion.

The movement did not escape Sir George: it alarmed him. He remembered what Mrs. Gaunt had said, — that this woman would be sure to hate Gaunt's lawful wife. But it was too late to go back. He did the next best thing, he rushed on.

He threw himself on his knees before Mercy Vint.

"O madam," he cried, piteously, "do not set your heart against the most unhappy lady in England. If you did but know her, her nobleness, her misery! Before you steel yourself against me, her friend, let me ask you one question. Do you know where Mrs. Gaunt is at this moment?"

Mercy answered coldly, "How should I know where she is?"

"Well, then, she lies in Carlisle jail."

"She — lies — in Carlisle jail?" repeated Mercy, looking all confused.

"They accuse her of murdering her husband."

Mercy uttered a scream, and, catching her child up off the floor, began to rock herself and moan over it.

"No, no, no," cried Sir George, "she is innocent, she is innocent."

"What is that to *me?*" cried Mercy, wildly. "He is murdered, he is dead, and my child an orphan." And so she went on moaning and rocking herself.

"But I tell you he is not dead at all," cried Sir George. "'T is all a mistake. When did you see him last?"

"More than six weeks ago."

"I mean, when did you hear from him last?"

"Never, since that day."

Sir George groaned aloud at this intelligence.

And Mercy, who heard him groan, was heart-broken. She accused herself of Griffith's death. "'T was I who drove him from me," she said. "'T was I who bade him go back to his lawful wife; and the wretch hated him. I sent him to his death." Her grief was wild, and deep. She could not hear Sir George's arguments.

But presently she said, sternly, "What does that woman say for herself?"

"Madam," said Sir George, dejectedly, "Heaven knows you are in no condition to fathom a mystery that hath puzzled wiser heads than yours or mine; and I am little able to lay the tale before you fairly; for your grief, it moves me deeply, and I could curse myself for putting the matter to you so bluntly and so uncouthly. Permit me to retire awhile and compose my own spirits for the task I have undertaken too rashly."

"Nay, George Neville," said Mercy, "stay you there. Only give me a moment to draw my breath."

She struggled hard for a little composure, and, after a shower of tears, she hung her head over the chair like a crushed thing, but made him a sign of attention.

Sir George told the story as fairly as he could; only of course his bias was in favor of Mrs. Gaunt; but as Mercy's bias was against her, this brought the thing nearly square.

When he came to the finding of the body, Mercy was seized with a deadly faintness; and though she did not become insensible, yet she was in no condition to judge, or even to comprehend.

Sir George was moved with pity, and would have called for help; but she shook her head. So then he sprinkled water on her face, and slapped her hand; and a beautifully moulded hand it was.

When she got a little better she sobbed faintly, and sobbing thanked him, and begged him to go on.

"My mind is stronger than my heart," she said. "I'll hear it all, though it kill me where I sit."

Sir George went on, and, to avoid repetition, I must ask the reader to understand that he left out nothing whatever which has been hitherto related in these pages; and, in fact, told her one or two little things that I have omitted.

When he had done, she sat quite still a minute or two, pale as a statue.

Then she turned to Neville, and said, solemnly, "You wish to know the truth in this dark matter : for dark it is in very sooth."

Neville was much impressed by her manner, and answered, respectfully, Yes, he desired to know, — by all means.

"Then take my hand," said Mercy, "and kneel down with me."

Sir George looked surprised, but obeyed, and kneeled down beside her, with his hand in hers.

There was a long pause, and then took place a transformation.

The dove-like eyes were lifted to heaven and gleamed like opals with an inward and celestial light ; the comely face shone with a higher beauty, and the rich voice rose in ardent supplication.

"Thou God, to whom all hearts be known, and no secrets hid from thine eye, look down now on thy servant in sore trouble, that putteth her trust in thee. Give wisdom to the simple this day, and understanding to the lowly. Thou that didst reveal to babes and sucklings the great things that were hidden from the wise, O show us the truth in this dark matter : enlighten us by thy spirit, for His dear sake who suffered more sorrows than I suffer now. Amen. Amen."

Then she looked at Neville ; and he said "Amen," with all his heart, and the tears in his eyes.

He had never heard real live prayer before. Here the little hand gripped his hard, as she wrestled ; and the heart seemed to rise out of the bosom and fly to Heaven on the sublime and thrilling voice.

They rose, and she sat down ; but it seemed as if her eyes once raised to Heaven in prayer could not come down again : they remained fixed and angelic, and her lips still moved in supplication.

Sir George Neville, though a loose liver, was no scoffer. He was smitten with reverence for this inspired countenance, and retired, bowing low and obsequiously.

He took a long walk, and thought it all over. One thing was clear, and consoling. He felt sure he had done wisely to disobey Mrs. Gaunt's instructions, and make a friend of Mercy, instead of trying to set his wits against hers. Ere he returned to the "Packhorse" he had determined to take another step in the right direction. He did not like to agitate her with another interview, so soon. But he wrote her a little letter.

"MADAM, — When I came here, I did not know you ; and therefore I feared to trust you too far. But, now I do know you for the best woman in England, I take the open way with you.

"Know that Mrs. Gaunt said the man would be here with you ; and she charged me with a few written lines to him. She would be angry if she knew that I had shown them to any other. Yet I take on me to show them to you ; for I believe you are wiser than any of us, if the truth were known. I do therefore entreat you to read these lines, and tell me whether you think the hand that wrote them can have shed the blood of him to whom they are writ.

"I am, madam, with profound respect,
"Your grateful and very humble servant,
"GEORGE NEVILLE."

He very soon received a line in reply, written in a clear and beautiful handwriting.

"Mercy Vint sends you her duty ; and she will speak to you at nine of the clock to-morrow morning. Pray for light."

At the appointed time, Sir George found her working with her needle. His letter lay on a table before her.

She rose and courtesied to him, and called the servant to take away the child for a while. She went with her to the door and kissed the bairn several times at parting, as if he was going away for good. "I 'm loath to let him go," said she to Neville ; "but it weakens a mother's mind to have her babe in the room, — takes her attention off each moment. Pray you be seated. Well, sir, I have read these lines of Mistress Gaunt, and wept over them. Methinks I had not done so, were they cunningly devised. Also I lay all night, and thought."

"That is just what she does."

"No doubt, sir; and the upshot is, I don't *feel* as if he was dead. Thank God."

"That is something," said Neville. But he could not help thinking it was very little; especially to produce in a court of justice.

"And now," said she, thoughtfully, "you say that the real Thomas Leicester was seen thereabouts as well as my Thomas Leicester. Then answer me one little question. What had the real Thomas Leicester on his feet that night?"

"Nay, I know not," was the half-careless reply.

"Bethink you. 'T is a question that must have been often put in your hearing."

"Begging your pardon, it was never put at all; nor do I see —"

"What, not at the inquest?"

"No."

"That is very strange. What, so many wise heads have bent over this riddle, and not one to ask how was yon pedler shod!"

"Madam," said Sir George, "our minds were fixed upon the fate of Gaunt. Many did ask how was the pedler armed, but none how was he shod."

"Hath he been seen since?"

"Not he; and that hath an ugly look; for the constables are out after him with hue and cry; but he is not to be found."

"Then," said Mercy, "I must e'en answer my own question. I do know how that pedler was shod. WITH HOB-NAILED SHOES."

Sir George bounded from his chair. One great ray of daylight broke in upon him.

"Ay," said Mercy, "she was right. Women do see clearer in some things than men. The pair went from my house to hers. He you call Griffith Gaunt had on a new pair of boots; and by the same token 't was I did pay for them, and there is the receipt in that cupboard: he you call Thomas Leicester went hence in hobnailed shoes. I think the body they found was the body of Thomas Leicester, the pedler. May God have mercy on his poor unprepared soul."

Sir George uttered a joyful exclamation. But the next moment he had a doubt. "Ay, but," said he, "you forget the mole! 'T was on that they built."

"I forget naught," said Mercy, calmly. "The pedler had a black mole over his left temple. He showed it me in this very room. You have found the body of Thomas Leicester, and Griffith Gaunt is hiding from the law that he hath broken. He is afeared of her and her friends, if he shows his face in Cumberland; he is afeared of my folk, if he be seen in Lancashire. Ah, Thomas, as if I would let them harm thee."

Sir George Neville walked to and fro in grand excitement. "O blessed day that I came hither! Madam, you are an angel. You will save an innocent, broken-hearted lady from death and dishonor. Your good heart and rare wit have read in a moment the dark riddle that hath puzzled a county."

"George," said Mercy, gravely, "you have gotten the wrong end of the stick. The wise in their own conceit are blinded. In Cumberland, where all this befell, they went not to God for light, as you and I did, George."

In saying this, she gave him her hand to celebrate their success.

He kissed it devoutly, and owned afterward that it was the proudest moment of his life, when that sweet Puritan gave him her neat hand so cordially, with a pressure so gentle yet frank.

And now came the question how they were to make a Cumberland jury see this matter as they saw it.

He asked her would she come to the trial as a witness?

At that she drew back with manifest repugnance.

"My shame would be public. I must tell who I am; and what. A ruined woman."

"Say rather an injured saint. You have nothing to be ashamed of. All good men would feel for you."

Mercy shook her head. "Ay, but the women. Shame is shame with us. Right or wrong goes for little. Nay, I hope to do better for you than that. I must find *him*, and send him to deliver her. 'T is his only chance of happiness."

She then asked him if he would draw up an advertisement of quite a different kind from those he had described to her.

He assented, and between them they concocted the following : —

"If Thomas Leicester, who went from the ' Packhorse ' two months ago, will come thither at once, Mercy will be much beholden to him, and tell him strange things that have befallen."

Sir George then, at her request, rode over to Lancaster, and inserted the above in the county paper, and also in a small sheet that was issued in the city three times a week. He had also handbills to the same effect printed, and sent into Cumberland and Westmoreland. Finally, he sent a copy to his man of business in London, with orders to insert it in all the journals.

Then he returned to the "Packhorse," and told Mercy what he had done.

The next day he bade her farewell, and away for Carlisle. It was a two days' journey. He reached Carlisle in the evening, and went all glowing to Mrs. Gaunt. "Madam," said he, " be of good cheer. I bless the day I went to see her; she is an angel of wit and goodness."

He then related to her, in glowing terms, most that had passed between Mercy and him. But, to his surprise, Mrs. Gaunt wore a cold, forbidding air.

"This is all very well," said she. "But 't will avail me little unless *he* comes before the judge and clears me; and she will never let him do that."

" Ay, that she will, — if she can find him."

"If she can find him ? How simple you are ! "

"Nay, madam, not so simple but I can tell a good woman from a bad one, and a true from a false."

"What! when you are in love with her? Not if you were the wisest of your sex."

" In love with her ? " cried Sir George ; and colored high.

"Ay," said the lady. "Think you I cannot tell ? Don't deceive yourself. You have gone and fallen in love with her. At your years ! Not that 't is any business of mine."

"Well, madam," said Sir George, stiffly, "say what you please on that score ; but at least welcome my good news."

Mrs. Gaunt begged him to excuse her petulance, and thanked him kindly for all he had just done. But the next moment she rose from her chair in great agitation, and burst out, " I 'd as lief die as owe anything to that woman."

Sir George remonstrated. " Why hate her ? She does not hate you."

"O, yes, she does. 'T is not in nature she should do any other."

" Her acts prove the contrary."

"Her acts ! She has *done* nothing, but make fair promises ; and that has blinded you. Women of this sort are very cunning, and never show their real characters to a man. No more ; prithee mention not her name to me. It makes me ill. I know he is with her at this moment. Ah, let me die, and be forgotten, since I am no more beloved."

The voice was sad and weary now, and the tears ran fast.

Poor Sir George was moved and melted, and set himself to flatter and console this impracticable lady, who hated her best friend in this sore strait, for being what she was herself, a woman ; and was much less annoyed at being hanged than at not being loved.

When she was a little calmer, he left her, and rode off to Houseman. That worthy was delighted.

"Get her to swear to those hobnailed shoes," said he, "and we shall shake them." He then let Sir George know that he had obtained private information which he would use in cross-examining a principal witness for the crown. "However," he added, "do not deceive yourself; nothing can make the prisoner really safe but the appearance of Griffith Gaunt. He has such strong motives for coming to light. He is heir to a fortune, and his wife is accused of murdering him. The jury will never believe he is alive till they see him. That man's prolonged disappearance is hideous. It turns my blood cold when I think of it."

"Do not despair on that score," said Neville. "I believe our good angel will produce him."

Three days only before the assizes, came the long-expected letter from Mercy Vint. Sir George tore it open, but bitter was his disappointment. The letter merely said that Griffith had not appeared in answer to her advertisements, and she was sore grieved and perplexed.

There were two postscripts, each on a little piece of paper.

First postscript, in a tremulous hand, "Pray."

Second postscript, in a firm hand, "Drain the water."

Houseman shrugged his shoulders impatiently. "Drain the water? Let the crown do that. We should but fish up more trouble. And prayers quo' she! 'T is not prayers we want, but evidence."

He sent his clerk off to travel post night and day, and subpœna Mercy, and bring her back with him to the trial. She was to have every comfort on the road, and be treated like a duchess.

The evening before the assizes, Mrs. Gaunt's apartments were Mr. Houseman's head-quarters, and messages were coming and going all day, on matters connected with the defence.

. Just at sunset, up · rattled a post-chaise, and the clerk got out and came haggard and bloodshot before his employer. "The witness has disappeared, sir. Left home last Tuesday, with her child, and has never been seen nor heard of since."

Here was a terrible blow. They all paled under it: it seriously diminished the chances of an acquittal.

But Mrs. Gaunt bore it nobly. She seemed to rise under it.

She turned to Sir George Neville, with a sweet smile. "The noble heart sees base things noble. No wonder then an artful woman deluded *you.* He has left England with her, and condemned me to the gallows, in cold blood. So be it. I shall defend myself."

She then sat down with Mr. Houseman, and went through the written case he had prepared for her, and showed him notes she had taken of full a hundred criminal trials great and small.

While they were putting their heads together, Sir George sat in a brown study, and uttered not a word. Presently he got up a little brusquely, and said, "I 'm going to Hernshaw."

"What, at this time of night? What to do?"

"To obey my orders. To drain the mere."

"And who could have ordered you to drain my mere?"

"Mercy Vint."

Sir George uttered this in a very curious way, half ashamed, half resolute, and retired before Mrs. Gaunt could vent in speech the surprise and indignation that fired her eye.

Houseman implored her not to heed Sir George and his vagaries, but to bend her whole mind on those approved modes of defence with which he had supplied her.

Being now alone with her, he no longer concealed his great anxiety.

"We have lost an invaluable witness in that woman," said he. "I was mad to think she would come."

Mrs. Gaunt shivered with repugnance. "I would not have her come, for all the world,' said she. "For Heaven's sake never mention her name to me. I want help from none but friends. Send Mrs. Houseman to me in the morning ; and do not distress yourself so. I shall defend myself far better than you think. I have not studied a hundred trials for naught."

Thus the prisoner cheered up her attorney, and soon after insisted on his going home to bed ; for she saw he was worn out by his exertions.

And now she was alone.

All was silent.

A few short hours, and she was to be tried for her life : tried, not by the All-wise Judge, but by fallible men, and under a system most unfavorable to the accused.

Worse than all this, she was a Papist ; and, as ill-luck would have it, since her imprisonment an alarm had been raised that the Pretender meditated another invasion. This report had set jurists very much against all the Romanists in the country, and had already perverted justice in one or two cases, espeeially in the North.

Mrs. Gaunt knew all this, and trembled at the peril to come.

She spent the early part of the night in studying her defence. Then she laid it quite aside, and prayed long and fervently. Towards morning she fell asleep from exhaustion.

When she awoke, Mrs. Houseman was sitting by her bedside, looking at her, and crying.

They were soon clasped in each other's arms, condoling.

But presently Houseman came, and took his wife away rather angrily.

Mrs. Gaunt was prevailed on to eat a little toast and drink a glass of wine, and then she sat waiting her dreadful summons.

She waited and waited, until she became impatient to face her danger.

But there were two petty larcenies on before her. She had to wait.

At last, about noon, came a message to say that the grand jury had found a true bill against her.

"Then may God forgive them !" said she.

Soon afterwards she was informed her time drew very near.

She made her toilet carefully, and passed with her attendant into a small room under the court.

Here she had to endure another chilling wait, and in a sombre room.

Presently she heard a voice above her cry out, "The King *versus* Catharine Gaunt."

Then she was beckoned to.

She mounted some steps, badly lighted, and found herself in the glare of day, and greedy eyes, in the felon's dock.

In a matter entirely strange, we seldom know beforehand what we can do, and how we shall carry ourselves. Mrs. Gaunt no sooner set her foot in that dock, and saw the awful front of Justice face to face, than her tremors abated, and all her powers awoke, and she thrilled with love of life, and bristled with all those fine arts of defence that Nature lends to superior women.

She entered on that defence before she spoke a word ; for she attacked the prejudices of the court, by deportment.

She courtesied reverently to the Judge, and contrived to make her reverence seem a willing homage, unmixed with fear.

She cast her eyes round and saw the court thronged with ladies and gentlemen she knew. In a moment she read in their eyes that only two or three were on her side. She bowed to those only ; and they returned her courtesy. This gave an impression (a false one) that the gentry sympathized with her.

After a little murmur of functionaries, the Clerk of Arraigns turned to the prisoner, and said, in a loud voice, "Catharine Gaunt, hold up thy hand."

She held up her hand, and he recited the indictment, which charged that, not having the fear of God before her eyes, but being moved by the instigation of the Devil, she had on the fifteenth of October, in the tenth year of the reign of his present Majesty, aided and abetted one Thomas Leicester in an assault upon one Griffith Gaunt, Esq., and him, the said Griffith Gaunt, did with force and arms assassinate and do to death, against the peace of our said Lord the King, his crown and dignity.

After reading the indictment, the Clerk of Arraigns turned to the prisoner: "How sayest thou, Catharine Gaunt; art thou guilty of the felony and murder whereof thou standest indicted, — or not guilty?"

"I am not guilty."

"Culprit, how wilt thou be tried?"

"Culprit I am none, but only accused. I will be tried by God and my country."

"God send thee a good deliverance."

Mr. Whitworth, the junior counsel for the crown, then rose to open the case ; but the prisoner, with a pale face, but most courteous demeanor, begged his leave to make a previous motion to the court. Mr. Whitworth bowed, and sat down. "My Lord," said she, " I have first a favor to ask ; and that favor, methinks, you will grant, since it is but justice, impartial justice. My accuser, I hear, has two counsel ; both learned and able. I am but a woman, and no match for their skill. Therefore I beg your Lordship to allow me counsel on my defence, to matter of fact as well as of law. I know this is not usual ; but it is just, and I am informed it has sometimes been granted in trials of life and death, and that your Lordship hath the *power*, if you have the *will*, to do me so much justice."

The Judge looked towards Mr. Serjeant Wiltshire, who was the leader on the other side. He rose instantly and replied to this purpose : " The prisoner is misinformed. The truth is, that from time immemorial, and down to the other day, a person indicted for a capital offence was never allowed counsel at all, except to matters of law, and these must be started by himself. By recent practice .the rule hath been so far relaxed that counsel have sometimes been permitted to examine and cross-examine witnesses for a prisoner ; but never to make observations on the evidence, nor to draw inferences from it to the point in issue."

Mrs. Gaunt. So, then, if I be sued for a small sum of money, I may have skilled orators to defend me against their like. But if I be sued for my life and honor, I may not oppose skill to skill, but must stand here a child against you that are masters. 'T is a monstrous iniquity, and you yourself, sir, will not deny it.

Serjeant Wiltshire. Madam, permit me. Whether it be a hardship to deny full counsel to prisoners in criminal cases, I shall not pretend to say ; but if it be, 't is a hardship of the law's making, and not of mine nor of my lord's ; and none have suffered by it (at least in our day) but those who had broken the law.

The Serjeant then stopped a minute, and whispered with his junior. After which he turned to the Judge. "My Lord, we that are of counsel for the crown desire to do nothing that is hard where a person's life is at stake. We yield to the prisoner any indulgence for which your Lordship can find a precedent in your reading ; but no more : and so we leave the matter to you."

The Clerk of Arraigns. Crier, proclaim silence.

The Crier. Oyez ! Oyez ! Oyez ! His Majesty's Justices do strictly charge all manner of persons to keep silence, on pain of imprisonment.

The Judge. Prisoner, what my Brother Wiltshire says, the law is clear in. There is no precedent for what you ask, and the contrary practice stares us in the face for centuries. What seems to you a partial practice, and, to be frank, some learned persons are of your mind, must be set against this, — that in capital cases the burden of proof lies on the crown, and not on the accused. Also it is my duty to give you all the assistance I can, and that I shall do. Thus then it is : you can be allowed counsel to examine your own witnesses, and cross-examine the witnesses for the crown, and speak to points of law, to be started by yourself, — but no further.

He then asked her what gentleman

there present he should assign to her for counsel.

Her reply to this inquiry took the whole court by surprise, and made her solicitor, Houseman, very miserable. "None, my Lord," said she. "Half-justice is injustice ; and I will lend it no color. I will not set able men to fight for me with their hands tied, against men as able whose hands be free. Counsel, on terms so partial, I will have none. My counsel shall be three, and no more, — Yourself, my Lord, my Innocence, and the Lord God Omniscient."

These words, grandly uttered, caused a dead silence in the court, but only for a few moments. It was broken by the loud mechanical voice of the crier, who proclaimed silence, and then called the names of the jury that were to try this cause.

Mrs. Gaunt listened keenly to the names, — familiar and bourgeois names, that now seemed regal ; for they who owned them held her life in their hands.

Each juryman was sworn in the grand old form, now slightly curtailed.

"Joseph King, look upon the prisoner. — You shall well and truly try, and true deliverance make, between our Sovereign Lord the King and the prisoner at the bar, whom you shall have in charge, and a true verdict give, according to the evidence. So help you God."

Mr Whitworth, for the crown, then opened the case, but did little more than translate the indictment into more rational language.

He sat down, and Serjeant Wiltshire addressed the court somewhat after this fashion : —

"May it please your Lordship, and you, gentlemen of the jury, this is a case of great expectation and importance. The prisoner at the bar, a gentlewoman by birth and education, and, as you must have already perceived, by breeding also, stands indicted for no less a crime than murder.

"I need not paint to you the heinousness of this crime : you have but to consult your own breasts. Who ever saw the ghastly corpse of the victim weltering in its blood, and did not feel his own blood run cold through his veins ? Has the murderer fled ? With what eagerness do we pursue ! with what zeal apprehend ! with what joy do we bring him to justice ! Even the dreadful sentence of death does not shock us, when pronounced upon him. We hear it with solemn satisfaction ; and acknowledge the justice of the Divine sentence, ' Whoso sheddeth man's blood, by man shall his blood be shed.'

" But if this be the case in every common murder, what shall be thought of her who has murdered her husband, — the man in whose arms she has lain, and whom she has sworn at God's altar to love and cherish ? Such a murderer is a robber as well as an assassin ; for she robs her own children of their father, that tender parent, who can never be replaced in this world.

"Gentlemen, it will, I fear, be proved that the prisoner at the bar hath been guilty of murder in this high degree ; and, though I will endeavor rather to extenuate than to aggravate, yet I trust [*sic*] I have such a history to open as will shock the ears of all who hear me.

" Mr. Griffith Gaunt, the unfortunate deceased, was a man of descent and worship. As to his character, it was inoffensive. He was known as a worthy, kindly gentleman, deeply attached to her who now stands accused of his murder. They lived happily together for some years ; but, unfortunately, there was a thorn in the rose of their wedded life : he was of the Church of England ; she was, and is, a Roman Catholic. This led to disputes ; and no wonder, since this same unhappy difference hath more than once embroiled a nation, let alone a single family.

"Well, gentlemen, about a year ago there was a more violent quarrel than usual between the deceased and the prisoner at the bar ; and the deceased left his home for several months.

"He returned upon a certain day in

this year, and a reconciliation, real or apparent, took place. He left home again soon afterwards, but only for a short period. On the 15th of last October he suddenly returned for good, as he intended; and here begins the tragedy, to which what I have hitherto related was but the prologue.

" Scarce an hour before he came, one Thomas Leicester entered the house. Now this Thomas Leicester was a creature of the prisoner's. He had been her gamekeeper, and was now a pedler. It was the prisoner who set him up as a pedler, and purchased the wares to start him in his trade.

" Gentlemen, this pedler, as I shall prove, was concealed in the house when the deceased arrived. One Caroline Ryder, who is the prisoner's gentlewoman, was the person who first informed her of Leicester's arrival, and it seems she was much moved: Mrs. Ryder will tell you she fell into hysterics. But, soon after, her husband's arrival was announced, and then the passion was of a very different kind. So violent was her rage against this unhappy man that, for once, she forgot all prudence, and threatened his life before a witness. Yes, gentlemen, we shall prove that this gentlewoman, who in appearance and manners might grace a court, was so transported out of her usual self that she held up a knife, — a knife, gentlemen, — and vowed to put it into her husband's heart. And this was no mere temporary ebullition of wrath. We shall see presently that, long after she had had time to cool, she repeated this menace to the unfortunate man's face. The first threat, however, was uttered in her own bedroom, before her confidential servant, Caroline Ryder aforesaid. But now the scene shifts. She has, to all appearance, recovered herself, and sits smiling at the head of her table; for, you must know, she entertained company that night, — persons of the highest standing in the county.

" Presently her husband, all unconscious of the terrible sentiments she entertained towards him, and the fearful purpose she had announced, enters the room, makes obeisance to his guests, and goes to take his wife's hand.

" What does she? She draws back with so strange a look, and such forbidding words, that the company were disconcerted. Consternation fell on all present; and erelong they made their excuses, and left the house. Thus the prisoner was left alone with her husband; but, meantime, curiosity had been excited by her strange conduct, and some of the servants, with foreboding hearts, listened at the door of the dining-room. What did they hear, gentlemen? A furious quarrel, in which, however, the deceased was comparatively passive, and the prisoner again threatened his life, with vehemence. Her passion, it is clear, had not cooled.

" Now it may fairly be alleged, on behalf of the prisoner, that the witnesses for the crown were on one side of the door, the prisoner and the deceased on the other, and that such evidence should be received with caution. I grant this —where it is not sustained by other circumstances, or by direct proofs. Let us then give the prisoner the benefit of this doubt, and let us inquire how the deceased himself understood her, — he, who not only heard the words, and the accents, but saw the looks, whatever they were, that accompanied them.

" Gentlemen, he was a man of known courage and resolution; yet he was found, after this terrible interview, much cowed and dejected. He spoke to Mrs. Ryder of his death as an event not far distant, and so went to his bedroom in a melancholy and foreboding state. And where was that bedroom? He was thrust, by his wife's orders, into a small chamber, and not allowed to enter hers, —he, the master of the house, her husband, and her lord.

" But his interpretation of the prisoner's words did not end there. He left us a further comment by his actions next ensuing. He dared not — (I beg pardon, this is my inference: receive it as such) — he *did* not, remain in that house a single night. He at all events bolted his chamber door inside; and in the very dead of night, notwithstanding the fatigues of the day's journey, (for he had ridden some distance,) he let himself out by the window, and reached the ground safely, though it was a height of fourteen feet, — a leap, gentlemen, that few of us would venture to take. But what will not men risk when destruction is at their heels? He did not wait even to saddle his horse, but fled on foot. Unhappy man, he fled from danger, and met his death.

"From the hour when he went up to bed, none of the inmates of the house ever saw Griffith Gaunt alive; but one Thomas Hayes, a laborer, saw him walking in a certain direction at one o'clock that morning; and behind him, gentlemen, there walked another man.

"Who was that other man?

"When I have told you (and this is an essential feature of the case) how the prisoner was employed during the time that her husband lay quaking in his little room, waiting an opportunity to escape, — when I have told you this, I fear you will divine who it was that followed the deceased, and for what purpose.

"Gentlemen, when the prisoner had threatened her husband in person, as I have described, she retired to her own room, but not to sleep. She ordered her maid, Mrs. Ryder, to bring Thomas Leicester to her chamber. Yes, gentlemen, she received this pedler, at midnight, in her bedchamber.

"Now, an act so strange as this admits, I think, but of two interpretations. Either she had a guilty amour with this fellow, or she had some extraordinary need of his services. Her whole character, by consent of the witnesses, renders it very improbable that she would descend to a low amour. Moreover, she acted too publicly in the matter. The man, as we know, was her tool, her creature: she had bought his wares for him, and set him up as a pedler. She openly summoned him to her presence, and kept him there about half an hour.

"He went from her, and very soon after is seen, by Thomas Hayes, following Griffith Gaunt, at one o'clock in the morning, — that Griffith Gaunt who after that hour was never seen alive.

"Gentlemen, up to this point, the evidence is clear, connected, and cogent; but it rarely happens in cases of murder that any human eye sees the very blow struck. The penalty is too severe for such an act to be done in the presence of an eyewitness; and not one murderer in ten could be convicted without the help of circumstantial evidence.

"The next link, however, is taken up by an ear-witness; and, in some cases, the ear is even better evidence than the eye, — for instance, as to the discharge of firearms, — for, by the eye alone, we could not positively tell whether a pistol had gone off or had but flashed in the pan. Well, then, gentlemen, a few minutes after Mr. Gaunt was last seen alive, — which was by Thomas Hayes, — Mrs. Ryder, who had retired to her bedroom, heard the said Gaunt distinctly cry for help; she also heard a pistol-shot discharged. This took place by the side of a lake or large pond near the house, called the mere. Mrs. Ryder alarmed the house, and she and the other servants proceeded to her master's room. They found it bolted from the inside. They broke it open. Mr. Gaunt had escaped by the window, as I have already told you.

"Presently in comes the prisoner from out of doors. This was at one o'clock in the morning. Now she appears to have seen at once that she must explain her being abroad at that time, so she told Mrs. Ryder she had been out — praying."

(Here some people laughed harshly, but were threatened severely, and silenced.)

"Is that credible? Do people go out of doors at one o'clock in the morning, to pray? Nay, but I fear it was to do an act that years of prayer and penitence cannot efface.

"From that moment Mr. Gaunt was seen no more among living men. And what made his disappearance the more mysterious was that he had actually at this time just inherited largely from his namesake, Mr. Gaunt of Biggleswade; and his own interest, and that of the other legatees, required his immediate presence. Mr. Atkins, the testator's solicitor, advertised for this unfortunate gentleman; but he did not appear, to claim his fortune. Then plain men began to put this and that together, and cried out, 'Foul play!'

"Justice was set in motion at last, but was embarrassed by the circumstance that the body of the deceased could not be found.

"At last, Mr. Atkins, the solicitor, being unable to get the estate I have mentioned administered, for want of proof of Griffith Gaunt's decease, entered heartily in this affair, on mere civil grounds. He asked the prisoner, before several witnesses, if she would permit him to drag that piece of water by the side of which Mr. Gaunt was heard to cry for help and, after that seen no more.

" The prisoner did not reply, but Mr. Houseman, her solicitor, a very worthy man, who has, I believe, or had, up to that moment, a sincere conviction of her innocence, answered for her, and told Mr. Atkins he was welcome to drag it or drain it. Then the prisoner said nothing. She fainted away.

"After this, you may imagine with what expectation the water was dragged. Gentlemen, after hours of fruitless labor, a body was found.

"But here an unforeseen circumstance befriended the prisoner. It seems that piece of water swarms with enormous pike and other ravenous fish. These had so horribly mutilated the deceased, that neither form nor feature remained to swear by; and, as the law wisely and humanely demands that in these cases a body shall be identified beyond doubt, justice bade fair to be baffled again. But lo! as often happens in cases of murder, Providence interposed and pointed with unerring finger to a slight, but infallible mark. The deceased gentleman was known to have a large mole over his left temple. It had been noticed by his servants and

his neighbors. Well, gentlemen, the greedy fish had spared this mole,—spared it, perhaps, by His command, who bade the whale swallow Jonah, yet not destroy him. There it was, clear and infallible. It was examined by several witnesses; it was recognized. It completed that chain of evidence, some of it direct, some of it circumstantial, which I have laid before you very briefly, and every part of which I shall now support by credible witnesses."

He called thirteen witnesses, including Mr. Atkins, Thomas Hayes, Jane Banister, Caroline Ryder, and others; and their evidence in chief bore out every positive statement the counsel had made.

In cross-examining these witnesses, Mrs. Gaunt took a line that agreeably surprised the court. It was not for nothing she had studied a hundred trials, with a woman's observation and patient docility. She had found out how badly people plead their own causes, and had noticed the reasons: one of which is that they say too much, and stray from the point. The line she took, with one exception, was keen brevity.

She cross-examined Thomas Hayes as follows.

CHAPTER XLI.

You say the pedler was a hundred yards behind my husband. Which of the two men was walking fastest?"

Thomas Hayes considered a moment. " Well, dame, I think the Squire was walking rather the smartest of the two."

" Did the pedler seem likely to overtake him?"

" Nay. Ye see, dame, Squire he walked straight on; but the pedler he took both sides of the road at onst, as the saying is."

Prisoner. Forgive me, Thomas, but I don't know what you mean.

Hayes (compassionately). How should

ye? You are never the worse for liquor, the likes of you.

Prisoner (very keenly). O, he was in liquor, was he?

Hayes. Come, dame, you do brew good ale at Hernshaw Castle. Ye need n't go to deny that; for, Lord knows, 't is no sin; and a poor fellow may be jolly, yet not to say drunk.

Judge (sternly). Witness, attend, and answer directly.

Prisoner. Nay, my lord, 't is a plain country body, and means no ill. Good Thomas, be so much my friend as to answer plainly. Was the man drunk or sober?

Hayes. All I know is he went from one side o' the road to t' other.

Prisoner. Thomas Hayes, as you hope to be saved eternally, was the pedler drunk or sober?

Hayes. Well, if I must tell on my neighbor or else be damned, then that there pedler was as drunk as a lord.

Here, notwithstanding the nature of the trial, the laughter was irrepressible, and Mrs. Gaunt sat quietly down (for she was allowed a seat), and said no more.

To the surgeon who had examined the body officially, she put this question: "Did you find any signs of violence?"

Surgeon. None whatever; but then there was nothing to go by, except the head and the bones.

Prisoner. Have you experience in this kind? I mean, have you inspected murdered bodies?

Surgeon. Yes.

Prisoner. How many?

Surgeon. Two before this.

Prisoner. O, pray, pray, do not say "before this"! I have great hopes no murder at all hath been committed here. Let us keep to plain cases. Please you describe the injuries in those two undoubted cases.

Surgeon. In Wellyn's the skull was fractured in two places. In Sherrett's the right arm was broken, and there were some contusions on the head; but the cause of death was a stab that penetrated the lungs.

Prisoner. Suppose Wellyn's murderers had thrown his body into the water, and the fishes had so mutilated it as they have this one, could you by your art have detected the signs of violence?

Surgeon. Certainly. The man's skull was fractured. Wellyn's, I mean.

Prisoner. I put the same question with regard to Sherrett's.

Surgeon. I cannot answer it; here the lungs were devoured by the fishes; no signs of lesion can be detected in an organ that has ceased to exist.

Prisoner. This is too partial. Why select one injury out of several? What I ask is this: could you have detected violence in Sherrett's case, although the fishes had eaten the flesh off his body.

Surgeon. I answer that the minor injuries of Sherrett would have been equally perceptible; to wit, the bruises on the head, and the broken arm; but not the perforation of the lungs; and that it was killed the man.

Prisoner. Then, so far as you know, and can swear, about murder, more blows have always been struck than one, and some of the blows struck in Sherrett's case, and Wellyn's, would have left traces that fishes' teeth could not efface?

Surgeon. That is so, if I am to be peevishly confined to my small and narrow experience of murdered bodies. But my general knowledge of the many ways in which life may be taken by violence —

The judge stopped him, and said that could hardly be admitted as evidence against his actual experience.

The prisoner put a drawing of the castle, the mere, and the bridge, into the witnesses' hands, and elicited that it was correct, and also the distances marked on it. They had, in fact, been measured exactly for her.

The hobnailed shoes were produced, and she made some use of them, particularly in cross-examining Jane Banister.

Prisoner. Look at those shoes. Saw

you ever the like on Mr. Gaunt's feet ?

Jane. That I never did, dame.

Prisoner. What, not when he came into the kitchen on the 15th of October ?

Jane. Nay, he was booted. By the same token I saw the boy a cleaning of them for supper.

Prisoner. Those boots, when you broke into his room, did you find them ?

Jane. Nay, when the man went his boots went ; as reason was. We found naught of his but a soiled glove.

Prisoner. Had the pedler boots on ?

Jane. Alas ! who ever seed a booted pedler ?

Prisoner. Had he these very shoes on ? Look at them.

Jane. I could n't say for that. He had shoon, for they did properly clatter on my bricks.

Judge. Clatter on her bricks ! What in the world does she mean ?

Prisoner. I think she means on the floor of her kitchen. 'T is a brick floor, if I remember right.

Judge. Good woman, say, is that what you mean ?

Jane. Ay, an 't please you, my lord.

Prisoner. Had the pedler a mole on his forehead ?

Jane. Not that I know on. I never took so much notice of the man. But, la, dame, now I look at you, I don't believe you was ever the one to murder our master.

Wiltshire. We don't want your opinion. Confine yourself to facts.

Prisoner. You heard me rating my husband on that night : what was it I said about the constables, — do you remember ?

Jane. La, dame, I would n't ask that if I was in your place.

Prisoner. I am much obliged to you for your advice ; but answer me — truly.

Jane. Well, if you will have it, I think you said they should be here in the morning. But, indeed, good gentlemen, her bark was always worse than her bite, poor soul.

Judge. Here. That meant at Hernshaw Castle, I presume.

Jane. Ay, my lord, an' if it please your lordship's honor's worship.

Mrs. Gaunt, husbanding the patience of the court, put no questions at all to several witnesses ; but she cross-examined Mrs. Ryder very closely. This was necessary ; for Ryder was a fatal witness. Her memory had stored every rash and hasty word the poor lady had uttered ; and, influenced either by animosity or prejudice, she put the worst color on every suspicious circumstance. She gave her damnatory evidence neatly, and clearly, and with a seeming candor and regret, that disarmed suspicion.

When her examination in chief concluded, there was but one opinion amongst the bar, and the auditors in general, namely, that the maid had hung the mistress.

Mrs. Gaunt herself felt she had a terrible antagonist to deal with, and, when she rose to cross - examine her, she looked paler than she had done all through the trial.

She rose, but seemed to ask herself how to begin ; and her pallor and her hesitation, while they excited some little sympathy, confirmed the unfavorable impression. She fixed her eyes upon the witness, as if to discover where she was most vulnerable. Mrs. Ryder returned her gaze calmly. The court was hushed ; for it was evident a duel was coming between two women of no common ability.

The opening rather disappointed expectation. Mrs. Gaunt seemed, by her manner, desirous to propitiate the witness.

Prisoner (very civilly). You say you brought Thomas Leicester to my bedroom on that terrible night ?

Ryder (civilly). Yes, madam.

Prisoner. And you say he stayed there half an hour ?

Ryder. Yes, madam ; he did.

Prisoner. May I inquire how you know he stayed just half an hour ?

Ryder. My watch told me that, madam. I brought him to you at a quarter past eleven ; and you did not ring for me till a quarter to twelve.

Prisoner. And when I did ring for you, what then ?

Ryder. I came and took the man away, by your orders.

Prisoner. At a quarter to twelve ?

Ryder. At a quarter to twelve.

Prisoner. This Leicester was a lover of yours ?

Ryder. Not he.

Prisoner. O, fie ! Why, he offered you marriage ; it went so far as that.

Ryder. O, that was before you set him up pedler.

Prisoner. 'T was so ; but he was single for your sake, and he renewed his offer that very night. Come, do not forswear yourself about a trifle.

Ryder. Trifle, indeed ! Why, if he did, what has that to do with the murder ? You 'll do yourself no good, madam, by going about so.

Wiltshire. Really, madam, this is beside the mark.

Prisoner. If so, it can do your case no harm. My lord, you did twice interrupt the learned counsel, and forbade him to lead his witnesses ; I not once, for I am for stopping no mouths, but sifting all to the bottom. Now, I implore you to let me have fair play in my turn, and an answer from this slippery witness.

Judge. Prisoner, I do not quite see your drift ; but God forbid you should be hampered in your defence. Witness, by virtue of your oath, reply directly. Did this pedler offer you marriage that night after he left the prisoner ?

Ryder. My lord, he did.

Prisoner. And confided to you he had orders to kill Mr. Gaunt ?

Ryder. Not he, madam : that was not the way to win me. He knew that.

Prisoner. What ! did not his terrible purpose peep out all the time he was making love to you ?

No reply.

Prisoner. You had the kitchen to your two selves ? Come, don't hesitate.

Ryder. The other servants were gone to bed. You kept the man so late.

Prisoner. O, I mean no reflection on your prudence. You went out of doors with your wooer ; just to see him off ?

Ryder. Not I. What for ? *I* had nobody to make away with. I just opened the door for him, bolted it after him, and went straight to my bedroom.

Prisoner. How long had you been there when you heard the cry for help ?

Ryder. Scarce ten minutes. I had not taken my stays off.

Prisoner. If you and Thomas Hayes speak true, that gives half an hour you were making love with the murderer after he left me. Am I correct ?

The witness now saw whither she had been led, and changed her manner: she became sullen, and watched an opportunity to stab.

Prisoner. Had he a mole on his brow ?

Ryder. Not that I know of.

Prisoner. Why, where were your eyes then, when the murderer saluted you at parting ?

Ryder's eyes flashed ; but she felt her temper tried, and governed it all the more severely. She treated the question with silent contempt.

Prisoner. But you pass for a discreet woman ; perhaps you looked modestly down when the assassin saluted you ?

Ryder. *If* he saluted me, *perhaps* I did.

Prisoner. In that case you could not see his mole ; but you must have noticed his shoes. Were these the shoes he wore ? Look at them well.

Ryder (after inspecting them). I do not recognize them.

Prisoner. Will you swear these were not the shoes he had on ?

Ryder. How can I swear that ? I know nothing about the man's shoes. If you please, my lord, am I to be kept here all day with her foolish, trifling questions ?

Judge. All day, and all night too, if Justice requires it. The law is not swift to shed blood.

Prisoner. My lord and the gentlemen of the jury were here before you, and will be kept here after you. Prithee, attend. Look at that drawing of Hernshaw Castle and Hernshaw Mere. Now take this pencil, and mark your bedroom on the drawing.

The pencil was taken from the prisoner, and handed to Ryder. She waited, like a cat, till it came close to her; then recoiled with an admirable scream. "Me handle a thing hot from the hand of a murderess! It makes me tremble all over!"

This cruel stab affected the prisoner visibly. She put her hand to her bosom, and, with tears in her eyes, faltered out a request to the judge that she might sit down a minute.

Judge. To be sure you may. And you, my good woman, must not run before the court. By law a prisoner is innocent till found guilty by his peers. How do you know what evidence she may have in store? At present we have only heard one side. Be more moderate.

The prisoner rose promptly to her feet. "My lord, I welcome the insult that has disgusted your lordship and the gentlemen of the jury, and won me those good words of comfort." To Ryder: "What sort of a night was it?"

Ryder. Very little moon, but a clear, starry night.

Prisoner. Could you see the Mere, and the banks?

Ryder. Nay, but so much of it as faced my window.

Prisoner. Have you marked your window?

Ryder. I have.

Prisoner. Now mark the place where you heard Mr. Gaunt cry for help.

Ryder. 'T was about here, — under these trees. And that is why I could not see him: along of the shadow.

Prisoner. Possibly. Did you see me on that side the Mere?

Ryder. No.

Prisoner. What colored dress had I on at that time?

Ryder. White satin.

Prisoner. Then you could have seen me, even among the trees, had I been on that side the Mere?

Ryder. I can't say. However, I never said you were on the very spot where the deed was done; but you were out of doors.

Prisoner. How do you know that?

Ryder. Why, you told me so yourself.

Prisoner. Then, that is my evidence, not yours. Swear to no more than you know. Had my husband, to your knowledge, a reason for absconding suddenly?

Ryder. Yes, he had.

Prisoner. What was it?

Ryder. Fear of you.

Prisoner. Nay, I mean, had he not something to fear, something quite different from that I am charged with?

Ryder. You know best, madam. I would gladly serve you, but I cannot guess what you are driving at.

The prisoner was taken aback by this impudent reply. She hesitated to force her servant to expose a husband, whom she believed to be living: and her hesitation looked like discomfiture; and Ryder was victorious in that encounter.

By this time they were both thoroughly embittered, and it was war to the knife.

Prisoner. You listened to our unhappy quarrel that night?

Ryder. Quarrel! madam, 't was all on one side.

Prisoner. How did you understand what I said to him about the constables?

Ryder. Constables! I never heard you say the word.

Prisoner. Oh!

Ryder. Neither when you threatened him with your knife to me, nor when you threatened him to his face.

Prisoner. Take care: you forget that Jane Banister heard me. Was her ear nearer the keyhole than yours?

Ryder. Jane! she is a simpleton.

You could make her think she heard anything. I noticed you put the words in her mouth.

Prisoner. God forgive you, you naughty woman. You had better have spoken the truth.

Ryder. My lord, if you please, am I to be miscalled — by a murderess ?

Judge. Come, come, this is no place for recrimination.

The prisoner now stooped and examined her papers, and took a distinct line of cross-examination.

Prisoner (with apparent carelessness). At all events, you are a virtuous woman, Mrs. Ryder?

Ryder. Yes, madam, as virtuous as yourself, to say the least.

Prisoner (still more carelessly). Married or single ?

Ryder. Single, and like to be.

Prisoner. Yes, if I remember right, I made a point of that before I engaged you as my maid.

Ryder. I believe the question was put.

Prisoner. Here is the answer in your handwriting. Is not that your handwriting ?

Ryder (after inspecting it). It is.

Prisoner. You came highly recommended by your last mistress, a certain Mrs. Hamilton. Here is *her* letter, describing you as a model.

Ryder. Well, madam, hitherto, I have given satisfaction to all my mistresses, Mrs. Hamilton among the rest. My character does not rest on her word only, I hope.

Prisoner. Excuse me ; I engaged you on her word alone. Now, who is this Mrs. Hamilton ?

Ryder. A worshipful lady I served for eight months before I came to you. She went abroad, or I should be with her now.

Prisoner. Now cast your eye over this paper.

It was the copy of a marriage certificate between Thomas Edwards and Caroline Plunkett.

" Who is this Caroline Plunkett ? "

Ryder turned very pale, and made no reply.

" I ask you who is this Caroline Plunkett ? "

Ryder (faintly). Myself.

Judge. Why, you said you were single !

Ryder. So I am ; as good as single. My husband and me we parted eight years ago, and I have never seen him since.

Prisoner. Was it quite eight years ago ?

Ryder. Nearly, 't was in May, 1739.

Prisoner. But you have lived with him since.

Ryder. Never, upon my soul.

Prisoner. When was your child born ?

Ryder. My child ! I have none.

Prisoner. In January, 1743, you left a baby at Biggleswade, with a woman called Church, — did you not ?

Ryder (panting). Of course I did. It was my sister's.

Prisoner. Do you mean to call God to witness that child was not your's ?

Ryder hesitated.

Prisoner. Will you swear Mrs. Church did not see you suckle that child in secret, and weep over it ?

At this question the perspiration stood visible on Ryder's brow, her cheeks were ghastly, and her black eyes roved like some wild animal's round the court. She saw her own danger, and had no means of measuring her inquisitor's information.

" My lord, have pity on me. I was betrayed, abandoned. Why am I so tormented ? *I* have not committed murder." So, catlike, she squealed and scratched at once.

Prisoner. What ! to swear away an innocent life, is not that murder ?

Judge. Prisoner, we make allowances for your sex, and your peril, but you must not remark on the evidence at present. Examine as severely as you will, but abstain from comment till you address the jury on your defence.

Sergeant Wiltshire. My lord, I submit that this line of examination is barbarous, and travels out of the case entirely.

Prisoner. Not so, Mr. Sergeant. 'T

is done by advice of an able lawyer. My life is in peril, unless I shake this witness's credit. To that end I show you she is incontinent, and practised in falsehood. Unchastity has been held in these courts to disqualify a female witness, hath it not, my lord?

Judge. Hardly. But to disparage her evidence it has. And wisely; for she who loses her virtue enters on a life of deceit; and lying is a habit that spreads from one thing to many. Much wisdom there is in ancient words. Our forefathers taught us to call a virtuous woman an honest woman, and the law does but follow in that track; still, however, leaving much to the discretion of the jury.

Prisoner. I would show her more mercy than she has shown to me. Therefore I leave that matter. Witness, be so good as to examine Mrs. Hamilton's letter, and compare it with your own. The "y's" and the "s's" are peculiar in both, and yet the same. Come, confess, Mrs. Hamilton's is a forgery. You wrote it. Be pleased to hand both letters up to my lord to compare; the disguise is but thin.

Ryder. Forgery there was none. There is no Mrs. Hamilton. (She burst into tears.) I had my child to provide for, and no man to help me! What was I to do? A servant must live.

Prisoner. Then why not let her mistress live, whose bread she has eaten? My lord, shall not this false witness be sent hence to prison for perjury?

Wiltshire. Certainly not. What woman on earth is expected to reveal her own shame upon oath? 'T was not fair nor human to put such questions. Come, madam, leave torturing this poor creature. Show some mercy; you may need it yourself.

Prisoner. Sir, 't is not mercy I ask, but justice according to law. But since you do me the honor to make me a request, I will comply, and ask her but one question more. Describe my apartment into which you showed Thomas Leicester that night. Begin at the outer door.

Ryder. First there is the anteroom; then the boudoir; then there's your bedchamber.

Prisoner. Into which of those three did you show Thomas Leicester?

Ryder. Into the anteroom.

Prisoner. Then why did you say it was in my chamber I entertained him?

Ryder. Madam, I meant no more than that it was your private apartment up stairs.

Prisoner. You contrived to make the gentlemen think otherwise.

Judge. That you did. 'T is down in my notes that she received the pedler in her bedchamber.

Ryder (sobbing). God is my witness I did not mean to mislead your lordship: and I ask my lady's pardon for not being more exact in that particular.

At this the prisoner bowed to the judge, and sat down with one victorious flash of her gray eye at the witness, who was in an abject condition of fear, and hung all about the witness-box limp as a wet towel.

Sergeant Wiltshire saw she was so thoroughly cowed she would be apt to truckle, and soften her evidence to propitiate the prisoner; so he asked her but one question.

"Were you and the prisoner on good terms?"

Ryder. On the best of terms. She was always a good and liberal mistress to me.

Wiltshire. I will not prolong your sufferings. You may go down.

Judge. But you will not leave the court till this trial is ended. I have grave doubts whether I ought not to commit you.

Unfortunately for the prisoner, Ryder was not the last witness for the crown. The others that followed were so manifestly honest that it would have been impolitic to handle them severely. The prisoner, therefore, put very few questions to them; and, when the last witness went down, the case looked very formidable.

The evidence for the crown being now complete, the judge retired for some refreshment; and the court buzzed like a hum of bees. Mrs. Gaunt's lips and throat were parched and her heart quaked.

A woman of quite the lower order thrust forth a great arm, and gave her an orange. Mrs. Gaunt thanked her sweetly; and the juice relieved her throat.

Also this bit of sympathy was of good omen, and did her heart good.

She buried her face in her hands, and collected all her powers for the undertaking before her. She had noted down the exact order of her topics, but no more.

The judge returned; the crier demanded silence; and the prisoner rose, and turned her eyes modestly but steadily upon those who held her life in their hands: and, true to the wisdom of her sex, the first thing she aimed at was — to please.

"My lord, and you gentlemen of the jury, I am now to reply to a charge of murder, founded on a little testimony, and a good deal of false, but, I must needs say, reasonable conjecture.

"I am innocent; but, unlike other innocent persons who have stood here before me, I have no man to complain of.

"The magistrates who committed me proceeded with due caution and humanity; they weighed my hitherto unspotted reputation, and were in no hurry to prejudge me; here, in this court, I have met with much forbearance; the learned counsel for the crown has made me groan under his abilities; that was his duty; but he said from the first he would do nothing hard, and he has kept his word; often he might have stopped me; I saw it in his face. But, being a gentleman and a Christian, as well as a learned lawyer, methinks he said to himself, 'This is a poor gentlewoman pleading for her life; let her have some little advantage.' As for my lord, he has promised to be my counsel, so far as his high station, and duty to the crown, admit; and he has supported and consoled me more than once with words of justice, that would not, I think, have encouraged a guilty person, but have comforted and sustained me beyond expression. So then I stand here, the victim, not of man's injustice, but of deceitful appearances, and of honest, but hasty and loose conjectures.

"These conjectures I shall now sift, and hope to show you how hollow they are.

"Gentlemen, in every disputed matter the best way, I am told, is to begin by settling what both parties are agreed in, and so to narrow the matter. To use that method, then, I do heartily agree with the learned counsel that murder is a heinous crime, and that, black as it is at the best, yet it is still more detestable when 't is a wife that murders her husband, and robs her child of a parent who can never be replaced.

"I also agree with him that circumstantial evidence is often sufficient to convict a murderer; and, indeed, were it not so, that most monstrous of crimes would go oftenest unpunished; since, of all culprits, murderers do most shun the eyes of men in their dark deeds, and so provide beforehand that direct testimony to their execrable crime there shall be none. Only herein I am advised to take a distinction that escaped the learned sergeant. I say that first of all it ought to be proved directly, and to the naked eye, that a man has been murdered; and then, if none saw the crime done, let circumstances point out the murderer.

"But here, they put the cart before the horse; they find a dead body, with no marks of violence whatever; and labor to prove by circumstantial evidence alone that this mere dead body is a murdered body. This, I am advised, is bad in law, and contrary to general precedents; and the particular precedents for it are not examples, but warnings; since both the prisoners so rashly convicted were proved innocent, after their execution."

(The judge took a note of this distinction.)

"Then, to go from principles to the

facts, I agree and admit that, in a moment of anger, I was so transported out of myself as to threaten my husband's life before Caroline Ryder. But afterwards, when I saw him face to face, then, that I threatened him with *violence*, that I deny. The fact is, I had just learned that he had committed a capital offence ; and what I threatened him with was the law. This was proved by Jane Banister. She says she heard me say the constables should come for him next morning. For what? to murder him ? "

Judge. Give me leave, madam. Shall you prove Mr. Gaunt had committed a capital offence ?

Prisoner. I could, my lord ; but I am loath to do it. For, if I did, I should cast him into worse trouble than I am in myself.

Judge (shaking his head gravely). Let me advise you to advance nothing you are not able and willing to prove.

Prisoner. "Then I confine myself to this : it was proved by a witness for the crown that in the dining-room I threatened my husband to his face with the law. Now this threat, and not that other extravagant threat, which he never heard, you know, was clearly the threat which caused him to abscond that night.

" In the next place, I agree with the learned counsel that I was out of doors at one o'clock that morning. But if he will use me as HIS WITNESS in that matter, then he must not pick and choose and mutilate my testimony. Nay, let him take the whole truth, and not just so much as he can square with the indictment. Either believe me, that I was out of doors praying, or do not believe me that I was out of doors at all.

"Gentlemen, hear the simple truth. You may see in the map, on the south side of Hernshaw Castle, a grove of large fir-trees. 'T is a reverend place, most fit for prayer and meditation. Here I have prayed a thousand times and more before the 15th of October. Hence 't is called 'The Dame's Haunt,' as I shall prove, that am the dame 't is called after.

"Let it not seem incredible to you that I should pray out of doors in my grove, on a fine, clear, starry night. For aught I know, Protestants may pray only by the fireside. But, remember, I am a Catholic. We are not so contracted in our praying. We do not confine it to little comfortable places. Nay, but for seventeen hundred years and more we have prayed out of doors as much as in doors. And this our custom is no fit subject for a shallow sneer. How does the learned sergeant know that, beneath the vault of heaven at night, studded with those angelic eyes, the stars, is an unfit place to bend the knee, and raise the soul in prayer ? Has he ever tried it ? "

This sudden appeal to a learned and eminent, but by no means devotional sergeant, so tickled the gentlemen of the bar, that they burst out laughing with singular unanimity.

This dashed the prisoner, who had not intended to be funny; and she hesitated, and looked distressed.

Judge. Proceed, madam ; these remarks of yours are singular, but quite pertinent, and no fit subject for ridicule. Gentlemen, remember the public looks to you for an example.

Prisoner. "My lord, 't was my fault for making that personal which should be general. But women they are so. 'T is our foible. I pray the good sergeant to excuse me.

"I say, then, generally, that when the sun retires, then earth fades, but heaven comes out in tenfold glory; and I say the starry firmament at night is a temple not built with hands, and the bare sight of it subdues the passions, chastens the heart, and aids the soul in prayer surprisingly. My lord, as I am a Christian woman, 't is true that my husband had wronged me cruelly and broken the law. 'T is true that I raged against him, and he answered me not again. 'T is true, as that witness said, that my bark is worse than my bite. I cooled, and then felt I had forgotten the wife and the Christian in my wrath. I repented, and, to be more earnest in my penitence, I did go and pray out o' doors beneath those holy eyes of heaven that seemed to look down with chaste reproach on my ungoverned heat. I left my fireside, my velvet cushions, and all the little comforts made by human hands, that adorn our earthly dwellings, but distract our eyes from God."

Some applause followed this piece of eloquence, exquisitely uttered. It was checked, and the prisoner resumed, with an entire change of manner.

"Gentlemen, the case against me is like a piece of rotten wood varnished all over. It looks fair to the eye; but will not bear handling.

"As example of what I say, take three charges on which the learned sergeant greatly relied in opening his case : —

"1st. That I received Thomas Leicester in my bedroom.

"2d. That he went hot from me after Mr. Gaunt.

"3d. That he was seen following Mr. Gaunt with a bloody intent.

"How ugly these three proofs looked at first sight! Well, but when we squeezed the witnesses ever so little, what did those three dwindle down to ?

"1st. That I received Thomas Leicester in an anteroom, which leads to a boudoir, and that boudoir leads to my bedroom.

"2d. That Thomas Leicester went from me to the kitchen, and there, for a good half-hour, drank my ale (as it appears), and made love to his old sweetheart, Caroline Ryder, the false witness for the crown ; and went abroad fresh from *her*, and not from *me*.

"3d. That he was not (to speak strictly) seen following Mr. Gaunt, but just walking on the same road, drunk, and staggering, and going at such a rate that, as the crown's own witness swore, he could not in the nature of things overtake Mr. Gaunt, who walked quicker, and straighter too, than he.

"So, then, even if a murder has been done, they have failed to connect Thomas Leicester with it, or me with

Thomas Leicester. Two broken links in a chain of but three.

"And now I come to the more agreeable part of my defence. I do think there has been no murder at all.

"There is no evidence of a murder.

"A body is found with the flesh eaten by fishes, but the bones and the head uninjured. They swear a surgeon, who has examined the body, and certainly he had the presumption to guess it looks like a murdered body. But, being sifted, he was forced to admit, that so far as his experience of murdered bodies goes, it is not like a murdered body ; for there is no bone broken, nor bruise on the head.

"Where is the body found ? In the water. But water by itself is a sufficient cause of death, and a common cause too ; and kills without breaking bones, or bruising the head. O perversity of the wise ! For every one creature murdered in England, ten are accidentally drowned ; and they find a dead man in the water, which is as much as to say they find the slain in the arms of the slayer ; yet they do not once suspect the water, but go about in search of a strange and monstrous crime.

"Mr. Gaunt's cry for help was heard *here*, if it was heard at all (which I greatly doubt), here by this clump of trees ; the body was found here, hard by the bridge ; which is, by measurement, one furlong and sixty paces from that clump of trees, as I shall prove. There is no current in the mere lively enough to move a body, and what there is runs the wrong way. So this disconnects the cry for help, and the dead body. Another broken link !

"And now I come to my third defence.

"I say the body is not the body of Griffith Gaunt.

"The body, mutilated as it was, had two distinguishing marks ; a mole on the brow, and a pair of hobnailed shoes on the feet.

"Now the advisers of the crown fix

their eyes on that mole; but they turn their heads away from the hobnailed shoes. But why? Articles of raiment found on a body are legal evidence of identity. How often, my lord, in cases of murder, hath the crown relied on such particulars, especially in cases where corruption had obscured the features!

"I shall not imitate this partiality, this obstinate prejudice; I shall not ask you to shut your eyes on the mole, as they do on the shoes, but shall meet the whole truth fairly.

"Mr. Gaunt went from my house that morning with boots on his feet, and with a mole on his brow.

"Thomas Leicester went the same road, with shoes on his feet, and, as I shall prove, with a mole on his brow.

"To be sure, the crown witnesses' did not distinctly admit this mole on him; but you will remember, they dared not deny it on their oaths, and so run their heads into an indictment for perjury.

"But, gentlemen, I shall put seven witnesses into the box, who will all swear that they have known Thomas Leicester for years, and that he had a mole upon his left temple.

"One of these witnesses is — the mother that bore him.

"I shall then call witnesses to prove that, on the 15th of October, the bridge over the mere was in bad repair, and a portion of the side rail gone; and that the body was found within a few yards of that defective bridge; and then, as Thomas Leicester went that way, drunk, and staggering from side to side, you may reasonably infer that he fell into the water in passing the bridge. To show you this is possible, I shall prove the same thing has actually occurred. I shall swear the oldest man in the parish, who will depose to a similar event that happened in his boyhood. He hath said it a thousand times before to-day, and now will swear it. He will tell you that on a certain day, sixty-nine years ago, the parson of Hernshaw, the Rev. Augustus Murthwaite, went to cross this bridge

at night, after carousing at Hernshaw Castle with our great-grandfather, my husband's and mine, the then proprietor of Hernshaw, and tumbled into the water; and his body was found gnawed out of the very form of humanity by the fishes, within a yard or two of the spot where poor Tom Leicester was found, that hath cost us all this trouble. So do the same causes bring round the same events in a cycle of years. The only difference is that the parson drank his death in our dining-room, and the pedler in our kitchen.

"No doubt, my lord, you have observed that sometimes a hasty and involuntary inaccuracy gives quite a wrong color to a thing. I assure you I have suffered by this. It is said that the moment Mr. Atkins proposed to drag my mere, I fainted away. In this account there is an omission. I shall prove that Mr. Atkins used these words: 'And underneath that water I undertake to find the remains of Griffith Gaunt.' Now, gentlemen, you shall understand that at this time, and indeed until the moment when I saw the shoes upon that poor corpse's feet, I was in great terror for my husband's life. How could it be otherwise? Caroline Ryder had told me she heard his cry for help. He had disappeared. What was I to think? I feared he had fallen in with robbers. I feared all manner of things. So when the lawyer said so positively he would find his body, I was overpowered. Ah, gentlemen, wedded love survives many wrongs, many angry words; I love my husband still; and when the man told me so brutally that he was certainly dead, I fainted away. I confess it. Shall I be hanged for that?

"But now, thank God, I am full of hope that he is alive; and that good hope has given me the courage to make this great effort to save my own life.

"Hitherto I have been able to contradict my accusers positively; but now I come to a mysterious circumstance that I own puzzles me. Most persons accused of murder could, if they chose, make a clean breast, and tell you the whole matter. But this is not my case. I know shoes from boots, and I know Kate Gaunt from a liar and a murderess. But, when all is said, this is still a dark, mysterious business, and there are things in it I can only deal with as you do, gentlemen, by bringing my wits to bear upon them in reasonable conjecture.

"Caroline Ryder swears she heard Mr. Gaunt cry for help. And Mr. Gaunt has certainly disappeared.

"My accusers have somewhat weakened this by trying to palm off the body of Thomas Leicester on you for the body of Mr. Gaunt. But the original mystery remains, and puzzles me. I might fairly appeal to you to disbelieve the witness. She is proved incontinent, and a practised liar, and she forswore herself in this court, and my lord is in two minds about committing her. But a liar does not always lie, and, to be honest, I think she really *believes* she heard Mr. Gaunt cry for help, for she went straight to his bedroom; and that looks as if she really thought she heard his voice. But a liar may be mistaken. Do not forget that. Distance affects the voice; and I think the voice she heard was Thomas Leicester's, and the place it came from higher up the mere.

"This, my notion, will surprise you less when I prove to you that Leicester's voice bore a family likeness to Mr. Gaunt's. I shall call two witnesses who have been out shooting with Mr. Gaunt and Tom Leicester, and have heard Leicester halloo in the wood, and taken it for Mr. Gaunt.

"Must I tell you the whole truth? This Leicester has always passed for an illegitimate son of Mr. Gaunt's father. He resembled my husband in form, stature, and voice: he had the Gaunt mole, and has often spoken of it by that name. My husband forgave him many faults for no other reason — and I bought wares and filled his pack for no other reason — than this; that he was my husband's brother by nature, though not in law. 'HONI SOIT QUI MAL Y PENSE.'

"Ah, that is a royal device; yet how often in this business have the advisers of the crown forgotten it?

"My lord, and gentlemen of the jury, I return from these conjectures to the indisputable facts of my defence.

"Mr. Gaunt may be alive, or he may be dead. He was certainly alive on the 15th of October, and it lies on the crown to prove him dead, and not on me to prove him alive. But as for the body that forms the subject of this indictment, it is the body of Thomas Leicester, who was seen on the 16th of October, at one in the morning, drunk and staggering, and making for Hernshaw Bridge, which leads to his mother's house; and on all his former visits to Hernshaw Castle he went on to his mother's, as I shall prove. This time, he never reached her, as I shall prove; but on his way to her did meet his death, by the will of God, and no fault of man or woman, in Hernshaw Mere.

"Call Sarah Leicester."

Judge. I think you say you have several witnesses.

Prisoner. More than twenty, my lord.

Judge. We cannot possibly dispose of them this evening. We will hear your evidence to-morrow. Prisoner, this will enable you to consult with your legal advisers, and let me urge upon you to prove, if you can, that Mr. Gaunt has a sufficient motive for hiding and not answering Mr. Atkins's invitation to inherit a large estate. Some such proof as this is necessary to complete your defence; and I am sorry to see you have made no mention of it in your address, which was otherwise able.

Prisoner. My lord, I think I can prove my own innocence without casting a slur upon my husband.

Judge. You *think?* when your life is at stake. Be not so mad as to leave so large a hole in your defence, if you can mend it. Take advice.

He said this very solemnly; then rose and left the court.

Mrs. Gaunt was conveyed back to prison, and there was soon prostrated

by the depression that follows an unnatural excitement.

Mr. Houseman found her on a sofa,
pale and dejected, and clasping the
jailer's wife convulsively, who applied
hartshorn to her nostrils.

He proved but a Job's comforter.
Her defence, creditable as it was to a
novice, seemed wordy and weak to him,
a lawyer; and he was horrified at the
admissions she had made. In her place
he would have admitted nothing he
could not thoroughly explain.

He came to insist on a change of
tactics.

When he saw her sad condition, he
tried to begin by consoling and encouraging her. But his own serious misgivings unfitted him for this task, and
very soon, notwithstanding the state
she was in, he was almost scolding her
for being so mad as to withstand the
judge, and set herself against his advice. "There," said he, "my lord
kept his word, and became counsel for
you. 'Close that gap in your defence,'
says he, 'and you will very likely be
acquitted.' 'Nay,' says you, 'I prefer
to chance it.' What madness! what
injustice!"

"Injustice! to whom?"

"To whom? why, to yourself."

"What, may I not be unjust to myself?"

"Certainly not; you have no right to
be unjust to anybody. Don't deceive
yourself; there is no virtue in this; it
is mere miserable weakness. What
right have you to peril an innocent life
merely to screen a malefactor from just
obloquy?"

"Alas!" said Mrs. Gaunt, "'t is
more than obloquy. They will kill
him; they will brand him with a hot
iron."

"Not unless he is indicted; and who
will indict him? Sir George Neville
must be got to muzzle the attorney-
general, and the Lancashire jade will
not move against him, for you say they
are living together."

"Of course they are; and, as you
say, why should I screen him? But
't will not serve; who can combat prej-

udice? If what I have said does not
convince them, an angel's voice would
not. Sir, I am a Catholic, and they
will hang me. I shall die miserably,
having exposed my husband, who loved
me once, O so dearly! I trifled with
his love. I deserve it all."

"You will not die at all, if you will
only be good and obedient, and listen
to wiser heads. I have subpœnaed Caroline Ryder as your witness, and given
her a hint how to escape an indictment
for perjury. You will find her supple
as a glove."

"Call a rattlesnake for my witness?"

"I have drawn her fangs. You will
also call Sir George Neville, to prove
he saw Gaunt's picture at the 'Packhorse,' and heard the other wife's tale.
Wiltshire will object to this as evidence, and say why don't you produce
Mercy Vint herself. Then you will call
me to prove I sent the subpœna to
Mercy Vint. Come now; I cannot eat
or sleep till you promise me."

Mrs. Gaunt sighed deeply. "Spare
me," said she; "I am worn out. O
that I could die before the trial begins
again!"

Houseman saw the signs of yielding, and persisted. "Come, promise
now," said he. "Then you will feel
better."

"I will do whatever you bid me,"
said she. "Only, if they let me off, I
will go into a convent. No power shall
hinder me."

"You shall go where you like, except
to the gallows. Enough, 't is a promise,
and I never knew you break one. Now
I can eat my supper. You are a good,
obedient child, and I am a happy attorney."

"And I am the most miserable woman in all England."

"Child," said the worthy lawyer,
"your spirits have given way, because
they were strung so high. You need
repose. Go to bed now, and sleep
twelve hours. Believe me, you will
wake another woman."

"Ah! would I could!" cried Mrs.
Gaunt, with all the eloquence of despair.

Houseman murmured a few more consoling words, and then left her, after once more exacting a promise that she would receive no more visits, but go to bed directly. She was to send all intruders to him at the "Angel."

Mrs. Gaunt proceeded to obey his orders, and though it was but eight o'clock, she made preparations for bed, and then went to her nightly devotions.

She was in sore trouble, and earthly trouble turns the heart heavenwards. Yet it was not so with her. The deep languor that oppressed her seemed to have reached her inmost soul. Her beads, falling one by one from her hand, denoted the number of her supplicacations; but, for once, they were *preces sine mente dictæ.* Her faith was cold, her belief in Divine justice was shaken for a time. She began to doubt and to despond. That bitter hour, which David has sung so well, and Bunyan, from experience, has described in his biography as well as in his novel, sat heavy upon her, as it had on many a true believer before her. So deep was the gloom, so paralyzing the languor, that at last she gave up all endeavor to utter words of prayer. She placed her crucifix at the foot of the wall, and laid herself down on the ground and kissed His feet, then, drawing back, gazed upon that effigy of the mortal sufferings of our Redeemer.

"O anima Christiana, respice vulnera morientis, pretium redemptionis."

She had lain thus a good half-hour, when a gentle tap came to the door.

"Who is that?" said she.

"Mrs. Menteith," the jailer's wife replied, softly, and asked leave to come in.

Now this Mrs. Menteith had been very kind to her, and stoutly maintained her innocence. Mrs. Gaunt rose, and invited her in.

"Madam," said Mrs. Menteith, "what I come for, there is a person below who much desires to see you."

"I beg to be excused," was the reply. "He must go to my solicitor at the 'Angel,' Mr. Houseman."

Mrs. Menteith retired with that message, but in about five minutes returned to say that the young woman declined to go to Mr. Houseman, and begged hard to see Mrs. Gaunt. "And, dame," said she, "if I were you, I'd let her come in; 'tis the honestest face, and the tears in her soft eyes, at you denying her: 'O dear, dear!' said she, 'I cannot tell my errand to any but her.'"

"Well, well," said Mrs. Gaunt; "but what is her business?"

"If you ask me, I think her business is your business. Come, dame, do see the poor thing; she is civil spoken, and she tells me she has come all the way out of Lancashire o' purpose."

Mrs. Gaunt recoiled, as if she had been stung.

"From Lancashire?" said she, faintly.

"Ay, madam," said Mrs. Menteith, "and that is a long road; and a child upon her arm all the way, poor thing!"

"Her name?" said Mrs. Gaunt, sternly.

"O, she is not ashamed of it. She gave it me directly."

"What, has she the effrontery to take my name?"

Mrs. Menteith stared at her with utter amazement. "*Your* name?" said she. "'Tis a simple, country body, and her name is Vint, — Mercy Vint."

Mrs. Gaunt was very much agitated, and said she felt quite unequal to see a stranger.

"Well, I'm sure I don't know what to do," said Mrs. Menteith. "She says she will lie at your door all night, but she will see you. 'Tis the face of a friend. She may know something. It seems hard to thrust her and her child out into the street, after their coming all the way from Lancashire."

Mrs. Gaunt stood silent awhile, and her intelligence had a severe combat with her deep repugnance to be in the same room with Griffith Gaunt's mistress (so she considered her). But a certain curiosity came to the aid of her good sense; and, after all, she was a brave and haughty woman, and her natural courage began to rise. She thought to herself, "What, dares she come to me all this way, and shall I shrink from *her?*"

She turned to Mrs. Menteith with a bitter smile, and she said, very slowly, and clenching her white teeth: "Since you desire it, and she *insists* on it, I will receive Mistress Mercy Vint."

Mrs. Menteith went off, and in about five minutes returned, ushering in Mercy Vint, in a hood and travelling-cloak.

Mrs. Gaunt received her standing, and with a very formal courtesy ; to which Mercy made a quiet obeisance, and both women looked one another all over in a moment.

Mrs. Menteith lingered, to know what on earth this was all about ; but as neither spoke a word, and their eyes were fixed on each other, she divined that her absence was necessary, and so retired, looking very much amazed at both of them.

CHAPTER XLII.

"BE seated, mistress, if you please," said Mrs. Gaunt, with icy civility, "and let me know to what I owe this extraordinary visit."

"I thank you, dame," said Mercy, "for indeed I am sore fatigued." She sat quietly down. "Why I have come to you? It was to serve you, and to keep my word with George Neville."

"Will you be kind enough to explain?" said Mrs. Gaunt, in a freezing tone, and with a look of her calm gray eye to match.

Mercy felt chilled, and was too frank to disguise it. "Alas !" said she, softly, "'t is hard to be received so, and me come all the way from Lancashire, with a heart like lead, to do my duty, God willing."

The tears stood in her eyes, and her mellow voice was sweet and patient.

The gentle remonstrance was not quite without effect. Mrs. Gaunt colored a little ; she said, stiffly : "Excuse me if I seem discourteous, but you and I ought not to be in one room a mo-

ment. You do not see this, apparently. But at least I have a right to insist that such an interview shall be very brief, and to the purpose. Oblige me, then, by telling me in plain terms why you have come hither."

"Madam, to be your witness at the trial."

"*You* to be *my* witness?"

"Why not? If I can clear you? What, would you rather be condemned for murder, than let me show them you are innocent? Alas ! how you hate me !"

"Hate you, child ? of course I hate you. We are both of us flesh and blood, and hate one another. And one of us is honest enough, and uncivil enough, to say so."

"Speak for yourself, dame," replied Mercy, quietly, "for I hate you not ; and I thank God for it. To hate is to be miserable. I 'd liever be hated than to hate."

Mrs. Gaunt looked at her. "Your words are goodly and wise," said she ; "your face is honest, and your eyes are like a very dove's. But, for all that, you hate me quietly, with all your heart. Human nature is human nature."

"'T is so. But grace is grace." She was silent a moment, then resumed : "I 'll not deny I did hate you for a time, when first I learned the man I had married had a wife, and you were she. We that be women are too unjust to each other, and too indulgent to a man. But I have worn out my hate. I wrestled in prayer, and the God of Love, he did quench my most unreasonable hate. For 't was the man betrayed me ; *you* never wronged me, nor I you. But you are right, madam ; 't is true that nature without grace is black as pitch. The Devil, he was busy at my ear, and whispered me, ' If the fools in Cumberland hang her, what fault o' thine ? Thou wilt be his lawful wife, and thy poor, innocent child will be a child of shame no more.' But, by God's grace, I did defy him. And I do defy him." She rose swiftly from her chair, and her dove's eyes gleamed with celestial light. "Get thee behind me, Satan. I tell thee the hangman shall never have her innocent body, nor thou my soul."

The movement was so unexpected, the words and the look so simply noble, that Mrs. Gaunt rose too, and gazed upon her visitor with astonishment and respect; yet still with a dash of doubt.

She thought to herself, "If this creature is not sincere, what a mistress of deceit she must be."

But Mercy Vint soon returned to her quiet self. She sat down, and said, gravely, and for the first time a little coldly, as one who had deserved well, and been received ill : " Mistress Gaunt, you are accused of murdering your husband. 'T is false ; for two days ago I saw him alive."

"What do you say?" cried Mrs. Gaunt, trembling all over.

"Be brave, madam. You have borne great trouble : do not give way under joy. He who has wronged us both — he who wedded you under his own name of Griffith Gaunt, and me under the false name of Thomas Leicester — is no more dead than we are.; I saw him two days ago, and spoke to him, and persuaded him to come to Carlisle town, and do you justice."

Mrs. Gaunt fell on her knees. " He is alive ; he is alive. Thank God! O, thank God! He is alive ; and God bless the tongue that tells me so. God bless you eternally, Mercy Vint."

The tears of joy streamed down her face, and then Mercy's flowed too. She uttered a little pathetic cry of joy. "Ah," she sobbed, " the bit of comfort I needed so has come to my heavy heart. *She* has blessed me."

But she said this very softly, and Mrs. Gaunt was in a rapture, and did not hear her.

"Is it a dream? My husband alive? and you the one to come and tell me so? How unjust I have been to you. Forgive me. Why does he not come himself?"

Mercy colored at this question, and hesitated.

"Well, dame," said she, "for one thing, he has been on the fuddle for the last two months."

"On the fuddle?"

"Ay; he owns he has never been sober a whole day. And that takes the heart out of a man, as well as the brains. And then he has got it into his head that you will never forgive him, and that he shall be cast in prison if he shows his face in Cumberland."

"Why in Cumberland more than in Lancashire?" asked Mrs. Gaunt, biting her lip.

Mercy blushed faintly. She replied with some delicacy, but did not altogether mince the matter.

"He knows I shall never punish him for what he has done to me."

"Why not? I begin to think he has wronged you almost as much as he has me."

"Worse, madam ; worse. He has robbed me of my good name. You are still his lawful wife, and none can point the finger at you. But look at me. I was an honest girl, respected by all the parish. What has he made of me? The man that lay a dying in my house, and I saved his life, and so my heart did warm to him, — he blasphemed God's altar, to deceive and betray me ; and here I am, a poor forlorn creature, neither maid, wife, nor widow ; with a child on my arms that I do nothing but cry over. Ay, my poor innocent, I left thee down below, because I was ashamed she should see thee ; ah me ! ah me !" She lifted up her voice, and wept.

Mrs. Gaunt looked at her wistfully, and, like Mercy before her, had a bitter struggle with human nature, — a struggle so sharp that, in the midst of it, she burst out crying with great violence ; but, with that burst, her great soul conquered.

She darted out of the room, leaving Mercy astonished at her abrupt departure.

Mercy was patiently drying her eyes, when the door opened, and judge her surprise when she saw Mrs. Gaunt glide into the room with her little boy asleep in her arms, and an expression upon her face more sublime than anything Mercy Vint had ever yet seen on earth. She kissed the babe softly, and, becoming infantine as well as angelic by this contact, sat herself down in a moment on the floor with him, and held out her hand to Mercy. " There," said she, "come, sit beside us, and see how I hate him, — no more than you do; sweet innocent."

They looked him all over, discussed his every feature learnedly, kissed his limbs and extremities after the manner of their sex, and, comprehending at last that to have been both of them wronged by one man was a bond of sympathy, not hate, the two wives of Griffith Gaunt laid his child across their two laps, and wept over him together.

Mercy Vint took herself to task. " I am but a selfish woman," said she, " to talk or think of anything but that I came here for." She then proceeded to show Mrs. Gaunt by what means she proposed to secure her acquittal, without getting Griffith Gaunt into trouble.

Mrs. Gaunt listened with keen and grateful attention, until she came to that part; then she interrupted her eagerly. " Don't spare him for me. In your place I 'd trounce the villain finely."

" Ay," said Mercy, "and then forgive him; but I am different. I shall never forgive him; but I am a poor hand at punishing and revenging. I always was. My name is Mercy, you know. To tell the truth, I was to have been called Prudence, after my good aunt; but she said, nay; she had lived to hear Greed, and Selfishness, and a heap of faults, named Prudence. ' Call the child something that means what it does mean, and not after me,' quoth she. So with me hearing ' Mercy, Mercy,' called out after me so many years, I do think the quality hath somehow got under my skin; for I cannot abide to see folk smart, let alone to strike the blow. What, shall I take the place of God, and punish the evil-doers, because 't is me they wrong ? Nay, dame, I

will never punish him, though he hath wronged me cruelly. All I shall do is to think very ill of him, and shun him, and tear his memory out of my heart. You look at me: do you think I cannot ? You don't know me; I am very resolute when I see clear. Of course I loved him, — loved him dearly. He was like a husband to me, and a kind one. But the moment I knew how basely he had deceived us both, my heart began to turn against the man, and now 't is ice to him. Heaven knows what I am made of; for, believe me, I 'd liever ten times be beside you than beside him. My heart it lay like a lump of lead till I heard your story, and found I could do you a good turn, — you that he had wronged, as well as me. I read your beautiful eyes; but nay, fear me not; I 'm not the woman to pine for the fruit that is my neighbor's. All I ask for on earth is a few kind words and looks from you. You are gentle, and I am simple; but we are both one flesh and blood, and your lovely wet eyes do prove it this moment. Dame Gaunt — Kate — I ne'er was ten miles from home afore, and I am come all this weary way to serve thee. O, give me the one thing that can do me good in this world, — the one thing I pine for, — a little of *your* love."

The words were scarce out of her lips, when Mrs. Gaunt caught her impetuously round the neck with both hands, and laid her on that erring but noble heart of hers, and kissed her eagerly.

They kissed one another again and again, and wept over one another.

And now Mrs. Gaunt, who did nothing by halves, could not make enough of Mercy Vint. She ordered supper, and ate with her, to make her eat. Mrs. Menteith offered Mercy a bed; but Mrs. Gaunt said she must lie with her, she and her child.

" What," said she, "think you I 'll let you out of my sight? Alas! who knows when you and I shall ever be together again ? "

" I know," said Mercy, thoughtfully. " In this world, never."

They slept in one bed, and held each

other by the hand all night, and talked to one another, and in the morning knew each the other's story, and each the other's mind and character, better than their oldest acquaintances knew either the one or the other.

CHAPTER XLIII.

THE trial began again; and the court was crowded to suffocation. All eyes were bent on the prisoner. She rose, calm and quiet, and begged leave to say a few words to the court.

Mr. Whitworth objected to that. She had concluded her address yesterday, and called a witness.

Prisoner. But I have not examined a witness yet.

Judge. You come somewhat out of time, madam; but, if you will be brief, we will hear you.

Prisoner. I thank you, my lord. It was only to withdraw an error. The cry for help that was heard by the side of Hernshaw Mere, I said, yesterday, that cry was uttered by Thomas Leicester. Well, I find I was mistaken: the cry for help was uttered by my husband, — by that Griffith Gaunt I am accused of assassinating.

This extraordinary admission caused a great sensation in court. The judge looked very grave and sad; and Sergeant Wiltshire, who came into court just then, whispered his junior, "She has put the rope round her own neck. The jury would never have believed our witness."

Prisoner. I will only add, that a person came into the town last night, who knows a great deal more about this mysterious business than I do. I purpose, therefore, to alter the plan of my defence; and to save your time, my lord, who have dealt so courteously with me, I shall call but a single witness.

Ere the astonishment caused by this sudden collapse of the defence was in any degree abated, she called "Mercy Vint."

There was the usual stir and struggle; and then the calm, self-possessed face and figure of a comely young woman confronted the court. She was sworn; and examined by the prisoner after this fashion.

"Where do you live?"

"At the 'Packhorse,' near Allerton, in Lancashire."

Prisoner. Do you know Mr. Griffith Gaunt?

Mercy. Madam, I do.

Prisoner. Was he at your place in October last?

Mercy. Yes, madam, on the thirteenth of October. On that day he left for Cumberland.

Prisoner. On foot, or on horseback?

Mercy. On horseback.

Prisoner. With boots on, or shoes?

Mercy. He had a pair of new boots on.

Prisoner. Do you know Thomas Leicester?

Mercy. A pedler called at our house on the eleventh of October, and he said his name was Thomas Leicester.

Prisoner. How was he shod?

Mercy. In hobnailed shoes.

Prisoner. Which way went he on leaving you?

Mercy. Madam, he went northwards; I know no more for certain.

Prisoner. When did you see Mr. Gaunt last?

Mercy. Four days ago.

Judge. What is that? You saw him alive four days ago?

Mercy. Ay, my lord; the last Wednesday that ever was.

At this the people burst out into a loud, agitated murmur, and their heads went to and fro all the time. In vain the crier cried and threatened. The noise rose and surged, and took its course. It went down gradually, as amazement gave way to curiosity; and then there was a remarkable silence; and then the silvery voice of the prisoner, and the mellow tones of the witness, appeared to penetrate the very walls of the building, each syllable of those two beautiful speakers was heard so distinctly.

Prisoner. Be so good as to tell the court what passed on Wednesday last between Griffith Gaunt and you, relative to this charge of murder.

Mercy. I let him know one George Neville had come from Cumberland in search of him, and had told me you lay in Carlisle jail charged with his murder. I did urge him to ride at once to Carlisle, and show himself; but he refused. He made light of the matter. Then I told him not so; the circumstances looked ugly, and your life was in peril. Then he said, nay, 't was in no peril; for if you were to be found guilty, then he would show himself on the instant. Then I told him he was not worthy the name of a man, and if he would not go, I would. "Go you, by all means," said he, "and I 'll give you a writing that will clear her. Jack Houseman will be there, that knows my hand; and so does the sheriff, and half the grand jury at the least."

Prisoner. Have you that writing?

Mercy. To be sure I have. Here 't is.

Prisoner. Be pleased to read it.

Judge. Stay a minute. Shall you prove it to be his handwriting?

Prisoner. Ay, my lord, by as many as you please.

Judge. Then let that stand over for the present. Let me see it.

It was handed up to him; and he showed it to the sheriff, who said he thought it was Griffith Gaunt's writing.

The paper was then read out to the jury. It ran as follows : —

"Know all men, that I, Griffith Gaunt, Esq., of Bolton Hall and Hernshaw Castle, in the county of Cumberland, am alive and well; and the matter which has so puzzled the good folk in Cumberland befell as follows : — I left Hernshaw Castle in the dead of night upon the fifteenth of October. Why, is no man's business but mine. I found the stable locked; so I left my horse, and went on foot. I crossed Hernshaw Mere by the bridge, and had got about a hundred yards, as I suppose, on the way, when I heard some one fall with a great splash into the mere, and soon after cry dolefully for help. I, that am no swimmer, ran instantly to the north side to a clump of trees, where a boat used always to be kept. But the boat was not there. Then I cried lustily for help, and, as no one came, I fired my pistol and cried murder! For I had heard men will come sooner to that cry than to any other. But in truth I was almost out of my wits, that a fellow-creature should perish miserably so near me. Whilst I ran wildly to and fro, some came out of the Castle bearing torches. By this time I was at the bridge, but saw no signs of the drowning man; yet the night was clear. Then I knew that his fate was sealed; and, for reasons of my own, not choosing to be seen by those who were coming to his aid, I hastened from the place. My happiness being gone, and my conscience smiting me sore, and not knowing whither to turn, I took to drink, and fell into bad ways, and lived like a brute, and not a man, for six weeks or more; so that I never knew of the good fortune that had fallen on me when least I deserved it: I mean by old Mr. Gaunt of Coggleswade making of me his heir. But one day at Kendal I saw Mercy Vint's advertisement; and I went to her, and learned that my wife lay in Carlisle jail for my supposed murder. But I say that she is innocent, and nowise to blame in this matter: for I deserved every hard word she ever gave me; and as for killing, she is a spirited woman with her tongue, but hath not the heart to kill a fly. She is what she always was, — the pearl of womankind; a virtuous, innocent, and noble lady. I have lost the treasure of her love by my fault, not hers; but at least I have a right to defend her life and honor. Whoever molests her after this, out of pretended regard for me, is a liar, and a fool, and no friend of mine, but my enemy, and I his — to the death.

"GRIFFITH GAUNT."

It was a day of surprises. This tribute from the murdered man to his assassin was one of them. People looked in one another's faces open-eyed.

The prisoner looked in the judge's, and acted on what she saw there. "That is my defence," said she, quietly, and sat down.

If a show of hands had been called at that moment, she would have been acquitted by acclamation.

But Mr. Whitworth was a zealous young barrister, burning for distinction. He stuck to his case, and cross-examined Mercy Vint with severity; indeed, with asperity.

Whitworth. What are you to receive for this evidence ?

Mercy. Anan.

Whitworth. O, you know what I mean. Are you not to be paid for telling us this romance ?

Mercy. Nay, sir, I ask naught for telling the truth.

Whitworth. You were in the prisoner's company yesterday ?

Mercy. Yes, sir, I visited her in the jail last night.

Whitworth. And there concerted this ingenious defence ?

Mercy. Well, sir, for that matter, I told her that her man was alive, and I did offer to be her witness.

Whitworth. For naught ?

Mercy. For no money or reward, if 't is that you mean. Why, 't is a joy beyond money to clear an innocent body, and save her life ; and that satisfaction is mine this day.

Whitworth (sarcastically). These are very fine sentiments for a person in your condition. Confess that Mrs. Gaunt primed you with all that.

Mercy. Nay, sir, I left home in that mind ; else I had not come at all. Bethink you ; 't is a long journey for one in my way of life ; and this dear child on my arm all the way.

Mrs. Gaunt sat boiling with indignation. But Mercy's good temper and meekness parried the attack that time. Mr. Whitworth changed his line.

Whitworth. You ask the jury to believe that Griffith Gaunt, Esquire, a gentleman, and a man of spirit and honor, is alive, yet skulks and sends you hither, when by showing his face in this court he could clear his wife without a single word spoken ?

Mercy. Yes, sir; I do hope to be believed, for I speak the naked truth. But, with due respect to you, Mr. Gaunt did not send me hither against my will. I could not bide in Lancashire, and let an innocent woman be murdered in Cumberland.

Whitworth. Murdered, quotha. That is a good jest. I 'd have you to know we punish murders here, not do them.

Mercy. I am glad to hear that, sir, on the lady's account.

Whitworth. Come, come. You pretend you discovered this Griffith Gaunt alive, by means of an advertisement. If so, produce the advertisement.

Mercy Vint colored, and cast a swift, uneasy glance at Mrs. Gaunt.

Rapid as it was, the keen eye of the counsel caught it.

"Nay, do not look to the culprit for orders," said he. "Produce it, or confess the truth. Come, you never advertised for him."

"Sir, I did advertise for him."

"Then produce the advertisement."

"Sir, I will not," said Mercy, calmly.

"Then I shall move the court to commit you."

"For what offence, if you please ? "

"For perjury and contempt of court."

"I am guiltless of either, God knows. But I will not show the advertisement."

Judge. This is very extraordinary. Perhaps you have it not about you.

Mercy. My lord, the truth is I have it in my bosom. But, if I show it, it will not make this matter one whit clearer, and 't will open the wounds of two poor women. 'T is not for myself. But, O my lord, look at her. Hath she not gone through grief enow ? "

The appeal was made with a quiet, touching earnestness, that affected every hearer. But the judge had a duty to perform. "Witness," said he, "you mean well ; but indeed you do the prisoner an injury by withholding this paper. Be good enough to produce it at once."

Prisoner (with a deep sigh). Obey my lord.

Mercy (with a patient sigh). There, sir, may the Lord forgive you the useless mischief you are doing.

Whitworth. I am doing my duty, young woman. And yours is to tell the whole truth, and not a part only.

Mercy (acquiescing). That is true, sir.

Whitworth. Why, what is this? 'T is not Mr. Gaunt you advertise for in these papers. 'T is Thomas Leicester.

Judge. What is that? I don't understand.

Whitworth. Nor I neither.

Judge. Let me see the papers. 'T is Thomas Leicester sure enough.

Whitworth. And you mean to swear that Griffith Gaunt answered an advertisement inviting Thomas Leicester?

Mercy. I do. Thomas Leicester was the name he went by in our part.

Whitworth. What? what? You are jesting.

Mercy. Is this a place or a time for jesting? I say he called himself Thomas Leicester.

Here the business was interrupted again by a multitudinous murmur of excited voices. Everybody was whispering astonishment to his neighbor. And the whisper of a great crowd has the effect of a loud murmur.

Whitworth. O, he called himself Thomas Leicester, did he? Then what makes you think he is Griffith Gaunt?

Mercy. Well, sir, the pedler, whose real name was Thomas Leicester, came to our house one day, and saw his picture, and knew it; and said something to a neighbor that raised my suspicions. When *he* came home, I took this shirt out of a drawer; 't was the shirt he wore when he first came to us. 'T is marked "G. G." (The shirt was examined.) Said I, "For God's sake speak the truth: what does G. G. stand for?" Then he told me his real name was Griffith Gaunt, and he

had a wife in Cumberland. "Go back to her," said I, "and ask her to forgive you." Then he rode north, and I never saw him again till last Wednesday.

Whitworth (satirically). You seem to have been mighty intimate with this Thomas Leicester, whom you now call Griffith Gaunt. May I ask what was, or is, the nature of your connection with him?

Mercy was silent.

Whitworth. I must press for a reply, that we may know what value to attach to your most extraordinary evidence. Were you his wife, — or his mistress?

Mercy. Indeed, I hardly know; but not his mistress, or I should not be here.

Whitworth. You don't know whether you were married to the man or not?

Mercy. I do not say so. But —

She hesitated, and cast a piteous look at Mrs. Gaunt, who sat boiling with indignation.

At this look, the prisoner, who had long contained herself with difficulty, rose, with scarlet cheeks and flashing eyes, in defence of her witness, and flung her prudence to the wind.

"Fie, sir," she cried. "The woman you insult is as pure as your own mother, or mine. She deserves the pity, the respect, the veneration of all good men. Know, my lord, that my miserable husband deceived and married her under the false name he had taken. She has the marriage-certificate in her bosom. Pray make her show it, whether she will or not. My lord, this Mercy Vint is more an angel than a woman. I am her rival, after a manner. Yet, out of the goodness and greatness of her noble heart, she came all that way to save me from an unjust death. And is such a woman to be insulted? I blush for the hired advocate who cannot see his superior in an incorruptible witness, a creature all truth, piety, purity, unselfishness, and goodness. Yes, sir, you began by insinuating that she was as venal as yourself; for you are one that can be bought by the first-comer; and now you would cast a slur on her chastity. For shame! for shame! This is one of those rare women that adorn our whole sex, and embellish human nature; and, so long as you have the privilege of exchanging words with her, I shall stand here on the watch, to see that you treat her with due respect: ay, sir, with reverence; for I have measured you both, and she is as much your superior as she is mine."

This amazing burst was delivered with such prodigious fire and rapidity that nobody was self-possessed enough to stop it in time. It was like a furious gust of words sweeping over the court.

Mr. Whitworth, pale with anger, merely said: "Madam, the good taste of these remarks I leave the court to decide upon. But you cannot be allowed to give evidence in your own defence."

"No, but in hers I will," said Mrs. Gaunt. "No power shall hinder me."

Judge (coldly). Had you not better go on cross-examining the witness?

Whitworth. Let me see your marriage-certificate, if you have one?

It was handed to him.

"Well, now how do you know that this Thomas Leicester was Griffith Gaunt?

Judge. Why, she has told you he confessed it to her.

Mercy. Yes, my lord; and, besides, he wrote me two letters signed Thomas Leicester. Here they are, and I desire they may be compared with the paper he wrote last Wednesday, and signed Griffith Gaunt. And more than that, whilst we lived together as man and wife, one Hamilton, a travelling painter, took our portraits, his and mine. I have brought his with me. Let his friends and neighbors look on this portrait, and say whose likeness it is. What I say and swear is, that on Wednesday last I saw and spoke with that Thomas Leicester, or Griffith Gaunt, whose likeness I now show you.

With that she lifted the portrait up, and showed it all the court.

Instantly there was a roar of recognition.

It was one of those hard daubs that are nevertheless so monstrously like the originals.

Judge (to Mr. Whitworth). Young gentleman, we are all greatly obliged to you. You have made the prisoner's case. There was but one weak point in it; I mean the prolonged absence of Griffith Gaunt. You have now accounted for that. You have forced a very truthful witness to depose that this Gaunt is himself a criminal, and is hiding from fear of the law. The case for the crown is a mere tissue of conjectures, on which no jury could safely convict, even if there was no defence at all. Under other circumstances I might decline to receive evidence at second-hand that Griffith Gaunt is alive. But here such evidence is sufficient, for it lies on the crown to prove the man dead; but you have only proved that he was alive on the fifteenth of October, and that since then somebody is dead with shoes on. This somebody appears on the balance of proof to be Thomas Leicester, the pedler; and he has never been heard of since, and Griffith Gaunt has. Then I say you cannot carry the case further. You have not a leg to stand on. What say you, brother Wiltshire?

Wiltshire. My lord, I think there is no case against the prisoner, and am thankful to your lordship for relieving me of a very unpleasant task.

The question of guilty or not guilty was then put to the jury, who instantly brought the prisoner in not guilty.

Judge. Catharine Gaunt, you leave this court without a stain, and with our sincere respect and sympathy. I much regret the fear and pain you have been put to: you have been terribly punished for a hasty word. Profit now by this bitter lesson; and may Heaven enable you to add a well-governed spirit to your many virtues and graces.

He half rose from his seat, and bowed courteously to her. She courtesied reverently, and retired.

He then said a few words to Mercy Vint.

"Young woman, I have no words to praise you as you deserve. You have shown us the beauty of the female character, and, let me add, the beauty of the Christian religion. You have come a long way to clear the innocent. I hope you will not stop there; but also punish the guilty person, on whom we have wasted so much pity."

"Me, my lord?" said Mercy. "I would not harm a hair of his head for as many guineas as there be hairs in mine."

"Child," said my lord, "thou art too good for this world; but go thy ways, and God bless thee."

Thus abruptly ended a trial that, at first, had looked so formidable for the accused.

The judge now retired for some refreshment, and while he was gone Sir George Neville dashed up to the Town Hall, four in hand, and rushed in by the magistrate's door, with a pedler's pack, which he had discovered in the mere, a few yards from the spot where the mutilated body was found.

He learned the prisoner was already acquitted. He left the pack with the sheriff, and begged him to show it to the judge; and went in search of Mrs. Gaunt.

He found her in the jailer's house. She and Mercy Vint were seated hand in hand.

He started at first sight of the latter. Then there was a universal shaking of hands, and glistening of eyes. And, when this was over, Mrs. Gaunt turned to him, and said, piteously: "She will go back to Lancashire tomorrow; nothing I can say will turn her."

"No, dame," said Mercy, quietly; "Cumberland is no place for me. My work is done here. Our paths in this world do lie apart. George Neville, persuade her to go home at once, and not trouble about me."

"Indeed, madam," said Sir George, "she speaks wisely: she always does. My carriage is at the door, and the people waiting by thousands in the street to welcome your deliverance."

Mrs. Gaunt drew herself up with fiery and bitter disdain.

"Are they so?" said she, grimly. "Then I'll balk them. I'll steal away in the dead of night. No, miserable populace, that howls and hisses with the strong against the weak, you shall have no part in my triumph; 't is sacred to my friends. You honored me with your hootings, you shall not disgrace me with your acclamations. Here I stay till Mercy Vint, my guardian angel, leaves me forever."

She then requested Sir George to order his horses back to the inn, and the coachman was to hold himself in readiness to start when the whole town should be asleep.

Meantime, a courier was despatched to Hernshaw Castle, to prepare for Mrs. Gaunt's reception.

Mrs. Menteith made a bed up for Mercy Vint, and at midnight, when the coast was clear, came the parting.

It was a sad one.

Even Mercy, who had great self-command, could not then restrain her tears.

To apply the sweet and touching words of Scripture, "They sorrowed most of all for this, that they should see each other's face no more."

Sir George accompanied Mrs. Gaunt to Hernshaw.

She drew back into her corner of the carriage, and was very silent and *distraite*.

After one or two attempts at conversation, he judged it wisest, and even most polite, to respect her mood.

At last she burst out, "I cannot bear it, I cannot bear it."

"Why, what is amiss?" inquired Sir George.

"What is amiss? Why, 't is all amiss. 'T is so heartless, so ungrateful, to let that poor angel go home to Lancashire all alone, now she has served my turn. Sir George, do not think I undervalue your company: but if you would but take her home, instead of taking me! Poor thing, she is brave; but when the excitement of her good action is over, and she goes back the weary road all alone, what desolation it will be ! My heart bleeds for her. I know I am an unconscionable woman, to ask such a thing ; but then you are a true chevalier ; you always were, and you saw her merit directly. O, do pray leave me to slip unnoticed into Hernshaw Castle, and do you accompany my benefactress to her humble home. Will you, dear Sir George ? 'T would be such a load off my heart."

To this appeal, uttered with trembling lip and moist eyes, Sir George replied in character. He declined to desert Mrs. Gaunt, until he had seen her safe home ; but, that done, he would ride back to Carlisle and escort Mercy home.

Mrs. Gaunt sighed, and said she was abusing his friendship, and should kill him with fatigue, and he was a good creature. " If anything could make me easy, this would," said she. " You know how to talk to a woman, and comfort her. I wish I was a man : I 'd cure her of Griffith before we reached the ' Packhorse.' And, now I think of it, you are a very happy man to travel eighty miles with an angel, a dove-eyed angel."

" I am a happy man to have an opportunity of complying with your desires, madam," was the demure reply. " 'T is not often you do me the honor to lay your orders on me."

After this, nothing of any moment passed until they reached Hernshaw Castle ; and then, as they drove up to the door, and saw the hall blazing with lights, Mrs. Gaunt laid her hand softly on Sir George, and whispered, " You were right. I thank you for not leaving me."

The servants were all in the hall, to receive their mistress ; and amongst them were those who had given honest but unfavorable testimony at the trial, being called by the crown. These had consulted together, and, after many pros and cons, had decided that they had better not follow their natural impulse, and hide from her face, since that might be a fresh offence. Accord-

ingly, these witnesses, dressed in their best, stood with the others in the hall, and made their obeisances, quaking inwardly.

Mrs. Gaunt entered the hall leaning on Sir George's arm. She scarcely bestowed a look upon any of her servants, but made them one sweeping courtesy in return, and passed on ; only Sir George felt her taper fingers just nip his arm.

She made him partake of some supper, and then this chevalier des dames rode home, snatched a few hours' sleep, put on the yeoman's suit in which he had first visited the " Packhorse," and, arriving at Carlisle, engaged the whole inside of the coach ; for his orders were to console, and he did not see his way clear to do that with two or three strangers listening to every word.

CHAPTER XLIV.

A great change was observable in Mrs. Gaunt after this fiery and chastening ordeal. In a short time she had been taught many lessons. She had learned that the law will not allow even a woman to say anything and everything with impunity. She had been in a court of justice, and seen how gravely, soberly, and fairly an accusation is sifted there ; and, if false, annihilated ; which, elsewhere, it never is. Member of a sex that could never have invented a court of justice, she had found something to revere and bless in that other sex to which her erring husband belonged. Finally, she had encountered in Mercy Vint a woman whom she recognized at once as her moral superior. The contact of that pure and well-governed spirit told wonderfully upon her. She began to watch her tongue and to bridle her high spirit. She became slower to give offence, and slower to take it. She took herself to task, and made some little excuses even for Griffith. She was resolved to retire from the world altogether ; but, meantime, she bowed her head to the lessons of adversity. Her features, always lovely, but somewhat too haughty, were now softened and embellished beyond description by a mingled expression of grief, humility, and resignation.

She never mentioned her husband; but it is not to be supposed she never thought of him. She waited the course of events in dignified and patient silence.

As for Griffith Gaunt, he was in the hands of two lawyers, Atkins and Houseman. He waited on the first, and made a friend of him. "I am at your service," said he; "but not if I am to be indicted for bigamy, and burned in the hand."

"These fears are idle," said Atkins. "Mercy Vint declared in open court she will not proceed against you."

" Ay, but there's my wife."

"She will keep quiet; I have Houseman's word for it."

" Ay, but there's the Attorney-General."

"O, he will not move, unless he is driven. We must use a little influence. Mr. Houseman is of my mind, and he has the ear of the county."

To be brief, it was represented in high quarters that to indict Mr. Gaunt would only open Mrs. Gaunt's wounds afresh, and do no good; and so Houseman found means to muzzle the Attorney-General.

Just three weeks after the trial, Griffith Gaunt, Esq. reappeared publicly. The place of his reappearance was Coggleswade. He came and set about finishing his new mansion with feverish rapidity. He engaged an army of carpenters and painters, and spent thousands of pounds on the decorating and furnishing of the mansion, and laying out the grounds.

This was duly reported to Mrs. Gaunt, who said — not a word.

But at last one day came a letter to Mrs. Gaunt, in Griffith's well-known handwriting.

With all her acquired self-possession, her hand trembled as she broke open the seal.

It contained but these words: —

"MADAM, — I do not ask you to forgive me. For, if you had done what I have, I could never forgive you. But for the sake of Rose, and to stop their tongues, I do hope you will do me the honor to live under this my roof. I dare not face Hernshaw Castle. Your own apartments here are now ready for you. The place is large. Upon my honor I will not trouble you; but show myself always, as now,

' "Your penitent and very humble servant,

"GRIFFITH GAUNT."

The messenger was to wait for her reply.

This letter disturbed Mrs. Gaunt's sorrowful tranquillity at once. She was much agitated, and so undecided that she sent the messenger away, and told him to call next day.

Then she sent off to Father Francis to beg his advice.

But her courier returned, late at night, to say Father Francis' was away from home.

Then she took Rose, and said to her, "My darling, papa wants us to go to his new house, and leave dear old Hernshaw; I know not what to say about that. What do *you* say?"

" Tell him to come to us," said Rose, dictatorially. "Only," (lowering her little voice very suddenly,) "if he is naughty and won't, why then we had better go to him; for he amuses me."

"As you please," said Mrs. Gaunt; and sent her husband this reply: —

"SIR, — Rose and I are agreed to defer to your judgment and obey your wishes. Be pleased to let me know what day you will require us; and I must trouble you to send a carriage.

"I am, sir,

"Your faithful wife and humble servant,

"CATHARINE GAUNT."

At the appointed day, a carriage and four came wheeling up to the door. The vehicle was gorgeously emblazoned, and the servants in rich liveries; all which finery glittering in the sun, and the glossy coats of the horses, did mightily please Mistress Rose. She stood on the stone steps, and clapped her hands with delight. Her mother just sighed, and said, "Ay, 't is in pomp and show we must seek our happiness now."

She leaned back in the carriage, and closed her eyes, yet not so close but now and then a tear would steal out, as she thought of the past.

They drove up under an avenue to a noble mansion, and landed at the foot of some marble steps, low and narrow, but of vast breadth.

As they mounted these, a hall door, through which the carriage could have passed, was flung open, and discovered the servants all drawn up to do honor to their mistress.

She entered the hall, leading Rose by the hand; the servants bowed and courtesied down to the ground.

She received this homage with dignified courtesy, and her eye stole round to see if the master of the house was coming to receive her.

The library door was opened hastily, and out came to meet her — Father Francis.

"Welcome, madam, a thousand times welcome to your new home," said he, in a stentorian voice, with a double infusion of geniality. "I claim the honor of showing you your part of the house, though 't is all yours for that matter." And he led the way.

Now this cheerful stentorian voice was just a little shaky for once, and his eyes were moist.

Mrs. Gaunt noticed, but said nothing before the people. She smiled graciously, and accompanied him.

He took her to her apartments. They consisted of a salle-à-manger, three delightful bedrooms, a boudoir, and a magnificent drawing-room, fifty feet long, with two fireplaces, and a bay-window thirty feet wide, filled with the choicest flowers.

An exclamation of delight escaped Mrs. Gaunt. Then she said, "One would think I was a queen." Then

she sighed, "Ah," said she, "'t is a fine thing to be rich." Then, despondently, "Tell him I think it very beautiful."

"Nay, madam, I hope you will tell him so yourself."

Mrs. Gaunt made no reply to that. She added: "And it was kind of him to have you here the first day: I do not feel so lonely as I should without you."

She took Griffith at his word, and lived with Rose in her own apartments.

For some time Griffith used to slip away whenever he saw her coming.

One day she caught him at it, and beckoned him.

He came to her.

"You need not run away from me," said she: "I did not come into your house to quarrel with you. Let us be *friends*," — and she gave him her hand sweetly enough, but O so coldly!

"I hope for nothing more," said Griffith. "If you ever have a wish, give me the pleasure of gratifying it, — that is all."

"I wish to retire to a convent," said she, quietly.

"And desert your daughter?"

"I would leave her behind, to remind you of days gone by."

By degrees they saw a little more of one another; they even dined together now and then. But it brought them no nearer. There was no anger, with its loving reaction. They were friendly enough, but an icy barrier stood between them.

One person set himself quietly to sap this barrier. Father Francis was often at the Castle, and played the peacemaker very adroitly.

The line he took might be called the innocent Jesuitical. He saw that it would be useless to exhort these two persons to ignore the terrible things that had happened, and to make it up as if it was only a squabble. What he did was to repeat to the husband every gracious word the wife let fall, and *vice versâ*, and to suppress all either said that might tend to estrange them.

In short, he acted the part of Mr.

Harmony in the play, and acted it to perfection.

Gutta cavat lapidem.

Though no perceptible effect followed his efforts, yet there is no doubt that he got rid of some of the bitterness. But the coldness remained.

One day he was sent for all in a hurry by Griffith.

He found him looking gloomy and agitated.

The cause came out directly. Griffith had observed, at last, what all the females in the house had seen two months ago, that Mrs. Gaunt was in the family way.

He now communicated this to Father Francis, with a voice of agony, and looks to match.

"All the better, my son," said the genial priest: "'t will be another tie between you. 1 hope it will be a fine boy to inherit your estates." Then, observing a certain hideous expression distorting Griffith's face, he fixed his eyes full on him, and said, sternly, "Are you not cured yet of that madness of yours?"

"No, no, no," said Griffith, deprecatingly; "but why did she not tell me?"

"You had better ask her."

"Not I. She will remind me I am nothing to her now. And, though 't is so, yet I would not hear it from her lips."

In spite of this wise resolution, the torture he was in drove him to remonstrate with her on her silence.

She blushed high, and excused herself as follows: —

"I should have told you as soon as I knew it myself. But you were not with me. I was all by myself — in Carlisle jail."

This reply, uttered with hypocritical meekness, went through Griffith like a knife. He turned white, and gasped for breath, but said nothing. He left her, with a deep groan, and never ventured to mention the matter again.

All he did in that direction was to redouble his attentions and solicitude for her health.

The relation between these two was now more anomalous than ever.

Even Father Francis, who had seen strange things in families, used to watch Mrs. Gaunt rise from the table and walk heavily to the door, and her husband dart to it and open it obsequiously, and receive only a very formal reverence in return, — and wonder how all this was to end.

However, under this icy surface, a change was gradually going on; and one afternoon, to his great surprise, Mrs. Gaunt's maid came to ask Griffith if he would come to Mrs. Gaunt's apartment.

He found her seated in her bay-window, among her flowers. She seemed another woman all of a sudden, and smiled on him her exquisite smile of days gone by.

"Come, sit beside me," said she, "in this beautiful window that you have given me."

"Sit beside you, Kate?" said Griffith. "Nay, let me kneel at your knees: that is my place."

"As you will," said she, softly; and continued, in the same tone: "Now listen to me. You and I are two fools. We have been very happy together in days gone by; and we should both of us like to try again; but we neither of us know how to begin. You are afraid to tell me you love me, and I am ashamed to own to you or anybody else that I love you, in spite of it all; — I do, though."

"You love me! a wretch like me, Kate? 'T is impossible. I cannot be so happy."

"Child," said Mrs. Gaunt, "love is not reason; love is not common sense. 'T is a passion; like your jealousy, poor fool. I love you, as a mother loves her child, all the more for all you have made me suffer. I might not say as much, if I thought we should be long together. But something tells me I shall die this time: I never felt so before. Bury me at Hernshaw. After all, I spent more happy years there than most wives ever know. I see you are very sorry for what you have done.

How could I die and leave thee in doubt of my forgiveness, and my love ? Kiss me, poor jealous fool; for I do forgive thee, and love thee with all my sorrowful heart." And even with the words she bowed herself and sank quietly into his arms, and he kissed her and cried bitterly over her : bitterly. But she was comparatively calm. For she said to herself, "The end is at hand."

Griffith, instead of pooh-poohing his wife's forebodings, set himself to baffle them.

He used his wealth freely, and, besides the county doctor, had two very eminent practitioners from London, one of whom was a gray-headed man, the other singularly young for the fame he had obtained. But then he was a genuine enthusiast in his art.

CHAPTER XLV.

GRIFFITH, white as a ghost, and unable to shake off the forebodings Catharine had communicated to him, walked incessantly up and down the room ; and, at his earnest request, one or other of the four doctors in attendance was constantly coming to him with information.

The case proceeded favorably, and, to Griffith's surprise and joy, a healthy boy was born about two o'clock in the morning. The mother was reported rather feverish, but nothing to cause alarm.

Griffith threw himself on two chairs and fell fast asleep.

Towards morning he found himself shaken, and there was Ashley, the young doctor, standing beside him with a very grave face. Griffith started up, and cried, "What is wrong, in God's name ? "

" I am sorry to say there has been a sudden hemorrhage, and the patient is much exhausted."

"She is dying, she is dying ! " cried Griffith, in anguish.

"Not dying. But she will infallibly sink, unless some unusual circumstance occur to sustain vitality."

Griffith laid hold of him. " O sir, take my whole fortune, but save her ! save her ! save her ! "

" Mr. Gaunt," said the young doctor, " be calm, or you will make matters worse. There is one chance to save her ; but my professional brethren are prejudiced against it. However, they have consented, at my earnest request, to refer my proposal to you. She is sinking for want of blood ; if you consent to my opening a vein and transfusing healthy blood from a living subject into hers, I will undertake the operation. You had better come and see her ; you will be more able to judge."

" Let me lean on you," said Griffith. And the strong wrestler went tottering up the stairs. There they showed him poor Kate, white as the bed-clothes, breathing hard, and with a pulse that hardly moved.

Griffith looked at her horror-struck.

" Death has got hold of my darling," he screamed. " Snatch her away ! for God's sake, snatch her from him ! "

The young doctor whipped off his coat, and bared his arm.

" There," he cried, " Mr. Gaunt consents. Now, Corrie, be quick with the lancet, and hold this tube as I tell you ; warm it first in that water."

Here came an interruption. Griffith Gaunt griped the young doctor's arm, and, with an agonized and ugly expression of countenance, cried out, " What, *your* blood ! What right have you to lose blood for her ? "

" The right of a man who loves his art better than his blood," cried Ashley, with enthusiasm.

Griffith tore off his coat and waistcoat, and bared his arm to the elbow. " Take every drop I have. No man's blood shall enter her veins but mine." And the creature seemed to swell to double his size, as, with flushed cheek and sparkling eyes, he held out a bare arm corded like a blacksmith's, and white as a duchess's.

The young doctor eyed the magnificent limb a moment with rapture; then fixed his apparatus and performed an operation which then, as now, was impossible in theory; only he did it. He sent some of Griffith Gaunt's bright red blood smoking hot into Kate Gaunt's veins.

This done, he watched his patient closely, and administered stimulants from time to time.

She hung between life and death for hours. But at noon next day she spoke, and, seeing Griffith sitting beside her, pale with anxiety and loss of blood, she said: "My dear, do not thou fret. I died last night. I knew I should. But they gave me another life; and now I shall live to a hundred."

They showed her the little boy; and, at sight of him, the whole woman made up her mind to live.

And live she did. And, what is very remarkable, her convalescence was more rapid than on any former occasion.

It was from a talkative nurse she first learned that Griffith had given his blood for her. She said nothing at the time, but lay, with an angelic, happy smile, thinking of it.

The first time she saw him after that, she laid her hand on his arm, and, looking Heaven itself into his eyes, she said, "My life is very dear to me now. 'T is a present from thee."

She only wanted a good excuse for loving him as frankly as before, and now he had given her one. She used to throw it in his teeth in the prettiest way. Whenever she confessed a fault, she was sure to turn slyly round and say, "But what could one expect of me? I have his blood in my veins."

But once she told Father Francis, quite seriously, that she had never been quite the same woman since she lived by Griffith's blood; she was turned jealous; and moreover it had given him a fascinating power over her, and she could tell blindfold when he was in the room. Which last fact, indeed, she once proved by actual experiment. But all this I leave to such as study

14

the occult sciences in this profound age of ours.

Starting with this advantage, Time, the great curer, gradually healed a wound that looked incurable.

Mrs. Gaunt became a better wife than she had ever been before. She studied her husband, and found he was not hard to please. She made his home bright and genial; and so he never went abroad for the sunshine he could have at home.

And he studied her. He added a chapel to the house, and easily persuaded Francis to become the chaplain. Thus they had a peacemaker, and a friend, in the house, and a man severe in morals, but candid in religion, and an inexhaustible companion to them and their children.

And so, after that terrible storm, this pair pursued the even tenor of a peaceful united life, till the olive-branches rising around them, and the happy years gliding on, almost obliterated that one dark passage, and made it seem a mere fantastical, incredible dream.

Mercy Vint and her child went home in the coach. It was empty at starting, and, as Mrs. Gaunt had foretold, a great sense of desolation fell upon her.

She leaned back, and the patient tears coursed steadily down her comely cheeks.

At the first stage a passenger got down from the outside, and entered the coach.

"What, George Neville!" said Mercy.

"The same," said he.

She expressed her surprise that he should be going her way.

"'T is strange," said he, "but to me most agreeable."

"And to me too, for that matter," said she.

Sir George observed her eyes were red, and, to divert her mind and keep up her spirits, launched into a flow of small talk.

In the midst of it, Mercy leaned back in the coach, and began to cry bitterly. So much for that mode of consolation.

Upon this he faced the situation, and begged her not to grieve. He praised the good action she had done, and told her how everybody admired her for it, especially himself.

At that she gave him her hand in silence, and turned away her pretty head. He carried her hand respectfully to his lips ; and his manly heart began to yearn over this suffering virtue, — so grave, so dignified, so meek. He was no longer a young man ; he began to talk to her like a friend. This tone, and the soft, sympathetic voice in which a gentleman speaks to a woman in trouble, unlocked her heart ; and for the first time in her life she was led to talk about herself.

She opened her heart to him. She told him she was not the woman to pine for any man. Her youth, her health, and love of occupation, would carry her through. What she mourned was the loss of esteem, and the blot upon her child. At that she drew the baby with inexpressible tenderness, and yet with a half-defiant air, closer to her bosom.

Sir George assured her she would lose the esteem of none but fools. "As for me," said he, "I always respected you, but now I revere you. You are a martyr and an angel."

"George," said Mercy, gravely, "be you my friend, not my enemy."

"Why, madam," said he, "sure you can't think me such a wretch."

"I mean, our flatterers are our enemies."

Sir George took the hint, given, as it was, very gravely and decidedly ; and henceforth showed her his respect by his acts ; he paid her as much attention as if she had been a princess. He handed her out, and handed her in ; and coaxed her to eat here, and to drink there ; and at the inn where the passengers slept for the night, he showed his long purse, and secured her superior comforts. Console her he could not ; but he broke the sense of utter desolation and loneliness with which she started from Carlisle. She told him so in the inn, and descanted on the goodness of God, who had sent her a friend in that bitter hour.

"You have been very kind to me, George," said she. "Now Heaven bless you for it, and give you many happy days, and well spent."

This, from one who never said a word she did not mean, sank deep into Sir George's heart, and he went to sleep thinking of her, and asking himself was there nothing he could do for her.

Next morning Sir George handed Mercy and her babe into the coach ; and the villain tried an experiment to see what value she set on him. He did not get in, so Mercy thought she had seen the last of him.

"Farewell, good, kind George," said she. "Alas ! there 's naught but meeting and parting in this weary world."

The tears stood in her sweet eyes, and she thanked him, not with words only, but with the soft pressure of her womanly hand.

He slipped up behind the coach, and was ashamed of himself, and his heart warmed to her more and more.

As soon as the coach stopped, my lord opened the door for Mercy to alight. Her eyes were very red ; he saw that. She started, and beamed with surprise and pleasure.

"Why, I thought I had lost you for good," said she. "Whither are you going ? to Lancaster ?"

"Not quite so far. I am going to the 'Packhorse.'"

Mercy opened her eyes, and blushed high. Sir George saw, and, to divert her suspicions, told her merrily to beware of making objections. "I am only a sort of servant in the matter. 'T was Mrs. Gaunt ordered me."

"I might have guessed it," said Mercy. "Bless her ; she knew I should be lonely."

"She was not easy till she had got rid of me, I assure you," said Sir George. "So let us make the best on 't, for she is a lady that likes to have her own way."

"She is a noble creature. George, I shall never regret anything I have done for *her.* And she will not be ungrateful.

O, the sting of ingratitude ! I have felt
that. Have you ?"

"No," said Sir George ; " I have escaped that, by never doing any good
actions."

"I doubt you are telling me a lie,"
said Mercy Vint.

She now looked upon Sir George
as Mrs. Gaunt's representative, and
prattled freely to. him. Only now and
then her trouble came over her, and
then she took a quiet cry without ceremony.

As for Sir George, he sat and studied,
and wondered at her.

Never in his life had he met such a
woman as this, who was as candid with
him as if he had been a woman. She
seemed to have a window in her bosom,
through which he looked, and saw the
pure and lovely soul within.

In the afternoon they reached a little
town, whence a cart conveyed them to
the "Packhorse."

Here Mercy Vint disappeared, and
busied herself with Sir George's comforts.

He sat by himself in the parlor, and
missed his gentle companion.

In the morning Mercy thought of
course he would go.

But instead of that, he stayed, and
followed her about, and began to court
her downright.

But the warmer he got, the cooler
she. And at last she said, mighty dryly,
"This is a very dull place for the likes
of you."

" 'T is the sweetest place in England," said he ; "at least to me ; for
it contains — the woman I love."

Mercy drew back, and colored rosy
red. "I hope not," said she.

"I loved you the first day I saw you,
and heard your voice. And now I love
you ten times more. Let me dry thy
tears forever, sweet Mercy. Be my
wife."

"You are mad;" said Mercy. "What,
would you wed a woman in my condition ? I am more your friend than to
take you at your word. And what must
you think I am made of, to go from one
man to another, like that ? "

"Take your time, sweetheart ; only
give me your hand."

"George," said Mercy, very gravely, "I am beholden to you ; but my
duty it lies another way. There is a
young man in these parts " (Sir George
groaned) "that was my follower for two
years and better. I wronged him for
one I never name now. I must marry
that poor lad, and make him happy, or
else live and die as I am."

Sir George turned pale. "One word :
do you love him ?"

"I have a regard for him."

"Do you love him ?"

"Hardly. But I wronged him, and
I owe him amends. I shall pay my
debts."

Sir George bowed, and retired sick
at heart, and deeply mortified. Mercy
looked after him and sighed.

Next day, as he walked disconsolate
up and down, she came to him and
gave him her hand. "You were a good
friend to me that bitter day," said she.
"Now let me be yours. Do not bide
here : 't will but vex you."

"I am going, madam," said Sir
George, stiffly. "I but wait to see the
man you prefer to me. If he is not
too unworthy of you, I 'll go, and trouble you no more. I have learned his
name."

Mercy blushed; for she knew Paul
Carrick would bear no comparison with
George Neville.

The next day Sir George took leave
to observe that this Paul Carrick did
not seem to appreciate her preference
so highly as he ought. "I understand
he has never been here."

Mercy colored, but made no reply;
and Sir George was sorry he had taunt-
ed her. He followed her about, and
showed her great attention, but not a
word of love.

There were fine trout streams in the
neighborhood, and he busied himself
fishing, and in the evening read aloud
to Mercy, and waited to see Paul Carrick.

Paul never came ; and from a word
Mercy let drop, he saw that she was
mortified. Then, being no tyro in love,

he told her he had business in Lancaster, and must leave her for a few days. But he would return, and by that time perhaps Paul Carrick would be visible.

Now his main object was to try the effect of correspondence.

Every day he sent her a long love-letter from Lancaster.

Paul Carrick, who, in absenting himself for a time, had acted upon his sister's advice, rather than his own natural impulse, learned that Mercy received a letter every day. This was a thing unheard of in that parish.

So then Paul defied his sister's advice, and presented himself to Mercy; when the following dialogue took place.

"Welcome home, Mercy."

"Thank you, Paul."

"Well, I 'm single still, lass."

"So I hear."

"I 'm come to say let bygones be bygones."

"So be it," said Mercy, dryly.

"You have tried a gentleman ; now try a farrier."

"I have ; and he did not stand the test."

"Anan."

"Why did you not come near me for ten days ? "

Paul blushed up to the eyes. "Well," said he, "I 'll tell you the truth. 'T was our Jess advised me to leave you quiet just at first."

"Ay, ay. I was to be humbled, and made to smart for my fault ; and then I should be thankful to take you. My lad, if ever you should be really in love, take a friend's advice ; listen to your own heart, and not to shallow advisers. You have mortified a poor sorrowful creature, who was going to make a sacrifice for you ; and you have lost her forever."

"What d' ye mean ? "

"I mean that you are to think no more of Mercy Vint."

"Then it is true, ye jade ; ye 've gotten a fresh lover already."

"Say no more than you know. If you were the only man on earth, I would not wed you, Paul Carrick."

Paul Carrick retired home, and blew up his sister, and told her that she had "gotten him the sack again."

The next day Sir George came back from Lancaster, and Mercy lowered her lashes for once at sight of him.

"Well," said he, "has this Carrick shown a sense of your goodness ? "

"He has come, — and gone."

She then, with her usual frankness, told him what had passed. "And," said she, with a smile, "you are partly to blame ; for how could I help comparing your behavior to me with his ? *You* came to my side when I was in trouble, and showed me respect when I expected scorn from all the world. A friend in need is a friend indeed."

"Reward me, reward me," said Sir George, gayly ; "you know the way."

"Nay, but I am too much *your* friend," said Mercy.

"Be less my friend then, and more my darling."

He pressed her, he urged her, he stuck to her, he pestered her.

She snubbed, and evaded, and parried, and liked him all the better for his pestering her.

At last, one day, she said : "If Mrs. Gaunt thinks it will be for your happiness, I *will* — in six months' time ; but you shall not marry in haste to repent at leisure. And I must have time to learn two things, — whether you can be constant to a simple woman like me, and whether I can love again, as tenderly as you deserve to be loved."

All his endeavors to shake this determination were vain. Mercy Vint had a terrible deal of quiet resolution.

He retired to Cumberland, and, in a long letter, asked Mrs. Gaunt's advice.

She replied characteristically. She began very soberly to say that she should be the last to advise a marriage between persons of different conditions in life. "But then," said she, "this Mercy is altogether an exception. If a flower grows on a dunghill, 't is still a flower, and not a part of the dunghill. She has the essence of gentility, and indeed her *manners* are better bred than most of our ladies. There is too much affectation abroad, and that is your true vulgarity. Tack 'my lady' on to 'Mercy Vint,' and that dignified and quiet simplicity of hers will carry her with credit through every court in Europe. Then think of her virtues," — (here the writer began to lose her temper,) — "where can you hope to find such another? She is a moral genius, and acts well, no matter under what temptation, as surely as Claude and Raphael paint well. Why, sir, what do you seek in a wife? Wealth? title? family? But you possess them already; you want something in addition that will make you happy. Well, take that angelic goodness into your house, and you will find, by your own absolute happiness, how ill your neighbors have wived. For my part, I see but one objection : the child. Well, if you are man enough to take the mother, I am woman enough to take the babe. In one word, he who has the sense to fall in love with such an angel, and has not the sense to marry it, if he can, is a fool.

" Postscript. — My poor friend, to what end think you I sent you down in the coach with her ? "

Sir George, thus advised, acted as he would have done had the advice been just the opposite.

He sent Mercy a love-letter by every post, and he often received one in return ; only his were passionate, and hers gentle and affectionate.

But one day came a letter that was a mere cry of distress.

" George, my child is dying. What shall I do ? "

He mounted his horse, and rode to her.

He came too late. The little boy had died suddenly of croup, and was to be buried next morning.

The poor mother received him up stairs, and her grief was terrible. She clung sobbing to him, and could not be comforted. Yet she felt his coming. But a mother's anguish overpowered all.

Crushed by this fearful blow, her strength gave way for a time, and she clung to George Neville, and told him she had nothing left but him, and one day implored him not to die and leave her.

Sir George said all he could think of to comfort her ; and at the end of a fortnight persuaded her to leave the " Packhorse," and England, as his wife.

She had little power to resist now, and indeed little inclination.

They were married by special license, and spent a twelvemonth abroad.

At the end of that time they returned to Neville's Court, and Mercy took her place there with the same dignified simplicity that had adorned her in a humbler station.

Sir George had given her no lessons ; but she had observed closely, for his sake ; and being already well educated, and very quick and docile, she seldom made him blush except with pride.

They were the happiest pair in Cumberland. Her merciful nature now found a larger field for its exercise, and, backed by her husband's purse, she became the Lady Bountiful of the parish and the county.

The day after she reached Neville's Court came an exquisite letter to her from Mrs. Gaunt. She sent an affectionate reply.

But the Gaunts and the Nevilles did not meet in society.

Sir George Neville and Mrs. Gaunt, being both singularly brave and haughty people, rather despised this arrangement.

But it seems that, one day, when they were all four in the Town Hall, folk whispered and looked ; and both Griffith Gaunt and Lady Neville surprised these glances, and determined, by one impulse, it should never happen again. Hence it was quite understood that the Nevilles and the Gaunts were not to be asked to the same party or ball.

The wives, however, corresponded, and Lady Neville easily induced Mrs. Gaunt to co-operate with her in her benevolent acts, especially in saving young women, who had been betrayed, from sinking deeper.

Living a good many miles apart, Lady Neville could send her stray sheep to service near Mrs. Gaunt; and *vice versa;* and so, merciful, but discriminating, they saved many a poor girl who had been weak, not wicked.

So then, though they could not eat nor dance together in earthly mansions, they could do good together; and methinks, in the eternal world, where years of social intercourse will prove less than cobwebs, these their joint acts of mercy will be links of a bright, strong chain, to bind their souls in everlasting amity.

It was a remarkable circumstance, that the one child of Lady Neville's unhappy marriage died, but her nine children by Sir George all grew to goodly men and women. That branch of the Nevilles became remarkable for high principle and good sense; and this they owe to Mercy Vint, and to Sir George's courage in marrying her. This Mercy was granddaughter to one of Cromwell's ironsides, and brought her rare personal merit into their house, and also the best blood of the old Puritans, than which there is no blood in Europe more rich in male courage, female chastity, and all the virtues.

THE END.

Cambridge: Electrotyped and Printed by Welch, Bigelow, & Co.